U0066617

CORE VOCABULARY

英文字彙王

核心
單字
2001 ~
4000

Levels 3 & 4

本系列套書依據大學入學考試中心於 109 年 7 月頒布之「高中英文參考詞彙表」重新編修，將原先的單字依使用者文化背景、日常用語及教學層面高頻用字考量，去除詞頻低、口語型詞彙及部分縮寫字與專有名詞等，將單字以**使用頻率**適度排序，另增補學習必備、各類考試重要字詞，除自學外，也適用**學測**、**高中英語聽力測驗**、**全民英檢中級**、**新制多益**……等考試。

內容方面，每單元單字除提供 K.K. 音標、詞性、實用例句、中文解釋外，亦嚴選補充該單字重要的**片語**、**衍生字**、**近似字**、**反義字**、**比較用字**、**延伸用法**及**文法說明**等，讓讀者在日常英語閱讀、聆聽、口說、寫作能力養成上，都能靈活運用這些字詞。

音檔設計上，我們特請專業美籍老師朗讀單字及例句，且為了結合科技、響應環保，全書採用 "QR Code"，讀者可依使用習慣，自由選擇聆聽**分頁式音檔**或**一次完整下載音檔**，邊聽邊朗讀單字及例句，可大幅改善發音並增進口語能力。

本系列《英文字彙王》套書，依單字難易程度分為基礎單字 2000（Levels 1 & 2）、核心單字 2001～4000（Levels 3 & 4）、進階單字 4001～6000（Levels 5 & 6）三套書，方便讀者循序漸進規劃學習。祝各位學習成功！

使用說明

每 1 ～ 2 頁皆有 QR Code 可下載該頁音檔分段學習，另有一個單元一個完整音檔，皆可於小書名頁掃描 QR Code 下載。

單字背熟後，可在框內打勾。

 0723-0730

23 widen [ˋwaɪdn̩] *vt.* 使變寬 & *vi.* 變寬

衍 (1) wide [waɪd] *a.* 廣泛的；寬的 ①
　(2) widely [ˋwaɪdlɪ] *adv.* 廣泛地
　(3) width [wɪdθ] *n.* 寬度 ②

▶ The construction crew spent several days widening the streets in town.
建築工人花了好幾天的時間拓寬鎮上的馬路。

▶ The gap between rich and poor in this country has widened.
該國的貧富差距已變大了。

補充單字的難度級數

與單字相關的重要片語、衍生字、近似字、反義字、比較用字、延伸用法及文法說明等補充。

代號說明

三 動詞三態
複 名詞的複數形
片 片語
衍 衍生字
似 近似字（含形音義）
比 多個近似字比較說明
反 反義字

用法 重要文法說明
延伸 相關補充
[美] 美式英語
[英] 英式英語

索 引

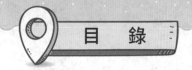

目　錄

Level ❸

Level ❹

| Level ❸ |

單字
New Words

衍生字
Derivatives

片語
Phrases

音檔下載
QR Code

近似字
Synonyms

延伸用法
Related
Words

重要
文法說明
Grammar

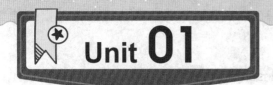

Unit 01

  0101-0102

1　unite [ju`naɪt] *vt.* 使聯合 & *vi.* 團結

衍 (1) unit [`junɪt] *n.* 單位 ②
　 (2) unify [`junə͵faɪ] *vt.* 統整；統一 ⑥

用法 過去分詞可作形容詞，表『團結的』。

▶ If we remain united, there will be nothing we can't achieve.
　我們若團結，什麼事都做得了。

▶ Our goal is to unite the labor unions to oppose the new policy.
　我們的目標是聯合這些勞工團體反對這項新政策。

▶ We should unite, or we'll be defeated by the enemy.
　我們要團結，否則會被敵人擊潰。
　＊defeat [dɪ`fit] *vt.* 擊敗

---

unity [`junətɪ] *n.* 一致；團結 (不可數)

似 teamwork [`tim͵wɜk] *n.* 團隊合作

用法 unity 可與介詞 with 及 in 並用，形成下列很好的句子：

▶ Without unity, we'll face failure.
　我們若不團結，就會面臨失敗。

▶ In unity there is strength.
　團結就是力量。

▶ The plot of the drama lacks unity.
　這齣戲的劇情缺乏一致性。

▶ The political party lost the election due to lack of unity.
　該政黨選舉失敗是因為不團結。

---

union [`junjən] *n.* 工會；聯合

衍 reunion [ri`junjən] *n.* 重聚，團圓 ④

延伸 (1) a labor union　工會，勞工聯盟
　 (2) a trade union　商會

▶ The union decided to go on strike due to the low wages.
　由於薪資偏低，因此該工會決定罷工。

▶ This car is a perfect union of beauty and technology.
　這輛車子是美與科技的完美結合。

2　remain [rɪ`men] *vi.* 繼續存在；仍是 (之後接名詞或形容詞作補語)

衍 remaining [rɪ`menɪŋ] *a.* 剩下的

似 stay [ste] *vi.* 仍保持是 ①

用法 (1) remain 作『仍保持是』解時，之後須接名詞或形容詞作補語。
　　 remain a puzzle　仍一直是個謎
　　 remain healthy　保持健康
　 (2) It remains to be seen + 疑問詞 (when、what、how……) 引導的名詞子句　……有待觀察

▶ No one remained in the hall soon after the concert was over.
　音樂會結束沒多久，大廳裡一個人影都不剩了。

▶ Though divorced, Anna and David still remain friends.
　雖然離婚了，安娜和大衛仍是朋友。

▶ The problem still remains unsolved.
　這個問題仍然一直沒被解決。

▶ It remains to be seen which team will win.
　哪一隊會贏尚有待觀察。

remains [rɪˋmenz] *n.* 遺跡 (恆用複數)

延伸 remains 亦可作『遺體』解，是 body (屍體) 的委婉語。

▶ The writer's remains are buried in his hometown.
這位作家的遺體被埋在他的故鄉。

▶ The remains are the most famous tourist attraction in the country.
這些遺跡是該國境內最有名的旅遊景點。

---

3 probable [ˋprɑbəbḷ] *a.* 很可能的

衍 probably [ˋprɑbəblɪ] *adv.* 很可能，或許 ①

似 likely [ˋlaɪklɪ] *a.* 很可能的 ②

用法 It is / seems probable that...
很可能……
= It is / seems likely that...

▶ It seems probable that this accident is the result of the driver's carelessness.
看來意外很可能是因為駕駛的粗心所致。

---

probability [ˏprɑbəˋbɪlətɪ] *n.* 可能性

似 likelihood [ˋlaɪklɪˏhʊd] *n.* 可能性 ⑤

▶ The probability is that the match will be postponed.
這場比賽很可能會延期。

---

4 situation [ˏsɪtʃʊˋeʃən] *n.* 處境，情勢

用法 本字常與介詞 in 並用。

▶ What would you do in such a situation?
在那種情況下你會怎麼做？

▶ This company's financial situation is getting more and more difficult.
這家公司的財務狀況越來越吃緊。

---

5 determine [dɪˋtɜmɪn] *vt.* 決定；確定

衍 determination [dɪˏtɜməˋneʃən] *n.* 決心 ④

似 resolve [rɪˋzɑlv] *vt.* 決定 ④

用法 determine to + V 下定決心要……
= resolve to + V
= make up one's mind to + V

▶ Lilly determined to leave for the hospital at once.
莉莉決定馬上動身去醫院。

▶ The police were finally able to determine the cause of the accident.
警方終於能確定這起意外的肇因了。

---

determined [dɪˋtɜmɪnd] *a.* 有決心的

片 be determined to + V 決心要……

▶ I'm determined to quit gambling.
我已下定決心要戒賭。

6　rate [ret] *n.* 比率 & *vt.* 評比為

片 (1) at any rate　無論如何
(2) rate sth as...　將某物評比為……
(3) At any rate, ...　無論如何，……
= Anyway, ...
= Anyhow, ...

▶ The rate of unemployment has been rising in recent years.
近年來的失業率逐漸上升。

▶ This resort is rated as the most beautiful place in the country.
這個觀光勝地被評為該國最美的地方。

▶ At any rate, their performance did not live up to our expectations.
無論如何，他們的表現並不如我們所預期。
＊live up to sb's expectations　符合某人的期望

7　political [pəˈlɪtɪkḷ] *a.* 政治的

衍 politically [pəˈlɪtɪkḷɪ] *adv.* 政治上地

▶ The writer fled abroad seeking political asylum.
這位作家逃到國外尋求政治庇護。
＊asylum [əˈsaɪləm] *n.* 庇護

politics [ˈpɑlətɪks] *n.* 政治

▶ Most youngsters are not interested in politics.
多數的年輕人都不熱衷政治。

politician [ˌpɑləˈtɪʃən] *n.* 政客

▶ I'd rather trust a hungry wolf than a politician.
我寧願相信一匹餓狼也不願意相信政客。

8　process [ˈprɑsɛs] *n.* 過程 & *vt.* 處理

片 be in the process of + N/V-ing
正在進行……中

延伸 (1) processed foods　加工食品
(2) meat processing　肉類加工

▶ I'm afraid getting things changed will be a slow process.
事情要改變恐怕會是一個緩慢的過程。

▶ We're still in the process of conducting a market survey.
我們尚在做市場調查中。

▶ It will take about 3 weeks to process your application.
處理您的申請約要 3 星期的時間。

9　majority [məˈdʒɔrətɪ] *n.* 大部分

片 the / a majority of...　大部分的……
衍 major [ˈmedʒɚ]
a. 大部分的；主要的，重要的 &
vi. 主修（與介詞 in 並用）&
n. 主修科目 ②

▶ The majority of residents on the island can only speak their own dialect.
這島上大部分的居民只會說他們自己的方言。
＊dialect [ˈdaɪəlɛkt] *n.* 方言

10 property [ˈprɑpətɪ] n. 財產 (不可數)；特性 (可數)

似 (1) possessions [pəˈzɛʃənz]
　　n. 財產 (恆用複數) ④
(2) assets [ˈæsɛts]
　　n. 資產 (恆用複數) ⑤
(3) quality [ˈkwɑlətɪ] n. 特性 (可數) ②

▶ They lost all their property in the fire.
他們在這場大火中失去了所有財產。

▶ One property of diamonds is hardness.
堅硬是鑽石的一項特性。

11 opportunity [ˌɑpəˈtjunətɪ] n. 機會，良機

似 chance [tʃæns] n. 機會 ①

延伸 a golden opportunity
千載難逢的良機

▶ This trip is a great opportunity to broaden your horizons and practice your English.
這趟旅行是個拓展視野以及練習英文的好機會。
＊broaden one's horizons　增廣見識，拓展視野
　horizon [həˈraɪzn̩] n. 地平線 (單)；範圍 (複)

12 actually [ˈæktʃʊəlɪ] adv. 事實上，實際上 (= in fact)

衍 actual [ˈæktʃʊəl]
　a. 真實的，確實的 ②
似 really [ˈrɪəlɪ] adv. 事實上；實際上 ①

▶ Nick likes to act like a teenager, but actually he's more than 30 years old.
尼克喜歡裝作青少年的樣子，但他事實上已經 30 多歲了。

13 recognize [ˈrɛkəɡˌnaɪz] vt. 認出；承認，認可

衍 (1) recognizable [ˈrɛkəɡˌnaɪzəbl̩]
　　a. 可分辨的，認得出的
(2) unrecognizable
　　[ʌnˈrɛkəɡˌnaɪzəbl̩] a. 認不出來的
(3) recognizably [ˈrɛkəɡˌnaɪzəblɪ]
　　adv. 可分辨地；顯著地
(4) recognition [ˌrɛkəɡˈnɪʃən]
　　n. 認出；承認，認可 ④

▶ After being separated for twenty years, Jack cannot recognize his daughter.
失散 20 年後，傑克認不出他的女兒來了。

▶ Professor Rollins is recognized as one of the best educators in the country.
羅林斯教授是該國公認為最優秀的教育家之一。

14 enjoyable [ɪnˈdʒɔɪəbl̩] a. 愉快的

衍 (1) enjoy [ɪnˈdʒɔɪ] vt. 享受
　　(之後接名詞或動名詞作受詞) ①
(2) enjoyment [ɪnˈdʒɔɪmənt]
　　n. 享受 ①
似 pleasant [ˈplɛzənt] a. 愉快的 ②
反 boring [ˈbɔrɪŋ] a. 令人無聊的 ①

▶ The party we had last Friday night was really enjoyable.
我們上星期五晚上那場派對實在愉快極了。

joyful [ˋdʒɔɪfəl] *a.* 喜悅的

衍 (1) joy [dʒɔɪ] *n.* 喜悅 ①
　　(2) joyfully [ˋdʒɔɪfəlɪ] *adv.* 喜悅地
　　(3) joyous [ˋdʒɔɪəs] *a.* 快樂的 ⑥

▶ We were excited and joyful, knowing that our team had won the game.
獲知我隊贏了比賽時，我們既興奮又高興。

15　unique [juˋnik] *a.* 與眾不同的；獨有的

片 be unique to + 地方
　　為某地方所獨有
= be native to + 地方
= be indigenous to + 地方
　*indigenous [ɪnˋdɪdʒənəs]
　　a. 土生的，土長的 ⑤

▶ Every person's fingerprints are unique. No two people's are alike.
每個人的指紋都是獨一無二的。沒有人是相同的。

▶ Kiwi birds are unique to New Zealand. Nowhere else can you find them.
鷸鴕為紐西蘭所獨有，其他地方都找不到。

---

terrific [təˋrɪfɪk] *a.* 很棒的

似 (1) excellent [ˋɛksələnt]
　　a. 極優秀的 ①
　　(2) fantastic [fænˋtæstɪk]
　　a. 很棒的 ④

▶ The restaurant on the corner serves terrific food.
轉角那間餐廳的餐點棒極了。

16　wed [wɛd] *vt. & vi.* 結婚

三 wed, wedded [ˋwɛdɪd] / wed, wedded / wed
似 marry [ˋmærɪ] *vt. & vi.* 結婚 ②
衍 the newlyweds 新婚夫婦

▶ Ken wedded his lover without his parents' consent.
肯未經父母同意便娶了他的情人。

▶ They wedded on a beautiful autumn day.
他們在一個美麗的秋日結為連理。

17　tough [tʌf] *a.* 堅韌的；嚴厲的；艱苦的，困難的

片 be tough on sb　對某人很嚴厲
似 (1) sturdy [ˋstɝdɪ] *a.* 堅韌的 ⑤
　　(2) difficult [ˋdɪfə͵kəlt] *a.* 困難的 ①
　　(3) harsh [hɑrʃ] *a.* 嚴厲的 ④

▶ This meat is too tough, Mom. I think you overcooked it.
媽，這塊肉好硬。我想妳把它煮得太老了。

▶ Tom is tough on his son because he thinks his child is a little too naughty.
湯姆對他兒子很嚴厲，因為他覺得他孩子有點太頑皮。

▶ Compared to last month's test, this one wasn't too tough.
= In comparison with last month's test, this one wasn't too difficult.
跟上個月的考試比起來，這次的考試不算太難。

18 hire [haɪr] *vt. & n.* 僱用;租用

囝 for hire   可供租用

似 (1) employ [ɪm'plɔɪ] *vt.* 僱用 ②
　(2) rent [rɛnt] *vt.* 租用;*n.* 租金 ②

▸ We hired a consultant to devise a new system for our company.
我們僱用一位顧問來幫公司設計一套新制度。

▸ Tina and her friends hired a limousine to drive them to the prom.
蒂娜和她朋友租了一臺加長型禮車載她們去學校舞會。
*limousine ['lɪmə,zin] *n.* 加長型禮車 (= limo)
prom [prɑm] *n.* (學期結束前舉辦的) 學校舞會

▸ The cabins over there are for hire.
那邊的小木屋可供租用。

19 homesick ['hom,sɪk] *a.* 思鄉的

似 nostalgic [nɑs'tældʒɪk] *a.* 鄉愁的

▸ I couldn't help feeling homesick on sleepless nights.
夜晚我睡不著時就忍不住會想家。

20 invitation [,ɪnvə'teʃən] *n.* 邀請;請帖,邀請卡

衍 (1) invite [ɪn'vaɪt]
　　vt. 邀請;引誘,招致 ①
　(2) inviting [ɪn'vaɪtɪŋ] *a.* 誘人的

▸ The food looks inviting.
這個食物看起來好好吃。

囝 at the invitation of sb   應某人之邀

▸ Mr. Lee joined the group at the invitation of the government.
李先生應政府的邀請加入這個小組。

▸ Have you received an invitation to the party?
你收到這次派對的邀請卡了嗎?

21 jealous ['dʒɛləs] *a.* 嫉妒的,吃醋的

囝 be jealous of...   嫉妒……

衍 jealousy ['dʒɛləsɪ] *n.* 嫉妒 ④

▸ Why are you so jealous of David's promotion?
為什麼大衛升遷你會那麼嫉妒?

envy ['ɛnvɪ] *n. & vt.* 嫉妒;羨慕

囝 (1) be the envy of sb
　　令某人羨慕的……

　(2) envy sb sth   羨慕某人某事

衍 envious ['ɛnvɪəs] *a.* 羨慕的 ⑤
be envious of...   羨慕……

▸ All the girls in Sally's class are envious of her beauty.
莎莉班上所有的女孩子都羨慕她的美貌。

▸ Peter's new cell phone is the envy of everyone in the office.
彼得的新手機羨煞辦公室內所有人。

▸ I sometimes envy the rich and famous whose lives seem so glamorous.
我有時候嫉妒有錢人和名人,他們的生活似乎很迷人。
*glamorous ['glæmərəs] *a.* 迷人的

▸ I don't envy Peter his success.
= I don't envy Peter's success.
我不羨慕彼得的成功。

22　fright [fraɪt] *n.* 驚嚇

片 (1) with fright　害怕地
(2) stage fright　怯場

似 (1) fear [fɪr] *n.* 恐懼 ②
(2) horror [ˈhɔrɚ] *n.* 恐怖 ③
(3) terror [ˈtɛrɚ] *n.* 恐怖，驚駭 ④

▶ Andy looked at the barking dog with fright.
安迪害怕地看著那隻狂吠的狗。

▶ Sarah has no stage fright; in fact, she enjoys making public speeches.
莎拉不會怯場；事實上，她很喜歡上臺演講。

---

frighten [ˈfraɪtṇ] *vt.* 使驚嚇

片 (1) be frightened to death
受到極度驚嚇
(2) frighten sb into + V-ing
脅迫某人從事……

衍 (1) frightened [ˈfraɪtṇd]
a. 受到驚嚇的
(2) frightening [ˈfraɪtṇɪŋ]
a. 令人害怕的

似 (1) scare [skɛr] *vt.* 使害怕 ②
(2) terrify [ˈtɛrəˌfaɪ] *vt.* 使害怕 ⑤

▶ You should not let your son watch that movie because it might frighten him.
你不應該讓你的兒子看那部電影，因為那有可能會嚇到他。

▶ I was frightened to death at the sight of the horrible accident.
目睹這起可怕的意外時，我嚇死了。

▶ Tom frightened Jim into keeping quiet.
湯姆威脅吉姆保持安靜。

23　locate [ˈloket / loˈket] *vt.* 位於 (用於被動語態)；找到……的位置；設置

用法 be located in / on / at...　位於……
= be situated in / on / at...
= lie in / on / at...
in 與大城市或區域並用
on 與街道或山峰並用
at 與轉角或某個有地址號碼的房舍並用

▶ Our school is located in that area.
我們學校位在那個區域。

▶ The leader was unable to locate the meeting point on the map.
隊長在地圖上找不到會合點。

▶ They located their new store on Second Avenue.
他們把新的商店設在第二大道上。

---

location [loˈkeʃən]

n. 地點；(找到) 位置

▶ Please come visit our store at its new location.
請到我們店的新址參觀。

▶ Finding the location of the escaped prisoner was difficult.
要找到這名逃犯的藏身處還真不容易。

24　costly [ˈkɔstlɪ] *a.* 昂貴的；代價高的

衍 cost [kɔst] *vt.* 花費 & *n.* 價錢 ①
似 expensive [ɪkˈspɛnsɪv] *a.* 昂貴的 ①

▶ Money is hard to earn, so I never buy costly clothes.
錢很難賺，因此我絕不買昂貴的衣服。

▶ George made a costly mistake by investing all his money in that project.
喬治把所有的錢全部投入那項企畫，犯了一個代價很高的錯誤。

25 mostly [ˈmostlɪ] *adv.* 主要地

似 (1) largely [ˈlɑrdʒlɪ] *adv.* 大大地；
　 大部分 ④
(2) mainly [ˈmenlɪ] *adv.* 主要地
(3) primarily [praɪˈmɛrəlɪ]
　 adv. 主要地

▶ John succeeded mostly because he worked hard and had great ambition.
約翰能夠成功主要是因為他努力工作又有強烈的企圖心。
＊ambition [æmˈbɪʃən] *n.* 企圖心；野心

26 lately [ˈletlɪ] *adv.* 最近

似 recently [ˈrisṇtlɪ] *adv.* 最近
用法 (1) lately 與 recently 須與現在完成式
　 或現在完成進行式並用。
(2) 中文的『最近』也可指『未來這段
　 期間』，此時應使用 in the near
　 future（最近，在最近的未來），與
　 未來式或未來進行式並用。

▶ Have you seen James lately?
你最近見到詹姆士了嗎？

▶ What have you been doing lately / of late?
你最近都在做什麼？

▶ I'll be taking a trip to Tokyo lately. (✕)
→ I'll be taking a trip to Tokyo in the near future. (○)
我最近要去東京旅行。

27 besides [bɪˈsaɪdz] *prep.* 除⋯⋯之外 & *adv.* 此外 (= additionally)

似 beside [bɪˈsaɪd] *prep.* 在⋯⋯旁邊 ①

▶ Besides math, Lucy is good at music.
露西除了精通數學以外，也精通音樂。

▶ I've seen the movie before. Besides, it isn't that good.
我以前看過那部電影。而且，它也沒那麼棒。

28 career [kəˈrɪr] *n.* 職業 (尤指終身職業) & *a.* 職業的

延伸 (1) a career soldier　　職業軍人
(2) a career woman　　職業婦女

▶ Ms. Wilson took up photography as her career.
魏爾遜女士以攝影作為她的終身職業。

▶ Though a career woman, Jane never ignores her duty as a mother.
阿珍雖然是職業婦女，卻從未忽略她身兼母親的責任。

painter [ˈpentɚ] *n.* 畫家；油漆匠
衍 (1) paint [pent] *n.* 繪畫顏料；油漆 ①
(2) painting [ˈpentɪŋ] *n.* 畫作
　 (尤指水彩畫、油畫等) ②

▶ My father used to be a painter but gave it up later.
我父親曾經是位畫家，不過後來放棄了。

▶ Michael worked as a house painter in the US.
邁可在美國時當過房屋的油漆工。

banker [ˈbæŋkɚ] *n.* 銀行家
衍 (1) bank [bæŋk] *n.* 銀行；河邊 ①
(2) banking [ˈbæŋkɪŋ] *n.* 銀行業務

▶ Mr. Emery is a successful banker, but he leads a simple life.
艾默瑞先生是成功的銀行家，卻過著簡樸的生活。

captain [ˈkæptɪn]

n. 船長；機長；連長；隊長

用法 在軍語中，captain 若用於陸軍或空軍，指『上尉』軍階，也分別指『連長』或『分隊長』；若用於海軍，captain 則指『上校』軍階或『艦長』。在民航用語中，captain 則指客機『機長』。

▶ The captain told the sailors to raise the sails.
船長要水手們將帆升起。

▶ The captain said that the plane would be landing soon.
機長宣布飛機即將著陸。

photographer [fəˈtɑgrəfə]

n. 照相師；攝影記者

延伸 cameraman [ˈkæmərəˌmæn]
n. 電影拍攝員／電視攝影記者

▶ The photographer won an award for his photos of war.
這名攝影記者因戰爭照片而獲獎。

producer [prəˈdjusə]

n. 生產者；製作人

似 (1) manufacturer [ˌmænjəˈfæktʃərə]
n. 廠商，製造業者 ④

(2) maker [ˈmekə] *n.* 製造者

▶ The firm is one of the main producers of laptop computers.
這家公司是筆記型電腦的主要製造商之一。

▶ Tina's ex-husband is a famous film producer.
提娜的前夫是有名的電影製作人。

professor [prəˈfɛsə] *n.* (大學) 教授

比 lecturer [ˈlɛktʃərə] *n.* 講師 ④

延伸 associate professor （大學）副教授

▶ Mr. Stevens is a professor of psychology.
史蒂芬先生是心理系的教授。

Unit 02

 0201-0206

---

1 permit [pɚˋmɪt] *vt.* & *vi.* 准許，允許 & [ˋpɝmɪt] *n.* 許可證

目 permit, permitted [pɚˋmɪtɪd],
permitted [pɚˋmɪtɪd]

片 (1) permit sb to + V　准許某人做……
　(2) permit + V-ing　允許從事……

衍 (1) permissive [pɚˋmɪsɪv] *a.* 許可的
　(2) permissible [pɚˋmɪsəbḷ]
　　　a. 可允許的 ⑥

似 (1) allow [əˋlaʊ] *vt.* 准許 ①
　(2) allow sb to + V　准許某人做……
　(3) allow + V-ing　　允許從事……

反 (1) ban [bæn]
　　　vt. 禁止 (以名詞或動名詞作受詞) &
　　　n. 禁令 ⑤
　(2) prohibit [prəˋhɪbɪt]
　　　vt. 禁止 (以名詞或動名詞作受詞) ⑤

▸ We are not permitted to smoke here.
　我們不能在此地抽菸。

▸ I'll contact you after the meeting if time permits.
　如果時間許可的話，開完會後我會跟你聯絡。

▸ You need a permit to go fishing here.
　你要有許可證才可以在這裡釣魚。

---

permission [pɚˋmɪʃən]
n. 許可，准許

片 without sb's permission
　未經某人的允許
= without sb's consent / agreement
　未經某人的同意

▸ You are not allowed to use the machine without my permission.
　沒有我的許可，你不能使用這臺機器。

---

2 volume [ˋvɑljəm] *n.* 量，容量；冊；音量

片 (1) turn the volume up / down
　　　把音量開大 / 關小
　(2) a large volume of + 不可數名詞
　　= a large amount of + 不可數名詞
　　　大量的……

▸ We need a large volume of money and manpower for this project.
　我們需要大量的財力及人力才能推動這個計畫。

▸ The volume of traffic reaches its peak during rush hour.
　交通流量在上下班尖峰時間會達到高峰。

▸ The history of the Roman Empire is in volumes 3 and 4.
　羅馬帝國的歷史收錄在第 3、4 冊中。

▸ Would you mind turning the volume down? I'm studying.
　你介意把音量關小嗎？我正在唸書。

3　represent [ˌrɛprɪˈzɛnt] vt. 代表；象徵

衍 representation [ˌrɛprɪzɛnˈteʃən]
n. 代表 ④

似 symbolize [ˈsɪmbḷˌaɪz] vt. 象徵 ⑥

用法 represent sth　代表某事物
= stand for sth
= be a representation of sth

▶ George represented his company at the press conference.
喬治代表公司出席記者會。

▶ This ring, though inexpensive, represents my love for you.
= This ring, though inexpensive, stands for my love for you.
這只戒指雖然不貴，卻代表著我對你的愛。

representative [ˌrɛprɪˈzɛntətɪv]
a. 代表性的 & n. 代表者

用法 be representative of...　代表……
= stand for...
= represent...
= be a representation of...

▶ The dove is representative of peace.
鴿子代表和平。

▶ The union sent a representative to negotiate with management.
工會派出一位代表和資方談判。
＊此處 management 表資方或公司管理高層，之前通常不置任何冠詞。

4　attitude [ˈætətjud] n. 態度

用法 本字之後多接介詞 to / toward(s)
an attitude to / toward(s) sth
對某事物的態度

▶ Tony has a positive attitude towards life.
東尼對人生持積極的態度。

5　reduce [rɪˈdjus] vt. 使減少；使淪為

片 reduce sb to + V-ing
使某人淪為……

衍 reduction [rɪˈdʌkʃən]
n. 減少；折扣 ④

似 decrease [dɪˈkris] vt. & vi. 減少 ③

反 increase [ɪnˈkris] vt. & vi. 增加 ②

▶ Despite Andy's pay cut, he won't reduce his standard of living.
儘管安迪被減薪，他仍不願降低他的生活水準。

▶ Bankruptcy reduced Bruce to begging.
= Bruce was reduced to begging after he went bankrupt.
布魯斯破產後淪為乞丐。
＊bankruptcy [ˈbæŋkrʌptsɪ] n. 破產
　bankrupt [ˈbæŋkrʌpt] a. 破產的
　go bankrupt　破產

6　fake [fek] a. 假的 & n. 贗品 & vt. 偽造；假裝

反 genuine [ˈdʒɛnjʊɪn] a. 真正的 ④

▶ Brian was caught using fake money.
布萊恩因為使用假鈔被抓。

▶ After careful examination, the experts revealed that the painting was a fake.
經過詳細檢驗，專家指出這幅畫是假畫。

▶ The teacher was angry when he found Gary had faked his father's signature.

老師發現蓋瑞偽造父親的簽名時很生氣。

▶ Ruth didn't want to go out with Tim, so she faked a stomachache.

茹絲不想和提姆約會，所以假裝胃痛。

7 religious [rɪ`lɪdʒəs] *a.* 虔誠的；宗教的

衍 religion [rɪ`lɪdʒən]
n. 宗教 (可數 / 不可數) ②

延伸 (1) a religious belief 　某宗教信仰
(2) different religious beliefs
不同的宗教信仰

▶ The rational scientist is very religious.

這位理性的科學家對宗教非常虔誠。

▶ Never talk about religious or political issues at social gatherings.

社交聚會千萬不要談論宗教或政治議題。

8 strength [strɛŋθ] *n.* 力量；優點

衍 (1) strong [strɔŋ] *a.* 強壯的 ①
(2) strengthen [`strɛŋθən]
vt. & vi. 加強 ④

▶ Operating this machine requires skill more than physical strength.

操作這臺機器需要的技巧比體力還多。

▶ Please analyze the strengths and weaknesses of this proposal.

請針對這個提案分析它的優缺點。

＊analyze [`ænḷˌaɪz] *vt.* 分析

weakness [`wiknɪs]
n. 虛弱；弱點

衍 (1) weak [wik] *a.* 虛弱的 ①
(2) weaken [`wikən] *vt.* 使虛弱 ③
用法 表『優點』、『缺點』有下列說法：
優點 / 強項：advantage、strong point、strength、forte
缺點 / 弱項：disadvantage、weak point、weakness、shortcoming

▶ You're not suitable for the job because of your physical weakness.

你身體虛弱，因此不適合這個工作。

▶ Math is my weakness, but music is my forte.

數學是我的弱項，不過音樂卻是我的強項。

＊forte [`fɔrˌte] *n.* 強處，優勢

9 vary [`vɛrɪ] *vi.* 變化 & *vt.* 改變

三 vary, varied [`vɛrɪd], varied
片 vary in... 　在……方面有所不同
似 (1) differ [`dɪfɚ] *vi.* 變化，不同 ④
(2) change [tʃendʒ] *vt.* 變化；改變 ①

▶ The weather here varies between cool and very hot.

這裡的天氣變化很大，忽而涼爽忽而酷熱。

▶ Tom varied the games he played with the children so as not to bore them.

湯姆更換和孩子們玩的遊戲，以免使他們感到無聊。

＊bore [bɔr] *vt.* 使無聊

various [ˈvɛrɪəs] *a.* 各式各樣的

衍 (1) variation [ˌvɛrɪˈeʃən] *n.* 變化 ⑤
(2) variable [ˈvɛrɪəbl]
   a. 易變的 & *n.* 變數 ⑤
(3) invariably [ɪnˈvɛrɪəblɪ]
   adv. 不變地 ⑥

▸ There have been various solutions to the problem.
這個問題有各式各樣的解決辦法。
＊solution [səˈluʃən] *n.* 解決之道 (與介詞 to 並用)
 a solution to a problem　某問題的解決之道

variety [vəˈraɪɪtɪ] *n.* 變化；種類

片 a variety of... 各式各樣的……

▸ Peter is a workaholic; his life lacks variety.
彼得是個工作狂；他的生活缺乏變化。
＊workaholic [ˌwɝkəˈhɔlɪk] *n.* 工作狂

▸ The library offers a wide variety of books to choose from.
圖書館有各類書可供選擇。

10　product [ˈprɑdʌkt] *n.* 產品；成果，結果

衍 (1) produce [ˈprɑdjus]
   n. 農產品 (集合名詞，不可數)
   & [prəˈdjus] *vt.* 生產；出版 ②
(2) producer [prəˈdjusɚ]
   n. 生產者；製片人 ③
(3) productivity [ˌprɑdʌkˈtɪvətɪ]
   n. 生產力 ⑤
(4) by-product [ˈbaɪˌprɑdəkt]
   n. 副產品

▸ Most of the produce on the island is exported to Japan.
島上的許多農產品都外銷日本。

▸ The country's main product is timber.
該國的主要產物是木材。
＊timber [ˈtɪmbɚ] *n.* 木材 (集合名詞，不可數)
= lumber [ˈlʌmbɚ] *n.*

▸ Nick's big muscles were the product of years spent in the gym.
尼克的結實肌肉是多年耗在健身房的成果。

11　imagination [ɪˌmædʒəˈneʃən] *n.* 想像力

衍 (1) image [ˈɪmɪdʒ]
   n. 形象；意象；影像，圖像 ②
(2) imagine [ɪˈmædʒɪn] *vt.* 想像 ②
(3) imaginative [ɪˈmædʒəˌnetɪv]
   a. 有想像力的 ④
(4) imaginary [ɪˈmædʒəˌnɛrɪ]
   a. 想像出來的，虛構的 ④
(5) imaginable [ɪˈmædʒɪnəbl]
   a. 可想得到的

▸ Use your imagination and see if you can come up with a better idea.
運用你的想像力，看看你能不能想出更好的辦法。

0212-0216

12 prevent [prɪˋvɛnt] *vt.* 阻止；預防，避免

片 prevent sb/sth from + N/V-ing / being p.p.　阻止某人 / 某物……；使某人 / 某物無法……

衍 (1) prevention [prɪˋvɛnʃən]
　　n. 阻止；預防，避免 ④
　　(2) preventive [prɪˋvɛntɪv]
　　a. 預防的 ⑥

似 (1) avoid [əˋvɔɪd] *vt.* 避免 ②
　　(2) stop [stɑp] *vt.* 阻止 ①

▶ Robert's sore legs prevented him from joining the marathon.
羅伯特腿痠使他無法參加馬拉松比賽。

▶ Taking necessary precautions will prevent many accidents from happening.
採取必要的預防措施能**防止**許多意外的發生。

13 response [rɪˋspɑns] *n.* 回應；回答；反應（與介詞 to 並用）

片 in response to...　對……做出回應

衍 (1) respond [rɪˋspɑnd]
　　vi. 回答；回應；反應（與介詞 to 並用）②
　　(2) responsive [rɪˋspɑnsɪv]
　　a. 有反應的；敏感的

似 (1) feedback [ˋfid͵bæk]
　　n. 反應；回饋 ④
　　(2) reply [rɪˋplaɪ] *n.* & *vt.* 回覆 ②

▶ Has there been any response to your letter?
你的信有回音了嗎？

▶ In response to your letter dated July 1, we regret to say that we'll have to cancel the deal.
茲回覆臺端 7 月 1 日的來信，我們很遺憾表示，我們不得不取消這個交易。

▶ Jason's response to my proposal was discouraging.
傑森對我的提議**反應**很令人沮喪。

responsibility [rɪ͵spɑnsəˋbɪlətɪ]
n. 責任

片 take responsibility for + N/V-ing
對……負責

衍 (1) responsible [rɪˋspɑnsəb!]
　　a. 負責的（與介詞 for 並用）②
　　(2) irresponsible [͵ɪrɪˋspɑnsəb!]
　　a. 沒責任感的

▶ You should take responsibility for what you've done.
= You should be responsible for what you've done.
你應該**對**自己做過的事**負責**。

14 **perform** [pə`fɔrm] *vt.* 執行；履行 & *vi.* 表演；表現

衍 performer [pə`fɔrmə] *n.* 表演者 ⑤

似 carry out... 執行……

用法 perform a mission　執行任務
= carry out a mission
　perform one's duties
　履行某人的義務

▶ The surgeon has performed this operation before.
該外科醫生以前動過這種手術。

▶ The teacher told us to perform our civic duties.
老師告訴我們要盡市民的義務。
*civic [`sɪvɪk] *a.* 市民的

▶ The young actor performed with such zest that there is no doubt that he will be awarded the prize for the most outstanding actor in the play.
這名年輕男演員的演出如此賣力,他將獲頒此劇的最佳男演員獎是無庸置疑的。
*zest [zɛst] *n.* 熱忱

▶ Much to my surprise, most of the students performed very well on the exam.
很讓我驚訝的是,大部分的學生這次考試表現得很好。

performance [pə`fɔrməns]
n. 表演；表現

用法 表某人在校成績優良,有下列說法:

▶ John does well in school.
= John's academic performance is good.
約翰在校成績優良。
*academic [͵ækə`dɛmɪk] *a.* 學術的 ④

▶ The famous actress gave a great performance in the play last night.
那位知名的女演員昨晚在舞臺劇中有精彩的演出。

▶ I'm pleased that my son's academic performance is very good.
= I'm pleased that my son does well in school.
我兒子的功課很好,這令我滿意。

15 **technique** [tɛk`nik] *n.* 技巧,手法

似 method [`mɛθəd] *n.* 方法 ②

▶ The artist was highly acclaimed for his painting techniques.
該藝術家的繪畫技巧受到高度讚揚。
*acclaim [ə`klem] *vt.* 稱讚
= praise [prez] *vt.*

technical [`tɛknɪkḷ]
a. 技術的；專門的

衍 a technical term　專業術語

▶ Frank studied auto repair at a technical school.
法蘭克在一所技術學校學汽車修護。

16 **normal** [`nɔrmḷ] *a.* 正常的

反 abnormal [æb`nɔrmḷ]
　a. 反常的；不規則的 ⑤

▶ It's normal to feel nervous before a test.
考前會感到緊張是正常的。

17　committee [kə'mɪtɪ] *n.* 委員會

補充	該字及 team (隊伍) 常與介詞 on 並用。	▶ How many members are there on your committee?
		你的委員會有多少人？

18　achieve [ə'tʃiv] *vt.* 達成；達到

似 (1) accomplish [ə'kʌmplɪʃ]
　　vt. 達成，完成 ④
　(2) attain [ə'ten]
　　vt. & vi. 獲得；到達 ⑥
　(3) obtain [əb'ten] *vt.* 獲得 ④

▶ If you work hard, you will eventually achieve your goals.
如果你努力，最後終將達成目標。

▶ At this time, this project is 95 percent achieved.
目前這項計畫已經完成了 95%。

achievement [ə'tʃivmənt] *n.* 成就
似 accomplishment [ə'kʌmplɪʃmənt]
　　n. 成就 ④

▶ The achievements of computer technology have been incredible.
電腦科技的成就令人難以置信。

▶ You've made it into Harvard, Jim. That's quite an achievement.
吉姆，你成功進入哈佛大學。這真是一項了不起的成就。

19　immediate [ɪ'midɪɪt] *a.* 立刻的；最接近的，直接的

▶ There was an immediate response to Mary's request.
瑪莉的要求立刻得到回應。

▶ The man's immediate heir was his son.
這位男子的直接繼承人就是他兒子。
*heir [ɛr] *n.* 繼承人 (h 不發音)

immediately [ɪ'midɪɪtlɪ]
adv. 立刻，馬上

🅷 immediately after...
　　……之後沒多久
= shortly after...
= instantly after...
似 instantly ['ɪnstəntlɪ] *adv.* 立刻
= shortly
= right away
= at once

▶ I went over immediately after I finished writing the letter.
= I went over shortly after I finished writing the letter.
我一寫完信就立刻過去。

20　magical ['mædʒɪkl] *a.* 魔術的，神奇的

衍 (1) magically ['mædʒɪklɪ]
　　adv. 魔術般地，神奇地
　(2) magic ['mædʒɪk]
　　n. 魔術 *a.* 魔術的 ①

▶ No medicine is so magical that it can cure all illnesses.
沒有一種藥神奇到什麼病都能治。

magician [məˈdʒɪʃən] *n.* 魔術師
似 (1) wizard [ˈwɪzəd] *n.* 男巫師 ④
　 (2) witch [wɪtʃ] *n.* 巫婆 ④

▶ The magician took out a rabbit from his hat.
魔術師從帽子裡抓出一隻兔子。

21 expectation [ˌɛkspɛkˈteʃən] *n.* 期望，預期 (常用複數)

片 meet sb's expectations
　 符合某人的期望
= live up to sb's expectations
= measure up to sb's expectations
衍 expect [ɪksˈpɛkt]
　 vt. 期待，等待；預料；要求 ①

▶ If you lower your expectations, you'll never be disappointed.
假使你不多所期待，就永遠不會失望。

▶ Without hard work, you can't meet your parents' expectations.
你若不努力就不能達到你父母的期望。

22 ongoing [ˈɑnˌɡoɪŋ] *a.* 前進的；不斷發展中的

▶ There is an ongoing crisis because that infectious disease is spreading quickly.
由於該傳染病蔓延得很快，因此危機一直存在。

▶ The lawyer refused to comment on the ongoing case.
這名律師拒絕就該審理中的案件發表評論。

underlying [ˌʌndəˈlaɪɪŋ]
a. 在下面的；隱含的；根本的

▶ The company drilled into the ground to get to the underlying reservoir of oil.
這間公司鑽入地面以便到達在其下的石油層。
*drill [drɪl] *vi.* & *vt.* 鑽洞
*reservoir [ˈrɛzəˌvɔr] *n.* 蘊藏；水庫

▶ It's difficult for such a young student to understand the underlying meaning of this novel.
要年紀這麼輕的學生了解這部小說隱含的意義是有難度的。

▶ What are the underlying causes of this problem?
這個問題的根本原因是什麼？

23 semester [səˈmɛstə] *n.* 學期 (分春季班和秋季班)

片 the spring / fall semester
　 春 / 秋季班
似 term [tɝm] *n.* 學期 ②

▶ I'm going to take 13 credits this semester.
我這學期要修 13 個學分。

24 pepper [ˈpɛpə] *n.* 胡椒粉 (不可數)；甜椒 (可數)

補充 (1) a red pepper　　紅椒
　　 (2) a green pepper　青椒

▶ Please pass me the salt and pepper.
請遞給我鹽和胡椒粉。

25 colorful [ˈkʌləfəl] *a.* 富有色彩的；生動的

似 (1) vivid [ˈvɪvɪd] *a.* 生動活潑的 ③
(2) animated [ˈænəˌmetɪd] *a.* 生動的
(3) graphic [ˈɡræfɪk] *a.* 生動的 ⑤

▶ The artist's paintings are very colorful.
這位畫家的畫作**色彩豐富**。

▶ I was attracted by Tom's colorful description of his life as a sailor.
湯姆將他當水手的生涯描述得很**生動**，令我嚮往。

---

fearful [ˈfɪrfəl] *a.* 害怕的
片 be fearful of... 懼怕……
= be afraid of...
衍 fear [fɪr] *n.* 恐懼 ②

▶ John was fearful of losing his job.
約翰**害怕**丟掉工作。

---

hateful [ˈhetfəl]
a. 憎恨的，充滿憎恨的
衍 (1) hate [het] *vt. & n.* 恨 ①
(2) hatred [ˈhetrɪd] *n.* 恨 ④

▶ Tom has been a hateful man ever since the accident.
自那場意外過後，湯姆的心中就**充滿了恨**。

---

hopeful [ˈhopfəl]
a. 充滿希望的，樂觀的

片 feel hopeful about...
對……抱持希望

衍 hopefully [ˈhopfəlɪ] *adv.* 但願
（置於句首，修飾全句）；滿懷希望地

▶ Hopefully the new system will significantly raise our productivity.
= It is my hope that the new system will significantly raise our productivity.
但願新系統會大大提高我們的生產力。

似 optimistic [ˌɑptəˈmɪstɪk] *a.* 樂觀的 ③
反 hopeless [ˈhoplɪs]
a. 不抱希望的，絕望的

▶ After watching the film, everyone feels hopeful about the future.
看完這部電影後，每個人**對未來都懷抱希望**。

---

playful [ˈplefəl] *a.* 愛玩的，貪玩的

▶ Healthy puppies and kittens are very playful animals.
健康的小狗和小貓是很**愛玩的**動物。

---

skillful [ˈskɪlfəl] *a.* 擅長的；高明的
衍 skillfully [ˈskɪlfəlɪ] *adv.* 巧妙地
反 unskillful [ʌnˈskɪlfəl] *a.* 技術不好的

▶ They are skillful at this game.
他們**擅長**這種遊戲。

▶ We need a skillful doctor.
我們需要一位**高明的**醫生。

26　skinny [ˈskɪnɪ] a. 皮包骨的

似 (1) bony [ˈbonɪ] a. 骨瘦如柴的；
　　　（魚）多刺的
　(2) thin [θɪn] a. 瘦的 ①
　(3) slim [slɪm] a. 細長的；微小的 ①

▸ Rosie is very skinny because she is an incredibly picky eater.
蘿西瘦到皮包骨，因為她挑食得要命。

slender [ˈslɛndɚ] a. 窈窕的，苗條的

▸ To have a slender figure, the fashion model went on a strict diet.
為了擁有窈窕身材，這位模特兒進行嚴格的節食。

27　downtown [ˌdaʊnˈtaʊn] a. 市中心的 & adv. 在市區，往市區

用法 downtown 作副詞時，之前不得置介詞。

▸ Let's go to downtown. (✗)
→ Let's go downtown. (○)
咱們去市區。

▸ The bank opened a new downtown branch last month.
該銀行上個月開了新的市中心分行。

▸ I am heading downtown.
我要到市中心去。

0301-0307

---

1 react [rɪˈækt] *vi.* 反應 (與介詞 to 並用)

⚑ react to sth　對某事物有反應	▶ Ted reacted calmly to the plaintiff's accusation. 泰德對原告的指控反應冷靜。 *plaintiff [ˈplentɪf] *n.* 原告 　accusation [ˌækjəˈzeʃən] *n.* 指控
reaction [rɪˈækʃən] *n.* 反應 (與介詞 to 並用)	▶ What's Tom's reaction to my proposal? 湯姆對我的提議有什麼表示？

---

2 fund [fʌnd] *n.* 基金；資金 (複數) & *vt.* 提供資金

⚑ raise funds for...　為……籌募資金 衍 **fundraiser** [ˈfʌndˌrezɚ] 　*n.* 募款人 / 募款機構；募款活動 　(如餐會)	▶ We contributed to the charity fund. 我們捐款給這個慈善基金。 ▶ The hospital is trying to raise funds for research into AIDS. 這家醫院正設法為愛滋病研究籌募資金。 ▶ The research was primarily funded by the government. 這項研究計畫大部分是由政府資助。 *primarily [ˌpraɪˈmɛrəlɪ] *adv.* 主要地

---

3 audience [ˈɔdɪəns] *n.* 觀眾 (集合名詞，通常不加 s，後接複數動詞)

⚑ an audience of 5,000 / 10,000 　5 千 / 1 萬名觀眾 用法 audience 為集合名詞，表多寡時，應 使用 large 或 small 來修飾。 　many / few audiences (✗) → a large / small audience (○) 　許多 / 很少觀眾 比 **spectator** [ˈspɛktetɚ] 　*n.* 觀眾 (可數名詞，複數需加 s) ⑤	▶ Because of the rain, the audience at the concert was small. 由於下雨的緣故，那場音樂會的觀眾很少。 ▶ The concert drew a large audience. 那場演唱會吸引了很多的觀眾。

---

4 moral [ˈmɔrəl] *a.* 教導明辨是非的；道德的 & *n.* 寓意

衍 **morality** [məˈrælətɪ] *n.* 道德；正義 ⑤ 似 **ethical** [ˈɛθɪkl̩] *a.* 道德的 ⑤	▶ The film has a good moral lesson. 這部影片有個很好的教訓，要我們明辨是非。 ▶ Tony is a true and moral man. 湯尼是一個真誠而有道德的人。 ▶ The moral of this story is that money cannot buy happiness. 這個故事的寓意就是：『金錢無法買到幸福。』

immoral [ɪˋmɔrəl] *a.* 不道德的
似 wicked [ˋwɪkɪd] *a.* 邪惡的 ③

▶ Taking advantage of other people's misfortune for one's own gain is immoral.
把自己的利益建築在別人的不幸上是不道德的。
*misfortune [mɪsˋfɔrtʃən] *n.* 不幸

5　announce [əˋnaʊns] *vt.* 公布；宣布

似 (1) declare [dɪˋklɛr] *vt.* 宣告 ④
　 (2) proclaim [proˋklem]
　　 vt. 聲明；表明 ⑤

▶ John will announce who will play the characters in the play.
約翰會公布該戲劇中的角色由哪些人擔綱。

▶ Their engagement was officially announced last June.
他們訂婚的消息在去年 6 月正式宣布。

announcement [əˋnaʊnsmənt] *n.* 公告；宣布

片 make an announcement that...
= announce that...　宣告……

▶ The announcement of the name of the winner will be made at three o'clock.
這次得獎人的名單將於 3 點鐘發布。

▶ The politician made a formal announcement that he would resign early next year.
這名政治人物正式宣告明年初他將辭職。

6　theory [ˋθiərɪ] *n.* 學說；理論

片 in theory　理論上
衍 theoretical [ˌθiəˋrɛtɪkḷ] *a.* 理論的 ⑤
反 in practice　實際上

▶ Many scientists believe the theory that the universe is getting larger.
很多科學家相信宇宙正在變大的這個說法。

▶ Developing a theory and proving it are very different things.
研發一套理論和加以證實是兩碼事。

▶ Well, that sounds good in theory, but I don't know if it will work in practice.
嗯，那在理論上聽起來不錯，但我不知道它實際上是否可行。

7　skate [sket] *n.* 溜冰鞋 & *vi.* 溜冰

片 go skating　去溜冰

▶ I've worn out these skates. I want to buy a new pair.
這雙溜冰鞋我穿壞了，我要買一雙新的。

▶ Would you like to join us in going skating this weekend?
這個週末你要不要跟我們溜冰去？

ski [ski] *n.* 滑雪板 & *vi.* 滑雪
三 ski, skied [skid], skied
片 go skiing　去滑雪

▶ That store specializes in imported skis.
那家店專賣進口的滑雪板。
*specialize in...　專門從事……

▶ Where will you go skiing this winter?
今年冬天你要到哪兒去滑雪？

8 structure [ˈstrʌktʃɚ] n. 結構；建築物

衍 structural [ˈstrʌktʃərəl] a. 結構的 ⑤

似 framework [ˈfrem,wɝk] n. 架構 ⑤

▶ The structure of the poem is very complicated.
這首詩的結構很複雜。

▶ The monument is a famous structure in town.
這座紀念碑是鎮上有名的建築。

9 staff [stæf] n. (全體) 職員 (集合名詞，不可數) & vt. 為……配備人員 (一般用被動)

片 (1) a staff of 20 / 500
20 / 500 名員工

= 20 / 500 staff members

(2) be staffed with...
配備 (有)……人員

▶ Our company has a staff of 500, working in both Canada and Taiwan.
我們公司有 500 名員工，分別在加拿大與臺灣工作。

▶ Our company is staffed with individuals from three different countries.
我們公司有分別來自三個不同的國家的職員。

crew [kru] n. (船上或飛機上的) 全體工作人員 (集合名詞，不可數)

片 a crew of 50　50 位工作人員

▶ We have a crew of twenty on our ship. (○)
= We have twenty crew members on our ship.
We have twenty crews on our ship. (×)
我們船上一共有 20 位工作人員。

10 suffer [ˈsʌfɚ] vt. 遭受 & vi. 受苦

片 suffer from...
飽受 (疾病) 之苦，罹患 (疾病)

▶ That company suffered a big loss because of poor management.
那家公司由於管理不善蒙受重大損失。

▶ My father suffers from diabetes.
我爸爸患有糖尿病。
*diabetes [ˌdaɪəˈbitis] n. 糖尿病

11 spite [spaɪt] n. 怨恨，恨意；儘管 (用於下列片語中)

片 in spite of...　儘管……
（之後須接名詞或動名詞作受詞）

= despite...

= notwithstanding [ˌnɑtwɪθˈstændɪŋ]
prep. 儘管

▶ Jason vandalized those cars out of spite.
傑森因怨恨而任意破壞那些車子。
*vandalize [ˈvændḷˌaɪz] vt. 任意破壞

▶ In spite of his dad's warning, Paul went fishing alone.

= Despite his dad's warning, Paul went fishing alone.

= Notwithstanding his dad's warning, Paul went fishing alone.
儘管他爸爸提出警告，保羅還是獨自一個人釣魚去。

12 lifestyle [ˈlaɪf,staɪl] n. 生活方式

▶ The topic of the magazine this month is living a healthy lifestyle.
這本雜誌這個月的主題談的是如何過健康的生活方式。

13　somehow [ˈsʌmˌhau] adv. 不知怎麼的；設法

似 somehow [ˈsʌmˌ(h)wɑt]
adv. 稍微，有幾分 ②
使用 somewhat 時，該字常置於形容
詞與副詞之間，修飾該形容詞或副詞。

▸ John is somewhat lazy, which is
why I don't like him.
約翰有點懶，這就是為什麼我不喜歡他
的原因。

▸ My blind date was beautiful, but somehow I didn't
find her attractive.
我相親的對象蠻美的，不過不知怎地我發現她並不吸引我。

▸ I know the job is difficult, but we have to finish it
somehow.
我知道這份工作很困難，但我們總得設法解決。

14　original [əˈrɪdʒənḷ] a. 原來的；原創的 & n. 原著，原文

衍 (1) origin [ˈɔrədʒɪn] n. 起源；出身 ②
(2) originality [əˌrɪdʒəˈnælətɪ]
n. 創意 (不可數) ⑤
(3) originate [əˈrɪdʒəˌnet] vi. 源自 ⑥
似 (1) initial [ɪˈnɪʃəl] a. 最初的 ④
(2) innovative [ˈɪnoˌvetɪv]
a. 創新的 ⑤

▸ The original plan was later changed.
最初的計畫後來有所更動。

▸ Kelly has a very original idea.
凱莉有一個非常有創意的點子。

▸ Have you read the original of the report?
這份報告的原文你看過了沒有？

originally [əˈrɪdʒənlɪ]
adv. 原本；最初地 (起先)
似 in the beginning　起先
反 eventually [ɪˈvɛntʃuəlɪ] adv. 最後

▸ We're originally from Texas.
我們原籍是德州。

▸ The town was originally quite small.
這個鎮最初規模相當小。

15　additional [əˈdɪʃənḷ] a. 額外的；另加的

片 an additional + 數字　額外若干……
= an extra + 數字
衍 (1) add [æd] vt. & vi. 增加 ①
(2) addition [əˈdɪʃən] n. 增加 ②

▸ So many children came to the party that additional
tables and chairs were required.
參加派對的孩子真多，以致於需要備用的桌椅。

▸ You have to pay an additional charge for overweight
baggage.
超重的行李你必須額外付費。

▸ Completion of this project calls for an additional
$500,000.
要完成這項計畫另需 50 萬美元。

additionally [əˈdɪʃənlɪ]
adv. 除此之外
(= in addition / on top of that)
似 (1) besides [bɪˈsaɪdz] adv. 此外 ③

▸ The rent is cheap. Additionally, the location is
perfect.
= The rent is cheap. In addition, the location is perfect.
= The rent is cheap. On top of that, the location is perfect.
除了房租便宜之外，地點更是棒得沒話講。

(2) **furthermore** [ˈfɝðɚˌmɔr]
adv. 而且 ④

(3) **moreover** [morˈovɚ] *adv.* 而且 ④

16 **advantage** [ədˈvæntɪdʒ] *n.* 優勢；優點；便利，益處

H (1) take advantage of sb
占某人的便宜

(2) take advantage of sth (to + V)
利用某物 (以⋯⋯)

衍 **disadvantage** [ˌdɪsədˈvæntɪdʒ]
n. 缺點 ④

▶ Bill's superior strength gave him an advantage over his opponents.
比爾的力氣比對手大多了，因此使他占了上風。
＊opponent [əˈponənt] *n.* 對手，敵手

▶ This book has the advantage of being easy to use.
這本書的優點在於它很容易使用。

▶ All students are invited to take advantage of our student discounts.
竭誠歡迎所有學生多加利用我們的學生折扣優待。

▶ Joseph lives by the principle that one should never take advantage of others.
喬瑟夫處世的原則就是永遠不占他人的便宜。

17 **specific** [spɪˈsɪfɪk] *a.* 特定的；特有的 (與介詞 to 並用)；明確的

H (1) be specific to + 地方
是某地所獨有的

(2) be specific about...
強調說明⋯⋯

衍 **specify** [ˈspɛsəˌfaɪ] *vt.* 具體指出 ⑤

似 (1) **particular** [pɚˈtɪkjələ]
a. 特定的 ②

(2) **accurate** [ˈækjərɪt] *a.* 精確的 ③

反 **general** [ˈdʒɛnərəl]
a. 一般的；籠統的 ②

▶ The man went there for a specific purpose.
那名男子到那兒去是有特定的目的。

▶ This problem is specific to big cities.
= This problem is unique to big cities.
這個問題是大城市所特有的。

▶ Please be more specific about what you want.
你要什麼請說明確一點。

specifically [spɪˈsɪfɪkl̩ɪ]
adv. 尤其，特別地

似 (1) **specially** [ˈspɛʃəlɪ] *adv.* 特別地

(2) **particularly** [pɚˈtɪkjələlɪ]
adv. 特別地

▶ The doctor warned Mark specifically not to eat eggs.
醫生特別警告馬克不要吃蛋。

18 **destroy** [dɪsˈtrɔɪ] *vt.* 毀壞；破壞

衍 (1) **destruction** [dɪˈstrʌkʃən]
n. 破壞 ④

(2) **destructive** [dɪˈstrʌktɪv]
a. 有破壞力的 ⑤

▶ The typhoon destroyed the whole area.
颱風把這一帶全部摧毀了。

似 (1) damage [ˋdæmɪdʒ] n. & vt. 破壞②
(2) ruin [ˋruɪn] vt. 破壞④

反 restore [rɪˋstor] vt. 重建④

▶ The bribery scandal destroyed the politician's reputation.

這次賄賂醜聞毀了該政客的名聲。

＊bribery [ˋbraɪbərɪ] n. 賄賂

19　column [ˋkaləm] n. 圓柱；專欄

衍 columnist [ˋkaləmnɪst]
n. 專欄作家⑤

▶ The wooden columns are severely decayed as a result of exposure to the elements.

由於受到風吹雨淋的關係，這些木製的柱子已經嚴重腐朽了。

▶ Nicole writes a weekly column for *The China Post*.

妮可每星期替《中國郵報》寫專欄。

20　mission [ˋmɪʃən] n. 任務

片 be on a mission　執行任務

衍 missionary [ˋmɪʃənˏɛrɪ] n. 傳教士⑤

▶ Rumor has it that Michael is on a secret mission in Syria.

謠傳麥可正在敘利亞執行一項祕密任務。

21　reveal [rɪˋvil] vt. 透露，揭露

衍 revelation [ˏrɛvl̩ˋeʃən]
n. 揭示；披露⑥

反 conceal [kənˋsil] vt. 隱瞞⑤

▶ The agent was jailed for revealing secrets to the enemy.

該名探員因洩密給敵方而入獄。

22　tropical [ˋtrɑpɪkl̩] a. 熱帶的

片 the tropical zone　熱帶地區

衍 subtropical [ˏsʌbˋtrɑpɪkl̩]
a. 亞熱帶的

延伸 (1) the subtropical zone
亞熱帶地區
(2) the temperate zone　溫帶地區
(3) the frigid zone　寒帶地區
＊frigid [ˋfrɪdʒɪd] a. 嚴寒的

▶ I have a liking for tropical fruits such as bananas and pineapples.

我很喜歡香蕉和鳳梨這類的熱帶水果。

23　agriculture [ˋægrɪˏkʌltʃɚ] n. 農業

衍 agricultural [ˏægrɪˋkʌltʃərəl]
a. 農業的⑤

似 farming [ˋfarmɪŋ] n. 農業

▶ We are developing new technology to improve our agriculture.

我們正在研發新科技來改善農業。

24 **drag** [dræg] *vt.* 拖曳 & *n.* (空氣) 阻力

似 (1) pull [pʊl] *vt.* 拉，拖 ①
(2) tow [to] *vt.* 拉，拖 ③
(3) haul [hɔl] *vt.* 拉，拖 ⑤

▶ Don't drag the chair around! It will leave marks on the wooden floor.
不要拖著椅子到處走。這樣會在木質地板上留下刮痕。

▶ The new design of the plane will help to reduce drag.
這架飛機的新設計能幫助減少阻力。

25 **drugstore** [ˈdrʌɡˌstɔr] *n.* 藥妝店

衍 drug [drʌɡ] *n.* 藥物；毒品②

▶ The drugstore is open 24 hours a day.
這家藥妝店全天候營業。

cough [kɔf] *vi.* & *n.* 咳嗽

片 have a cough   咳嗽

延伸 have a runny nose   流鼻水
不可寫成：have a running nose
(有個正在跑步的鼻子)

▶ Cover your mouth when you cough.
咳嗽時要用手搗著嘴。

▶ I had a bad cough and couldn't sleep last night.
我昨晚咳得很厲害，無法入眠。

dizzy [ˈdɪzɪ] *a.* 暈眩的

▶ After three glasses of beer, I felt slightly dizzy.
喝了 3 杯啤酒後，我感覺有一點暈眩。

26 **tasty** [ˈtestɪ] *a.* 好吃的

衍 taste [test]
n. 味道 & *vt.* 品嚐 & *vi.* 嚐起來 ①
似 (1) delicious [dɪˈlɪʃəs] *a.* 好吃的 ②
(2) yummy [ˈjʌmɪ] *a.* 好吃的 (口語)

▶ My mother makes very tasty cakes.
我媽媽做的蛋糕很好吃。

27 **weapon** [ˈwɛpən] *n.* 武器

片 (1) a nuclear weapon   核武
(2) a lethal / deadly weapon
致命武器
*lethal [ˈliθəl] *a.* 致命的 ⑥

▶ The police found a large number of weapons in the deserted warehouse.
警方在廢置的倉庫裡查獲大批武器。

28 **anxious** [ˈæŋkʃəs] *a.* 焦慮的；渴望的

片 (1) be anxious about...
對……感到焦慮
= be worried about...
(2) be anxious to + V   渴望……
= be eager to + V

▶ Today, more than ever, college students are anxious about their future.
今日，更甚於以往，大學生對前途感到焦慮不安。

衍 (1) anxiously [ˈæŋkʃəslɪ]
　　　adv. 焦急地
　　(2) anxiety [æŋˈzaɪətɪ] *n.* 焦慮 ④
似 (1) worried [ˈwɜɪd] *a.* 擔心的
　　(2) apprehensive [ˌæprɪˈhɛnsɪv]
　　　a. 憂慮的
　　(3) longing [ˈlɔŋɪŋ] *a.* 渴望的
　　(4) eager [ˈigɚ] *a.* 渴望的 ③

▶ The government is anxious to improve the investment environment.
政府迫切想改善投資環境。

29　flash [flæʃ] *n.* 閃光 & *vt.* & *vi.* (使) 閃光

似 (1) blaze [blez]
　　　vi. 閃耀；燃燒 & *n.* 大火 ⑥
　　(2) flesh [flɛʃ] *n.* (人或動物的) 肉 ③

▶ The flash of lightning scared those birds away.
那道閃電的閃光把那群鳥嚇走了。

▶ That taxi driver flashed his lights impatiently.
那個計程車司機不耐煩地閃了車燈。

▶ The stars are flashing in the sky.
群星在天空中閃耀著。

flashlight [ˈflæʃˌlaɪt] *n.* 手電筒
似 torch [tɔrtʃ] *n.* 火把 ⑤
延伸 lantern [ˈlæntɚn] *n.* 燈籠 ②

▶ The flashlight doesn't work when the batteries are dead.
電池沒電時，手電筒就不亮了。

30　naked [ˈnekɪd] *a.* 赤裸的

片 to the naked eye　對肉眼而言
似 (1) nude [njud] *a.* 裸的 ⑥
　　(2) bare [bɛr] *a.* 裸的 ③

▶ At some beaches in Spain, you can swim naked.
在西班牙若干海灘，你可以裸泳。

▶ Germs are not visible to the naked eye.
對肉眼而言，細菌是看不見的。

31　sink [sɪŋk] *n.* (廚房內的) 水槽 & *vi.* 沉

三 sink, sank [sæŋk], sunk [sʌŋk]
反 float [flot] *vi.* 浮 ③

▶ Put the dishes in the sink, and I'll wash them later.
把碗盤放在水槽裡，我等會兒去洗。

▶ Two boats sank off the coast of the island during the storm.
暴風雨中，兩艘船在島嶼的外海沉沒。

32　passenger [ˈpæsndʒɚ] *n.* 乘客

片 a passenger plane　客機
似 rider [ˈraɪdɚ] *n.* 乘坐者

▶ Several passengers were injured during the bumpy flight.
好幾名乘客在顛簸的飛行途中受傷了。
＊bumpy [ˈbʌmpɪ] *a.* 顛簸的

33 lock [lɑk] *n.* 鎖 & *vt.* 鎖好

衍 (1) lockable [ˈlɑkəbḷ] *a.* 可鎖起來的
(2) locker [ˈlɑkɚ] *n.* 衣物櫃 ⑥

反 unlock [ʌnˈlɑk] *vt.* 開鎖 ⑤

▸ Turn the key in the lock to make sure it is secure.
把鑰匙插到鎖裡轉一下，確定上鎖了。
＊secure [sɪˈkjʊr] *a.* 牢固的

▸ Always make sure that the door is locked when you leave.
離開時務必要確認門是上鎖的。

34 juicy [ˈdʒusɪ] *a.* 多汁的

衍 juice [dʒus] *n.* 果汁 ①

▸ The apples are big and juicy at this time of the year.
每年這個時候蘋果總是又大又多汁。

35 neat [nit] *a.* 整齊的，整潔的

片 neat and tidy 乾淨整潔的

似 tidy [ˈtaɪdɪ]
a. 整潔的 & *vt.* & *vi.* 整理 ①

反 (1) sloppy [ˈslɑpɪ]
a. 懶散的；草率的 ⑥
(2) untidy [ʌnˈtaɪdɪ] *a.* 凌亂的

▸ Judy's handwriting is very neat.
茱蒂的筆跡非常整齊。

▸ Everything in my bedroom is neat and tidy.
我臥室的每樣東西都乾淨整潔。

Unit 04

0401-0405

1　pretend [prɪˋtɛnd] *vt.* 假裝

用 (1) pretend + that... 　假裝……
　= make believe + that...
　(2) pretend to + V　假裝要……

▶ Mary has broken up with John, but he pretends that nothing has happened.
　瑪莉和約翰分手了，但約翰假裝什麼事都沒發生。

▶ When I passed by, Peter pretended not to see me.
　我走過時，彼得假裝沒看到我。

2　frequent [ˋfrikwənt] *a.* 經常的 & [friˋkwent] *vt.* 經常造訪

衍 frequency [ˋfrikwənsɪ] *n.* 頻率 ④
似 (1) constant [ˋkɑnstənt]
　　a. 持續的 ③
　(2) continual [kənˋtɪnjuəl]
　　a. 頻頻的 ④

▶ Nick is a frequent visitor to our house.
　尼克是我們家的常客。

▶ This restaurant is frequented by celebrities.
　這家餐廳經常有社交名流光顧。
　＊celebrity [səˋlɛbrətɪ] *n.* 名人

3　connect [kəˋnɛkt] *vt.* & *vi.* 連結；關聯

用 (1) connect A with B
　　將 A 與 B 聯想在一起
　= associate A with B
　(2) connect A to B
　　將 A 與 B 連結，使 A 與 B 有關聯
衍 connection [kəˋnɛkʃən]
　n. 關係，關聯 ②

▶ The railway connects Paris and Nice.
　這條鐵路連接巴黎和尼斯。

▶ Whenever I see that handsome young man, I connect him with my ex-boyfriend.
　我每次見到那位大帥哥就聯想到我前男友。

▶ There is no evidence to connect David to the murder.
　沒有證據顯示大衛和這樁謀殺案有關。

4　occasion [əˋkeʒən] *n.* 特殊的大事；場合 (與介詞 on 並用)

用 on occasion　偶爾
　= occasionally
衍 (1) occasional [əˋkeʒənḷ] *a.* 偶爾的 ④
　(2) occasionally [əˋkeʒənḷɪ] *adv.* 偶爾
似 event [ɪˋvɛnt] *n.* 事件 ②

▶ This wedding is a great occasion.
　這場婚禮是一件大事。

▶ On occasion, I go to see a movie alone.
　= Occasionally, I go to see a movie alone.
　我偶爾會一個人去看電影。

▶ Behave yourself on formal occasions.
　在正式場合你要守規矩。

5　faith [feθ] *n.* 信心，信任

用 have faith in...　對……有信心
　= have trust in...
　= have belief in...

▶ I have faith in your honesty.
　我信任你的誠實。

衍 **faithful** [ˈfeθfl] *a.* 忠實的；守信的 ④

似 (1) **assurance** [əˈʃʊrəns]
n. 信心；保證 ④

(2) **belief** [bɪˈlif] *n.* 相信 ②

(3) **trust** [trʌst] *n.* 相信 ②

6　experiment [ɪkˈspɛrəmənt] *n. & vi.* 實驗，試驗

片 (1) conduct / perform / carry out / do an experiment　做實驗

(2) experiment on sth
對某物做實驗

(3) experiment with sth
用某物做實驗

衍 (1) **experimental** [ɪkˌspɛrəˈmɛntl]
a. 實驗性的 ④

(2) **experimentation**
[ɪkˌspɛrəmɛnˈteʃən] *n.* 實驗 (不可數)

▸ This product is the result of long experiments.
這個產品是長期實驗的結果。

▸ The group opposed any experiments on living animals.
該團體反對用動物活體做任何的實驗。

▸ Some researchers were experimenting on the rabbits.
一些研究人員正在對那些兔子做實驗。

▸ This time I'll experiment with a different chemical.
這次我要用不同的化學藥劑做實驗。

7　aware [əˈwɛr] *a.* 知道的；察覺的 (與介詞 of 並用)

片 be aware of...
知道⋯⋯；察覺到⋯⋯

= be conscious of...

似 **conscious** [ˈkɑnʃəs]
a. 察覺到的；有知覺的 ③

反 **unaware** [ˌʌnəˈwɛr] *a.* 未察覺到的

▸ You should always be aware of your surroundings.
你隨時要了解周遭的環境。

▸ Mary was aware of Tom's bad intentions, so she refused to go out with him.
瑪莉察覺出湯姆不懷好意，所以拒絕和他約會。

---

awareness [əˈwɛrnɪs]
n. 意識；察覺

片 (1) raise awareness of / about...
喚起關於⋯⋯的意識

(2) environmental / protection / political / social awareness
環保 / 政治 / 社會意識

似 **consciousness** [ˈkɑnʃəsnɪs]
n. 知覺，意識

▸ The government is trying to raise public awareness about environmental protection.
政府正設法提高民眾的環保意識。

8　security [sɪˈkjʊrətɪ] *n.* 安全

衍 **secure** [sɪˈkjʊr] *a.* 安全的 ④

似 **safety** [ˈseftɪ] *n.* 安全 ②

▸ Many workers see the policy as a major threat to their job security.
許多員工都認為這項政策是他們工作保障的一大威脅。

9　considerable [kənˈsɪdərəb̩l] a. 相當大的

衍 (1) consider [kənˈsɪdə]
　　　vt. & vi. 衡量；考慮 ②
　　(2) considerate [kənˈsɪdərɪt]
　　　a. 體貼的 ⑤
　　(3) consideration [kənˌsɪdəˈreʃən]
　　　n. 考慮 ②

▶ The rice crop suffered considerable damage as a result of the typhoon.
由於這場颱風，稻米作物遭受相當大的損失。

10　replace [rɪˈples] vt. 取代

片 replace A with B
　　以 B 取代 A，把 A 換成 B
衍 replaceable [rɪˈplesəb̩l] a. 可取代的

▶ I'm considering replacing my old PC with a notebook.
我正考慮把舊的個人電腦換成一臺新的筆記型電腦。

replacement [rɪˈplesmənt]
n. 替代人選；替代品
似 substitute [ˈsʌbstəˌtjut]
　　vt. 取代 & n. 代替者 ⑤

▶ We need a replacement for the waiter who left last week.
我們需要一個人來接替上週離職的服務生。

11　conclusion [kənˈkluʒən] n. 結束；結論

片 (1) come to a / the conclusion
　　　得到結論
　　= reach a / the conclusion
　　(2) In conclusion, ...　總之，……
　　= To sum up, ...
衍 conclude [kənˈklud]
　　vi. & vt. 作結論，結束；斷定 ②

▶ Mr. Williams thanked his audience at the conclusion of his speech.
威廉斯先生在演講結束時向聽眾表示謝意。

▶ The committee came to the conclusion that the plan was not feasible.
該委員會得到的結論是這個計畫不可行。
*feasible [ˈfizəb̩l] a. 可行的

▶ In conclusion, Tom is a man you can count on.
總之，湯姆是個你可信賴的人。

12　collection [kəˈlɛkʃən] n. 蒐集物

片 (1) a collection of...　……的收藏
　　(2) a large collection of...
　　　……的大量收藏
衍 (1) collect [kəˈlɛkt]
　　　vt. 蒐集 (郵票等) & vi. 集合 ①
　　(2) collective [kəˈlɛktɪv]
　　　a. 共同的；集體的 & n. 企業集團 ⑤
　　(3) collector [kəˈlɛktə]
　　　n. 收藏家；收稅員 ⑤

▶ Bill showed us a very fine collection of old coins.
比爾向我們展示了非常珍貴的古錢收藏。

13 **inform** [ɪnˈfɔrm] *vt.* 通知，告知

(1) inform sb of sth　通知某人某事
　= notify sb of sth
(2) keep sb informed of / about sth
　將某事隨時通知某人

informative [ɪnˈfɔrmətɪv]
　a. 有內容的；能增進知識的 ④

▸ Please inform us of any change of schedule.
若排程表有異動請告知我們。

▸ Please keep me informed about what you're doing.
你們正在做什麼事，請隨時讓我知道。

information [ˌɪnfəˈmeʃən]
n. 消息，資料
（不可數，有時縮寫成 info [ˈɪnfo]）

▸ Thank you for giving us all the information we need.
謝謝你提供我們一切想要的資訊。

▸ John is a mine of information about music.
約翰是個音樂通。
*mine [maɪn] *n.* 礦山（此處指寶庫）

14 **elect** [ɪˈlɛkt] *vt.* 選舉 & *a.* 當選的（與名詞並用，形成複合字）

elect sb + (as) + 職位
　選舉某人擔任某職位

select [səˈlɛkt] *vt.* 挑選 & *a.* 精選的 ②

▸ We elected John (as) our class leader.
我們推選約翰擔任本班班長。

▸ The president-elect is ready to take office next week.
總統當選人已經準備好在下星期就職。

election [ɪˈlɛkʃən] *n.* 選舉

▸ The election results will be broadcast tomorrow morning.
這次的選舉結果將於明天早上廣播。

elective [ɪˈlɛktɪv]
a. 選舉的 & *n.* 選修

option [ˈɑpʃən] *n.* 選修科目 ④

▸ The mayor is an elective official.
市長是經由選舉產生的官員。

▸ Peter took art as an elective in college.
彼得大學時曾選修藝術。

15 **signal** [ˈsɪgn̩] *n.* 號誌；信號 & *vt.* 發出信號

signal sb to + V
　向某人打手勢，要某人……

(1) sign [saɪn] *n.* 表示；信號 &
　vt. 簽署 & *vi.* 簽名 ①
(2) signature [ˈsɪgnətʃə]
　n. 簽訂；簽名 ④

▸ You must obey the traffic signals.
你必須遵守交通號誌。

▸ The referee gave the signal to stop.
裁判做出停止的手勢。

▸ The traffic cop signaled us to pull over.
交通警察對我們打手勢要我們靠邊停車。

gesture [ˈdʒɛstʃɚ]
n. 手勢；表示 & *vi.* 做手勢

片 (1) make a... gesture
做出……的手勢
(2) in a gesture of... 表示……

▶ The foreigner used gestures to convey his idea.
這名外國人使用手勢傳達他的意思。

▶ Ron made a vulgar gesture and got into a fight.
朗恩比了一個粗俗的手勢而與人打起架來。
＊vulgar [ˈvʌlgɚ] *a.* 粗俗的

▶ Rebecca shook her head in a gesture of disappointment.
蕾貝嘉搖了搖頭表示失望。

▶ When asked who she was talking about, Anna gestured at the handsome man sitting alone in the corner.
當安娜被問到她在談論的人是誰時，她用手勢表示是那位獨坐角落的帥哥。

16　civil [ˈsɪvl̩] *a.* 國內的；公民的；文明的，有禮的

片 (1) a civil war 內戰
(2) civil rights
公民的權利 (恆用複數)

衍 (1) civilize [ˈsɪvəˌlaɪz]
vt. 教化，使開化 ⑥
(2) civilized [ˈsɪvəˌlaɪzd]
a. 文明的，開化的
(3) civilization [ˌsɪvələˈzeʃən]
n. 文明 (不可數) ④
(4) civilian [sɪˈvɪljən]
a. 平民的 & *n.* 平民 ④

▶ The incident led to a civil war that lasted twenty years.
這個事件導致了一場持續 20 年之久的內戰。

▶ Protesters expressed their concern about the government's recent violation of civil rights.
抗議群眾表達了他們對政府近日違反公民權行徑的關切。

▶ Despite their mutual dislike, the two men remained civil in public.
儘管這兩個人彼此不喜歡對方，他們在公開場合仍保持禮貌。

17　scary [ˈskɛrɪ] *a.* 可怕的

衍 (1) scare [skɛr] *vt.* 嚇 & *n.* 驚嚇 ②
(2) scared [skɛrd] *a.* 感到害怕的 ②
= afraid [əˈfred] *a.* 害怕的 ①

▶ The scary scene of the accident shocked all of us.
這起意外的可怕景象讓我們大家都感震驚。

18　edit [ˈɛdɪt] *vt.* 編輯

片 edit sth for publication
編輯某物以供出版

▶ Tom edited the manuscripts for publication.
湯姆編輯這些手稿準備出版。

---

editor [ˈɛdɪtɚ] *n.* 編者，編輯
衍 (1) edition [ɪˈdɪʃən] *n.* 版本 ②
(2) editorial [ˌɛdəˈtorɪəl]
n. (報紙的) 社論 & *a.* 編輯上的 ⑥
(3) editor-in-chief 總編輯

▶ Bill is the editor-in-chief of that magazine.
比爾是那本雜誌的總編輯。

19 governor [ˈɡʌvɚnɚ] *n.* 州長；省長

衍 (1) govern [ˈɡʌvɚn] *vt.* 統治；控制②
  (2) government [ˈɡʌvɚnmənt]
    n. 政府②

▶ The governor of the state is said to have been involved in the scandal.
  據傳該州州長涉及此一醜聞。

20 expressive [ɪkˈsprɛsɪv] *a.* 表示的；善於表達的

片 be expressive of... 表示……
衍 (1) express [ɪkˈsprɛs]
    vt. 表達（思想、感情等）& *n.* 快車；快遞 & *a.* 快遞的，快速的 & *adv.* 用快遞寄送地②
  (2) expression [ɪkˈsprɛʃən]
    n. 表達；表情；用語②

▶ A baby's cry can be expressive of hunger.
  嬰兒哭鬧可能表示他／她餓了。

▶ Todd is not a very expressive person.
  陶德不是個善於表達的人。

21 familiar [fəˈmɪljɚ] *a.* 熟悉的

片 (1) be familiar with... 熟悉……
  (2) be familiar to sb
    對某人而言是熟悉的
衍 (1) family [ˈfæməlɪ]
    n. 家庭 & *a.* 家庭的①
  (2) familiarity [fəˌmɪlɪˈærətɪ]
    n. 親密；熟悉⑥
反 unfamiliar [ˌʌnfəˈmɪljɚ]
    a. 不熟悉的，生疏的

▶ Are you familiar with my boss?
  你和我老闆熟嗎？

▶ The story is familiar to most students in Taiwan.
  大部分臺灣的學生都熟悉這個故事。

22 sexy [ˈsɛksɪ] *a.* 性感的

衍 sex [sɛks] *n.* 性別；性②

▶ Latin dances often involve sexy movements.
  拉丁舞經常會出現性感的舞步。

sexual [ˈsɛkʃʊəl] *a.* 性的；性別的

片 (1) sexual harassment 性騷擾
    *harassment [həˈræsmənt]
    n. 騷擾⑥
  (2) sexual discrimination 性別歧視
    *discrimination [dɪˌskrɪməˈneʃən]
    n. 歧視⑤

▶ Parents and school teachers should teach kids how to deal with sexual harassment.
  家長和學校老師應該教導孩童如何處理性騷擾。

▶ We do not tolerate any sexual discrimination in this office.
  這間辦公室內不允許任何的性別歧視。

23 **explore** [ɪk`splɔr] *vt.* 探尋，探索；尋找

衍 (1) explorer [ɪk`splɔrə] *n.* 探險家
(2) exploration [ˌɛksplə`reʃən]
　　 n. 探尋 ⑤

似 (1) search [sɜtʃ] *vt.* & *vi.* 搜索 ②
(2) investigate [ɪn`vɛstə,get]
　　 vt. & *vi.* 調查 ③

▶ It is said that Columbus arrived here but did not explore the area.
據說哥倫布到過這裡，但沒有**探索**這個地區。

▶ The captain explored the causes of the leak.
船長**尋找**造成進水的原因。
＊leak [lik] *n.* 滲漏

24 **coach** [kotʃ] *n.* (運動) 教練；長途巴士 & *vt.* 指導

似 (1) bus [bʌs] *n.* 巴士；公車 ①
(2) train [tren] *vt.* 訓練 ①
(3) instruct [ɪn`strʌkt] *vt.* 指導 ④

▶ When did Tom become a baseball coach?
湯姆何時當起棒球**教練**的？

▶ We toured around the US by coach.
我們**搭長途巴士**在美國境內旅行。

▶ Kim coaches a basketball team in her leisure time.
小金利用閒暇時間**指導**籃球隊。

▶ I'll find a top-notch trainer to coach me.
＝ I'll find a top-notch trainer to instruct me.
我要找一位一流的訓練員來指導我。
＊top-notch [`tap`natʃ] *a.* 最好的

25 **bowling** [`bolɪŋ] *n.* 保齡球運動

片 (1) go bowling　　打保齡球
(2) a bowling ball　　保齡球
(3) a bowling alley
　　保齡球館；保齡球道

延伸 pin [pɪn] *n.* 保齡球瓶 ①

▶ I seldom go bowling because I think it's a waste of time and money.
我很少去**打保齡球**，因為我認為這很浪費時間和金錢。

▶ A regular bowling alley is 60 feet long.
正規的**保齡球球道**長 60 呎。

golf [gɑlf] *n.* 高爾夫球運動 & *vi.* 打高爾夫球

片 (1) go golfing　　打高爾夫球
(2) a golf course　　高爾夫球場
(3) a golf club
　　高爾夫球桿；高爾夫俱樂部

似 gulf [gʌlf] *n.* 海灣；鴻溝 ④

▶ Golf is very popular among businessmen.
高爾夫球運動在商人間非常盛行。

▶ Tammy and I will go golfing this afternoon.
塔米和我今天下午要**去打高爾夫球**。

volleyball [`vɑlɪ,bɔl] *n.* 排球
片 play volleyball　　打排球

▶ Helen was tired out after the volleyball game.
海倫在**排球**比賽以後整個人累垮了。

26 vocabulary [vəˋkæbjəˌlɛrɪ] *n.* 字彙 (量)

▶ John has a very large vocabulary.
= John knows many words.
約翰懂很多單字。

▶ Extensive reading will increase your vocabulary.
廣泛閱讀可以增進你的字彙量。

27 tend [tɛnd] *vi.* 傾向，易於 (之後接不定詞片語) & *vt.* 照顧

片 (1) tend to + V
容易……，往往會……
= be apt / inclined / prone to + V
(2) tend sth　照顧某物
= take care of sth
衍 tendency [ˋtɛndənsɪ] *n.* 傾向 ④
似 tent [tɛnt] *n.* 帳篷 ③

▶ We tend to take natural resources for granted nowadays.
現今，我們往往將自然資源視為理所當然。

▶ Mary tended the shop for her father while he was sick.
父親生病時瑪莉替她父親看店。

28 scissors [ˋsɪzəz] *n.* 剪刀 (因有兩個刀片，故恆用複數)

片 a pair of scissors　一把剪刀

▶ Please hand me the scissors on the table.
請遞給我桌上的剪刀。

29 overseas [ˌovəˋsiz] *a.* 海外的，國外的 & *adv.* 在國外地

片 (1) an overseas student　僑生
(2) an overseas Chinese　華僑
似 foreign [ˋfɔrɪn] *a.* 國外的 ①

▶ Our overseas division has been doing very well over the past three years.
過去三年來我們的海外部門一直都表現得很好。

▶ Jenny is going to work overseas this summer.
珍妮今年夏天要到國外工作。

30 peanut [ˋpiˌnʌt] *n.* 花生；很小的金額 (恆用複數)

片 peanut butter　花生醬

▶ Mom spread peanut butter on each slice of bread.
媽媽把花生醬塗在每片麵包上。

▶ Nancy's boss is stingy. He pays her peanuts.
南西的老闆很小器，只支付她微薄的薪資。
*stingy [ˋstɪndʒɪ] *a.* 小器的

31 kindergarten [ˋkɪndəˌgartn̩] *n.* 幼兒園

似 (1) nursery [ˋnɝsərɪ]
n. 托兒所，托嬰中心 ④
(2) a day care center　日間托兒所

▶ We sent our child to kindergarten last September.
我們去年九月把小孩送到幼兒園就讀。

32 oral [ˋɔrəl] *a.* 口語的

(似) **spoken** [ˋspokən] *a.* 口語的

(延伸) (1) an oral test　　口試
(2) a written test　　筆試

▶ Our language teacher gave us an oral test instead of a written one.
我們語言老師考我們口試而非筆試。

33 oven [ˋʌvən] *n.* 烤箱

(似) **microwave** [ˋmaɪkro͵wev]
n. 微波爐 & *vt.* 微波
（= microwave oven）③

▶ I used an oven to bake the cakes.
我用烤箱烤蛋糕。

stove [stov] *n.* 爐子

▶ The kettle is boiling on the gas stove.
瓦斯爐上的水壺燒開了。

34 shrimp [ʃrɪmp] *n.* 蝦子

(複) shrimp 或 shrimps 皆可

(延伸) (1) prawn [prɔn] *n.* 明蝦
(2) lobster [ˋlɑbstɚ] *n.* 龍蝦 ④

▶ The fishermen cast a net and caught a lot of shrimp.
漁夫撒網捕了很多蝦子。

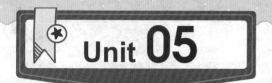

 0501-0509

1 previous [ˈprivɪəs] *a.* 先前的

似 (1) early [ˈɝlɪ] *a.* 早先的 & *adv.* 早先
(2) former [ˈfɔrmɚ]
  a. 從前的，以前的 ②

反 subsequent [ˈsʌbsɪˌkwɛnt]
 a. 隨後的 ⑤

▶ Do you have any previous experience in this job?
你之前有沒有這種工作經驗？

2 background [ˈbækˌɡraʊnd] *n.* 背景

片 (1) a family background　家庭背景
(2) background information
  背景知識

▶ Because of his background, John got the job very easily.
由於他的背景，約翰輕易就得到了那份工作。

3 aside [əˈsaɪd] *adv.* 一旁地

片 (1) step aside　　　站在一旁
(2) put sth aside　將某物擱置一旁

▶ Please step aside. You're blocking my view.
請站到旁邊。你擋住我的視線了。

▶ Peter and Mary put their differences aside and made up with each other.
彼得和瑪莉放下歧見，言歸於好。

apart [əˈpɑrt] *adv.* 分開

片 (1) apart from...　除了……
 = aside from...
 = except for...
(2) tell... apart　分辨出……的不同

▶ Kathy and her husband decided to live apart for a while.
凱西和她老公決定分居一段時間。

▶ John occasionally goes hiking. Apart from that, he hardly has any hobbies.
約翰偶爾會健行。除此之外，他幾乎沒有什麼嗜好。

▶ It is quite hard to tell these ducklings apart.
要分辨出這些小鴨間的差異相當不容易。

4 decade [ˈdɛked] *n.* 10 年

延伸 score [skɔr] *n.* 20 個 (左右) ②
six decades ago　60 年前
= three score years ago
= sixty years ago

▶ The company has been in business for three decades.
這間公司已經營運 30 年了。

5 spill [spɪl] *vt.* 灑出；洩密 & *n.* 灑出物

spill, spilled / spilt [spɪlt], spilled / spilt

▶ I got mad when the careless waiter spilled coffee on my shirt.
粗心的服務生把咖啡灑在我襯衫上時，我便發火了。

▶ Tell me exactly who spilled the secret.
告訴我到底是誰洩露了這個祕密。

▶ I need some tissue paper to dry the coffee spill.
我需要一些衛生紙把濺灑出來的咖啡漬擦乾。

6 fashionable [ˋfæʃənəbl̩] *a.* 流行的；時髦的

延伸 **old-fashioned** [ˌoldˋfæʃənd]
a. 舊式的；過時的

▶ Don't concern yourself merely with what's fashionable.
不要只關心現在流行什麼。

▶ Though old, the woman likes to wear fashionable dresses.
這名婦人雖有年紀，卻喜歡穿著時髦的洋裝。

7 relief [rɪˋlif] *n.* (痛苦等) 解除，減輕；救濟，救濟物資 (集合名詞，不可數)

片 (1) a relief organization　救濟組織
(2) relief materials　救濟物資
(3) a lot of relief　許多救濟物資
= a lot of relief materials

▶ Doctors work for the relief of their patients' suffering.
醫生們致力解除病人們的痛苦。

▶ A lot of relief is being sent to the disaster area.
許多救濟物資正被送往災區。

8 solid [ˋsalɪd] *a.* 固體的；堅固的 & *n.* 固體

衍 (1) consolidate [kənˋsalə͵det]
vt. 鞏固；統一 & *vi.* 合併
(2) solidarity [͵saləˋdærətɪ] *n.* 團結 ⑥
似 (1) gas [gæs] *n.* 氣體；瓦斯，汽油
(gasoline 的縮寫) ③
(2) liquid [ˋlɪkwɪd]
a. 液體 / 態的 & *n.* 液體 ②

▶ The water froze into a solid block of ice.
水凝結成一團冰塊。

▶ The desk is made of solid wood.
這張桌子是用堅固的木頭製成的。

▶ Wood is a solid while water is a liquid.
木頭是固體，水則是液體。

9 democratic [͵dɛməˋkrætɪk] *a.* 民主的；〔美〕民主黨的 (大寫)

衍 **democrat** [ˋdɛmə͵kræt]
n. 民主主義者：(美) 民主黨員 (大寫) ⑤
延伸 the Democratic Party　〔美〕民主黨
the Republican Party　〔美〕共和黨

▶ The president was elected through a democratic process.
該總統是經由民主程序選出來的。

▶ The Democratic and Republican Parties are the two major political parties in the US.
民主黨與共和黨是美國的兩個主要政黨。

democracy [dɪˋmakrəsɪ]
n. 民主 (不可數)；民主國家 (可數)

反 **tyranny** [ˋtaɪrənɪ]
n. 專制政府，暴政

▶ That country has moved steadily toward true democracy.
該國已穩定地邁向真正的民主。

▶ Freedom of speech is guaranteed in Western democracies.
在西方的民主國家中，言論自由是有保障的。

10 neighborhood [ˈnebɚˌhʊd] *n.* 鄰近地區

片 in sb's neighborhood
在某人住處附近
= near where sb lives

衍 (1) neighbor [ˈnebɚ] *n.* 鄰居 ②
(2) neighboring [ˈnebərɪŋ] *a.* 鄰近的

似 area [ˈɛrɪə] *n.* 地區 ①

▶ There is a big department store in my neighborhood.
我家附近有一家大型百貨公司。

11 tricky [ˈtrɪkɪ] *a.* 狡猾的；微妙的，難以處理的

衍 trick [trɪk]
vt. 欺騙 & *n.* 惡作劇；竅門；把戲 ②

似 (1) cunning [ˈkʌnɪŋ] *a.* 狡猾的 ④
(2) sly [slaɪ] *a.* 狡猾的 ⑥
(3) crafty [ˈkræftɪ] *a.* 狡猾的

▶ No one likes to deal with a tricky person.
誰都不喜歡與狡猾的人打交道。

▶ The teacher put me on the spot by asking me a few tricky questions.
老師問了我一些難以回答的問題讓我很難堪。
＊put sb on the spot 讓某人出糗／下不了臺

12 significant [sɪgˈnɪfəkənt] *a.* 重要的；顯著的

衍 (1) signify [ˈsɪgnəˌfaɪ] *vt.* 表示；預示
(2) significance [sɪgˈnɪfəkəns]
n. 意義；重要性 ④

反 insignificant [ˌɪnsɪgˈnɪfəkənt]
a. 不重要的

▶ Hard work plays a significant role in achieving success.
努力在獲致成功方面扮演了重要的角色。

▶ There is a significant difference in personality between the twin sisters.
這對雙胞胎姐妹的個性有明顯的不同。

13 scientist [ˈsaɪəntɪst] *n.* 科學家

衍 science [ˈsaɪəns] *n.* 科學 ①

▶ The boy wants to be a scientist when he grows up.
這名小男孩長大後要當科學家。

scientific [ˌsaɪənˈtɪfɪk]
a. 科學的；合乎科學的

衍 (1) science [ˈsaɪəns]
n. 科學；一門學問 ①
(2) scientist [ˈsaɪəntɪst] *n.* 科學家 ③

▶ Ben compiled a lot of scientific data.
班彙編了大量的科學資料。

▶ Hank's approach to the matter was not very scientific.
漢克對這個問題所採取的方法不太合乎科學。

14 wage [wedʒ] *n.* 工資 (尤指時薪) & *vt.* 發動 (活動、戰爭等)

片 wage war on... 向……宣戰

▶ The workers went on strike in protest against low wages.
工人發動罷工抗議工資低廉。

► The government vowed to wage war on drug trafficking.
政府誓言向販毒宣戰。

salary [ˈsælərɪ] *n.* (按月發放的) 薪水
似 pay [pe] *n.* 薪資 ①

► How can you live on such a small salary?
這麼微薄的薪水你如何賴以為生？

15　resource [rɪˈsɔrs / ˈrisɔrs] *n.* 資源 (常用複數)

片 natural resources　天然資源
衍 source [sɔrs] *n.* 來源 ②

► We must use natural resources wisely—many of them cannot be replenished.
我們必須善用天然資源 —— 它們有很多是無法再補足的。
＊replenish [rɪˈplɛnɪʃ] *vt.* 補充

16　motor [ˈmotɚ] *n.* 馬達

衍 motorcycle [ˈmotɚˌsaɪkl̩]
　n. 摩托車 ②

► The machine is powered by two electric motors.
這臺機器是由兩個電動馬達提供電力的。

17　engage [ɪnˈgedʒ] *vi.* 從事，忙於 (與介詞 in 並用)

衍 engaged [ɪnˈgedʒd] *a.* 已訂婚的
片 (1) be engaged to sb　與某人訂婚
　(2) engage in + N/V-ing　從事某事

► The two sides engaged in peace talks.
雙方從事和平談判。
► My eldest son is engaged to his classmate from college.
我大兒子和他大學同班同學訂婚了。

engagement [ɪnˈgedʒmənt]
n. 訂婚；(尤指公務上的) 預約，約會
似 appointment [əˈpɔɪntmənt]
　n. (公務或正式的) 約會 ④

► The couple announced their engagement at the dinner party.
這對情人在這場晚宴上宣布他們已訂婚。
► Ted has an engagement for dinner with his boss tonight.
泰德今晚和他的上司有約吃晚飯。

18　capable [ˈkepəbl̩] *a.* 有能力的；做得出……的 (與介詞 of 並用)

片 be capable of + N/V-ing
　= be able to + V
　有能力……的；可以……的
衍 capability [ˌkepəˈbɪlətɪ] *n.* 能力 ⑤
似 capacity [kəˈpæsətɪ] *n.* 容量 ④
反 incapable [ɪnˈkepəbl̩] *a.* 無能的

► The firm was not capable of handling such a large order.
= The firm was unable to handle such a large order.
那家公司沒有能力處理如此龐大的訂單。
► Ben is capable of any act when he's angry.
班生氣時什麼事都做得出來。

0518-0524

enable [ɪnˈebl̩] *vt.* 使能夠

🔑 enable sb to + V　使某人能夠……

衍 (1) able [ˈebl̩] *a.* 能夠的 ①
　(2) unable [ʌnˈebl̩]
　　 a. 無法勝任的；不會的
　(3) ability [əˈbɪlətɪ] *n.* 能力 ①
　(4) inability [ˌɪnəˈbɪlətɪ]
　　 n. 無力；不能

▶ Knowledge enables one to solve one's own problems.
知識**使人有能力**自行解決難題。

19　portion [ˈpɔrʃən] *n.* 部分 & *vt.* 分配

🔑 (1) a large portion of...
　　大部分的……
　(2) a small portion of...
　　少部分的……
　(3) portion sth out
　　分配某物 (通常使用被動)

▶ A large portion of the money will go to charity.
這筆錢**大部分**要捐給慈善機構。

▶ The cake had to be portioned out among the large number of guests at the party.
這個蛋糕需要**分配**給派對上的眾多賓客。

20　passage [ˈpæsɪdʒ] *n.* 通道；一段 (文字)；(時間) 消逝

▶ There was a dark passage leading to a secret room.
有一條黑暗的**通道**通往一間密室。

▶ This is my favorite passage in the book.
這是本書中我最喜歡的**一段**。

▶ With the passage of time, the little girl has grown into a beautiful lady.
隨著時間的**消逝**，這個小女孩已長大，變成漂亮的小姐了。

21　honor [ˈɑnɚ] *n.* 名譽，榮譽 & *vt.* 尊重；給予榮譽；實踐

🔑 (1) on one's honor
　　以某人的人格名譽
　(2) Your Honor
　　閣下 (對法官、市長等的尊稱語)
　(3) honor one's promise　實踐承諾
　　= fulfill one's promise
衍 (1) honorary [ˈɑnəˌrɛrɪ]
　　 a. (稱號等) 名譽上的 ⑥
　(2) honorable [ˈɑnərəbl̩] *a.* 可敬的 ⑤
似 (1) respect [rɪˈspɛkt] *n.* & *vt.* 敬重 ②
　(2) prestige [prɛsˈtiʒ] *n.* 聲望 ⑥

▶ Thomas Edison won honor for inventing the light bulb.
湯瑪士・愛迪生因發明電燈泡而贏得**殊榮**。

▶ We should all honor justice.
我們大家都應**尊重**司法。

▶ I feel honored to have the opportunity to deliver this speech to you.
有此機會對諸位演講，本人深感**榮幸**。

▶ I honored my promise by buying my girlfriend a ring.
我**實踐**了我的諾言，買了戒指給我女友。

▶ I promise you on my honor—I won't let you down.
我以我的人格向你保證 —— 我不會讓你失望的。

▶ "Yes, Your Honor," I replied to the judge.
我回答法官說:『是的,法官閣下。』

glory [ˋglɔrɪ] *n.* 光榮,榮耀
衍 (1) glorify [ˋglɔrɪ͵faɪ] *vt.* 光耀
(2) glorious [ˋglɔrɪəs] *a.* 光榮的 ④

▶ The castle reminds us of the past glory of the kingdom.
這座城堡使我們想起該王國往日的榮耀。

22　appeal [əˋpil] *vi. & n.* 吸引;請求;上訴 (均與介詞 to 並用)

用 (1) appeal to sb　吸引某人
(2) appeal to sb for sth
　　懇請某人給與某物
(3) appeal to sb to + V
　　請求某人……
= beg sb to + V
衍 appealing [əˋpilɪŋ] *a.* 動人的
似 (1) attract [əˋtrækt] *vt.* 吸引 ③
(2) request [rɪˋkwɛst] *n. & vt.* 請求 ③

▶ I'm sure this program will appeal to children of all ages.
我相信這個節目一定可以吸引各年齡層的小朋友。

▶ The police are appealing to the public for any information about the robbery.
警方懇請大眾提供與搶案相關的任何訊息。

▶ Not satisfied with the judge's decision, Gary is planning to appeal to a higher court.
蓋瑞對法官的判決不滿,計劃要上訴到高等法院。

▶ The new variety show has a wide appeal.
這個新的綜藝節目非常吸引人。

▶ I sent an appeal to the board, asking for extra funding.
我向董事會提出請求,希望可以得到額外補助金。

▶ The victim's family made a public appeal for help to catch the murderer.
受難者家屬公開訴求希望協助逮捕殺人兇手。

23　steep [stip] *a.* 陡峭的;急劇升降的

▶ The hill was so steep that it took us almost two hours to reach the top.
這座山丘真陡,我們花了將近兩個小時才爬到山頭。

▶ The steep rise in living costs makes life tougher.
生活費用的急劇上升讓日子更不好過了。

24　desert [dɪˋzɝt] *vt.* 拋棄 & [ˋdɛzɚt] *n.* 沙漠

似 (1) abandon [əˋbændən] *vt.* 丟棄 ④
(2) dessert [dɪˋzɝt]
　　n. 餐後甜點 (不可數) ③
▶ What would you like for dessert?
你想要什麼甜點?

▶ People who desert their pets on the street are really heartless.
把寵物丟棄在街上的人真的很無情。

▶ The camel is called the ship of the desert.
駱駝被稱為沙漠之舟。

25 detect [dɪˋtɛkt] vt. 發現，查出

衍 (1) detective [dɪˋtɛktɪv]
　　　n. 偵探；刑警 ④
　 (2) detection [dɪˋtɛkʃən] n. 偵查
　 (3) detector [dɪˋtɛktɚ] n. 探測器

▶ This dog detected drugs in the man's baggage.
這隻狗在該男子的行李中發現毒品。

26 ambulance [ˋæmbjələns] n. 救護車

片 call an ambulance　叫救護車

▶ Wait here. I'll go and call an ambulance.
你在此等候。我去打電話叫救護車。

27 confirm [kənˋfɝm] vt. 確認；證實

衍 confirmation [͵kɑnfɚˋmeʃən]
　 n. 證實；認可
似 verify [ˋvɛrə͵faɪ] vt. 確認
反 deny [dɪˋnaɪ] vt. 否認 ②

▶ I would like to confirm my dinner reservation.
我想要確認晚餐的訂位資料。

▶ The police confirmed that the man was murdered.
警方證實這名男子是被謀殺的。

28 loser [ˋluzɚ] n. 失敗者

衍 lose [luz] vt. 失敗；失去 ①
反 winner [ˋwɪnɚ] n. 勝者；得獎者

▶ Losers always find excuses for their failure.
失敗者永遠會為自己的失敗找藉口。

29 handkerchief [ˋhæŋkɚ͵tʃɪf] n. 手帕

複 handkerchiefs [ˋhæŋkɚ͵tʃɪfs]

▶ The old man blew his nose on a handkerchief.
老先生用手帕擤鼻涕。

napkin [ˋnæpkɪn] n. 餐巾
似 towel [ˋtauəl] n. 毛巾 ①

▶ I need a napkin to wipe my mouth.
我需要一條餐巾來擦嘴。

30 frank [fræŋk] a. 坦白的

片 To be frank, ...　坦白說
= Frankly speaking, ...
似 honest [ˋɑnɪst] a. 誠實的 ①

▶ To be frank, I don't trust you.
= Frankly speaking, I don't trust you.
坦白說，我不信任你。

31 elevator [ˋɛlə͵vetɚ] n. 電梯 (= lift〔英〕)

片 take an elevator　搭電梯
似 escalator [ˋɛskə͵letɚ] n. 電扶梯 ⑤

▶ We took the elevator to the tenth floor.
我們搭電梯到 10 樓。

32　shorten [ˈʃɔrtn̩] *vt.* 使變短；縮短

反 lengthen [ˈlɛŋθən]
vt. 使變長，加長 ④

▶ I asked the tailor to shorten the sleeves of my shirt.
我要裁縫師將我襯衫的袖子改短。

▶ The lengthy original was shortened to two short paragraphs.
冗長的原文被縮短為兩小段。

33　talkative [ˈtɔkətɪv] *a.* 多話的

衍 talk [tɔk] *vi.* 談話 ①

▶ Sara isn't very talkative, is she?
莎拉不多話，是不是？

34　lover [ˈlʌvɚ] *n.* 情人，愛人 (= sweetheart)

片 a secret / underground lover
地下情人

▶ Ben and Naomi were friends for years before they became lovers.
班跟奈歐蜜成為情侶前當了好幾年朋友。

35　apologize [əˈpɑləˌdʒaɪz] *vi.* 道歉，賠罪

片 apologize to sb for sth
因某事向某人道歉

似 sorry [ˈsɔrɪ] *a.* 抱歉的，難過的 ①

▶ I must apologize to you for not answering your letter immediately.
= I'm sorry for not answering your letter immediately.
我必須為未立即回信給你而向你道歉。

36　clothe [kloð] *vt.* 使穿上衣服 (通常用於被動語態) (= dress)

片 (1) clothe sb in sth　使某人穿上某物
(2) be clothed in sth　穿上某物

▶ Since it was very cold outside, Teresa clothed / dressed her children in warm clothing before they went out.
因為外邊天氣冷，泰瑞莎讓小孩穿上保暖的衣物後才出門。

▶ Make sure Johnny is properly clothed, or he'll catch a cold.
務必幫強尼穿夠衣服，否則他會感冒的。

closet [ˈklɑzɪt] *n.* 衣櫥
似 (1) wardrobe [ˈwɔrdˌrob] *n.* 衣櫥 ⑥
(2) cupboard [ˈkʌbɚd]
　n. 櫥櫃；壁櫥 ③

▶ Most of the clothes in my closet are black.
我衣櫥裡大部分的衣服是黑色的。

Unit 06

0601-0607

---

1 **murder** [ˈmɝdɚ] *vt.* 謀殺 & *n.* 謀殺 (案)

片 (1) commit murder　犯謀殺罪
　(2) commit attempted murder
　　　犯意圖謀殺 / 謀殺未遂罪
　(3) get away with murder
　　　做錯事而不被懲處

衍 murderer [ˈmɝdərɚ] *n.* 兇手 ④

▶ The man committed murder and was sentenced to thirty years in prison.
這個男子犯了殺人罪，被判 30 年有期徒刑。

▶ Two suspects were arrested soon after that girl was murdered.
那個女孩遭到殺害沒多久，就有兩名嫌犯就被逮捕了。
＊suspect [ˈsʌspɛkt] *n.* 嫌犯

▶ Although all of the evidence was against him, Frank still got away with murder.
雖然所有證據都對犯下謀殺案的法蘭克不利，但他仍逍遙法外。

---

2 **roast** [rost] *vt.* & *vi.* 烤 (肉) & *a.* 烘烤的 (= roasted) & *n.* (大塊的) 烤肉

▶ Mom roasted some lamb chops for dinner.
媽媽烤了一些羊排當晚餐。

▶ One famous dish from Germany is roast / roasted pork knuckle.
烤豬腳是一道有名的德國菜。
＊knuckle [ˈnʌkḷ] *n.* (豬) 蹄；(人) 指關節

▶ Peter ate the entire roast by himself.
彼得一個人吃了一整塊烤肉。

---

3 **reasonable** [ˈriznəbḷ] *a.* 合理的；講理的

衍 reason [ˈrizṇ] *n.* 理由 & *vt.* 推斷 ①
反 unreasonable [ʌnˈriznəbḷ]
　a. 不合理的

▶ I bought this piece of furniture at a reasonable price.
我以合理的價格買了這件傢俱。

▶ I don't think Susan's being reasonable about this.
我認為蘇珊對這件事不講道理。

---

4 **missing** [ˈmɪsɪŋ] *a.* 失蹤的；缺的

衍 miss [mɪs] *vt.* 想念；錯過，沒趕上 ①
似 lost [lɔst] *a.* 遺失的

▶ The hiker was reported missing three days ago and was found this morning.
這名健行者於 3 天前據報失蹤，在今晨被尋獲。

▶ Several pages of the first chapter were missing.
第一章缺了好幾頁。

5　benefit [ˈbɛnəfɪt] n. 利益 & vt. 有益於 & vi. 獲益 (與介詞 from 並用)

片 benefit from...　從……中獲益
衍 beneficial [ˌbɛnəˈfɪʃəl]
　　a. 有益的，有用的 ⑤

▶ My trip to the US was a benefit of my job.
我的美國之旅是工作上的一項福利。

▶ The doctor said a long rest would benefit the patient.
醫生說長時間休息將會有益於該病患。

▶ Everyone will benefit from the new road.
那條新路會造福每個人。

profit [ˈprɑfɪt]
n. 利潤 & vt. 對……有利 & vi. 獲利

片 (1) make a profit　獲利
　　(2) profit from...　從……中獲利
衍 (1) profitable [ˈprɑfɪtəbl̩]
　　a. 有利的 ④
　　(2) nonprofit [ˌnɑnˈprɑfɪt]
　　a. 不是以賺錢為目標的 ⑤

▶ Tom made a handsome profit from the sale.
湯姆從這次買賣中得到可觀的利潤。

▶ It will not profit you at all to do such a thing.
做這樣的事將對你毫無益處。

▶ A wise person profits from his mistakes.
聰明的人會從錯誤中獲益。── 諺語

6　muscle [ˈmʌsl̩] n. 肌肉 (可數)

衍 muscular [ˈmʌskjələ] a. 肌肉的 ⑤

▶ To tone up your muscles, you should exercise on a regular basis.
為了鍛鍊你的肌肉，你應該規律地運動。
*tone up a muscle　強化肌肉

flesh [flɛʃ] n. (人或動物的) 肉
比 meat [mit]
　　n. (可供食用的動物的) 肉 ①

▶ Eating human flesh is considered barbarous.
吃人肉被認為很野蠻。

7　dust [dʌst] n. 灰塵 & vt. 除去……的灰塵

衍 (1) dusty [ˈdʌstɪ] a. 滿是灰塵的 ④
　　(2) duster [ˈdʌstə] n. 撢子

▶ There is so much dust on the table.
桌上有很多灰塵。

▶ I used a feather duster to dust the table.
我用雞毛撢子把桌上的灰塵撢掉。

dirt [dɝt] n. 泥土；髒東西；灰塵
比 dirty [ˈdɝtɪ]
　　a. 髒的；卑鄙的，差勁的 & vt. 弄髒 ①

▶ I'm afraid your sneakers need to be washed because they're covered with dirt.
你的球鞋都是泥巴，恐怕得洗了。
*sneaker [ˈsnikə] n. 運動鞋；球鞋
　a pair of sneakers　一雙球鞋

8 automobile [ˈɔtəməˌbil] *n.* 汽車 (= auto)

> I can't afford a brand-new automobile, so I'm going to buy a used one.
> 我買不起全新的汽車,因此我打算要買一臺中古的。

vehicle [ˈviɪkl̩]
n. 車輛;任何有輪子的運載工具

> The number of motor vehicles on the roads rose by 30% last year.
> 去年道路車輛的數量成長了 30%。

9 headquarters [ˈhɛdˌkwɔrtɚz] *n.* 總部 (單複數同形;縮寫為 HQ)

反 **branch** [bræntʃ]
　 n. 分部;樹枝 & *vt.* 分岔;長出新枝 ②

> Gangsters surrounded the police headquarters last night.
> 幫派分子昨晚包圍警備總部。

10 vision [ˈvɪʒən] *n.* 視力;影 / 幻像;眼光,先見,遠見

片 a person of vision　有遠見的人

衍 (1) **visual** [ˈvɪʒuəl] *a.* 視力的 ④
　 (2) **envision** [ɪnˈvɪʒən] *vt.* 想像 ⑤
　 (3) **provision** [prəˈvɪʒən]
　　 n. 準備,供應 (不可數);乾糧 (恆用複數) ⑤
　 (4) **supervision** [ˌsupɚˈvɪʒən]
　　 n. 監督,管理 ⑤

> I wear glasses to improve my vision.
> 我戴眼鏡以改善我的視力。
> It is said that the children saw a vision of an angel here.
> 據說這些孩子在這裡看到天使的影像。
> The mayor had a vision of changing this area into a lovely park.
> 這位市長很有眼光要把這個地區改建成一座美麗的公園。
> A great leader must be a person of vision.
> 偉大的領袖必須是個有遠見的人。

visible [ˈvɪzəbl̩]
a. 肉眼可見的;顯而易見的

反 **invisible** [ɪnˈvɪzəbl̩] *a.* 無形的

> The building was visible through the trees.
> 從這片樹林望出去可看見那棟建築物。
> There's been a visible change in Hank since he started exercising.
> 自從開始運動後,漢克有了明顯的改變。

11 exchange [ɪksˈtʃendʒ] *vt.* & *n.* 交換

片 (1) exchange sth with sb
　　 和某人交換某物
　 (2) exchange A for B　以 A 交換 B
　 (3) in exchange for...　交換……

衍 (1) **change** [tʃendʒ]
　　 vt. & *n.* 變換;改變 ①
　 (2) **exchangeable** [ɪksˈtʃendʒəbl̩]
　　 a. 可替換的

> I love to exchange stamps with my friends.
> 我喜歡和朋友交換郵票。
> Peter exchanged his toy car for a toy gun.
> 彼得用玩具車換了一把玩具槍。
> I gave Allen a pen in exchange for his watch.
> 我用一支筆和艾倫換一只手錶。

12　practical [ˈpræktɪkl̩] a. 實際的

衍 practice [ˈpræktɪs]
　n. 練習；常規，習俗；實踐 & vt. 練習 ①

反 impractical [ɪmˈpræktɪkl̩]
　a. 不切實際的

▶ This job calls for at least five years of practical experience.
這份工作需要至少 5 年的實際經驗。

▶ Tom is a practical person and never does things beyond his ability.
湯姆是很務實的人，超過自己能力的事他從不會去做。

---

practically [ˈpræktɪkl̩ɪ] adv. 實際地

片 Practically speaking, ...
　說得實際一點，……
　＊practically 亦等於 almost（幾乎），
　修飾 all、every、any、no 等 4 個字。

▶ Ken comes here almost every single day.
肯幾乎每一天都會來這裡。

▶ Practically speaking, Jason isn't cut out for the job.
講得實際一點，這份工作傑森不能勝任。
＊be not cut out for sth　生來就不適合某事物

13　mend [mɛnd] vt. 修理，修補；改正

似 (1) repair [rɪˈpɛr] vt. 修理 ②
　(2) fix [fɪks] vt. 修理 ②

▶ The thrifty man mends his own clothes, including torn socks.
這個節儉的男子會修補自己的衣服，包括穿破的襪子。

▶ Least said, soonest mended.
少說為妙，越描越黑。── 諺語

14　constant [ˈkɑnstənt] a. 持續的；穩定的 & n. 恆久不變的數量（常數）；不變的事物

衍 constancy [ˈkɑnstənsɪ]
　n. 恆久不變；忠貞不渝

▶ The constant noise of the machine is driving me crazy.
機器不斷發出的噪音快把我逼瘋了。

▶ The weather has been constant this week.
這星期的天氣很穩定。

▶ The temperature in the fish tank remains a constant.
水族箱裡的溫度維持恆溫。

▶ No matter what life threw at them, their love for each other remained a constant.
不論遇到什麼困難，他們仍對彼此堅貞不移。

15　dramatic [drəˈmætɪk] a. 戲劇的；戲劇性的；強烈的

衍 drama [ˈdrɑmə] n. 戲劇 ②
似 drastic [ˈdræstɪk] a. 激烈的 ⑥

▶ Would you like to read the dramatic piece I wrote recently?
你想看我最近寫的這個劇本嗎？

▶ Peter made an impassioned and dramatic speech.
彼得用慷慨激昂且戲劇性的口吻發表了一段話。
＊impassioned [ɪmˋpæʃənd] *a.* 慷慨激昂的

▶ Dramatic changes have swept Taiwan in the last twenty years.
臺灣在過去 20 年來經歷了強烈的改變。

16 warn [wɔrn] *vt.* 警告；告誡

片 (1) warn sb not to + V
　　警告某人不要……
　= warn sb against + N/V-ing
　(2) warn sb of / about...
　　就……方面警告某人

▶ Our teacher warned us not to cheat on the test.
= Our teacher warned us against cheating on the test.
老師警告我們考試不可作弊。

warning [ˋwɔrnɪŋ] *n.* 警告

▶ Thank you for your timely warning.
謝謝你適時的警告。

17 definition [ˌdɛfəˋnɪʃən] *n.* 定義；(錄音、電視等的) 清晰度

衍 (1) define [dɪˋfaɪn]
　　vt. 下定義；解釋 ①
　(2) definite [ˋdɛfənɪt]
　　a. 明確的，肯定的 ④
　(3) definitive [dɪˋfɪnətɪv]
　　a. 明確的；最終的 ⑥

延伸 HDTV　高解析度 / 高畫質 / 高清電視
　＊HDTV 是 high definition television
　的縮寫。

▶ There are several definitions listed under the word.
這個字底下列有好幾個定義。

▶ I want a TV with better definition.
我要一臺解析度較高的電視機。

18 afford [əˋfɔrd] *vt.* 買得起；負擔得起

衍 affordable [əˋfɔrdəbl]
　a. 負擔得起的

用法 afford 通常與 can 或 cannot 並用，
形成下列片語：
　(1) can afford to + V
　　有能力從事……
　(2) can afford sth
　　買得起某物 / 有能力負擔某事物

▶ Being poor, I can't afford to take a trip to Thailand.
因為很窮，所以到泰國旅遊我玩不起。

▶ I can't imagine how such a poor man could afford such an expensive car.
我無法想像那樣窮的人竟買得起那麼貴的車。

19 missile [ˈmɪsḷ] *n.* 飛彈

▶ They will launch the missile as scheduled.
他們會按既定時間發射飛彈。
＊launch [lɔntʃ] *vt.* 發射

rocket [ˈrɑkɪt] *n.* 火箭

▶ The scientists launched a rocket with a communications satellite on it.
這群科學家發射了一枚火箭，上面搭載了一顆通訊衛星。

20 credit [ˈkrɛdɪt] *n.* 信譽 (不可數)；學分 (可數) & *vt.* 將功勞歸因於……(常用被動)

片 (1) on credit　賒帳，信用貸款
(2) a credit card　信用卡
(3) sb is credited with sth
= sth is credited to sb
某事要歸因於某人的功勞

衍 (1) credible [ˈkrɛdəbḷ] *a.* 可信的 ⑥
(2) credibility [ˌkrɛdəˈbɪlətɪ]
n. 可信度，信任 (不可數) ⑤

▶ Buying on credit is getting popular in Taiwan.
在臺灣有越來越多的人使用信用卡購物。

▶ How many credits are you planning to take this semester?
你這學期打算修幾學分？

▶ Mr. Wang is credited with the success of this project.
= The success of this project is credited to Mr. Wang.
這項計畫的成功是王先生的功勞。

21 educate [ˈɛdʒə͵ket] *vt.* 教育，栽培

衍 (1) educator [ˈɛdʒə͵ketɚ]
n. 教育學家
(2) education [͵ɛdʒəˈkeʃən] *n.* 教育 ②

▶ Peter was born in Taiwan but educated in the United States.
彼得在臺灣出生但在美國受教育。

educational [͵ɛdʒəˈkeʃnḷ]
a. 教育的；教育性的

▶ The educational / education system in the US is somewhat different from that in Taiwan.
美國的教育制度和臺灣的有些不同。

▶ The family all watched an educational show on TV.
這家人一同觀賞一個教育性的節目。

22 preparation [͵prɛpəˈreʃən] *n.* 準備，預備

片 (1) in preparation for...　以準備……
(2) make preparations for...
為……做準備

衍 prepare [prɪˈpɛr]
vt. & *vi.* 準備，預備 ①

▶ Education should be a preparation for life after graduation.
教育應是為畢業後的人生做準備。

▶ Many students are studying in the library in preparation for the upcoming finals.
許多學生正在圖書館念書以準備即將來臨的期末考。

▶ They're making preparations for the prince's birthday party.
他們正在為王子生日派對的事宜做準備。

23 airline [ˈɛrˌlaɪn] n. 航空公司

衍 airliner [ˈɛrˌlaɪnɚ] n. 大型客機

▶ Lufthansa is one of the most popular airlines in Europe.
德航是歐洲最有名的航空公司之一。

▶ A: Which airline are you flying with tomorrow?
= Who are you flying with tomorrow?
B: China Airlines.
A：你明天搭哪家航空公司的飛機？
B：華航。

24 anyhow [ˈɛnɪˌhaʊ] adv. 無論如何

似 anyway [ˈɛnɪˌwe] adv. 無論如何 ②

▶ We did our best, but the other team won anyhow.
我們全力以赴，但無論如何另一隊還是贏了。

25 dinosaur [ˈdaɪnəˌsɔr] n. 恐龍；古板的人

▶ Dinosaurs ruled the earth millions of years ago.
恐龍幾百萬年前曾主宰地球。

▶ Johnny is a dinosaur! He doesn't even know how to take the MRT.
強尼真是老古板！他甚至不會搭捷運。

26 puppet [ˈpʌpɪt] n. 玩偶，木偶；傀儡

似 doll [dɑl] n. 玩偶，洋娃娃 ①

▶ The students made puppets out of socks in art class.
學生在美術課用襪子做玩偶。

27 squirrel [ˈskwɝəl] n. 松鼠

▶ City squirrels eat a variety of foods, including nuts, snacks, and insects.
城市的松鼠吃很多食物，包括核果、餅乾和昆蟲。

koala [koˈɑlə] n. 無尾熊
(= koala bear)

▶ Children love koalas because they think these little animals are cute.
小孩喜歡無尾熊，因為他們認為這些小動物很可愛。

donkey [ˈdɑŋkɪ] n. 驢子

用法 donkey 及 ass 均指驢子。但俚語中，ass 亦表『笨蛋』或『屁股』之意，是粗俗的字眼，宜避免使用。

▶ Typically, donkeys are used as work animals.
驢子是很典型的勞役動物。

ox [ɑks] *n.* (去勢的) 公牛
複 oxen [ˋɑksən]
似 bull [bʊl] *n.* 公牛 ③

▶ My sister was born in the Year of the Ox.
我妹妹是牛年出生的。

leopard [ˋlɛpɚd] *n.* 豹
延伸 (1) cheetah [ˋtʃitə] *n.* 獵豹
(2) jaguar [ˋdʒægwɑr] *n.* 美洲豹

▶ Leopards are very good at climbing trees, but they rarely do so.
豹很擅長爬樹，但是牠們不常這麼做。

dolphin [ˋdɑlfɪn] *n.* 海豚
延伸 porpoise [ˋpɔrpəs]
n. 鼠海豚 (體型比 dolphin 小)

▶ Dolphins have a very complicated communication system.
海豚有一套複雜的溝通系統。

penguin [ˋpɛngwɪn] *n.* 企鵝

▶ Penguins are birds; however, they don't fly but they can swim like fish.
企鵝是鳥類；然而牠們不會飛但卻能像魚一樣游泳。

owl [aʊl] *n.* 貓頭鷹

▶ Owls have large eyes and hunt at night.
貓頭鷹有一雙大眼，在夜間獵食。

parrot [ˋpærət]
n. 鸚鵡 & *vt.* 機械式地模仿
延伸 (1) eagle [ˋigl] *n.* 鷹 ②
(2) swallow [ˋswɑlo] *n.* 燕子 ②

▶ The parrot likes to imitate my words.
這隻鸚鵡喜歡學我講話。
▶ I have no idea why this little kid keeps parroting me.
我實在搞不懂這小子為何一直在模仿我的一舉一動。

pigeon [ˋpɪdʒən]
n. 灰鴿，鴿子 (比 dove 大)

▶ Can you tell the difference between a pigeon and a dove?
你能分辨灰鴿與白鴿的不同嗎？

---

1 **trend** [trɛnd] *n.* 趨勢；潮流

片 (1) keep up with the trends
　　趕上潮流
　(2) follow the trends　跟著潮流走

衍 trendy [ˈtrɛndɪ] *a.* 時髦的

▶ Business leaders have to keep track of the latest economic trends.
企業領袖必須隨時掌握最新的經濟趨勢。

▶ Reading newspapers and watching TV enable you to keep up with the trends.
看報及看電視可以讓你趕上潮流。

---

tide [taɪd] *n.* 潮汐，潮流 &
vt. 幫助 (某人) 渡過 (難關)

片 tide sb over　幫某人度過難關

▶ Time and tide wait for no man.
歲月不饒人。── 諺語

▶ I wonder if you could lend me $200 to tide me over until payday.
我想知道你是否可借我 200 美元，讓我撐到發薪水的那一天。

---

2 **attract** [əˈtrækt] *vt.* 吸引；引起⋯⋯的注意或興趣

片 (1) be attracted to / by...
　　對⋯⋯著迷，被⋯⋯深深吸引
　(2) attract attention from...
　　吸引⋯⋯的注意力
　= draw attention from...

衍 attraction [əˈtrækʃən]
　n. 吸引力；誘惑；吸引人的事物 ④

▶ I must admit that I'm very attracted to David.
我必須承認我對大衛十分著迷。

▶ The new policy attracted attention from minorities.
這項新政策引起弱勢族群的關切。

---

attractive [əˈtræktɪv]
a. 誘人的，有吸引力的

似 (1) charming [ˈtʃɑrmɪŋ] *a.* 迷人的
　(2) appealing [əˈpilɪŋ] *a.* 吸引人的

▶ Unlike her sister, Liz was extremely attractive.
和她姊姊不同的是，莉絲十分嫵媚動人。

▶ I find the idea of rail travel attractive.
我發覺鐵道旅遊的構想頗具吸引力。

---

3 **historic** [hɪsˈtɔrɪk] *a.* 有歷史性的；歷史上著名的

衍 (1) history [ˈhɪstrɪ] *n.* 歷史 ①
　(2) historical [hɪsˈtɔrɪkḷ]
　　a. 與歷史有關的 ②

▶ This invention is of historic significance.
這件發明具有歷史性的意義。

▶ It was on this historic spot that the battle was fought.
那場戰役就是在這歷史上很著名的地方開打的。

---

historian [hɪsˈtɔrɪən] *n.* 歷史學家

▶ This historian wrote a book, revealing the mysteries of the dynasty.
這位歷史學家寫了一本書，揭開該朝代神祕的面紗。

4　avenue [ˈævəˌnu] *n.* 大道；方法

▣ explore every avenue
遍尋各種方法

▸ They established a branch office on Fifth Avenue.
他們在第五大道上開了一間分公司。

▸ They explored every avenue to find a cure for the disease.
他們試了各種方法，要找到這個疾病的療方。

alley [ˈælɪ] *n.* 巷

似 (1) valley [ˈvælɪ] *n.* 山谷 ②
(2) rally [ˈrælɪ] *n.* 集會 & *vi.* & *vt.* 召集 ⑤
(3) ally [ˈælaɪ] *n.* 同盟者 & [əˈlaɪ] *vt.* 使結盟 ⑤

▸ A car got stuck in the narrow alley.
有輛車困在這條窄巷裡。

5　threat [θrɛt] *n.* 威脅，恐嚇；惡兆，兆頭

▣ pose a threat to...　對……構成威脅

▸ Poverty is a threat to society.
貧困對社會是一種威脅。

▸ Global warming is posing a threat to human survival.
全球暖化對人類的生存正構成威脅。

▸ The dark clouds are a threat of heavy rain.
這些烏雲是大雨將至的前兆。

threaten [ˈθrɛtn̩]
vt. 威脅……；有……的前兆

▣ threaten sb with sth
以某事威脅某人

▸ Todd threatened his wife with divorce.
陶德以離婚威脅他老婆。

▸ These clouds threaten rain.
這些雲是下雨的前兆。

6　paradise [ˈpærəˌdaɪs] *n.* 天堂（= heaven）；樂園

似 heaven [ˈhɛvən]
n. 天堂（不與 the 並用）②

▸ They say Singapore is a shopping paradise.
據說新加坡是個購物天堂。

hell [hɛl] *n.* 地獄（不與 the 並用）

▣ go to hell　下地獄

▸ Bad people go to hell after they die.
壞人死後會下地獄。

7　remind [rɪˈmaɪnd] *vt.* 提醒；使想起

▣ (1) remind sb of sth/sb
使某人想起某事物 / 某人
(2) remind sb to + V
提醒某人要……

▸ The lullaby reminds me of my childhood.
這首搖籃曲使我想起我的童年。

▸ Please remind me to call Jason at seven.
請提醒我 7 點時打電話給傑森。

衍 **reminder** [rɪˋmaɪndɚ]
　　n. 提醒物；提示；令人回憶之物 ⑤

8　inner [ˋɪnɚ] *a.* 內部的；內心的

片 an inner circle　核心集團；內圈人士
似 internal [ɪnˋtɝn̩] *a.* 內部的 ②

▶ Beauty is only skin deep. It is inner beauty that counts.
美貌是膚淺的。重要的是內在美。

▶ They believe the religious faith can bring them inner peace.
他們相信宗教信仰能帶給他們內心的平靜。

▶ One figure in the dictator's inner circle was executed this morning.
該獨裁者身邊的核心人士其中一位今晨遭到處決了。
*dictator [ˋdɪk͵tetɚ / dɪkˋtetɚ] *n.* 獨裁者
　execute [ˋɛksɪ͵kjut] *vt.* 處死

---

outer [ˋautɚ] *a.* 外在的；外面的
片 in outer space　在外太空
似 external [ɪksˋtɝn̩] *a.* 外部的 ⑤

▶ Some people believe that there are intelligent beings like mankind in outer space.
有些人相信，在外太空有像人類一樣的智慧型生物。

9　hollow [ˋhɑlo] *a.* 中空的 & *n.* 坑洞 & *vt.* 陷落，挖洞

反 solid [ˋsɑlɪd]
　　a. 實心的；固體的 & *n.* 固體 ③
片 hollow out (sth) / hollow (sth) out
　　把……挖空

▶ Bamboo is light because it is hollow.
竹子因為是中空的所以很輕。

▶ Their car got stuck in a muddy hollow in the middle of nowhere.
他們的車子卡在一個很荒涼的地方的泥巴坑洞裡。

▶ Rex hollowed out a log to make a canoe.
雷克斯把一根木頭挖空做成獨木舟。

---

vacant [ˋvekənt]
a. 空缺的，未被占用的
似 available [əˋveləb̩] *a.* 空著的 ②

▶ We'll keep this position vacant until you come back.
我們會把這個職位空著直到你回來為止。

10　pilot [ˋpaɪlət] *n.* 飛行員；(船舶的) 領航員 & *vt.* 駕駛 (飛機)

衍 copilot [ˋko͵paɪlət]
　　n. (飛機的) 副駕駛員
片 pilot a plane　開飛機
　= fly a plane
　　不可說：drive a plane

▶ Brian is a licensed pilot and owns his own plane.
布萊恩是位有執照的飛行駕駛，而且還有一架私人飛機。

▶ I can drive a car and pilot a plane.
我會開車也會開飛機。

11　slave [slev] n. 奴隸 (與介詞 to 並用) & vi. 像奴隸般地工作

用 (1) be a slave to...　被……所奴役
= be enslaved by...
(2) slave away at...　為……賣命工作

衍 (1) slavery [ˈslevərɪ] n. 奴隸制度 ⑤
(2) enslave [ɪnˈslev] vt. 奴役

▶ Peter is a slave to his work and often works himself to exhaustion.
彼得是工作的奴隸，常工作到筋疲力盡。

▶ Henry slaved away at the company for fifteen years, and then he got laid off.
亨利為公司賣命工作十五年後被裁員了。

▶ I feel sorry for John because he is a slave to money.
= I feel sorry for John because he is enslaved by money.
我為約翰感到難過，因為他是金錢的奴隸。

12　advise [ədˈvaɪz] vt. 勸告，忠告；通知

用法 advise sb (not) to + V
勸某人 (不要) 從事……

衍 advice [ədˈvaɪs]
n. 勸告，忠告，建議 (不可數) ②

▶ The doctor advised Grandfather not to climb too many stairs.
醫生建議爺爺別爬太多樓梯。

▶ Travelers have been advised that they should avoid going out alone after dark.
遊客們已被告知天黑後要避免單獨外出。

adviser [ədˈvaɪzɚ]
n. 顧問 (= advisor)

衍 advisory [ədˈvaɪzərɪ]
a. 提供意見的 ⑥

▶ I think you need a financial adviser to help you plan your investments.
我想你需要一位理財顧問來幫助你規劃你的投資。

13　stare [stɛr] vi. 凝視；瞪視 (與介詞 at 並用) & n. 凝視

用 stare at...　凝視著……

▶ Why are you staring at me, John? Is there something wrong with me?
約翰，你為什麼這樣瞪著我？我有什麼不對勁嗎？

▶ Alice gave Ted a long stare but didn't say anything.
艾莉絲一直凝視著泰德卻一語不發。

glance [glæns] vi. 瞥視 & n. 一瞥
用 (1) glance at...　匆匆一瞥
(2) at first glance　乍看之下
似 peep [pip]
vi. 偷窺 (也與介詞 at 並用) ④

▶ I glanced at the girl one more time before I left.
我對那個女孩子匆匆再看了一眼便離開了。

▶ At first glance, the painting was average. But the more I looked at it, the more I liked it.
乍看之下，這幅畫沒啥了不起。不過，我越看則越愛。

14 sum [sʌm] *n.* 合計，總額；數目；金額 & *vt.* 概述

目 sum, summed [sʌmd], summed
片 (1) a large / small sum of money
巨額 / 小額金錢
(2) To sum up, ... 總之，……
= In sum, ...

▶ 54 is the sum of 17, 18 and 19.
17、18 和 19 合計是 54。

▶ Harry has a large sum of money in a bank account in Switzerland.
哈利在瑞士某家銀行戶頭內有大筆存款。

▶ To sum up, the plan to raise taxes is a terrible idea.
總之，這項增稅計畫是個很差勁的想法。

summary [ˈsʌmərɪ] *n.* 概述，概要

片 In summary, ... 概括來說，……
= In sum, ...
衍 summarize [ˈsʌməraɪz]
vt. 摘要；摘錄大意 ④

▶ Please give me a summary of what was decided at the meeting.
請就會議的決議事項給我一個概述。

▶ In summary, the meeting last Friday was quite fruitful.
概括來說，上星期五的會議成果豐碩。

15 necessity [nəˈsɛsə,tɪ] *n.* 需要 (不可數)；必需品 (可數)

片 basic necessities 生活必需品
衍 (1) necessary [ˈnɛsə,sɛrɪ]
a. 必須的；不可避免的 ②
(2) necessarily [ˈnɛsə,sɛrəlɪ]
adv. 必然地

▶ Necessity is the mother of invention.
需要為發明之母。── 諺語

▶ Water is a basic necessity of life.
水是生命中不可或缺的基本要素。

▶ Most families ran out of basic necessities during the natural disaster.
在這場天災期間，多數家庭耗盡了他們的生活必需品。

16 sensible [ˈsɛnsəbḷ] *a.* 明智的；顯著的

衍 (1) sense [sɛns] *n.* 感覺 & *vt.* 察覺 ②
(2) sensitivity [ˌsɛnsəˈtɪvətɪ]
n. 靈敏；易生氣；靈敏度 ⑤
(3) sensor [ˈsɛnsɚ] *n.* 感應器 ⑤
(4) insensible [ɪnˈsɛnsəbḷ]
a. 失去意識的
(5) sensation [sɛnˈseʃən]
n. 感覺；轟動 ⑤

▶ That's a sensible approach to the problem.
那是一個解決問題的明智辦法。

▶ There's a sensible difference between red and blue.
紅色和藍色之間有顯著的差別。

17 sufficient [səˈfɪʃənt] *a.* 充分的，足夠的

片 be sufficient for sth 足以應付某事
衍 sufficiency [səˈfɪʃənsɪ] *n.* 充足

▶ Those poor children do not have sufficient food for the winter.
那些窮孩子沒有足夠的食物過冬。

反 insufficient [ˌɪnsəˈfɪʃnt̩] *a.* 不足的
似 enough [ɪˈnʌf] *a.* 充分的，足夠的 ①

▶ This sum will be sufficient for our living expenses.
　這筆金額將足夠應付我們的生活開銷。

18　**crispy** [ˈkrɪspɪ] *a.* 脆的

用法 本字亦可寫成 crisp [krɪsp]，意思相同。
似 crunchy [ˈkrʌntʃɪ] *a.* 鮮脆的 ④

▶ These crackers are crispy and tasty.
　這些餅乾又脆又好吃。

19　**almond** [ˈɑmənd] *n.* 杏仁

H almond eyes　杏眼
似 apricot [ˈeprɪˌkɑt] *n.* 杏桃

▶ Almond eyes are not unique to Asians.
　杏眼並非是亞洲人所獨有的特徵。

▶ Eating a handful of almonds or walnuts can help control cholesterol levels.
　吃點杏仁或核桃有助於控制膽固醇指數。
　＊cholesterol [kəˈlɛstəˌrol] *n.* 膽固醇

20　**crop** [krɑp] *n.* 農作物 & *vt.* (牛羊等) 吃(草)；把(頭髮等) 剪得很短

三 crop, copped [krɑpt], cropped
H (1) have one's hair cropped
　　(某人) 把頭髮剪得很短
　(2) a crop circle　麥田圈

▶ Our crops are doing poorly because of the drought.
　因為乾旱，我們的農產欠收。

▶ A flock of sheep are cropping grass on the prairie.
　有一群羊在草原上吃草。

▶ Julie had her hair closely cropped yesterday.
　茱莉昨天去剪了超級短髮。

21　**lettuce** [ˈlɛtɪs] *n.* 生菜，萵苣

似 cabbage [ˈkæbɪdʒ]
　n. 高麗菜，包心菜 ②

▶ Have some lettuce. It's good for your health.
　吃點萵苣吧。對你的健康會有益的。

onion [ˈʌnjən] *n.* 洋蔥
H (1) peel an onion　剝洋蔥
　(2) green onion　(青) 蔥
　(3) a green onion pancake　蔥油餅

▶ Do you know how to peel onions without shedding tears?
　你知道怎麼剝洋蔥而不流眼淚嗎？

spinach [ˈspɪnɪtʃ] *n.* 菠菜

▶ Popeye eats spinach every day to gain strength.
　大力水手卜派每天吃菠菜獲取體力。

22　**bamboo** [bæmˈbu] *n.* 竹子

H a bamboo shoot　竹筍

▶ Pandas only eat a certain kind of bamboo.
　熊貓只吃某一類的竹子。

23 widen [ˈwaɪdn̩] vt. 使變寬 & vi. 變寬

衍 (1) wide [waɪd] a. 廣泛的；寬的 ①
(2) widely [ˈwaɪdlɪ] adv. 廣泛地
(3) width [wɪdθ] n. 寬度 ②

▶ The construction crew spent several days widening the streets in town.
建築工人花了好幾天的時間拓寬鎮上的馬路。

▶ The gap between rich and poor in this country has widened.
該國的貧富差距已變大了。

24 weaken [ˈwikən] vt. & vi. 減弱，削弱

衍 weakness [ˈwiknəs] n. 虛弱；弱點

▶ One of John's weaknesses is that he is afraid of heights.
約翰的弱點之一就是懼高。

▶ Tina's absence has weakened my interest in attending the party tonight.
由於蒂娜不克出席，使得我對今晚的派對興趣缺缺。

▶ My grandfather's ability to beat anyone at chess has weakened over the last few years.
過去幾年來，爺爺打遍天下無敵手的棋藝漸趨退步。

25 tent [tɛnt] n. 帳篷

片 pitch a tent   搭帳篷
= put up a tent

▶ We pitched our tent by the lake.
我們在湖邊搭帳篷。

延伸 camp [kæmp] n. 營地 & vi. 露營 ①

26 purse [pɝs] n. 女用手提包 (= handbag)；女用小錢包

用法 在英式英語中，purse 指女用小錢包，類似男用的皮夾子 (wallet)。在美式英語中，purse 就是女用手提包。

▶ Where did you get this purse? It looks absolutely fantastic.
妳這個包包是哪兒買的？看起來棒透了。

▶ I left my purse in the taxi.
我把小錢包掉在計程車上了。

27 observe [əbˈzɝv] vt. 觀察；遵守

衍 (1) observation [ˌɑbzɚˈveʃən]
    n. 觀察 ④
(2) observer [əbˈzɝvɚ] n. 觀察員 ⑤
(3) observant [əbˈzɝvənt]
    a. 有觀察力的；嚴格遵守的

似 obey [əˈbe] vt. 服從 ②

▶ Have you observed any changes in Sam's behavior?
你觀察到山姆的行為有所改變嗎？

▶ A good citizen should always observe the law.
= A good citizen should always abide by the law.
= A good citizen should always comply with the law.
好國民應始終守法。

28　junior [ˈdʒunjɚ] *n.* 大三學生；年少者 & *a.* 資淺的

片 (1) **be junior to sb**
　　階級 / 職位比某人低
　 (2) **be sb's junior by three / five years**　比某人小 3 / 5 歲

▶ All juniors have to take two science classes.
所有的大三學生都要上兩門理化課。

▶ In my company, my wife is junior to me, but back home, she is my boss.
我太太在我公司的職位比我低，可是回家後，她卻是我的老闆。

▶ Junior officers must salute senior officers when meeting or passing.
低階軍官在見到高階軍官或擦肩而過時，必須向他們敬禮。
*salute [səˈlut] *vt.* 向……敬禮

▶ Peter is my junior by five years.
= Peter is younger than I by five years.
彼得比我小 5 歲。

senior [ˈsinjɚ]
n. 大四學生；年長者 & *a.* 地位較高的

片 **be senior to sb**　階級 / 職位比某人高
be sb's senior by three / five years　比某人大 3 / 5 歲

▶ During my first year in college, I dated a senior.
我大一的時候和一個大四學生約會。

▶ Jane is my senior by five years.
= Jane is older than I by five years.
珍比我大 5 歲。

▶ Patty is a senior sales manager at Asia Motors.
派蒂是亞洲汽車的資深業務經理。

29　marker [ˈmarkɚ] *n.* 奇異 / 馬克筆；標誌

▶ Dennis soiled the wall with a marker.
阿丹用奇異筆把牆弄髒。

▶ Greg left a marker on the path so he would know the way back to the campsite.
葛瑞格在路上留下標誌，這樣他才認得出回營地的路。

30　pile [paɪl] *n.* 一堆 & *vi.* 堆積 (與介詞 up 並用) & *vt.* 累積，堆積

片 (1) **a pile of...**　一堆……
　 (2) **pile up (sth) / pile (sth) up**
　　(將某物) 堆積起來

似 (1) **stack** [stæk] *n.* 一疊；一堆 & *vt.* 把……疊起來 ⑤
a stack of...　一疊……；一堆……
　 (2) **mound** [maʊnd] *n.* 堆 ⑥
　 (3) **heap** [hip] *n.* 一堆 ③

▶ There is a pile of books in Lucy's study.
露西的書房有一堆書。

▶ Peter had been on sick leave for two days, and his work at the office really piled up.
彼得請了兩天病假，結果辦公室的工作堆積如山。

▶ Paul's desk is piled high with books.
保羅的桌子堆滿了書。

)) 0731

31　steal [stil] *vt.* 偷竊

steal, stole [stol], stolen [ˋstolən]　▶ The cop caught the thief stealing a car.
警察當場抓到小偷在偷車。

Unit 08

0801-0804

---

1 protection [prəˈtɛkʃən] n. 保護

衍 (1) protect [prəˈtɛkt]
　　vt. 保護；防禦 ②
　(2) protective [prəˈtɛktɪv]
　　a. 保護的 ②

▸ Jack was wearing a heavy coat as protection against the cold.
傑克穿著一件厚外套禦寒。

▸ These kittens ran to their mother for protection.
這些小貓跑去找母貓尋求保護。

---

2 stormy [ˈstɔrmɪ] a. 暴風雨的；激烈的

衍 storm [stɔrm] *n.* 暴風雨 &
　vi. & *vt.* 怒罵；攻占 ②

似 vehement [ˈviəmənt] *a.* 激烈的
　a vehement argument
　激烈的爭論
　= a stormy argument

▸ We had a blackout during the stormy night.
暴風雨夜晚我們停電了。
*blackout [ˈblækˌaʊt] *n.* 停電

▸ After a stormy argument, we finally reached an agreement.
經過一番激烈的爭論後我們終於達成了協議。

---

3 pure [pjʊr] a. 純粹的；純潔的

片 (1) pure silk　純絲
　(2) pure cotton　純棉

衍 (1) purify [ˈpjʊrəˌfaɪ] *vt.* 淨化 ⑥
　(2) purity [ˈpjʊrətɪ] *n.* 純淨 ⑥

▸ The pajamas are made of pure cotton.
這件睡衣是純棉製的。
*pajamas [pəˈdʒɑməz] *n.* 睡衣 (衣褲成套，故用複數)
　a pair of pajamas　一套睡衣

▸ The water is clean and pure. It has been tested over and over again.
這水質清潔而純淨，它可是經過一再測試的。

---

4 native [ˈnetɪv] a. 祖國的；本地的，土生的 & n. 本地人；原住民

片 (1) sb's native language / tongue
　　某人的母語
　(2) be native to + 地方
　　為某地方所獨有
　= be unique to + 地方
　= be indigenous to + 地方
　　*indigenous [ɪnˈdɪdʒənəs]
　　　a. 土生的，土長的 ⑤

似 domestic [dəˈmɛstɪk]
　a. 國內的；家庭的 ②

▸ Chinese is Ken's native language, but he is more fluent in Spanish.
中文是肯的母語，但是他的西班牙文比較流利。

▸ Kiwi birds are native to New Zealand.
鷸鴕是紐西蘭的原產。

▸ The natives were required to relocate to a safer area.
當地的人被要求遷居到一處更安全的地區。

---

5 **cattle** [`ˋkætḷ`] *n.* 牛群

用法 cattle 如同 people，視作複數名詞，可被 two (2) 以上的數詞 (如 three、four、many 等) 修飾。
There is a people in the room. (✕)
→ There are two / five / many people in the room. (○)
房間裡有 2 個 / 5 個 / 許多人。
同理：There is a cattle in the field. (✕)
→ There are two / five / many cattle in the field. (○)
牧場裡有 2 隻 / 5 隻 / 許多隻牛。

▶ In New Zealand, there are more than 13,000 sheep and cattle farms.
紐西蘭有 1 萬 3 千多座飼養綿羊和牛群的農場。

---

bull [`bʊl`] *n.* 公牛
延伸 cow [`kaʊ`] *n.* 母牛 ①

▶ During the festival, many bulls will run through the narrow streets in the city.
在慶典期間，許多公牛會狂奔於該城市狹窄的街道。

---

buffalo [`ˋbʌfə͵lo`] *n.* 野牛；水牛
(= water buffalo)
複 buffalo 或 buffaloes

▶ The American buffalo is one of the largest land animals in North America.
美洲野牛是北美陸地上體型最大的動物之一。

---

6 **lord** [`lɔrd`] *n.* 貴族；君主；(大寫) 上帝

延伸 在教會基督徒對上帝祈禱時，即用 Lord 一字。

▶ Oh, Lord, forgive me for cheating on my wife. I'll never do it again.
哦，主啊，原諒我對內人不忠。我下次再也不會做這樣的事了。

▶ A knight should pledge loyalty to his lord.
騎士應該向他的君主效忠。
*pledge [`plɛdʒ`] *vt.* 誓言，保證

▶ If you feel lost, let the Lord guide you.
如果你很茫然，就讓上帝來指引你方向。

---

7 **shadow** [`ˋʃædo`] *n.* 陰影 & *vt.* 以影籠罩

片 (1) cast a shadow on...
投影在⋯⋯之上
(2) live in sb's shadow
活在某人的陰影 / 光環之下
似 shade [`ʃed`] *n.* 陰涼處，(樹) 蔭；窗 / 卷簾 & *vt.* 遮擋 & *vi.* 逐漸改變 ④

▶ Winnie sat in the shadows.
溫妮坐在暗處。

▶ The cottage was shadowed by palm trees.
這間小屋被棕櫚樹的陰影遮蔽著。

▶ The tree cast a shadow on the wall.
這棵樹投影在牆上。

▶ Not wanting to live in his father's shadow, Babe Ruth's son quit baseball.
貝比・魯斯的兒子不願活在父親的陰影下，便不再打棒球。

8 advertise [ˋædvɚ͵taɪz] vt. 將……登廣告 & vi. 登廣告

片 advertise for sb　登廣告徵人

▶ You should advertise your car in the local newspaper if you want to sell it quickly.
你如果想快點把車賣掉，應該在本地的報紙登廣告。

▶ On the wall there was a small poster advertising a new magazine.
牆上有張替新雜誌打廣告的小海報。

▶ They advertised for someone to look after the garden.
他們登廣告徵人照顧花園。

advertiser [ˋædvɚ͵taɪzɚ]
n. 刊登廣告者；廣告商

▶ Super Bowl advertisers have to pay lots of money for their commercial time.
超級盃的廣告商要花很多錢來支付他們打廣告的時間。

advertisement [͵ædvɚˋtaɪzmənt]
n. 廣告 (可數，常縮寫成 ad [æd])

片 put / place an advertisement in the newspaper　在報上刊登廣告

衍 advertising [ˋædvɚ͵taɪzɪŋ]
n. 廣告；廣告業 (皆不可數)

▶ No one replied to the advertisement Mary put in the paper.
瑪莉在報上登的廣告沒有回音。

9 liberty [ˋlɪbɚtɪ] *n.* 自由

衍 (1) liberal [ˋlɪbərəl]
　　a. 自由的；開明的 ②
　　(2) liberate [ˋlɪbəret]
　　vt. 解放，使自由 ⑥

延伸 the Statue of Liberty　自由女神像

▶ Give me liberty, or give me death!
不自由，毋寧死！── 諺語

10 confuse [kənˋfjuz] *vt.* 使困惑；混淆，弄錯

片 (1) confuse A with B　將 A 與 B 混淆
　　(2) get confused　搞迷糊了

▶ Please slow down—you are confusing me.
請說慢一點 ── 你把我搞糊塗了。

▶ Our teacher sometimes confuses John with Lee.
我們老師有時會把約翰當作是李。

▶ Sophie saw the sign and got confused.
蘇菲看到這標示就搞不清楚了。

11 suspect [səˋspɛkt] vt. 懷疑；猜想

用 (1) suspect sb of + N/V-ing
懷疑某人犯了⋯⋯之罪

(2) be suspected of + N/V-ing
涉嫌⋯⋯

▶ The police suspected Bob of the crime.
警方懷疑鮑伯犯了這個罪行。

▶ Ted was suspected of stealing Mary's watch.
泰德涉嫌偷了瑪莉的手錶。

suspect [ˋsʌspɛkt]
n. 嫌疑犯 & a. 可疑的

▶ Robert was one of the main suspects in the murder case.
羅伯特是這宗謀殺案的主嫌之一。

▶ A suspect package was delivered to the government minister's office.
一件可疑的包裹被送到部長辦公室。

suspicion [səˋspɪʃən]
n. 嫌疑；疑心

用 be under suspicion 遭受懷疑

衍 suspicious [səˋspɪʃəs]
a. 可疑的；多疑的，猜疑的 ④

▶ Daniel is under suspicion by the police for robbery.
警方懷疑丹尼爾犯下搶案。

▶ I have a suspicion that Ben is somewhere around here.
= I suspect that Ben is somewhere around here.
我懷疑班就在這附近的某個地方。

12 beneath [bɪˋniθ] prep. & adv. 在⋯⋯正下方

似 (1) underneath [ˌʌndəˋniθ]
prep. & adv. 在⋯⋯下方 ⑥

(2) below [bəˋlo]
prep. & adv. 在下方 ①

反 above [əˋbʌv] prep. & adv. 在上方 ①

▶ The money was hidden beneath a stack of newspapers.
錢藏在一堆報紙下面。

▶ Beneath his inconspicuous appearance, Tom is a talented pianist.
在不起眼的外表下，湯姆其實是個很有才氣的鋼琴家。
*inconspicuous [ˌɪnkənˋspɪkjuəs] a. 不顯眼的

13 onto [ˋɑntu] prep. 到 / 向⋯⋯之上

▶ The chef squeezed some lemon juice onto the fish to bring out its flavor.
主廚把檸檬擠出汁液滴到魚上頭，以帶出魚的風味。

14 comfort [ˋkʌmfət] n. 舒適 & vt. 安慰

用 find / take comfort in + N/V-ing
在⋯⋯中尋找安慰

衍 comfortable [ˋkʌmfətəbḷ]
a. 舒適的 ①

▶ Despite all the material comforts, the rich man isn't happy.
這個富翁儘管有種種的物質享受，卻仍不快樂。

反 **discomfort** [dɪsˋkʌmfɚt]
n. 不適 & *vt.* 使不舒服（常用被動）⑥

▶ I find comfort in listening to music whenever I feel troubled.
每當我心煩時就會在聽音樂中找到慰藉。

▶ We comforted the woman when her child was killed in a car accident.
這位婦人的孩子在車禍中喪生，我們便安慰她。

---

15 comparison [kəmˋpɛrəsn̩] *n.* 相較；相比

片 in comparison with... 　與……相較

衍 (1) **compare** [kəmˋpɛr]
　　vt. & *vi.* 比較 ②

　　(2) **comparable** [ˋkɑmpərəbḷ]
　　　a. 可相比的 ⑤

　　(3) **comparative** [kəmˋpærətɪv]
　　　a. 比較的，相對的 ⑥

▶ A comparison of the two teams indicates that the game should be close.
兩隊實力相較，可預見那場比賽會勝負難分。

▶ In comparison with my old one, my new motorcycle is really fast.
與我那臺舊摩托車比起來，新的跑得真是快。

---

16 chest [tʃɛst] *n.* 胸

片 get something off one's chest
把心中的某事一吐為快

▶ Don't keep the secret to yourself. You should tell me and get it off your chest.
別把祕密藏在自己心裡，你應告訴我，心中一吐為快。

breast [brɛst] *n.* 胸部；乳房

衍 **abreast** [əˋbrɛst] *adv.* 並排

▶ Breast cancer can be cured if detected early.
乳癌若能及早診斷出來是可以治癒的。

---

17 scale [skel] *n.* 規模；等級；磅秤

片 on a... scale 　……規模的

▶ Pollution has caused changes to weather patterns on a large scale.
汙染已經大幅造成天氣型態的改變。

▶ We should start out testing on a small scale before we move on to a larger one.
我們應該先做小規模的測試，再做較大型的實驗。

▶ Nuclear weapons cause destruction on a massive scale.
核武造成大規模的破壞。

▶ The scale determined the weight of the package.
磅秤測出包裹的重量。

18 conscious [ˈkɑnʃəs] *a.* 有所察覺的；清醒的

🄗 be conscious of...　察覺到……
= be aware of...

▸ Conscious of the dangers of smoking, Benny decided to give up the bad habit.

班尼察覺到抽菸的危險，決定要戒掉這個壞習慣。

▸ The soldier was wounded but still conscious.

這士兵受了傷，但仍然清醒。

consciousness [ˈkɑnʃəsnɪs]
n. 知覺；了解，知道

🄗 regain consciousness　恢復意識

衍 (1) awareness [əˈwɛrnɪs]
　　　n. 察覺；意識
　　(2) conscience [ˈkɑnʃəns] *n.* 良心 ④

▸ The patient regained consciousness shortly after treatment.

這個病人經過治療後不久就恢復了意識。

▸ My consciousness of their suffering urged me to offer help.

我知道他們的痛苦遭遇後，就有一股伸出援手的衝動。

19 troop [trup] *n.* 軍隊 (恆用複數)

▸ The commander gave his troops a pep talk to boost their morale.

指揮官對他的部隊做精神喊話以提振他們的士氣。

★a pep talk　精神喊話，鼓舞士氣的談話
　　morale [məˈræl] *n.* 士氣

20 cricket [ˈkrɪkɪt] *n.* 蟋蟀；板球 (運動)

▸ Do you hear a cricket? It's keeping me awake.

你有沒有聽到蟋蟀在叫？它讓我睡不著。

▸ Let's play cricket this afternoon at the park.

咱們今天下午去公園玩板球吧。

grasshopper [ˈgræsˌhɑpɚ]
n. 蚱蜢

▸ Did you know that a grasshopper can leap 20 times the length of its own body?

你知道蚱蜢一跳可跳過多達自己身長 20 倍的高度嗎？

21 fairly [ˈfɛrlɪ] *adv.* 相當地，蠻

衍 fair [fɛr] *a.* 公平的；相當多的 &
　 n. 市集 & *adv.* 遵守規定地 ②

似 (1) fairy [ˈfɛrɪ] *n.* 妖精，仙子 ③
　　(2) quite [kwaɪt] *adv.* 相當地 ①
　　(3) rather [ˈræðɚ] *adv.* 相當 ②

▸ It's fairly difficult to tell the difference between Sandy and her twin sister.

要區分珊蒂跟她的雙胞胎姊姊相當困難。

22　substance [ˈsʌbstəns] n. 物質

衍 substantial [səbˈstænʃəl]
　 a. 相當大的；重大的 ⑤

▶ This colorless, odorless substance is actually quite toxic.
這種無色無味的物質事實上有劇毒。
＊odorless [ˈodə<ləs] a. 無氣味的
　toxic [ˈtɑksɪk] a. 有毒的

23　pour [pɔr] vt. & vi. 傾注；下大雨

▶ Please pour water into the jug and then place it on the table.
請把水倒到罐子裡，然後把罐子放在桌上。
＊jug [dʒʌg] n. 罐子 (多指裝水用的玻璃或塑膠罐)

▶ It's pouring now. You may as well stay here for the night.
＝ It's raining hard now. You may as well stay here for the night.
＝ It's raining cats and dogs. You may as well stay here for the night.
現在正在下大雨，你不妨留下來過夜。
＊may as well ＋ V　不妨……，倒如……

▶ When it rains, it pours.
＝ It never rains but it pours.
每次下雨，就會下傾盆大雨。/ 禍不單行。

24　promote [prəˈmot] vt. 促進，提倡；升遷

片 (1) promote peace　提倡和平
　 (2) promote sales　促銷
　 (3) be promoted to ＋ 職位
　　　 獲得升任……一職
衍 promotion [prəˈmoʃən]
　 n. 促進；提倡；升遷 ④

▶ Our company promotes education by offering scholarships to the poor.
本公司提供窮困的人獎學金，以提倡教育。

▶ Peter was promoted to general manager last week.
彼得上星期晉升總經理一職。

25　pad [pæd] n. 襯墊 & vt. (用柔軟物質) 填塞

三 pad, padded [ˈpædɪd], padded
片 a mouse pad　滑鼠墊

▶ There is a pad on every corner of the table so that you won't get hurt if you bump into one.
桌角都有安全護墊，所以如果你撞到其中之一都不會受傷。

▶ The pillow is padded with duck feathers to make it extra soft.
這枕頭使用鴨毛填塞來增加柔軟度。

0826-0836

26 cinema [ˈsɪnəmə] n. 電影院

片 go to the cinema 〔英〕看電影
= go to the movies 〔美〕

似 movie theater [ˈmuvɪ ˌθɪətə]
n. 電影院〔美〕

▶ They are building a cinema in our town.
我們鎮上正在蓋一座電影院。

▶ I've been working too long. I need to go to the cinema tonight for a change.
我工作太久了。今晚我得看場電影調適一下。

27 clay [kle] n. 黏土

▶ My daughter made me a flower with clay.
我的女兒用黏土做了一朵花給我。

28 fence [fɛns] vt. 圍起來 & n. 籬笆，柵欄

片 fence... in
用籬笆／柵欄將……圍起來

▶ The farmer fenced in all his cattle.
那個農夫把他的牛都圍了起來。

▶ I want to live in a house with white fences.
我想要住在有白色籬笆的房子裡。

29 garage [gəˈrɑdʒ] n. 車庫；汽車修理廠

片 a garage sale
在自家車庫舉辦的家中舊貨拍賣會

▶ My garage can only accommodate one car.
我的車庫只容得下一輛車。

▶ I have to ride my motorcycle because my car is in the garage.
我的車在修理廠，所以我必須騎摩托車。

30 fuel [ˈfjuəl] n. 燃料 vt. & vi. 填加燃料 & vt. 激起 (憤怒等)

片 (1) add fuel to the fire 火上加油
(2) fuel up （給汽車等）加油
(3) fuel sb's anger 激起某人的憤怒

衍 biofuel [ˌbaɪəˈfjuəl]
n. 生質／生物燃料，生質能 (從動植物或其廢棄物製成的燃料)

▶ Your criticism will only add fuel to the fire.
你的批評只會火上加油而已。

▶ We're running out of gas, so we have to fuel up at the next gas station.
我們汽油快用完了，因此我們得在下個加油站加油了。

▶ Stop talking! Your remarks will only fuel Paul's anger.
別再說了！你的話只會激起保羅的憤怒。

31 decorate [ˈdɛkəˌret] vt. 裝飾

片 (1) decorate A with B 用 B 布置 A
(2) be decorated with...
被……裝飾著

衍 decoration [ˌdɛkəˈreʃən]
n. 裝飾 (不可數)；裝飾品 (可數) ④

▶ Ken decorated his bedroom with his favorite band's posters.
肯用他最喜歡的樂團的海報布置他的房間。

▶ The small table was decorated with roses.
這張小桌子以玫瑰花裝飾著。

32 decrease [dɪˈkris] vt. & vi. 減少 & [ˈdikris] n. 下降，減少

片 be on the decrease / decline
下降中 / 減少
= be decreasing
反 increase [ɪnˈkris] vt. & vi. 增加
& [ˈɪnkris] n. 增加 ②
be on the increase 增加中
= be increasing

▶ Mary's fear decreased as she calmed down.
瑪莉鎮定下來時，就不那麼害怕了。
▶ The company has decreased the number of its staff members because of the recession.
因為經濟不景氣，公司已裁減了員工人數。
▶ The birthrate in Taiwan has been on the decrease in recent years.
近年來臺灣的出生率都在下降。
▶ There has been a decrease in the unemployment rate ever since the new policy was carried out.
自從新政策開始執行後，失業率已經降低了。

33 emotional [ɪˈmoʃənl] a. 感情激動的；情緒的

片 emotional quotient
情緒商數，情商 (縮寫為 EQ)

▶ My mom became emotional upon reading the card I sent her.
我媽看了我寄給她的卡片深受感動。
▶ A person with a high EQ usually gets along with other people well.
情商高的人通常都和別人處得很好。

34 lick [lɪk] vt. & n. 舔

延伸 (1) suck [sʌk] vt. & vi. 吸 ③
(2) chew [tʃu] vt. 咀嚼 ④
(3) swallow [ˈswɑlo] vt. 吞 ②

▶ My dog jumped onto the sofa and licked my face.
我的狗跳到沙發上並舔了我的臉。
▶ Sammy wants to have a lick of my ice cream.
珊米想要舔一口我的冰淇淋。

35 nest [nɛst] n. 巢，窩

▶ There's a bird's nest in the tree.
樹上有個鳥巢。

36 element [ˈɛləmənt] n. 要素

衍 (1) elemental [ˌɛləˈmɛntl] a. 基本的
(2) elementary [ˌɛləˈmɛntərɪ]
a. 基礎的 ④
an elementary school 小學

▶ The book has all the elements of a good suspense novel.
這本書具備所有懸疑小說的成功要素。

1 bang [bæŋ] *n.* 發出砰的一聲 & *vt.* 猛然撞擊 & *adv.* 準確地〔英〕

■ with a bang　砰然一聲

用法 with a bang 除表『砰然一聲』外，亦可表『很成功地』，用於下列結構：

go off with a bang　極為成功
= start off with a bang

似 bump [bʌmp] *vt.* 猛然撞擊 ③

▶ The police officer heard a loud bang and quickly grabbed his gun.
這名警官聽到一聲砰然巨響，便迅速掏槍。

▶ The angry man shut the door with a bang.
這名生氣的男子砰地一聲把門關上。

▶ The meeting went off with a bang.
會議開得很成功。

▶ The little boy cried when he banged his head against the table.
= The little boy cried when he bumped his head against the table.
那個小男孩頭撞到桌子哭了起來。

▶ Kelly always arrives at work bang on time.
凱莉總是準時上班。

2 quote [kwot] *vt.* 引用 & *n.* 引文

■ quote sb as saying...
引用某人的話稱……

衍 quotation [kwoˋteʃən] *n.* 引文 ④

似 quota [ˋkwotə] *n.* 配額 ⑤

▶ The newspaper quoted the mayor as saying, "Two more parks will be built in this city next year."
該報引用市長的話稱：『明年本市將再興建兩座公園。』

▶ I like this famous quote, "As you sow, so shall you reap."
我喜歡這句名言：『一分耕耘，一分收穫。』

3 raw [rɔ] *a.* 生的；未加工的

■ (1) eat sth raw　生吃某物
(2) a raw material　原料

似 (1) uncooked [ʌnˋkʊkt] *a.* 未煮過的
(2) unprocessed [ʌnˋprɑsɛst]
a. 未加工的

▶ Some vegetables can be eaten raw.
有些蔬菜可以生吃。

▶ Indonesia used to export a lot of raw materials to Japan, including rubber and timber.
印尼過去曾輸出許多原料到日本，包括橡膠及木材。

4 freeze [friz] *vi.* 結冰，凝固 & *n.* (暫時) 停止

三 freeze, froze [froz], frozen [ˋfrozn]

■ freeze to death　凍死

▶ The water froze on the road, making it dangerous to drive.
水在馬路上結成冰，因此在上面開車很危險。

▶ The lake freezes in winter.
這座湖在冬天都會結冰。

> It was so cold on the hilltop that I nearly froze to death.
> 山頂好冷，我幾乎快凍死了。

> The struggling company is considering a pay freeze for its staff.
> 那間陷入財務困難的公司正考慮暫時停發員工薪水。

freezer [ˈfrizɚ]
n. (冰箱內的) 冷凍庫；冷凍櫃

> Put the beef in the freezer.
> 把牛肉存放在冷凍庫內。

freezing [ˈfrizɪŋ]
a. 冷到快要結冰似的 (喻『極冷的』)

日 (1) be freezing cold
　　極冷的 (此處 freezing 視作副詞，
　　專用以修飾 cold)
　 (2) the freezing point　　冰點
　　　the boiling point　　　沸點

> The freezing weather during the holiday kept most people indoors.
> 假日時天寒地凍，大部分的人只好待在家裡。

> It's freezing cold today.
> 今天實在冷極了。

> Water becomes ice when the temperature drops below the freezing point.
> 溫度降至冰點以下時，水就會結冰。

frozen [ˈfrozən] a. 冷凍的
日 be frozen with fear　嚇得動彈不得

> Mom took the frozen fish from the freezer, so it would defrost.
> 媽媽把冷凍魚肉從冰箱拿出來解凍。
> *defrost [diˈfrɔst] vt. 將……除霜

> The girl was frozen with fear at the sight of the bandit.
> 這女孩子看到匪徒時嚇得動彈不得。
> *bandit [ˈbændɪt] n. 匪徒

5　request [rɪˈkwɛst] n. & vt. 請求；要求

日 (1) at sb's request　應某人的要求
　 (2) on request　　　　備索
　　 = for the asking
似 require [rɪˈkwaɪr] vt. 要求；需要 ②

> My boss thought my report was too lengthy, so I had to cut it short at his request.
> 老闆認為我的報告過於冗長，所以我只好應他要求把報告裁短一些。

> For those who are interested in this investment, we have a lot of booklets on request.
> 對於本投資有興趣的人，我們準備了許多小冊子備索。

> May we request the honor of your presence at our gathering?
> 我們可否有此榮幸邀您出席我們的聚會？

> Since the holiday is drawing near, I request that the meeting (should) be put off until sometime next month.
> 由於假期在即，我要求會議延到下個月其他時間另行召開。

6 mental [ˋmɛntḷ] a. 心理的

衍 mentality [mɛnˋtælətɪ] n. 心態 ⑥

似 psychological [ˏsaɪkəˋlɑdʒɪkḷ]
　a. 心理的 ④

反 physical [ˋfɪzɪkḷ]
　a. 生理的 & n. 健康檢查
　(= physical examination) ④

▸ Lucy is said to have some mental problems. She is a little bit weird.
據說露西有些精神方面的問題。她有點兒怪怪的。
＊weird [wɪrd] a. 怪異的

7 victim [ˋvɪktəm] n. 受害者

片 fall victim to... 成為……的受害者
　＊本片語中的 victim 不可使用複數形。

＝ fall prey to...
　＊本片語中的 prey [pre] 是集合名詞，
　不可數，泛指『被捕食的動物』。

▸ Many teenagers fall victim to drugs.
許多青少年都成了毒品的受害者。

▸ I hope there are no victims of racial discrimination in our company.
我希望我們公司沒有任何種族歧視的受害者。
＊discrimination [dɪˏskrɪməˋneʃən] n. 歧視

8 republic [rɪˋpʌblɪk] n. 共和國

衍 republican [rɪˋpʌblɪkən]
　a. & n. 共和國的；(大寫) 共和黨員 ⑤

延伸 the Republican Party〔美〕共和黨
　the Democratic Party〔美〕民主黨
　＊democratic [ˏdɛməˋkrætɪk]
　　a. 民主的 ③

▸ ROK stands for the Republic of Korea, which is commonly known as South Korea.
ROK 是『大韓民國』的縮寫，也就是我們一般所知的『南韓』。

9 opposite [ˋɑpəzɪt] prep. 在……的對面 (= across from) & a. 相對的；相反的 & n. 相反的情形 & adv. 在對面

片 (1) hold the opposite view
　　持相反的看法
　(2) quite the opposite 正好相反

衍 opposition [ˏɑpəˋzɪʃən] n. 反對 ⑤

延伸 opposite 作介詞時，等於 across
　from (在……的對面)。

▸ I live next to the bank opposite the train station.
我住在火車站對面的銀行旁邊。

▸ Everyone says that Jane is a nice girl, but I hold the opposite view.
每個人都說珍是好女孩，不過我卻持相反的看法。

▸ I didn't mean to hurt you — quite the opposite. I was trying to help you.
我並非故意要傷害你 —— 事實正好相反。我一直想幫你。

▸ Ted finally told the woman sitting opposite to put out her cigarette.
泰德最後要坐在對面的女子把菸熄掉。

10　superior [sə`pɪrɪɚ] a. 較優的；上等的 & n. 上級長官

片 be superior / inferior to...
比……優秀 / 差

用法 英文中若干以 –ior 結尾的形容詞有比較級的意味，但不可與 than 並用，只可與介詞 to 並用（如上述片語）。

▶ John is five years senior / junior to me.
= John is older / younger than I by five years.
約翰比我大 / 小五歲。

▶ This car is far superior to that one in terms of comfort.
就舒適性而言，這輛車要比那一輛棒多了。
*in terms of... 就……而言

▶ Judy's winery stored a wide range of superior wines.
茱蒂的釀酒廠貯藏了許多上等好酒。
*winery [`waɪnərɪ] n. 釀酒廠

▶ Larry was fired for being rude to his superiors.
賴瑞因為對長官無禮而被開除。

---

inferior [ɪn`fɪrɪɚ] a. 較差的 & n. 下屬
片 be inferior to...　比……差

▶ Confucius once said, "Do not make friends with those who are inferior to us."
孔子曾說：『無友不如己者。』

▶ Kent is the kind of person who is nice to all of his inferiors.
肯特是一個對所有下屬都好的人。

11　emergency [ɪ`mɝdʒənsɪ] n. 緊急事件，緊急狀況

片 in case of emergency
如遇緊急狀態

用法 emergency 雖為名詞，卻常作形容詞，修飾名詞。

(1) the emergency room
急診室（常縮寫成 ER）
(2) the emergency exit　緊急出口
(3) make an emergency landing
（飛機）緊急降落

似 crisis [`kraɪsɪs] n. 危機 ②

▶ In Taiwan, in case of emergency, please dial 119.
在臺灣，如遇緊急狀況，請撥打 119。

▶ Because of the bad weather, the pilot had to make an emergency landing.
由於天候不佳，飛行員不得不緊急降落。

12　creative [krɪ`etɪv] a. 有創造力的

衍 (1) create [krɪ`et] vt. 創造 ②
(2) creativity [ˌkrie`tɪvətɪ]
n. 創造力 ④

似 (1) imaginative [ɪ`mædʒə͵netɪv]
a. 有想像力的 ④
(2) inventive [ɪn`vɛntɪv]
a. 善於創造的

▶ A creative advertisement requires intelligence and imagination.
有創意的廣告需要智力與想像力。

▶ Mr. Brown is a creative and prolific writer.
布朗先生是個有創意且多產的作家。
*prolific [prə`lɪfɪk] a. 多產的

(3) innovative [ˈɪnəˌvetɪv]
　　a. 創新的 ⑤
(4) original [əˈrɪdʒn̩l]
　　a. 有獨特性的 ③

creature [ˈkritʃɚ] *n.* 生物
囮 living thing　生物

▶ Humans are creatures of habit.
　人類是慣性動物。

creator [krɪˈetɚ] *n.* 創造者
囮 (1) maker [ˈmekɚ] *n.* 創造者
　　(2) inventor [ɪnˈvɛntɚ] *n.* 發明者 ③
囝 destroyer [dɪˈstrɔɪɚ]
　　n. 破壞者；驅逐艦

▶ Walt Disney was the creator of Mickey Mouse.
　華德・迪士尼是創造米老鼠的人。

13　media [ˈmidɪə] *n.* 媒體 (複數)

單 medium [ˈmidɪəm]
　　n. 媒體 (單數) & *a.* 中等的 ①
囲 the mass media　大眾傳播媒體

▶ The political party accused the media of being biased.
　該政黨指控媒體是偏頗的。
　＊biased [ˈbaɪəst] *a.* 有偏見的

14　extreme [ɪkˈstrim] *a.* 極度的 & *n.* 極端

囲 go to extremes　走極端
囮 excessive [ɪkˈsɛsɪv]
　　a. 過度的，極度的 ⑤

▶ You should handle the problem with extreme caution.
　你應極為謹慎地來處理這個問題。
▶ Work and play are both important. But in either case, do not go to extremes.
　工作和玩樂都很重要，但兩樣都不能過頭。

extremely [ɪkˈstrimlɪ]
adv. 極端地；非常地
囮 (1) exceedingly [ɪkˈsidɪŋlɪ]
　　adv. 極度地
　　(2) exceptionally [ɪkˈsɛpʃənlɪ]
　　adv. 格外地

▶ I was extremely happy upon hearing the good news.
　我一聽到這個好消息便高興得不得了。
▶ Street violence is an extremely common problem in big cities.
　在各大城市，街頭暴力是非常普遍的問題。

15　plenty [ˈplɛntɪ] *pron.* 充分 (與介詞 of 並用) & *n.* 富足 & *adv.* 非常地

囲 plenty of + 複數名詞 / 不可數名詞
　　很多……
衍 plentiful [ˈplɛntɪfəl] *a.* 充分的 ④

▶ There are plenty of activities to do on the beach during the summertime.
　夏天在海灘可做很多的活動。

▶ In times of plenty, you should remember to save for a rainy day.
你應該在富足之時未雨綢繆。

▶ There are plenty more fish in the sea. You can find someone better than your ex-boyfriend.
天涯何處無芳草。你會找到比你前男友更好的人。

16　**wagon** [ˈwæɡən] *n.* 運貨馬車

▶ Tom plans to journey across America in a covered wagon.
湯姆計劃要駕著遮篷馬車周遊美國。

van [væn] *n.* 廂型車，麵包車

▶ I'm moving to my new apartment this Sunday. Would you lend me your van?
我要在這星期天搬到新公寓。你的廂型車可以借我嗎？

17　**dare** [dɛr] *aux. & vi.* 膽敢 & *vt.* 向……挑戰

片 dare sb to + V
向某人挑戰，諒某人不敢……

= challenge sb to + V

用法 (1) dare 作『膽敢』解釋時，可當不及物動詞，在肯定句中，dare 之後接 to 引導的不定詞片語；在否定句中，don't／doesn't／didn't dare 之後也接 to 引導的不定詞片語，但 to 可省略。

▶ Ben dares to do it.
班敢做這件事。

▶ Ben doesn't dare (to) do it.
班不敢做這件事。

(2) dare 作助動詞時，常用於直述否定句，故恆與 not 並用，另外也可用於疑問句，不管第幾人稱皆使用 dare，過去式則為 dared。dare not 或 dared not（不敢）之後一律接原形動詞。

▶ Tim's brother dares not swim across the river. (✗)

→ Tim's brother dare not swim across the river. (○)
提姆的哥哥不敢游過這條河。

▶ I dare not tell my parents that I'm getting married soon.
我不敢跟我爸媽說我快結婚了。

▶ Though Jerry wants to ask Holly to the prom, he doesn't dare.
雖然傑瑞想邀荷莉參加舞會，他卻不敢行動。
＊prom [prɑm] *n.* 學校班級舞會

▶ I dare you to swim across the river.
我向你挑戰，諒你不敢游過這條河。

18 scholar [ˈskɑlɚ] n. 學者

衍 scholarly [ˈskɑlɚlɪ] a. 有學者風範的
a scholarly statesman
有學者風範的政治家

▶ The author of this book is also a famous scholar in his country.

在他的國家裡，本書的作者同時也是一位知名的學者。

scholarship [ˈskɑlɚˌʃɪp] n. 獎學金

片 study on a scholarship
靠獎學金唸書

▶ The intelligent young girl is studying at Harvard on a government scholarship.

那位聰明的女孩正在哈佛公費留學。

19 risk [rɪsk] n. 風險 & vt. 冒……的風險

片 (1) take / run the risk of + V-ing
冒險從事……

(2) at risk   處於危險之中

衍 risky [ˈrɪskɪ] a. 冒險的 ⑤

用法 risk 作及物動詞時，需以名詞或動名詞作受詞。

不可說：Never risk to swim alone.
(✕)

應說：Never risk swimming alone.
(○)

千萬不要冒險獨自去游泳。

▶ Parents shouldn't run the risk of leaving their children alone.

父母不應冒讓小孩獨處的風險。

▶ The soldier risked his life trying to save his friend.

那位士兵冒著生命危險，企圖拯救他的朋友。

▶ Jane's father warns her not to risk traveling alone.

珍的爸爸警告她不要冒險獨自去旅行。

20 loose [lus] a. 寬鬆的；鬆脫的；不受控制的

片 come loose   鬆動

反 tight [taɪt] a. 緊的 ③

▶ My brother likes to wear loose clothes and pants.

我弟弟喜歡穿寬鬆的衣褲。

▶ The air crash took place because a screw on the plane's wing came loose.

空難發生的原因是機翼上的一支螺絲鬆脫了。

▶ Minnie's dog is running loose in the park.

米妮的狗在公園裡四處亂跑。

21 persuade [pɚˈswed] vt. 說服

片 (1) persuade sb to + V
說服某人做……

= talk sb into + V-ing

(2) persuade sb not to + V
說服某人不要……

= dissuade sb from + V-ing

= talk sb out of + V-ing

▶ Try to persuade Jerry to apologize to the teacher.

試著說服傑瑞去向老師道歉。

▶ Could you persuade Kurt not to cancel the pop concert?

你可以說服柯特不要取消這場流行音樂演唱會嗎？

▶ Could you dissuade Tom from talking so loudly?
你能不能說服阿湯哥別說話那麼大聲？

衍 (1) persuasion [pɚˋsweʃən]
　　 n. 說服；說服力 ④
　 (2) persuasive [pɚˋswesɪv]
　　 a. 有說服力的 ④
= convincing [kənˋvɪnsɪŋ]
　　 a. 使人信服的

22　cone [kon] *n.* 圓錐體　▢

句 an ice cream cone　蛋捲冰淇淋

▶ I set a warning cone behind the car to avoid further accidents.
我在車後放了一個警示圓錐，以防意外再度發生。

23　odd [ɑd] *a.* 奇怪的；奇數的；不成對的　▢

衍 odds [ɑdz] *n.* 機會；不和，相爭 ⑤
似 strange [strendʒ] *a.* 奇怪的 ①

▶ Paul looks odd today. What's wrong with him?
保羅今天看起來怪怪的。他怎麼了？

▶ One and three are odd numbers, while two and four are even numbers.
1 和 3 是奇數，2 及 4 則是偶數。

▶ Maggie overslept and rushed to work this morning. She wasn't aware that she was wearing odd socks.
瑪姬早上睡過頭又趕著上班。她沒發現自己穿著不成對的襪子。

24　breath [brɛθ] *n.* 呼吸；一絲 (微風)　▢

句 (1) take a deep breath　　深呼吸
　 (2) catch one's breath　　喘口氣
　 (3) a breath of wind　　　一絲微風
衍 breathtaking [ˋbrɛθ͵tekɪŋ] *a.* 驚人的

▶ I always take a deep breath before going on the stage.
我每次上臺前都會深呼吸。

▶ I could hardly catch my breath after trying to catch up with you.
我為了要追上你，幾乎快要喘不過氣了。

▶ There is not a breath of wind here at all.
這裡連一絲風也沒有。

---

breathe [brið] *vi.* & *vt.* 呼吸

延伸 (1) inhale [ɪnˋhel] *vt.* & *vi.* 吸入
= breathe in
　 (2) exhale [ɛksˋhel] *vt.* & *vi.* 呼出
= breathe out

▶ Breathe in. Breathe out. Try to relax yourself.　▢
吸氣。吐氣。設法讓自己放鬆。

▸ Upon hearing the good news, everyone breathed a sigh of relief.
一聽到這個好消息，大家都歎了口氣，如釋重負。
＊relief [rɪˋlif] *n.* 紓解；寬心

25　release [rɪˋlis] *vt.* & *n.* 釋出，釋放 (= let go of)；發行，發布

▸ After ten years in prison, the prisoner was released this morning.
坐了 10 年牢後，那名囚犯今早獲釋。

▸ The authorities concerned have released the names of those killed in the crash.
有關當局已發布這次空難的罹難者名單。

▸ Simon's good behavior earned him early release from prison.
賽門表現良好，因此可以提早出獄。

▸ Marilyn Manson's latest release again topped the charts.
瑪莉蓮・曼森發行的最新專輯再次橫掃排行榜冠軍。
＊top the charts　登上排行榜冠軍
　chart [tʃɑrt] *n.* 圖表 (此處指『排行榜』，在上列片語中恆用複數)

26　temper [ˋtɛmpɚ] *n.* 脾氣

片 keep / lose sb's temper
耐著性子 / 發脾氣

▸ I've never seen Victoria lose her temper.
我從來沒看過維多莉亞發脾氣。

27　cotton [ˋkɑtn̩] *n.* 棉

延伸 (1) a cotton ball　棉花球
　　(2) a cotton swab　棉花棒

▸ All of our T-shirts are made of pure cotton.
我們所有的 T 恤都是純棉製的。

28　lily [ˋlɪlɪ] *n.* 百合

▸ The lilies in the garden are in full bloom.
花園裡的百合花正盛開。

29　straw [strɔ] *n.* 稻草 (不可數)；吸管 (可數)

片 the last straw　忍無可忍的地步
似 hay [he] *n.* 乾草 ③

▸ Make hay while the sun shines.
打鐵趁熱 / 趁著好時機幹活。
—— 諺語

▸ You look very charming when you wear that straw hat.
妳戴著那頂草帽時模樣真迷人。

▸ The little boy used a straw to drink his juice.
小男孩用一根吸管來喝果汁。

▶ Finding the missing ring here is like looking for a needle in the hay.

在這裡尋找丟失的戒指就像大海撈針一般極為困難。

▶ When the boss asked him to work overtime again, John said, "That's the last straw! I quit!"

老闆要他再加班時，約翰便說：『我已到了忍無可忍的地步了！老子不幹了！』

30　flour [flaʊr] *n.* 麵粉 & *vt.* 撒麵粉

用法 flour 與 flower (花) 是同聲字，意思卻不相同，故使用時宜注意拼法。

▶ To make a cake, you need flour and eggs.

做蛋糕需要麵粉和雞蛋。

▶ Flour the bottom of the bowl before you put in the meat.

先將麵粉撒在碗底再把肉放進去。

31　tunnel [ˈtʌnḷ] *n.* 隧道

▶ A tunnel is being built between the two cities.

兩座城市間正在興建一條隧道。

32　quit [kwɪt] *vt.* 停止；戒除；辭 (職) & *vi.* 辭職 (= resign [rɪˈzaɪn])

三 三態同形

片 quit smoking　戒菸
= give up smoking

似 (1) stop [stɑp] *vt.* 停止 ①
　 (2) halt [hɔlt] *vt.* 停止 ④

反 continue [kənˈtɪnjʊ] *vt.* & *vi.* 繼續 ②

▶ Paula announced that she will quit show business next year.

寶拉宣布明年將退出演藝圈。

▶ The old man quit smoking at last.

這位老先生終於戒菸了。

▶ I quit my job because I have to take care of my sick father.

為了照顧生病的父親，我把工作辭掉了。

▶ John no longer works here. He quit two years ago.

約翰已不在這兒工作了。他兩年前就辭職了。

33　intelligent [ɪnˈtɛlədʒənt] *a.* 聰明的

衍 intelligence [ɪnˈtɛlədʒəns]
　 n. 聰明才智；情報 ④

似 (1) clever [ˈklɛvɚ] *a.* 聰明的 ②
　 (2) bright [braɪt] *a.* 睿智的 ①

▶ Lisa is intelligent and hardworking, which is why all her teachers like her.

莉莎既聰明又用功，難怪她的老師們都喜歡她。

34　exhibition [ˌɛksəˈbɪʃən] *n.* 展覽會

片 be on exhibition　展出中
= be on display

▶ There will be an exhibition of modern sculpture next month.

下個月將有一場現代雕塑展覽會。

*sculpture [ˈskʌlptʃɚ] *n.* 雕塑，雕刻

動 exhibit [ɪɡˋzɪbɪt]
  vt. 顯示，現出；展示，陳列 &
  n. 展覽會（= exhibition）④

▶ All the works of the artist are currently on exhibition at the gallery.
那位藝術家的全部作品正在畫廊展出中。

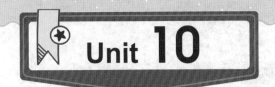

1 electronic [ɪˌlɛk`trɑnɪk] *a.* 電子的

衍 (1) electric [ɪ`lɛktrɪk]
　　　a. 電的；電動的 ②
　　　an electric appliance
　　　家用電器 (冰箱、電視機等)
　　 (2) electrical [ɪ`lɛktrɪkḷ]
　　　a. 與電有關的 ②
　　 (3) electrician [ɪ,lɛk`trɪʃən]
　　　n. 技工，電工 ⑥

▶ To our surprise, Penny plays the electronic organ very well.
令我們驚訝的是，佩妮電子琴彈得非常好。

electricity [ɪˌlɛk`trɪsətɪ] *n.* 電；電力

▶ This commuter train runs on electricity.
這班通勤列車是以電驅動的。

2 shiny [`ʃaɪnɪ] *a.* 發亮的，有光澤的

似 glossy [`glɔsɪ] *a.* 有光澤的，光滑
衍 shine [ʃaɪn]
　　vt. 擦亮 & *vi.* 發亮，照耀 & *n.* 光亮 ②

▶ I found a shiny new coin on the ground and picked it up.
我在地上發現一枚發亮的新硬幣，把它撿了起來。

3 palace [`pælɪs] *n.* 皇宮

似 place [ples] *n.* 地方 & *vt.* 放置 ①

▶ Buckingham Palace is one of the Queen's six homes.
白金漢宮是英國女皇 6 個住所的其中一個。

4 rank [ræŋk] *n.* 等級 & *vi.* 排名

片 the rank and file
　　所有 (機構或部隊) 基層成員
似 (1) grade [gred] *n.* 等級 ①
　　 (2) class [klæs] *n.* 級別 ①

▶ People from all ranks of society deserve equal treatment.
社會各階層的人士都應獲得平等的對待。

▶ Ever since he was found involved in a scandal, the leader has lost the support of the rank and file.
領導者自從被發現涉入醜聞後，就失去基層的支持了。

▶ When it comes to giving aid to countries in need, the US ranks first.
= When it comes to giving aid to countries in need, the US comes in first.
說到援助有難的國家，美國排名第一。

5 rough [rʌf] *a.* 粗糙的；粗略的；粗暴的 & *n.* 草圖 & *adv.* 粗魯地

用 (1) have a rough idea of sth
　　　對某事略知一二
　　(2) be rough on sb　對某人很兇
　　 = be hard on sb

似 (1) uneven [ʌnˋivən] *a.* 不平坦的
　　(2) coarse [kɔrs] *a.* 粗糙的 ④
　　(3) brutal [ˋbrutl] *a.* 粗野的 ④
　　(4) violent [ˋvaɪələnt] *a.* 粗暴的 ③

▶ Mom's hands are rough from hard work.
　媽媽的雙手因為辛勤工作而變得粗糙。

▶ This is just a rough translation and not ready to use.
　這只是粗略的翻譯，還不能用。

▶ I have a rough idea of the proposal you came up with at the meeting.
　你在會議上提出的方案我略知一二。

▶ Michael is a man of little patience, and he is often rough on his children.
　麥可是一個很沒耐心的人，他時常粗暴地對待他的孩子。

▶ When can I see the rough draft of the proposal?
　我何時能看提案的草圖？

▶ Be careful because this team likes to play rough.
　小心一點，這隊打球很粗暴。

roughly [ˋrʌflɪ] *adv.* 約略地，大致上

似 briefly [ˋbriflɪ] *adv.* 簡略地
延伸 roughly 亦可修飾數字。

▶ John is going to stay in Hong Kong for roughly / some / about / approximately / around ten days.
　約翰大約要在香港待 10 天。

▶ Nicole described roughly to me the planned course of action.
　妮可向我概略地描述預定的活動行程。

6 entry [ˋɛntrɪ] *n.* 入口

似 entrance [ˋɛntrəns]
　n. 入口（與介詞 to 並用）②

▶ There is only one entrance to this building.
　這棟大樓只有一個入口。

反 exit [ˋɛksɪt]
　n. 出口（與介詞 from 並用）②

▶ There are two exits from that building.
　那棟大樓有兩個出口。

▶ The main entry to the stadium is across the road.
　體育場的主要入口在馬路對面。

7　proof [pruf] *n.* 證明（集合名詞，不可數）& *a.* 防……的（多用於『名詞 -proof』的複合字）

衍 **prove** [pruv]
　　vt. 證明 & *vi.* 結果顯示 ②

似 **evidence** [ˈɛvədəns]
　　n. 證據，證明（集合名詞，不可數）④

延伸 (1) **waterproof** [ˈwɑtɚˌpruf]
　　　　a. 防水的 ⑥
　　(2) **soundproof** [ˈsaʊndˌpruf]
　　　　a. 隔音的
　　(3) **bulletproof** [ˈbʊlɪtˌpruf]
　　　　a. 防彈的

▶ I wouldn't demand proof of loyalty from a friend.
　 我不會向朋友要求忠誠的證明。

▶ The judge required proof of what the defendant said.
　 法官要求被告提出說辭的證據。
　 *defendant [dɪˈfɛndənt] *n.* 被告

▶ Most banks' safes are proof against fire.
= Most banks' safes are fireproof.
　 大部份銀行的保險箱都是防火的。

8　owe [o] *vt.* 欠（債）；歸功

片 (1) **owe sb sth**　欠某人某物
　　(2) **owe A to B**　將 A 歸功於 B
　 = **attribute A to B**

▶ You still owe me NT$1,000, and you seem to have forgotten it.
　 你仍欠我新臺幣 1,000 元，而你似乎已忘了這碼事。

▶ I owe what I am to my parents.
= I attribute what I am to my parents.
　 我要把我現有的成就歸功於父母。

---

owing [ˈoɪŋ] *a.* 欠著的，未付清的

片 **owing to**　　由於

用法 **owing to**　　之後接名詞作受詞。
　 owing to...　由於……
　 = **because of...**
　 = **due to...**
　 = **on account of...**
　 = **as a result of...**

▶ Owing to poor management, the factory shut down 2 years after it was established.
　 由於管理不善，工廠建立兩年後就關門大吉了。

▶ You've paid most of the rent, but NT$1,000 is still owing.
　 你房租已付了一大半，不過尚欠新臺幣 1,000 元。

9　sin [sɪn] *n.* 罪惡 & *vi.* 犯罪

三 **sin, sinned** [sɪnd], **sinned**

衍 **sinful** [ˈsɪnfəl] *a.* 有（違背良心）罪的

比 crime 及 sin 均指「罪」，前者指與刑法有關的罪（如搶劫、偷竊），而後者指良心上的罪（如拋棄家庭）。

▶ In the eyes of my boss, wasting time is a sin.
　 我的老闆認為浪費時間就是一種罪惡。

▶ You have sinned and brought great shame on the family.
　 你犯了罪並且使家族蒙羞。

10　navy [ˈnevɪ] *n.* 海軍

衍 **naval** [ˈnevḷ] *a.* 海軍的

▶ Nancy's grandfather was in the navy during the war.
　 南西的祖父於戰爭期間在海軍服役。

air force [`ɛr,fɔrs`] *n.* 空軍

延伸 (1) army [`armɪ`] *n.* 陸軍 ②
marine corps [`mə,rin ˋkɔr`]
n. 海軍陸戰隊

*注意 corps 的發音，不要唸成
[`kɔrps`]；但 corpse 則唸成
[`kɔrps`]，表人的『屍體』。

(2) 雄哥 (賴老師) 的老爸曾是空軍的老
兵，因此雄哥從小就對空軍很熟，
以下是有關空軍的一些用語。

① an air base　空軍基地
② the barracks [`bærəks`]
營房，兵營
③ the PX　福利社
(是 the post exchange 的縮寫)

▶ The air force general was charged with bribery and corruption.

該名空軍將軍將被控貪汙收賄。

*bribery [`braɪbərɪ`] *n.* 賄賂
corruption [kə`rʌpʃən`] *n.* 貪汙，腐敗

---

11 violence [`vaɪələns`] *n.* 暴力；猛烈

似 (1) cruelty [`kruəltɪ`] *n.* 殘忍 ④
(2) brutality [bru`tælətɪ`] *n.* 殘暴

▶ You can't resort to violence just because you can't reason with someone.

你不能只是因為無法跟別人理論就訴諸暴力。

*not... just because...　不要只是因為……而就……
resort to...　訴諸……

▶ The violence of the storm was frightening.

暴風雨的猛烈令人害怕。

---

violent [`vaɪələnt`] *a.* 粗暴的

似 (1) cruel [`kruəl`] *a.* 殘忍的 ③
(2) brutal [`brutl`] *a.* 殘暴的 ④

▶ Beethoven's father was a violent and dangerous man.

貝多芬的父親是一個粗暴而又危險的人。

---

violently [`vaɪələntlɪ`]
adv. 激烈地；粗暴地

似 (1) fiercely [`fɪrslɪ`] *adv.* 強烈地
(2) vehemently [`viəməntlɪ`]
adv. 激烈地
(3) cruelly [`kruəlɪ`] *adv.* 殘忍地
(4) brutally [`brutlɪ`] *adv.* 粗暴地

▶ All the villagers in this town violently objected to the proposed construction of a nuclear power plant.

整個鎮上的村民都激烈地反對興建核電廠的提議。

▶ Parents should never treat their children violently.

父母絕不可粗暴地對待孩子。

---

12 concert [`kansət`] *n.* 一致，協調 (不可數)；音樂會 (可數)，演唱會

片 (1) work in concert with...
與……同心協力

▶ We should work in concert with one another to improve the quality of our lives.

我們應該同心協力改善生活品質。

(2) put on a concert　舉辦演唱會
= hold a concert

▶ The band is going to put on a concert this weekend.
該樂團這個週末將舉辦一場演唱會。

13　poll [pol] *n.* 民意測驗 & *vt.* 做問卷調查

▶ A nationwide poll revealed different opinions among young voters.
一項全國調查顯示了年輕選民不同的意見。
＊reveal [rɪ'vil] *vt.* 顯露

▶ Two thousand people were polled about the upcoming election.
有 2,000 人針對即將到來的選舉接受問卷調查。

survey ['sɝve] *n.* 調查 & [sɚ've] *vt.* 勘察

衍 surveyor [sɚ'veɚ] *n.* 調查員

▶ According to a recent survey, the quality of life in Taiwan is deteriorating.
根據最近的一項調查，臺灣的生活品質正逐漸惡化。
＊deteriorate [dɪ'tɪrɪə,ret] *vi.* 惡化

▶ The burglar surveyed the house before entering it.
竊賊在進入屋子前先在四周勘察一番。
＊burglar ['bɝglɚ] *n.* 夜賊

investigate [ɪn'vɛstə,get] *vt.* 調查（案件）

片 investigate a case　調查案件
= look into a case

衍 investigation [ɪn,vɛstə'geʃən] *n.* 調查 ④

似 probe [prob] *vt.* 調查、探查 ⑥

▶ The police are still investigating the case.
警方還在調查這個案子。

14　automatic [,ɔtə'mætɪk] *a.* 自動的

衍 automated ['ɔtə,metɪd] *a.* 自動化的

▶ Automatic cameras are getting more and more popular these days.
自動照相機現在越來越流行了。

automatically [,ɔtə'mætɪklɪ] *adv.* 自動地

用法 automatically 亦可被下列片語取代：
on one's own　靠……自己

▶ The dishwasher will stop automatically when the dishes are clean.
= The dishwasher will stop on its own when the dishes are clean.
盤子洗乾淨時洗碗機會自動停止。

15　bullet ['bulɪt] *n.* 子彈

片 (1) fire a bullet at...　向……開一槍

▶ The police fired a bullet at the thief as he ran away.
竊賊脫逃時，警察朝他開了一槍。

(2) the bullet train
子彈列車 (高速火車)

(3) a bullet hole　彈孔

似 bulletin [ˈbʊlətɪn]
n. 告示，公告；新聞快報 ④

▶ I see some bullet holes in the wall. What happened here?
我在牆上看到一些彈孔。這裡發生了什麼事？

16　ownership [ˈonɚˌʃɪp] n. 所有權

衍 (1) own [on] vt. 擁有 ①
(2) owner [ˈonɚ] n. 擁有者，主人 ②

▶ Tom and John had a fight over the ownership of the land.
湯姆和約翰為了這塊土地的所有權而爭吵。

17　similarity [ˌsɪməˈlærətɪ] n. 相似 (不可數)，相似之處 (可數)

片 bear (a) similarity to...　與……相似
= bear a resemblance to...

衍 similar [ˈsɪmələ] a. 相似的 ②

似 resemblance [rɪˈzɛmbləns]
n. 相似 ⑤

反 difference [ˈdɪfərəns]
n. 差異，不同 ②

▶ There is little similarity between the two sisters.
這兩姊妹長得不太像。

▶ This city bears some similarity to San Francisco.
這個城市和舊金山有點相似。

18　relax [rɪˈlæks] vt. 使放鬆；使寬鬆 & vi. 放鬆，休息

衍 relaxation [ˌrilæksˈeʃən]
n. 放鬆；緩和 ④

似 unwind [ʌnˈwaɪnd]
vt. & vi. (使) 放鬆 (三態為：unwind, unwound [ʌnˈwaʊnd], unwound)

▶ Listening to music can help me relax.
聽音樂可以幫助我放鬆。

▶ The rules are usually relaxed a bit around Christmas.
聖誕節前後這段時間，規定通常會變寬鬆一點。

▶ Let's stop working and relax for a while.
咱們停工放鬆一下吧。

relaxed [rɪˈlækst]
a. 寬鬆的；覺得放鬆的

衍 relaxing [rɪˈlæksɪŋ] a. 令人放鬆的

似 (1) loose [lus] a. 寬鬆的 ③
(2) carefree [ˈkɛrˌfri]
　a. 無憂無慮的，輕鬆愉快的 ⑥

▶ School regulations have become more and more relaxed.
校規變得越來越寬鬆了。

▶ I always feel relaxed around you.
和你在一起我總是覺得很輕鬆。

19　stir [stɝ] vt. & n. 攪拌；騷動

目 stir, stirred [stɝd], stirred

▶ I stirred my coffee with a spoon.
我用湯匙攪拌咖啡。

片 (1) stir up... 激起……
(2) stir up trouble 鬧事，惹麻煩
(3) cause a stir 引起騷動 / 混亂
似 mixture [ˋmɪkstʃɚ] n. 混和；混和物 ②

▶ Behave yourself and don't stir up trouble.
你要守規矩，別惹麻煩。
▶ The war in Iraq has caused a stir around the world.
伊拉克戰爭在全球引起騷動。

20　territory [ˋtɛrəˌtɔrɪ] n. 地盤；區域；領土，屬地

衍 territorial [ˌtɛrəˋtɔrɪəl] a. 領土的
延伸 流氓的地盤則使用 turf [tɝf]。
▶ The gangsters do their best to protect their turf.
這群幫派分子會盡全力來保護他們的地盤。

▶ It is not uncommon for dogs to fight over food and territory.
狗為了搶食物及地盤而打架是屢見不鮮的事。
▶ Tom and Jerry formed a team to explore the territory around the South Pole.
湯姆和傑利組了一支隊伍前往探索南極附近的區域。
▶ Guam is a territory of the US.
關島是美國的屬地。

21　sip [sɪp] vt. & n. 啜飲

三 sip, sipped [sɪpt], sipped
片 take a sip of... 小喝一口……

▶ The guy sitting at the bar sipping coffee is my boyfriend.
那個坐在吧臺喝咖啡的男生是我男友。
▶ Julie took a sip of her tea and went on reading.
茱莉品了一口茶後繼續閱讀。

22　wisdom [ˋwɪzdəm] n. 智慧

衍 wise [waɪz] a. 聰明的，有智慧的 ①
似 intelligence [ɪnˋtɛlədʒəns] n. 智能，智慧 ④
比 wisdom 指的是『生活經驗上的智慧』，而 intelligence 指的是『課業、學術上的智慧』。

▶ Aristotle was a man of great wisdom.
亞里斯多得是一個很有智慧的人。

23　meanwhile [ˋminˌ(h)waɪl] adv. & n. 同時

似 meantime [ˋminˌtaɪm] adv. & n. 同時 ⑤
用法 meanwhile 及 meantime 作名詞時，用於下列片語：
in the meanwhile 在此同時
= in the meantime
= meanwhile / meantime (adv.)

▶ I'll do the cooking; meanwhile, you can do the laundry for me.
= I'll do the cooking; in the meanwhile, you can do the laundry for me.
我來煮飯；在此同時你可幫我洗衣服。

24 wheat [(h)wit] n. 小麥

延伸 (1) oat [ot] n. 燕麥
(2) barley [ˈbɑrlɪ] n. 大麥
(3) rye [raɪ] n. 黑麥，裸麥
(4) buckwheat [ˈbʌkˌ(h)wit] n. 蕎麥
(5) grain [gren] n. 穀物 ②

▶ Flour is made from wheat.
麵粉由小麥製成。

25 compete [kəmˈpit] vi. 競爭

片 compete with sb for sth
與某人競爭某物

衍 (1) competition [ˌkɑmpəˈtɪʃən]
n. 競爭 ④
(2) competitive [kəmˈpɛtətɪv]
a. 競爭的 ④
(3) competitor [kəmˈpɛtətɚ]
n. 競爭者，參賽者 ④
(4) competent [ˈkɑmpətənt]
a. 有能力的，能勝任的 ⑤
(5) competence [ˈkɑmpətəns]
n. 能力，稱職 ⑤

▶ No computer can compete with this one in terms of speed.
說到速度，沒有一臺電腦能比得上這臺。

▶ There will be 50 basketball teams competing for the championship.
將有 50 支籃球隊角逐冠軍寶座。

26 ton [tʌn] n. 噸；許多

片 tons of work　許多工作
= a lot of work

▶ The truck weighs over two tons and cannot cross the bridge.
這輛卡車超過兩噸重，因此不能過橋。

▶ Sherry's got tons of work to do, so she's not going to the movies with us tonight.
雪莉有很多工作要做，所以她今晚不跟我們去看電影了。

27 pea [pi] n. 豌豆

延伸 (1) mung bean [ˈmʌŋˌbin] n. 綠豆
(2) soybean [ˈsɔɪˌbin] n. 黃豆
(3) adzuki bean [æˈdzukɪˌbin]
n. 紅豆

▶ My favorite dish is roast chicken with peas and vegetables.
我最喜歡的一道菜是烤雞加豌豆和蔬菜。

28 controller [kənˈtrolɚ] n. 控制器；控制人員

▶ Please press the controller to turn the machine on.
請按控制器來開機。

▶ Flight traffic controllers track hundreds of planes in the air over the country every day.
航管人員每天監控數以百計飛過該國領空的飛機。

29 county [ˈkauntɪ] *n.* 縣；郡

比 (1) province [ˈprɑvɪns] *n.* 省；州 ⑤
　 (2) city [ˈsɪtɪ] *n.* 城市 ①

▶ John grew up in Taichung County.
　約翰在臺中縣長大。

30 awkward [ˈɔkwəd] *a.* 笨拙的，不熟練的；令人尷尬的

似 clumsy [ˈklʌmzɪ] *a.* 笨拙的 ④

▶ Sue is quite awkward and falls over a lot.
　蘇相當笨拙，而且時常跌倒。
▶ I felt awkward when I saw my ex-boyfriend yesterday.
　昨天我看到前任男友時渾身不自在。

31 talent [ˈtælənt] *n.* 天分；天才

片 have a talent for...
　在……方面有才能
= be talented in...

▶ Mary has a talent for drawing.
= Mary is talented in drawing.
　瑪莉有繪畫天分。

talented [ˈtæləntɪd] *a.* 有天分的

似 (1) gifted [ˈgɪftɪd] *a.* 有天分的 ④
　 (2) versatile [ˈvɝsətḷ]
　　 a. 多才多藝的 ⑥

▶ The lack of talented people makes it hard for the government to carry out the project.
　由於缺乏有才幹的人，政府很難執行這項計畫。

32 shortly [ˈʃɔrtlɪ] *adv.* 不久，立刻

片 shortly after / before...
　……不久之後 / 不久之前
= immediately after / before

▶ Mary successfully found a well-paid job shortly after she graduated from college.
　瑪莉大學畢業後不久，就順利地找到一份待遇不錯的工作。

33 organize [ˈɔrgəˌnaɪz] *vt.* 組織

衍 (1) organized [ˈɔrgənˌaɪzd]
　　 a. 有組織的
　 (2) organizer [ˈɔrgəˌnaɪzɚ]
　　 n. 組織者，主辦人 ⑥

▶ Ted organized these workers into a union.
　泰德將這些工人組織成一個工會。

34 pronounce [prəˈnauns] *vt.* 發音；宣布

衍 pronunciation [prəˌnʌnsɪˈeʃən]
　 n. 發音 ④

▶ How do you pronounce your last name?
　請問您的姓要怎樣發音？
▶ I now pronounce you man and wife.
　我現在宣布你們成為夫妻。

35 assume [əˈsum] *vt.* 假定，認為（以 that ... 作受詞）；負起（責任）

片 assume the burden of...
　　挑起……的重擔
= shoulder the burden of...

衍 assumption [əˈsʌmpʃən] *n.* 假定 ⑤

▶ Paul assumed that his girlfriend was joking when she said he was ugly.
　保羅的女友說他很醜時，他認定她一定是在開玩笑。

▶ After his parents passed away, the boy assumed the burden of raising the family.
　男孩的父母雙亡後，他便負起養家的責任。

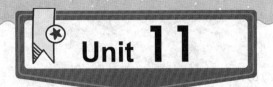

Unit 11

1101-1103

1 forever [fə`ɛvə] adv. 永遠

用法 forever 之後亦可加 a day，形成誇大的用法。

比 forever 與 for good 及 permanently [`pɜmənəntlɪ] 同義，均表『永遠』，使用時多置於句尾，修飾之前的動詞。

▸ Those good old days have gone for good.
過去的那些美好時光永不再返。

▸ After working 20 years in New York, John is planning on going back to his hometown in Minneapolis and staying there forever.
在紐約工作二十年後，約翰計劃要回到明尼亞波里斯老家，永遠待在那裡。

▸ I'll love you forever and a day.
我會永遠愛你，而且還多愛你一天 —— 我會愛你到海枯石爛。

---

temporary [`tɛmpə,rɛrɪ] a. 暫時的

片 on a temporary basis　暫時地
= temporarily

反 permanent [`pɜmənənt] a. 永久的 ④

▸ The hunter made a temporary shelter out of branches.
獵人用樹枝做了一個臨時的避難小屋。

▸ I'm teaching on a temporary basis for the time being, but I hope I can find a permanent job as a computer engineer.
我目前暫時教書，不過我希望能找到一份當電腦工程師的永久性工作。

---

temporarily [`tɛmpə,rɛrəlɪ] adv. 暫時地

似 momentarily [`momən,tɛrəlɪ] adv. 臨時地

反 permanently [`pɜmənəntlɪ] adv. 永久地

▸ After taking the medicine, Amber felt temporarily relieved.
吃了藥之後，安柏暫時感到舒坦一些。
*relieved [rɪ`livd] a. 舒緩的

2 maid [med] n. 侍女

似 servant [`sɜvənt] n. 僕人 ②

▸ Having a butler, three maids, and two gardeners to take care of his needs, the millionaire leads a luxurious life.
這個百萬富翁有一個管家、三個女僕及兩個園丁來照顧他的需求，過著奢侈的生活。
*butler [`bʌtlə] n. 男管家
　luxurious [lʌg`ʒurɪəs] a. 豪華的，奢侈的

3 resist [rɪ`zɪst] vt. & vi. 抗拒

片 cannot resist + V-ing　忍不住……
= cannot help + V-ing
= cannot help but + V

▸ How can you resist chocolate cake? Whenever I see some, I must have a piece.
你怎麼抗拒得了巧克力蛋糕？我每次看到都非來一塊不可。

衍 (1) resistant [rɪˈzɪstənt] *a.* 抵抗的 ⑥
　　be resistant to sth　抗拒某物
　(2) resistance [rɪˈzɪstəns] *n.* 抵抗 ④

▶ You can try to resist, but you know you can't ignore your deepest desire.
你可以試著抗拒，但你知道你無法忽視你最深層的渴望。

▶ I couldn't resist taking a look at that beautiful girl when she passed by.
= I couldn't help taking a look at that beautiful girl when she passed by.
= I couldn't help but take a look at that beautiful girl when she passed by.
那個美女經過時，我忍不住看了她一眼。

4　guidance [ˈɡaɪdəns] *n.* 指導 (不可數)

H under sb's guidance
　在某人指導下

衍 guide [ɡaɪd] *vt.* 引導 ②

似 instruction [ɪnˈstrʌkʃən] *n.* 教導 ②

▶ Under Coach Lee's guidance and leadership, I'm sure we'll win the contest.
在李教練的指導及帶領下，我有把握我們一定會贏得這場比賽。
*contest [ˈkɑntɛst] *n.* 比賽；競賽

5　accurate [ˈækjərɪt] *a.* 精準的

衍 accuracy [ˈækjərəsɪ] *n.* 準確性 ④

似 precise [prɪˈsaɪs] *a.* 精確的 ④

反 inaccurate [ɪnˈækjərɪt] *a.* 不精準的

▶ Though the clock is old, it is still accurate.
這個時鐘雖然老舊，卻依然準確。

▶ These figures are not accurate. I'm afraid you'll have to work them out again.
這些數據不準。恐怕你得重算一遍。

6　sake [sek] *n.* 理由，緣故

H (1) for the sake of...　為了……的緣故
　(2) for sb's sake　為了某人的緣故

▶ For the sake of your health, you should break the habit of smoking immediately.
= For your health's sake, you should break the habit of smoking immediately.
為了你的健康著想，你應立刻戒掉抽菸的習慣。

▶ I hope Jerry has taken your advice for his own sake.
我希望傑瑞能為自己著想，接受你的建議。

7　toss [tɔs] *vt.* 扔，擲 & *n.* 扔，擲；擲幣賭勝負

H (1) toss and turn　輾轉難眠
　(2) a toss of a coin　擲硬幣決定

似 throw [θro] *vt.* 投，擲 ①

▶ After reading the letter, David crumpled it up and tossed it into the fire.
大衛看完信之後，就把信揉成一團丟到火裡去了。
*crumple [ˈkrʌmpl] *vt.* 弄皺

▶ I tossed and turned in bed last night, wondering why my girlfriend would leave me.

我昨晚輾轉難眠，一直在想我女友為何要離我而去。

▶ Paul threw an empty bottle in the trash can with a quick toss.

保羅迅速地將一個空瓶子扔進垃圾桶裡。

▶ The venue of the contest was decided with a toss of a coin.

比賽的場地是以擲硬幣決定的。

＊venue [ˈvɛnju] n. 地點

8　reserve [rɪˈzɜv] vt. 預訂 & n. 儲備；保護區

⊞ keep sth in reserve　儲備某物

衍 (1) reservation [ˌrɛzəˈveʃən] n. 預訂 ④

(2) reservoir [ˈrɛzəˌvwɑr] n. 水庫 ⑤

似 preserve [prɪˈzɜv] vt. 保護；保存 & n. 果醬；蜜餞（常用複數）④

▶ I'd like to reserve a room for three nights.

= I'd like to make a reservation for three nights.

= I'd like to book a room for three nights.

我要訂房住三晚。

▶ You should keep some money in reserve for a rainy day.

你應儲備一些錢以備不時之需。

▶ This area is a wildlife reserve and hunting is strictly prohibited.

這裡是野生動物保護區，嚴禁打獵。

＊prohibit [prəˈhɪbɪt] vt. 禁止

9　harbor [ˈharbɚ] n. 港口 & vt. 窩藏，庇護；心懷

⊞ (1) a harbor city　港都
　= a port city

(2) harbor a grudge against sb　對某人懷恨
　= bear a grudge against sb
　＊grudge [grʌdʒ] n. 怨恨

似 port [port] n. 港口 ②

▶ Hong Kong is a harbor city.

香港是個港都。

▶ Cindy is accused of harboring an escaped outlaw.

辛蒂被控窩藏逃犯。

＊outlaw [ˈautˌlɔ] n. 亡命之徒

▶ Since quarreling with Tom last week, John has harbored a grudge against him.

自從上星期跟湯姆吵過架之後，約翰對他就一直心懷憤恨。

＊quarrel [ˈkwɔrəl] vi. 爭吵

dock [dak] n. 碼頭 & vt. 減少

⊞ (1) in dock　靠碼頭

(2) dock sb's pay / wages / salary　減某人的薪資

似 wharf [(h)wɔrf] n. 碼頭（複數形為 wharves [(h)wɔrvz]）⑥

▶ The ships were all in dock before the typhoon approached.

颱風來襲前，所有船隻全都停靠到碼頭。

▶ The boss threatened to dock Peter's salary if he was late again.

老闆威脅彼得，如果他再遲到就要扣他薪水。

10 trail [trel] vt. 跟蹤；拖 & n. 小徑

片 trail sb to + 地方　跟蹤某人到某地
= track sb to + 地方
= follow sb to + 地方
似 (1) track [træk] vt. 跟蹤 ②
(2) path [pæθ] n. 小徑 ②

▶ The policeman trailed the suspect to the house he lived in.
那名警察跟蹤嫌犯到他住的地方。

▶ Lucy walked down the stairs slowly, trailing a coat behind her.
= Lucy walked down the stairs slowly, tugging a coat behind her.
露西身後拖了一件外套，緩緩地走下樓梯。
＊tug [tʌg] vt. 拖，拉

▶ The trail leads to a beautiful valley.
這條小徑通往一個很美的山谷。

11 faint [fent] a. 頭暈的；微弱的 & vi. 暈倒 & n. 昏厥 (恆為單數)

片 (1) feel faint　感到暈暈的
= feel dizzy
(2) not have the faintest idea
毫不知情
= not have the foggiest idea
＊foggiest [ˈfɑgɪst] a. 最模糊的
= not have the slightest idea
= have no idea
似 pass out　昏倒

▶ I didn't eat anything today and I feel faint with hunger now.
我今天什麼也沒吃，現在餓得發昏。

▶ Patrick spoke in a very faint voice, so no one could hear him.
派翠克講話的聲音很微弱，所以沒人聽到他說什麼。

▶ I don't have the faintest idea what you're talking about.
我一點都不明白你們在談些什麼。

▶ When I saw my favorite singer in person, I nearly fainted in excitement.
我親眼看到最喜愛的歌手時，興奮得幾乎要昏倒。

▶ Upon hearing the news, Jennifer fell into a faint.
珍妮佛一聽到這個消息就昏倒了。

12 trace [tres] vt. 追蹤 & n. 蹤跡

片 disappear without a trace
消失得無影無蹤
比 track [træk]
vt. 追蹤 & n. 小徑；軌道 ②

▶ It isn't easy to trace your ancestors, especially your female relatives.
要追溯祖先並非易事，尤其是女性的親屬。
＊ancestor [ˈænsɛstɚ] n. 祖先

▶ The bank robber disappeared without a trace.
銀行大盜消失得無影無蹤。

13 steady [ˈstɛdɪ] a. 穩定的 & vt. 使穩定 & adv. 穩定地 & n. (關係確定的) 情侶

三 steady, steadied [ˈstɛdɪd], steadied

▶ It's hard to find a steady job these days.
這年頭要找一份穩定的工作很難。

片 go steady （男女）穩定交往
（與介詞 with 並用）

▶ James leaned on the wall in order to steady himself.
詹姆士靠在牆上以穩住自己的身體。
＊lean [lin] vi. 倚，靠

▶ John is going steady with Mary, and they will probably get married one day.
約翰和瑪莉穩定交往，他們很可能有一天會結婚。

▶ Tammy has been dating Chris for six months. He's her steady.
塔米跟克里斯約會六個月了。他已是她的穩定男友。

---

steadily [ˈstɛdəlɪ]
adv. 不斷地，漸漸地

似 (1) progressively [prəˈgrɛsɪvlɪ]
adv. 不斷地

(2) gradually [ˈgrædʒuəlɪ]
adv. 漸漸地

▶ With the breeze blowing steadily from the window, I couldn't help but fall asleep.
微風從窗口徐徐吹來，我忍不住睡著了。

---

stable [ˈstebl̩] *a.* 穩定的

片 be in stable / critical condition
（病人）處於穩定 / 危急的狀況
＊critical [ˈkrɪtɪkl̩] *a.* 危急的

衍 stabilize [ˈstebl̩ˌaɪz] *vt.* 使穩定 ⑥

▶ The company is currently stable and doing well.
這家公司目前狀況穩定，運作良好。

▶ Shortly after treatment, the patient was in stable condition.
經過治療之後不久，病人的情況就穩定了。

---

14 **injury** [ˈɪndʒərɪ] *n.* （身體）傷害（可數）；（名譽）損壞（不可數）

複 injuries [ˈɪndʒərɪz]

衍 injure [ˈɪndʒɚ] *vt.* 使受傷 ④

▶ It took three weeks for Sam to recover from his sports injury.
山姆的運動傷害花了三個星期才康復。
＊recover from... 從……復原

▶ The sex scandal caused terrible injury to Jill's reputation.
這樁性醜聞讓吉兒的名譽嚴重受損。
＊scandal [ˈskændl̩] *n.* 醜聞
reputation [ˌrɛpjəˈteʃən] *n.* 名譽，名聲

---

15 **dealer** [ˈdilɚ] *n.* 業者

片 (1) a car dealer 汽車商
(2) an antique dealer 古董商

衍 deal [dil] *vi. & n.* 交易 ①
deal in used cars 買賣中古汽車
= buy and sell used cars

似 merchant [ˈmɝtʃənt] *n.* 商人 ④

▶ Paul has made a lot of money as an antique dealer.
保羅是古董商，賺了不少錢。
＊antique [ænˈtik] *n.* 古董，古玩

▶ A used car dealer is one who deals in used cars.
中古汽車商就是從事中古汽車買賣的人。

trader [`tredə] *n.* 交易商，業者

衍 trade [tred] *n.* 交易 ②

▶ Jane's husband is a diamond trader.
阿珍的老公是鑽石商人。

---

16 admire [əd`maɪr] *vt.* 欣賞，欽佩

片 admire sb for sth
因某事物而欣賞某人

衍 (1) admirable [`ædmərəbḷ]
　　a. 值得讚賞的 ④
　　＊不要將本字誤唸成 [əd`maɪrəbḷ]。
　　(2) admiration [ˌædmə`reʃən]
　　n. 欽佩；羨慕 ④

似 (1) appreciate [ə`priʃɪˌet] *vt.* 欣賞 ②
　　(2) think highly of... 看得起……

▶ I admire Justin for his proficiency in English.
= I think highly of Justin for his proficiency in English.
賈斯汀的英文造詣令我折服。
＊proficiency [prə`fɪʃənsɪ] *n.* 精通

---

17 heel [hil] *n.* 腳後跟；高跟鞋 & *vt.* 修理（鞋跟）；裝鞋跟 & *vi.* 緊跟

片 (1) hard on one's heels　緊跟某人
　　(2) high heels　高跟鞋
　　　　a pair of high heels　一雙高跟鞋

▶ With the enemy army hard on his heels, the soldier had no choice but to jump off the cliff.
由於後頭敵軍窮追不捨，這名士兵別無選擇，只好跳下懸崖。
＊cliff [klɪf] *n.* 懸崖

▶ Walking gracefully in high heels is never an easy task.
穿著高跟鞋優雅地行走絕非易事。
＊gracefully [`gresfəlɪ] *adv.* 優雅地

▶ Jack took his old shoes to the shop to get them heeled.
傑克把他的一雙舊鞋拿去鞋店修理鞋跟。

▶ When you tell your dog to heel, you are telling it to come close to you.
你叫你的狗緊跟上來時，你是在告訴牠要跟到你身邊。

---

18 satisfactory [ˌsætɪs`fæktərɪ] *a.* 令人滿意的

衍 (1) satisfy [`sætɪsˌfaɪ]
　　vt. 使滿足；符合（要求、條件）②
　　(2) satisfying [`sætɪsˌfaɪɪŋ]
　　　　a. 令人愉悅的；令人飽足的
　　(3) satisfied [`sætɪsˌfaɪd]
　　　　a. 感到滿意的
　　　　be satisfied with...
　　　　對……感到滿意
　　(4) satisfaction [ˌsætɪs`fækʃən]
　　　　n. 滿足，滿意 ④

▶ I couldn't get a satisfactory explanation for what had occurred.
對於所發生的事我找不到滿意的解釋。

satisfactorily [ˌsætɪs'fæktərɪlɪ]
adv. 令人滿意地

▸ The conference has been progressing satisfactorily so far.
這場會議至今進行得還算令人滿意。

19　splash [splæʃ] *vt.* 潑水 & *vi.* 濺起水花 & *n.* 濺起的水花聲

(1) splash water on sb
　　把水潑到某人身上
(2) splash about / around
　　到處潑水
(3) make a splash　引起轟動
= cause a sensation
　　*sensation [sɛn'seʃən] *n.* 轟動

▸ The baby splashed water on her mother as her mother bathed her.
小寶寶在媽媽幫她洗澡的時候，潑水到媽媽身上。
*bathe [beð] *vt.* 為……洗澡

▸ The two children had a good time taking a bath and splashing about in the bathtub.
那兩個小孩洗澡洗得很高興，還在浴缸中到處潑水。

▸ Tammy jumped into the swimming pool with a splash.
塔米噗通一聲跳進游泳池裡。

▸ Rose's debut made a big splash on Broadway.
蘿絲初次登臺亮相就在百老匯造成大轟動。
*debut [de'bju / 'debju] *n.* 初次露面

20　impress [ɪm'prɛs] *vt.* 使印象深刻；使銘記

(1) be impressed with sth
　　對某事物有深刻的印象
(2) impress sb with sth
= impress sth on / upon sb
　　使某人對某事物有深刻的印象
(1) impressive [ɪm'prɛsɪv]
　　a. 令人印象深刻的 ②
(2) impression [ɪm'prɛʃən]
　　n. 印象；想法，感覺；痕跡 ④

▸ I was deeply impressed with the city's boulevard.
我對該市的林蔭大道印象極為深刻。
*boulevard ['bulə,vɑrd] *n.* 林蔭大道

▸ The teacher impressed the importance of honesty upon the class.
老師讓班上的同學銘記誠實的重要。

21　melt [mɛlt] *vt.* 融化；熔化 & *vi.* 心軟

(1) melt away　融化殆盡
(2) a melting pot　鎔爐

▸ The sun melted the ice in the buckets before the party even started.
派對都還沒開始，太陽就把好幾桶的冰塊融化了。
*bucket ['bʌkɪt] *n.* 桶子，小桶

▸ The snow melted away soon after the sun rose.
太陽出來後不久雪就融化了。

▸ With a diversity of immigrants from across the world, the United States is properly called a big melting pot.
美國擁有來自世界各地的移民，堪稱是個大鎔爐。
*diversity [daɪ'vɜsətɪ] *n.* 多樣性

▶ Peter's heart melted when he saw tears rolling down his girlfriend's face.
彼得看到女友淚流滿面就心軟了。

22 desirable [dɪˈzaɪrəbḷ] *a.* 適合的，妥當的；值得嚮往的，合意的

用法 It is desirable that + S + (should) + V 最好……

▶ That busy corner is a desirable place for a restaurant.
那個車水馬龍的角落很適合開一家餐廳。

▶ Ted tried to seek a desirable alternative to make up for his wrongdoing.
泰德試圖尋求好方法來彌補他的過錯。

▶ It is desirable that the report (should) be finished today.
這份報告最好今天就完成。

desire [dɪˈzaɪr]
vt. 渴望，想要 & *n.* 慾望

片 (1) leave nothing to be desired
無懈可擊
(2) leave much to be desired
尚待改進
(3) a desire for... 對……的慾望
(4) have a desire to + V 想要……

▶ Everyone desires happiness.
每個人都渴望幸福。

▶ The article Nick wrote leaves nothing to be desired.
這篇尼克所寫的文章完美無缺。

▶ Our educational system leaves much to be desired.
我們的教育制度仍有很大的改善空間。

▶ Tom had a great desire for a sports car.
湯姆很渴望擁有一部跑車。

▶ Most of us have a desire to live as long as possible.
我們大部分的人都想活得越久越好。

23 badly [ˈbædlɪ] *adv.* 拙劣地，差勁地；嚴重地；非常

片 need sth badly
迫切 / 非常需要某事物
= be badly in need of sth

▶ Kelly plays the piano very badly.
凱莉的鋼琴彈得很糟。

▶ Johnny fell down the steps and sprained his ankle badly.
強尼跌下樓梯，嚴重地扭傷了腳踝。

I need your advice badly.
= I'm badly in need of your advice.
我非常需要你的建議。

24 colony [ˈkɑlənɪ] *n.* 殖民地；一群同類且有組織的動物

複 colonies [ˈkɑlənɪz]
片 a colony of ants / bees
一群螞蟻 / 蜜蜂

▶ New York was originally a Dutch colony.
紐約原本是荷蘭的殖民地。

衍 (1) colonial [kəˈlonjəl]
　　　a. 殖民地的，殖民的 ⑤
　　(2) colonize [ˈkɑləˌnaɪz]
　　　vt. 將……開拓為殖民地

▶ I found a large colony of ants in the hole.
我發現洞內有一大群螞蟻。

25　efficient [ɪˈfɪʃənt] a. 有效率的

比 effective [ɪˈfɛktɪv] a. 有效的 ②

▶ A boss likes nothing more than a faithful and efficient worker.
老闆最喜歡忠心且有效率的員工。

inefficient [ɪnəˈfɪʃənt] a. 無效率的

▶ The machine is inefficient; in addition, it consumes too much fuel.
這臺機器效率不彰，除此之外，它又很耗油。
*consume [kənˈsjum] vt. 消耗

26　stale [stel] a. 不新鮮的；無新意的；倦怠的

片 (1) go stale　變得索然無味 / 沒有興趣
　　(2) stale bread　不新鮮的麵包
　　(3) a stale joke　老掉牙的笑話
似 (1) decayed [dɪˈked] a. 腐壞的
　　(2) flat [flæt] a. 單調的 ②
　　(3) boring [ˈborɪŋ] a. 令人無聊的 ①
反 fresh [frɛʃ] a. 新鮮的 ①

▶ The man left his wife when he found their marriage had gone stale.
這個男子發現跟太太的婚姻已變得索然無味時，便離她而去。

▶ Professor Brown always tells stale jokes in class.
布朗教授老是在課堂上講一些老掉牙的笑話。

▶ After ten years at the company, Jack was becoming stale and lacking enthusiasm.
在公司服務 10 年後，傑克漸漸變得倦怠、缺乏熱忱。

27　ambassador [æmˈbæsədɚ] n. 大使 (與介詞 to 並用)

似 (1) consul [ˈkɑnsl̩] n. 領事
　　(2) diplomat [ˈdɪpləmæt] n. 外交官 ④
衍 embassy [ˈɛmbəsɪ] n. 大使館 ④

▶ Who is the Japanese ambassador to South Africa?
日本駐南非大使是誰？

28　alphabet [ˈælfəˌbɛt] n. 字母 (總稱)

用法 alphabet 指某語言的整組字母，而 letter 則指整組字母中的每個字母。

衍 alphabetical [ˌælfəˈbɛtɪkl̩]
　　a. 按字母順序的

▶ There are 26 alphabets in English. (×)
→ There are 26 letters in the English alphabet. (○)
英文字母表共有二十六個字母。

29　crab [kræb] n. 螃蟹

衍 crabbed [ˈkræbɪd]
　　a. (字跡) 潦草難讀的
　　crabbed handwriting　字跡潦草

▶ A crab has two large claws.
螃蟹有兩隻巨螯。

30 global [ˈglobḷ] *a.* 全球的，全世界的

片 global warming　全球暖化

衍 globe [glob] *n.* 地球儀；地球 ④

▶ This could become a global problem.
這可能成為全球的問題。

▶ Global warming is an issue which we can't pay too much attention to.
全球暖化是個我們再注意也不為過的議題。

31 foggy [ˈfɑgɪ] *a.* 多霧的

衍 fog [fɑg] *n.* 霧 ②

延伸 (1) sunny [ˈsʌnɪ] *a.* 晴朗的 ①

(2) cloudy [ˈklaʊdɪ]
a. 多雲的，陰的 ②

(3) rainy [ˈrenɪ] *a.* 下雨的 ①

(4) snowy [ˈsnoɪ] *a.* 下雪的 ②

(5) windy [ˈwɪndɪ] *a.* 多風的 ②

▶ It's dangerous to drive on foggy days.
在霧天開車很危險。

32 dumb [dʌm] *a.* 啞的；愚笨的

片 play dumb　裝傻

似 (1) stupid [ˈstjupɪd] *a.* 愚蠢的 ①

(2) mute [mjut] *a.* 啞的 ⑥

延伸 (1) blind [blaɪnd] *a.* 盲的 ①

(2) deaf [dɛf] *a.* 失聰的 ②
deaf and dumb　又聾又啞

▶ People who can't speak used to be called "dumb"; now we call them "mute".
不能說話的人以前會被稱作 "dumb"，現在則用 "mute" 一字形容。

▶ The dumb thief left his fingerprints at the crime scene.
那位笨賊把他的指紋留在犯罪現場。

▶ Don't play dumb with me. I know what you did.
不要跟我裝傻。我知道你幹了什麼事。

33 pump [pʌmp] *vt. & vi.* 抽取；灌注 & *n.* 幫浦

片 (1) pump... up / pump up...
將……充氣

(2) pump sth into...　將某物灌入……

衍 pumper [ˈpʌmpɚ] *n.* 抽水機

▶ We need to pump the water out of the basement.
我們必須把水從地下室抽出去。

▶ First of all, we need to pump up the balloons.
首先，我們必須將汽球充氣。

▶ The government has pumped millions of dollars into the health service.
政府已挹注數百萬元到醫療照護上。

▶ The gas pump is broken, so be careful with it.
汽油幫浦故障了，所以要小心。

34 **subtract** [səbˈtrækt] *vt.* 減

片 subtract A from B　B 減 A
反 (1) add [æd] *vt.* 增加 ①
　 (2) plus [plʌs] *prep.* (算數) 加 ②

▸ Subtract five from ten, and you'll get five.
10 減 5 等於 5。

minus [ˈmaɪnəs]
prep. (算數) 減 & *a.* 零以下的，負數的
延伸 the minus sign　減號；負號

▸ Six minus five is / equals one.
6 減 5 等於 1。
▸ The temperature is now minus 3 degrees.
現在氣溫是零下三度。

multiply [ˈmʌltəˌplaɪ] *vt.* 乘
三 multiply, multiplied
　 [ˈmʌltəˌplaɪd], multiplied
片 multiply A by B　A 乘 B
　 = multiply A and B
似 times [taɪmz] *prep.* & *vt.* 數字相乘
▸ What is three times two?
3 乘 2 是多少？
反 divide [dəˈvaɪd] *vt.* 除以 ②

▸ If you multiply five by two, you get ten.
= If you multiply five and two, you get ten.
5 乘 2 得 10。

1 capture [ˈkæptʃɚ] *vt.* 逮捕；獲得，引起 (注意) & *n.* 逮捕

片 (1) capture / catch sb's attention
吸引某人的注意力

(2) capture the headlines
獲得媒體的大篇幅報導

似 (1) arrest [əˈrɛst] *vt.* 逮捕 ③
(2) seize [siz] *vt.* 捉住 ④
(3) apprehend [ˌæprɪˈhɛnd] *vt.* 逮捕

▶ Police have finally captured the leader of the criminal organization.
警方終於逮捕了該犯罪組織的首腦。

▶ The singer captured the audience's attention with her good looks and beautiful voice.
這位歌手以其亮麗外型與美妙歌聲獲得觀眾注目。

▶ J.K. Rowling captured the headlines shortly after the release of her novel *Harry Potter*.
J.K. 羅琳發表她的小說《哈利波特》之後，旋即獲得媒體大篇幅報導。

▶ The capture of the rebel leader is a great victory for the government troops.
俘虜叛軍領袖是政府軍的一大勝利。
*rebel [ˈrɛbl̩] *a.* 反叛的 & *n.* 反叛者

2 ambition [æmˈbɪʃən] *n.* 野心，抱負

似 (1) drive [draɪv] *n.* 幹勁，衝勁 ①
▶ John is full of drive.
約翰充滿幹勁。

(2) determination [dɪˌtɜməˈneʃən]
n. 決心 ④

衍 ambitious [æmˈbɪʃəs] *a.* 有野心的 ④

▶ Mike's ambition is to become the chess champion.
麥可的野心是成為西洋棋冠軍。

▶ A man with great ambition is more likely to succeed.
有遠大抱負的人較容易成功。

3 rely [rɪˈlaɪ] *vi.* 依賴；信賴

三 rely, relied [rɪˈlaɪd], relied

片 rely on / upon...
依賴……；信賴……

= depend on / upon...

▶ A happy marriage relies on mutual trust.
幸福的婚姻端賴互相信任。
*mutual [ˈmjutʃʊəl] *a.* 相互的

▶ I trust Steve very much. I know he is a man I can always rely on.
我很信任史提夫。我知道他是一個可信賴的人。

reliable [rɪˈlaɪəbl̩] *a.* 可信賴的

似 dependable [dɪˈpɛndəbl̩]
a. 可信賴的

▶ The weather forecast is not always reliable, so you'd better carry an umbrella with you just in case.
天氣預報並不總是可靠，因此你最好帶把傘以防萬一。
*forecast [ˈforˌkæst] *n.* 預測，預報

4　holy [ˈholɪ] a. 神聖的

似 (1) divine [dɪˈvaɪn] a. 神聖的 ④
　 (2) sacred [ˈsekrɪd] a. 神聖的 ⑤

▶ Nothing is holy for Paul; he only believes in money.
對保羅來說，沒什麼是神聖的；他眼裡只有錢。

5　survivor [səˈvaɪvɚ] n. 生還者

衍 (1) survive [səˈvaɪv]
　　vi. 生存 & vt. 從……中存活；比
　　(某人) 活得久 ②
　 (2) survival [səˈvaɪvl̩]
　　n. 倖存；生存 ②

▶ No survivors were found in this airplane crash.
這起空難無任何生還者。

6　wicked [ˈwɪkɪd] a. 惡毒的；缺德的

衍 wickedness [ˈwɪkɪdnɪs] n. 邪惡
似 evil [ˈivl̩] a. 邪惡的 ②

▶ Snow White's wicked stepmother is very jealous of her stepdaughter's beauty.
白雪公主的惡毒繼母非常嫉妒她繼女的美貌。

▶ The wicked shopkeeper tried to rip off his customers whenever he got the chance.
這個缺德的店主一逮到機會就敲客人竹槓。
＊rip sb off　敲某人竹槓

7　innocent [ˈɪnəsn̩t] a. 清白的，無罪的；純真的

片 be innocent of... 　無……的罪
衍 innocence [ˈɪnəsn̩s] n. 清白；純真 ④

▶ The suspect claimed to be innocent of the robbery, but no one believed him.
該嫌犯聲稱這起搶案他是清白的，但沒人相信他。

▶ I believe Susan is incapable of this crime because she is such an innocent girl.
我相信蘇珊不可能犯下這起案件，因為她是個非常純真的女孩。
＊be incapable of... 　沒有能力 (做)……

8　restrict [rɪˈstrɪkt] vt. 限制，制止

片 restrict A to B
　 將 A 約束在 B 的限度內
衍 (1) restricted [rɪˈstrɪktɪd] a. 受限的
　 (2) restriction [rɪˈstrɪkʃən] n. 限制 ④
似 limit [ˈlɪmɪt] vt. 限制 ②

▶ Hoping that she could eventually quit smoking, Mary started restricting her smoking to half a pack a day.
瑪莉希望終究能把菸戒掉，便開始限制自己一天抽半包菸。

▶ Because of martial law, many activities are restricted.
因為戒嚴，很多活動都遭到限制。
＊martial law [ˌmɑrʃəl ˈlɔ] n. 戒嚴令

9 pause [pɔz] *n.* 沈默，中斷 & *vi.* 停頓

片 pause to + V 停頓片刻再……

似 (1) silence [`saɪləns] *n.* 沉默 ②
(2) break [brek] *n.* 中斷 ①

▶ There was a long, embarrassing pause after Tommy asked a stupid question.
湯米問了個笨問題後，便是一陣漫長、尷尬的沈默。

▶ Howard paused to think about his answer.
霍華德停頓了一下，思索該如何回答。

10 darkness [`dɑrknɪs] *n.* 黑暗

片 leave... in darkness
使……陷入一片漆黑

衍 dark [dɑrk]
n. 暗處；天黑 & *a.* 黑暗的 ①

比 darkness 與 dark 均可做名詞；
darkness 純指『黑暗』，而 dark 則表
『暗處』或『天黑』。有下列重要片語：
(1) after dark 天黑後

▶ Don't go out after dark.
天黑後不要外出。

(2) keep sb in the dark about sth
把某事將某人蒙在鼓裡

▶ John kept me in the dark about his wedding.
約翰把我蒙在鼓裡，不讓我知道他的婚事。

▶ It's very dangerous to drive in such darkness without headlights.
在如此的黑暗中沒開頭燈開車真是非常危險。

▶ The power failure left the whole town in darkness.
停電讓整個城鎮陷入一片漆黑。
＊a power failure 停電

darken [`dɑrkn̩]
vt. & vi. (使) 變暗；(使) 變得不樂觀

▶ The theater room darkened and then the film began.
電影放映廳暗了下來，接著影片便開始了。

▶ The loss of a big deal darkened the future of this company.
失去一筆大買賣使得該公司的前途一片茫茫。

11 fortune [`fɔrtʃən] *n.* 命運 (可數)；運氣 (不可數)；財富

片 (1) make a fortune 發財
(2) cost sb a fortune 花某人不少錢

衍 (1) fortunate [`fɔrtʃənɪt] *a.* 幸運的 ④
(2) misfortune [mɪsˋfɔrtʃən]
n. 不幸 ④

▶ Frank always says it's his good fortune to work with so many brilliant and talented people here in this company.
法蘭克總是說他運氣好，能在這間公司跟這麼多優秀有才氣的人共事。

延伸 a fortune teller　命理師，算命師
似 fate [fet] *n.* 命運 ②

▶ Uncle Peter made a small fortune selling hot dogs.
彼得叔叔賣熱狗發了一筆小財。

▶ What a superb bike! It must've cost you a fortune.
這臺腳踏車真棒！一定花了你一大筆錢吧。
＊superb [suˋpɝb] *a.* 很棒的

12　remote [rɪˋmot] *a.* 偏僻的；久遠的

片 (1) a remote control　遙控器
　 (2) a remote relative　遠房親戚
　 (3) a remote chance
　　　機會渺茫，機會很小
似 distant [ˋdɪstənt] *a.* 遙遠的 ②

▶ No gas station can be found in such a remote town.
在如此偏遠的小鎮，一間加油站都找不到。

▶ Aunt Susan is a remote relative of mine.
蘇珊姑媽是我的遠親。

▶ There's not even a remote chance that Porter will pass the driving test. He's color-blind.
波特要考到駕照根本是機會渺茫。他是個色盲。
＊color-blind [ˋkʌlə‚blaɪnd] *a.* 色盲的

13　assist [əˋsɪst] *vt.* & *vi.* 幫助

片 assist sb in + V-ing　幫助某人做……
　 = help sb (to +) V
衍 assistance [əˋsɪstəns] *n.* 幫助 ④
　 come to sb's assistance
　　前來幫助某人

▶ I assist Mom in doing the housework on weekends.
= I help Mom do the housework on weekends.
每逢週末我都會幫老媽做家事。

▶ If everybody assists, the job will get done quickly.
如果大家都能來幫忙，我們很快就能完工。

---

assistant [əˋsɪstənt]
n. 助理 & *a.* 助理的

▶ The boss always hires attractive personal assistants.
老闆總是僱用迷人的私人助理。

▶ I was promoted to assistant manager last month.
我上個月被升為協理。

14　scatter [ˋskætə] *vt.* 撒；使分散 & *vi.* 分散 & *n.* 零星散布的東西

似 spread [sprɛd]
　 vt. 撒，散布 (三態同形) ②

▶ You can scatter some sand on the ice so you don't slip.
在冰上撒點沙子，這樣你就不會滑倒了。
＊slip [slɪp] *vi.* 滑動

▶ The strong wind scattered the leaves all around.
一陣強風把葉子吹得四散。

▶ The mob began to scatter in all directions after riot police fired tear gas.
鎮暴警察發射催淚瓦斯後，暴民開始四散離開。
＊mob [mɑb] *n.* (一群) 暴徒
　 mobster [ˋmɑbstə] *n.* (一個) 暴徒

▶ There were no people in the square; just a scatter of birds.
廣場上沒有人,只有零星的鳥兒。

---

15 regional [ˋridʒənl̩] *a.* 區域的,局部的

衍 region [ˋridʒən] *n.* 地區,局部 ②

▶ Economic recession in these countries is partly caused by regional conflicts.
區域性的衝突是這幾個國家經濟不景氣的部分原因。
＊recession [rɪˋsɛʃən] *n.* 不景氣

---

zone [zon]
n. 地區 & *vt.* 將……劃作特殊地區

似 (1) area [ˋɛrɪə] *n.* 地區 ①
(2) district [ˋdɪstrɪkt] *n.* 地區;區域 ④

▶ Louise volunteered to go to the war zone to report on the war.
路易斯自願前往戰區報導戰事。

▶ The land has been zoned for industrial use.
該土地已被劃為工業用地。

---

16 grab [græb] *vt.* 抓取 & *n.* 攫取,搶奪

三 grab, grabbed [græbd], grabbed
片 (1) grab a bite to eat 隨便抓東西吃
(2) make a grab for sth 搶奪某物
似 seize [siz] *vt.* 抓住;突然感到……;奪取,占領 ④

▶ I grabbed a bite to eat this morning and then went to work.
早上我隨便抓了點東西吃,便去上班了。

▶ The criminal made a grab for the old woman's purse.
該名罪犯搶了那個老婦人的手提包。

---

grasp [græsp]
vt. 緊抓;理解 & *n.* 抓,緊握

片 grasp the meaning of...
理解……的意思
= understand the meaning of...

▶ A man in a black suit grasped Paul by the arm and shook him violently, telling him to stay out of their business.
一名黑衣人抓住保羅的手臂大力搖晃,要他別再管他們的事。

▶ Most readers found it hard to grasp the meaning of this poem.
大部分的讀者都覺得難以理解這首詩的意思。

▶ Kelly held her husband's hand in a tight grasp.
凱莉緊緊握住她先生的手。

---

17 horn [hɔrn] *n.* 角;號角 (= trumpet);(汽車的) 喇叭

片 (1) honk the horn 按喇叭
(2) blow one's own horn / trumpet 自吹自擂

▶ Some goats have large and magnificent horns.
某些山羊有著又大又雄偉的角。

▶ Nicole drove off honking the horn and threatening to hit anyone who got in her way.
妮可把車開走的同時猛按喇叭,威脅要撞倒任何擋路的人。

比 表樂器的『喇叭』應使用 trumpet
[ˈtrʌmpɪt]；表音響的『喇叭』應使用
loudspeaker [ˈlaud͵spikɚ]。

▶ I don't like Peter because he likes to blow his own horn most of the time.

我不喜歡彼得，因為大部分時間他都愛自吹自擂。

---

whistle [ˈ(h)wɪsḷ]

n. 口哨；哨子 & *vi.* 吹口哨；吹哨子

片 (1) blow a whistle　吹哨子
　　(2) whistle at sb　　對某人吹口哨

▶ I knew Uncle George was around when I heard that tuneless whistle of his.

一聽到喬治叔叔那不成調的口哨聲，我就知道他來了。
*tuneless [ˈtunləs] *a.* 不成曲調的；不悅耳的

▶ The police officer blew his whistle and asked the crowd to leave immediately.

警官吹著哨子，要求群眾立刻離開。

▶ Jimmy whistled at the beautiful girl but was rewarded with a cold stare.

吉米對著那美麗女孩吹口哨，卻得到她冷冷回瞪一眼。

▶ The referee whistled and the game started.

裁判吹起哨子，比賽開始了。
*referee [͵rɛfəˈri] *n.* 裁判

18　dine [daɪn] *vi.* 用餐

片 (1) dine in　在家吃飯
　　(2) dine out　外出進餐

▶ Who are you going to dine out with tonight?

你今晚要跟誰一塊兒外出用餐？

19　suburb [ˈsʌbɝb] *n.* 郊區 (常用複數)

片 in the suburbs of...　在……的郊區
似 outskirts [ˈaut͵skɝts] *n.* 郊區 ⑥

▶ Judy used to live in the suburbs of London.
= Judy used to live on the outskirts of London.

茱蒂曾在倫敦的郊區住過。

---

urban [ˈɝbən] *a.* 都市的

衍 (1) urbanize [ˈɝbən͵aɪz] *vt.* 都市化
　　(2) urbanization [͵ɝbənɪˈzeʃən]
　　　n. 都市化
反 rural [ˈrurəl] *a.* 鄉下的 ④

▶ I'd rather live in a rural area than in an urban area.

我寧願住在鄉下也不願住在都會區。

20　strip [strɪp] *vt.* 移除；*vt.* & *vi.* 剝除 (衣物) & *n.* 條，帶

三 strip, stripped [strɪpt], stripped
片 (1) strip sb of sth
　　　剝奪 (頭銜、財產等) 作為懲罰
　　(2) strip off　脫光衣服
　　= take off one's clothes

▶ We'll have to strip the posters off the wall before we start painting.

上油漆之前，我們得先把海報從牆上弄下來。

▶ The prisoner was stripped naked and beaten up.

囚犯被剝光衣服毒打一頓。
*naked [ˈnekɪd] *a.* 赤裸的

似 **stripe** [straɪp] *n.* 條紋 ④

▶ The children stripped off and jumped into the swimming pool.
孩子們脫光衣服，跳進游泳池裡。

▶ Nick was stripped of his scholarship after he was found cheating on the exam.
考試作弊被發現後，尼克的獎學金被取消以示懲罰。

▶ Cut the meat into strips, please.
請幫我把肉切成條狀。

---

21 **graduate** [ˈɡrædʒʊ͵et] *vi.* 畢業 & [ˈɡrædʒʊɪt] *n.* 大學畢業生 & *a.* 研究生的

片 (1) graduate from...　從 (某校) 畢業
(2) a graduate school　研究所
(3) a graduate student　研究所學生
(4) an undergraduate student
大學部學生

衍 (1) graduation [͵ɡrædʒʊˈeʃən]
n. 畢業 (與介詞 from 並用) ④
(2) undergraduate
[͵ʌndəˈɡrædʒʊɪt] *n.* 大學生 &
a. 大學部的 ⑤

▶ Mary graduated in history from Yale University last year.
瑪莉去年自耶魯大學歷史系畢業。

▶ Benjamin's father is a Cambridge graduate.
班哲明的爸爸是劍橋畢業生。

▶ I am currently a graduate student at that university.
我目前是那所大學的研究生。

---

22 **coconut** [ˈkokə͵nət] *n.* 椰子

▶ Coconut milk is an important ingredient of Thai cuisine.
椰奶是泰式料理的重要食材。
＊ingredient [ɪnˈɡridɪənt] *n.* 成分，(烹飪) 原料
cuisine [kwɪˈzin] *n.* 料理，烹飪

---

23 **hesitate** [ˈhɛzə͵tet] *vi.* 猶豫

片 (1) hesitate about / over sth
對某事感到猶豫
(2) don't hesitate to + V
不假思索就……

衍 (1) hesitant [ˈhɛzə͵tənt] *a.* 猶豫的
(2) hesitation [͵hɛzəˈteʃən] *n.* 猶豫 ④

▶ Katherine is still hesitating about whether or not to marry Kevin.
凱瑟琳還在猶豫是否要嫁給凱文。

▶ Should you have any problems, don't hesitate to call me.
你萬一有什麼問題，別猶豫立刻打電話給我。
＊Should you / If you should...　萬一你……

---

24 **fist** [fɪst] *n.* 拳頭 & *vt.* 用拳頭打

片 shake sb's fist
揮舞拳頭 (表示十分生氣)

▶ The angry driver shook his fist at the slow-moving pedestrian.
憤怒的駕駛向那位行動緩慢的行人揮舞拳頭。

▶ John fisted the wall in anger.
約翰憤怒地揮拳打牆壁。

wrist [rɪst] *n.* 手腕

延伸 (1) a wristband　護腕
(2) a knee band　護膝
＊以上是打網球、羽毛球所戴的護具。

▶ I sprained my wrist bowling.
我玩保齡球時扭傷了手腕。

elbow [ˋɛlbo] *n.* 手肘 & *vt.* 以肘推擠

片 (1) elbow one's way
用手肘推擠前進
(2) elbow sb out of the way
用手肘把某人推開

▶ Jenny hurt her elbow when playing tennis.
珍妮打網球時手肘受傷了。

▶ I elbowed my way through the crowd and successfully got on the train.
我用手肘在群眾中殺出一條路，成功地上了火車。

▶ I tried to stop that guy, but he elbowed me out of the way.
我想要制止那個傢伙，但他用手肘把我推開了。

25 buzz [bʌz] *vi.* (蜜蜂) 嗡嗡地飛；忙進忙出；機器發出聲響 & *n.* 嗡嗡聲

片 (1) buzz around
(蜜蜂) 嗡嗡地四處飛來飛去；
(人) 忙進忙出
(2) give sb a buzz　打電話給某人
= give sb a call
= give sb a ring
= call sb (up)

▶ Bees were buzzing around the flowers in the garden.
蜜蜂在花園裡嗡嗡地圍繞著花叢飛。

▶ Reporters were buzzing around at the crime scene, trying to get more information about the case.
記者在犯罪現場忙進忙出，試圖得到更多該案的消息。

▶ Steve pulled the car over when he heard something buzzing in the engine.
史提夫聽見引擎發出怪聲後，便把車子開到路邊停下來。

▶ I had a bad sleep last night because of the buzz of mosquitoes.
我昨晚因為蚊子的嗡嗡聲睡得很不好。

▶ Give me a buzz if you need help.
你若需要幫忙就打電話給我。

hum [hʌm] *vt.* & *vi.* 哼唱 & *n.* 嗡嗡聲

三 hum, hummed [hʌmd], hummed
似 sing [sɪŋ] *vt.* & *vi.* 唱歌 ①

▶ Jeff was humming a song while taking a shower.
傑夫一邊淋浴一邊哼歌。

▶ The annoying hum from the speakers almost drove me nuts.
擴音器發出的擾人嗡嗡聲快讓我發瘋了。

26 **waterfall** [ˈwɑtɚˌfɔl] *n.* 瀑布

似 cascade [kæsˈked] *n.* 小瀑布

▶ The boat went over the waterfall, and no one survived.
那艘船從瀑布掉下去,無人生還。

27 **flood** [flʌd] *n.* 水災;大批⋯⋯ & *vt.* & *vi.* 淹沒;湧入

片 (1) a flood of... 一大批⋯⋯
(2) be flooded with... 被⋯⋯淹沒

▶ The flood ruined hundreds of houses and claimed twenty lives.
這場水災毀了好幾百棟房舍,奪走了二十條人命。

▶ A flood of vehicles congests the streets of downtown at rush hour.
大批車輛在交通尖峰時刻塞爆了市中心的街道。

▶ The storm left the whole area flooded.
暴風雨使整個地區都淹水了。

▶ The area flooded often, so most residents moved out.
這個地區經常淹水,所以居民大多搬走了。
＊resident [ˈrɛzədənt] *n.* 居民

▶ The TV station was flooded with emails after the interview.
那個訪談播出後,電視臺收到如潮水般湧來的電子郵件。

28 **cafeteria** [ˌkæfəˈtɪrɪə] *n.* 自助餐廳

似 café [kəˈfe] *n.* 兼賣簡餐的咖啡廳

▶ I've heard that the cafeteria over there has excellent food.
聽說那邊那家自助餐廳的菜色極佳。

29 **dawn** [dɔn] *n.* 黎明;開端 & *vi.* 開始明白

片 (1) at dawn 在黎明時
(2) since the dawn of history
有史以來
(3) it dawns on sb that...
某人開始明白⋯⋯

似 daybreak [ˈdeˌbrek] *n.* 黎明
at daybreak 在黎明時分

反 dusk [dʌsk] *n.* 黃昏 ⑥
at dusk 在黃昏時分

▶ The couple got up at dawn to watch the sunrise together.
這對夫妻黎明起床,一起欣賞日出。

▶ Since the dawn of history, man has been searching for immortality.
自古以來,人類都在尋求長生不老。
＊immortality [ˌɪmɔrˈtælətɪ] *n.* 永生

▶ When Carl lost that game, it dawned on him that he could never make it.
輸掉了那場比賽的時候,卡爾開始明白自己永遠都贏不了。

30　bind [baɪnd] *vt.* 綁；束縛

- bind, bound [baʊnd], bound
- bind A to B　將 A 綁在 B 上
- bound [baʊnd] *a.* 注定的；開往的 ⑤

▶ I think you should bind the old papers into a bundle before putting them outside.
我認為你應先把這些舊報紙綁成一捆，然後再把它們放在外頭。

▶ The villagers bound the thief to a tree with a heavy rope.
村民們用一根粗繩把這個賊綁在樹上。

31　dishonest [dɪsˈɑnɪst] *a.* 不誠實的

- (1) untruthful [ʌnˈtruθfəl] *a.* 不實的
  (2) deceitful [dɪˈsitfəl]
  　a. 騙人的；虛假的
- honest [ˈɑnɪst] *a.* 誠實的；坦白的 ①

▶ I can see Tom has been doing things in a dishonest manner.
我看得出湯姆一直以不誠實的方式在做事。

32　operation [ˌɑpəˈreʃən] *n.* 操作；營運；手術

- perform an operation on...
  對……做手術
= perform surgery on...
  (surgery 是不可數名詞，之前不加 a)
- (1) operate [ˈɑpəˌret] *vt.* 操作 ②
  (2) operator [ˈɑpəˌretɚ]
  　n. 操作人員；接線生，總機
  (3) operational [ˌɑpəˈreʃən̩]
  　a. 操作上的 ⑤

▶ Are you familiar with the operation of this machine?
你熟悉這臺機器的操作方式嗎？

▶ Three doctors were performing an operation on the patient.
三位醫生正為病人動手術。

33　crane [kren] *n.* 起重機；鶴 & *vt.* & *vi.* 伸(頸)

- crane one's neck　引頸
- 與鶴長得有點像但體積都較小的鷺鷥，英文稱作 egret [ˈigrət]。

▶ You have to get a license to operate a crane.
你必須取得執照，才能操作起重機。

▶ I saw a crane spread its wings and take off gracefully.
我看到一隻鶴張開雙翅，優雅地飛了起來。

▶ People craned their necks to see the accident scene as they passed by.
人們路過時都引頸觀看事故現場。

34　basement [ˈbesmənt] *n.* 地下室

- cellar [ˈsɛlɚ] *n.* 地窖

▶ During the storm, everyone went to the basement for safety.
暴風雨來襲時，大家都到地下室避難。

35 bet [bɛt] *vt.* 打賭，敢肯定 & *vt.* & *vi.* 打賭，下注 & *n.* 賭注

三態同形

(1) bet money on sth
　　在某物上下賭注
(2) place / put a bet (on sth)
　　（在某物上）下賭注

▶ I bet you Betty is still in the office.
我跟你打賭，貝蒂還在公司。

▶ John bet all of his money on the black horse.
約翰把他所有的錢全部押注在那匹黑馬上。

▶ The inexperienced gambler placed a bet on a horse that had no chance of winning.
那個沒經驗的賭客下注給那匹不可能獲勝的賽馬。
*inexperienced [ˌɪnɪkˋspɪrɪənst] *a.* 經驗不足的

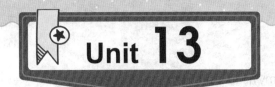

Unit 13

1　cast [kæst] *vt.* 扔，擲 & *n.* 演員陣容；石膏 (= plaster cast)

目 三態同形

用 (1) cast the die　擲骰子
　　＊die [daɪ]
　　　n. 骰子 (單數，複數為 dice [daɪs])
　　(2) cast a ballot　投票
　　＝ cast a vote
　　　＊ballot [ˋbælət] *n.* 選票 ⑤
　　(3) cast a(n)... look at...
　　　對……投以……的眼光

似 throw [θro] *vt.* 扔，擲 ①

▶ James cast the die to start the game.
　詹姆士擲了骰子來開始遊戲。

▶ We will cast a ballot to decide who will lead our team in the future.
　我們將投票決定未來由誰來領導我們的團隊。

▶ The students cast a puzzled look at their math teacher.
　學生們一臉疑惑地看著數學老師。

▶ This movie has an all-star cast, but the plot is terrible.
　這部電影全是大牌卡司，但故事情節卻很糟。
　＊plot [plɑt] *n.* (小說、電影) 情節，布局

▶ The doctor said the plaster cast would help my broken leg to heal more quickly.
　醫生說石膏可以幫助我的斷腿較快復原。
　＊heal [hil] *vi.* 痊癒

2　squeeze [skwiz] *vt.* & *vi.* 擠；壓；緊握 & *n.* 壓榨；緊握

用 (1) squeeze into...　擠進 / 擠入……
　　(2) squeeze sth out　將某物擠出來
　　(3) squeeze sb's hand
　　　緊握某人的手

似 press [prɛs] *vt.* 壓 ②

▶ Don't squeeze your pimples unless you want scars on your face.
　除非你希望臉上有疤痕，否則不要擠青春痘。
　＊pimple [ˋpɪmpl] *n.* 青春痘
　　scar [skɑr] *n.* 疤痕

▶ The six of us squeezed into a car that had four seats only.
　我們 6 個人擠入只有 4 個座位的車子。

▶ I squeezed out the last bit of toothpaste from the tube.
　我把這條牙膏的最後一點牙膏全擠出來了。

▶ The chef put a squeeze of lemon juice on the fish to bring out its flavor.
　廚師擠了一點檸檬汁在魚肉上來引出它的味道。

▶ Henry gave my hand a little squeeze and wished me good luck.
　＝ Henry squeezed my hand and wished me good luck.
　亨利緊握著我的手，祝我好運。

twist [twɪst] *vt.* 扭轉；曲解，扭曲 & *n.* 扭轉；扭扭舞 (與 the 並用)

- (1) twist one's head around　轉頭
  (2) twist the truth　扭曲真相
  (3) twist sb's words　曲解某人的話
- (1) distort [dɪˈstɔrt] *vt.* 扭曲，曲解
  (2) sprain [spren] *vt.* 扭到 ③

▶ I twisted my head around to see what was going on.
我轉頭看發生了什麼事。

▶ Be honest. Don't twist the truth.
要老實。別扭曲事實。

▶ I don't like John because he tends to twist people's words.
我不喜歡約翰，因為他常曲解大家的話。

▶ Terry gave the cap of the jar another twist to open it.
泰瑞又扭轉了罐子的瓶蓋一次，試圖打開它。

▶ When Jerry heard the music, he rushed onto the dance floor to do the twist.
傑瑞一聽到音樂就衝進舞池跳扭扭舞。

3　**award** [əˈwɔrd] *n.* 獎品 & *vt.* 授予，給予

- prize [praɪz] *n.* 獎賞，獎品 ②
- (1) award sb sth　頒發給某人某物
  (2) be awarded sth　被頒發某物

▶ Many celebrities attended the awards ceremony.
許多名人都出席了該頒獎典禮。
*celebrity [səˈlɛbrətɪ] *n.* 名人

▶ The university awarded Joy a scholarship.
該大學頒給喬伊獎學金。

▶ Tim was awarded a statue for Best Actor.
提姆獲頒最佳演員獎一座。

medal [ˈmɛdḷ] *n.* 獎章；獎牌

- (1) a gold medal　金牌
  (2) a silver medal　銀牌
  (3) a bronze medal　銅牌

▶ Officer Smith was given a medal for his brave deeds.
史密斯警官因其英勇行徑獲頒一枚獎章。

▶ The athlete won two gold medals in the Athens Olympic Games.
這名運動員在雅典奧運贏了兩面金牌。

4　**drip** [drɪp] *vi.* & *vt.* 滴下 & *n.* 滴水聲

- drip, dripped [drɪpt], dripped
- (1) drop [drɑp] *vi.* 滴下 & *n.* (一) 滴 ①
  (2) dribble [ˈdrɪbḷ] *vi.* 滴下 & *n.* (一) 滴

▶ Water dripped from my ceiling during rainstorms.
暴風雨時，水從我家天花板上滴了下來。

▶ The injured man dripped blood all over the floor.
這位受傷的男子血滴得滿地都是。

▶ Jane didn't sleep well last night because of the endless drip of the rain from the roof.
因為屋頂上不停傳來的滴水聲，珍昨晚一夜沒睡好。

5   journey [ˋdʒɝnɪ] *n.* 旅行 (尤指長途旅行) & *vi.* 旅行

似 trip [trɪp] *n.* 旅行 ①

片 journey to + 地方　到某地去旅遊
= go on a journey / trip to + 地方
= take a trip to + 地方
= travel to + 地方

▶ Peter has decided to go on a journey to southern Taiwan next month.
彼得已決定下個月到南臺灣旅遊。

▶ I journeyed to Japan last summer and had a fantastic time there.
= I went on a journey / trip to Japan last summer and had a fantastic time there.
= I took a trip to Japan last summer and had a great time there.
= I traveled to Japan last summer and had a wonderful time there.
去年夏天我到日本旅遊，在那兒我玩得很愉快。

6   client [ˋklaɪənt] *n.* 客戶

比 client 多指大宗買賣或與銀行有來往的『客戶』，而 customer [ˋkʌstəmɚ] 則指到一般商店買東西的『顧客』。client 也指請律師打官司的『委託訴訟人』。

▶ We can't afford to lose Mr. Johnson. He's a very important client of ours.
我們萬萬不能失去強森先生。他可是我們非常重要的客戶。

7   precious [ˋprɛʃəs] *a.* 珍貴的

似 valuable [ˋvæljʊəbl̩] *a.* 珍貴的 ②

▶ Time is precious, and we cannot afford to waste it.
時間很寶貴，我們浪費不起。

8   jet [dʒɛt] *n.* 噴射機 & *vi.* 搭飛機旅行 & *vt.* 噴出

三 jet, jetted [ˋdʒɛtɪd], jetted

片 (1) a passenger jet　噴射客機
(2) a jet fighter　　噴射戰鬥機
(3) jet lag [ˋdʒɛt ˌlæg]
　　n. (長途飛行所造成的) 時差感

▶ Mr. Stevenson is so rich that he even has his own jet.
史帝文森先生很有錢，甚至擁有自己的噴射機。

▶ Jet lag makes you feel tired, so I don't like long flights.
時差感會讓人有疲勞感，因此我不喜歡長途飛行。

▶ Jessica is jetting off to New Zealand next week.
潔西卡下週搭飛機到紐西蘭旅行。

▶ The fire hose jetted water onto the burning building.
消防水柱朝燃燒的大樓噴水。

9   mystery [ˋmɪstərɪ] *n.* 神祕，神祕難解的事物

衍 mysterious [mɪsˋtɪrɪəs] *a.* 神祕的 ④
似 riddle [ˋrɪdl̩] *n.* 謎 ④

▶ The reasons behind Dr. Todd's murder have remained a mystery for many years.
陶德醫師命案的犯罪動機多年來一直成謎。

10 mankind [ˌmænˈkaɪnd] *n.* 人類 (前面不加冠詞)

比 mankind 及 man 均表『人類』，視作集合名詞，不可數，且之前不置任何冠詞 (a 或 the)，與單數動詞並用。human being 亦表『人類』，卻是可數名詞，單數為 a human being，複數則為 human beings (之前不置 the)。

▸ Television is one of the most popular inventions in the history of mankind.
電視是人類史上最普及的發明之一。

humankind [ˈhjumənˌkaɪnd]
n. 人類

用法 humankind 與 mankind 意思及用法完全相同。

▸ All humankind will benefit from the scientist's discovery.
該科學家的發現將使全體人類獲益。
＊benefit [ˈbɛnəfɪt] *vi.* 獲益
benefit from... 從……獲益

11 campus [ˈkæmpəs] *n.* (大學) 校園

片 (1) on campus 在校園內
(2) off campus 在校園外

▸ Mary didn't live on campus while in college. She lived off campus with her aunt and uncle.
瑪莉念大學時不住校內。她在校外與阿姨及姨丈同住。

12 scream [skrim] *vi.* 發出尖叫聲 & *n.* 尖叫

似 shriek [ʃrik] *vi.* & *n.* 尖叫 ⑥
比 (1) shout [ʃaut] 表『大叫』，我們想提高音量讓遠處的人們聽見我們的聲音時，就可使用本字。我們生氣時，對某人吼叫也使用 shout。

▸ They shouted for help.
他們大聲求救。
▸ Don't shout at me.
別對我大吼。

(2) yell [jɛl] 則多指生氣時所發出的大吼聲。

▸ Don't yell at me.
別對我大吼。

▸ It is horrible to hear someone screaming in the middle of the night.
半夜聽到有人尖叫真恐怖。

▸ When Sandra opened her birthday present, she let out a scream of joy.
當珊卓拉打開她的生日禮物時，開心地尖叫了一聲。

roar [rɔr]
n. 吼聲 & *vi.* 大吼，發出很大聲響

片 roar with laughter 大聲爆笑

▸ The roar of a lion can be quite scary.
獅子的吼聲挺嚇人的。

▸ They all roared with laughter after John told the joke.
約翰講完笑話時，大家全都笑翻了。

yell [jɛl] *vi.* 大聲說，喊叫 & *n.* 叫喊

片 (1) yell at sb　對某人大吼，大罵某人
(2) let out a yell　發出一聲大吼

▶ Dad yelled at me when I made the same mistake again.
我又犯同樣的錯時，老爸就開口罵我。

▶ James let out a yell of frustration and then walked out of the room.
詹姆士在大吼一聲吐出鬱悶後，便走出了房外。
＊frustration [frʌˋstreʃən] *n.* 挫折

13　harm [hɑrm] *n.* & *vt.* 傷害

片 do sb harm　對某人有害
反 do sb good　對某人有益
延伸 wouldn't harm / hurt a fly
連蒼蠅都不願傷害，喻心地非常善良。

▶ Smoking will do you great harm. Why don't you just quit?
抽菸對你傷害很大。你幹嘛不乾脆戒掉？

▶ Mary wouldn't even harm a fly. How could she commit such a crime?
瑪莉心地非常善良。她怎麼可能會犯下這起案子呢？

---

harmful [ˋhɑrmfəl] *a.* 有害的

片 be harmful / detrimental to sb / sth
對某人 / 某物有害
似 detrimental [ˌdɛtrəˋmɛntl] *a.* 有害的

▶ Anything can be harmful when carried to extremes.
任何事做得過火都可能變得有害。
＊extreme [ɪkˋstrim] *n.* 極端
carry sth to extremes　將某事做得過火

14　budget [ˋbʌdʒɪt] *n.* 預算 & *vt.* 安排 (開支)；規劃 (時間等)

片 (1) on a tight budget　預算吃緊
(2) budget one's time / money
審慎規劃時間 / 金錢

▶ We have to carry out the project on a tight budget.
我們必須在有限的預算下完成案子。

▶ We budgeted $3,000 for our month-long trip to Europe.
我們要到歐洲旅遊一個月，預算為 3 千美金。

▶ To get the work done on time, you need to learn how to budget your time.
要準時完工的話，你就得學習如何審慎規劃你的時間。

15　flame [flem] *n.* 火焰 & *vi.* 燃燒

片 (1) be in flames　在火焰之中
(2) flame with envy
（眼睛）展現強烈的羨慕之情
衍 inflame [ɪnˋflem] *vt.* 使激動；激起
似 (1) fire [faɪr] *n.* 火；火災；熱情
& *vt.* 開除；發射 & *vi.* 發射 ①
(2) arouse [əˋraʊz] *vt.* 激起 ⑤

▶ The barn was already in flames by the time the fire engine arrived.
等到消防車抵達時，整個穀倉已陷在一片火海中。

▶ Mary's eyes flamed with envy when she saw her friend's designer purse.
瑪莉看到她朋友的名牌包時，眼裡滿是羨慕。
＊designer purse　名牌包包

16 wipe [waɪp] vt. 擦拭；消滅 & n. 擦，拭，抹

🅗 wipe sth out	▸ The waitress wiped the table with a damp cloth.
將某物破壞無遺 / 掃蕩殆盡	這個女服務生用一塊溼抹布擦拭桌子。
	▸ The typhoon wiped out the whole village.
	颱風將整座村莊破壞殆盡。
	▸ The waiter gave the table in the café a quick wipe.
	服務生很快地擦拭咖啡廳的桌面。

17 angel [ˈendʒḷ] n. 天使

| 🅢 angle [ˈæŋgḷ] n. 角度；觀點 ② | ▸ Helen has a perfect voice and sings just like an angel. |
| | 海倫有副好歌喉，唱起歌來就像是天使一樣。 |

devil [ˈdɛvḷ] n. 魔鬼	▸ Stay away from that guy! He is a real devil!
	離那人遠點！他是個不折不扣的惡魔！
	▸ Speak of the devil, and he shall appear.
	說到曹操，曹操就到了。——諺語

18 barrel [ˈbærəl] n. 大桶；槍枝的槍管

🅑 barrel 指裝石油的大鐵桶或裝啤酒的大木桶。一般裝水的水桶稱作 bucket。	▸ These oak barrels are used for wine storage.
	這些橡木桶是用來貯藏酒的。
	*storage [ˈstɔrɪdʒ] n. 貯藏，存放
	▸ The bullet shot through the barrel of the gun and hit a nearby tree.
	子彈穿過槍管，擊中附近的樹。

bucket [ˈbʌkɪt] n. 水桶	▸ Can you help me fill these buckets with water?
🅗 kick the bucket	你可以幫我把這些水桶裝滿水嗎？
翹辮子，死去 (幽默用語)	▸ Old Henry hasn't kicked the bucket yet. He's still alive and kicking.
	老亨利還沒死。他老兄還硬朗得很。
	*be alive and kicking　生龍活虎

pail [pel] n. 桶，提桶	▸ It took several pails of water to put out the fire.
🅢 pale [pel] a. (臉色) 蒼白的 ③	用了好幾桶水才把火熄滅。
	▸ After a two-hour walk, my dog drank a whole pail of water.
	走了兩小時後，我的狗狗喝下了一整桶的水。

19　clue [klu] n. 線索，端倪，頭緒

片 do not have a clue　一點都不知道

用法 clue 之後若要接名詞，常與介詞 to、about 或 as to 並用。

▶ Do you have any clues to the robber's whereabouts?
你有任何搶匪下落的線索嗎？
*whereabouts [ˌ(h)wɛrəˈbaʊts] n. 下落，行蹤

▶ I didn't have a clue why Roger yelled at me.
我一點都不知道為什麼羅傑對我大叫。

---

hint [hɪnt] n. & vt. & vi. 暗示

片 take / get a / the hint
得到暗示，識相，知趣

用法 hint 作及物動詞時，須接 that 子句作受詞；若作不及物動詞時，與介詞 at 並用。
(1) hint that...　暗示……
(2) hint at...　暗示……

似 suggest [səgˈdʒɛst / səˈdʒɛst]
vt. 暗示 ②

▶ Tammy hoped Steven would take the hint and stop bothering her.
塔米希望史蒂芬識相點，別再煩她。

▶ Emily glanced at her watch, hinting that she had to leave.
= Emily glanced at her watch, suggesting that she had to leave.
艾蜜莉看了一下錶，暗示她得走了。

▶ Tom hinted that he might buy Jane a diamond ring for their anniversary.
湯姆暗示他可能會買一只鑽戒送給珍當作結婚週年紀念禮物。

▶ Our general manager hinted at the possibility of opening a new branch next summer.
總經理暗示了來年夏天開設新分公司的可能性。

20　eager [ˈiɡɚ] a. 渴望的

片 (1) be eager to + V　渴望做……
= be longing to + V
= be dying to + V
(2) be eager for + sth　渴望得到某物
= be longing for + sth
= be dying for + sth

▶ Mary is eager to start her new job.
瑪莉渴望開始新工作。

▶ Children are always eager for the arrival of Christmas.
孩子們總是期待聖誕節的到來。

21　spin [spɪn] vt. 紡紗；編造 (故事) & vi. 旋轉 & n. 旋轉

三 spin, spun [spʌn], spun

片 (1) spin a story / yarn
編造故事 (尤指誇大、吹牛的冒險故事)
*yarn [jɑrn] n. 紗線
(2) spin around　旋轉

似 rotate [ˈrotet] vt. & vi. (地球) 自轉 ⑥

▶ The factory has a reputation for spinning fine wool yarn.
這座工廠紡的細緻羊毛線相當有名。
*reputation [ˌrɛpjəˈteʃən] n. 名聲

▶ The sailor spun a story about his trip to Egypt.
這位水手編了一個他到埃及的冒險故事。

▶ The dancer spun around and around but never fell over.
這名舞者不停地轉圈，卻不會摔倒。

▶ The dancer took the woman by the hand and gave her a spin.

舞者用手挽著女子並讓她旋轉。

22 romantic [roˈmæntɪk] a. 不切實際的；浪漫的 & n. 浪漫主義者

衍 romance [roˈmæns / ˈromæns]
　n. 戀情；浪漫；愛情小說 ④

似 (1) impractical [ɪmˈpræktɪkḷ]
　　a. 不切實際的

　(2) dreamy [ˈdrimɪ] a. 夢幻般的

反 realistic [rɪəˈlɪstɪk] a. 切合實際的 ④

▶ Many girls have romantic ideas about becoming a model.

關於當模特兒，許多女孩都有不切實際的想法。

▶ It would be romantic for us to go to Venice together.

咱們一起去威尼斯一定會很浪漫的。

▶ They say Bob is a hopeless romantic who indulges in his own fantasies.

他們說鮑伯是個無可救藥的浪漫主義者，他老愛沉浸在自己的幻想裡。

＊indulge [ɪnˈdʌldʒ] vi. 沉浸於（與介詞 in 並用）

23 passion [ˈpæʃən] n. 熱情，熱愛

片 have a passion for...　熱愛……
衍 passionate [ˈpæʃənɪt] a. 熱愛的 ⑤

▶ Amy has a passion for clothes. She always wears stylish things.

＝ Amy has a liking for clothes. She always wears stylish things.

艾咪熱愛服飾。她的穿著一向很時髦。

＊stylish [ˈstaɪlɪʃ] a. 時髦的，流行的

warmth [wɔrmθ] n. 溫暖

衍 warm [wɔrm] a. 溫暖的 ①

▶ Seeing Jane smile brings me warmth and makes my day.

看到珍的笑容會帶給我溫暖，讓我開心一整天。

＊make sb's day　令某人整天很愉快

24 adventure [ədˈvɛntʃɚ] n. 冒險，奇遇

衍 venture [ˈvɛntʃɚ]
　n. & vt. & vi. (使) 冒險 ⑤

▶ Nothing ventured, nothing gained.
＝ If you venture nothing, you'll gain nothing.

不入虎穴，焉得虎子。── 諺語

▶ That old man often tells us of his many adventures in Africa.

那個老伯伯常告訴我們他在非洲的許多冒險經歷。

adventurous [ədˈvɛntʃərəs]
a. 大膽的；充滿危險和刺激的

似 (1) daring [ˈdɛrɪŋ]
　　a. 大膽的，敢冒險的

▶ George is not very adventurous when it comes to food.

談到食物，喬治就不是那麼大膽了。

(2) **risk-taking** [ˋrɪskˏtekɪŋ]
a. 冒險的

▶ Roger wants to climb Mt. Everest, but I'd prefer a less adventurous trip.
羅傑想攀登聖母峰，我則比較想要冒險性沒那麼高的旅行。

25　studio [ˋstjudɪˏo] *n.* 播音室；工作室；攝影棚

▶ This recording studio is fully equipped.
這間錄音室的設備很齊全。

▶ The artist used this abandoned warehouse as his studio.
這名藝術家把這座廢棄的倉庫當作工作室。
*warehouse [ˋwɛrˏhaʊs] *n.* 倉庫

26　verse [vɝs] *n.* 韻文，詩

衍 (1) **version** [ˋvɝʒən] *n.* 版本；說法 ⑤
(2) **versed** [vɝst] *a.* 擅長的；精通的
be versed in... 精通……

▶ The poet expressed his ideas in verse.
這位詩人用詩來表達他的想法。

▶ Peter is versed in Chinese calligraphy.
彼得精通中國書法。

27　bride [braɪd] *n.* 新娘

衍 **bridegroom** [ˋbraɪdˏgrum]
n. 新郎（= groom [grum]）④

▶ Kent introduced us to his young bride.
肯特介紹我們認識他年輕的新娘。

28　bore [bɔr] *vt.* 使厭煩 & *n.* 令人厭煩的人或物（可數）

H **bore sb to death / tears**
令某人覺得無聊透頂
衍 (1) **bored** [bɔrd] *a.* 感到無聊的 ①
(2) **boring** [ˋbɔrɪŋ]
a. 令人厭煩的，無趣的 ①
(3) **boredom** [ˋbɔrdəm]
n. 厭煩（不可數）⑤

▶ People who talk too much about themselves bore everyone else.
大家都對滔滔不絕談論自己的人感到厭煩。

▶ The old professor's lecture really bored me to death.
這位老教授的講課讓我覺得無聊死了。

▶ Helen considers Hank a bore.
海倫覺得漢克是個討厭鬼。

29　presence [ˋprɛzəns] *n.* 出席；在場

H **in the presence of...** 當著……的面
衍 **present** [ˋprɛzənt]
a. 目前的，出席的 & *n.* 禮物（= gift）①
反 **absence** [ˋæbsn̩s] *n.* 缺席，不在場

▶ Your presence is requested at this afternoon's meeting.
今天下午的會議你必須出席。

▶ The girl was so quiet that her presence was hardly noticed.
這女孩太安靜了，因此幾乎沒有人注意到她在場。

▸ Parents shouldn't argue in the presence of their children.
父母親不應該當著孩子的面爭吵。

30 doughnut [ˈdoˌnʌt] *n.* 甜甜圈 (= donut)

▸ We ate doughnuts for breakfast this morning.
我們今天早上吃甜甜圈當早餐。

31 rush [rʌʃ] *vi.* & *vt.* 衝；匆促行動 & *n.* 衝；搶購熱潮

片 (1) rush into... 衝進……
(2) rush out of... 從……衝出
(3) be rushed to... 很快被送到……
(4) in a rush 匆忙
　 = in a hurry
　 = in haste
(5) rush hour 尖峰時刻
似 rash [ræʃ] *n.* 疹子 & *a.* 草率的 ⑥

▸ Everyone rushed into the street when a fire broke out.
失火時，所有人全都衝到街上。

▸ Tom was rushed to the hospital because he was bleeding severely.
湯姆因為大量失血，很快地被送到醫院。

▸ Why are you in such a rush to leave?
你為何這麼急著要離開？

▸ There was a big rush for that toy last summer.
去年夏天那款玩具造成了搶購熱潮。

▸ I was stuck in traffic during rush hour.
尖峰時刻時，我被卡在車陣中動彈不得。

32 bitter [ˈbɪtɚ] *a.* (味道) 苦的；引起痛苦或悲傷的；極為不滿的

片 be bitter about... 對……極為不滿
衍 (1) bitterly [ˈbɪtɚlɪ]
　　 adv. 痛苦地；殘酷地
　　 bitterly criticize sb
　　 把某人批評得體無完膚
(2) bitterness [ˈbɪtɚnɪs] *n.* 苦味

▸ Some Chinese medicines taste quite bitter.
某些中藥吃起來相當苦。

▸ The bitter truth is that my sweetheart has married someone else.
令人悲痛的事實是我的心上人已嫁給別人。

▸ Leon was bitter about not being picked for the team.
沒被選入球隊使里昂極為不滿。

33 bookcase [ˈbʊkˌkes] *n.* 書櫃

似 bookshelf [ˈbʊkˌʃɛlf] *n.* 書架

▸ Lisa pulled out a book from her bookcase.
麗莎從她的書櫃抽出一本書。

Unit 14

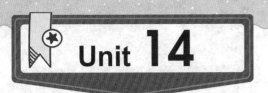

1401-1403

1　swear [swɛr] vt. 發誓 & vi. 說髒話

- swear, swore [swɔr], sworn
  [sworn]
- (1) swear to God + that...
  發誓……
- (2) to be sworn in as...
  (被大法官或其他高級官員帶領) 宣
  誓就任……

▶ I swear to God that I didn't take your pen!
我對天發誓我沒拿你的筆！

▶ Mr. Johnson was sworn in as mayor of the city
yesterday.
強森先生昨天宣誓就任市長。

▶ Don't swear in front of the children.
不要在孩子面前說髒話。

2　parade [pəˋred] vi. & n. 遊行

- be on parade　列隊前進

▶ Those soldiers were parading in front of the
presidential palace.
= Those soldiers were on parade in front of the
presidential palace.
那些士兵正在總統府前做分列式遊行。

march [mɑrtʃ]
vi. 前進 & n. 行軍，行進，遊行

- be on the march　行軍

▶ Thousands of demonstrators marched toward
City Hall at 2:00 yesterday afternoon.
昨天下午兩點，數千名示威者往市政府方向前進。
*demonstrator [ˋdɛmən͵stretɚ] n. 示威者

▶ The troops were on a long march into the mountains.
部隊往深山長途行軍。

3　cigarette [͵sɪgəˋrɛt] n. 香菸

- (1) be addicted to cigarettes /
  smoking　有菸癮
  *addicted [əˋdɪktɪd]
    a. 有癮頭的 (與介詞 to 並用)
- (2) get addicted to cigarettes /
  smoking　抽菸上癮

▶ Please put out your cigarette, sir. This is a non-smoking
area.
先生，請把香菸熄掉。這裡是禁菸區。

▶ I got addicted to cigarettes while I was in college.
我念大學時染上菸癮。

tobacco [təˋbæko] n. 菸草
似 cigar [sɪˋgɑr] n. 雪茄 ⑥

▶ The nicotine in tobacco is an addictive and harmful
substance.
菸草內的尼古丁是種會使人上癮且有害的物質。
*nicotine [ˋnɪkə͵tin] n. 尼古丁，菸鹼
　addictive [əˋdɪktɪv] a. 易上癮的

4 plastic [`plæstɪk] *n.* 塑膠 & *a.* 塑膠的

片 (1) a plastic bag　　塑膠袋
(2) plastic surgery　　美容整型手術

▶ Bags made of plastic are harmful to the environment.
塑膠製的袋子對環境有害。

▶ Stores no longer give customers plastic bags for the sake of environmental protection.
為了環保的緣故，商店不再供應塑膠袋給顧客了。

leather [`lɛðɚ] *n.* 皮革

片 (1) a leather coat　　皮外套
(2) leather boots　　皮靴

▶ Leather coats are back in fashion.
皮革外套又再度流行了。

5 float [flot] *vi.* 漂浮 & *n.* 浮板

反 sink [sɪŋk] *vi.* 沉 ③

▶ The first step in learning how to swim is to learn how to float.
學游泳的第一步就是學會如何漂浮。

▶ The man used a piece of wood as a float to get back to shore.
該男子用了一塊木頭當浮板回到岸邊。

6 pole [pol] *n.* 極，磁極；竿子

片 (1) a fishing pole　　釣竿
= a fishing rod
(2) be poles apart
完全相反，完全不同
= be completely different
(3) the North Pole / South Pole
北極 / 南極

▶ Place the positive pole of the battery in the toy first and then the negative one.
先將電池正極的那一端放進玩具裡，再放進負極。

▶ If you want to catch a big fish, the right kind of fishing pole and bait are a must.
想要釣大魚，就必須要選對釣竿及釣餌。
*bait [bet] *n.* 魚餌
be a must　是必要條件

▶ Both of the sisters are great artists, though they are poles apart in artistic styles.
這對姐妹都是很傑出的藝術家，但她們的藝術風格截然不同。

7 casual [`kæʒuəl] *a.* 偶然的；無心的；非正式的 (指服裝)

片 casual wear　非正式衣著，休閒裝
（集合名詞，不可數）

似 informal [ɪn`fɔrml] *a.* 非正式的

反 formal [`fɔrml] *a.* 正式的 ②

▶ Peter and Bruce's long friendship began with a casual meeting at a party.
彼得與布魯斯長久的友誼始於派對上的一次偶遇。

▶ Mr. Lee's casual remark caused a political storm.
李先生無心的言論引發了一場政治風暴。

▶ You can find casual wear on the sixth floor.
六樓是休閒服裝區。

casually [ˈkæʒʊəlɪ]

adv. 悠閒地；隨便地

▶ On weekends, I enjoy strolling casually in the park near where I live.
週末我喜歡在我住處附近的公園悠閒地漫步。

▶ Much to our surprise, Mary was casually dressed for the formal party.
令我們大感驚訝的是，那是個正式宴會，瑪莉卻穿得很隨便。

8　doubtful [ˈdaʊtfəl] *a.* 起疑的；可疑的

片 be doubtful about...　對⋯⋯起疑
衍 (1) doubt [daʊt] *vt.* 懷疑 & *n.* 疑問 ②
　　 without (a) doubt　毫無疑問
　　(2) doubtfully [ˈdaʊtfəlɪ] *adv.* 可疑地
似 (1) unsure [ʌnˈʃʊr] *a.* 不確定的
　　(2) uncertain [ʌnˈsɝtn̩] *a.* 不確定的
　　(3) unconvinced [ˌʌnkənˈvɪnst]
　　　　 a. 不信的，懷疑的

▶ I was doubtful about the old man's good intentions.
這個老頭的好意令我起疑。

▶ It is doubtful whether Ted will keep his promise.
泰德會不會履行諾言令人懷疑。

---

doubtless [ˈdaʊtlɪs]

adv. 無疑地，必定地

用法 doubtless 雖有表形容詞的字尾 -less，但為副詞，等於 doubtlessly、undoubtedly、without (a) doubt 或 certainly（必然）。

▶ Bill has been studying so hard that he will doubtless pass the exam.
= Bill has been studying so hard that he will doubtlessly pass the exam.
比爾一直是那麼用功，所以他必定會通過這次考試。

9　stuff [stʌf] *n.* 東西（不可數）& *vt.* 塞滿

片 be stuffed with sth　塞滿了某物
衍 stuffy [ˈstʌfɪ] *a.* 通風不良的，窒悶的
比 thing 與 stuff 均表『東西』，前者為可數名詞，後者為不可數名詞。
　　have a lot of things to do
　　有很多事要做
= have a lot of stuff to do

▶ Leave your stuff in the car while we check if the hotel has any rooms available.
我們去確認飯店還有沒有房間的時候，把你的東西留在車內。

▶ This closet is stuffed with clothes I don't wear anymore.
這個衣櫥塞滿我再也不穿的衣服。

10　bare [bɛr] *a.* 空的；赤裸的 & *vt.* 露出

衍 (1) barehanded [ˈbɛrˌhændɪd]
　　　　 a. 赤手空拳的
　　(2) barefoot [ˈbɛrˌfʊt] *a.* 赤腳的
　　= barefooted [ˈbɛrˌfʊtɪd]
　　　 walk barefoot　赤腳走路

▶ Our fridge is bare, so we must do some shopping this afternoon.
我們的冰箱空了，因此下午我們得買些東西。

▶ Don't walk around barefoot because there are pieces of broken glass on the floor.

地板上有玻璃碎片，所以不要光著腳到處走。

似 empty [ˈɛmptɪ] *a.* 空的 ②

▶ Sue put her shorts on so she could bare her legs to the hot sun.

蘇換上短褲把腳露出來曬曬太陽。

---

barely [ˈbɛrlɪ]
adv. 僅僅；勉強，幾乎不

似 (1) only [ˈonlɪ] *adv.* 僅僅 ①
(2) hardly [ˈhɑrdlɪ] *adv.* 幾乎不 ②
(3) scarcely [ˈskɛrslɪ] *adv.* 幾乎不 ④

▶ Linda is barely 18 years old and yet has two children.

琳達只有 18 歲，卻已經有 2 個小孩了。

▶ With such a meager income, John is barely able to make ends meet.

約翰的收入很少，收支勉強過得去。

＊meager [ˈmigɚ] *a.* 微薄的，不足的
make ends meet　收支平衡

11　tourist [ˈturɪst] *n.* 觀光客，遊客 & *a.* 觀光的

片 tourist attraction　　觀光勝地
衍 tour [tur] *n.* & *vt.* 遊覽，觀光 ②
be on a tour of a city　遊覽城市
= tour a city

▶ This scenic spot draws tens of thousands of tourists every month.

這個景點每個月都會吸引好幾萬名遊客。

▶ Eluanbi is a famous tourist attraction in southern Taiwan.

鵝鑾鼻是臺灣南部知名的觀光勝地。

---

tourism [ˈturɪzm̩] *n.* 觀光業，觀光

▶ The country heavily depends on tourism to support its economy.

該國的經濟極度仰賴觀光業。

12　leap [lip] *vi.* 跳躍 & *n.* 跳

三 leap, leapt [lɛpt], leapt
片 (1) by leaps and bounds　突飛猛進
(2) a leap year　　　　　閏年
似 jump [dʒʌmp] *vi.* & *n.* 跳 ①

▶ You'd better look before you leap. I don't think you really understand the situation.

你最好三思而後行。我覺得你還沒真正了解狀況。

▶ The dog made a leap for the cat, but it managed to get away.

這隻狗跳向這隻貓，但牠設法逃脫了。

▶ Since I moved to America, my English has improved by leaps and bounds.

我搬到美國後，我的英文就突飛猛進了。

13　fade [fed] *vi.* 褪色；漸弱

片 (1) fade away　消逝；褪色
(2) fade out　（聲音）漸弱

▶ General MacArthur once said, "Old soldiers never die; they just fade away."

麥克阿瑟將軍曾說：『老兵不死，只是凋零。』

▶ When the music faded out, the show host walked onto the stage.
音樂漸弱時，節目主持人走上舞臺。

vanish [`vænɪʃ] *vi.* 消失
似 disappear [ˌdɪsə`pɪr] *vi.* 消失 ②

▶ Many ancient civilizations have vanished mysteriously.
許多古文明都已神祕消失了。

14　cabin [`kæbɪn] *n.* (在森林或山中搭建的) 小木屋；船艙，機艙

片 the passenger cabin　客艙

▶ Nobody lives in that log cabin.
那個圓木搭建的小木屋沒有住人。
＊log [lɔg / lɑg] *n.* 圓木

▶ Even though the ship was sinking, the captain refused to leave his cabin.
雖然船即將下沉，船長還是拒絕離開他的船艙。

hut [hʌt] *n.* 小屋
延伸 hut 指『小屋』，通常只有一、兩個房間，由木頭、泥土、草或石頭搭建而成。

▶ Jim built a wooden hut all by himself.
吉姆靠一己之力蓋了一間小木屋。

15　powder [`paudɚ] *n.* 粉末 & *vt.* 灑粉

片 powder one's face　補妝

▶ Slowly grind these ingredients into a powder.
慢慢地將這些原料磨成粉末。

▶ Mary went to the restroom to powder her face.
瑪莉去洗手間補妝。

pill [pɪl] *n.* 藥丸

▶ Judy has to rely on sleeping pills in order to fall asleep.
茱蒂要靠安眠藥才能睡著。

tablet [`tæblɪt] *n.* 藥片；平板電腦
用法 表藥物的名稱，如 medicine（藥）、pill（藥丸）、tablet（藥片），均與動詞 take 並用，此處 take 表『吃』或『服用』。

▶ Take this medicine, and you'll feel better.
服用這個藥，你就會覺得好多了。

▶ Take those pills according to the instructions.
按照說明指示服用那些藥丸。

▶ The doctor gave me some tablets to help control my frequent headaches.
醫師給了我一些藥片幫助我控制經常性的頭痛。

▶ Jack bought the latest model of the tablet with his annual bonus.
傑克用年度獎金買了最新型的平板電腦。

16 deck [dɛk] *n.* 甲板

▶ Let's go up on deck and take a look at the night view.
我們上甲板去看看夜景吧。

17 limb [lɪm] *n.* 四肢之一

似 limp [lɪmp]
n. (因為腿、腳受傷或疼痛) 艱難緩慢地行走 & *vi.* 跛行 ⑥

▶ In that country, many children lost limbs because of stepping on landmines.
在那個國家，許多孩子因為踩到地雷而失去四肢。

18 mayor [ˈmeɚ] *n.* 市長

似 major [ˈmedʒɚ]
a. 大部分的；重要的 & *vi.* 主修 (與介詞 in 並用) & *n.* 主修科目 ②

延伸 county magistrate
[ˈkaʊntɪ ˌmædʒɪsˌtret] *n.* 縣長

▶ The mayor offered his condolences to the victims of the earthquake.
市長對地震受災戶表達慰問之意。
*offer one's condolences　某人表達慰問之意
condolence [kənˈdoləns] *n.* 慰問

19 disk [dɪsk] *n.* 光碟片 (= disc)

衍 a disk drive　光碟機

▶ Jimmy took out a disk and put it into his computer's disk drive.
吉米拿出一張光碟片放進他的電腦光碟機裡。

20 strategy [ˈstræˌtədʒɪ] *n.* 策略，謀略

衍 strategic [strəˈtidʒɪk]
a. 謀略的，戰略的 ⑤
strategic weapons　戰略性武器

▶ We're working on new marketing strategies for the product.
我們正在為這項產品研擬新的行銷策略。

21 crawl [krɔl] *vi.* 爬 & *n.* 緩慢的行進

似 creep [krip] *vi.* 爬行；緩慢前進 ④

▶ A child crawls before it learns to walk.
嬰孩先學會爬才會走路。

▶ Jeff became frustrated when the traffic slowed down to a crawl.
車輛減速放慢行進時，傑夫變得很沮喪。

22 barn [bɑrn] *n.* 穀倉

▶ The farmer keeps his cows and horses in the barn.
那位農夫把他的乳牛和馬養在穀倉裡。

hay [he] *n.* 乾草 (不可數)

片 **hit the hay** 上床睡覺 (口語)
= hit the sack
= go to bed

衍 **haystack** [ˈheˌstæk] *n.* 乾草堆

▶ The homeless man was found sleeping on the hay in the barn.
那名無家可歸的男子被發現睡在穀倉的乾草上。

▶ Jimmy was so tired that he hit the hay straight after he got home.
吉米太累了，一回家馬上倒頭就睡。

▶ Make hay while the sun shines.
曬草要趁陽光好 / 行事要趁機會好 / 打鐵趁熱。── 諺語

---

23 routine [ruˈtin] *n.* 慣例，例行公事 & *a.* 例行公事的

片 **a daily routine** 每天的例行公事

▶ Reading English papers in the morning has become part of my daily routine.
在早上看英文報紙已經成為我日常作息的一部分。

▶ Bill conducts a routine inspection of our copier once a month.
比爾每個月來公司一次做影印機的例行檢查。
＊inspection [ɪnˈspɛkʃən] *n.* 視察；檢查

---

24 carpet [ˈkɑrpɪt] *n.* 地毯 & *vt.* 在……鋪地毯

片 **be carpeted with...**
覆蓋著一層……

似 **rug** [rʌg] *n.* 地毯 ③

▶ Use the brush to clean the carpet.
用這支刷子來清掃地毯。

▶ Jane wants to carpet the living room, but her husband prefers a wooden floor.
珍想要在客廳鋪上地毯，但她的先生比較喜歡木製的地板。

▶ The meadow was carpeted with thousands of beautiful, colorful flowers.
草地布滿了數千朵色彩鮮豔的美麗花朵。

---

cleaner [ˈklinɚ] *n.* 清潔工；清潔劑

片 (1) the cleaner's 洗衣店
(2) the dry cleaner's 乾洗店

▶ My boss was once a street cleaner when he was young.
我老闆年輕時一度當過掃馬路的清潔工。

▶ Take all of the food out of your cabinet, and clean it with kitchen cleaner.
把櫃子裡所有食物拿出來，再用廚房清潔劑清理乾淨。

---

cooker [ˈkʊkɚ] *n.* 炊具

衍 **a rice cooker** 電鍋

似 **cook** [kʊk] *n.* 廚師 ①

▶ Almost every Chinese family has a rice cooker.
幾乎每個華人家庭都有電鍋。

---

cupboard [ˈkʌbɚd] *n.* 碗櫥

用法 注意本字的發音，不要唸成
[ˈkʌpˌbɔrd]。

▶ Put these plates on the top shelf of the kitchen cupboard.
把這些盤子放到廚房廚櫃的最上層。

hammer [ˈhæməˈ]

n. 榔頭 & vt. 用榔頭敲

🔡 hammer a nail into...
把釘子釘進……
= drive a nail into...

▶ I drove the nail into the wall with a hammer.
我用榔頭把釘子釘到牆上。

▶ Joyce hammered the nails into the wall.
喬依斯用榔頭把釘子敲進牆壁。

---

hanger [ˈhæŋəˈ] n. 衣架

▶ Dry your clothes on hangers.
把衣服掛在衣架上晾乾。

---

heater [ˈhitəˈ] n. 暖氣機

延伸 air-conditioner [ˈɛrkənˌdɪʃənəˈ]
n. 冷氣機

▶ We need a heater to keep us warm in winter.
我們冬天需要暖氣機保暖。

---

25 **broadcast** [ˈbrɔdˌkæst] vt. & n. 廣播

三 三態同形

似 (1) cast [kæst]
vt. (三態同形) & n. 投 ③
(2) forecast [ˈfɔrˌkæst]
vt. (三態同形) & n. 預測 ④

▶ The show was broadcast live.
這個節目現場播出。

▶ I listen to the news broadcast every morning.
我每天早上收聽新聞廣播。

---

26 **brunch** [brʌntʃ] n. 早午餐 (由 breakfast 與 lunch 兩字結合而成)

▶ I eat brunch on weekends because I sleep late.
週末的時候我會睡得很晚才起床，因此我都吃早午餐。

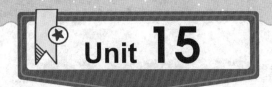

1 dislike [dɪsˈlaɪk] n. 嫌惡 & vt. 討厭

片 have a dislike for... 厭惡……

用法 dislike 作及物動詞時，之後須以名詞或動名詞作受詞。like 之後則可接名詞、動名詞或不定詞作受詞。

dislike doing sth 討厭做某事
不可說：I dislike to do it. (×)
應 說：I dislike doing it. (○)
　　 = I don't like to do it.
　　 = I don't like doing it.
　　　 我不喜歡做這件事。

▸ Tanya has a dislike for grapes.
坦雅討厭吃葡萄。

▸ Albert dislikes keeping a low profile on the issue.
亞伯特討厭對此一問題採取低姿態。

＊keep a low profile　保持低調
　profile [ˈprofaɪl] n. 形象；側影

2 patience [ˈpeʃəns] n. 耐心

衍 (1) patient [ˈpeʃənt]
　 a. 有耐心的 & n. 病患 ②
　 be patient with sb
　 對某人有耐心
(2) impatient [ɪmˈpeʃənt] a. 不耐煩的
　 be impatient with sb
　 對某人無耐心
反 impatience [ɪmˈpeʃəns] n. 不耐煩

▸ Can't you walk a little faster? I'm losing my patience.
你難道不能走快一點嗎？我快沒耐性了。

▸ Patience is a virtue.
耐心是一種美德。—— 諺語

3 bubble [ˈbʌbl] n. 泡沫 & vi. 冒泡

片 bubble over　興奮
= feel excited

▸ There are many bubbles in the bathtub.
浴缸裡有好多肥皂泡泡。

▸ When the soup starts to bubble, it is nearly ready.
湯開始冒泡時，它就快煮好了。

▸ I was bubbling over with joy after Jane gave me a kiss.
珍吻了我後，我真是樂翻了。

4 mushroom [ˈmʌʃrum] n. 洋菇，蘑菇 & vi. 急速增加或快速發展

似 flourish [ˈflɝɪʃ] vi. 茂盛 ⑥

▸ Mushroom soup is my favorite.
蘑菇湯是我的最愛。

▸ Coffee shops are mushrooming all over the island.
咖啡廳在全島如雨後春筍般設立。

1505-1512

5 mobile [ˈmobaɪl / ˈmobḷ] *a.* 可動的，流動的

似 movable [ˈmuvəbḷ] *a.* 可移動的
延伸 a mobile phone　行動電話，手機
= a cellular phone
= a cellphone
a smartphone　智慧型手機

▶ A business person cannot do without a mobile phone.
= A business person cannot do without a cellphone.
生意人沒有行動電話就無法工作。

6 nickname [ˈnɪkˌnem] *n.* 綽號 & *vt.* 取綽號

延伸 pen name [ˈpɛn ˌnem] *n.* 筆名

▶ Every student in my class has a nickname.
我班上的每位學生都有一個綽號。

▶ Hank Aaron was nicknamed "Hammer" because of his hitting power.
漢克・阿倫由於他打擊的爆發力，被人們取了『槌頭』的綽號。
＊hammer [ˈhæmə] *n.* 槌頭

7 vivid [ˈvɪvɪd] *a.* 生動的

衍 vividly [ˈvɪvɪdlɪ] *adv.* 生動地
似 graphic [ˈgræfɪk] *a.* 生動的 ⑤
反 dull [dʌl] *a.* 無聊的 ②

▶ Mary's description of the party was so vivid that I felt as though I had been there.
瑪莉把派對描述得那麼生動，讓我覺得我也曾在現場似的。

lively [ˈlaɪvlɪ] *a.* 有生氣的，生動的

似 (1) energetic [ˌɛnəˈdʒɛtɪk] *a.* 精力旺盛的 ③
(2) vigorous [ˈvɪgərəs] *a.* 精力充沛的 ⑥
反 feeble [ˈfibḷ] *a.* 虛弱的 ⑥

▶ A good night's sleep helped me feel lively again.
一夜好眠後，我又感到朝氣蓬勃。

▶ In his speech, Mr. Johnson gave a lively description of his experience as a sailor.
強森先生在演講中生動地描述他當水手的生涯經驗。

8 bury [ˈbɛrɪ] *vt.* 埋葬；使投入，使埋首

三 bury, buried [ˈbɛrɪd], buried
片 (1) bury sb alive　活埋某人
(2) be buried alive　被活埋
(3) be buried in...　埋首於……
衍 burial [ˈbɛrɪəl] *n.* 埋葬；葬禮 ⑤

▶ Because of the earthquake, hundreds of people were buried alive.
數百人因為這場地震被活埋。

▶ John is a devoted employee. Whenever you see him, he is buried in his work.
約翰是個很認真的員工。你看到他的時候，他都是在埋首工作。

134

9　continent [ˈkɑntənənt] *n.* 大陸；洲

衍 continental [ˌkɑntəˈnɛntl̩]
a. 洲的，大陸的 ⑤

似 mainland [ˈmenˌlənd] *n.* 大陸 ⑥

用法 表『中國大陸』多使用 mainland，表
『歐美大陸』則多使用 continent，兩
字均與介詞 on 並用。

on the Chinese mainland
在中國大陸（mainland 為小寫）

on the European Continent
在歐洲大陸（Continent 為大寫）

▶ Australia is a continent; New Zealand isn't.
澳洲是一塊大陸，紐西蘭不是。

▶ There used to be many Native American tribes on the American Continent.
美洲大陸一度曾有許多美國原住民部落。

10　farther [ˈfɑrðɚ] *a.* (時間、距離) 更遠的 & *adv.* 更遠地

似 further [ˈfɝðɚ] *a.* 進一步的 &
adv. 進一步地；更遠地 (= farther) ②

▶ We won't take any action until further notice.
我們在獲得進一步的通知後才會採取行動。

▶ Walk two blocks further down, and you'll see the post office on your right-hand side.
= Walk two blocks farther down and you will see the post office on your right-hand side.
往下再走兩個街區，你就可看到郵局在你的右手邊。

▶ You'll find the bookcase at the farther end of the living room.
你會在客廳較遠的那一端看到書櫃。

▶ The farther away you live, the longer it will take to get home.
你住得越遠，回家就越費時。

11　weep [wip] *vi.* 流淚，哭泣

三 weep, wept [wɛpt], wept

似 sob [sɑb] *vi.* 啜泣 ⑤

▶ The mourners silently wept at the old man's funeral.
哀悼者在老先生的葬禮上靜靜地哭著。
＊mourner [ˈmɔrnɚ] *n.* 哀悼者

12　ripe [raɪp] *a.* (農作物、時機) 成熟的

衍 ripen [ˈraɪpən] *vi.* (農作物) 成熟

似 mature [məˈtʃʊr] *a.* 成熟的 ②

▶ You can't eat those oranges until they are ripe.
那些柳橙熟了才能吃。

▶ The time is ripe for investing in this company.
現在正是投資這家公司的成熟時機。

13 boot [but] *n.* 長靴 & *vt.* & *vi.* 使電腦啟動 (= boot up) & *vt.* 猛踢

片 (1) a pair of boots　一雙長靴
　(2) give sb the boot　開除某人
　= fire sb

▶ I need to buy a new pair of boots for my hiking trip.
我需要買雙新的靴子以便健行之旅用。

▶ Boot up the computer and let me take a look at it.
啟動電腦然後讓我看一下。

▶ The player was sent off for booting another player in the leg.
這位選手因猛踢另一位選手的腿而被罰退場。
*send sb off　罰某人下場

▶ The employee was given the boot for being tardy too often.
這名員工因為經常遲到而被炒魷魚了。
*tardy [ˋtɑrdɪ] *a.* 遲到的

14 complain [kəmˋplen] *vt.* & *vi.* 抱怨

片 (1) complain that + ...　抱怨……
　(2) complain about + N/V-ing
　　抱怨……

▶ Kevin complained that the food was terrible.
凱文抱怨食物很難吃。

▶ Every time I see Christine, she complains about her job.
每次我看到克莉絲汀，她都在抱怨她的工作。

complaint [kəmˋplent]
n. 抱怨；投訴

片 make complaints about...
　抱怨……
　= complain about...
似 grievance [ˋgrivəns] *n.* 抱怨

▶ Stop making complaints about life and learn to appreciate what you have.
= Stop complaining about life and learn to appreciate what you have.
別再抱怨人生，學習感激你現有的一切。
*appreciate [əˋpriʃɪˌet] *vt.* 感激

▶ We've received a lot of customer complaints about our new products lately.
最近我們收到許多客戶對我們新產品的投訴。

15 cheek [tʃik] *n.* 臉頰 (因有兩片，故常用複數)；厚顏

片 have the cheek to + V
　居然有臉做……，厚臉皮做……

▶ The little girl has rosy cheeks and blue eyes.
這個小女孩有紅潤的臉頰及一雙碧藍的眼睛。

▶ I was surprised that the new employee had the cheek to yell at the boss.
我很訝異這位新來的員工竟然有臉對老闆大吼。

jaw [dʒɔ] *n.* 下顎
片 escape from the jaws of death
　死裡逃生

▶ Your jaw is the lower part of your face below your mouth.
你的下顎就是指你臉部嘴巴下方的部位。

▶ The hero's quick thinking enabled him to escape from the jaws of death.
這位英雄的機智使他能死裡逃生。

chin [tʃɪn] *n.* 下巴

▶ Peter has a big chin, but it is hidden under his thick beard.
彼得的下巴很長，不過被他的大鬍子遮住了。

forehead [ˈfɔrˌhɛd] *n.* 前額
似 brow [braʊ] *n.* 額頭 ②

▶ Helen's got a large forehead and a pointy chin.
海倫的額頭高、下巴尖。
＊pointy [ˈpɔɪntɪ] *a.* 尖的

16　cocktail [ˈkɑkˌtel] *n.* 雞尾酒

片 a cocktail party　雞尾酒會

▶ We will host a cocktail party tonight in celebration of John's birthday.
我們今晚會辦一個雞尾酒會以慶祝約翰的生日。

bartender [ˈbɑrˌtɛndɚ] *n.* 酒保

▶ The successful businessman used to work as a bartender while in college.
這位成功的商人念大學時曾當過酒保。

pub [pʌb] *n.* 酒吧
似 (1) bar [bɑr] *n.* 酒吧 ②
　　(2) tavern [ˈtævən] *n.* 小酒館

▶ Many foreigners frequent that pub because of its homey atmosphere.
那間酒吧有家的氣氛，因此許多老外常會到那兒光顧。
＊frequent [friˈkwɛnt] *vt.* 常去
　homey [ˈhomɪ] *a.* 像家一樣的

17　wander [ˈwɑndɚ] *vi.* 漫遊；閒逛 ＆ *n.* 閒逛

衍 wanderer [ˈwɑndərɚ] *n.* 閒蕩者
似 (1) roam [rom] *vi.* 漫步，遊蕩 ⑥
　　(2) wonder [ˈwʌndɚ]
　　　vt. 想知道 ＆ *n.* 驚奇；奇蹟 ②
　　(3) stroll [strol] *vi.* ＆ *n.* 散步 ⑥

▶ The confused old man wandered through the streets, unsure of where he was.
這位困惑的老先生在街頭遊蕩，不知自己身在何處。

▶ The runaway girl wandered along the street, looking in the shop windows.
這個蹺家的女孩在街上閒逛，瀏覽商店的櫥窗。
＊runaway [ˈrʌnəˌwe] *a.* 逃跑的；失控的

▶ Nick likes to go for a wander around the park during his lunch break.
尼克喜歡在他午休期間到公園附近閒逛。

18　miracle [ˈmɪrəkl] *n.* 奇蹟

片 work / perform miracles
　產生奇蹟，有效

▶ It's a miracle that no one was killed or injured in that accident.
那起意外無人傷亡，真是個奇蹟。

衍 **miraculous** [mɪˋrækjələs]
a. 不可思議的，如奇蹟般的 ⑥

似 **wonder** [ˋwʌndɚ] *n.* 奇蹟 ②

▶ Maybe you should try this medicine for your headache—it worked miracles for me.
也許你該試試這種藥來治頭痛 —— 它對我蠻有效的。

19 **whip** [(h)wɪp] *n.* 鞭子 & *vt.* 用鞭子抽打；攪打（食材）

三 **whip, whipped** [(h)wɪpt], **whipped**

似 **lash** [læʃ] *vt.* 用鞭子抽打

▶ The cowboy picked up his hat and whip, and then he went to find the horse.
這個牛仔撿起他的帽子和鞭子，然後去找那匹馬。

▶ Some states in the US have banned jockeys from whipping their horses.
美國某些州已禁止騎師鞭打馬匹。
＊jockey [ˋdʒɑkɪ] *n.* 騎師

▶ Cindy likes to whip the cream when her mother bakes a cake.
辛蒂喜歡在媽媽烤蛋糕時打奶油。

20 **wealthy** [ˋwɛlθɪ] *a.* 富有的

衍 **wealth** [wɛlθ]
n. 財富，富裕（不可數）；豐富 ②

似 (1) **rich** [rɪtʃ] *a.* 有錢的 ①
(2) **affluent** [ˋæfluənt] *a.* 富裕的

▶ The wealthy are not necessarily happy; likewise, the poor are not necessarily sad.
有錢人未必快樂；同樣地，窮人未必悲傷。

poverty [ˋpɑvɚtɪ]
n. 貧窮；缺乏；貧瘠

衍 (1) **poor** [pʊr]
a. 貧困的；糟糕的；可憐的 ①
(2) **poverty-stricken**
[ˋpɑvɚtɪˏstrɪkən]
a. 備受貧窮打擊的
(3) **impoverished** [ɪmˋpɑvərɪʃt]
a. 赤貧的

▶ The poverty of his family made it impossible for Paul to attend college.
保羅家境清寒，這使他不能念大學。

▶ The student's writing showed a poverty of imagination.
＝ The student's writing showed a shortage of imagination.
這位學生寫作的內容顯示他缺乏想像力。

▶ The poverty of the soil caused a bad rice harvest.
這塊土壤很貧瘠導致稻米歉收。

21 **drunk** [drʌŋk] *a.* 酒醉的 & *n.* 醉漢

片 **get drunk** 喝醉了

似 **intoxicated** [ɪnˋtɑksəˏketɪd]
a. 喝醉的

▶ Sam got drunk at the party, so I drove him home.
山姆在派對上喝醉了，因此我便開車送他回家。

▶ You should cut down on your drinking, or you'll turn into a drunk.
你應該少喝酒，不然你會變成酒鬼。

22　lawn [lɔn] *n.* 草坪

片 (1) mow the lawn　修剪草坪
　(2) a lawn mower　剪草機

▶ Peter spent all morning helping his father mow the lawn.
彼得整個早上都在幫他父親剪草坪。

---

meadow [ˋmɛdo] *n.* 草地

似 (1) grassland [ˋɡræs͵lənd] *n.* 草地
　(2) pasture [ˋpæstʃɚ] *n.* 牧草地

▶ Some sheep were grazing in the meadow.
有幾隻羊在草地上吃草。
＊graze [ɡrez] *vi.* (牛羊等) 吃草

---

weed [wid]
n. 雜草 & *vt.* & *vi.* (為……) 除草

片 grow like weeds
如雜草般快速成長

▶ Is this a healthy plant or is it a weed?
這是棵健康植物還是株雜草？

▶ Kids grow like weeds. In less than three years, Johnny has grown into a tall teenager.
小孩長得真快。不到三年的時間，強尼已經長成高個子的青少年了。

▶ Hannah asked her son to help her weed the garden.
漢娜要她兒子幫她為花園除草。

23　portrait [ˋpɔrtret] *n.* 肖像，畫像

衍 portray [pɔrˋtre] *vt.* 描繪；描述 ④

▶ Mary's great-grandmother's portrait still hangs in her father's house.
瑪莉的曾祖母畫像還掛在她爸爸家裡。

24　marble [ˋmarbl̩] *n.* 大理石 (不可數)；玻璃彈珠 (可數)

片 play marbles　打彈珠

▶ The monument is made of marble and granite.
這座紀念碑是由大理石和花崗石製成的。
＊granite [ˋɡrænɪt] *n.* 花崗石

▶ Peter was good at playing marbles when young.
彼得年輕時很會打彈珠。

---

bead [bid] *n.* (有孔的) 珠子

▶ I'm making a necklace for my niece using colorful beads.
我正在用彩色的珠珠為我姪女做項鍊。

25　comma [ˋkamə] *n.* 逗號

似 coma [ˋkomə] *n.* 昏睡狀態
　be left in a coma　陷入昏睡狀態

▶ The only mistake was a missing comma in this sentence.
這裡唯一的錯誤就是這個句子裡少了一個逗號。

26 laughter [ˈlæftɚ] *n.* 笑，笑聲

🅗 burst into laughter　突然大笑
= burst out laughing

▶ Laughter is the best medicine.
笑是最好的良藥。── 諺語

▶ Linda burst into laughter after hearing Michael's joke.
= Linda burst out laughing after hearing Michael's joke.
琳達聽完麥可的笑話後大笑出聲。

grin [grɪn]
vi. & *n.* 露齒微笑，開心地微笑

🅔 grin, grinned [grɪnd], grinned

🅗 grin at sb　對著某人開心地微笑

🅢 giggle [ˈgɪgl̩]
vi. & *n.* 喀喀地笑，傻笑 ④

▶ Mary grinned at her boyfriend the moment she saw him.
瑪莉一看到男友就對他眉開眼笑。

▶ The winner stepped down the stage with a wide grin on his face.
優勝者走下舞臺，臉上帶著大大的笑容。

27 bless [blɛs] *vt.* 祝福；保佑

🅗 be blessed with...　幸運擁有……

🅥 blessing [ˈblɛsɪŋ]
n. 祝福；保佑 (可數) ④

▶ The priest blessed the children as they left.
那位牧師在孩子離開之際祈神祝福他們。

▶ Jim is blessed with a good sense of humor.
吉姆受到老天眷顧，天生就有幽默感。

28 crash [kræʃ] *n.* 墜毀；撞擊聲 & *vi.* 衝撞，撞擊

🅗 (1) a plane crash　空難
= an air crash
(2) crash into...　撞上……

🅢 (1) crush [krʌʃ] *vt.* 擠壓 ④
(2) clash [klæʃ] *n.* & *vi.* 打架，衝突 ④

▶ While driving through the intersection, we heard a loud crash.
當開車經過十字路口時，我們聽到一陣很大的撞擊聲。

▶ At least 100 people were killed in the plane crash.
這場空難中至少有 100 人罹難。

▶ The car crashed into the tree, killing the driver on the spot.
這輛車撞上樹，駕駛當場死亡。
*on the spot　當場，立刻

29 cruel [ˈkruəl] *a.* 殘忍的

🅗 be cruel to...　對……很殘忍

🅥 (1) cruelty [ˈkruəltɪ] *n.* 殘忍 ④
(2) cruelly [ˈkruəlɪ] *adv.* 殘忍地

▶ Children should be taught from an early age not to be cruel to animals.
孩子們應該要從小就被教導不應殘忍對待動物。

似 (1) violent [`vaɪələnt] *a.* 粗暴的 ③
　　(2) brutal [`brutḷ] *a.* 粗暴的 ④
　　(3) nasty [`næstɪ] *a.* 惡毒的 ⑤
　　(4) unkind [ʌn`kaɪnd] *a.* 刻薄的
反 kind [kaɪnd] *a.* 善良的 ①

30　database [`detə,bes] *n.* 資料庫

衍 data [`detə] *n.* 資料 (複數形) ②

延伸 information [,ɪnfə`meʃən]
n. 資料 (不可數，有時縮寫成 info
[`ɪnfo]) ③

▶ The researcher entered the survey results into the database.
那位研究人員將問卷調查結果輸入資料庫裡。
＊researcher [rɪ`sɝtʃɚ] *n.* 研究人員

31　grassy [`græsɪ] *a.* 長滿草的

衍 grass [græs] *n.* 草 ①

▶ Eric likes to lie down on grassy fields and watch the clouds float by.
艾瑞克喜歡躺在草地上看著空中的雲飄過。

32　dumpling [`dʌmplɪŋ] *n.* 餃子

▶ Would you like some more dumplings?
你想要再來一點餃子嗎？

33　geography [dʒɪ`agrəfɪ] *n.* 地理

衍 geographic [,dʒɪə`græfɪk] *a.* 地理的
= geographical [,dʒɪə`græfɪkḷ] ⑥

▶ In high school, my worst subject was geography.
我念高中的時候，最差的一科就是地理了。

1 **amaze** [ə'mez] *vt.* 使驚訝

似 (1) surprise [sə'praɪz] *vt.* 使驚訝 ①
(2) astonish [ə'stɑnɪʃ] *vt.* 使吃驚 ⑤
(3) astound [ə'staʊnd] *vt.* 使震驚

▶ Joe's violin-playing skills amazed everyone at the concert.
喬的小提琴演奏技巧讓演奏會上的所有人大吃一驚。

amazed [ə'mezd] *a.* 感到驚訝的
用 be amazed at / by...
對⋯⋯感到驚訝
似 (1) be surprised at / by...
對⋯⋯感到訝異
(2) be astonished at / by...
(3) be astounded at / by...

▶ We were all amazed at Peter's ability to handle the problem.
我們對彼得處理問題的能力感到驚訝。

amazing [ə'mezɪŋ] *a.* 令人驚訝的
似 (1) surprising [sə'praɪzɪŋ]
a. 令人吃驚的
(2) astonishing [ə'stɑnɪʃɪŋ]
a. 令人驚訝的
(3) astounding [ə'staʊndɪŋ]
a. 令人震驚的

▶ It's amazing that an ant can carry objects many times heavier than itself.
螞蟻搬得動比自己身體重好幾倍的物體，真令人驚奇。

amazement [ə'mezmənt]
n. 訝異，驚愕
用 To one's amazement, ...
令某人吃驚的是，⋯⋯
似 (1) surprise [sə'praɪz] *n.* 驚訝 ①
(2) astonishment [ə'stɑnɪʃmənt]
n. 驚訝 ⑤

▶ I thought my father would get angry, but to my amazement, he tried to comfort me.
我以為父親會生氣，但令我吃驚的是，他卻試著要安慰我。

2 **acceptable** [ək'sɛptəbḷ] *a.* 可接受的；尚可的

衍 (1) accept [ək'sɛpt] *vt.* 接受 ②
(2) acceptance [ək'sɛptəns] *n.* 接受 ④
似 (1) satisfactory [ˌsætɪs'fæktərɪ]
a. 令人滿意的 ③
(2) good enough 還算不錯的
反 unacceptable [ˌʌnək'sɛptəbḷ]
a. 不能接受的

▶ The plan we made should be acceptable to them.
我們擬的計畫對他們而言應該是可以接受的。

▶ Your performance in the game was acceptable, but it could have been better.
你比賽中的表現勉強可以，但可以更好一點。

3 charm [tʃɑrm] n. 魅力；符咒 & vt. 使著迷

片 (1) be charmed by... 為……著迷
 = be fascinated by / with...
 = be attracted by / to...
 (2) work like a charm
 正如預期的效果

似 (1) attraction [əˈtrækʃən] n. 吸引 ④
 (2) charisma [kəˈrɪzmə] n. 魅力
 (3) fascination [ˌfæsnˈeʃən]
 n. 魅力，迷戀 ⑥

▶ The actor is not very handsome but has great charm.
 這名演員不是很帥但是魅力十足。

▶ This ring is my lucky charm.
 這只戒指是我的幸運符。

▶ I tried your idea, and it worked like a charm.
 我嘗試你的點子，效果正如預期。

▶ Rachel is charmed by AhXiong's sense of humor.
 瑞秋為阿雄的幽默感所吸引。

charming [ˈtʃɑrmɪŋ] a. 迷人的

似 (1) attractive [əˈtræktɪv]
 a. 吸引人的 ③
 (2) appealing [əˈpilɪŋ] a. 迷人的

延伸 Prince Charming 白馬王子

▶ I'm under Jane's spell because she is so charming.
 我對珍意亂情迷因為她真迷人。

4 meaningful [ˈminɪŋfəl] a. 有意義的；意義深長的

衍 (1) mean [min]
 a. 小器的；心地壞的 & vt. 表示 ①
 a mean guy 壞心眼的傢伙
 (2) means [minz] n. 方法；手段
 (單複數同形)；財富 (不可數) ②
 by means of... 藉由……
 a man of means 有錢人
 (3) meaning [ˈminɪŋ] n. 意思 ②

似 significant [sɪgˈnɪfəkənt]
 a. 有意義的；重大的 ③

▶ We had a meaningful and constructive meeting this afternoon.
 今天下午我們開了一場有意義且具建設性的會議。

▶ Patricia gave her husband a meaningful look as he hugged her.
 派翠莎的老公擁抱她時，她意味深長地看了他一眼。

meaningless [ˈminɪŋlɪs]
a. 無意義的；不重要的

似 insignificant [ˌɪnsɪgˈnɪfəkənt]
 a. 無意義的；不重要的

▶ I find this essay utterly meaningless.
 我覺得這篇文章完全沒有意義。
 *utterly [ˈʌtəlɪ] adv. 完全地 (= completely)

5 statue [ˈstætʃu] n. 雕像

似 sculpture [ˈskʌlptʃɚ] n. 雕像 ④

延伸 the Statue of Liberty　自由女神像

▶ The Statue of Liberty is probably America's most famous landmark.
自由女神像很可能是美國最知名的地標。

▶ The city government erected a statue in the park in honor of the hero.
市政府在公園內豎立一座雕像以記念這位英雄。
＊erect [ɪˈrɛkt] vt. 豎立
　in honor of...　以記念……；向……致敬

6 living [ˈlɪvɪŋ] n. 生計 & a. 活著的，現在的

片 earn / make a living + V-ing
　　以……維生

＝ earn / make a living as + 職業

衍 (1) live [laɪv] a. 現場的 & [lɪv] vi. & vt. 活著；過日子 ①
　　a live show　現場播出的節目
　　(2) alive [əˈlaɪv]
　　a. 活著的 (置於名詞後) ②

▶ The rescuers found no one alive in the cave-in.
此次礦坑災變中救難人員未發現有任何生還者。

似 livelihood [ˈlaɪvlɪˌhʊd] n. 生計

▶ Joseph makes a living teaching English.
= Joseph makes a living as an English teacher.
喬瑟夫以教英文維生。

▶ Mr. Akins is one of the few living WWII veterans.
亞金斯先生是少數僅存的二次世界大戰老兵之一。
＊veteran [ˈvɛtərən] n. 老兵

7 communicate [kəˈmjunəˌket] vt. 傳達 (意見、感受等) & vi. 溝通

片 communicate with sb　與某人溝通

衍 (1) communication
　　[kəˌmjunəˈkeʃən] n. 聯絡；傳播，傳播學 (複數) ④
　　(2) communicative
　　[kəˈmjunəˌketɪv] a. 愛交際的，很會說話的 ⑥
　　(3) communicable [kəˈmjunəkəbl̩]
　　a. 可溝通的

▶ Richard always communicates his ideas clearly.
理查總能清楚地表達他的意見。

▶ The deaf communicate through sign language.
失聰者透過手語溝通。
＊deaf [dɛf] a. 聾的
　the deaf　聽障人士
　=deaf people

▶ I have difficulty communicating with a stubborn man like Tony.
我很難與像東尼那樣固執的人溝通。
＊stubborn [ˈstʌbɚn] a. 固執的

8 swell [swɛl] vi. 腫大；膨脹 & n. 隆起

swell, swelled [swɛld], swelled /
swollen [ˋswolən]

▶ The man's finger swelled after the snake bit it.
該男子的手指被蛇咬後腫了起來。

▶ The audience swelled to 50,000 before the concert came to an end.
演唱會結束前，觀眾人數暴增到五萬人。

▶ A large swell appeared in the middle of the road.
路中央出現了一大片路面隆起。

---

shrink [ʃrɪŋk] vi. & vt. (使) 縮小

shrink, shrank [ʃræŋk], shrunk
[ʃrʌŋk]

延伸 在口語中，shrink 也可作名詞，表
『精神科醫生』，等於 psychiatrist
[saɪˋkaɪətrɪst]。

▶ Cotton clothes usually shrink in the dryer.
棉質衣服烘乾後通常會縮小。

▶ Hot water shrinks woolen clothes.
熱水會使毛線衣縮水。

9 knight [naɪt] n. 騎士

▶ That knight betrayed his country for his lover.
那名騎士為了情人而背叛國家。
＊betray [brɪˋtre] vt. 背叛

---

crown [kraʊn]
n. 皇冠 & vt. 為……加冕

片 (1) crown sb king / queen
將某人加冕為國王 / 王后
(2) be crowned king / queen
被加冕為國王 / 王后

▶ Queen Elizabeth's crown is on display in the Jewel House in the Tower of London.
伊麗莎白女皇的皇冠在倫敦塔內的珠寶屋展示。

▶ How long will it be before Prince Charles is crowned king?
要多久查爾斯王子才會被加冕為國王？

10 gang [gæŋ] n. 幫派 & vi. 成群結隊

片 gang up against / on sb
因對付某人而成群結隊

衍 gangster [ˋgæŋstɚ]
n. 幫派分子，流氓 ⑥

似 clan [klæn]
n. (為共同利益而結合的) 幫派

延伸 幫派所占的『地盤』稱作 turf [tɝf]，他
們向人所索取的保護費稱作 protection
fee。

▶ Rumor has it that Peter joined a street gang when he was young.
＝ Word has it that Peter joined a street gang when he was young.
謠傳彼得年輕時曾加入某街頭幫派。

▶ The shop owners ganged together to resist the increase in rent.
這些商家店主集結起來抵制租金調漲。

▶ The older prisoners would often gang up against / on the younger ones.
這些較資深的囚犯通常聯合對付較菜的囚犯。

mob [mɑb]

n. (一群) 暴民 & *vt.* (人群) 圍住

目 mob, mobbed [mɑbd], mobbed

片 a mob of + 數字

一群為數……的暴民

衍 mobster [`mɑbstə] *n.* 暴民中的一員

▶ The demonstrators got out of control and became a mob.

那些示威群眾失控，變成一群暴民。

▶ A mob of some sixty occupied the building and destroyed everything they saw.

一群為數約 60 人的暴徒占據大樓，看到什麼就全加以破壞。

▶ The actress was mobbed by her fans as soon as she went out of the airport.

該女演員一出機場時，就被她的影迷團團圍住。

---

11 thread [θrɛd] *n.* (縫衣服的) 線；頭緒 & *vt.* 穿線於

片 (1) lose the thread of...

理不出……的頭緒

(2) a thread of hope 一線希望

似 (1) cord [kɔrd]

n. 有插頭的電線；細繩 ④

(2) rope [rop] *n.* 粗繩 ①

▶ Do you have a needle and thread I can borrow?

你有針和線可以借我嗎？

▶ I missed a few words, so I lost the thread of what you were saying.

有幾個字我沒聽到，因此我不懂你在說什麼。

▶ There is a thread of hope that the boy is still alive.

對小男孩仍存活著一事我們還抱持一線希望。

▶ No one in the class knew how to thread a needle.

班上沒有人知道怎麼穿針線。

---

stitch [stɪtʃ] *n.* 一針 & *vt.* 縫

▶ A stitch in time saves nine.

及時一針可省下九針 / 亡羊補牢，時猶未晚。—— 諺語

▶ Jack was wounded in a fight and needed 10 stitches.

傑克因打架受了傷，需要縫 10 針。

▶ This jacket has our brand name stitched across the back.

這件外套後面繡上了我們的品牌名稱。

---

12 explode [ɪk`splod] *vt.* & *vi.* 爆炸，炸掉 & *vi.* 激增

衍 (1) explosion [ɪk`sploʒən]

n. 爆炸聲；爆炸 ④

(2) explosive [ɪk`splosɪv]

a. 爆炸 (性) 的；爆發的 &

n. 爆炸物 ④

似 blow up... 炸掉……

▶ In 1949, the Soviet Union exploded its first atomic bomb.

1949 年，蘇聯引爆它的第一顆原子彈。

*atomic [ə`tɑmɪk] *a.* 原子的

▶ The newspapers showed pictures of the plane after it exploded.

報紙登出這架飛機爆炸後的照片。

▶ We exploded the bridge so the enemy troops couldn't cross it.

= We blew up the bridge so the enemy troops couldn't cross it.

我們把橋炸掉，好讓敵軍無法通過。

▶ The population of this town has exploded in recent years.
該鎮的人口近年來激增。

13 horror [ˈhɔrə] *n.* 恐怖，恐懼

片 (1) To one's horror, ...
嚇壞某人的是，……

(2) a horror movie　恐怖片

衍 horrify [ˈhɔrəˌfaɪ] *vt.* 使恐懼 ④

似 (1) fear [fɪr] *n.* 害怕 ②

(2) panic [ˈpænɪk] *n.* 驚恐 ③

延伸 (1) a tearjerker [ˈtɪrˌdʒɜkə]
賺人眼淚的電影

(2) a blockbuster [ˈblɑkˌbʌstə]
賣座片

(3) a detective movie　偵探片

(4) a romantic movie　愛情片

(5) a comedy movie　喜劇片

(6) a tragedy movie　悲劇片

▶ To my horror, I realized a stranger was in my house.
嚇壞我的是，我發現家裡有個陌生人。

▶ Horror movies do not appeal to me. I hate to be scared.
恐怖片並不吸引我。我討厭被嚇的感覺。
＊appeal to sb　吸引某人
＝attract sb

horrible [ˈhɔrəbl̩] *a.* 可怕的；很糟的

似 terrible [ˈtɛrəbl̩] *a.* 可怕的；很糟的 ①

▶ The horrible accident was the worst one we've had this year.
這起可怕的意外是今年我們經歷最嚴重的一件。

14 gap [gæp] *n.* 裂縫；歧異

片 the generation gap　代溝

似 (1) difference [ˈdɪfərəns] *n.* 差異 ②

(2) crack [kræk] *n.* 裂縫 ④

▶ Because of the generation gap, my mom doesn't share my interest in this type of music.
因為有代溝，我媽並不和我一樣喜歡這類的音樂。

▶ There is a wide gap in the views of the two opposing parties.
兩個對立的政黨看法之間有很大的歧異。

15 fountain [ˈfauntn̩] *n.* 噴泉，噴水池

片 (1) a fountain machine　飲水機

(2) a fountain pen　鋼筆

▶ Some people throw coins into fountains and make a wish, believing that their wish will come true.
有些人會擲銅幣到池子裡並許個願，他們相信這些願望會成真。

16 **youngster** [ˈjʌŋstɚ] *n.* 年輕人

衍 (1) young [jʌŋ] *a.* 年輕的 ①
(2) youth [juθ]
　　n. 青春 (不可數)；青年 (可數) ②

▸ These youths are my friends.
　這些年輕人是我的朋友。

(3) youthful [ˈjuθfəl] *a.* 青春的 ④

▸ More and more youngsters are becoming concerned about the environment.
越來越多的年輕人開始關心環境問題。

---

elderly [ˈɛldɚlɪ] *a.* 年老的

片 the elderly　老年人 (泛指所有老年人)
= elderly people

衍 elder [ˈɛldɚ]
　　n. 年長者 & *a.* 血緣關係中年長的 ②
one's elder brother / sister
= one's older brother / sister
　某人的哥哥 / 姊姊

▸ Please give your seat to elderly passengers on the bus.
在公車上請讓座給年長的乘客。

▸ We should learn to respect the elderly.
我們應學習尊重長者。

---

17 **tap** [tæp] *n.* 水龍頭〔英〕& *vt.* 輕拍 & *vi.* 輕敲

三 tap, tapped [tæpt], tapped
片 (1) tap water　自來水
(2) tap sb on the + 身體部位
　　　輕拍某人某部位

似 tab [tæb] *n.* (帳簿等邊緣供翻開的) 標籤；(易開罐的) 拉環；(電腦鍵盤上的) 跳位鍵 & *vt.* 在……上貼標籤

▸ This tap water is not potable; it's polluted.
不能飲用這自來水；它被汙染了。
＊potable [ˈpotəbl̩] *a.* 可飲用的

▸ I tapped John on the shoulder to get his attention.
我輕拍約翰的肩膀，想引起他的注意。

▸ Paul tapped on the window of the room to wake up his brother.
保羅輕敲房間的窗戶，要叫醒他弟弟。

---

faucet [ˈfɔsɪt] *n.* 水龍頭〔美〕

用法 表『打開 / 關掉水龍頭』：
應　　說：turn on / off the faucet
不可說：open / close the faucet
　　　　(拆開 / 封閉水龍頭)

▸ I turned on the faucet, but no water came out.
我打開水龍頭，卻沒有水流出來。

---

18 **racial** [ˈreʃəl] *a.* 種族的

片 racial discrimination
[dɪˌskrɪməˈneʃən]　種族歧視
衍 race [res] *n.* 種族 ①

▸ Racial discrimination is something that shouldn't be tolerated.
種族歧視不應被容忍。
＊tolerate [ˈtɑləˌret] *vt.* 容忍

19　summit [ˈsʌmɪt] n. 頂峰；頂點

片 (1) summit talks　高峰會議
　　(2) the summit of one's career
　　　　是某人事業的最高峰

似 peak [pik] n. 山頂；最高峰 ②

▶ The world leaders held summit talks in Manila last month.
上個月各國領袖在馬尼拉舉行高峰會議。

▶ Winning the heavyweight title was the summit of Albert's professional career.
贏得重量級冠軍是亞伯特職業生涯的最高峰。

20　follower [ˈfaloɚ] n. 擁護者，信徒

衍 follow [ˈfalo] vt. 追隨 ①

反 leader [ˈlidɚ] n. 領導者 ①

▶ The followers of the church all participated in the annual celebration.
該教會的信徒全部參與這個年度盛典。

21　traveler [ˈtrævl̩ɚ] n. 旅行者

衍 travel [ˈtrævl̩] vi. 旅行 ②

▶ Because of her work, Cindy is a frequent traveler to Europe.
因為工作的關係，辛蒂常常到歐洲旅行。

22　champion [ˈtʃæmpɪən] n. 得到冠軍者

衍 championship [ˈtʃæmpɪənˌʃɪp]
　　n. 冠軍頭銜 ④
　　win the championship　贏得冠軍

▶ John was the champion of the contest.
約翰是這次比賽的冠軍。

23　interrupt [ˌɪntəˈrʌpt] vt. 打斷

片 interrupt sb　打斷某人的話
= cut in on sb

衍 interruption [ˌɪntəˈrʌpʃən]
　　n. 中斷；干擾 ④

▶ Do not interrupt us while we're talking.
= Do not cut in on us while we're talking.
我們在講話時不要插嘴。

24　glow [glo] n. 光輝 & vi. 發光；(眼睛) 發亮

片 glow with pleasure / pride / passion
散發出愉快 / 驕傲 / 熱情的光芒

▶ The oil lamp gives off a soft glow.
油燈散發出柔和的光。

▶ The shirt glows in the dark.
這件襯衫在暗處會發光。

▶ Mary's eyes glowed with passion when she saw me.
瑪莉見到我時，雙眼散發出熱情的光芒。

ray [re] *n.* 光線

衍 X-ray [ˈɛks͵re] *n.* X 光，X 光片

▶ The sun's rays shone through the gap between the walls.
太陽光束從牆壁間的縫隙射進來。

---

beam [bim]
vt. 播送，廣播 & *vi.* 高興地微笑（與介詞 at 並用）& *n.* 愉快的微笑；光束

片 beam at sb　對某人微笑
= smile at sb

▶ This program will be beamed to Japan.
本節目將對日本播送。

▶ Who is that girl beaming at you?
那位對你開心微笑的女孩子是誰？

▶ Robert greeted his old friend with a beam of delight.
羅伯特笑容滿面地迎接老朋友。

▶ A single beam of light shone through the skylight in the roof.
一條光束射穿過屋頂的天窗。
＊skylight [ˈskaɪ͵laɪt] *n.* 天窗

---

25 **twin** [twɪn] *n.* 雙胞胎之一 & *a.* 孿生的

延伸 Siamese twins [͵saɪəmiz ˈtwɪnz]
n. 連體嬰

▶ The two girls are twins, but they look nothing alike.
這兩個女孩是雙胞胎，但她們看起來一點也不像。

▶ Simon is my twin brother.
賽門是我的孿生兄弟。

---

26 **tight** [taɪt] *a.* 緊的 & *adv.* 緊地

片 keep a tight budget
抓緊預算 / 節儉過日
反 loose [lus] *a.* 鬆的 ③

▶ Now that I plan to study abroad, I keep a tight budget.
我既然計劃要出國深造，就要省吃儉用。
＊now that...　既然……
　　now that 視為連接詞，等於 since，表『既然』，由於有 now 一字，故所引導的副詞子句應採現在式或現在完成式。

▶ Jane asked her husband to make sure the door was shut tight.
珍請她老公確認這扇門有關緊。

---

tighten [ˈtaɪtn̩] *vt.* 拉緊
片 tighten one's grip on sth
緊抓某物
＊grip [grɪp] *n.* 握住
反 loosen [ˈlusn̩] *vt.* 鬆開 ④

▶ The little girl tightened her grip on her mom's hand when she saw the dog.
小女孩看到那隻狗時緊抓著她媽媽的手。

27　sigh [saɪ] *n.* & *vi.* 歎氣

片 let out a sigh　歎一口氣
= heave a sigh
= utter a sigh

▶ Olivia let out a sigh of relief when she received a call from her son.
奧莉維亞接到兒子的電話時，放心地歎了口氣。
＊relief [rɪˋlif] *n.* 寬心；解除

▶ Michael sighed deeply as he hung up the phone.
麥可掛上電話時深深地歎了一口氣。

28　citizen [ˋsɪtəzn̩] *n.* 公民；市民

衍 citizenship [ˋsɪtəzn̩ˏʃɪp] *n.* 公民權 ⑤
似 resident [ˋrɛzədənt] *n.* 居民 ⑤

▶ Tom is an Australian citizen but grew up in Taiwan.
湯姆是澳洲公民，但卻是在臺灣長大的。

▶ The mayor urged citizens to prepare for the typhoon season.
市長呼籲市民為颱風季節做好準備。

29　holder [ˋholdɚ] *n.* 保持者；持有人

片 (1) a record holder　紀錄保持者
(2) set a record　創下紀錄
(3) keep the record　保持紀錄
(4) break the record　破紀錄

▶ Mr. Smith is the current record holder in this game.
史密斯先生是這項比賽目前的紀錄保持者。

▶ Credit card holders, please sign at the bottom of the receipt.
信用卡的持有人請在該收據下方簽名。

30　hunger [ˋhʌŋgɚ] *vi.* 渴望 & *n.* 飢餓；渴望

片 hunger for...　渴望……
= have a hunger for...
= yearn for...
= crave for...
衍 hungry [ˋhʌŋgrɪ] *a.* 飢餓的 ①

▶ After years of war, we all hunger for peace.
經過多年的戰爭，我們都渴望和平。

▶ Many people in Africa are dying from hunger.
在非洲有許多人因飢餓而死亡。

▶ Mr. Rogers has a hunger for fame.
羅傑斯先生渴望成名。

1 knit [nɪt] *vt.* (用毛線) 針織 & *n.* 編織衣物

目 knit, knitted [`nɪtɪd], knitted

似 sew [so] *vt.* 縫製 ④

▶ Jenny knitted her son a pair of blue socks.
珍妮替她兒子織了一雙藍襪子。

▶ The clothes shop sells many different kinds of winter knits.
這間服飾店販售很多不同種類的冬天針織衣物。

---

weave [wiv]

vt. & *vi.* 穿梭而行；編織 & *n.* 織法

目 weave, wove [wov], woven [`wovən]

片 (1) weave one's way through
某人穿梭而行

= worm one's way through

(2) weave in and out of traffic
在車陣中蛇行

▶ Alan had to weave his way through the crowd to get to the other end of the mall.
艾倫得穿過人群才能到賣場的另一邊。

▶ In the city of Taipei, there are always a lot of motorcycles weaving through the traffic.
在臺北市總是有很多機車在車陣間穿梭。

▶ It's dangerous to weave in and out of traffic.
在車陣中蛇行很危險。

▶ Many women in this town make their living by weaving rugs.
該鎮許多婦女靠編織地毯維生。

▶ Lucy learned how to weave from her grandmother.
露西向她外婆學習編織。

▶ The rug that Sharon has chosen features a tight weave.
雪倫選好的地毯以密實織法為其特色。

2 monk [mʌŋk] *n.* (天主教) 修士；和尚

似 priest [prist] *n.* 神父 ②

延伸 monastery [`mɑnəsˌtɛrɪ] *n.* 修道院

▶ The millionaire converted to Buddhism and became a monk after his wife passed away.
這個百萬富翁在太太過世後皈依佛門做和尚去了。
*convert [kən`vɝt] *vi.* 皈依 (某宗教) (與介詞 to 並用)

---

nun [nʌn] *n.* 修女；尼姑

延伸 sister 亦表『修女』，冠於名字之前，以示尊敬。

Sister Maria 瑪麗亞修女

▶ The nun is a volunteer in that hospital.
這位修女是那家醫院的義工。
*volunteer [ˌvɑlən`tɪr] *n.* 志工

3 breeze [briz] *n.* 微風 & *vi.* 飄然而行；輕鬆贏得

片 (1) shoot the breeze 閒聊 (口語)
= chitchat [`tʃɪtˌtʃæt] *n.* & *vi.* 閒聊

(2) breeze through 輕鬆贏得

▶ I felt great as a gentle breeze blew over my face.
一陣輕柔的微風吹拂我的臉時，我感到舒服極了。

似 wind [wɪnd] *n.* 風 ①

▶ Peter and John did nothing but shoot the breeze all afternoon.

彼得和約翰整個下午啥事都不幹，只顧著閒聊。

* do nothing but V　除了從事……外其他事都不做

▶ The president breezed into the room and shook everyone's hands.

總統如風似地走到房間裡並跟每一位握手。

▶ John breezed through the math exam and left with half an hour to go.

約翰輕鬆地考完數學並在剩 30 分鐘時離開。

4　mathematical [ˌmæθəˈmætɪkl̩] *a.* 數學的 (= math) ☐

片 a mathematical / math formula
數學公式

衍 (1) mathematics / math
[ˌmæθəˈmætɪks / mæθ] *n.* 數學 ①

(2) mathematician
[ˌmæθəməˈtɪʃən] *n.* 數學家

(3) arithmetic [əˈrɪθmətɪk]
n. 算術；計算 ⑥

▶ The mathematical formula was named after the great mathematician.

= The math formula was named after the great mathematician.

這道數學公式是以這位偉大數學家的名字命名的。

5　postpone [postˈpon] *vt.* 延期，延緩 ☐

片 postpone + N/V-ing　暫緩……
= put off + N/V-ing

似 delay [dɪˈle] *vt.* 延期；延宕 ②

用法 postpone、delay 及 put off 均使用動名詞作受詞，不可接 to 引導的不定詞片語作受詞。

不可說：We'll postpone to hold the meeting.

應　說：We'll postpone holding the meeting.　我們將延期開會。

▶ Because of the approaching typhoon, we decided to postpone holding the meeting until next Friday.

由於颱風逼近，我們決定將會議延至下週五再舉行。

* approaching [əˈprotʃɪŋ] *a.* 即將來臨的

---

postponement [postˈponmənt]
n. 延期，延緩

似 delay [dɪˈle] *n.* 延期；延宕 ②

▶ The client seemed unsatisfied with the postponement of the delivery.

該客戶似乎對於送貨時間延宕很不滿意。

6　emperor [ˈɛmpərɚ] *n.* 皇帝 ☐

衍 (1) empress [ˈɛmprɪs] *n.* 皇后；女皇
(2) empire [ˈɛmpaɪr] *n.* 帝國 ④

▶ Naruhito became the emperor of Japan on May 1st, 2019.

德仁在 2019 年 5 月 1 日成為日本天皇。

7 feather [ˈfɛðɚ] n. 羽毛

▸ After the pillow fight, the two children were covered in feathers.
在打完枕頭仗後，這兩個小朋友弄得滿身都是羽毛。

▸ Birds of a feather flock together.
物以類聚。—— 諺語

fur [fɝ] n. (動物的) 皮毛
囲 a fur coat　皮草大衣

▸ Conservationists discourage people from wearing fur coats.
保育人士勸阻大家不要穿皮草大衣。

＊conservationist [ˌkɑnsɚˈveʃənɪst] n. 保育人士

8 wrap [ræp] vt. 包裝，包 & n. 覆蓋物 (不可數)；披肩

囯 wrap, wrapped [ræpt], wrapped
囲 (1) wrap (sth) up　包裝某物
　 (2) be wrapped up in sth
　　　專注於某事
　 (3) wrap up　結束 (= finish)

▸ The little girl wrapped some coins in her handkerchief.
小女孩用手帕包了一些硬幣。

▸ Hannah covered the sandwiches in plastic wrap to keep them fresh.
漢娜用塑膠膜包好三明治為了讓它們保鮮。

▸ Claire likes to wear a wrap in the office to keep herself warm.
克萊兒喜歡在辦公室披著披肩來保持自身溫暖。

▸ Can you wrap up the food so we can take it home?
你可以把食物包起來好讓我們帶回家嗎？

▸ Peter was so wrapped up in his work that he didn't notice me coming.
＝ Peter was so absorbed in his work that he didn't notice me coming.
彼得非常專心地在工作，因此沒發現我的到來。

▸ The speaker wrapped up his speech with a joke.
演講人說了一個笑話就結束演講了。

9 dose [dos] n. 藥劑 & vt. (按劑量) 給……服藥 (常與介詞 with 並用)

衍 dosage [ˈdosɪdʒ] n. (藥的) 劑量

▸ One dose of this medicine will put the dog to sleep.
這種藥只要一劑就能讓這隻狗死去。

＊put an animal to sleep
讓某動物死掉 (是 kill an animal 的委婉用語)

▸ Helen dosed herself up with vitamin pills to get rid of her cold.
為了擺脫感冒，海倫服用了維他命藥丸。

10 drown [draʊn] vt. 使溺斃；淹沒 & vi. 淹死

🔲 drown one's sorrows　借酒澆愁

▶ George kept drowning his sorrows after breaking up with Ellen.

和艾倫分手後，喬治就一直就借酒澆愁。

▶ The farmer's crops were drowned when the river burst its banks.

當河水沖破河岸時，該農夫的農作物被淹沒。

▶ The fisherman almost drowned when his little boat overturned.

小船翻覆，那漁夫差點淹死。

▶ A drowning man will clutch at a straw.

飢不擇食 / 狗急跳牆。── 諺語

11 bunch [bʌntʃ] n. 一束；一群（人）

🔲 a bunch of...　一束 / 一群⋯⋯

🔲 bouquet [buˋke] n. 花束

▶ Oliver gave me a bouquet of roses on Valentine's Day.

奧利佛在情人節那一天送我一束玫瑰花。

▶ I sent Mary a bunch of flowers, but she didn't seem delighted.

我送給瑪莉一束花，但她看起來並沒有很高興。

▶ I've got a bunch of friends coming over on Friday evening, so we have to buy more food for a big dinner.

星期五晚上我有一群朋友要來，因此我們得多買些吃的準備一頓豐盛的晚餐。

bundle [ˋbʌndḷ] n. 捆，束 & vt. 捆

🔲 (1) a bundle of...

　　一捆 / 束⋯⋯；一堆⋯⋯

(2) bundle up...　將⋯⋯捆起來

(3) be a bundle of nerves

　　緊張兮兮的

▶ Richard gave Judie a bundle of flowers on their first date.

理查和茱蒂第一次約會時送了她一束花。

▶ I found a bundle of typos in Lorita's paper.

我在蘿莉塔的報告裡發現一堆打字錯誤。

*typo [ˋtaɪpo] n. (打字排版的) 錯誤

▶ Bob bundled up these magazines and put them away.

鮑伯把這些雜誌捆起來，然後把它們收好。

▶ Helen has been a bundle of nerves recently because her book's deadline is drawing near.

海倫最近緊張兮兮的，因為她的書的截稿日快到了。

12 motel [moˋtɛl] n. 汽車旅館

🔲 (1) hotel [hoˋtɛl] n. 飯店，旅館 ①
(2) hostel [ˋhɑstḷ] n. 便宜的旅社 ⑥

▶ When I'm on business, I stay in a motel instead of a hotel because it's a lot cheaper.

我出差時都會住汽車旅館而不住飯店，因為那便宜多了。

inn [ɪn] *n.* 酒店；小旅館

▶ An inn is a small hotel that provides room and board for travelers.
小酒店就是為旅客提供膳宿的小旅館。
＊board [bɔrd] *n.* 伙食，膳食

---

13 suicide [`suə͵saɪd] *n.* 自殺

⊞ commit suicide　自殺

▶ It's shocking that Larry committed suicide. He seemed like a very happy man.
賴瑞自殺的事很令人震驚。他看起來像是個非常快樂的人。

---

14 mess [mɛs] *n.* 混亂 & *vt.* 使混亂 & *vi.* 胡鬧，鬼混

⊞ (1) be a mess　一團糟
＝ be in a mess
(2) make a mess of...
　使……成一團亂，弄糟
(3) mess sth up　將某事搞砸
(4) mess around　胡鬧，鬼混

衍 messy [`mɛsɪ] *a.* 雜亂的 ④

似 (1) confusion [kən`fjuʒən] *n.* 混亂 ④
(2) chaos [`keas] *n.* 混亂 ⑤
(3) mass [mæs] *n.* 群眾；大量；團 ②

▶ The room is a mess. Clean up before you go.
房間亂七八糟。你先整理好再出門。

▶ Our two-year-old boy is a real "explorer;" he makes a mess of the house several times a day.
我們家的兩歲小子真是個『探險家』，一天會把屋子搞亂好幾次。

▶ I spent a lot of time preparing a party for you. I hope you won't mess it up.
我花了很多時間為你準備這個派對。希望你不要把它搞砸了。

▶ Stop messing around, John. We need to get back to work.
不要在一旁鬧了，約翰。我們得繼續工作。

---

15 separation [͵sɛpə`reʃən] *n.* 分離，別離

衍 separate [`sɛpə͵ret ] *vt.* 使分開；區分 & *vi.* 分開 & [ `sɛpərət] *a.* 分開的 ②

▶ Separation from his homeland made the young soldier sad.
離開他的家鄉使這個年輕士兵感到悲傷。

---

16 bush [buʃ] *n.* 灌木

⊞ beat around the bush
（講話）拐彎抹角

似 shrub [ʃrʌb] *n.* 矮樹，灌木 ⑥

▶ This website provided detailed information on how to plant rose bushes.
這個網站提供種植玫瑰叢的詳細資訊。

▶ Don't beat around the bush. Just tell me what happened.
別拐彎抹角了。快告訴我發生了什麼事。

17　panic [ˈpænɪk] n. & vi. 驚恐

目 panic, panicked [ˈpænɪkt],
panicked (動名詞及現在分詞為
panicking [ˈpænɪkɪŋ])

似 (1) fear [fɪr] n. 恐懼 & vt. 害怕 ②
　(2) fright [fraɪt] n. 驚嚇 ③
　(3) scare [skɛr] n. & vt. 驚嚇 ②

▶ Panic does not help when one is in a dangerous situation.
陷入險境時，驚恐是無濟於事的。

▶ I panicked at the sight of the poisonous snake.
我一看到那條毒蛇就驚慌起來。

18　seal [sil] vt. 密封 & n. 封條；海豹

片 seal off...　封鎖某處

似 close [kloz] vt. 關閉 ①

▶ Police sealed off all the exits so the bank robbers couldn't escape.
警方封鎖所有出口，讓銀行搶匪無處可逃。

▶ You need to break the seal in order to open the box.
你要把箱子打開就要先把封條折掉。

▶ Most seals live near the Arctic and the Antarctic and feed on smaller fish.
大多數的海豹棲息在南北極，以小魚為主食。
＊the Arctic [ˈɑrktɪk] n. 北極
　the Antarctic [ænˈtɑrktɪk] n. 南極

19　recorder [rɪˈkɔrdɚ] n. 錄音機，記錄器

衍 record [ˈrɛkɚd] n. 唱片；紀錄 &
[rɪˈkɔrd] vt. 錄音／影；記錄 ②

延
伸 (1) a tape recorder　錄音機
　(2) a flight data recorder
　　飛航情報記錄器 (俗稱 a black box
　　『黑盒子』)

▶ The tape recorder is a user-friendly machine.
這臺錄音機是臺很容易使用的機器。
＊user-friendly [ˈjuzɚˌfrɛndlɪ] a. 使用者容易上手的

20　afterward(s) [ˈæftɚwɚd(z)] adv. 之後

似 thereafter [ðɛrˈæftɚ] adv. 之後 ⑥

反 beforehand [bɪˈfɔrˌhænd]
adv. 事先 ⑥

▶ First, we went to the movies. Afterwards, we went to dinner together.
首先，我們先去看電影，之後，又一起去吃晚餐。

▶ It drizzled at first, but afterwards it rained cats and dogs.
起初只是下毛毛雨，後來變成傾盆大雨。
＊drizzle [ˈdrɪzl̩] vi. 下毛毛雨

21　ladder [ˈlædɚ] n. 梯子

似 stair [stɛr] n. 階梯 ①
climb a flight of stairs
爬一排／層樓梯

▶ Andy fell down the ladder and broke his ankle and wrist.
安迪從梯子上摔下來，把腳踝和手腕都摔斷了。

22 skip [skɪp] *vt.* 省略 & *n.* 跳；省略

- skip, skipped [skɪpt], skipped
- skip class　翹課
= cut class
= play hooky
  *hooky [ˋhʊkɪ] *n.* 逃學
= play truant
  *truant [ˋtruənt] *n.* 逃學者
似 (1) jump [dʒʌmp] *n.* 跳 ①
   (2) hop [hɑp] *n.* 單腳跳 ②
   (3) leap [lip] *n.* 跳 ③

▸ Jerry skipped lunch in order to get his work done.
   傑瑞略過午餐沒吃以把工作做完。
▸ Tom's mother gave him a good spanking because he skipped class.
   湯姆的媽媽因為他蹺課狠狠打了他的屁股。
   *spanking [ˋspæŋkɪŋ] *n.* 打屁股
▸ The little girl gave a skip of joy when she got her new puppy.
   當這個小女孩獲得她的新小狗時，她快樂地跳起來。
▸ The final part of the tour sounded boring so we gave it a skip.
   因為這趟旅程最後一段聽起來很無趣，所以我們跳過。

23 plug [plʌg] *n.* 插頭 & *vt.* 將……插入 (插頭)

- plug, plugged [plʌgd], plugged
- plug sth in　將某物插入插頭
衍 socket [ˋsɑkɪt] *n.* 插座 ④

▸ I need to change the plug on the stereo.
   我需要替換音響的插頭。
▸ I plugged the hairdryer in and began drying my hair.
   我將吹風機插頭插上，開始吹乾頭髮。

earplug [ˋɪr͵plʌg] *n.* 耳塞
用法 a pair of earplugs　一副耳塞

▸ This pair of earplugs helps me sleep better.
   這副耳塞讓我睡得更安穩。

24 humor [ˋhjumɚ] *n.* 幽默；心情，情緒 & *vt.* 遷就，寵愛 (= spoil [spɔɪl])

- (1) a sense of humor　幽默感
   (2) be in a good / bad humor
      心情好 / 壞
    = be in a good / bad mood

▸ Mark has a great sense of humor.
   馬克非常有幽默感。
▸ Kent was in a very bad humor this morning.
   肯特今天早上心情很糟。
▸ It's not always wise to humor a child.
   遷就孩子有時是不智的。

humorous [ˋhjumərəs]
a. 幽默的，風趣的

▸ John is well liked by us because of his humorous personality.
   約翰個性幽默，因此很受我們的喜愛。

25 deed [did] *n.* 行為 (可數)

似 behavior [bɪˋhevjɚ]
   n. 行為 (不可數) ④

▸ Scouts need to do at least one good deed a day.
   童子軍至少需日行一善。

> Deeds are more important than empty words.
= Actions speak louder than words.
行動勝於空談。── 諺語

26　stomach [ˈstʌmək] *n.* 胃

🔲 turn one's stomach　使某人反胃
🔲 stomachache [ˈstʌməkˌek]
　n. 胃痛 ②

> The smell of stinky tofu always turns Billy's stomach.
聞到臭豆腐的味道總是讓比利反胃。

belly [ˈbɛlɪ] *n.* 肚子
🔲 (1) tummy [ˈtʌmɪ] *n.* 肚子 (口語)
　(2) abdomen [ˈæbdəmən] *n.* 腹部 (醫)
🔲 belly button [ˈbɛlɪ ˌbʌtn̩]
　n. 肚臍 (口語)
= navel [ˈnevl̩] *n.* 肚臍 (正式)

> The top is too tight and your belly button is showing.
你這件上衣太緊，肚臍露出來了。

> The man has a pot belly because he drinks lots of beer every day.
這男子每天都喝很多啤酒，因此肚子很大。
*a pot belly　大肚皮

27　misery [ˈmɪzərɪ] *n.* 悲慘，窮困

🔲 miserable [ˈmɪzərəbl̩]
　a. 不幸的；令人不快的 ④

> The homeless man lives in hunger and misery.
這個無家可歸的男子活在飢餓與窮困中。

28　fold [fold] *vt.* 折疊 & *n.* 摺線

🔲 with one's arms folded
　雙臂交叉地
🔲 (1) unfold [ʌnˈfold] *vt.* 攤開 ⑤
　(2) folder [ˈfoldɚ] *n.* 文件夾

> Fold up the towels like this.
將毛巾折成像這樣。

> The man talked to me with his arms folded.
這男子和我說話時雙臂交叉著。

> Our address is printed on the paper, just under the fold.
我們的住址印在這張紙上，就在這條摺線下面。

29　punch [pʌntʃ] *n.* & *vt.* 用拳重擊

🔲 (1) land a punch on sth
　一拳打在某物上
　(2) punch sb in the face
　一拳打在某人臉上

> That boxer landed a punch on his opponent's head.
那位拳擊手一拳擊中對手的頭部。

> Why did you punch that reporter in the face? He was only doing his job.
你為何打那個記者的臉？他不過是盡本分而已。

30　label [ˈlebl̩] *n.* 標籤 & *vt.* 貼標籤；歸類

🔲 label A as B
　將 A 歸類為 B；將 A 稱為 B

> Mom put labels on the medicine bottles so that we could easily distinguish them.
媽媽在藥瓶上貼標籤以利我們辨認。

1730-1733

▶ The doctor labeled the expired bottle of pills as poisonous.

醫生在過期的藥瓶上貼上標籤以示有毒。

*expired [ɪk'spaɪrd] *a.* 過期的

▶ The press labeled the politician as a liar.

媒體把這名政客歸類為一個騙子。

---

tag [tæg] *n.* 標籤 & *vt.* 給……加上標籤

目 tag, tagged [tægd], tagged

用法 tag 常與名詞 price 或 name 並用，形成下列固定用語：

(1) a price tag　價格標籤，標價

(2) a name tag　名牌，胸牌

衍 hashtag ['hæʃ,tæg] *n.* 電話 (或電腦鍵盤) 上的 # 號；在社群網路上發文時用來描述主題的 # 號

▶ The price tag on the package says US$25.

該套裝產品的標價是 25 美元。

▶ All the staff members in the office are required to wear name tags.

辦公室所有職員都被要求要配戴名牌。

▶ Make sure all your suitcases are tagged with your name and address.

要確實將你所有的行李加上你的姓名及住址的標籤。

31　regret [rɪ'grɛt] *vt.* 後悔；遺憾，抱歉 & *n.* 遺憾；惋惜

目 regret, regretted [rɪ'grɛtɪd], regretted

片 (Much) To one's regret, ...

令某人 (很) 遺憾的是，……

用法 regret 作及物動詞，表『後悔』時，之後接動名詞作受詞；regret 亦可表『遺憾』或『抱歉』，之後要接不定詞片語作受詞，句型如下：

(1) regret + V-ing　後悔曾經……

(2) regret to + V　抱歉 / 遺憾要……

▶ I regret having made such a mistake.

= I regret making such a mistake.

我後悔曾犯下這樣的錯誤。

▶ I regret to tell you that your answer is wrong.

我很抱歉告訴你，你的答案是錯的。

▶ I regret to tell you that you didn't meet our requirements.

我很抱歉要告訴你，你未達到我們的要求。

▶ There are things we regret doing and things we regret not having done.

我們會後悔做了某些事，也有些事我們後悔沒去做。

▶ I regret to say that I can't come to the party.

很遺憾，我得告訴你我不能來參加派對。

▶ I regret to inform you that you flunked three subjects this semester.

我很遺憾要通知你，你這學期被當 3 科。

▶ Much to my regret, I didn't have enough money with me then.

令我很遺憾的是，當時我沒帶夠錢。

▶ I heard of Mr. Wilson's death with deep regret.

我對威爾遜先生的死訊深感惋惜。

---

regretful [rɪ'grɛtfəl]

a. 後悔的 (修飾人)

▶ I'm regretful that I made such a mistake.

很遺憾我犯了這樣的錯。

regrettable [rɪˋgrɛtəbḷ]
a. 令人遺憾的 (修飾事物)

▶ It is regrettable that John failed the test.

= John's failure to pass the test is regrettable.
約翰考試未及格真令人遺憾。

32 jazz [dʒæz] *n.* 爵士樂

▶ Patrick sang in a jazz band before he became a popular singer.
派翠克在成為流行歌手之前，曾在一個爵士樂團裡擔任歌手。

33 jeep [dʒip] *n.* 吉普車

▶ A military jeep got stuck in the mud.
一輛軍用吉普車陷在泥淖中。

1801-1805

1 outdoor [ˈaʊtˌdɔr] a. 戶外的，露天的

用法 本字須置於名詞前，修飾該名詞。
outdoor activities　戶外活動

▶ A lot of outdoor activities will take place in the park tomorrow.
公園明天會舉辦很多戶外活動。

outdoors [ˌaʊtˈdɔrz] adv. 在戶外

用法 outdoors 為副詞，在句中應置於動詞之後，修飾該動詞。outdoors 亦可作名詞，之前置定冠詞 the。
the outdoors　戶外生活 / 活動

▶ I want to stay outdoors because I enjoy the scenery.
我想待在外頭，因為我喜歡看風景。

▶ I live in the countryside because I enjoy the outdoors.
我喜歡戶外生活，所以我住在鄉間。

indoor [ˈɪnˌdɔr] a. 室內的

用法 本字須置於名詞之前，修飾該名詞。

▶ An indoor flower market is regularly held here on Sunday mornings.
這裡每個禮拜天早上都有室內花市。

indoors [ˌɪnˈdɔrz] adv. 在室內

用法 indoors 為副詞，在句中應置於動詞之後，修飾該動詞。

▶ People must stay indoors for their safety during a typhoon.
颱風期間，大家一定要待在室內以保安全。

2 bold [bold] a. 大膽的，勇敢的

片 be as bold as brass　厚顏無恥
＊brass [bræs] n. 黃銅 ③
似 (1) brave [brev] a. 勇敢的 ①
(2) courageous [kəˈredʒəs] a. 勇敢的 ④
反 (1) timid [ˈtɪmɪd] a. 膽小的 ④
(2) cowardly [ˈkaʊədlɪ] a. 膽小的 ⑥

▶ The attempt was bold but reckless as well.
這個嘗試很大膽也很魯莽。
＊reckless [ˈrɛklɪs] a. 魯莽的

▶ Ted is as bold as brass and would do anything you can imagine.
泰德臉皮厚得很，會做出任何你想像的到的事。

3 spit [spɪt] vt. 吐出 & vi. 吐痰 & n. 唾液，口水

三 spit, spat [spæt] / spit, spat / spit
片 spit sth out　將某物吐出來
延伸 phlegm [flɛm] n. 痰

▶ Eric spat his food out when he saw a cockroach on the dish.
艾瑞克看到菜上面有蟑螂時，就把食物吐了出來。

▶ I thought the gangster was going to hit me; however, he just spat and left.
我以為那個幫派分子會打我，結果他吐了口痰就走了。

▶ Donald woke up on the sofa with spit all round his mouth.
唐納在沙發上醒來滿嘴口水。

suck [sʌk] *vi.* & *vt.* & *n.* 吸 & *vi.* 糟糕，很爛 (俚語)

🄷 suck on　吸、舔

▸ The little boy is sucking on a lollipop.
小男孩在舔棒棒糖。
＊lollipop [ˈlɑlɪ͵pɑp] *n.* 棒棒糖

▸ The little boy sat on the ground in silence and sucked his thumb.
那個小男孩安靜地坐在地上吸大拇指。

▸ The little girl asked for a suck of her sister's popsicle.
這個小女孩求她姊姊讓她舔一舔她的冰棒。
＊popsicle [ˈpɑpsɪk!] *n.* 冰棒

▸ The concert I went to last night really sucked.
我昨天晚上去的那場演唱會爛透了。

4　timber [ˈtɪmbɚ] *n.* 木材 (不可數)

🄲 (1) lumber [ˈlʌmbɚ] *n.* 木材 (不可數)
(2) log [lɔg] *n.* 圓木 (可數) ③

▸ In this country, over 80 percent of its export earnings come from timber.
這個國家 80% 以上的外銷收益來自木材。
＊earnings [ˈɝnɪŋz] *n.* 收益 (恆用複數)

---

oak [ok] *n.* 橡木

🄲 oat [ot] *n.* 燕麥

▸ This antique table is made of red oak.
這張古董桌是紅橡木製的。
＊antique [ænˈtik] *a.* 古董的 & *n.* 古董

---

pine [paɪn] *n.* 松樹 (= pine trees) & *vi.* 憔悴

🄷 pine away　消瘦，憔悴

▸ The lumberjacks decided to chop down dead pine trees in the forest.
伐木工們決定把這片森林中凋零的松樹砍掉。
＊lumberjack [ˈlʌmbɚ͵dʒæk] *n.* 伐木工人

▸ The widow was pining away after her husband's death.
這名寡婦自先生過世之後便日漸憔悴。

5　jail [dʒel] *n.* 監獄 & *vt.* 使入獄

🄷 be put in jail / prison　入獄服刑
= be jailed
= be imprisoned
🄲 prison [ˈprɪzn̩] *n.* 監獄 ②

▸ Alex was put in jail for drug trafficking.
= Alex was jailed for drug trafficking.
艾力克斯因販賣毒品而鋃鐺入獄。

---

criminal [ˈkrɪmən!] *n.* 罪犯 & *a.* 犯法的 (= illegal [ɪˈligl])；刑法方面的

▸ The judge put the criminal in prison.
法官判決那名罪犯入獄服刑。

▸ Stealing is a criminal act.
偷竊是犯法的行為。

衍 (1) crime [kraɪm]
   n. 罪行，犯罪活動 ②
  (2) criminal law　刑法
    civil law　民法

似 convict [ˈkɑnvɪkt]
   n. 已被定罪的犯人 ⑤

▶ The lawyer specializes in criminal law.
這位律師專精刑法。
＊specialize [ˈspɛʃəl͵aɪz] *vi.* 專攻（與介詞 in 並用）

6　flavor [ˈflevɚ] *n.* 口味 & *vt.* 給……調味

片 flavor A with B　用 B 將 A 調味
似 taste [test] *n.* 味道 & *vt.* 嚐味道 ①

▶ Chocolate and vanilla are two different flavors.
巧克力和香草是兩種不同的口味。

▶ This dish is flavored with garlic and herbs.
這道菜用蒜頭和香草調味。
＊herb [(h)ɝb] *n.* 藥草

7　transport [trænsˈpɔrt] *vt.* 運送，運輸 & [ˈtræns͵pɔrt] *n.* 運輸

似 transportation [͵trænspɚˈteʃən]
   n. 交通運輸 ④

▶ In the past, people used trains to transport coal.
過去人們利用火車運送煤炭。

▶ To save money, we'll have to transport these goods to Spain by ship.
為了省錢，我們必須以海運將這些貨物運往西班牙。

▶ This city boasts a good public transport system.
= This city boasts a good public transportation system.
這座城市以擁有順暢的大眾運輸系統而自豪。
＊boast [bost] *vt.* （某城市／地區）以擁有……而自豪

8　hourly [ˈaʊrlɪ] *a.* 每小時的 & *adv.* 每小時地

片 on an hourly basis
   以每小時為基礎
= hourly　每小時（*adv.*）
= every hour

▶ I get an hourly wage of $20 at my job.
我做這工作可獲得時薪 20 美元。

▶ Students in our school take a 10-minute break hourly.
= Students in our school take a 10-minute break on an hourly basis.
我們學校的學生每 1 小時就休息 10 分鐘。

---

weekly [ˈwiklɪ]
a. 每週的 & *adv.* 每週地 & *n.* 週刊（報）

片 on a weekly basis　以每週為基礎
= weekly　每週（*adv.*）
= every week

▶ The employee's weekly wage was reduced by 10%.
這名員工的週薪被扣了 10%。

▶ A meeting is held weekly in our company.
= A meeting is held on a weekly basis in our company.
我們公司每個禮拜舉行一次會議。

延伸 biweekly [baɪˋwiklɪ] *a.* 雙週的；
每週兩次的 & *adv.* 兩週地；每週兩次地

▶ Due to poor sales, the newspaper will be turned into a weekly.
因銷售不佳，這份報紙將轉型為週報。

---

monthly [ˋmʌnθlɪ]
a. 每月的 & *adv.* 每月地 & *n.* 月刊

片 on a monthly basis　以每月為基礎
= monthly　每月（*adv.*）
= every month

▶ Roger usually spends his monthly allowance on clothes.
羅傑通常把他每個月的零用錢都拿去買衣服。

▶ I pay my phone bill monthly.
= I pay my phone bill on a monthly basis.
我每個月付一次電話費。

▶ *National Geographic* is a famous monthly that is published in many languages.
《國家地理雜誌》是一份以多種語言出版的著名月刊。

---

quarterly [ˋkwɔrtəlɪ]
a. 每一季的 & *adv.* 每季地 & *n.* 季刊

▶ The quarterly meeting is a big event in Jerry's company.
一季一次的會議是傑瑞所屬公司的一件大事。

▶ This periodical is published quarterly.
這本期刊每季發行一次。
＊periodical [ˌpɪrɪˋɑdɪk!] *n.* 期刊

▶ That publishing company publishes four quarterlies every three months.
那家出版公司每 3 個月就出版 4 本季刊。

---

yearly [ˋjɪrlɪ] *a.* 每年的 & *adv.* 每年地

片 on a yearly basis　以年為基礎
= yearly　每年（*adv.*）
= every year
似 (1) annual [ˋænjʊəl] *a.* 每年的 ④
(2) annually [ˋænjʊəlɪ] *adv.* 每年地

▶ The doctor advised my parents to have a yearly checkup.
醫生建議我父母每年做一次健康檢查。

▶ This sports event attracts thousands of tourists yearly.
這項運動盛事每年都會吸引上千名遊客。

9　stiff [stɪf] *a.* 硬的；激烈的

片 身體部位 + be stiff from + V-ing
某身體部位因從事……而變得僵硬
衍 stiffen [ˋstɪfən] *vt.* & *vi.* (使) 變僵硬
▶ My neck stiffened after hours of reading.
看了幾個小時的書之後，我的脖子僵硬了。

▶ My legs are stiff from sitting too long.
我坐得太久，兩腳都僵硬了。

▶ After a long day's work, my back was stiff and sore.
在一天漫長的工作後，我的背又僵硬又痠痛。

▶ Small motels are going out of business in the face of stiff competition.
面對激烈的競爭，小型的汽車旅館都快關門大吉了。

10 rag [ræg] n. 破布

片 from rags to riches 從赤貧到富有

衍 ragged ['rægɪd]
   a. 破爛的;衣衫襤褸的 ⑤

▶ I felt sorry for those children in rags.
那些穿著破爛的孩子令我感到心酸。

▶ The beggar went from rags to riches overnight by winning the lottery.
那個乞丐贏了彩券後一夕間由赤貧變為富有。

---

rug [rʌg] n. 小地毯

比 rug 是指小地毯,尤指放在壁爐前客廳地板上的方毯;carpet ['kɑrpɪt] 是指覆蓋全部地板的地毯;blanket ['blæŋkɪt] 是指蓋在身上的小毯子;tapestry ['tæpɪstrɪ] 則指掛在牆上有圖像供裝飾用的掛毯。

▶ A good rug can add a cozy atmosphere to your living room.
好地毯可以為府上的客廳增添舒適的氣氛。
＊cozy ['kozɪ] a. 舒適的 (＝ comfortable)

11 rob [rɑb] vt. 搶奪 & vi. 搶劫

三 rob, robbed [rɑbd], robbed

用法 rob 作及物動詞時,以人作受詞,接介詞 of,再接被搶奪的東西,採下列結構:
   rob sb of sth 搶奪某人某物

似 mob [mɑb] vt. (人群) 圍住 ③

▶ The bandit robbed Ted of all the money he had.
這名土匪搶了泰德身上所有的錢。
＊bandit ['bændɪt] n. 土匪,強盜

▶ These pirates rob and kill whenever and wherever they want.
這批海盜肆無忌憚,隨時隨地搶劫殺人。

---

robbery ['rɑbərɪ] n. 搶劫,搶案

片 commit robbery 犯搶劫罪

衍 robber ['rɑbɚ] n. 強盜,搶匪 ④

▶ Mark was charged with armed robbery.
馬克被控武裝搶劫。

▶ The young man committed robbery and was put in jail.
這個年輕人犯了搶案被關入牢內。

12 aboard [ə'bɔrd] prep. & adv. 在 (車、船或飛機) 上

片 go aboard + 交通工具
   登上某交通工具

似 abroad [ə'brɔd] adv. 在國外 ①

▶ We went aboard the ship at 6:00 this morning.
我們今早 6 點登船。

▶ All the people aboard the plane are celebrities.
機上的乘客都是名人。
＊celebrity [sə'lɛbrətɪ] n. 名人

13 athlete ['æθlit] n. 運動員

片 athlete's foot 香港腳 (不可數)

衍 (1) athletic [æθ'lɛtɪk] a. 運動的 ④
   (2) an athletic meet 運動會

▶ An athlete should know the importance of warming up.
運動員應該知道暖身的重要性。

▶ It seems that there is no cure for athlete's foot.
香港腳似乎沒有治癒方法。

14　ribbon [ˈrɪbən] *n.* 彩帶，緞帶

団 tie a ribbon around...
　繞著……綁一條緞帶

▶ Mom tied a beautiful purple ribbon around my birthday gift.
　媽媽在我的生日禮物上繫了一條漂亮的紫色緞帶。

---

knot [nɑt] *n.* 繩結 & *vt.* 把……打結
目 knot, knotted [ˈnɑtɪd], knotted
団 tie the knot with sb　與某人結婚

▶ Mary tied the wires together into a knot.
　瑪莉把電線綁起來打成一個結。

▶ Jane is going to tie the knot with her high school sweetheart this weekend.
　珍這個週末就要和她高中時期的情人結婚了。

▶ Graham took the rope and knotted it around a nearby tree.
　格林漢拿了一條粗繩並在附近的一棵樹上把它打結。

15　tune [tjun] *n.* 曲調，旋律 & *vi.* 轉到……的頻道 & *vt.* 為……調音

団 (1) sing out of tune　唱歌走音
　 (2) sing in tune　唱歌不走音，音很準
　 (3) tune in to...
　　　將電臺／電視轉至某頻道
似 melody [ˈmɛlədɪ] *n.* 旋律 ②

▶ The girl was singing out of tune because of stage fright.
　由於怯場，這女孩唱歌走音了。

▶ Don't forget to tune in to our program every day.
　別忘了每天收聽本節目。

▶ David tuned his guitar before the performance.
　大衛在表演前替吉他調音。

16　dim [dɪm] *a.* 微暗的 & *vt.* & *vi.* (使) 變暗

目 dim, dimmed [dɪmd], dimmed
反 bright [braɪt] *a.* 明亮的 ①

▶ You will hurt your eyes working in such dim light.
　在這樣暗淡的燈光下工作有損你的視力。

▶ Katrina dimmed the light in the living room to create a romantic mood.
　卡崔娜調暗客廳的燈以營造浪漫的氣氛。

17　carriage [ˈkærɪdʒ] *n.* 馬車

似 carrier [ˈkærɪɚ]
　n. 運輸公司；(疾病) 帶原者 ④

▶ I still remember riding in Grandpa's carriage when I was small.
　我還記得小時候坐在祖父馬車裡的情景。

18　thankful [ˈθæŋkfəl] *a.* 感謝的，感激的

団 be thankful / grateful / obliged / indebted to sb for sth
　因某事感激某人
衍 thank [θæŋk] *n.* & *vt.* 感謝 ①
似 grateful [ˈgretfəl] *a.* 感激的 ④

▶ I'm really thankful to you for all the support you gave me and my family.
　我真的很感激你對我和我家人的支持。

19 brass [bræs] n. 黃銅 & a. 銅管樂器的

延伸 (1) copper [ˋkɑpɚ] n. (紅) 銅 ④
(2) bronze [brɑnz] n. 青銅 ⑤

▶ The medal the commander gave me was made of brass.
指揮官頒發給我的獎章是黃銅打造的。

▶ The trumpet is just one example of a brass instrument.
小號只是銅管樂器的其一實例。

20 shallow [ˋʃælo] a. 淺的；膚淺的

似 superficial [͵supɚˋfɪʃəl] a. 表面的 ⑥
反 deep [dip] a. 深的 ①

▶ Kids should play in the shallow end of the pool.
小朋友們應該待在泳池淺的那一端玩水。

▶ I don't like to deal with shallow people.
我不喜歡和膚淺的人打交道。

21 kidney [ˋkɪdnɪ] n. 腎臟

片 a kidney transplant [ˋtrænsplænt] 腎臟移植

▶ Johnny will die if he doesn't have a kidney transplant soon.
如果強尼不趕快進行腎臟移植，他很快就會死掉。

lung [lʌŋ] n. 肺臟
用法 人體因有兩個肺，故本字常用複數。

▶ Research has proven that smoking leads to lung cancer.
研究證實抽菸會導致肺癌。

22 saucer [ˋsɔsɚ] n. 茶托，淺碟

片 a flying saucer　飛碟

▶ I gave Mike a set of cups and saucers for his birthday.
我送麥克一組茶杯和茶托作為生日禮物。

sauce [sɔs] n. 醬汁
片 soy sauce [ˋsɔɪ ͵sɔs] n. 醬油

▶ Pour the tomato sauce over the noodles and then add cheese.
將番茄醬倒在麵條上，然後加上起司。

23 receiver [rɪˋsivɚ] n. (電話) 聽筒

衍 receive [rɪˋsiv] vt. 收到；接待 ②

▶ The receptionist picked up the telephone receiver and said, "Hello."
接待員拿起電話聽筒說：『哈囉。』

receipt [rɪˋsit] n. 收據，發票
注意 本字的 p 不發音，因此不要唸成 [rɪˋsipt]。

▶ When you pay the bill, don't forget to ask for a receipt.
你付錢時，別忘了要發票。

24　**mighty** [`maɪtɪ] *a.* 強大的，強力的

衍 almighty [ɔl`maɪtɪ] *a.* 全能的
（大寫，修飾上帝，祈禱的用語）
God Almighty　萬能的主

似 powerful [`paʊɚfəl] *a.* 強而有力的 ②

衍 might [maɪt] *n.* 力量 & *aux.* 可能，
說不定 (是 may 的過去式)

▶ The mighty lion roared from the hilltop.
勇猛的獅子從山頂發出怒吼。

25　**swift** [swɪft] *a.* 迅速的，敏捷的

似 (1) prompt [prɑmpt] *a.* 敏捷的 ④
(2) quick [kwɪk] *a.* 快速的 ①

▶ A swift current carried the little boat down the river.
一道急流將小船順著河流沖走。

26　**approve** [ə`pruv] *vt.* 批准，核可 & *vi.* 贊同 (與介詞 of 並用)

片 approve of...　贊同……
= agree to...

▶ The manager didn't approve our plan.
經理沒有核准我們的計畫。

▶ I felt very happy when the boss approved my proposal.
老闆核准我的提案時我感到很高興。

▶ Father does not approve of our staying up late at night.
老爸不贊同我們熬夜。
＊stay up　熬夜

▶ I felt upset when nobody approved of my idea at the meeting.
會議上沒有人贊同我的點子，我感到很難過。

27　**lightning** [`laɪtnɪŋ] *n.* 閃電

片 a bolt of lightning　一道閃電

延伸 thunder [`θʌndɚ] *n.* 雷；雷聲 ②
a crash of thunder　一陣雷聲

▶ The farmer was struck by lightning but fortunately he survived.
農夫被閃電擊中，所幸他活了下來。

28　**pitch** [pɪtʃ] *vt.* 投 (球)；紮 (營) & *n.* 瀝青；音調

片 (1) pitch-black
像瀝青一樣黑，全黑的
(2) perfect pitch　絕對音感

衍 pitcher [`pɪtʃɚ]
n. (棒球) 投手；有把手的水瓶 ⑤

▶ Dad pitched the ball to my sister, and she swung the bat.
老爸投球給我妹妹，她便揮棒。

▶ Let's pitch our tent by the river.
咱們在河邊紮營吧。

▶ I dare not go downstairs myself. It's pitch-black down there.
我不敢自己一個人下樓。那裡烏漆抹黑的。

1828

延伸 a high-pitched voice 高音

▶ The girl can sing in a high-pitched voice.

這個女孩可以唱高音。

▶ Andrew has perfect pitch; he can sing any note correctly without the help of instruments.

安德魯有絕對音感，他不用樂器輔助就能準確地唱出任何音調。

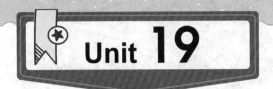

1 ash [æʃ] n. 灰

田 turn to ashes
(夢想) 化成灰燼，變成泡影

衍 ashtray [ˈæʃˌtre] n. 煙灰缸

▶ Mary emptied the ashes in the trash can.
瑪莉把垃圾筒裡的灰清掉。

▶ John felt that all his dreams turned to ashes when his girlfriend left him.
約翰的女友離他而去時，他感覺夢想全都化成泡影了。

2 rumor [ˈrumɚ] n. 謠言，傳言 & vt. 散播謠言

田 (1) Rumor has it that...　謠傳……
(本句構中 Rumor 恆為不可數)

= It is rumored that...

= It is said that...

(2) Rumors spread that...
有關……的謠言四處傳播 (本句構中 Rumors 應採複數)

▶ Rumor has it that Gatsby is going to marry a rich widow.

= It is rumored that Gatsby is going to marry a rich widow.

= It is said that Gatsby is going to marry a rich widow.
謠傳蓋茲比要迎娶一位有錢的寡婦。

▶ Rumors spread that the mayor is going to step down.
市長就要下臺的傳聞四處散播。

3 echo [ˈɛko] n. 回音 & vt. 重複

似 (1) repeat [rɪˈpit] vt. 重複 ①
(2) reiterate [rɪˈɪtəˌret] vt. 重申

▶ I heard vague echoes of someone's footsteps.
我隱約聽見某人腳步聲的回音。
*vague [veg] a. 模糊不清的

▶ Our teacher echoed what the report stated.
我們老師把報告上寫的東西重述一遍。

4 sweat [swɛt] vi. 出汗 & n. 汗

田 (1) sweat a lot　大量流汗
= sweat heavily
= sweat like a pig (俚語)
(2) No sweat.　沒問題。(俚語)
= No problem.
(3) break a sweat　冒汗

似 perspire [pɚˈspaɪr] vi. 出汗

▶ I sweat a lot on hot days.
大熱天我會流很多汗。

▶ A: Can you help me carry these books?
B: No sweat.
A：你可以幫我搬這些書嗎？
B：沒問題。

▶ After jogging for 10 minutes, Jim started to break a sweat.
慢跑 10 分鐘後，吉姆就開始冒汗了。

5 tub [tʌb] n. 澡盆，浴缸

似 bathtub [ˈbæθˌtʌb]
n. 浴缸 (= bath [bæθ] ①)

▶ My apartment, sadly, does not have a tub.
遺憾的是，我的公寓沒有浴缸。

6　peel [pil] *n.* 水果皮 & *vt.* 剝 / 削 (果皮)

衍 peeler [`pilɚ] *n.* 削皮器

▸ Scientists have discovered that banana peels contain alcohol.
科學家發現香蕉皮含有酒精。

▸ I think it's rather troublesome to peel grapes.
我認為剝葡萄皮很麻煩。

7　handy [`hændɪ] *a.* 在手邊的；方便的

H come in handy　隨時可以派上用場

▸ You'd better carry an umbrella with you; it may come in handy.
你最好帶把傘，它可能隨時會派得上用場。

▸ This new kitchen gadget is very handy.
這個新的廚房器具使用方便。
＊gadget [`gædʒɪt] *n.* 小器具 (如開罐器、果汁機等)

handful [`hændfəl] *n.* 一把
H a handful of...　一把……

▸ The boy grabbed a handful of berries and tucked them in his pocket.
這男孩抓了一把莓果塞進口袋。
＊tuck [tʌk] *vt.* 塞

8　outline [`aut͵laɪn] *n.* 大綱；輪廓 & *vt.* 重點說明

似 (1) sketch [skɛtʃ] *n.* & *vt.* 概述 ④
(2) summarize [`sʌmə͵raɪz]
vt. 概括說明；總結 ④

▸ Our teacher asked us to write an outline before writing our research papers.
老師要求我們先擬大綱再寫研究報告。

▸ Jessie knows the outline of the lecture, but not the details.
潔西知道這堂課的大概，但對細節並不了解。

▸ At the interview, Nancy outlined the requirements for the position.
面試的時候，南西就這個職位的必要條件做了重點說明。

9　tray [tre] *n.* 托盤

▸ The waitress brought the drinks we ordered on a tray.
那名女侍用托盤送上我們點的飲料。

10　hasty [`hestɪ] *a.* 急忙的

衍 (1) hasten [`hesn̩] *vt.* 催促 &
vi. 急忙，趕快 ④

▸ A hasty decision is often regretted later.
草率的決定經常讓人事後感到懊悔。

(2) haste [hest] *n.* 匆忙，急促 ④
　　in haste　匆促地
　　= in a hurry
　　= in a rush
似 hurried [ˋhɝɪd] *a.* 急忙的

hastily [ˋhestɪlɪ] *adv.* 倉促地，匆忙地
似 in haste　倉促地，匆忙地
　= hurriedly [ˋhɝɪdlɪ] *adv.*

▶ Don't do things hastily, or you're likely to make mistakes.
做事別過急，否則你可能會出錯。

11　saving(s) [ˋsevɪŋ(z)] *n.* 存款 (恆用複數)；節省 (費用)

片 open a savings account
開儲蓄帳戶 / 開定期戶頭
open a checking account
開支票帳戶 / 開活存戶頭

▶ Karen opened a new savings account so she could begin saving for college.
凱倫新開了一個定存戶頭，這樣就可開始存錢念大學了。

▶ We made a huge saving by booking the hotel early.
我們提早訂了這間飯店而省下一大筆費用。

---

earnings [ˋɝnɪŋz]
n. 收入 (恆用複數，不可數)
似 (1) income [ˋɪnˌkʌm] *n.* 收入 ②
　　(2) revenue [ˋrɛvəˌnju] *n.* 營收 ⑤
　　(亦可作 revenues，均不可數)

▶ Thanks to our successful marketing strategies, our company's earnings increased by 20% last quarter.
由於我們的行銷策略奏效，本公司上一季的收入增加了 20%。
＊strategy [ˋstræˌtədʒɪ] *n.* 謀略，策略

---

deposit [dɪˋpɑzɪt]
vt. 存放 (銀行) & *n.* 蘊藏量；訂金
反 withdraw [wɪðˋdrɔ] *vt.* 提領 (金錢) ④
比 deposit 作及物動詞表『存放』時，與介詞 in 或 into 並用。withdraw 作及物動詞時表『提領』，與介詞 from 並用。
deposit money in / into a bank (account)
將錢存放在某銀行 (戶頭) 內
withdraw money from a bank (account)
將錢從某銀行 (戶頭) 內提領出來

▶ Jason deposits 200 dollars in the bank each month.
傑森每個月存 200 美元到銀行。

▶ The country has quite a few oil deposits.
那個國家蘊藏豐富的石油。

▶ The hotel requires that guests pay a deposit of 5% to book a room.
這間旅館要求房客支付 5% 的房間訂金。

12　sincere [sɪnˋsɪr] *a.* 誠懇的，誠摯的

片 express one's sincere thanks / apologies to sb
向某人表達誠摯的謝意 / 歉意

▶ John was sincere in his apology, so his mom forgave him.
約翰很誠懇地道歉，所以媽媽就原諒他了。

衍 sincerity [sɪn'sɛrətɪ] n. 誠懇 ④
似 honest ['ɑnɪst] a. 誠實的 ①
反 insincere [,ɪnsɪn'sɪr] a. 不誠懇的

▸ I'd like to express my sincere thanks to you for all the help you've given me.
我想向您表達誠摯的謝意，感謝您對我種種的幫助。

13 inspect [ɪn'spɛkt] vt. 檢查；視察

衍 inspection [ɪn'spɛkʃən]
   n. 檢查；查驗 ④
似 (1) examine [ɪg'zæmɪn] vt. 檢驗 ②
   (2) investigate [ɪn'vɛstə,get]
       vt. 調查 ③

▸ The police inspected the bloodstains at the crime scene.
警方檢查犯罪現場中的血跡。
*bloodstain ['blʌd,sten] n. 血跡

▸ The fire department inspects all pubs and KTVs in the city on a monthly basis.
消防局每個月視察該市所有的酒吧和 KTV。

inspector [ɪn'spɛktɚ] n. 檢查員
似 examiner [ɪg'zæmɪnɚ] n. 檢查員 ⑥

▸ Those inspectors were busy checking our products for defects before shipment.
那些檢查人員正忙著檢查我們準備運送前的產品，看看有什麼瑕疵。
*defect ['dɪfɛkt] n. 瑕疵，缺點

14 spray [spre] vt. 噴灑 & n. 噴霧劑

似 sprinkle ['sprɪŋkl] vt. 灑；撒 ④

▸ Mary sprayed herself with perfume before going out on a date.
瑪莉在出門約會前噴了香水。

▸ I'd like to try this new styling spray.
我想試用這款新的髮型噴霧劑。

15 lobby ['lɑbɪ] n. 大廳 & vt. & vi. 遊說 (國會議員等)

衍 lobbyist ['lɑbɪɪst] n. 說客
似 persuade [pɚ'swed] vt. 說服 ③

▸ Harry and I will meet in the hotel lobby tomorrow morning.
哈利和我明天早上要在飯店的大廳碰面。

▸ Those people were lobbying some congressmen to support their proposal.
那些人正在遊說若干國會議員支持他們的提案。
*proposal [prə'pozl] n. 提案

hallway ['hɔl,we] n. 走廊
似 (1) passage ['pæsɪdʒ] n. 通道 ③
   (2) corridor ['kɔrɪdɚ] n. 走廊 ⑤

▸ The restroom is at the end of the hallway on the right-hand side.
洗手間在走廊盡頭的右手邊。

16　halfway [ˌhæfˈwe] a. 中途的 & adv. 在半路上

囝 (1) a halfway house　中途之家
　　(2) meet sb halfway　和某人妥協

▶ A halfway house is a place aimed at helping former prisoners turn over a new leaf.
中途之家旨在幫助更生人改過自新。
＊turn over a new leaf　翻開新的一頁
（喻改過自新，重新做人）

▶ I called John an hour ago, and he said he was halfway here.
我一小時前打給約翰，他說他還在來這裡的半路上。

▶ Nick chose to meet Dave halfway on the business deal.
尼克決定和戴夫妥協，搞定這筆生意。

17　fond [fɑnd] a. 喜好的

囝 be fond of...　喜愛……

▶ Kim is really fond of heavy metal.
金真的很喜歡重金屬樂。

18　harvest [ˈhɑrvɪst] vt. & n. 收穫

囮 reap [rip] vt. & vi. 收割；收穫 ⑥

▶ The farmers had to harvest the rice before the typhoon came.
農人必須在颱風來臨之前收割稻穀。

▶ The farm owner gave his farmhands a share of profits from the harvest.
這個農場主人讓他的工人從收益中分錢。
＊farmhand [ˈfɑrmˌhænd] n. 農場工人

19　gamble [ˈɡæmbḷ] vt. & vi. & n. 賭博

囝 (1) gamble A on B　將 A 賭在 B 之上
　　(2) take a gamble　賭博；冒險而為
囮 bet [bɛt] vt. 打賭 & n. 賭注 ③
（三態同形）

▶ James loves to gamble by buying lottery tickets each week.
詹姆斯喜歡每個禮拜買彩券來賭一賭。

▶ Jessica gambled all her savings on the stock market.
潔西卡拿她畢生的積蓄賭在股市上。

▶ Ricky decided to take a gamble and quit his comfortable job.
瑞奇決定要冒險一搏並辭去他安穩的工作。

20　sleeve [sliv] n. 袖子

囝 (1) have sth up one's sleeve
　　　藏了一手
　　(2) roll up one's sleeves　捲起袖子

▶ It looks like the boxer is going to lose the fight, but I believe he still has some tricks up his sleeve.
這位拳擊手看來好像快輸了，但我認為他還留了幾手。

> Judy rolled up her sleeves and did the dishes.
> 茱蒂捲起衣袖開始洗碗。

collar [ˋkɑlɚ] *n.* 衣領

衍 (1) white-collar [ˏ(h)waɪtˋkɑlɚ]
    a. 白領階級的 (指坐辦公室的上班族)
  (2) blue-collar [ˏbluˋkɑlɚ]
    a. 藍領階級的 (勞動階級的)

似 color [ˋkʌlɚ] *n.* 顏色 ①

> Todd grabbed George by the collar and punched him in the face.
> 陶德揪住喬治的衣領，往他臉上揍了一拳。

> A mechanic is a blue-collar worker, whereas an editor is a white-collar worker.
> 技師是藍領勞工，編輯則是白領勞工。

---

21 truthful [ˋtruθfəl] *a.* 誠實的；真實的

似 (1) honest [ˋɑnɪst] *a.* 誠實的 ①
  (2) true [tru] *a.* 真實的 ②
衍 truth [truθ] *n.* 真相；真理 ②

> You can trust Jim; he is a truthful and upright man.
> 你可以信任吉姆，他為人誠實又正直。

> The boy's account of what happened seems to be truthful.
> 這個男孩對事件發生經過的說詞似乎是真的。

---

22 kilometer [kɪˋlɑmətɚ / ˋkɪləˏmitɚ] *n.* (長度單位) 公里

用法 本字亦可寫成 km。
10 kilometers　10 公里
= 10 km

延伸 (1) meter [ˋmitɚ]
    n. (長度單位) 公尺 (= m) ②
    (1,000 公尺 = 1 公里)
  (2) centimeter [ˋsɛntəˏmitɚ]
    n. (長度單位) 公分 (= cm) ②
    (100 公分 = 1 公尺)

> The Great Wall is thousands of kilometers long.
> 萬里長城有數千公里長。

---

23 awful [ˋɔful] *a.* 可怕的；很差的

似 (1) horrible [ˋhɔrəbl]
    a. 恐怖的；很差的 ③
  (2) terrible [ˋtɛrəbl]
    a. 可怕的；很差的 ①

> Denny's handwriting was so awful that the teacher asked him to rewrite his report.
> 丹尼的字跡非常潦草，所以老師要他重寫一次報告。

---

24 discount [dɪsˋkaʊnt] *vt.* 打折 & [ˋdɪskaʊnt] *n.* 折扣

片 give sb a 20% / 40% discount on sth
就某物幫某人打八 / 六折

> Shops discount everything around holidays.
> 商店會在假日前後大減價。

似 reduction [rɪ`dʌkʃən] *n.* 減少 ④

▶ Since I was a regular customer at this fashion boutique, they gave me a 30% discount on that dress.
因為我是這家精品店的老顧客，所以那套洋裝他們幫我打了七折。
*boutique [bu`tik] *n.* 時裝精品店

---

25 drain [dren] *vt. & n.* 排掉 (液體)

片 brain drain 人才外流

▶ The water in the bathtub should be drained first.
浴缸的水應該先放掉。

▶ Many African countries have had a problem with brain drain over the years.
多年來，非洲許多國家一直都有人才外流的問題。

---

26 pit [pɪt] *n.* 坑

似 hole [hol] *n.* 洞 ②

▶ We dug a pit for the campfire.
為了生營火，我們挖了一個坑。

---

27 chip [tʃɪp] *n.* 碎片，屑片；電腦晶片 & *vt.* 撞成碎片

目 chip, chipped [tʃɪpt], chipped
片 be a chip off the old block
是從老木塊掉下來的木屑
(喻像極了某人)

▶ The detective found some chips of wood on the floor.
那位偵探在地板上找到了一些木屑。

▶ Peter looks very much like his father. He is indeed a chip off the old block.
彼得跟他爸爸很像，簡直就是一個模子刻出來似的。

▶ Our computer uses the smallest silicon chip ever invented.
我們的電腦使用有史以來最小的晶片。

▶ Dennis chipped his tooth when he fell down.
丹尼斯跌倒時撞碎了一顆牙。

---

28 tug [tʌg] *vt. & vi. & n.* 突然拉扯

目 tug, tugged [tʌgd], tugged
片 (1) tug sb's arm 拉某人的手臂
　 (2) tug on / at sb's sleeve
　　　 拉扯某人的袖子
延伸 a tug boat 拖船

▶ My girlfriend gently tugged my arm, asking me to give her a kiss.
我女友輕輕拉了拉我的手臂，要我給她一個吻。

▶ My grandson tugged on my sleeve and pointed at the toy he wanted me to buy.
我孫子扯了扯我的袖子，指著他要我買的玩具。

tug-of-war [ˏtʌgəv`wɔr]
n. 拔河比賽 (可數)

▶ My class played against Christine's in a tug-of-war.
我這班和克莉絲汀她那班比賽拔河。

29 beetle [`bitl] *n.* 甲蟲

▶ My brother keeps a beetle as a pet.
我弟弟養一隻甲蟲當寵物。

dragonfly [`drægən,flaɪ] *n.* 蜻蜓
複 dragonflies [`drægən,flaɪz]

▶ Different species of dragonflies can be found near the lake.
靠近湖的地方可以發現各種不同的蜻蜓。

moth [mɔθ] *n.* 蛾
延伸 moth 與 butterfly (蝴蝶) 屬同一科。牠們的蛹稱作 pupa [`pjupə ]，牠們織的繭則稱 cocoon [ kə`kun]。

▶ Can you distinguish between a moth and a butterfly?
你會分辨蛾和蝴蝶的不同嗎？

30 apron [`eprən] *n.* 圍裙

延伸 小朋友穿在身上的『圍兜』則稱作 bib [bɪb]。

▶ Mother put on her kitchen apron and cooked us a meal.
媽媽穿上廚房圍裙為我們做飯。

31 cock [kɑk] *n.* 公雞 (= rooster [`rustɚ])

用法 cock 在俚語中是髒話，表『男性生殖器』，故宜用 rooster 表『公雞』。

▶ Cocks usually crow in the early morning.
公雞通常一大早就會啼叫。

32 fighter [`faɪtɚ] *n.* 戰鬥機；鬥士

片 a jet fighter 噴射戰鬥機

▶ The fighter plane crashed, killing its two pilots.
這架戰鬥機墜毀了，機上兩名駕駛員均罹難。

▶ Such crime fighters only live in comic books.
這種打擊犯罪的鬥士只會出現在漫畫書中。

33 brick [brɪk] *n.* 磚頭

延伸 a bricklayer 水泥工，砌磚者

▶ Tom built a house of bricks.
湯姆用磚頭蓋了棟房子。

34 spaghetti [spə`gɛtɪ] *n.* 細條義大利麵 (不可數)

延伸 macaroni [,mækə`ronɪ] *n.* 義大利通心粉

▶ I ate two plates of spaghetti at the party.
派對上我吃了兩盤義大利麵。

35 steam [stim] *n.* 水蒸氣 & *vt.* 蒸煮 (食物)

片 (1) run out of steam 精疲力盡

▶ Steam engines were developed in the 18th century.
蒸氣引擎是在 18 世紀發展出來的。

(2) let / blow off steam
紓解壓力 / 發洩怒氣

(3) steam up sth　使某物蒙上霧氣

衍 steamer [ˈstimɚ] n. 蒸汽船

▸ I have been working so hard for months. Now I'm running out of steam.
我為工作拼了好幾個月了。現在我快精疲力盡了。

▸ After a hard day at the office, Jack went to the gym to let off some steam.
一整天辛苦工作之後，傑克上健身房來紓解壓力。

▸ It is healthy to steam food as no oil is used in the cooking process.
因為蒸煮食物在烹調過程中不使用油，所以是健康的。

▸ Walking into the hot kitchen steamed up my glasses.
走進充滿熱氣的廚房，把我的眼鏡蒙上了一層霧氣。

1 import [ɪmˋpɔrt] vt. 進口 & [ˋɪmpɚt] n. 進口品

(1) import sth to + 地方
將某物進口至某地

(2) import sth from + 地方
從某地進口某物

► Most cheeses in that store are imported from France.
那家店的起司大多是從法國進口。

► Millions of cheap imports from India enter European markets each year.
每年都有大量的廉價進口品從印度進入到歐洲市場。

export [ɪksˋpɔrt] vt. 出口
& [ˋɛkspɔrt] n. 輸出品

(1) export sth to + 地方
出口某物至某地

(2) export sth from + 地方
從某地出口某物

► Cheap toys made in that country are exported to the US in large numbers every year.
由那個國家製造的便宜玩具每年都會大量出口到美國去。

► Oil is the major export to Saudi Arabia.
石油是沙烏地阿拉伯主要的出口品。

2 tribe [traɪb] n. 部落

衍 tribal [ˋtraɪbl̩] a. 部落的 ④

► Each of the tribes has its distinctive tribal traditions and cultures.
每個部落都有其獨特的部落習俗與文化。
*distinctive [dɪˋstɪŋktɪv] a. 特殊的，獨特的

3 leisure [ˋliʒɚ] n. 閒暇，空閒時間

片 at one's leisure   在某人從容的時候

衍 leisurely [ˋliʒɚlɪ]
adv. 從容不迫地 & a. 休閒的 ④
lead / live a leisurely life
過著悠閒的生活

► John decided to pack his things at his leisure.
約翰決定要慢慢收拾行李。

► Playing chess is a leisure activity that requires a lot of mental effort.
下棋是個需要許多心力的休閒活動。

4 gum [gʌm] n. 牙齦 (複數)；口香糖 (不可數)

片 chewing gum / bubble gum
口香糖

a stick / piece of chewing gum
一片口香糖

a pack of chewing gum
一條口香糖

► I went to see a dentist for my sore gums.
因為牙齦疼痛，我去看了牙醫。

► The driver chewed gum to keep himself awake.
司機嚼著口香糖，好保持清醒。

5 awake [ə`wek] *vi.* 醒來 & *a.* 清醒的

☰ awake, awoke [ə`wok], awoken
　[ə`wokən]

☐ be awake to sth　了解某事

似 wake up　醒來
　wake 的三態為：wake, woke [wok],
　woken [`wokən]

▶ It was raining outside when Dylan awoke.
　狄倫醒來時，外頭正在下雨。

▶ Lisa was wide awake the whole night, fearing the worst.
　麗莎整晚都沒睡，擔心最壞的情況會發生。

▶ John doesn't seem to be awake to the dangers of smoking.
　約翰似乎不了解抽菸的危險。

awaken [ə`wekən] *vt.* 喚醒

☐ awaken sb to sth
　喚醒某人注意某事

似 waken [`wekən] *vi.* 醒來 & *vt.* 喚醒 ④

▶ Bill was awakened by a strange noise in the middle of the night.

= Bill was woken up by a strange noise in the middle of the night.
　比爾在半夜被奇怪的聲響吵醒。

▶ We should awaken Brad to the dangers of taking drugs.
　我們應喚醒布萊德了解吸毒的危險。

6 heap [hip] *n.* 一堆 & *vt.* 堆滿

☐ a heap of...　一堆……
= a pile of...

▶ There is a heap of dirty clothes on Jack's bed.
　傑克床上有一堆髒衣服。

▶ The teenager heaped her dirty clothes in the corner instead of washing them.
　這名少女把她的髒衣服堆在角落卻不把它們拿去洗。

7 ivory [`aɪvərɪ] *n.* 象牙；象牙材質 (不可數)；象牙製品 (常用複數) & *a.* 乳白色的

複 ivories [`aɪvərɪz]

☐ live in an ivory tower　住在象牙塔裡 (喻某人很封閉，不知外面的世界)

延伸 tusk [tʌsk] *n.* (象、野豬的) 長牙 (可數)

▶ A grown male elephant has two long tusks of ivory.
　成年公象有兩條長牙。

▶ The politician lives in an ivory tower and has no understanding of ordinary people's problems.
　這名政客活在象牙塔裡，無視普通老百姓的問題。

▶ The rich man has a collection of ivories from all over the world.
　這位有錢人擁有來自全世界的象牙製品。

▶ Darren wanted to use ivory paint, but his wife wanted to use white.
　戴倫想漆乳白色的，但他太太想漆白色的。

8　stubborn [ˋstʌbən] *a.* 頑固的

片 be as stubborn as a mule
像騾一樣固執，非常固執

*mule [mjul]
n. 騾（馬與驢雜交所生的後代）④

▶ Jane wanted to try traveling abroad all by herself, but her stubborn parents wouldn't let her.
珍想要試試獨自一人出國旅行，但她固執的父母親不答應。

▶ Can someone help me talk some sense into this man? He's as stubborn as a mule!
有人能幫我說說這個人，讓他明理一點嗎？他簡直像騾一樣固執！

*talk some sense into sb　跟某人講理

---

greedy [ˋgridɪ] *a.* 貪心的，貪吃的

片 be greedy for...　貪圖⋯⋯

衍 greed [grid] *n.* 貪心 ⑤

▶ The young man is greedy for power.
那個年輕人貪圖權力。

---

optimistic [ˌɑptəˋmɪstɪk]
a. 樂觀的（與介詞 about 並用）

片 be optimistic about...
對⋯⋯表示樂觀

衍 optimism [ˋɑptəmɪzəm] *n.* 樂觀 ⑤

▶ Investors are still relatively optimistic about the company's prospects.
投資人對該公司的前景仍舊相當樂觀。

9　rid [rɪd] *vt.* 使擺脫 & *a.* 擺脫的

三 三態同形

片 (1) rid sb/sth of sth　使某人／某物
擺脫、免於某事物（rid 是動詞）

(2) get rid of sb/sth　擺脫某人／某物
（此處 get 是連綴動詞，相當於 be；
rid 是過去分詞，表『被擺脫』）

▶ The police chief promised he would do whatever he could to rid the city of crime.
警察局長承諾將竭盡所能讓該城免於犯罪侵擾。

▶ We all felt it was a great relief to get rid of Bob. He was such a nuisance.
能擺脫鮑伯，大家都鬆了口氣。他真的很惹人厭。

*nuisance [ˋnjusn̩s] *n.* 令人討厭的事物或人

10　moist [mɔɪst] *a.* 潮溼的，溼潤的

似 damp [dæmp] *a.* 潮溼的 ④
humid [ˋhjumɪd] *a.* 溼度高的 ③

比 moist 與 damp 皆為『潮溼的』意思，
moist 常指不會令人不舒服的潮溼，
如 moist soil（溼潤的土壤），而 damp
則常指令人感覺不舒服的潮溼，如 a
damp shirt（溼掉的襯衫）。

▶ The warm and moist climate here makes it a perfect place for tropical fruits.
該地溫暖且溼潤的氣候很適合種熱帶水果。

▶ Frogs live near wet places to keep their skin moist.
青蛙靠近溼地居住以保持表皮溼潤。

moisture [ˈmɔɪstʃɚ] *n.* 溼氣，水分
似 dampness [ˈdæmpnɪs] *n.* 潮溼

▶ Moisture is taken out of the air by this machine, after which it turns into water.
溼氣被這臺機器從空氣裡抽出，之後便轉變成水。
*turn into...　轉變為……
=change into...

11　laundry [ˈlɔndrɪ] *n.* 待洗衣物 (集合名詞，不可數)

片 do the laundry　洗衣服
延伸 do the dishes　洗碗

▶ I used to do the laundry once a week when I lived in a dormitory.
我以前住宿舍時一星期洗一次衣服。

12　chill [tʃɪl] *n.* 寒冷；感冒；恐懼，寒意 & *vt.* & *vi.* (使) 冷卻 & *a.* 寒冷的

片 (1) catch a chill　著涼
= catch a cold
(2) a chill of fear
一陣恐懼引起的寒意
(3) chill sb to the bone　使某人凍僵
(4) chill out　放鬆

▶ I felt the chill in the air when I left home this morning and realized that winter was around the corner.
今天早上我出門時感到一陣寒意，知道冬天就要到了。
*be around the corner　即將來臨
=be coming soon

▶ Dry your hair before you go out, or you'll catch a chill.
把你頭髮吹乾再出門，不然你會著涼的。

▶ David suddenly realized, with a chill of fear, that his business partners had been plotting against him.
大衛倒抽一口涼氣，突然發現自己的生意合夥人一直對他圖謀不軌。
*plot against...　密謀對抗……

▶ After playing in the snow all morning, Jeff was chilled to the bone.
傑夫玩了一個早上的雪後，他凍僵了。

▶ Emma told her friend to chill the white wine before drinking it.
艾瑪告訴她的朋友在飲用白酒前要冰鎮一下。

▶ Chill out! We've got loads of time to get to the airport.
放鬆點！我們有很多時間能抵達機場。

▶ When I left the front door open, a chill wind blew through the house.
我讓前門開啟時，一陣冷風吹進屋內。

chilly [ˈtʃɪlɪ] *a.* 寒冷的
似 cold [kold] *a.* 寒冷的 ①

▶ It is getting chilly in here. Let's turn the heater on.
這裡頭越來越冷了。把暖氣打開吧。

13 headline [ˈhɛdˌlaɪn] n. (報紙) 標題 & vt. 給……加標題

H be in the headlines
被媒體大肆報導
= hit the headlines
= grab the headlines
= make the headlines

▶ The financial scandal has been in the headlines for weeks.
這則財經醜聞已被媒體大肆報導了好幾個禮拜。

▶ The front-page story was headlined, "Political Crisis at City Hall."
這個頭版報導下的標題是：『市政府的政治危機。』

heading [ˈhɛdɪŋ] n. 標題
似 title [ˈtaɪtl̩] n. 標題 ②

▶ What's the heading of that article you mentioned?
你提到的那篇文章標題是什麼？

14 bleed [blid] vi. 流血

三 bleed, bled [blɛd], bled
H bleed like a stuck pig　像被刺到的
豬那樣流血 (喻流很多血)
= bleed heavily
衍 bleeding [ˈblidɪŋ]
n. 流血 & a. 出血的；沉痛的

▶ After being hit in the face with a volleyball, Tom's nose kept bleeding.
被排球打中臉部後，湯姆的鼻子一直流血不停。

▶ The criminal fell down on his back after being shot by police, bleeding like a stuck pig.
被警方射擊後，該名罪犯仰天倒地，流了很多血。

bloody [ˈblʌdɪ] a. 流血的；血腥的
衍 blood [blʌd] n. 血液 ②

▶ The driver's bloody leg was tied up immediately.
司機流血的那條腿馬上就被包紮起來了。

▶ Many people consider boxing to be a bloody and violent sport.
許多人認為拳擊是一項血腥且殘暴的運動。
*violent [ˈvaɪələnt] a. 兇暴的

15 dash [dæʃ] vt. & n. 衝撞，急奔 & n. 短跑比賽

H (1) dash to...　急奔到……
= make a dash for...
(2) dash sb's dreams
破壞某人的夢想
似 sprint [sprɪnt] vt. 急奔 & n. 短跑比賽

▶ Frank dashed to the toilet as soon as the film was over.
= Frank made a dash for the toilet as soon as the film was over.
電影一結束，法蘭克馬上急奔廁所。

▶ Mary dashed John's dreams when she told him she had no interest in him at all.
瑪莉告訴約翰她對他一點興趣都沒有，讓約翰的夢想全都落空了。

▶ Phoebe won first prize in the women's 100-meter dash.
菲比贏得女子一百公尺短跑比賽第一名。

16 robe [rob] n. 長袍；浴袍

似 bathrobe [ˈbæθˌrob]
n. 浴袍 (= dressing gown)

▶ The judge was wearing a black robe.
那位法官穿著黑色長袍。

▶ Bryan put on his robe / bathrobe before he went to answer the door.
布萊恩去應門前，先穿上了他的浴袍。

17　icy [ˈaɪsɪ] *a.* 結冰的；冰涼的

囲 icy cold　非常寒冷的
似 iced [aɪst] *a.* 冰過的

▶ Be careful! The sidewalk is icy.
小心點！人行道上都結冰了。

▶ Nothing beats a glass of iced / icy tea on a hot day.
大熱天一杯冰茶比什麼都好。
＊beat [bit] *vt.* 勝過

18　screw [skru] *n.* 螺絲 & *vt.* 用螺絲鎖 (常與介詞 to / onto / into 並用) & *vt.* & *vi.* 搞砸，毀掉

囲 (1) screw A to B
　　用螺絲將 A 鎖到 B 上
　(2) screw up / mess up　搞砸
延伸 (1) a screwdriver　螺絲起子
　(2) a wrench　扳手
　(3) a hammer　榔頭

▶ I used strong screws to fix the shelf to the wall.
我用大螺絲釘把這個架子固定在牆上。

▶ The benches in the park are screwed to the ground.
公園內的長凳被用螺絲鎖到地面上。

▶ Handle this problem with care. Don't screw up.
謹慎處理這個問題。別搞砸了。

▶ Toby screwed up his life with drugs.
＝ Toby messed up his life with drugs.
托比的人生讓毒品給毀了。

19　pottery [ˈpɑtərɪ] *n.* 陶器 (集合名詞，不可數)

▶ Bill has a fine collection of pottery.
比爾收藏了一批很棒的陶器。

porcelain [ˈpɔrs(ə)lɪn]
n. 瓷器 (集合名詞，不可數)

▶ I bought this porcelain vase at an auction.
我在一場拍賣會上買了這只瓷花瓶。
＊auction [ˈɔkʃən] *n.* 拍賣會

20　vitamin [ˈvaɪtəmɪn] *n.* 維他命

▶ Vitamin C is crucial for healthy gums.
維他命 C 對牙齦的健康很重要。
＊crucial [ˈkruʃəl] *a.* 重要的 (＝ important)

21　ache [ek] *vi.* 疼痛；渴望 & *n.* 疼痛

囲 (1) ache for sth　渴望得到某物
　＝ long for sth

▶ My heart ached when I saw images of bony-faced children in refugee camps on TV.
看著電視畫面中難民營裡臉頰削瘦的幼童，我很心痛。

(2) have a headache 頭痛
(3) have a toothache 牙痛
(4) have a backache 背痛
(5) have a stomachache 胃痛

▶ I'm so tired that I'm aching for a good sleep.
我好累，因此好想要好好睡一下。

▶ Nick had an ache in his shoulder when he woke up yesterday morning.
昨天早上尼克醒來時，他肩膀痛。

▶ I had a toothache and didn't sleep a wink last night.
我牙痛，昨晚都沒睡。
＊not sleep a wink　沒闔過眼

22　sometime [ˋsʌmˏtaɪm] *adv.* 某個時候（與明確的時間並用）

似 (1) some time　一段時間
▶ I'm planning to stay here for some time.
我計劃要在這裡待上一段時間。

(2) sometimes　有時候
（= at times / on occasion / occasionally）
▶ I call on my grandparents in the country sometimes.
我有時候會到鄉下看我爺爺奶奶。

▶ Let's meet sometime next week to discuss the details of our plan, all right?
我們下星期找個時間見面，討論一下計畫的細節，好嗎？
＊本句 sometime 之後有明確的時間 next week（下星期）。

▶ I met John sometime last week.
上星期某個時候我曾見到約翰。

---

someday [ˋsʌmˏde] *adv.* 某天，
有朝一日（= some day，與未來式並用）

似 one day 可指『未來有一天』，等於 someday，與未來式並用；也可指『過去某一天』，與過去式並用。

▶ I'm busy now, but I'll do it one day.
我現在很忙，不過我有一天會做這件事。

▶ I ran into John downtown one day.
有一天我在城裡碰見了約翰。

▶ Ryan always believes he'll become a millionaire someday.
萊恩總是認為他有朝一日會成為百萬富翁。

23　heal [hil] *vi.* & *vt.* (使身體或心理的) 傷口痊癒

似 cure [kjur] *vt.* 治癒 ②

▶ My broken leg is gradually healing, but the doctor said it'll take me three more weeks to fully recover.
我斷掉的腿正慢慢在復原，不過醫生說還要再三個禮拜才會完全康復。

▶ Some people claim they can heal the sick by simply touching them with their hands.
有些人宣稱他們藉著用手碰觸病患便能使他們復原。

▶ Time heals all wounds.
時間可癒合所有的傷口。—— 諺語

24 jungle [ˈdʒʌŋɡl̩] n. 叢林；競爭激烈的環境 (可數)

片 a concrete jungle　水泥叢林
　　(指都市內醜陋的水泥建築) (可數)

似 (1) forest [ˈfɔrɪst] n. 森林 (可數) ②
　　(2) woods [wʊdz]
　　　　n. 樹林 (恆用複數，不可數)

▶ They said the rebels had a stronghold deep in the jungle.
據說叛軍在叢林深處有個據點。
＊stronghold [ˈstrɔŋ,hold] n. 據點

▶ Many people consider big cities to be jungles because you have to watch out for yourself.
許多人認為大都市就像叢林，因為你必須要時時提防以求自保。

▶ After trekking through the wilderness of New Zealand, Peter returned to his life in the concrete jungle.
經過一趟紐西蘭野外之旅後，彼得又重回都市的水泥叢林生活。
＊trek [trɛk] vi. 徒步長途行走，跋涉
　 wilderness [ˈwɪldənɪs] n. 荒野

25 pave [pev] vt. 鋪 (路)

片 pave the way for...
　　為……鋪路；為……奠基

▶ The construction workers were busy paving the road.
建築工人正忙著鋪路。

▶ The decision paved the way for a future merger with another company.
這個決定為日後與別家公司的合併案打下基礎。
＊merger [ˈmɝdʒɚ] n. (公司) 合併

pavement [ˈpevmənt]
n. 人行道〔英〕

衍 sidewalk [ˈsaɪd,wɔk] n. 人行道〔美〕②

▶ David fell from his bike and his head hit the pavement.
大衛從腳踏車上摔下來，頭撞到了人行道。

26 sword [sɔrd] n. 劍

延伸 swordsman [ˈsɔrdzmən] n. 劍客

▶ The young man drew his sword and challenged the knight to a duel.
年輕人拔出了他的劍，向騎士要求決鬥。
＊knight [naɪt] n. 騎士，武士
　 duel [ˈdjuəl] n. 決鬥

▶ The pen is mightier than the sword.
文勝於武。—— 諺語
＊mighty [ˈmaɪtɪ] a. 強而有力的 (= powerful)

27 armed [ɑrmd] *a.* 武裝的

片 (1) be armed with...
持有……(武器)

(2) armed robbery 持械搶劫

反 unarmed [ʌnˈɑrmd] *a.* 沒有武裝的

▶ The bank robber was armed with only a knife.
那個銀行搶匪僅持有一把刀。

▶ The armed robbery took place this morning.
那宗持械搶案發生在今天早上。

28 canyon [ˈkænjən] *n.* 峽谷

似 (1) gorge [gɔrdʒ] *n.* (小而深的) 峽谷
the Taroko Gorge （花蓮）太魯閣

(2) crayon [ˈkreən] *n.* 蠟筆

▶ Have you ever visited the Grand Canyon in Arizona?
你有去看過亞利桑納州的大峽谷嗎？

29 sprain [spren] *vt.* 扭到 & *n.* 扭傷

似 (1) twist [twɪst] *vt.* 扭 ③
(2) wrench [rɛntʃ] *vt.* 扭

▶ Paula tripped on her shoelaces and sprained her ankle.
寶拉踩到自己的鞋帶，因而扭傷了腳踝。

▶ Larry suffered a bad wrist sprain during the basketball game.
賴瑞在籃球比賽中手腕嚴重扭傷。

30 dive [daɪv] *vi.* & *n.* 跳水

三 dive, dived / dove [dov], dived

片 (1) dive into... 跳入 (水中)
(2) take a dive 大幅下跌

延伸 skydive [ˈskaɪˌdaɪv] *vi.* 高空跳傘
go skydiving 從事高空跳傘

▶ The boys took off their clothes and dived into the river.
男孩們脫下衣服跳進河裡去。

▶ The swimmer got ready for her dive into the water.
這位女泳者準備好跳水。

▶ Global markets took a dive last night after the US election results.
昨晚全球市場在美國選舉結果公布後重挫。

31 violet [ˈvaɪəlɪt] *n.* 紫羅蘭 & *a.* 紫羅藍色的

▶ Violets are my grandmother's favorite flowers.
紫羅蘭是我祖母最愛的花。

▶ The violet carpet in the bedroom made Kelly feel relaxed.
臥室的紫羅蘭色地毯讓凱莉覺得很放鬆。

tulip [ˈtjuləp] *n.* 鬱金香

▶ Tulips are on sale today at the flower shop.
這家花店今天鬱金香特價。

Unit 21

2101-2103

1　luggage [ˈlʌɡɪdʒ] n. 行李〔英〕(不可數)

用法 不可說：a luggage / two luggages / many luggages (✕)

應　說：a piece of luggage (○)
一件行李

two pieces of luggage (○)　兩件行李

a lot of luggage (○)
許多行李

▸ Don't forget to claim your luggage before you leave the airport.

在你離開機場前，別忘了領取行李。

*claim one's luggage　領取行李

baggage [ˈbæɡɪdʒ]

n. 行李〔美〕(不可數，用法同 luggage)

▸ Be sure to check the baggage allowance for your airline.

記得要確認你搭乘的航空公司行李允載重量限制。

▸ How many pieces of baggage / luggage do you have with you?

你隨身帶了多少件行李？

2　excellence [ˈɛksləns] n. 傑出，優異

衍 (1) excellent [ˈɛksələnt]
　　a. 極好的，特優的 ①

(2) excel [ɪkˈsɛl] vi. 善於，擅長於
　　(與介詞 in 或 at 並用) ⑥

excel in / at painting　擅長繪畫
= be good at painting

▸ Professor Burton is well-known for his academic excellence.

波頓教授因其學術優異表現廣為人知。

▸ I'm amazed at Peter's excellence in Chinese calligraphy.

我很驚訝地發現彼得書法寫得真棒。

3　spoil [spɔɪl] vi. (食物) 腐敗；vt. 寵壞；破壞

三 spoil, spoiled [spɔɪld] /
spoilt [spɔɪlt], spoiled / spoilt

似 ruin [ˈruɪn] vt. 破壞 ④

▸ Spare the rod, spoil the child.
省著竿子不用，就會寵壞孩子。/ 孩子不打不成器。── 諺語

▸ Food tends to spoil quickly in summer.
= Food tends to go bad quickly in summer.
夏天食物容易腐敗。

▸ You will spoil your children if you give them whatever they want.

如果小孩要什麼就給什麼，你會把他們寵壞的。

▸ The continuous rain has spoiled our plan to go fishing today.

持續下雨破壞了我們今天要去釣魚的計畫。

2104-2112

4 novelist [ˈnɑvl̩ɪst] n. 小說家

衍 novel [ˈnɑvl̩] n. 小說 ②

▶ Ken was just an average Joe until he wrote the book. He is a famous novelist now.

在寫那本書之前，肯不過是個無名小卒。他現在可是位名小說家了。

＊an average Joe　無名小卒

5 invent [ɪnˈvɛnt] vt. 發明；捏造 (= make up)

用 invent a story　捏造故事
= make up a story

衍 (1) invention [ɪnˈvɛnʃən]
　　n. 發明 (不可數)；發明物 (可數) ④

(2) inventive [ɪnˈvɛntɪv]
　　a. 有創意的，點子多的

▶ Some people claim that Bell didn't invent the telephone.

某些人主張電話不是貝爾發明的。

▶ Al invented many stories to cover his lies.
= Al made up many stories to cover his lies.

艾爾編造出許多故事來掩飾謊言。

▶ The criminal invented an alibi to deceive the judge.

那名犯人捏造了不在場證明欺騙法官。

＊alibi [ˈæləbaɪ] n. 不在場証明

inventor [ɪnˈvɛntɚ] n. 發明家

▶ Edison was one of the greatest inventors of the twentieth century.

愛迪生是二十世紀最偉大的發明家之一。

6 cheerful [ˈtʃɪrfəl] a. 愉快的

▶ Ruth can speak in a cheerful tone even when she is really mad.

即使茹絲很生氣，她還是可以用愉快的語調說話。

7 gossip [ˈgɑsəp] n. 八卦，閒言閒語 (不可數) & vi. 聊八卦

用 gossip about...
　閒聊有關……的八卦

似 (1) rumor [ˈrumɚ] n. 謠言 ③
(2) hearsay [ˈhɪrˌse] n. 傳聞，謠言

▶ My friend Ruby always keeps me up to date with the latest gossip about celebrities.

我的朋友露比總是會告訴我最新的名人八卦。

▶ The staff members spent a whole afternoon in the office doing nothing but gossiping about their boss.

這些職員花了一整個下午在辦公室啥都沒做，盡聊老闆的八卦。

8 dump [dʌmp] vt. 丟棄，隨意扔；甩，分手 & n. 垃圾集中處

用 dump sb　(男女交往) 甩掉某人
法 = walk out on sb

▶ The police finally found the stolen car, which had been dumped near the beach.

警方最後尋獲了這輛失竊的車子，它被丟棄在海灘附近。

> That guy is really a jerk. I'm glad Lucy dumped him.
> 那個傢伙是個渾球。我很高興露西甩了他。
> ＊jerk [dʒɝk] *n.* 蠢蛋，渾球

> Mom asked me to take the garbage bag to the dump.
> 媽媽要我把那包垃圾拿去丟在垃圾集中處。

---

ditch [dɪtʃ]
n. 溝渠 & *vt.* 丟棄；甩，分手

片 ditch sb　（男女交往）甩掉某人
= dump sb
= walk out on sb

> Farmers use ditches for draining water.
> 農夫利用溝渠來排水。
> ＊drain [dren] *vt.* 排除（水）

> The boss ditched the project because it was impractical.
> 老闆丟棄了該企畫案，因為它不切實際。

> Judy was heartbroken when Johnny ditched her at the party last night.
> 茱蒂很傷心，強尼在昨晚的派對上把她給甩了。

9　dairy [ˈdɛrɪ] *n.* 乳酪業

複 dairies [ˈdɛriz]
似 diary [ˈdaɪərɪ] *n.* 日記 ②
　keep a diary
　寫日記（非 write a diary）
延伸 dairy products　乳酪產品

> Dairy products, such as cheese and butter, are produced from milk.
> 像是起司和奶油等的酪農產品，是由牛奶做成的。

10　jar [dʒɑr] *n.* 罐（尤指玻璃罐）

似 container [kənˈtenɚ] *n.* 容器 ④

> I bought a jar of peanut butter at the supermarket.
> 我在超市買了一罐花生醬。

11　sticky [ˈstɪkɪ] *a.* 黏的；（天氣）溼熱的

衍 stick [stɪk] *vt.* 黏 & *n.* 枝條，手杖 ②

> I was sweating like a pig because it was hot and sticky.
> 因為天氣又溼熱又黏，我流了滿身大汗。
> ＊sweat like a pig　流了很多汗，汗如雨下

12　advanced [ədˈvænst] *a.* 先進的；進階的；年高的

衍 advance [ədˈvæns]
　vi. 前進，行進 & *vt.* 促進 & *n.* 進步 ②
　in advance　事前，預先
= beforehand [bɪˈfɔr,hænd]
　adv. 事先 ⑥

> This digital camera is the most advanced model on the market.
> 這臺數位相機是市面上最先進的機種。

> This dictionary is for advanced learners of English.
> 這本字典適用於進階的英文學習者。

▶ The landlord told us to pay the rent a week in advance.
房東要我們提前一週付房租。

▶ Mrs. Anderson died at an advanced age.
安德森太太高齡過世。

13 bacon [ˈbekən] n. 培根

🔗 bring home the bacon　養家餬口
= support one's family
= be responsible for the livelihood of one's family

▶ A typical English breakfast includes eggs, bacon, sausages, baked beans, and a cup of tea.
典型的英式早餐包括蛋、培根、香腸、烤豆跟一杯茶。

▶ Who brings home the bacon in your house?
= Who is responsible for the livelihood of your family?
你們家是誰負責維持生計的？

14 bait [bet] n. 餌 (集合名詞，不可數) & vt. 設誘餌

🔗 (1) take the bait
(魚) 吃魚餌；(人) 上鉤，上當
(2) bait sth with
用……在某物上設誘餌

▶ The con artist used a small amount of money as bait to cheat the old man out of all his life savings.
這名金光黨用一小筆錢做餌，把老翁的畢生積蓄全騙走了。
＊con [kɑn] n. 騙術
　a con artist　專搞騙術的人
＝a conman [ˈkɑnmæn] n. 金光黨，騙徒

▶ Do you think you can have the car for free? Don't take the bait!
你以為你可以免費得到那輛車嗎？別上當！

▶ My father baited the trap with a piece of meat.
我父親用一塊肉來當陷阱的餌。

15 beast [bist] n. 野獸；凶殘的人

▶ The power of reason is believed to be the chief difference between man and beasts.
理性被認為是人跟獸的主要區別。

▶ Stay away from that beast. He might hurt you.
遠離那個凶巴巴的傢伙。他可能會傷害你。

monster [ˈmɑnstɚ] n. 怪獸

衍 monstrous [ˈmɑnstrəs]
　a. 似怪物的；可怕的 ⑥

▶ The witch turned the animal into a monster.
巫婆把那隻動物變成了怪物。

16 berry [ˈbɛrɪ] n. 莓，果子

延伸 (1) strawberry [ˈstrɔˌbɛrɪ] n. 草莓 ②
(2) blueberry [ˈbluˌbɛrɪ] n. 藍莓
(3) cranberry [ˈkrænˌbɛrɪ] n. 蔓越莓
(4) mulberry [ˈmʌlˌbɛrɪ] n. 桑椹

▶ Tom picked some berries from that bush and popped them into his mouth.
湯姆從樹叢裡採了一些果子塞進嘴裡。

cherry [ˈtʃɛrɪ]
n. 櫻桃 & *a.* 櫻桃紅的，鮮紅色的

▶ Mr. Brown grew a cherry tree in his backyard.
布朗先生在後院種了一棵櫻桃樹。

▶ Tina's cherry lips left a bright mark on the little boy's cheek.
提娜的鮮紅色嘴唇在小男孩的臉頰上留下一抹鮮明的印記。

17　best-seller [ˌbɛstˈsɛlɚ] *n.* 暢銷貨（尤指書）

似 sell like hot cakes　熱賣

▶ The writer's latest novel has been a best-seller for over 20 weeks.
該作家最新出版的小說二十多週以來都很暢銷。

18　pancake [ˈpænˌkek] *n.* 煎餅

▶ Can I have some of your pancakes? I'm starving.
我可以吃點你的煎餅嗎？我好餓喔。

jelly [ˈdʒɛlɪ] *n.* 果凍

▶ Tonight we'll have some jelly for dessert.
今晚我們的甜點是果凍。

19　brake [brek] *n.* 煞車，制動器 & *vi.* 煞車

片 put on / apply the brakes　踩煞車
（由於汽車有四個輪子，而每個輪子都有煞車裝置，故在本片語中 brakes 採複數形。）

似 break [brek] *vt.* 破壞；打破 & *vi.* 破，裂；破曉 & *n.* 休息；裂口 ①

▶ We found a break in the pipe.
我們發現水管有一道裂痕。

▶ Nicole put on the brakes all of a sudden and my head almost hit the windshield.
妮可突然踩煞車，害我的頭差點撞上擋風玻璃。
*windshield [ˈwɪndˌʃild] *n.* 擋風玻璃

▶ Wendy braked to avoid hitting a stray dog.
溫蒂煞車以避免撞到流浪狗。

20　bud [bʌd] *n.* 芽，花苞 & *vi.* 發苞，結苞

三 bud, budded [ˈbʌdɪd], budded

片 (1) be in bud　結苞
(2) nip sth in the bud　防患於未然
*nip [nɪp] *vt.* 掐，捏

▶ The roses in my backyard are in bud.
我後院的玫瑰結苞了。

▶ You'd better nip the problem in the bud before it worsens.
你最好在問題惡化前解決它。

▶ Global warming has caused plants in this area to bud early in recent years.
全球暖化造成該區植物近年提早發苞。

21 yolk [jok] *n.* 蛋黃

比 egg white [ˈɛgˌ(h)waɪt] 蛋白

▶ An egg is made up of the yolk and the white.
蛋是由蛋黃和蛋白所組成。

---

22 buffet [bəˈfe] *n.* 自助餐 & [ˈbʌfɪt] *vt.* 打擊

用法 buffet 作及物動詞表『打擊』時，常使用被動語態。

be buffeted by... 被……打擊

似 strike [straɪk] *vt.* 打擊 ②

▶ It's an all-you-can-eat buffet, so take whatever you want and pig out!
這是吃到飽的自助吧，所以想吃什麼儘管拿，吃個痛快吧！
*pig out 大吃特吃

▶ Many African countries are buffeted by civil war.
許多非洲國家都受到內戰摧殘。

---

23 bump [bʌmp] *vi.* 衝撞 & *n.* 腫塊；隆起之處；重擊

片 (1) bump into sb 巧遇某人
= run across sb
(2) bump into sth/sb
撞到某物 / 某人

衍 (1) bumper [ˈbʌmpɚ]
n. (汽車前後的) 保險桿
(2) bumpy [ˈbʌmpɪ]
a. 顛簸不平的，晃動的
a bumpy road 顛簸不平的路

▶ I bumped into an old friend of mine on the street last night.
我昨晚在街上巧遇老友。

▶ The brakes suddenly failed, and the car bumped into a tree.
煞車突然失靈，然後車子撞上了樹。

▶ How did you get that bump on your head?
你頭上腫一塊是怎麼來的？

▶ James got a bad bump on his head when he fell down the stairs.
詹姆士從樓梯上摔下來時，他的頭部受到重擊。

---

24 carpenter [ˈkɑrpəntɚ] *n.* 木匠

衍 carpentry [ˈkɑrpəntrɪ] *n.* 木匠業
延伸 (1) mason [ˈmesən] *n.* 水泥工
(2) plumber [ˈplʌmɚ] *n.* 水管工 ④

▶ A few carpenters were hired by the government to reconstruct the temple.
政府僱用了幾名木匠進行寺廟的重建工作。

---

tailor [ˈtelɚ] *n.* 裁縫師

延伸 a tailor-made suit 訂做的西裝
= a custom-made suit
a ready-made suit 現成的西裝

▶ The tailor makes the man.
人靠衣裳，佛靠金裝。── 諺語

---

25 chat [tʃæt] *vi.* & *n.* 聊天，閒談

三 chat, chatted [ˈtʃætɪd], chatted

▶ We had a good time chatting over dinner last night.
= We had a pleasant chat over dinner last night.
我們昨晚吃晚餐邊吃邊聊很愉快。
*chat over dinner 邊吃晚餐邊聊天

片 chat with sb　與某人聊天
= have a chat with sb
延伸 the chat room　（網路）聊天室

26　chop [tʃɑp] *vt.* 切，砍 & *n.* 切，砍；帶骨的肉塊

三 chop, chopped [tʃɑpt], chopped
片 (1) get the chop　被開除〔英〕
　 = get the boot
　 = get the sack
　 = be fired
　 (2) a pork chop　豬排
　　 a lamb chop　羊排
延伸 chop 做名詞時亦可表示我們常用的『圖章』、『印章』。

▶ Workers were busy chopping down trees in the forest.
　工人正在樹林裡忙著砍樹。
▶ Wendy got the chop after she was found stealing from the company.
　溫蒂被發現偷公司錢後遭到開除。
▶ That restaurant serves the finest grilled lamb chops in town.
　那家餐廳提供鎮上最好的烤羊排。

27　slice [slaɪs] *n.* 一片 & *vt.* 削，切

片 a slice of bread / cheese / pizza / ham
= a piece of bread / cheese / pizza / ham
一片麵包 / 起司 / 披薩 / 火腿

▶ Jerry grabbed a slice of bread and then rushed to work.
　傑瑞抓了片麵包後就匆匆去上班了。
▶ Mom sliced some onions and dumped them into the cooking pot.
　媽媽切了一些洋蔥然後丟進鍋裡。

---

loaf [lof] *n.* (一條、一塊) 麵包 & *vi.* 閒混
複 loaves [lovz]
片 (1) a loaf of bread　一條麵包
　 (2) loaf around　虛度時光
　 = play around

▶ We bought a loaf of bread at the bakery.
　我們在麵包店買了一條麵包。
▶ Billy and I loafed around in the park after school.
　比利和我放學後在公園裡閒晃。

28　circus [ˈsɝkəs] *n.* 馬戲團

▶ Sammy was so happy when her father promised to take her to the circus on Saturday night.
　爸爸答應星期六晚上帶她去看馬戲團表演時，珊米高興極了。

---

clown [klaʊn] *n.* 小丑
似 (1) crow [kro] *n.* 烏鴉 ②
　 (2) crown [kraʊn] *n.* 王冠 ③

▶ The funny clown made all of the children happy.
　滑稽的小丑讓所有的孩子很開心。

29 clinic [ˈklɪnɪk] n. 診所

片 a dental clinic 牙科診所

▶ Have you made an appointment with the local clinic?
你有沒有跟當地那家診所先預約看診？

30 stool [stul] n. 凳子；高腳椅

比 couch [kaʊtʃ] n. 長沙發

▶ Roger sat on the bar stool drinking beer and talking to the bartender.
羅傑坐在酒館高腳椅上，邊喝酒邊跟酒保聊天。

31 zipper [ˈzɪpɚ] n. 拉鍊 & vt. 拉上拉鍊（= zip）

▶ The zipper of the jacket I just bought is not working. What a piece of junk!
這件夾克的拉鍊剛買就壞掉。真是爛貨！
*junk [dʒʌŋk] n. （用不到的）廢棄物；垃圾（集合名詞，不可數）

▶ My keys fell out of my backpack because I forgot to zipper it shut.
我忘了把背包的拉鍊拉上，所以鑰匙掉出來了。

zip [zɪp] vt. 拉上拉鍊（常與介詞 up 並用）
三 zip, zipped [zɪpt], zipped
片 zip up a coat 把外套的拉鍊拉起來

▶ Can you help me zip up my dress?
你可以幫我把洋裝拉鍊拉上嗎？

32 cable [ˈkebl] n. 電纜

延伸 a cable car 纜車

▶ We have to pay to watch cable TV.
我們得付費才能收看有線電視。

33 cart [kɑrt] n. 手推車；（馬、牛等動物拉的）貨運車

片 put the cart before the horse
本末倒置

▶ The cart was full of fruit and vegetables.
手推車上滿是蔬果。

▶ The horse-drawn cart is loaded with fruit and vegetables.
這輛馬車載滿了蔬果。

▶ Brushing your teeth before eating is putting the cart before the horse.
吃東西前刷牙是本末倒置。

Unit 22

2201-2204

1 bravery [ˈbrevərɪ] n. 勇敢

衍 brave [brev] a. 勇敢的 ①

似 courage [ˈkɜɪdʒ] n. 勇氣 ②

反 cowardice [ˈkaʊədɪs] n. 膽小；懦弱

▶ Peter's bravery and loyalty led him to complete the mission.
彼得的勇氣和忠誠促使他完成這項任務。

2 cradle [ˈkredl̩] n. 搖籃；發源地 & vt. 輕抱

片 from (the) cradle to (the) grave
從生到死；(某人的) 一生

似 (1) hug [hʌg] vt. 擁抱 ③
(2) embrace [ɪmˈbres] vt. 擁抱 ⑤

▶ Thanks to the sound welfare system, everyone in this country is well taken care of from cradle to grave.
由於健全的福利制度，該國所有的人一生都受到良好的照顧。
＊welfare [ˈwɛl͵fɛr] n. 福利

▶ Archaeological evidence has shown that Mesopotamia was the cradle of civilization.
考古學上的證據顯示，美索不達米亞是人類文明的發源地。
＊archaeological [͵ɑrkɪəˈlɑdʒɪkl̩] a. 考古學的

▶ Cathy cradled the baby in her arms as she fed it.
凱西把小寶寶抱在懷裡餵他牛奶。
＊此處 baby 指小嬰兒，因看不出是男是女，故以代名詞 it 代替。

3 dam [dæm] n. 水壩 & vt. 在 (河上) 築壩攔水

三 dam, dammed [dæmd], dammed

比 reservoir [ˈrɛzə͵vɔr] n. 水庫 ⑤

▶ The government is building a dam in that area, but conservationists are strongly against it for fear that it might spoil the environment.
政府正在該區興建一座水壩，但保育人士強烈反對，害怕這麼做將對環境造成危害。
＊conservationist [͵kɑnsəˈveʃənɪst] n. 保育人士

▶ The government decided to dam the river to prevent further floods.
政府決定在河上築壩攔水，以防止再有洪水氾濫。

4 darling [ˈdɑrlɪŋ] n. 親愛的 (對情人或配偶的暱稱) & a. 可愛的

似 (1) dear [dɪr]
n. 親愛的 (對情人或配偶的暱稱)
& a. 親愛的 ①
(2) honey [ˈhʌnɪ]
n. 親愛的 (對情人或配偶的暱稱) ①

▶ Oh my darling! How I have missed you!
噢，親愛的！我真是想死你了！

▶ What a darling little puppy you have, Lisa.
麗莎，妳這隻小狗狗真是可愛。
＊puppy [ˈpʌpɪ] n. 小狗

5 deepen [ˈdipən] vt. & vi. (使) 變深；(使) 強烈

衍 (1) deep [dip] a. 深的 ①
　　a deep river　很深的一條河
　(2) deeply [ˈdiplɪ] adv. 深深地

▶ I'm deeply moved by the story.
　我深受這故事感動。

　(3) depth [dɛpθ] n. 深度 ②
　　in-depth　詳細的，深入的
　　an in-depth report
　　一則深入的報導

似 lengthen [ˈlɛŋθən] vt. 使變長，加長

▶ The expert suggested that we deepen the river to prevent flooding.
該專家建議我們把河加深以防水災。

▶ The water deepens suddenly beyond this point.
越過這個地點後水位會突然加深。

▶ You'll find more interesting facts as you deepen your research into this subject.
你對這個主題有了更深入的研究後，就會發現更多有趣的事實。

▶ After being classmates for three years, George and Betty's friendship deepened into love.
在當了三年的同學後，喬治與貝蒂之間的友誼逐漸深化成愛情。

6 dime [daɪm] n. (美金) 一角 (硬幣)

片 be a dime a dozen
　稀鬆平常的 (一毛錢就可買到一打的)

似 dine [daɪn]
　vi. 用餐 & n. 晚餐 (= dinner)

▶ A dime is worth one tenth of a United States dollar.
美金一角值十分之一美元。

▶ MP3 players are a dime a dozen nowadays.
= MP3 players are very common nowadays.
MP3 播放器現在很普遍。

---

penny [ˈpɛnɪ] n. 一便士〔英〕

複 pence [pɛns]

片 be worth every penny〔英〕
= be worth every cent〔美〕
　每一分錢都很值得

延伸 pound [paʊnd] n. (英) 鎊 ②

▶ The postcards are on sale for 99 pence each.
這些明信片特價一張九十九便士。

▶ This car is expensive but is worth every penny—it has all the top-of-the-line devices you can find.
這輛車很貴，不過花的每一分錢都很值得 —— 它有所有你能找到的一流裝置。
*top-of-the-line　一流的，最棒的

7 dip [dɪp] vt. 浸泡 & vi. 沉下，下降 & n. 游泳 (一會兒)；下跌；蘸醬

三 dip, dipped [dɪpt], dipped

片 (1) dip in / into...　浸入……
　(2) take a dip　游一會泳

似 (1) sink [sɪŋk] vi. 下沉 ③
　(2) immerse [ɪˈmɝs] vt. 使浸入

▶ Mary dipped her handkerchief in soapy water and gently washed it.
瑪莉把手帕浸在肥皂水裡，輕柔地洗滌。
*soapy [ˈsopɪ] a. 沾滿肥皂的

▶ The price of airline tickets dips between September and November.
九月到十一月間，機票價格會下跌。

▶ Fiona decided to take a dip in the swimming pool before dinner.
費歐娜決定在吃晚餐前先在游泳池裡游一會兒。

▶ There was a dip in sales towards the end of the year.
銷售量接近年底時下滑了。

▶ Helen's favorite dip is made from tomatoes and onions.
海倫最喜歡的蘸醬是用番茄和洋蔥調製成的。

8 arrest [əˋrɛst] *n. & vt.* 逮捕

(1) be under arrest　　　　被逮捕
(2) be under house arrest　被軟禁

▶ "Freeze! You're under arrest!" shouted the policeman.
『不許動，你被捕了！』警員喊道。

▶ The young boy was arrested for robbing the bank.
這小子因搶銀行被逮捕。

▶ The political activist has been placed under house arrest for three days.
這名政治活躍分子已經被軟禁三天了。
＊activist [ˋæktɪvɪst] *n.* 活躍分子

9 erase [ɪˋres] *vt.* 擦掉，消除

erase sth from one's mind
從腦海中刪除對某事的記憶

(1) eraser [ɪˋresɚ]
n. 黑板擦；橡皮擦 ①
(2) erasable [ɪˋresəbḷ] *a.* 可消除的
(1) cancel [ˋkænsḷ] *vt.* 刪去，取消 ②
(2) delete [dɪˋlit] *vt.* 刪除

▶ John helped his teacher erase the blackboard after class.
約翰下課後幫老師擦黑板。

▶ Years have gone by, but I still can't erase the image of my first girlfriend from my mind.
事隔多年，不過我第一任女友在我心中的影像仍然揮之不去。

10 fancy [ˋfænsɪ] *n.* 愛好；想像力 & *a.* 別緻的 & *vt.* 想要 / 做……；想像

fancy, fancied [ˋfænsɪd], fancied
(1) have a fancy for...　喜歡……
= have a liking for...
= like...
(2) fancy + N/V-ing　想要 / 做……

▶ Tom has a fancy for spicy Mexican food.
湯姆喜歡吃味道重的墨西哥食物。

▶ Dragons, fairies, and giants are creatures of fancy.
龍、精靈、巨人都是想像出來的。

▶ Sarah dreamed that she was getting married to John while wearing a fancy dress.
莎拉夢見她穿著一件別緻的洋裝跟約翰結婚了。

▶ I don't fancy living on a desert island all by myself.
我不想要自己一個人住在荒島上。

11 fare [fɛr] *n.* 交通費

fee [fi] *n.* (手續) 費用 ②

▶ How much is the bus fare from New York to Washington D.C.?
從紐約到華府坐公車車費是多少錢？

用法 fare 指『交通費』，包含乘坐公車、計程車、火車、船隻、飛機等費用，如 the bus fare、the taxi fare、the train fare 等。

12　flock [flɑk] *n.* (羊) 群；群眾 & *vi.* (成群) 聚集

片 (1) a flock of sheep / goats
　　一群綿羊 / 山羊
(2) a flock of people　一群人
(3) come in flocks　成群結隊前來

▶ Birds of a feather flock together.
　羽毛相似的鳥會聚在一塊兒 / 物以類聚。—— 諺語

▶ I see a flock of sheep on the hillside.
　我看到山坡上有一群綿羊。

▶ People came in flocks to see their favorite singer.
　群眾湧進來看他們喜愛的歌手。

▶ Swallows are flocking together to fly south.
　燕子正群集準備一起飛向南方。

13　pint [paɪnt] *n.* 品脫，一品脫的量

延伸 一品脫約半公斤重。

▶ Lee accidentally spilled about 10 pints of cream on the ground.
　小李一不小心把約十品脫的奶油打翻在地上。

quart [kwɔrt] *n.* 夸脫，一夸脫的量

延伸 一夸脫約兩品脫重 (約一公斤)。

▶ Milk comes in quart and gallon sized jugs.
　牛奶都是以夸脫或加崙為單位的瓶罐裝填。

gallon [ˋgælən] *n.* 加侖，一加侖的量

延伸 一加侖約 3.8 公升。

▶ A gallon is a unit for measuring liquids.
　加侖是測量液體的單位。

14　gasoline [ˋgæsə͵lin] *n.* 汽油 (常縮寫成 gas)

似 (1) gas [gæs] *n.* 汽油；氣體；瓦斯 ③
　= petrol [ˋpɛtrol] *n.* 汽油〔英〕⑥
(2) petroleum [pəˋtrolɪəm] *n.* 石油 ⑥

延伸 a gas station〔美〕　加油站
= a petrol station〔英〕

▶ We ran out of gasoline while in the middle of nowhere.
　我們在荒郊野外時汽車沒油了。

15　grocery [ˋgrosərɪ] *n.* 食品雜貨 (常用複數)

複 groceries [ˋgrosərɪz]
延伸 a grocery store　食品雜貨店

▶ I need to pick up some groceries on my way home.
　我回家時要順道買些食品雜貨。
　*pick up...　購買……
　= buy...

16 stadium [ˈstedɪəm] *n.* 體育場

似 **gymnasium** [dʒɪmˈnezɪəm]
n. 體育館；健身房

比 stadium 大部分為室外的場館，也有少數為室內的，其周圍設有觀眾席，常用來舉辦體育賽事或演唱會。gymnasium 則通常為室內的場館，裡面有運動設施供人健身。

▸ The concert will be held in a large stadium.
演唱會將於一座大型運動場舉行。

17 helmet [ˈhɛlmɪt] *n.* 頭盔；安全帽

片 **wear a helmet**　戴安全帽

▸ Always wear a helmet when you ride a motorcycle.
騎乘機車一定要戴安全帽。

18 hometown [ˈhomˌtaun] *n.* 故鄉；家鄉

衍 **homesick** [ˈhomˌsɪk] *a.* 想家的 ③
似 **homeland** [ˈhomˌlænd]
n. 祖國，故鄉 ④

▸ William Shakespeare's memorial is located in his hometown.
莎士比亞紀念館蓋在莎翁的故鄉。
＊memorial [məˈmorɪəl] *n.* 紀念碑；紀念堂

19 honesty [ˈɑnɪstɪ] *n.* 誠實

衍 **honest** [ˈɑnɪst] *a.* 誠實的 ①
反 **dishonesty** [dɪsˈɑnɪstɪ] *n.* 不誠實 ③
▸ Honesty is the best policy.
誠實為上策。—— 諺語

▸ John has won my respect not because of his competence but because of his honesty.
約翰贏得我的尊敬不是因為他有能力，而是因為他誠實。
＊competence [ˈkɑmpətəns] *n.* 能力，稱職

20 jewel [ˈdʒuəl] *n.* 寶石，珠寶；可貴的東西 (可數)

似 **gem** [dʒɛm] *n.* 寶石

▸ The billionaire keeps most of his jewels in the bank lest they should be stolen.
因深怕被竊，那個億萬富翁把大部分的珠寶放在銀行裡。
＊lest [lɛst] *conj.* 以免，免得

jewelry [ˈdʒuəlrɪ] *n.* 珠寶，首飾
(集合名詞，不可數)

用法 可　說：a jewel　　　一件珠寶
　　　　　two jewels　　兩件珠寶
　　不可說：a jewelry (×)
　　　　　two jewelries (×)

▸ Zack gave his wife a piece of jewelry to celebrate their wedding anniversary.
查克給了他太太一件珠寶以慶祝結婚週年。

應　說：a piece of jewelry　一件珠寶
　　　two pieces of jewelry
　　　兩件珠寶
　　　a lot of jewelry　許多件珠寶

21　junk [dʒʌŋk] *n.* 垃圾，廢物 & *vt.* 丟棄（廢棄物品）

片 junk food　垃圾食物
（尤指漢堡、炸雞等不營養的速食）

衍 junkyard [ˋdʒʌŋkˌjɑrd]
n. 廢材料（尤指廢汽車）堆積場

用法 junk 指用不到或不能使用的東西，是集合名詞，不可數。
不可說：a junk　一個廢物
應　說：a piece of junk　一件廢物

似 (1) trash [træʃ] *n.* 垃圾（不可數）②
(2) garbage [ˋgɑrbɪdʒ]
n. 垃圾（不可數）〔美〕②
(3) rubbish [ˋrʌbɪʃ]
n. 垃圾（不可數）〔英〕；無意義的話或想法（= nonsense）⑥

▶ That bicycle I bought yesterday is really a piece of junk.
我昨天買的那輛腳踏車真是個爛貨。

▶ Marty decided to junk his old car and get a new one.
馬蒂決定丟掉舊車，然後買輛新車。

22　litter [ˋlɪtɚ] *n.* 垃圾（集合名詞，不可數）；一窩（剛生下來的小動物，如狗、貓等）& *vt.* 把……弄亂 & *vi.* 亂丟垃圾

片 (1) a litter of...　一窩（小動物）
(2) be littered with...
到處散布……的垃圾

用法 litter、trash、garbage、rubbish 皆表『垃圾』，且均為不可數名詞。如表一件垃圾，均需與 a piece of 並用。
不可說：a trash (×)
應　說：a piece of trash (○)

延伸 a litterbug　亂丟垃圾的人，討厭鬼

▶ A litterbug is one who litters public places with garbage.
垃圾鬼指的就是在公共場所亂丟垃圾的人。

▶ After the fair, litter was everywhere.
展覽會之後，到處都是垃圾。
＊fair [fɛr] *n.* 展覽會
a book fair　書展

▶ On hearing a strange sound, I walked over to the bushes and found a litter of puppies.
我聽到奇怪的聲音，走到樹叢去，發現了一窩小狗。

▶ Some people litter by throwing garbage out of their car windows.
有些人會亂丟垃圾，把它們直接丟出車窗外。

▶ Don't litter, or you'll be fined.
別亂丟垃圾，否則你會被罰款。

▶ John is sloppy, and his room is always littered with old newspapers.
約翰很邋遢，他的房間到處都是舊報紙。
＊sloppy [ˋslɑpɪ] *a.* 邋遢的

23 **lifetime** [ˈlaɪfˌtaɪm] *n.* 一生 & *a.* 終生的

片 (1) a chance of a lifetime
　　　千載難逢的機會
　(2) in one's lifetime　某人的一生中

似 lifelong [ˈlaɪfˌlɔŋ] *a.* 終生的 ⑥

▶ For Tammy, going on a trip to India was a chance of a lifetime.
對塔米來說，印度之行是個千載難逢的機會。

▶ Russell married three times in his lifetime.
羅素一生中結過三次婚。

▶ Marriage used to be thought of as a lifetime commitment.
婚姻曾經被視為是一種終生的承諾。
＊commitment [kəˈmɪtmənt] *n.* 承諾

---

24 **mall** [mɔl] *n.* 大型購物中心

延伸 a shopping mall　購物商場

▶ I usually hang around at the mall with friends on weekends.
我週末通常和朋友在購物中心閒晃。

---

25 **marvelous** [ˈmɑrvələs] *a.* 不可思議的，了不起的 (= marvellous〔英〕)

衍 marvel [ˈmɑrvl] *n.* 令人驚歎的事物
　& *vi.* 感到讚歎 (與 at 並用) ⑥
　marvel at...　對……讚歎

似 wonderful [ˈwʌndəfəl]
　a. 了不起，很棒的 ①

▶ John is famous for his marvelous achievements in computer science.
約翰因為在電腦科學方面有了不起的成就而聞名。

---

26 **merry** [ˈmɛrɪ] *a.* 愉快的

似 (1) happy [ˈhæpɪ] *a.* 快樂的 ①
　(2) cheerful [ˈtʃɪrfəl] *a.* 開心的 ③

▶ The park was full of smiling parents and merry children.
整個公園都是笑容滿面的父母與高興的小朋友。

---

27 **queer** [kwɪr] *a.* 古怪的

似 (1) strange [strendʒ] *a.* 奇怪的 ①
　(2) weird [wɪrd] *a.* 怪異的 ⑤

▶ Last night, I heard a queer noise coming from the basement.
昨晚我聽見地下室傳來奇怪的噪音。

---

28 **voter** [ˈvotɚ] *n.* 選民

衍 vote [vot] *vi.*, *vt.* 選舉；投票 ②

▶ The voters lined up at the polling station to get the ballots.
選民在投票所排隊領取選票。
＊ballot [ˈbælət] *n.* 選票

Level 3　Unit 22

29 **underwear** [ˋʌndɚ͵wɛr] *n.* 內衣（集合名詞，不可數）

▸ When Jack opened his suitcase, he realized that he'd forgotten to pack his underwear.
傑克打開手提箱時，他才意識到他忘記把內衣放進去了。

30 **trumpet** [ˋtrʌmpɪt] *n.* 小號

☐ blow one's own trumpet / horn
某人自吹自擂

衍 trumpeter [ˋtrʌmpɪtɚ] *n.* 小號手

▸ The young man seemed to keep blowing his own trumpet in the interview.
在這段訪談中，這位年輕人好像不停地在自吹自擂。

▸ Roger is a talented trumpet player.
羅傑是個很有天分的小號手。

31 **tower** [ˋtaʊɚ] *n.* 塔

▸ The tower is about 100 meters high.
這座塔約有一百公尺高。

32 **tangerine** [ˋtændʒə͵rin] *n.* 橘子

▸ What's the difference between an orange and a tangerine?
柳橙和橘子的差別是什麼？

pineapple [ˋpaɪn͵æpḷ] *n.* 鳳梨

▸ Pineapples make great snacks and desserts.
鳳梨很適合做各類點心和甜點。

melon [ˋmɛlən] *n.* 甜瓜

延伸 cantaloupe [ˋkæntḷ͵op] *n.* 哈蜜瓜

▸ There are many kinds of melons in this market.
這個市場有很多種類的甜瓜。

lemonade [͵lɛmənˋed] *n.* 檸檬水

衍 lemon [ˋlɛmən] *n.* 檸檬①

▸ My uncle made a small fortune selling lemonade.
我叔叔靠著賣檸檬水發了一筆小財。

33 **surround** [səˋraʊnd] *vt.* 環繞

☐ be surrounded with / by...
被……所環繞

衍 surroundings [səˋraʊndɪŋz]
n. (住處) 環境 (恆用複數) ④

▸ All the classmates surrounded Tom, praising him for his musical talent at the concert.
所有班上同學都圍繞著湯姆，讚美他在演唱會所展現的音樂天賦。

▸ I live in a small village which is surrounded by lush hills.
我住在青山環繞的一座小村莊裡。
*lush [lʌʃ] *a.* 綠意盎然的

34 **snap** [snæp] *vt.* (啪擦一聲) 折斷；快速拍攝 & *n.* (啪擦一聲) 折斷；快照

目 snap, snapped [snæpt], snapped

H (1) snap one's fingers
　　(某人) 彈響指

　　(2) take a snap of... 替……拍張照

田 snappy [ˋsnæpɪ] *a.* 快速的
　　make it snappy 快一點
= hurry up

▸ It's really impolite for you to snap your fingers at a waiter.
對服務生彈指是件很沒禮貌的事。

▸ During our visit to the Eiffel Tower, Lucy snapped over 100 pictures.
我們去參觀艾菲爾鐵塔時，露西猛拍了一百多張相片。

▸ There was a loud snap and the tree branch hit the ground.
那根樹枝啪擦一聲斷掉，然後掉落到地上。

▸ We took a few snaps of the happy couple.
我們替那對開心的夫婦拍了幾張照片。

1 microphone [ˈmaɪkrəˌfon] n. 麥克風 (= mike)

延伸 a wireless microphone
無線麥克風
*wireless [ˈwaɪrlɪs] a. 無線的

▶ Speak into the microphone so everyone can hear you.
對著麥克風講話這樣大家才可以聽得到。

2 microwave [ˈmaɪkroˌwev] n. 微波爐 & vt. 以微波爐烹調

延伸 microwave 原指『微波』，a microwave oven 才是『微波爐』正式的說法，但現今許多英美人士均將微波爐簡稱為 a microwave。
*oven [ˈʌvən] n. 烤箱，烤爐 ③

▶ Reheat the pizza in the microwave oven for two minutes.
把比薩放到微波爐再加熱兩分鐘。
*reheat [riˈhit] vt. 再加熱

▶ Before we start to watch the movie, I'd like to microwave some popcorn.
我們開始看電影前，我想先用微波爐弄點爆米花。

3 nap [næp] vi. 打瞌睡 & n. 打盹，小睡

三 nap, napped [næpt], napped
片 take a nap   小睡一會
= take a siesta
*siesta [sɪˈɛstə] n. 小睡 (西班牙語，已為英美人士使用)
似 snap [snæp] vi. & n. 突然折斷

▶ Grandfather napped in the armchair while the TV was still on.
爺爺在單人座沙發上打起瞌睡，而電視還開著。

▶ You look exhausted. Why don't you take a nap?
你看來累極了。何不小睡一下？

4 necktie [ˈnɛkˌtaɪ] n. 領帶

用法 本字常可縮寫成 tie，與動詞 wear 並用。
wear a necktie / tie   繫領帶

▶ You are required to wear a necktie if you want to get into that restaurant.
要進入那間餐廳，你得繫領帶才行。

blouse [blaʊz] n. (女用) 罩衫，短衫
比 shirt [ʃɝt] n. (男用) 襯衫 ①

▶ Alice looks absolutely stunning in that blouse.
穿著那件罩衫的艾麗絲看起來美極了。
*look beautiful in + 衣服   穿著某衣服看起來很美
stunning [ˈstʌnɪŋ] a. 極美的，美得要冒泡似的

vest [vɛst] n. 背心
延伸 vest 可指搭配西裝穿著的無袖厚背心，亦可指當內衣的無袖汗衫。

▶ You can buy a vest to match your new shirt.
你可以買件背心搭配你這件新的襯衫。

5 pal [pæl] n. 夥伴，哥兒們 (口語)

似 (1) companion [kəmˈpænjən]
n. 同伴 (正式) ④

▶ Hey, pal! Want to go see a movie?
嘿，哥兒們，想不想去看場電影？

(2) buddy [ˈbʌdɪ]
　　 n. 老兄；哥兒們（口語）

延伸 a pen pal　筆友

▶ Susan has several pen pals, some of whom she has known for ages but has never met in person.
蘇珊有幾個筆友，其中有的認識很多年了，但從沒實際見過面。

6　parcel [ˈpɑrsḷ] n. 包裹〔英〕& vt. 分配（與介詞 out 並用）

似 package [ˈpækɪdʒ] n. 包裹〔美〕①

▶ Please take this parcel to the post office and have it sent immediately.
請把這個包裹拿到郵局立刻把它寄掉。

▶ They plan to parcel the food out to different charities.
他們打算把食物分給不同的慈善機構。
＊charity [ˈtʃærətɪ] n. 慈善機構

7　passport [ˈpæsˌpɔrt] n. 護照

延伸 visa [ˈvizə] n. 簽證⑤
▶ Your visa is about to expire, so you must have it renewed at once.
你的簽證快到期了，因此你必須得立刻加簽。

▶ You have to present your passport as you go through customs.
你出入海關必須出示護照。
＊customs [ˈkʌstəmz] n. 海關（恆用複數）
　 go through customs　通關，通過出入境檢查過程

8　pity [ˈpɪtɪ] n. 同情；可惜，遺憾 & vt. 同情，憐憫

三 pity, pitied [ˈpɪtɪd], pitied
片 (1) take / have pity on sb　同情某人
　 (2) It is a pity that...　很遺憾……
　 = It is too bad that...
　 = It is a shame that...
衍 (1) pitiful [ˈpɪtɪfəl] a. 可憐的
　　 look pitiful　一副可憐的樣子
　 (2) pitiless [ˈpɪtɪlɪs]
　　 a. 無憐憫心的，無情的
似 sympathy [ˈsɪmpəθɪ]
　 n. 同情，憐憫④

▶ Mr. Green took pity on me and let me postpone my presentation until Friday.
葛林老師同情我的處境，讓我延到星期五再做報告。

▶ It is a pity that John didn't come to the party.
約翰沒來派對真可惜。

▶ We pitied the boy who lost his parents.
我們很同情那個失去雙親的男孩。

9　pollute [pəˈlut] vt. 汙染

衍 pollutant [pəˈlutənt] n. 汙染物

▶ The exhaust from our cars pollutes the air and causes asthma in children.
我們汽車排放的廢氣會汙染空氣，使幼童罹患氣喘。
＊asthma [ˈæzmə] n. 氣喘病

pollution [pəˋluʃən]
n. 汙染 (不可數)

📆 air / noise / water pollution
空氣 / 噪音 / 水汙染

▶ Pollution control has become one of the country's major concerns.
汙染防制已成為該國關切的重要議題之一。

---

10 rot [rɑt] *vt.* 使腐敗 & *vi.* 腐化 & *n.* 腐爛；腐敗

📋 rot, rotted [ˋrɑtɪd], rotted
似 decay [dɪˋke] *vt.* 侵蝕 & *vi.* 腐爛 ⑤

▶ Sweets will rot your teeth if you eat too many of them.
如果你吃太多甜食，可是會蛀牙的。

▶ Fruit rots quickly on such hot days.
大熱天水果會腐爛得很快。

▶ The wood has been weakened by rot.
這塊木頭因為一直腐爛而變得不結實。
＊weaken [ˋwikən] *vt.* 使衰弱

---

rotten [ˋrɑtn̩] *a.* 腐敗的；貪腐的

▶ One rotten apple spoils the barrel.
一粒老鼠屎壞了一鍋粥。—— 諺語
＊barrel [ˋbærəl]
n. (中間鼓起的) 木製大圓桶

▶ The smell of rotten food disgusts me.
腐敗的食物味道令我作嘔。

▶ The rotten official was sentenced to five years in prison.
該貪腐官員被判處五年徒刑。

---

11 rust [rʌst] *n.* 鏽，銹 & *vt.* 使生鏽 & *vi.* 生鏽；荒廢

衍 rusty [ˋrʌstɪ] *a.* 生鏽的；生疏的 ④
似 (1) corrode [kəˋrod] *vt.* 腐蝕
(2) corrosion [kəˋroʒən] *n.* 腐蝕
(3) erode [ɪˋrod] *vt.* 腐蝕
(4) erosion [ɪˋroʒən] *n.* 腐蝕

▶ The old bike is covered with a lot of rust.
這輛老舊的腳踏車上生滿了鏽。
＊be covered in / with...　被⋯⋯覆蓋

▶ The lock on this old safe is rusted. We will have to saw it open.
舊保險箱上的鎖已經生鏽了。我們必須鋸開它。

▶ Iron and gold are different because iron rusts and gold does not.
鐵和黃金不同，因為鐵會生鏽，而黃金不會。

▶ Don't let your talent rust. As they say, use it or lose it.
別讓你的才華荒廢了。誠如大家說的，要好好利用它，否則就會失去它。

---

12 sack [sæk] *n.* 大袋子

📆 (1) hit the sack　睡覺 (口語)
＝ hit the hay (口語)
＝ turn in (口語)
＝ go to bed (正式)

▶ I'm so tired that I think I'll just hit the sack.
我好累，所以我想乾脆去睡覺。

(2) get the sack　被開除
= be sacked
= be fired

▶ Eric got the sack for stealing money from the company.
= Eric was sacked for stealing money from the company.
= Eric was fired for stealing money from the company.
　艾瑞克因為偷公司的錢被開除了。

---

13 **shampoo** [ʃæmˋpu] *n.* 洗髮精 (物質名詞，不可數) & *vt.* 用洗髮精洗髮

延伸 **conditioner** [kənˋdɪʃənɚ]
n. 潤絲精 (物質名詞，不可數)

▶ You should buy a special kind of shampoo for your damaged hair.
　你應該買受損髮質專用的洗髮精。

▶ This brand of shampoo can help get rid of your dandruff.
　這種牌子的洗髮精可幫助你去除頭皮屑。
　＊dandruff [ˋdændrəf] *n.* 頭皮屑

▶ Mary took a shower and shampooed her hair.
　瑪莉淋浴並用洗髮精洗了頭髮。

---

14 **shepherd** [ˋʃɛpɚd] *n.* 牧羊人

延伸 a shepherd dog　牧羊犬

▶ The young shepherd led a flock of sheep up the hill.
　那個年輕的牧羊人把一群羊帶到山坡上。

---

15 **slippery** [ˋslɪpərɪ] *a.* 滑溜溜的

衍 (1) slip [slɪp] *vi.* 滑倒 ②
(2) slipper [ˋslɪpɚ] *n.* 拖鞋 ②

▶ Be careful! The sidewalk is slippery.
　小心！人行道很滑。

---

16 **sorrow** [ˋsoro] *n.* 悲傷

衍 (1) sorrowful [ˋsorəfəl] *a.* 悲傷的 ⑥
(2) sorry [ˋsorɪ] *a.* 難過的 ①
似 grief [grif] *n.* 悲痛，悲傷 ④

▶ To our great sorrow, the doctor said Edward has only another five months to live.
　令我們很難過的是，醫生說愛德華只剩五個月可活。

---

17 **spy** [spaɪ] *n.* 間諜 & *vi.* 偵察 (與介詞 on 並用)

三 spy, spied [spaɪd], spied
片 spy on sb　監視某人
似 detective [dɪˋtɛktɪv] *n.* 偵探；刑警 ④

▶ The spy was caught providing information to the enemy.
　這名間諜在提供情報給敵方時被逮到。

▶ Celebrities always worry about people spying on them.
　名人們總是擔心著有人在監視他們。

- - - - - - - -

scout [skaʊt] *vi.* 偵察，尋找 &
n. 童子軍
似 search [sɝtʃ] *vi.* 尋找 (與 for 並用) ②

▶ I'm scouting around for a school that has a good English learning program.
= I'm looking around for a school that has a good English learning program.
　我在找尋有優良英語學習課程的學校。

209

片 (1) scout for... 尋找……
= search for...
(2) a boy scout 男童軍
a girl scout 女童軍

▶ The boy scouts are taught to do a good deed a day.
這些男童軍被教導要日行一善。
＊deed [did] n. 行為

---

18 tease [tiz] vt. 揶揄

用法 tease sb 揶揄某人
= laugh at sb
= make fun of sb
= pull sb's leg
愚弄某人 (非『扯某人後腿』)

▶ I couldn't help getting angry when I found out John was teasing me.
我發現約翰在揶揄我時，就忍不住生氣了。

---

19 tender [ˈtɛndɚ] a. 溫柔的；(年紀) 稚嫩的

片 at the tender age of + 年齡
以……歲的稚齡

似 gentle [ˈdʒɛntl̩] a. 溫和的 ②

▶ The tender look my mother gave made me smile.
我媽媽溫柔的眼神讓我笑了。

▶ Michael joined the circus at the tender age of seven.
麥可以 7 歲的稚齡就加入馬戲團了。
＊circus [ˈsɝkəs] n. 馬戲團

---

20 trunk [trʌŋk] n. 樹幹；(汽車) 後行李箱；象鼻

延伸 (1) bough [baʊ] n. 大樹枝
branch [bræntʃ] n. 中樹枝 ②
twig [twɪg] n. 小樹枝，嫩枝 ④
(2) 複數形 trunks 則可指籃球員或游泳選手穿的運動褲。
a pair of trunks 一件短運動褲

▶ Some mountain climbers like to carve their names on tree trunks.
有些登山客喜歡把自己的名字刻在樹幹上。

▶ I always keep a first-aid kit in the trunk in case of emergency.
我都會在後車箱放置一個急救箱，以防緊急事故。
＊a first-aid kit 急救箱

▶ An elephant's trunk is flexible, and is used to drink and eat.
象鼻極富彈性，大象用它來喝水及進食。
＊flexible [ˈflɛksəbl̩] a. 有彈性的

---

21 tutor [ˈtjutɚ] n. 家庭教師 & vt. 教導；給……當家庭教師

▶ John's parents are looking for a private tutor to help him with his English.
約翰的父母正在找私人家教來幫助他學英文。

▶ To help support the family, I'm tutoring two junior high school students.
為了幫助養家，我目前擔任家教，教導兩個國中生。

22　**wax** [wæks] *n.* 蠟 & *vt.* 打蠟

延伸 (1) styling wax　髮臘
(2) earwax [ˈɪrˌwæks]
　　n. 耳屎 (不可數)

▶ Wax will become liquid when it is heated.
加熱後的蠟會變成液體狀。

▶ Father reminded me to wax his car after I finished washing it.
老爸提醒我車子洗完後要記得打蠟。

23　**web** [wɛb] *n.* 全球資訊網 (字首大寫) (= the World Wide Web)；蜘蛛網

似 (1) net [nɛt] *n.* 網際網路 (字首大寫)
　　(= the internet)；(捕捉魚、昆蟲
　　等的) 網子 ①
(2) website [ˈwɛbˌsaɪt]
　　n. 網站 (= site) ④
(3) internet [ˈɪntɚˌnɛt]
　　n. 網際網路 ②

▶ Nowadays you can find almost anything you'd like to know on the Web.

= Nowadays you can find almost anything you'd like to know on the Net.
現今你幾乎可在全球資訊網 / 網際網路上找到所有你想知道的東西。

▶ The spider sits back and waits for its prey on the web.
蜘蛛會在蜘蛛網上坐等獵物上門。
＊prey [pre] *n.* 獵物 (集合名詞，不可數)

24　**bulb** [bʌlb] *n.* 電燈泡 (= light bulb)

似 a lamp　一盞燈 (含燈泡及燈罩)

▶ This light bulb gives off purple light, which is creepy.
這個燈泡會發出紫色的光，令人毛骨悚然。
＊creepy [ˈkripɪ] *a.* 令人毛骨悚然的

25　**mist** [mɪst] *n.* 薄霧 & *vt.* 使蒙上薄霧 (與介詞 up 並用)

衍 misty [ˈmɪstɪ] *a.* 陰霾的，模糊不清的
似 (1) fog [fɑg] *n.* 厚霧 ②
(2) foggy [ˈfɑgɪ] *a.* 起大霧的 ③
(3) frost [frɔst] *n.* 霜 ④
(4) smog [smɑg] *n.* 煙霧 ⑤

▶ Because of the mist, we didn't have a clear view of the mountains.
我們因為霧氣而看不清楚山景。

▶ The steam from the kettle misted up the window.
從水壺冒出的水蒸氣使窗戶起霧了。
＊kettle [ˈkɛtl̩] *n.* (煮開水用的) 水壺

26　**organic** [ɔrˈgænɪk] *a.* 有機的

衍 (1) organ [ˈɔrgən] *n.* 器官 ②
(2) organism [ˈɔrgənˌɪzəm]
　　n. 生物，有機體 ⑤

▶ More and more people are eating organic food for the sake of their health.
為了健康的緣故，吃有機食物的人越來越多了。

27　**palm** [pɑm] *n.* 手掌；棕櫚 (樹)

片 (1) palm reading　看手相
(2) read sb's palms　看某人的手相

▶ John gripped the coins tightly in his palm.
約翰把這些錢幣緊緊地握在掌中。

似 fist [fɪst] *n.* 拳 ③

▶ Betty and Tom were strolling under palm trees near the beach.
貝蒂和湯姆在海灘附近的棕櫚樹下散步。

▶ My friend makes a living by practicing astrology and palm reading.
我朋友以占卜及看手相謀生。

28 pat [pæt] *vt. & n.* 輕拍

三 pat, patted [`pætɪd], patted

用 (1) pat sb on the + 身體部位
    拍某人的……

(2) pat sb on the back　鼓勵某人

= give sb a pat on the back

似 tap [tæp] *vt.* 輕拍，輕敲 ③

▶ Stop patting me on the head. I have had enough of it.
別再拍我的頭，我受夠了。

▶ After the presentation, the teacher patted me on the back.

= After the presentation, the teacher gave me a pat on the back.
做完報告之後，老師拍拍我的背給我鼓勵。

29 learning [`lɝnɪŋ] *n.* 學識 (不可數)

衍 (1) learn [lɝn] *vt.* 學習 ①

(2) learned [`lɝnɪd] *a.* 學問淵博的 ④

似 knowledge [`nɑlɪdʒ] *n.* 知識 ①

▶ Professor Koss is a man of great learning.

= Professor Koss is a man of great knowledge.
寇斯教授是一個博學的人。

30 kingdom [`kɪŋdəm] *n.* 王國

衍 king [kɪŋ] *n.* 國王，君主 ①

似 empire [`ɛmpaɪr] *n.* 帝國 ④

延伸 the United Kingdom　大英聯合王國

▶ The king ruled the kingdom for 50 years.
那位國王統治那個王國有五十年之久。

31 industrial [ɪn`dʌstrɪəl] *a.* 工業的

衍 (1) industry [`ɪndəstrɪ] *n.* 工業 ②

(2) industrious [ɪn`dʌstrɪəs]
    a. 勤奮的

= diligent [`dɪlədʒənt] ④

(3) industrialize [ɪn`dʌstrɪəl,aɪz]
    vt. & vi. (使) 工業化 ⑥

(4) industrialist [ɪn`dʌstrɪəlɪst]
    n. 企業家，實業家

延伸 the Industrial Revolution
工業革命

▶ That area of the country is industrial rather than agricultural.
該國那個地區是工業區而非農業區。

＊agricultural [,ægrɪ`kʌltʃərəl] *a.* 農業的

32　humid [ˋhjumɪd] *a.* 溼氣重的

衍 humidity [hjuˋmɪdətɪ]
　　n. 溼氣，溼度 ④

似 (1) damp [dæmp] *a.* 潮溼的 ④
　　(2) moist [mɔɪst] *a.* 潮溼的 ③

▶ In the summer, the weather is generally hot and humid.
夏季時，天氣通常又熱又潮溼。

33　rectangle [ˋrɛktæŋ!] *n.* 長方形

衍 rectangular [rɛkˋtæŋgjələ]
　　a. 長方形的

延伸 (1) square [skwɛr] *n.* 正方形 ①
　　(2) circle [ˋsɝk!] *n.* 圓形 ①
　　(3) triangle [ˋtraɪˏæŋg!] *n.* 三角形 ②
　　(4) diamond [ˋdaɪəmənd] *n.* 菱形 ②

▶ The table is in the shape of a rectangle.
這個餐桌是長方形的。

34　scarce [skɛrs] *a.* 稀少的

衍 (1) scarcely [ˋskɛrslɪ] *adv.* 幾乎不 ④
　　(2) scarcity [ˋskɛrsətɪ] *n.* 稀罕，缺乏

▶ Natural resources, such as timber and oil, are becoming scarce.
像木材和石油等這類的天然資源正日漸稀少。

35　silk [sɪlk] *n.* 絲

衍 silky [ˋsɪlkɪ] *a.* 像絲一樣的

▶ Jessica wore a blue silk dress to the wedding party.
潔西卡穿一件藍色絲質洋裝參加結婚派對。

36　slope [slop] *n.* 斜坡；山坡

用 (1) a steep slope　　陡坡
　　(2) a gentle slope　　緩坡

▶ It is difficult to ride a small motorcycle up a steep slope.
沿著陡坡騎摩托車是很困難的一件事。

37　swan [swɑn] *n.* 天鵝

▶ To everyone's surprise, the ugly duckling has grown up into a beautiful swan.
令大家驚奇的是，那隻醜小鴨已經長大變成了一隻漂亮的天鵝。

38　log [lɔg] *n.* 圓木 & *vt.* 伐 (木)，砍 (樹)

三 log, logged [lɔgd], logged
片 sleep like a log　　睡得很沉
似 (1) wood(s) [wud(z)] *n.* 樹林 ②
　　(2) timber [ˋtɪmbə]
　　　　n. 木材 (= lumber) ③

▶ Dad slept like a log and I couldn't wake him up.
老爸睡得很沉，我叫不醒。

▶ Hundreds of trees have been logged in that forest.
那座森林裡有上百棵樹被砍掉了。

---

1 **chimney** [`tʃɪmnɪ] *n.* 煙囪

片 smoke like a chimney　菸抽個不停

▶ Charlie smoked like a chimney all night, worrying about his missing daughter.
查理整晚菸抽個不停，擔心他失蹤的女兒。

---

2 **clip** [klɪp] *n.* 迴紋針，紙夾 & *vt.* 夾住；剪去，修剪

目 clip, clipped [klɪpt], clipped

延伸 clip 作名詞時指『迴紋針』。pin 指『大頭針』。這些都屬文具。『文具』的英文說法是 stationery [`steʃən,ɛrɪ]，此為集合名詞，不可數。

▶ We need more office stationery for our work.
我們的工作需要更多的文具。

▶ I need some clips to hold these papers together.
我需要一些迴紋針 / 紙夾把這些文件夾在一起。

▶ Mother asked me to clip the receipts together for her.
媽媽要我幫她把這些收據夾起來。

▶ Mr. Smith spent the whole afternoon clipping rose bushes in his backyard.
史密斯先生整個下午都在後院修剪玫瑰叢。

......

tack [tæk] *n.* 圖釘 & *vt.* 用圖釘釘

片 press a tack / thumbtack to the wall
把圖釘按到牆上

似 thumbtack [`θʌm,tæk] *n.* 圖釘

▶ Jack used a tack to fix the note onto the bulletin board.
傑克用圖釘將字條釘在布告欄上。

▶ George got hurt when he tried to tack the letter to the wall.
喬治試著用圖釘把那封信按到牆上的時候弄傷了自己。

---

3 **countable** [`kaʊntəbḷ] *a.* 可數的

衍 countless [`kaʊntlɪs]
a. 難以計算的，數不盡的

反 uncountable [ʌn`kaʊntəbḷ]
a. 不可數的

▶ The word *dog* is a countable noun, whereas the word *water* is an uncountable noun.
*狗*這個字是可數名詞，而*水*這個字則是不可數名詞。

---

4 **dearly** [`dɪrlɪ] *adv.* 非常；昂貴地，付出很大代價地

片 cost sb dearly　花了某人很多錢
= cost sb greatly

似 (1) greatly [`gretlɪ] *adv.* 很，大大地
(2) deeply [`diplɪ] *adv.* 深深地

▶ Henry loves his family dearly. He is willing to do anything for them.
亨利非常愛他的家人。他願意為他們做任何事。

▶ John's arrogance and laziness cost him dearly—he has no job, nor does he have any friends.
約翰的自大和懶惰令他付出慘痛代價 —— 他沒工作，也沒什麼朋友。
＊arrogance [`ærəgəns] *n.* 自大，傲慢

5 energetic [ˌɛnɚˈdʒɛtɪk] *a.* 精力充沛的

衍 energy [ˈɛnɚdʒɪ]
　n. 能源；體力；活力 ②

似 (1) active [ˈæktɪv] *a.* 好動的 ②
　(2) dynamic [daɪˈnæmɪk]
　　a. 有活力的 ④
　(3) vigorous [ˈvɪgərəs]
　　a. 精力充沛的 ⑥

▶ Modern women are energetic, ambitious and, most of all, persistent in the pursuit of their goals.
現代女性有活力，有雄心，而且最重要的是，有毅力追求自己的目標。
*persistent [pɚˈsɪstənt] *a.* 堅持不懈的

6 fairy [ˈfɛrɪ] *n.* 妖精，仙子 & *a.* 妖精 (似) 的，仙子 (似) 的

複 fairies [ˈfɛrɪz]
片 a fairy tale　童話

▶ Fairies are often described in folklore as tiny, mysterious creatures.
民間傳說常把妖精描繪成體型極小且神祕的生物。
*folklore [ˈfokˌlɔr] *n.* 民間傳說 (集合名詞，不可數)
　tiny [ˈtaɪnɪ] *a.* 極小的

▶ Children love to hear fairy tales.
孩子們喜歡聽童話故事。

▶ Jessica liked to dress up as a fairy princess when she was little.
潔西卡小時候喜歡裝扮成仙女般的公主。

7 fireworks [ˈfaɪrˌwɜks] *n.* 煙火 (恆用複數)

片 set off fireworks　放煙火
似 firecrackers [ˈfaɪrˌkrækɚz]
　n. 鞭炮 (恆用複數) ⑥
　set off firecrackers　放鞭炮
用法 通常 firecracker 與 firework 使用於句中時，都要加 s，以表示多數而熱鬧之意。如用單數，則表示只放一個，『碰』的一聲，就無下文，未免單調而小器，故通常無此用法。

▶ Last night's fireworks were really impressive.
昨晚的煙火秀真讓人印象深刻。

▶ In the evening, colorful fireworks were set off along the river in celebration of the National Day.
晚間時分，有人沿著河畔施放五彩繽紛的煙火慶祝國慶。

8 greenhouse [ˈgrinˌhaus] *n.* 溫室

片 the greenhouse effect　溫室效應

▶ The greenhouse effect is raising ocean temperatures worldwide.
溫室效應使得全球海洋持續升溫。

lighthouse [ˈlaɪtˌhaus] *n.* 燈塔

▶ The lighthouse cast a light onto the sea to guide the ships.
燈塔投射一道光到海面上，以指引船隻。
*cast [kæst] *vt.* 投射 (光、影) (三態同形)

9 housekeeper [ˈhaʊsˌkipɚ] *n.* 管家；家庭主婦

似 (1) housewife [ˈhaʊsˌwaɪf]
　　n. 家庭主婦（複數形為 housewives
　　[ˈhaʊsˌwaɪvz]）①
　　(2) butler [ˈbʌtlɚ] *n.* 男管家

▶ Since you are so busy, you should hire a housekeeper to take care of your house.
既然你這麼忙碌，你應該要僱用一名管家照顧你的房子。

10 hairdresser [ˈhɛrˌdrɛsɚ] *n.* 美髮師

衍 (1) hair [hɛr] *n.* 頭髮 ①
　　(2) haircut [ˈhɛrˌkʌt] *n.* 理髮 ②
　　　get a haircut　去理髮 / 剪髮
　　(3) hairdo [ˈhɛrˌdu] *n.* 髮式，髮型
　　= hairstyle [ˈhɛrˌstaɪl] *n.* 髮型

▶ A hairdresser is one whose job is to cut, style, and color people's hair.
美髮師的工作就是為人剪髮、做造型及染髮。

barbershop [ˈbɑrbɚˌʃɑp]
n. (男) 理髮店

衍 barber [ˈbɑrbɚ] *n.* (男) 理髮師 ②
延伸 (1) a beauty parlor　美容院
　　(2) a hair salon　髮廊

▶ Bob swore he would never go to that barbershop again because none of his friends seemed to appreciate his new haircut.
鮑伯發誓再也不去那家理髮店了，因為他朋友似乎都不欣賞他的新髮型。

11 hatch [hætʃ] *vi.* 孵 (蛋) & *vt.* 祕密擬定 & *n.* (飛機、船等的) 艙口，艙門

複 hatches [ˈhætʃɪz]
片 hatch a plan / plot　祕密策劃

▶ The hen is sitting on the eggs waiting for them to hatch.
母雞正坐在蛋上孵這些蛋。

▶ Don't count your chickens before they hatch.
勿打如意算盤。── 諺語

▶ Those people hatched a plan to overthrow the government.
那些人策劃要推翻政府。

▶ The bad guy in the movie opened the hatch and jumped out of the plane.
電影裡的歹徒打開艙門，然後跳出了飛機。

12 hug [hʌg] *n.* & *vt.* 擁抱

三 hug, hugged [hʌgd], hugged
片 give sb a big / warm hug
　　熱情擁抱某人
= give sb a big / warm embrace
似 embrace [ɪmˈbrɛs] *n.* & *vt.* 擁抱 ⑤

▶ John gave his girlfriend a big hug when they met at the airport.
在機場見到女友時，約翰熱情地擁抱她。

▶ Dan's parents hugged him as soon as he returned home after several years' traveling in Asia.
丹在亞洲旅行多年之後，一回到家，他的父母便立刻擁抱他。

13 kangaroo [ˌkæŋgəˈru] *n.* 袋鼠

複 kangaroos [ˌkæŋgəˈruz]

延伸 kangaroo 是澳洲的土生動物，與另一土生動物 koala [koˈɑlə]（無尾熊）已成澳洲的代名詞。

▶ Many tourists have been attacked by wild kangaroos recently.
近來有許多遊客遭到野生袋鼠攻擊。

14 keyboard [ˈkiˌbɔrd] *n.* (電腦、樂器) 鍵盤

片 (1) a computer keyboard　電腦鍵盤
(2) an electronic keyboard　電子琴

▶ This computer keyboard is designed to reduce wrist strain.
這組電腦鍵盤是專門為減少手腕壓力所設計的。
＊wrist [rɪst] *n.* (手) 腕
　strain [stren] *n.* 壓力，過勞

15 kit [kɪt] *n.* 成套工具

片 (1) a first-aid kit　急救箱
(2) a tool kit　工具箱

▶ When you're at home, it's always a good idea to have a first-aid kit handy in case of emergency.
你在家裡隨時都要準備好急救箱以備緊急之需，這種作法一向是個好點子。
＊handy [ˈhændɪ] *a.* 手邊的
　have sth handy　將某物準備妥當可隨時供拿取

16 lace [les] *n.* 蕾絲，花邊 (不可數)；鞋帶 (可數，等於 shoelace) & *vi.* 用花邊等裝飾

片 (1) be trimmed with lace
被以蕾絲裝飾鑲邊
＊trim [trɪm] *vt.* 裝飾 ⑤
(2) a pair of shoelaces　一雙鞋帶

▶ Peggy is wearing a beautiful evening gown which is trimmed with black lace.
佩姬穿著一件有黑色蕾絲鑲邊的美麗晚禮服。

▶ Be careful! Your laces are undone.
小心點！你的鞋帶沒綁好。
＊undone [ʌnˈdʌn] *a.* 未綁緊的，鬆開的

▶ Mary's favorite clothing is a blouse that laces at the front.
瑪莉最喜歡的衣服是前面有花邊的上衣。

17 leak [lik] *vi.* & *n.* 漏 (水、油、瓦斯等)

衍 leaky [ˈlikɪ] *a.* 漏水的

用法 leaking 及 leaky 均表『漏水的』，但前者只能置於 be 動詞之後，作主詞補語；而後者只能用以修飾名詞。

▶ The roof is leaking.
這屋頂漏水。

▶ This is a leaky roof.
這是漏水的屋頂。

▶ Oil was leaking out of the truck.
那輛卡車正在漏油。

▶ Over 50 factory workers were rushed to the hospital due to a gas leak.
由於瓦斯外洩，有五十多名工廠員工被緊急送醫。

18 scrub [skrʌb] vt. 用力擦 & n. 擦洗，擦淨 (恆為單數)

目 scrub, scrubbed [skrʌbd], scrubbed

片 give the floor / the table a good scrub
使勁擦地板 / 桌子

似 mop [mɑp] vt. 用拖把拖 & n. 拖把 ②

▶ Julie was busy scrubbing the floor while her husband prepared dinner.
茱莉忙著刷洗地板，而老公則在煮晚餐。

▶ Jane told her husband to give the floors a good scrub.
珍叫她先生要使勁擦地板。

19 scarf [skɑrf] n. 圍巾

複 scarfs [skɑrfs] / scarves [skɑrvz]

▶ The scarf you're wearing looks great. Where did you get it?
你戴的這條圍巾真好看。哪兒買的？

20 pearl [pɝl] n. 珍珠

片 (1) a string of pearls 一串珍珠
(2) cast pearls before swine
對牛彈琴；暴殄天物

*swine [swaɪn] n. 豬 (單複數同形，複數亦可寫成 swines；本片語中的 swine 是複數) 本片語字面的意思為『在豬前面投擲珍珠而豬卻不識貨』。

衍 pearly [ˋpɝlɪ] a. 如珍珠般的

▶ Susan has pearly white teeth.
蘇珊有一口潔白的牙齒。

▶ I bought this pearl necklace at a bargain price.
我用很便宜的價錢買到了這串珍珠項鍊。

▶ I bought John a very good English dictionary, and he now uses it as a pillow. It was just like casting pearls before swine.
我買了本很好的英文字典給約翰，他現在卻把它當枕頭用，真是暴殄天物啊。

21 poster [ˋpostɚ] n. 海報

片 put up a poster 貼海報

▶ Mary put up a poster of Madonna on the wall.
瑪莉在牆上貼上瑪丹娜的海報。

22 sausage [ˋsɔsɪdʒ] n. 香腸

▶ This restaurant is famous for its German sausages and beer.
這家餐廳以它的德國香腸和啤酒聞名。

23 shovel [ˋʃʌvl] n. 鏟子 & vt. 鏟 (雪)

衍 shove [ʃʌv] vt. 推，撞 ⑤
shove sb out of the way
把某人推開使他不擋路

似 spade [sped] n. 鏟子 ④

▶ John used a shovel to shovel the snow away from his front door.
約翰用鏟子把前門的積雪剷除。

24 spice [spaɪs] *n.* 香料；情趣，風味 & *vt.* 加香料於……；為……增添趣味 (與介詞 up 並用)

衍 spicy [ˈspaɪsɪ] *a.* 辛辣的；加香料的 ⑤
spicy food　辛辣的食物

▶ The chef told Peter that he could add some spices to his foods.
廚師告訴彼得可以在食物中添加一些香料。

▶ The cook spiced the food with cinnamon.
廚師用肉桂來為這食物調味。
*cinnamon [ˈsɪnəmən] *n.* 肉桂

▶ Lisa and Steve are trying to spice up their marriage.
麗莎和史提夫想為他們的婚姻生活增添一些情趣。

▶ Variety is the spice of life.
變化是人生的香料 / 生活應有變化才有情趣。── 諺語

25 starve [stɑrv] *vt.* 使飢餓 & *vi.* 挨餓

片 be starving / starved to death
快要餓死了 (誇張用語，喻『很餓』)

衍 starvation [stɑrˈveʃən]
n. 飢餓；飢荒 ⑥

▶ All the prisoners of war here have been starved and ill-treated.
這裡所有的戰犯都沒飯可吃，而且還被虐待。

▶ These poor kids are starving to death. Do you have any food?
這些可憐的孩子餓壞了。你有什麼吃的嗎？

26 sting [stɪŋ] *vt.* 刺，螫，叮 & *n.* 螫針；刺；螫傷處〔英〕

三 sting, stung [stʌŋ], stung
衍 stinger [ˈstɪŋɚ]
n. (昆蟲或動物的) 刺，螫針〔美〕

▶ Stay away from the bees. They might sting you.
離那些蜜蜂遠一點。牠們可能會螫你。

▶ The insect may be small, but it has a powerful sting.
這隻昆蟲也許體型很小，不過牠有一根強而有力的螫針。

▶ Robert had several bee stings after his walk in the park.
羅伯特在公園散步後被蜜蜂螫了幾下。

27 tame [tem] *a.* 溫馴的 & *vt.* 馴服

似 (1) obedient [əˈbidjənt] *a.* 服從的 ④
(2) docile [ˈdɑsl] *a.* 馴服的
反 wild [waɪld] *a.* 野的 ②

▶ Strange to say, the wild horse became very tame as soon as it saw me.
說來奇怪，那頭野馬一見到我就變得溫馴極了。

▶ It takes skill and a lot of energy to tame a wild horse.
馴服野馬需要技巧和充沛的體力。

28 thirst [θɝst] *n.* 口渴 (不可數)；渴望 (恆為單數) & *vi.* 渴望

片 (1) quench one's thirst　止渴
(2) thirst for sth　渴望獲得某物
= long for sth

▶ I need a glass of water to quench my thirst.
我需要一杯水止渴。

219

衍 **thirsty** [ˈθɝstɪ] *a.* 口渴的；渴望的 ②

▸ Rebecca goes to the library in her free time to quench her thirst for knowledge.

= Rebecca goes to the library in her free time to satisfy her thirst for knowledge.

蕾貝卡有空時就到圖書館去，以滿足其求知慾。

▸ We all thirst for peace.

我們大家都渴望和平。

---

29 tow [to] *vt.* 拖，拉 & *n.* 拖，拉；牽引

用 (1) tow sth away 將某物拖 (吊) 走
(2) give sb / sth a tow 把……拖走

▸ All illegally parked cars are to be towed away.

違規停車的車輛全部要被拖吊。

▸ When my car broke down, a kind man offered to give me a tow.

我的汽車拋錨時，有個好心人幫忙把我的車拖走。

---

30 vase [ves / vɑs] *n.* 花瓶

用 a vase of flowers 一瓶花

▸ I bumped into a table and broke a vase.

我撞到桌子，打破了一個花瓶。

---

31 lollipop [ˈlɑlɪˌpɑp] *n.* 棒棒糖

▸ You should brush your teeth after eating the lollipop, Johnny.

強尼，吃完棒棒糖後應該要去刷牙。

---

32 teenage [ˈtinˌedʒ] *a.* 青少年的 (= teenaged [ˈtinˌedʒd])

衍 (1) teenager [ˈtinedʒɚ] *n.* 青少年 ①
(2) teen(s) [tin(z)] *n.* 青少年時代 (複數) & *a.* 青少年的 ②

似 adolescent [ˌædlˈɛsn̩t] *a.* 青少年的 & *n.* 青少年 ⑤

▸ My teenage daughter loves rock 'n' roll.

我正值青春期的女兒熱愛搖滾樂。

---

33 tank [tæŋk] *n.* 坦克車；槽；油箱

用 (1) a water tank 水箱
(2) a fuel tank 燃料箱
(3) a gas tank 油箱

衍 tanker [ˈtæŋkɚ] *n.* 油輪

▸ The tank smashed through the building at a high speed.

坦克車以高速衝進大樓。

▸ We need to clean the water tank this weekend.

這個週末我們要清洗水塔。

▸ We should fill the tank with gas before we set out.

出發前我們應該把油箱加滿。

34 bacteria [bæk`tɪrɪə] *n.* 細菌 (複數)

單 bacterium [bæk`tɪrɪəm]
似 (1) germ [dʒɝm] *n.* 細菌，病菌 ④
(2) virus [`vaɪrəs]
　　n. 病毒，濾過性病毒 ④

▶ Handrails are covered in / with bacteria.
扶手上都是細菌。
＊handrail [`hænd͵rel] *n.* 扶手

35 bay [be] *n.* 海灣

片 keep sb at bay　與某人保持距離
= keep sb at a distance
似 gulf [gʌlf] *n.* 海灣 (複數形為 gulfs)

▶ Polly lives in a beautiful mansion overlooking the bay.
波莉住在一棟美麗的豪宅，可以俯瞰整個海灣。
＊mansion [`mænʃən] *n.* 豪宅

▶ Believing that Peter is not a nice guy, Mary's father asked her to keep him at bay.
瑪莉的父親認為彼得不是個好人，要她與他保持距離。

36 bomb [bam] *n.* 炸彈 & *vt.* 轟炸

片 a bomb squad　炸彈拆除小組
衍 (1) bomber [`bamɚ]
　　n. 轟炸機；炸彈客
(2) bombard [bam`bard] *vt.* 轟炸
似 (1) mine [maɪn] *n.* 地雷 ①
(2) missile [`mɪsl̩] *n.* 飛彈 ③

▶ The time bomb went off at 10, killing all the people around.
那枚定時炸彈在 10 點鐘引爆，周圍所有的人全部喪生。

▶ The terrorists bombed the city again.
恐怖分子又再次轟炸這座城市。

37 cave [kev] *n.* 山洞

延 a cave-in　礦坑崩塌；礦坑災變

▶ The cave was dark and scary.
這個山洞既黑且嚇人。

38 flute [flut] *n.* 長笛

片 play the flute　吹笛子

▶ John plays the flute very well.
約翰笛子吹得很好。

39 razor [`rezɚ] *n.* 剃刀；刮鬍刀

片 a razor blade　刮鬍刀 (片)
似 shaver [`ʃevɚ]
　　n. 刮鬍刀 (尤指電動刮鬍刀)
延 blade [bled] *n.* 刀鋒 ④

▶ I bought some disposable razors for my trip overseas.
為了要海外旅遊，我買了一些拋棄式刮鬍刀。
＊disposable [dɪ`spozəbl̩] *a.* 用過即丟的
　disposable chopsticks　免洗筷

▶ The razor blade is dull, so you have to replace it with a new one.
這片刮鬍刀片鈍了，你需要更換一片新的。

40 magnet [ˈmægnɪt] *n.* 磁鐵

衍 magnetic [mæɡˈnɛtɪk]
a. 磁石的；磁場的；有吸引力的 ④

▶ The boy picked up the nails with a magnet.
男孩子用一塊磁鐵吸起這些釘子。

| Level ④ |

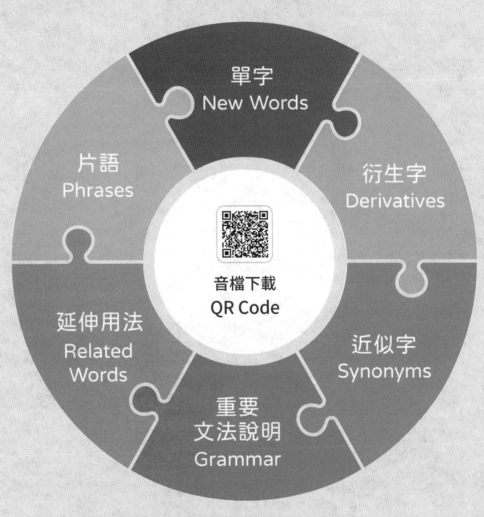

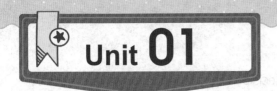

0101-0104

1 involve [ɪnˋvɑlv] *vt.* 使涉入；包含，需要

片 **be involved in...** 涉入……

▶ The evidence shows that Paul is involved in that murder.
證據顯示保羅涉入那起謀殺案。

▶ Kyle's plan involves some creative ideas.
凱爾的計畫中包含一些有創意的點子。

involvement [ɪnˋvɑlvmənt]
n. 牽涉 (不可數)

▶ Employee involvement is a big step for the company.
員工投入是這家公司的一大進展。

participation [pɑr͵tɪsəˋpeʃən]
n. 參加

衍 (1) **participate** [pɑrˋtɪsə͵pet]
vi. 參加 ②
(2) **participant** [pɑrˋtɪsəpənt]
n. 參與者 ⑤

▶ Teachers encourage student participation in school affairs.
老師都會鼓勵學生參與學務。

2 community [kəˋmjunətɪ] *n.* 社區；界，共同利益團體

比 **neighborhood** [ˋnebɚ͵hʊd]
n. 鄰近地區 ③

▶ There is a shopping mall in my neighborhood.
我住的附近有一家購物中心。

▶ I live in a small community outside the city.
我住在城外的一個小社區裡。

▶ The medical community is sparing no effort to promote human health.
醫學界正不遺餘力提升人類的健康。

3 informative [ɪnˋfɔrmətɪv] *a.* 有內容的；能增進知識的

衍 **information** [͵ɪnfɚˋmeʃən]
n. 消息，資料 (不可數，有時縮寫成 info [ˋɪnfo]) ③

似 **educational** [͵ɛdʒʊˋkeʃənḷ]
a. 有教育意義的 ③

= **illuminating** [ɪˋlumə͵netɪŋ]
a. 有啟發性的

= **inspiring** [ɪnˋspaɪrɪŋ] *a.* 激勵人心的

▶ Mr. Johnson's speech was quite informative.
強森先生的演講頗有內容。

▶ Tom found the television program quite informative.
湯姆發現這個電視節目蠻具教育性的。

4 economy [ɪˋkɑnəmɪ] *n.* 經濟；節儉

似 **frugality** [fruˋgælətɪ] *n.* 節儉

▶ The economy of this country seems to be improving.
這個國家的經濟似乎正在好轉。

▶ Several decisions about the economy were made by us in order to save money.
為了節省開支，我們做了好幾樣省錢的決定。

economic [ˌɛkəˈnɑmɪk]
a. 與經濟有關的

⚑ an economic development
　經濟發展

▶ Mary's economic problems started when she got divorced.
瑪莉離婚時，經濟方面的問題就產生了。

economical [ˌɛkəˈnɑmɪkḷ]
a. 合乎經濟效益的，節省的

似 frugal [ˈfrugḷ] *a.* 節省的

▶ It's more economical to buy food in large quantities.
大量購買食物比較划算。

economics [ˌɛkəˈnɑmɪks]
n. 經濟學

延伸 也有人將 economic、economical、economics 分別唸成 [ˌikəˈnɑmɪk]、[ˌikəˈnɑmɪkḷ]、及 [ˌikəˈnɑmɪks]。

▶ I majored in economics while I was in college.
我念大學時主修經濟學。

economist [ɪˈkɑnəmɪst]
n. 經濟學家

▶ Economists estimate a slow growth in the global economy.
經濟學家預估全球經濟將有緩慢的成長。

5　facial [ˈfeʃəl] *a.* 臉的，面部的 & *n.* 面部美容護理

⚑ (1) a facial massage　臉部按摩
　 (2) do a facial　　　做臉

▶ Sue had a strange facial expression when she tasted this dish.
蘇吃這道菜時臉上有奇怪的表情。

▶ To keep young and beautiful, the lady goes to the beauty parlor for a facial massage every week.
為了永保青春美麗，這位女士每週都到美容院做臉部按摩。

▶ My wife does a facial every now and then.
我太太偶爾會做臉。

6　evidence [ˈɛvədəns] *n.* 證據（集合名詞，不可數）& *vt.* 證明

⚑ ..., as (is) evidenced by...
　……可以作證

用法 an evidence (×)
→ a piece of evidence (○)　一項證據

▶ We have found a lot of evidence against John.
我們發現很多不利於約翰的證據。

▶ The king loves the queen very much, as evidenced by a large palace he built for her.
國王非常愛皇后，他為她建造的這座大皇宮可以作證。

evident [`ˈɛvədənt`] *a.* 明顯的

衍 **evidently** [`ˈɛvədəntlɪ`] *adv.* 明顯地

似 (1) **obvious** [`ˈɑbvɪəs`] *a.* 明顯的 ②
(2) **apparent** [`əˈpærənt`] *a.* 顯然的 ④

▶ It's evident that Alan committed the murder.
顯然艾倫犯了這樁謀殺案。

7　establish [`ɪˈstæblɪʃ`] *vt.* 建立，創立

片 **establish sth**　建立某物
= **set up sth**

衍 **established** [`ɪˈstæblɪʃt`]
a. 名聲穩固的
an established writer
名聲屹立不搖的作家

▶ The company was established in 1988.
這家公司於 1988 年創立。

establishment [`ɪˈstæblɪʃmənt`]
n. 建立

似 **foundation** [`faʊnˈdeʃən`] *n.* 建立 ④

▶ The establishment of Mike's own business was the turning point in his life.
自行創業是麥克人生的轉捩點。

8　including [`ɪnˈkludɪŋ`] *prep.* 包括 (= inclusive of)

衍 (1) **include** [`ɪnˈklud`] *vt.* 包含，包括 ②
(2) **inclusive** [`ɪnˈklusɪv`] *a.* 包含的，
包括的 (與介詞 of 並用) ⑥

反 **excluding** [`ɪkˈskludɪŋ`] *prep.* 不包括
= **exclusive of...**

▶ Five passengers were injured in the accident, including a pregnant woman.
= Five passengers were injured in the accident, inclusive of a pregnant woman.
= Five passengers were injured in the accident, a pregnant woman included.
5 名乘客在意外中受傷，包括一名孕婦在內。
＊換言之，上列句中名詞前可使用 including 或 inclusive of，名詞後則使用過去分詞 included。

9　defend [`dɪˈfɛnd`] *vt.* 防禦；辯護

片 **defend sb/sth against...**
保護某人 / 某事物免受……；為……替
某人 / 某事物做辯護

衍 **defendant** [`dɪˈfɛndənt`] *n.* 被告 ⑤

反 (1) **attack** [`əˈtæk`] *vt.* 攻擊 ①
(2) **offend** [`əˈfɛnd`] *vt.* 冒犯 ④

▶ The villagers struggled to defend their homeland.
村民們奮力保衛家園。

▶ The singer held a press conference to defend herself against the rumor.
這名歌手召開記者會，為流言替她自己做辯護。

defense [`dɪˈfɛns`] *n.* 防禦；辯護

片 **in defense of...**　以保護 / 辯護……

反 **offense** [`əˈfɛns`] *n.* 攻擊；犯罪 ④

▶ The best defense is offense.
攻擊是最佳的防禦。—— 諺語

▶ The lawyer spoke in defense of his client's innocence.
律師發話為委託訴訟人的無辜做辯護。

Level 4　Unit 01

defensive [dɪˈfɛnsɪv] *a.* 防禦性的
反 **offensive** [əˈfɛnsɪv] *a.* 攻擊性的 ④

▶ We need both defensive and offensive weapons to face attacks from neighboring countries.
我們需要防禦性及攻擊性的武器以對抗鄰國的攻擊。

defensible [dɪˈfɛnsəbḷ] *a.* 可防禦的

▶ A castle built on a high mountain is easily defensible.
興建在高山上的城堡容易防禦。

10 **associate** [əˈsoʃɪˌet] *vt.* 使有關聯 & *vi.* 交往

片 (1) be associated with...
與……有關
= be connected to / with...
(2) associate with sb　與某人來往

▶ Lung cancer is mostly associated with smoking.
肺癌大多與吸菸有關。

▶ If I were you, I wouldn't associate with that guy. He's a gangster.
如果我是你的話，我不會和那名男子有所往來。他是幫派分子。

associate [əˈsoʃɪt] *n.* 合夥人 & *a.* 副的
似 **partner** [ˈpɑrtnɚ] *n.* 夥伴，合夥人 ②

▶ Jason is one of my business associates.
傑森是我的事業夥伴之一。

▶ Maggie is the associate editor of that magazine.
瑪姬是那本雜誌的副編輯。

association [əˌsosɪˈeʃən] *n.* 協會；聯合

片 in association with...
與……聯合 / 合作
= in cooperation with...

▶ We decided to set up an association of photography lovers.
我們決定成立一個攝影愛好者協會。

▶ The exhibition was sponsored by the government in association with local businesses.
這場展覽是由政府聯合當地企業贊助舉辦的。

11 **equip** [ɪˈkwɪp] *vt.* 配備 (常用被動語態)

變 equip, equipped [ɪˈkwɪpt], equipped
片 be equipped with...　配備有……

▶ All the classrooms are equipped with state-of-the-art facilities.
所有的教室都配有最先進的設備。

equipment [ɪˈkwɪpmənt] *n.* 裝備 (集合名詞，不可數)

片 (1) a piece of equipment　一件裝備
(2) a lot of equipment　很多裝備

▶ This camera is the most important piece of equipment I have.
這臺相機是目前我擁有最重要的一項配備。

12 **research** [ˈrisɝtʃ / rɪˈsɝtʃ] *n.* 研究 (不可數)

片 do / conduct research about / on...
做有關……的研究

▶ Scientists are still conducting research on global warming.
科學家仍在進行全球暖化的研究。

research [rɪˈsɝtʃ] *vt.* 研究
似 study [ˈstʌdɪ] *vt.* 研究 ①

▸ Pam researched her family's history, tracing it back to the 1500s.
小潘研究她的家族史，可追溯到 16 世紀。
＊the 1500s　16 世紀

researcher [rɪˈsɝtʃɚ] *n.* 研究員

▸ Researchers have found that eating more vegetables is conducive to good health.
研究人員已經發現多吃青菜有益健康。
＊conducive [kənˈdusɪv] *a.* 有益的

13　physical [ˈfɪzɪkl] *a.* 身體的，生理的；物理的 & *n.* 健康檢查

片 (1) a physical law　物理定律
(2) have a physical checkup
　　做身體檢查
＝ have a physical
反 mental [ˈmɛntl] *a.* 心理的 ③

▸ Laura has been suffering from constant physical pain.
蘿拉飽受持續不斷的身體病痛。

▸ The Law of Gravity is one of the most basic physical laws you should know.
萬有引力定律是你應該知道的最基本物理定律之一。
＊gravity [ˈɡrævətɪ] *n.* 地心引力

▸ You should have a physical (checkup) regularly.
你應該要定期做健康檢查。

physically [ˈfɪzɪklɪ] *adv.* 身體上
片 stay physically and mentally healthy　保持身心健康
反 mentally [ˈmɛntlɪ] *adv.* 心理上

▸ To stay physically and mentally healthy, you need to exercise regularly.
＝ To stay healthy in both body and mind, you need to exercise regularly.
要保持身心健康，你就必須規律運動。

physician [fɪˈzɪʃən]
n. 醫師 (尤指內科)
似 surgeon [ˈsɝdʒən] *n.* 外科醫師 ④

▸ The physician ordered the patient to stay in bed for 3 days.
醫師囑咐病人必須待在床上 3 天。

physics [ˈfɪzɪks] *n.* 物理學

▸ The Nobel Prize winner used to teach physics at a famous university in California.
這位諾貝爾獎得主曾在加州某知名大學教過物理學。

physicist [ˈfɪzɪsɪst] *n.* 物理學家

▸ Through hard work, Marvin finally became a world-famous physicist.
馬文經由努力終於成了世界知名的物理學家。

14　authority [əˈθɔrətɪ] *n.* 權威 (不可數)；權威人士 (可數)；有關當局 (恆用複數)

片 (1) have authority over...
　　有支配……的權力 / 權威

▸ Our parents have authority over us when we are young.
小時候，父母可完全支配我們。

(2) an authority on...
在……方面的權威人士

▶ My cousin is an authority on photography.
我表哥在攝影方面是個權威。

(3) the authorities (concerned)
有關當局

▶ The authorities concerned should take immediate action to deal with the problem.
有關當局應立刻採取行動處理此問題。

衍 authorize [ˈɔθəˌraɪz]
vt. 授權；認可 ⑤

15 district [ˈdɪstrɪkt] n. (行政) 區

似 (1) zone [zon] n. 地帶，地區 ③
(2) area [ˈɛrɪə] n. 地區 ①

▶ Which district of the city do you live in?
你住在這座城市的哪一區？

16 labor [ˈlebɚ] n. 勞動，勞力；分娩 & vi. 勞動，工作

片 be in labor   分娩中

衍 laborer [ˈlebərɚ] n. 勞動者

似 (1) work [wɝk] n. & vi. 工作 ①
(2) toil [tɔɪl] n. & vi. 辛苦工作，苦幹

▶ Wages for unskilled labor are usually not very high.
非技術性勞力的薪資通常不會很高。

▶ Kate was in labor for almost four hours before she gave birth to a healthy baby boy.
凱特分娩了將近四個小時才生下一個健康的男寶寶。

▶ George labored late into the night in order to finish his report.
為了完成他的報告，喬治工作到很晚。

17 extend [ɪkˈstɛnd] vt. 延伸；擴大

衍 (1) extension [ɪkˈstɛnʃən]
n. 延長；電話分機 ⑤

▶ Call me at 1234567, extension 10.
請撥電話給我，電話是 1234567，分機 10。

(2) extensive [ɪkˈstɛnsɪv]
a. 廣泛的；大量的 ⑤

似 lengthen [ˈlɛŋθən]
vt. 延長，使加長 ④

▶ I'd like to extend my stay another two days.
我想多待兩天。

▶ We have decided to extend our house by adding a dining room.
我們已決定增加飯廳擴建房子。

extent [ɪkˈstɛnt] n. 程度

片 to a(n)... extent / degree
到……的程度

衍 (1) degree [dɪˈgri] n. 程度 ②
(2) level [ˈlɛvl] n. 程度 ①

▶ I love Connie to such an extent that without her I couldn't live.
我愛康妮到沒有她我就活不下去的程度。

230

18 productive [prəˈdʌktɪv] *a.* 多產的；富有成效的

衍 (1) produce [prəˈdjus] *vt.* 生產 ②
(2) producer [prəˈdjusɚ]
n. 生產者；製作人 ③
(3) production [prəˈdʌkʃən]
n. 生產；(電影) 製片 ②
(4) product [ˈprɑdʌkt]
n. 產品；成果，結果 ③
(5) productivity [ˌprɑdʌkˈtɪvətɪ]
n. 生產力 ⑤

似 prolific [prəˈlɪfɪk] *a.* 多產的

▶ All bosses like productive employees.
所有的老闆都喜歡有生產力的員工。

▶ Nick had a productive day at work, so he treated himself to a beer.
尼克因工作富有成效，所以他請自己喝一杯啤酒。

19 obtain [əbˈten] *vt.* 獲得，把……弄到手

似 get [gɛt] *vt.* 獲得 ①

▶ The latest bus timetable can be obtained at the tourist center.
最新的公車時刻表可在遊客中心索取。

acquire [əˈkwaɪr] *vt.* 獲得

衍 (1) acquisition [ˌækwəˈzɪʃən]
n. 獲得；獲得物 ⑤
(2) acquired [əˈkwaɪrd]
a. 後天習得的；後天獲得的

▶ Dancing is an acquired skill.
跳舞是後天習得的技巧。

▶ AIDS is short for acquired immune deficiency syndrome.
愛滋病是後天性免疫不全症候群的縮寫。

▶ David acquired the skills needed to become a surgeon.
大衛習得了當外科醫生所必備的技術。

20 mere [mɪr] *a.* 僅僅的

片 a mere + 數字   僅僅若干……
= merely + 數字
= only + 數字

衍 merely [ˈmɪrlɪ] *adv.* 僅僅

▶ Lucy was a mere child when her parents got divorced.
露西的父母離婚時她還只是個小孩子。

▶ We need a mere $30,000 to set up a radio station.
我們設立一座廣播電臺只需要 3 萬美元就行了。

21 persuasive [pɚˈswesɪv] *a.* 有說服力的

似 convincing [kənˈvɪnsɪŋ]
a. 使人信服的

▶ John made a powerful and persuasive speech at the meeting.
會議中約翰發表了一篇措詞有力且具說服力的演講。

Level 4 Unit 01

persuasion [pəˈsweʒən]
n. 說服（不可數）；信念（可數）

衍 persuade [pəˈswed] *vt.* 說服 ③

▶ Paul is skilled in the art of persuasion and always gets what he wants.
保羅精通說服的藝術，總是會得到他想要的東西。

▶ The club is famous for welcoming people of all political persuasions.
這間俱樂部因歡迎所有政治理念的人而聞名。

22 relieve [rɪˈliv] *vt.* 減輕；緩和

衍 relief [rɪˈlif] *n.* 解除；減輕 ③
似 soothe [suð] *vt.* 緩和；安慰 ⑥

▶ Aspirin will relieve your headache.
阿斯匹靈會減輕你的頭痛。

▶ The government will take steps to relieve unemployment.
政府將採取措施來緩和失業的現象。

23 addict [əˈdɪkt] *vt.* 使上癮（與介詞 to 並用）& [ˈædɪkt] *n.* 上癮的人

片 be / become addicted to + N/V-ing 對……上癮
似 addiction [əˈdɪkʃən] *n.* 上癮 ⑥

▶ The movie star became addicted to alcohol after her divorce and the death of her son.
這名影星自從離婚加上她兒子過世後，就沉迷於嗜酒了。

▶ Drug addicts pose potential threats to society as a whole.
吸毒者對整個社會造成潛在的威脅。
＊pose a threat to... 對……造成威脅

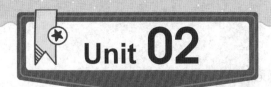

Level 4　Unit 02

1 observation [ˌɑbzɚˈveʃən] *n.* 觀察

衍 (1) observe [əbˈzɝv] *vt.* 觀察；遵守 ③
(2) observer [əbˈzɝvɚ] *n.* 觀察員 ⑤
(3) observance [əbˈzɝvəns]
　　n. 遵守；慶祝
　　in observance of the holiday
　　慶祝節日
= in celebration of the holiday

► Ray is a man of keen observation but of few words.
雷是個觀察敏銳卻不多言的人。

2 proceed [prəˈsid] *vi.* 前進；繼續

衍 (1) process [ˈprɑsɛs] *n.* 過程 ③
(2) proceedings [prəˈsidɪŋz]
　　n. (一系列的) 活動 / 事件；會議紀錄 (皆恆用複數)
(3) proceeds [ˈprosidz] *n.* 收益 (複數)

► All passengers should proceed to Gate 2 for boarding.
所有乘客應前往 2 號登機門登機。

► Please proceed with your explanation.
= Please continue with your explanation.
請繼續你的說明。

procedure [prəˈsidʒɚ] *n.* 程序

► What is the procedure for replacing a lost passport?
辦理護照遺失申請的手續為何？

3 congress [ˈkɑŋgrəs] *n.* 國會 (大寫，尤指美國國會)；代表大會

衍 (1) congressman [ˈkɑŋgrəsmən]
　　n. (美國) 國會議員 ⑥
(2) congresswoman
　　[ˈkɑŋgrəsˌwumən] *n.* (美國) 女國會議員 ⑥

似 parliament [ˈpɑrləmənt]
n. 議會；英國國會 (大寫) ⑥

► The United States Congress consists of the House of Representatives and the Senate.
美國國會是由眾議院及參議院組成。

► Dr. Brown's speech at the medical congress won the respect of his peers.
布朗博士在醫學代表大會上的演講贏得了同儕的尊敬。

council [ˈkaʊnsl] *n.* 議會

片 a city council　市議會

衍 councilman [ˈkaʊnslmən] *n.* 議員

► Rita sent an email to the council to complain about air pollution.
麗塔寄了封電子郵件給議會，抱怨空氣汙染一事。

► The City Council met every day last week to discuss how to cut down on water pollution.
上星期市議會每天都開會討論減少水汙染之道。

4 demand [dɪˈmænd] *vt. & n.* 要求，請求

片 (1) sb demand / require / request that S (+ should) + V
某人要求……

► The teacher demands / requires / requests that his students (should) be quiet when he speaks.
老師要求學生在他講話時要保持安靜。

(2) **meet one's demands**
達到某人的要求

▶ The firm does all it can to meet its customers' demands.
這家公司盡其所能以達到顧客的需求。

(3) **be in demand** 有需求

(4) **on demand** 備索，有人要求就給

▶ Good software engineers are in great demand these days.
這年頭需要大量優秀的軟體工程師。

▶ We have a lot of free pamphlets on demand.
我們有很多免費小冊子備索。
＊pamphlet [ˋpæmflɪt] *n.* 小冊子

demanding [dɪˋmændɪŋ] *a.* 苛求的

似 (1) **strict** [strɪkt] *a.* 嚴格的 ②

(2) **tough** [tʌf] *a.* 嚴厲的 ③

(3) **harsh** [harʃ] *a.* 嚴厲的 ④

▶ The demanding boss frightens all his employees.
這位苛求的老闆令他所有的員工害怕。

5　reflect [rɪˋflɛkt] *vt.* 反射；反應 & *vi.* 思考（與介詞 on 並用）

片 **reflect on...** 思考／反省……

衍 **reflective** [rɪˋflɛktɪv]
a. 反光的；反映的 ⑥

▶ The mirror reflects sunlight.
鏡子會反射陽光。

▶ The polls have reflected that welfare is the top issue with voters.
這些民調反應出福利制度才是選民關注的首要議題。

▶ We took a moment to reflect on what we were about to do.
我們花了片刻時間思考我們要怎麼做。

---

reflection [rɪˋflɛkʃən]
n. 反射；熟思

似 **consideration** [kənˏsɪdəˋreʃən]
n. 考慮 ②

▶ An echo is a reflection of sound.
回音是聲音的反射作用。

▶ After some reflection, I decided to accept Benjamin's offer.
經過一番考慮後，我決定接受班傑明的提議。

6　refer [rɪˋfɝ] *vi.* 言及，提到；查（字典）（皆與介詞 to 並用）

三 **refer, referred** [rɪˋfɝd], **referred**

片 **refer to the dictionary / phone book**
= **consult the dictionary / phone book** 查字典／電話簿

衍 **referee** [ˏrɛfəˋri] *n.* 裁判 ⑥

似 (1) **mention** [ˋmɛnʃən] *vt.* 提及 ②

(2) **look up sth**
查某事物（以被查的對象作受詞）

▶ Professor Wright didn't like anyone referring to his artificial arm.
萊特教授不喜歡任何人提到他的義肢。
＊artificial [ˏartəˋfɪʃəl] *a.* 人工的

▶ I referred to the dictionary for a definition.
= I consulted the dictionary for a definition.
我查字典找一個字的定義。

▶ If you don't know the word, you can look it up in the dictionary.
你若不懂這個字，可以在字典裡查它。

---

reference [ˈrɛfərəns]
n. 參考；言及，提到

🔑 (1) a reference book　參考書
(2) make reference to...
提到，言及……
= refer to...
= mention...

衍 referendum [ˌrɛfəˈrɛndəm]
n. 公投 ⑥

▶ A dictionary is a reference book.
字典是一種參考書。

▶ The speaker made reference to some events of the past year.
演講者提到去年發生的一些大事。

7　conference [ˈkɑnfərəns] *n.* 會議

🔑 a press conference　記者會
= a news conference

似 meeting [ˈmitɪŋ] *n.* 會議 ①

▶ The press conference is scheduled for 2 p.m. today.
記者會預定在今天下午 2 點召開。

8　circumstance [ˈsɝkəmˌstæns] *n.* 情況，環境 (常用複數)

🔑 Under no circumstances + 倒裝句
絕不……
= By no means + 倒裝句
= In no way + 倒裝句
= On no account + 倒裝句

▶ James only lies under certain circumstances.
詹姆士只會在特定情況下說謊。

▶ Under no circumstances will I apologize to that guy.
我絕對不會向那個傢伙道歉。
＊apologize [əˈpɑləˌdʒaɪz] *vi.* 道歉
apologize to sb (for sth)　(因某事) 向某人道歉

9　profession [prəˈfɛʃən] *n.* 職業 (尤指需要高等教育的職業，如律師、編輯、工程師等)

衍 professor [prəˈfɛsɚ] *n.* (大學) 教授 ③
似 (1) career [kəˈrɪr]
n. 職業 (尤指終身職業) ③
(2) occupation [ˌɑkjəˈpeʃən]
n. 一般職業 ④

▶ In the medical profession, it is common for doctors to work very long hours.
在醫療專業領域，醫師工時長是很正常的。

---

professional [prəˈfɛʃənl]
a. 專業的，職業的 ＆ *n.* 專家；職業選手
(作名詞時，縮寫為 pro [pro])

反 amateur [ˈæməˌtʃɚ / ˈæməˌtʃur]
a. 業餘的 ＆ *n.* 業餘從事者 ④

▶ Though Mr. Bagnell was once a professional TV comedian, he is now a politician in California.
巴格諾先生曾是職業的電視諧星，不過現在卻成了加州的政治人物。

▶ I'm a professional. It won't take me long to fix your computer.
我是專家。修理你的電腦我兩三下就搞定了。

10   aspect [ˈæspɛkt] n. 方面

片 in all aspects　在各方面
= in every aspect

▶ Alcoholism will affect all aspects of your life.
酗酒會全面影響你的生活。
＊alcoholism [ˈælkəhɔlˌɪzəm] n. 酗酒

▶ Brian outdistances John in all aspects, including math.
布萊恩在各方面都領先約翰，包括數學在內。
＊outdistance [ˌautˈdɪstəns] vt. 超越

11   publish [ˈpʌblɪʃ] vt. 出版；發表，公開

衍 (1) public [ˈpʌblɪk]
　　　a. 大眾的 & n. 民眾，大眾（與定冠詞 the 搭配使用）①
(2) publicize [ˈpʌblɪˌsaɪz] vt. 宣傳 ⑥
(3) publishing [ˈpʌblɪʃɪŋ] n. 出版業

▶ That company publishes a variety of educational books.
那家公司出版各種教育用書。

▶ Don't publish what I said today—it's off the record.
不要公開我今天說的話 —— 這是非正式的。

publisher [ˈpʌblɪʃɚ]
n. 出版社；發行人

▶ I'll write to the publisher for a copy of that book.
我將寫信向該出版社要那一本書。

▶ Sam has been a publisher in that textbook company for over ten years.
山姆在那間教科書公司擔任發行人已超過十年。

publication [ˌpʌblɪˈkeʃən]
n. 刊物（可數）；發表，公布（不可數）

▶ Peter's company has produced numerous publications.
彼得的公司出版了不少書刊。

▶ The news is not fit for publication.
這個消息不適合公開。

publicity [pʌbˈlɪsətɪ]
n. 名氣；（公眾的）關注；宣傳

似 (1) promotion [prəˈmoʃən] n. 宣傳 ④
(2) exposure [ɪkˈspoʒɚ]
　　　n. 宣傳，曝光 ④
(3) advertising [ˈædvɚˌtaɪzɪŋ]
　　　n. 廣告

▶ The hero's actions brought him a lot of publicity.
這位英雄的事跡為他帶來很大的名氣。

▶ The two stars didn't want any publicity about their wedding.
這兩個大明星不想公開他倆的婚禮。

▶ Few attended the concert because of bad publicity.
因為宣傳不夠，來聽這場音樂會的人並不多。

12   literature [ˈlɪtərətʃɚ] n. 文學（不可數）；文獻

片 Western / Chinese literature
西洋 / 中國文學

似 writings [ˈraɪtɪŋz]
　　n. （文學）作品（複數）

▶ Mary majored in Western literature while in college.
瑪莉念大學時主修西洋文學。

► Paul didn't have time to read all the available literature on the subject.
保羅沒有時間看完有關這主題所有的現存文獻。

literary [ˈlɪtəˌrɛrɪ] *a.* 文學的

衍 (1) literate [ˈlɪtərɪt]
　　a. 識字的 & *n.* 能讀寫的人 ⑥
　(2) literacy [ˈlɪtərəsɪ] *n.* 識字 ⑥

► The literary scholars met in the library.
文學界的學者在圖書館開會。

13　consist [kənˈsɪst] *vi.* 由……組成 (與介詞 of 並用)；在於…… (與介詞 in 並用)

片 (1) consist of...　由……組成
　= be made up of...
　= be composed of...
　(2) consist in...　在於……
　= lie in...

► This delegation consists of 50 government officials.
= This delegation is made up of 50 government officials.
= This delegation is composed of 50 government officials.
該代表團由 50 名政府官員組成。
＊delegation [ˌdɛləˈgeʃən] *n.* 代表團

► Well goes the saying, "Happiness consists in contentment."
俗語說得好：『快樂在於知足 / 知足常樂。』
＊contentment [kənˈtɛntmənt] *n.* 滿足

---

consistent [kənˈsɪstənt]
a. 前後一致的；一貫的；符合的

片 (1) be consistent in...
　　　對……始終如一
　(2) be consistent with...
　　　與……一致 / 沒有矛盾
　= be in accord with...
　= correspond with...

衍 (1) consistency [kənˈsɪstənsɪ] *n.* 一致
　(2) consistently [kənˈsɪstəntlɪ]
　　　adv. 一致地；一向

反 inconsistent [ˌɪnkənˈsɪstənt]
　　a. 不一致的

► Raymond is not consistent in his opinions.
雷蒙的意見前後不一致。

► The author has a consistent style of writing.
這位作者保有一貫的寫作風格。

► John's actions are consistent with his words.
= John's actions are in accord with his words.
= John's actions correspond with his words.
約翰言行一致。

14　assure [əˈʃʊr] *vt.* 向 (某人) 保證

片 (1) assure sb that...　向某人保證……
　(2) assure sb of sth　向某人保證某事

衍 reassure [ˌriəˈʃʊr]
　　vt. 使放心；向……再三保證 ⑤

► I can assure you that this is the best restaurant in town.
我向你保證，這是鎮上最棒的一家餐廳。

► Sam wasn't able to assure Sophie of his support.
山姆無法向蘇菲保證會支持她。

assurance [ə`ʃʊrəns]
n. 保證;自信,把握,胸有成竹

似 (1) guarantee [ˌgærən`ti] *n.* 保證 ④
　　(2) pledge [plɛdʒ] *n.* 保證 ⑤
　　(3) self-confidence [ˌsɛlf`kɑnfədəns]
　　　 n. 自信

▶ Tom gave me his assurance that he would show up on time.
湯姆向我保證他會準時出現。

▶ In spite of all her assurances, Jane did not do the job as promised.
雖然珍信誓旦旦,卻未做到她所承諾的工作。

▶ "John will like that," Lisa said with assurance.
麗莎胸有成竹地說:『約翰一定會喜歡的。』

ensure [ɪn`ʃʊr] *vt.* 確保

似 insure [ɪn`ʃʊr] *vt.* 投保
insure sth against...
為某物保⋯⋯的險

▶ Have you insured your house against fire?
你有為你的房子投保火險了嗎?

▶ The airline took precautions to ensure flight safety.
航空公司採取預防措施以確保飛航安全。
＊precaution [prɪ`kɔʃən] *n.* 預防措施

▶ Hard work does not necessarily ensure success. Sometimes good luck counts.
努力工作並不確保成功。有時候好運蠻重要的。
＊count [kaʊnt] *vi.* 很重要

15　timid [`tɪmɪd] *a.* 膽小的

衍 intimidate [ɪn`tɪməˌdet] *vt.* 威嚇 ⑥
似 (1) chicken [`tʃɪkɪn] *a.* 膽怯的 ①
　　(2) yellow [`jɛlo] *a.* 膽小的 ①
　　(3) cowardly [`kaʊədlɪ]
　　　 a. 膽小的,如懦夫般的 ⑥
反 bold [bold] *a.* 大膽的 ③

▶ The timid boy rarely speaks up in class.
這個膽怯的男孩在班上很少開口說話。

16　tendency [`tɛndənsɪ] *n.* 傾向

片 have a tendency to + V
　　有⋯⋯的傾向
＝ tend to + V

衍 tend [tɛnd] *vi.* 傾向,易於
　　(之後接不定詞 to) & *vt.* 照顧 ③

▶ Henry has a tendency to look at the ground when he is telling a lie.
亨利說謊時往往會看地面。

17　contribute [kən`trɪbjut] *vt.* 捐助,貢獻 & *vi.* 促成,導致 (與介詞 to 並用)

片 contribute to...　　導致⋯⋯
＝ lead to...
＝ result in...
＝ give rise to...
＝ bring about...

▶ The generous man contributed a large sum of money to charity.
這位慷慨人士捐了一大筆錢給慈善事業。

衍 contributor [kənˈtrɪbjətɚ]
　n. 捐助者；投稿人

▶ Hard work alone does not necessarily contribute to success.
　光靠努力不一定就會成功。

contribution [ˌkɑntrəˈbjuʃən]
n. 捐獻；貢獻

片 make a contribution to...
　對⋯⋯貢獻

▶ Any contribution, large or small, will be appreciated.
　任何捐獻，不論金額大小，我們都感激。

▶ The ceasefire agreement would certainly make a great contribution to peace in that area.
　該停火協定肯定會對該區的和平有重大貢獻。

18　agency [ˈedʒənsɪ] n. 代辦處，機關

片 a news / travel agency
　通訊社 / 旅行社

▶ My dad works at a travel agency.
　我老爸在旅行社工作。

agent [ˈedʒənt] n. 代理商，經紀人
似 broker [ˈbrokɚ] n. 經紀人，掮客

▶ A real estate agent came by to talk to my father about selling our house.
　一位房地產經紀人前來和父親談論出售房子的事。

19　facility [fəˈsɪlətɪ] n. 設施，設備 (常用複數)

衍 facilitate [fəˈsɪləˌtet]
　vt. 使便利；促進 ⑤

▶ The facilities in that building are of the highest quality.
　那棟建築物的設備品質棒極了。

20　otherwise [ˈʌðɚˌwaɪz] adv. 否則；以相反的方式

用法 otherwise 與 or 同義，均表『否則』。or 是連接詞，之前置逗點，而 otherwise 是副詞，之前置分號，用以連接兩個主要子句。

▶ Be quiet, or I'll punish you.
= Be quiet; otherwise I'll punish you.
　要安靜，否則我會處罰你。

▶ You should listen to me; otherwise, you'll be sorry.
　你應聽我的話，否則你會後悔。

▶ I'll stay here until Dad tells me otherwise.
　我會待在這裡直到老爸要我不要繼續待為止。

21　capacity [kəˈpæsətɪ] n. 容量；能力；職位

片 (1) have a capacity of + 數字
　　可容納若干⋯⋯
　(2) in one's capacity as + 職位
　　某人以某職位的身分
衍 (1) capable [ˈkepəbḷ] a. 有能力的；做得出⋯⋯的 (與介詞 of 並用) ③
　(2) capability [ˌkepəˈbɪlətɪ] n. 能力 ⑤

▶ The stadium has a seating capacity of 1,000.
　該體育場可以容納一千人。

▶ Everyone is born with an immense capacity for love.
　每個人生來就有無限去愛的能力。
＊immense [ɪˈmɛns] a. 巨大的，廣大的

▶ In my capacity as general manager of this company, I would like to recommend Mr. Peter M. Johnson to you.
　本人以本公司總經理的身分向您推薦彼得 ·M· 強森先生。

Level 4　Unit 02

22 communication [kə͵mjunə`keʃən] *n.* 聯絡，通訊；傳播，傳播學 (恆用複數)

衍 (1) communicate [kə`mjunə͵ket]
　　　　vt. 傳達 & *vi.* 溝通 ③
　　(2) communicative [kə`mjunə͵ketɪv]
　　　　a. 善於溝通的；對話的 ⑥

▶ Native Americans used smoke signals as means of communication.
　美國原住民過去用煙幕訊號作為聯絡的方式。

▶ My sister studied communications at university.
　我姊姊念大學時曾修傳播學。

23 status [`stetəs / `stætəs] *n.* 地位，身分；狀態，情況

片 the status quo　現狀
似 situation [͵sɪtʃu`eʃən] *n.* 情況 ③

▶ The status of a teacher is not high in many countries.
　在許多國家中老師的地位並不高。

▶ What is the present status of the negotiations?
　這次協商目前的情況如何？

▶ Most people want to maintain their status quo and are reluctant to make any changes.
　大部分的人都想要維持現狀，很不願做任何改變。

24 atmosphere [`ætməs͵fɪr] *n.* 大氣；空氣；氛圍

似 (1) feeling [`filɪŋ] *n.* 感覺 ②
　　(2) mood [mud] *n.* 氣氛 ②

▶ The satellite is fixed at a point just outside the Earth's atmosphere.
　那枚衛星被安置在地球大氣層外的某個定點上。

▶ Mildew easily forms in my room because of the damp atmosphere.
　因為空氣很潮溼，我的房間很容易長黴。
　＊mildew [`mɪl͵d(j)u] *n.* 黴

▶ I like the warm and pleasant atmosphere in that coffee shop.
　我喜歡那家咖啡廳溫暖又愉快的氣氛。

25 tribal [`traɪbl̩] *a.* 部落的

衍 tribe [traɪb] *n.* 部落 ③

▶ As this area was becoming increasingly civilized, many of the tribal rituals were lost.
　這個地區日趨文明時，許多部落的習俗也跟著不見了。
　＊ritual [`rɪtʃuəl] *n.* 儀式

26 combination [͵kɑmbə`neʃən] *n.* 結合，聯合

片 (1) a combination lock　密碼鎖
　　(2) a combination of...　……的結合
衍 combine [kɑm`baɪn] *vt.* & *vi.* 結合 ②

▶ This accident resulted from a combination of errors.
　許多錯誤的結合導致了這個意外。

27 jealousy [ˈdʒɛləsɪ] *n.* 忌妒

衍 jealous [ˈdʒɛləs] *a.* 忌妒的 ③

▸ I'm sick of Linda's petty jealousies.
我厭煩了琳達那小心眼的忌妒。
＊petty [ˈpɛtɪ] *a.* 小的，瑣碎的

28 prevention [prɪˈvɛnʃən] *n.* 阻止；預防，避免

片 (1) crime prevention　　犯罪預防
　　(2) disaster prevention　災難預防

衍 (1) prevent [prɪˈvɛnt] *vt.* 避免 ③
　　(2) preventive [prɪˈvɛntɪv]
　　　　a. 預防的 ⑥

▸ They organized an association for the prevention of child abuse.
他們組織了一個防止虐童的協會。

▸ Prevention is better than cure.
＝ An ounce of prevention is worth a pound of cure.
預防勝於治療。── 諺語

29 measure(s) [ˈmɛʒɚ(z)] *n.* 度量單位；衡量標準；措施，手段（常用複數）

片 take measures　採取措施
＝ take action
＝ take steps

衍 (1) measure [ˈmɛʒɚ]
　　　　vt. 測量；衡量 & *vi.* 量起來有⋯⋯②
　　(2) measurement [ˈmɛʒɚmənt]
　　　　n. 測量；尺寸 ②

▸ A yard is a measure of length.
碼是一種長度的度量單位。

▸ Age is not an accurate measure of maturity.
年齡並非衡量成熟的精確標準。

▸ We should take measures right now before it's too late.
我們應立刻採取措施，以免太遲。

measurable [ˈmɛʒərəbļ]
a. 可測量的；相當多／大的

反 immeasurable [ɪˈmɛʒərəbļ]
　　a. 無法測量的

▸ The pollution in this area is not measurable.
這地區的汙染是無法測量的。

▸ We have made measurable progress in three months.
3 個月來我們已有相當大的進展。

30 occasional [əˈkeʒənļ] *a.* 偶爾的

衍 (1) occasion [əˈkeʒən]
　　　　n. 特殊的大事；場合 ③
　　(2) occasionally [əˈkeʒənļɪ] *adv.* 偶爾

似 irregular [ɪˈrɛgjələ] *a.* 不常的

反 regular [ˈrɛgjələ]
　　a. 經常的；定期的 ②

▸ Irene takes occasional trips to Hong Kong for shopping.
艾琳偶爾會到香港購物。

---

1 **device** [dɪˈvaɪs] *n.* 裝置；設計

似 (1) machine [məˈʃin] *n.* 機器 ①
(2) gadget [ˈgædʒɪt] *n.* 小機器
(3) mechanism [ˈmɛkəˌnɪzəm]
　　n. 機械裝置；結構 ⑤

▶ This machine has a safety device.
　這臺機器有一個安全裝置。

▶ The girl on the magazine cover is a device to get everyone's attention.
　雜誌上的封面女郎是用來引起大家注意的一種設計。

---

devise [dɪˈvaɪz] *vt.* 發明，想出；設計

似 (1) create [krɪˈet] *vt.* 創造 ②
(2) invent [ɪnˈvɛnt] *vt.* 發明 ③
(3) think up... 　想出......

▶ For safety's sake, we'll have to devise a new secret code.
　為了安全起見，我們必須想出一個新的密碼。

▶ It is necessary that we devise a new system to improve our productivity.
　我們有必要設計一套新系統以提升我們的生產力。

---

gear [gɪr]
n. 裝備 (不可數)；齒輪 (可數) & *vt.* 使適合 & *vi.* 準備好

片 (1) be geared to + V
　　　被設計適合......
　 = be designed to + V
(2) gear up for... 　為......做好準備

▶ Uncle George spent a lot of money on his fishing gear.
　喬治叔叔花了很多錢在釣魚的裝備上。

▶ The gears can transmit force from one machine to another.
　齒輪可以把動力從一臺機器傳到另一臺機器。

▶ This book is geared to teach students how to use words correctly.
　本書旨在教導學生如何正確使用單字。

▶ The couple is gearing up for their wedding in June.
　這對情侶正在為他們六月的婚禮做準備。

---

2 **concept** [ˈkɑnsɛpt] *n.* 觀念，想法

衍 (1) conceive [kənˈsiv]
　　vt. 構想出，懷有 (某想法) ⑤
(2) conception [kənˈsɛpʃən]
　　n. 看法；概念 ⑤

▶ It is difficult to grasp some of the concepts in Buddhism.
　有些佛學的觀念很難理解。

---

3 **moreover** [mɔrˈovə] *adv.* 並且，此外

似 (1) in addition 　此外
(2) besides [bɪˈsaɪdz]
　　prep. 除......之外 & *adv.* 此外 ③

▶ I love John. He has a heart of gold. Moreover, he is very handsome.

= I love John. He has a heart of gold. In addition, he is very handsome.
　我愛約翰。他有仁慈的心。此外，他也很英俊。

furthermore [ˈfɝðɚ͵mɔr]
adv. 而且

▶ I'm upset with your behavior; furthermore, your grades are terrible.
你的行為讓我生氣，而且你的成績也很糟。

---

4 declare [dɪˈklɛr] *vt.* 宣布；宣稱

▶ 片 (1) declare independence
宣布獨立

(2) declare war on... 向……宣戰

衍 declaration [͵dɛkləˈreʃən]
n. 宣布；宣言 ⑤

似 (1) claim [klem] *vt.* 宣稱 ②

(2) announce [əˈnaʊns]
vt. 公布；宣布 ③

▶ The American colonies declared independence in 1776.
美洲殖民地於 1776 年宣布獨立。

▶ The suspect declared that he was innocent.
該嫌犯宣稱他是無辜的。

---

5 nuclear [ˈn(j)uklɪɚ] *a.* 核子的

片 nuclear war 核子戰爭

衍 nucleus [ˈn(j)uklɪəs] *n.* (原子) 核；
細胞核 (複數為 nuclei [ˈn(j)uklɪ͵aɪ]
或 nucleuses) ⑥

▶ When nuclear war breaks out, humans are doomed.
核子大戰爆發時，人類注定要毀滅。
＊doomed [dumd] *a.* 注定滅亡的

atom [ˈætəm] *n.* 原子

▶ One hundred million atoms laid side by side are about an inch long.
一億個原子並排放在一起約有一寸長。

atomic [əˈtɑmɪk] *a.* 原子的

▶ Most people oppose the use of atomic energy in Taiwan.
臺灣大多數人反對使用原子能。

---

6 tension [ˈtɛnʃən] *n.* 緊張

似 nervousness [ˈnɝvəsnəs] *n.* 緊張

▶ There was a lot of tension between the two countries after the terrorist attack.
發生恐攻後，兩國之間的關係很緊張。

tense [tɛns]
a. 緊張的；繃緊的 & *vi.* 變緊張

似 (1) nervous [ˈnɝvəs] *a.* 緊張的 ②

(2) tight [taɪt] *a.* 緊的 ③

(3) tighten [ˈtaɪtən]
vt. & vi. (使) 變緊 ③

▶ It was a tense situation when the two rivals met.
這兩個敵手碰面時，情況緊張了起來。

▶ Are the wires tense enough?
這些繩索拉得夠緊嗎？

▶ Whenever someone gets near, Linda tenses.
只要一有人靠近琳達，她就會緊張。

7 **campaign** [kæmˋpen] *n.* (社會、宣傳) 運動 & *vi.* 從事運動

片 (1) launch a campaign
發起一項運動 / 活動

(2) campaign against...
發起活動反對……

▶ They are going to launch a campaign against corruption.
他們準備要發起肅貪運動。

▶ These groups campaigned against child abuse.
這些團體展開對抗虐童的活動。

8 **identify** [aıˋdɛntəˌfaı] *vt.* 指認，認定；視為同一 & *vi.* 對……感同身受 (與介詞 with 並用)

三 identify, identified [aıˋdɛntəˌfaıd], identified

片 (1) identify A as B　將 A 認定為 B

(2) identify A with B
將 A 與 B 視為相等

(3) identify with...　對……感同身受，
對……產生認同感

衍 identity [aıˋdɛntətı] *n.* 身分 ②

▶ Tammy identified the purse as hers by telling what it contained.
塔米藉著說出手提包內的東西指認這個手提包是她的。

▶ The good mayor identified the well-being of his citizens with his own.
這位善良的市長把市民的幸福當作是自己的幸福。

▶ The audience identified with the sorrow of the hero.
觀眾對這位男主角的悲痛感同身受。

identical [aıˋdɛntık!] *a.* 相同的

片 be identical to...　與……相同

似 similar [ˋsımələ] *a.* 相似的 ②
A is similar to B
A 與 B 類似 (但並非完全相同)

▶ The houses in that area are all identical.
那個地區的房子全都是一個樣。

▶ Surprisingly enough, Jack's answer was identical to yours.
令人驚訝的是，傑克的答案跟你的完全一樣。

identification [aıˌdɛntəfəˋkeʃən]
n. 身分證明 (不可數，縮寫為 ID)

▶ The policeman asked us to show him some identification.
這名警員要求我們給他看身分證明。

9 **construct** [kənˋstrʌkt] *vt.* 興建，建造；創造 (故事)

似 (1) build [bıld] *vt.* 建造 ①

(2) create [krıˋet] *vt.* 創造 ②

▶ A new highway is being constructed.
一條新的高速公路正在興建中。

▶ This story is constructed out of several legends.
這個故事由好幾個傳說創造而成。

construction [ˌkənˋstrʌkʃən]
n. 施工，建造

片 (1) a construction site　工地

(2) under construction　在興建中

▶ Traffic was slow due to road construction.
由於道路施工，車輛通行緩慢。

▶ We were told to wear helmets at the construction site.
在工地時，我們被吩咐要戴上安全帽。

▶ There are three new apartments under construction.
有三棟新的公寓正在興建中。

constructive [kənˈstrʌktɪv]
a. 有建設性的

🔲 constructive criticism
　有建設性的批評

🔲 destructive [dɪˈstrʌktɪv]
　a. 破壞的；破壞性的 ⑤

▶ There is nothing constructive in Peter's opinion.
　彼得的意見一點建設性也沒有。

▶ We welcome any constructive criticism.
　任何有建設性的批評我們都很歡迎。

10　application [ˌæpləˈkeʃən] *n.* 應用；用途；申請（表格）

衍 (1) apply [əˈplaɪ] *vt.* 應用；塗，擦（藥膏）& *vi.* 適用；應徵，申請 ②
　apply for admission to a university　申請入學某大學
　(2) appliance [əˈplaɪəns]
　　n. 用具（尤指家電用品）⑤
　(3) applicable [ˈæplɪkəbḷ]
　　a. 適用的，合適的 ⑥

▶ The application of the new data led to the success of the mission.
　這些新資訊的運用使得任務順利達成。

▶ It seems that this information has no practical application.
　這項訊息似乎沒有實際效用。

▶ Could you tell me how to fill out this application (form) for admission to that university?
　你可以告訴我怎麼填寫那所大學的入學申請表格嗎？

applicant [ˈæpləkənt] *n.* 申請者

▶ There were more than 100 applicants for the job as a bodyguard.
　這份保鑣的工作有 100 多名申請者。

11　recall [rɪˈkɔl] *vt.* 回想，憶起，記得；召回 & [ˈrikɔl / rɪˈkɔl] *n.* 回想（不可數）；收回

🔲 (1) recall + N/V-ing　記得⋯⋯
　(2) total recall
　　（所學或過去事件）過目不忘

似 remember [rɪˈmɛmbɚ]
　vt. 記得；記住 ①

▶ I don't recall seeing that girl before.
= I don't remember seeing that girl before.
　我不記得以前曾見過那個女孩子。

▶ Toyota has decided to recall all the cars produced in 2004 because of some mechanical problems.
　由於若干機械毛病，豐田汽車公司決定召回所有在 2004 年生產的車輛。

▶ James has total recall of the events of that night.
　詹姆士對那晚發生的事記得清清楚楚。

▶ The company ordered a recall of the dictionary, as the book contained several errors.
　公司命令把那本字典全部收回，因為書裡面有好幾處錯誤。

12　remark [rɪˈmɑrk] *vt.* 說，談到（用 that 子句作受詞）& *vi.* & *n.* 評論，談論

🔲 (1) remark that...　說⋯⋯
　= say that...

▶ Harry remarked that John wasn't cut out for the job.
= Harry said that John wasn't cut out for the job.
　哈利表示約翰並不能勝任那份工作。

(2) remark on... 評論有關……

(3) make a remark on...
評論 / 批評……

▶ David remarked on my wife's hairstyle.
大衛評論我太太的髮型。

▶ The film critic made some bitter remarks on the film.
這位影評人對這部電影做了一些嚴厲的批評。

---

remarkable [rɪˋmɑrkəbl]
a. 了不起的，非凡的

似 (1) unusual [ʌnˋjuʒʊəl] *a.* 非凡的

(2) wonderful [ˋwʌndəˌfəl]
a. 了不起的，很棒的 ①

▶ Joe's performance in the speech contest was truly remarkable.
喬在演講比賽的表現實在了不起。

---

13 relaxation [ˌrilæksˋeʃən] *n.* 放鬆

衍 relax [rɪˋlæks] *vt.* 放鬆 ③

▶ Occasional relaxation is very important for efficient work.
偶爾放鬆一下對工作有效率至為重要。

---

14 nevertheless [ˌnɛvəðəˋlɛs] *adv.* 然而

似 (1) nonetheless [ˌnʌnðəˋlɛs]
adv. 但是

(2) however [haʊˋɛvə] *adv.* 然而 ①

用法 nevertheless、nonetheless 及 however 均為連接性副詞，換言之，這些字仍只是副詞，故之前應置分號用以連接兩個子句；而 but (但是) 是連接詞，之前置逗點即可。

▶ George is nice; nevertheless, I don't like him.
= George is nice; however, I don't like him.
= George is nice, but I don't like him.
喬治人不錯，然而我並不喜歡他。

---

15 misunderstand [ˌmɪsʌndəˋstænd] *vt.* 誤會，誤解

≡ misunderstand, misunderstood [ˌmɪsʌndəˋstʊd], misunderstood

衍 (1) misunderstanding
[ˌmɪsʌndəˋstændɪŋ] *n.* 誤會

(2) understand [ˌʌndəˋstænd]
vt. 懂；知道 ①

(3) understanding [ˌʌndəˋstændɪŋ]
n. 理解力 & *a.* 善解人意的

▶ Kelly misunderstood my compliment and took it as an insult.
凱莉誤解我的讚美而視之為侮辱。
＊insult [ˋɪnsʌlt] *n.* 侮辱
compliment [ˋkɑmpləmənt] *n.* 讚美；恭維

16 arise [əˋraɪz] vi. 產生，形成

目 arise, arose [əˋroz], arisen [əˋrɪzn̩]
片 arise from...　起因於……
　= result from...
似 (1) raise [rez] vt. 舉起；提升；養育 ①
　(2) rise [raɪz] vi. 上升；起立 ①

▸ Tony's failure arose from laziness.
= Tony's failure resulted from laziness.
　東尼的失敗起因於懶惰。

17 behavior [brˋhevjɚ] n. 行為 (不可數)

衍 behave [brˋhev] vi. 行為舉止 ②
似 deed [did] n. 行為 (可數) ③

▸ Stealing is bad behavior.
　偷竊是不好的行為。

18 annual [ˋænjuəl] a. 每年的；年度的，一年的

衍 annually [ˋænjuəlɪ] adv. 每年
似 yearly [ˋjɪrlɪ]
　a. 一年一度的 & adv. 每年 ③

▸ Labor Day is an annual holiday in many countries.
　在許多國家，勞動節每年都有放假。
▸ What's your annual income?
　你年收入是多少？

anniversary [ˌænəˋvɚsərɪ]
n. 週年紀念

▸ My parents invited their friends to their 30th wedding anniversary.
　我父母親邀請朋友來參加他倆的結婚 30 週年紀念。

19 frame [frem] n. 框架；畫框 & vt. 裝框；陷害

片 frame sb　陷害某人
　= set sb up
似 flame [flem] n. 火焰 & vi. 燃燒 ③

▸ The frame of the window is made of iron.
　這扇窗戶的框架是鐵做的。
▸ The frame is prettier than the picture.
　畫框要比畫作漂亮。
▸ I framed my portrait and hung it in my room.
　我把我的畫像裝框掛在房間裡。
▸ Tom was framed for Angela's murder.
　湯姆被誣陷謀殺安琪拉。
▸ I was furious upon learning that my best friend had framed me.
= I was furious upon learning that my best friend had set me up.
　一獲知我最好的朋友陷害我時，我氣瘋了。

20 generation [ˌdʒɛnəˈreʃən] *n.* 世代

片 a generation gap　代溝

▶ If the generation gap between parents and their children could be narrowed, there wouldn't be so many social problems.

假使父母與子女間的代溝能縮小，就不會有那麼多的社會問題了。

21 oppose [əˈpoz] *vt.* 反對，反抗

片 oppose + N/V-ing　反對……
= be opposed to + N/V-ing
= object to + N/V-ing

衍 (1) opposition [ˌɑpəˈzɪʃən] *n.* 反對 ⑤
(2) opposite [ˈɑpəzɪt]
a. 相對的；相反的 & *prep.* 在……對面 ③

▶ I oppose adopting Tim's proposal because I don't think it is feasible.

= I'm opposed to adopting Tim's proposal because I don't think it is feasible.

= I object to adopting Tim's proposal because I don't think it is feasible.

我反對採納提姆的方案，因為我認為那行不通。
＊feasible [ˈfizəbl̩] *a.* 可行的

objection [əbˈdʒɛkʃən]
n. 異議，反對

片 take objection to...　反對……
= object to...

衍 object [əbˈdʒɛkt] *vt.* & *vi.* 反對 ②

▶ Does anyone have any objections to this suggestion?

有沒有人對這個提議有任何異議？

▶ My boss took objection to what was decided in the meeting.

我老闆反對此次會議所做的決定。

22 embarrass [ɪmˈbærəs] *vt.* 使困窘，使尷尬

▶ We were embarrassed by our companion's rudeness to our host.

我們同伴對主人的無禮使我們很尷尬。

embarrassing [ɪmˈbærəsɪŋ]
a. 令人尷尬的

似 awkward [ˈɔkwəd] *a.* 尷尬的 ③

▶ What is the most embarrassing thing that's ever happened to you?

你遇過最令人尷尬的事情是什麼？

embarrassed [ɪmˈbærəst]
a. 感到尷尬的

▶ Sean was quite embarrassed when he found a big hole in the back of his pants.

尚恩發現他的褲子後頭破了一個大洞時，他尷尬極了。

embarrassment
[ɪmˈbærəsmənt] *n.* 困窘，尷尬(不可數)；令人困窘的人或事 (可數)

▶ Patty couldn't hide her embarrassment when the event occurred.

這事件發生時，派蒂無法掩飾她的困窘。

▶ That naughty boy was a complete embarrassment to the host at the party last night.
昨晚派對上的頑皮男孩真是令主人尷尬。

23 disappoint [ˌdɪsəˈpɔɪnt] vt. 使失望

片 disappoint sb　使某人失望
= let sb down
衍 (1) disappointing [ˌdɪsəˈpɔɪntɪŋ]
　　 a. 令人失望的
(2) disappointed [ˌdɪsəˈpɔɪntɪd]
　　 a. 感到失望的

▶ My son disappointed me when he cheated at chess.
= My son let me down when he cheated at chess.
我兒子下棋作弊，令我失望。

disappointment
[ˌdɪsəˈpɔɪntmənt] n. 失望；失望之情

片 To sb's disappointment, ...
令某人失望的是，……

▶ To our disappointment, it rained on the day of the field trip.
令我們失望的是，校外教學那天下雨了。

▶ Ned couldn't hide his disappointment when Jane refused his proposal.
當珍拒絕他的求婚時，奈德難掩失望之情。

24 attraction [əˈtrækʃən] n. 吸引力；愛慕；誘惑；吸引人的事物

片 (1) hold no attraction for sb
　　 對某人沒有吸引力
(2) a tourist attraction
　　 觀光勝地 / 景點
衍 (1) attract [əˈtrækt] vt. 吸引，引起
　　 (某人的) 注意或興趣 ③
(2) attractive [əˈtræktɪv]
　　 a. 誘人的；有吸引力的 ③

▶ The movie's greatest attraction for me is the all-star cast.
這部電影對我最大的吸引力是全明星的演員陣容。

▶ Wealth and fame hold no attraction for Tom.
名利對湯姆毫無吸引力。

▶ Chris could barely conceal his attraction to Melody.
克里斯很難隱藏自己對美樂蒂的愛戀。

▶ Our main attraction tonight is the lucky draw.
我們今晚的重頭戲是摸彩。

▶ The prison was turned into a tourist attraction after the government shut it down.
政府關閉了這座監獄後，它就變成了一個觀光景點。

25 accidental [ˌæksəˈdɛntḷ] a. 意外的；突發的

衍 (1) accident [ˈæksədənt]
　　 n. 意外 (尤指車禍) ②
(2) accidentally [ˌæksəˈdɛntḷɪ]
　　 adv. 無意間
= by accident
似 unexpected [ˌʌnɪkˈspɛktɪd]
　　 a. 料想不到的

▶ I'm sorry, but the mistake was completely accidental.
很抱歉，這個錯誤完全是無心之過。

▶ Police are investigating the accidental death of the millionaire.
警方正在調查這位百萬富翁暴斃的原因。

26 **ambitious** [æm`bɪʃəs] *a.* 有野心的

似 (1) **determined** [dɪ`tɝmɪnd]
    a. 有決心的
(2) **motivated** [`motɪ͵vetɪd]
    a. 有動機的，積極的

▶ Jack has always been very ambitious, believing that he was born to be a leader.
傑克總是很有野心，覺得自己天生就是領袖的料。

▶ The government has made some highly ambitious plans to end poverty.
政府擬了一些野心十足的計畫以解決貧困。

27 **fasten** [`fæsn̩] *vt.* 繫緊

反 **loosen** [`lusn̩] *vt.* 鬆開 ④

▶ For your safety, always fasten your seatbelt while driving.
為了安全起見，開車上路一定要繫安全帶。

28 **injure** [`ɪndʒɚ] *vt.* 傷害 (尤指車禍、天災等意外事件造成的受傷)

片 (1) **be slightly injured**   受到輕傷
(2) **be seriously injured**   受到重傷

衍 **injury** [`ɪndʒərɪ]
    n. (身體) 傷害；(名譽) 損壞 ③

似 **hurt** [hɝt] *vt.* 傷害 (三態同形) ①

▶ Charles injured his foot during the hockey game.
查理斯在曲棍球比賽中傷到了腳。

▶ The car turned over, but fortunately no one was seriously injured.
= The car turned over, but fortunately no one was seriously hurt.
車子翻覆，所幸無人受重傷。

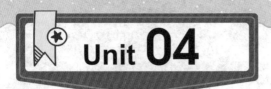

0401-0403

1 **devote** [dɪˈvot] *vt.* 致力於

片 (1) devote A to B　將 A 奉獻在 B 之上
(2) devote oneself to + N/V-ing
= dedicate oneself to + N/V-ing
　　某人奉獻／致力於……

衍 devotion [dɪˈvoʃən] *n.* 奉獻 ⑤

似 dedicate [ˈdɛdə,ket] *vt.* 奉獻 ⑤

▶ Richard has devoted his whole life to his career as a surgeon.
理查將一生奉獻在外科醫師的志職上。

▶ Denny has devoted himself to helping the poor.
丹尼一直都致力於幫助窮人。

devoted [dɪˈvotɪd] *a.* 忠實的

似 (1) faithful [ˈfeθfəl] *a.* 忠實的 ④
(2) loyal [ˈlɔɪəl] *a.* 忠誠的 ④

▶ Mr. Parker is a devoted husband and loving father.
派克先生既是忠實的丈夫，也是慈愛的父親。

2 **analyze** [ˈænə,laɪz] *vt.* 分析，解析

似 (1) examine [ɪgˈzæmɪn] *vt.* 檢查 ②
(2) evaluate [ɪˈvælju,et] *vt.* 評估 ④

▶ In science class, we analyzed water from a nearby river.
我們在上自然課時，分析取自附近河裡的水。

▶ Why don't we analyze the problem and see what's wrong?
我們何不分析這個問題，看看毛病出在哪裡？

analysis [əˈnæləsɪs] *n.* 分析

複 analyses [əˈnælə,siz]

衍 (1) analyst [ˈænl̩ɪst] *n.* 分析師 ⑤
(2) analytical [,ænəˈlɪtɪkl̩]
　　a. 分析的 ⑥

▶ Our final analysis is that your wife's health is perfectly normal.
我們最後的分析結果是夫人的健康狀況一切正常。

3 **essential** [ɪˈsɛnʃəl] *a.* 必要的，不可或缺的 & *n.* 要素，要點 (常用複數)

片 be essential to...
　　對……是不可或缺的

衍 essence [ˈɛsn̩s] *n.* 要點；精髓 ⑤

似 necessary [ˈnɛsə,sɛrɪ] *a.* 必要的 ②

▶ Water and air are essential to us.
水和空氣對我們而言都是不可或缺的。

▶ The teacher taught us the essentials of good health.
老師教導我們健康的要素。

essentially [ɪˈsɛnʃəlɪ]
adv. 本質上；基本上

似 (1) basically [ˈbesɪklɪ] *adv.* 基本上
(2) fundamentally [,fʌndəˈmɛntl̩ɪ]
　　adv. 基本上
(3) in essence　基本上

▶ Tim's got his flaws, but he is essentially a nice guy.
提姆是有他的缺點，但他本質上是個好人。

▶ We are essentially concerned with ending the conflict, not with discovering who started it.
基本上我們關心的是化解這場衝突，而不是探究是誰先引起的。

Level 4　Unit 04

251

4 vital [`vaɪtl̩] *a.* 維持生命必需的;極重要的

片 play a vital role in...
　　在……方面扮演極重要的角色

衍 vitality [vaɪ`tælətɪ] *n.* 生命力,活力 ⑥

似 extremely important　極為重要的

▸ Digestion is a vital function.
　消化是維持生命必需的功能。

▸ Police officers play a vital role in maintaining social stability.
　在維持社會治安方面,警察扮演了至為重要的角色。
　＊stability [stə`bɪlətɪ] *n.* 穩定

---

5 sorrowful [`sɑrəfəl] *a.* 悲傷的

似 sad [sæd] *a.* 悲傷的,難過的 ①

反 joyful [`dʒɔɪfəl] *a.* 充滿喜悅的 ③

▸ The sorrowful old man missed his wife, who recently passed away.
　那位悲傷的老先生很思念他最近過世的老伴。

---

6 accomplish [ə`kɑmplɪʃ] *vt.* 完成(任務);達到(目標)

片 accomplish a goal　達到目標
　= achieve a goal
　= attain a goal

似 (1) achieve [ə`tʃiv] *vt.* 達成 ③
　(2) attain [ə`ten] *vt.* 達到 ⑥

▸ Through teamwork, we finally accomplished the mission required of us.
　透過團隊合作,我們終於完成了被要求的任務。

▸ Unfortunately, we have not accomplished our goal this year.
　很不幸地,我們今年沒有達到目標。

---

accomplished [ə`kɑmplɪʃt]
a. 熟練(於某種才藝)的,有造詣的

似 (1) skillful [`skɪlfəl] *a.* 熟練的 ③
　(2) adept [ə`dɛpt] *a.* 熟練的
　(3) proficient [prə`fɪʃənt] *a.* 精通的

▸ At the age of fifteen, Sandy was already an accomplished pianist.
　珊蒂在 15 歲時就已是位出色的鋼琴家。

---

accomplishment
[ə`kɑmplɪʃmənt] *n.* 完成,實現(不可數);
成就;才華

片 a person of many accomplishments
　= a versatile person　有多樣才華的人

▸ The accomplishment of the task will take more than ten years.
　要完成這項任務需費時 10 年以上。

▸ The first landing on the moon was a great accomplishment for humanity.
　第一次登陸月球是人類一項偉大的成就。

▸ Though a man of many accomplishments, John is never arrogant.
　約翰是個多才多藝的人,卻從不驕傲。
　＊arrogant [`ærəgənt] *a.* 傲慢的,自負的

7 intend [ɪnˈtɛnd] *vt.* 意欲，想要；意指，意謂；針對

用 (1) intend sb to + V
想要叫某人做……

(2) intend to + V　想要做……
= desire to + V

衍 intent [ɪnˈtɛnt] *a.* 下定決心的 ⑤
be intent on + V-ing　一心要……

▶ John is intent on traveling around the world.
約翰一心想要環遊世界。

▶ Father intends me to be a doctor.
父親想要我當醫生。

▶ I didn't intend to do that.
我不想那麼做。

▶ Whatever I did, I intended no harm.
= No matter what I did, I meant no harm.
不論我做了什麼，我都是沒有惡意的。

▶ These toys are intended for children aged 3 to 5.
= These toys are meant for children aged 3 to 5.
這些玩具是針對 3 至 5 歲的兒童設計的。

---

intention [ɪnˈtɛnʃən] *n.* 意圖

衍 intentionally [ɪnˈtɛnʃənlɪ]
adv. 有意地，故意地

▶ It was not my intention to upset you.
我無意要惹你生氣。

---

8 emerge [ɪˈmɜdʒ] *vi.* 出現，冒出（常與介詞 from 並用）

用 emerge from...　從……冒出來
似 appear [əˈpɪr] *vi.* 出現 ①
反 submerge [səbˈmɜdʒ] *vi.* 沉入

▶ Ben suddenly emerged from behind the door, which frightened me.
班突然從門後冒出來，嚇了我一跳。

---

9 objective [əbˈdʒɛktɪv] *n.* 目標 & *a.* 客觀的

似 (1) goal [gol] *n.* 目標 ②
(2) target [ˈtɑrgɪt] *n.* 目標 ②
(3) aim [em] *n.* 目標 ②
反 subjective [səbˈdʒɛktɪv] *a.* 主觀的 ⑥

▶ Our objective was to reach the next town by sunset.
我們的目標是在日落前抵達下一個城鎮。

▶ Scientists must be objective in their research.
科學家在做研究時必須要很客觀。

---

10 finance [ˈfaɪnæns] *n.* 財政，財務；財力，財務狀況（恆用複數）& *vt.* 向……提供資金

▶ The Minister of Finance was forced to resign after he was found involved in a scandal.
財政部長經人發現涉入某項醜聞後被迫請辭。

▶ The government is worried about the state of the nation's finances.
政府很擔心國家的財務狀況。

▶ We need more businesses to finance our project.
我們需要更多的企業金援我們的企畫。

financial [faɪˈnænʃəl]
a. 金融的；財務的

▶ London and New York are financial centers.
倫敦和紐約都是金融中心。

用 (1) a financial center　金融中心
(2) a financial problem　財務問題

▶ The business closed due to financial problems.
這個企業由於財務問題而關閉了。

11　philosophy [fəˈlɑsəfɪ] *n.* 哲學 (不可數)；人生觀 (可數)

似 (1) viewpoint [ˈvju,pɔɪnt]
n. 觀點，見解 ⑤
(2) belief [bɪˈlif] *n.* 信念 ②

▶ All the freshmen must take a course in philosophy.
所有的大一學生都必須修哲學課。

▶ It is my philosophy that we should never take advantage of others.
我的人生觀就是我們絕不可占別人的便宜。

---

philosopher [fəˈlɑsəfɚ]
n. 哲學家；哲人

似 thinker [ˈθɪŋkɚ] *n.* 思想家

▶ It is not too much to say that Confucius was the greatest philosopher in ancient China.
孔子是中國古代最偉大的哲學家，這種說法並不為過。

▶ Many people become philosophers in old age.
許多人年邁時都成了很有哲理的人。

---

philosophical [,fɪləˈsɑfɪkl̩]
a. 哲學的；理智的，看得開的

似 (1) calm [kɑm] *a.* 鎮靜的 ②
(2) thoughtful [ˈθɔtfəl]
a. 很有思想的 ④
(3) rational [ˈræʃənl̩] *a.* 理智的 ⑤

▶ The students stayed up late discussing many philosophical questions.
學生們熬夜到很晚，討論許多哲學的問題。

▶ Jane was quite philosophical about her recent bad luck.
珍對她最近的霉運相當看得開。

12　contrast [ˈkɑntræst] *n.* 對比，差異 & [kənˈtræst] *vt.* 對比

用 (1) By contrast, ...　相對之下，……
(2) in contrast to...　與……成對比
(3) contrast A with B
將 A 與 B 做對照

▶ Tom is introverted. By contrast, his brother John is extroverted.
湯姆很內向。相對之下，他哥哥約翰就很外向。
*introverted [ˈɪntrə,vɝtɪd] *a.* 內向的
extroverted [ˈɛkstrə,vɝtɪd] *a.* 外向的

▶ The puppy appears small in contrast to its mother.
這隻小狗和母狗比起來模樣小多了。

▶ When you contrast Edward with Henry, you'll find a big difference between them in terms of personality.
你將愛德華與亨利對比時，會發現兩人的個性有很大的差異。
*in terms of...　就……而言

contrary [ˈkɑntrɛrɪ]

a. 相反的，對立的 & *n.* 相反

H (1) be contrary to...　與……相反
　(2) On the contrary, ...
　　　相反地，……

▶ The new regulations are contrary to the public interest.
　新規定和公共利益相對立。

▶ The camera was far from a bargain; on the contrary, it was too expensive.
　這臺相機一點也不划算。相反地，它的價格太貴了。
　*be far from...　一點也不……
　=be not... at all

13　accompany [əˈkʌmpənɪ] *vt.* 陪伴

H accompany sb　陪伴某人
衍 company [ˈkʌmpənɪ] *n.* 同伴
　（集合名詞，不可數）；公司（可數）②

▶ One is known by the company one keeps.
　觀其友而知其人。── 諺語

▶ Let me accompany you to your house.
　讓我陪你回家吧。

---

companion [kəmˈpænjən]

n. 伴侶，同伴（可數）

衍 companionship [kəmˈpænjənʃɪp]
　n. 友誼（不可數）

▶ The dog is man's faithful companion.
　狗是人類忠實的同伴。

14　assign [əˈsaɪn] *vt.* 分配；指派

H (1) assign sb sth　　分配某人某事
　(2) assign sb to + V　指派某人做……

▶ Our teacher will assign us tasks for the morning.
　老師將會為我們分配早上的工作。

▶ The trained cadets have been assigned to their places of duty.
　那些受過專業訓練的軍校生被派到不同的崗位上履職。
　*cadet [kəˈdɛt] *n.* 軍校生

▶ The sheriff assigned someone to watch the suspect twenty-four hours a day.
　警長指派某人 1 天 24 小時看守該嫌犯。
　*sheriff [ˈʃɛrɪf] *n.* 警長

---

assignment [əˈsaɪnmənt]

n. 任命，派定的工作；指定作業或功課

似 (1) task [tæsk] *n.* 工作 ②
　(2) mission [ˈmɪʃən] *n.* 任務 ③

▶ We are going to Tokyo on a special assignment for our magazine.
　我們將為我們的雜誌到東京出一趟特別任務。

▶ My first assignment in the company was to serve my colleagues coffee.
　我在公司的第一項工作就是替我的同事們倒咖啡。

(3) appointment [əˋpɔɪntmənt]
  n. 任命 ④

(4) schoolwork [ˋskulˏwɝk]
  n. 課堂作業

比 表『作業』時，schoolwork 是不可數
名詞，assignment 則為可數名詞。

▸ Please complete your assignment before our next class.
  請在下次上課前完成指定的作業。

▸ Our English teacher gives us more reading assignments than we can handle.
  我們英文老師交給我們的閱讀作業太多使我們吃不消。

---

15 preserve [prɪˋzɝv] vt. 保存；維持；醃製 & n. 果醬，蜜餞 (常用複數)

似 (1) reserve [rɪˋzɝv] vt. 預訂 ③
  reserve a ticket / room
  訂票 / 訂房

(2) conserve [kənˋsɝv]
  vt. 保留；節約使用 ⑥
  conserve water / energy
  節約水 / 能源

▸ The local residents want the ancient temple to be preserved for future generations.
  當地居民希望能為後代子孫維護這座歷史悠久的寺廟。

▸ The police must preserve public order.
  警方必須維持公共秩序。

▸ What is the best method of preserving plums?
  醃製梅子最好的方法是什麼？

▸ I like peach preserves on toast.
  我喜歡吐司抹上桃子果醬吃。

---

preservation [ˏprɛzɚˋveʃən]
  n. 保存，保護

衍 preservative [prɪˋzɝvətɪv]
  a. 防腐的，保存的 & n. 防腐劑

▸ All the books in the library are in a good state of preservation.
  圖書館所有的書都被保存得很好。

▸ The preservation of our national parks is important.
  保護我們的國家公園很重要。

---

16 distinguish [dɪˋstɪŋgwɪʃ] vt. 分辨，區別；使揚名

片 (1) distinguish A from B
  = tell A from B 區別 A 與 B 的不同
(2) distinguish oneself 使自己揚名

▸ It took me months to distinguish my girlfriend's voice from her sister's on the telephone.
  我花了好幾個月才能在電話上分辨出我女友和她姊姊的聲音。

▸ Dolly distinguished herself by her profound scholarship.
  多莉因學術造詣很深而揚名。
  ＊profound [prəˋfaʊnd] a. 淵博的，深的
    scholarship [ˋskɑlɚˏʃɪp] n. 學識 (不可數)；獎學金 (可數)

---

distinguished [dɪˋstɪŋgwɪʃt]
  a. 傑出的；著名的

片 be distinguished for...
  因……而出名
= be renowned for...
= be famous for...

▸ The award went to a distinguished movie director.
  這座獎項由一位傑出的電影導演獲得。

▸ Dr. Kahn is distinguished for his knowledge of classical Chinese literature.
  康博士以其中國古典文學的知識而著稱。

似 (1) famous [ˈfeməs] *a.* 著名的 ①
　 (2) outstanding [aʊtˈstændɪŋ]
　　　 a. 傑出的 ④
　 (3) renowned [rɪˈnaʊnd] *a.* 著名的 ⑥

---

distinct [dɪˈstɪŋkt]

a. 清楚的；不同的，獨特的

片 be distinct from... 不同於……

衍 (1) distinctive [dɪˈstɪŋktɪv]
　　　 a. 特殊的 ⑤
　 (2) distinction [dɪˈstɪŋkʃən]
　　　 n. 差別，區別；特色 ⑤

▶ Rebecca has very distinct handwriting.
蕾貝卡的字跡非常清晰。

▶ Taiwanese is a dialect which is completely distinct from Mandarin.
臺語是完全不同於國語的一種方言。

---

17 exception [ɪkˈsɛpʃən] *n.* 例外，除外

片 with the exception of...
　 除了……之外
= except (for)...

衍 exceptional [ɪkˈsɛpʃənḷ]
　　 a. 例外的，罕見的；優異的 ⑤

▶ There is no rule without exceptions.
所有規則皆有例外。

▶ Most boys in that school like football, but my son is an exception.
那間學校大部分男孩都喜歡足球，但我兒子卻是個例外。

▶ With the exception of his ill temper, John is quite a nice person.
= Except for his ill temper, John is quite a nice person.
約翰除了脾氣壞之外，為人倒是挺不錯的。

---

18 comment [ˈkɑmɛnt] *n.* 評語，批評 & *vi.* 評論 (與介詞 on 並用)

片 make a comment on...
= comment on...
　 對……評論 / 發表意見

衍 (1) commentary [ˈkɑmənˌtɛrɪ]
　　　 n. 評論 (針對球賽或文藝作品) ⑤
　 (2) commentator [ˈkɑmənˌtetɚ]
　　　 n. 時事評論家 ⑤

▶ Did the teacher make any comments on your speech?
= Did the teacher comment on your speech?
老師對你的演說有什麼評論嗎？

▶ I was unhappy when Ray commented on my new shoes.
瑞評論我的新鞋時，我很不高興。

---

19 impact [ˈɪmpækt] *n.* 影響，衝擊 (常與介詞 on 並用) & [ɪmˈpækt] *vt.* 對……產生影響

片 have an impact on...
　 對……有影響 / 衝擊

似 (1) influence [ˈɪnflʊəns]
　　　 n. & *vt.* 影響 ②
　 (2) affect [əˈfɛkt] *vt.* 影響 ②
　 (3) effect [ɪˈfɛkt] *n.* 影響 ②

▶ The writer's style had a deep impact on his literary successors.
這位作家的風格對後世文人有深遠的影響。

▶ Many experts believe the new policy will greatly impact the society.
許多專家都認為那項新政策會對社會帶來巨大衝擊。

20 **investigation** [ɪn͵vɛstə`geʃən] *n.* 調查

衍 (1) investigate [ɪn`vɛstə͵get]
　　 vt. 調查 ③
　 (2) investigator [ɪn`vɛstə͵getɚ]
　　 n. 調查者 ⑤

▸ The police started the investigation into the murder three years ago, but nothing has been found yet.
　 警方 3 年前展開這宗謀殺案的調查，不過迄今仍一無所獲。

inspection [ɪn`spɛkʃən]
n. 檢查，查驗

衍 (1) inspect [ɪn`spɛkt]
　　 vt. 檢查；視察 ③
　 (2) inspector [ɪn`spɛktɚ] *n.* 檢查員 ③

▸ Those business establishments that have failed to pass safety inspections will lose their licenses.
　 凡是沒有通過安全檢查的營業場所將被吊銷執照。

21 **rejection** [rɪ`dʒɛkʃən] *n.* 拒絕，推辭

衍 reject [rɪ`dʒɛkt] *vt.* 回絕，拒絕 ②
似 refusal [rɪ`fjuzḷ] *n.* 拒絕，推卻 ④

▸ Willie kept asking Jane for a date, but constant rejections had discouraged him.
　 威利一直找珍約會，但不斷的碰壁使他洩了氣。

22 **vast** [væst] *a.* 廣闊的；巨大的

似 (1) big [bɪg] *a.* 大的 ①
　 (2) large [lɑrdʒ] *a.* 巨大的 ①
　 (3) huge [hjudʒ] *a.* 巨大的 ②
　 (4) immense [ɪ`mɛns] *a.* 巨大的 ⑤

▸ A vast number of students attended the rally.
　 有好多學生參加這次的集會遊行。

▸ This university has a vast library.
　 這所大學裡有間大圖書館。

gigantic [dʒaɪ`gæntɪk]
a. 巨大的，龐大的

▸ Scientists found gigantic stone statues on Easter Island.
　 科學家在復活島上發現巨大的石雕像。

tremendous [trɪ`mɛndəs]
a. 龐大的

▸ Peter's company has achieved tremendous success this year.
　 彼得的公司今年大獲成功。

enormous [ɪ`nɔrməs] *a.* 巨大的

▸ John has an enormous amount of money.
　 約翰有一大筆錢。

23 **urge** [ɝdʒ] *vt.* 力勸，激勵 & *n.* 強烈的欲望，衝動

用 urge sb to + V　激勵某人做……
　 = call on sb to + V
似 desire [dɪ`zaɪr] *n.* 欲望 ③

▸ Tom's mother urged him to study every day.
　 湯姆的母親激勵他每天讀書。

▸ Rick felt a sudden urge to call Monica to tell her he was sorry.
　 瑞克突然很想打電話給莫妮卡，告訴他很抱歉。

urgent [ˋɝdʒənt] *a.* 緊急的；迫切的

衍 urgency [ˋɝdʒənsɪ] *n.* 緊急，急迫 ⑥

▶ I'm sorry I can't go out with you because I have something urgent to deal with.
很抱歉我無法跟你們出去，因為我有要事要處理。

---

24 minister [ˋmɪnɪstɚ] *n.* 部長；牧師

似 pastor [ˋpæstɚ] *n.* 牧師

▶ After the scandal, the Minister of Foreign Affairs was forced to step down.
醜聞事件後，外交部長被迫下臺。

▶ Susan's husband is the minister at a local church.
蘇珊的先生是當地某教會的牧師。

---

ministry [ˋmɪnɪstrɪ]
n. (政府) 部；牧師職務

片 (1) the Ministry of Education
教育部
(2) the Ministry of National Defense　國防部
(3) the Ministry of Foreign Affairs
外交部
(4) the Ministry of Internal Affairs
內政部

▶ The Ministry of National Defense is in charge of overall national defense.
國防部掌管整體的國防事務。

▶ There are three candidates for the Baptist ministry.
浸信會教會的牧師職位有三個候選人。

---

25 potential [pəˋtɛnʃəl] *n.* 潛力 & *a.* 潛在的

片 (1) have the potential for + N
有……的潛力
(2) have the potential to + V
有做……的潛力
(3) a potential customer　潛在客戶
衍 potentially [pəˋtɛnʃəlɪ] *adv.* 潛在地

▶ Howard has the potential to become one of the best centers in the basketball league.
霍華德有潛力成為該籃球聯盟裡其中一位頂尖的中鋒。
＊center [ˋsɛntɚ] *n.* (籃球、足球等的) 中鋒；中心

▶ The earlier you identify potential problems, the sooner you can take action to avoid them.
你越早發現那些潛在的問題，就能越快採取行動去避免它們發生。

1 occupy [ˈɑkjəˌpaɪ] *vt.* 擁有 (某職務)；占據；使忙碌

- ▤ occupy, occupied [ˈɑkjəˌpaɪd], occupied
- ⽚ be occupied with + N/V-ing
  忙於做……
  = be busy with + N
  = be busy + V-ing
- ⾐ occupied [ˈɑkjəˌpaɪd] *a.* 忙碌的
- ⾣ busy [ˈbɪzɪ] *vt.* 使忙於 & *a.* 忙碌的 ①

- ▶ Mr. White occupies an important position in the government.
  懷特先生在政府裡身居要職。
- ▶ The building occupies an entire block.
  這棟建築占據了一整個街區。
- ▶ Those workers were occupied with building a new road.
  = Those workers were busy building a new road.
  那些工人正忙著建造一條新路。

occupation [ˌɑkjəˈpeʃən] *n.* 職業；占領

- ⽚ be a(n)... by occupation
  職業是……
- ⾐ occupational [ˌɑkjəˈpeʃənl̩] *a.* 職業的
- ⾣ career [kəˈrɪr]
  n. 職業 (尤指終身職業) ③

- ▶ I'm a teacher by occupation.
  我的職業是教書。
- ▶ My ideal occupation is teaching at an elementary school because being with little children makes me feel young.
  我理想的職業是在小學教書，因為跟小朋友在一起讓我有年輕的感覺。
- ▶ The occupation of the country by the enemy lasted six years.
  敵人占領該國達 6 年之久。

2 explanation [ˌɛkspləˈneʃən] *n.* 解釋，說明

- ⾐ explain [ɪkˈsplen] *vt.* 說明，解釋 ①

- ▶ The teacher gave a satisfactory explanation of the process.
  這位老師把這程序作了令人滿意的說明。

3 initial [ɪˈnɪʃəl] *a.* 初期的 & *n.* (姓名的) 第一個字母 & *vt.* 在……上簽署姓名的首字母

- ⾐ (1) initiate [ɪˈnɪʃɪˌet] *vt.* 發起；
  使入會 & [ɪˈnɪʃɪət] *n.* 新加入者 ⑤
  (2) initiative [ɪˈnɪʃɪˌetɪv]
  n. 率先，主動 ⑤
  take the initiative in + V-ing
  率先做……

- ▶ Paul's initial effort was a failure, but he kept trying and finally succeeded.
  保羅最初的努力失敗了，但他繼續嘗試最後終於成功。
- ▶ The picture was signed with the initials "J.B.," which stood for James Brown.
  這幅畫落款的姓名縮寫是 J.B.，代表詹姆士・布朗。
- ▶ Please read the contract carefully and then initial here.
  請仔細閱讀合約後，接著在這裡簽下你姓名的開頭字母。

initially [ɪˈnɪʃəlɪ] *adv.* 開始時，最初
- ⾣ in the beginning 起先

- ▶ Initially, Andy was nice to Nancy, but eventually he left her.
  剛開始安迪對南西蠻好的，但後來卻離開她。

4 estimate [ˈɛstəˌmet] vt. 估計 & [ˈɛstəmɪt] n. 估計

用 (1) It is estimated that...
據估計……

(2) an estimated + 數字
估計有……

衍 (1) estimation [ˌɛstəˈmeʃən]
n. 評價;預算

(2) underestimate [ˌʌndəˈɛstəˌmet]
vt. 低估 ⑥

▶ It is estimated that 20,000 people will participate in the demonstration.

= An estimated 20,000 people will participate in the demonstration.
估計將有 2 萬人參與這次的示威遊行。

▶ Please give me a rough estimate of how much time you'll need to complete the project.
你需要花多久時間完成這件案子,請給我一個大約的數字。

5 expand [ɪkˈspænd] vt. & vi. (使)(尺寸或數量) 擴大,增加

似 (1) develop [dɪˈvɛləp] vt. & vi. 發展 ②
(2) grow [gro] vi. 成長 ①

反 shrink [ʃrɪŋk] vt. & vi. 縮小 ③

▶ We've expanded our business by opening two more restaurants lately.
我們最近擴大營業,新開了兩家餐廳。

▶ Thanks to teamwork and sound strategies, our sales expanded by 20% last year.
由於團結合作且策略得當,我們的業績去年增加了 20%。

---

expansion [ɪkˈspænʃən] n. 擴大

似 development [dɪˈvɛləpmənt]
n. 發展 ②

▶ The building's expansion took two years to complete.
該棟大樓的擴建花了兩年的時間才完成。

6 consequence [ˈkɑnsəˌkwəns] n. 結果;重要性 (= importance)

用 (1) in consequence of... 因為……
= as a consequence of...
= as a result of...
= because of...
= on account of...

(2) be of no / little / some / great consequence
= be of no / little / some / great importance
不 / 不太 / 有些 / 非常重要

▶ In consequence of your continual tardiness, I will dock your pay.

= As a consequence of your continual tardiness, I will dock your pay.
因為你常遲到,所以我要扣你薪水。

*tardiness [ˈtɑrdɪnəs] n. 遲到
dock [dɑk] vt. 扣除 (薪水)

▶ Don't worry about the matter. It's of no consequence to you.
別擔心這件事,它對你不重要。

---

consequent [ˈkɑnsəˌkwənt]
a. 由……的原因而發生的;必然的

用 be consequent on... 因……而起的
= be caused by...

▶ The landslide was consequent on the heavy rains.
這次坍方乃是因大雨所造成的。

▶ David didn't work hard, so his consequent failure was inevitable.
大衛不努力,因此他必然的失敗在所難免。

consequently [ˈkɑnsəˌkwəntlɪ]
adv. 因此，所以

似 therefore [ˈðɛrˌfɔr] *adv.* 因此 ②
= as a result
= as a consequence

▶ It rained, and consequently our picnic was postponed.
那天下雨，因此我們的野餐延期了。

▶ The mayor is very popular; consequently, he is likely to be reelected.
這位市長非常受歡迎；因此，他很可能再次當選。

---

7 convince [kənˈvɪns] *vt.* 使確信；說服

片 (1) convince sb of sth
使某人確信某事
(2) convince sb to + V
說服某人做……
= persuade sb to + V

似 persuade [pəˈswed] *vt.* 說服 ③

▶ How can I convince Ted of the dangers of running a red light?
我要怎樣才能讓泰德相信闖紅燈的危險性呢？

▶ It seems I can do nothing to convince my husband to quit smoking.
我似乎拿不出辦法說服我老公戒菸。

convinced [kənˈvɪnst] *a.* 確信的

片 (1) be convinced of sth 相信某事
(2) be convinced that... 相信……

衍 convincing [kənˈvɪnsɪŋ]
a. 令人信服的

▶ I'm convinced of John's innocence.
= I'm sure of John's innocence.
= I'm convinced that John is innocent.
我相信約翰是無辜的。

---

8 illustrate [ˈɪləstret] *vt.* 為……畫插圖；說明

衍 illustrator [ˈɪləsˌtretə] *n.* 插畫家

▶ Jane illustrates children's books for a living.
珍替兒童書籍畫插畫維生。

▶ The graphs illustrate the growth of our business.
這些圖表說明了我們事業的成長。
*graph [græf] *n.* 圖表

illustration [ˌɪləˈstreʃən]
n. 圖解（不可數）；插圖（可數）

片 (1) an illustration magazine
插畫雜誌
(2) illustration art 插畫藝術

▶ Illustration is often more useful in teaching than mere words.
在教學時，圖解常比光用文字解釋要來得有用。

▶ This book is full of beautiful illustrations.
這本書充滿了美麗的插圖。

---

9 surroundings [səˈraʊndɪŋz] *n.* (住處) 環境 (恆用複數)

衍 surround [səˈraʊnd] *vt.* 環繞 ③

▶ It took me a couple of days to get used to my new surroundings.
我花了好幾天才習慣新的環境。

似 (1) environment [ɪnˈvaɪrənmənt]
    n. (生態) 環境 (常用單數) ②

(2) circumstances [ˈsɚkəmˌstænsɪz]
    n. (抽象) 環境 (常用複數，常與介詞 under 並用) ④

under such circumstances
在這樣的環境下

---

10   **eliminate** [ɪˈlɪməˌnet] *vt.* 殲滅；剔除，淘汰

衍 elimination [ɪˌlɪməˈneʃən]
    n. 殲滅；淘汰

似 (1) eradicate [ɪˈrædɪˌket]
    vt. 連根拔出，剷除

(2) annihilate [əˈnaɪəˌlet] *vt.* 殲滅

▶ Our troops made a surprise attack and eliminated the enemy.
我軍發動奇襲，把敵人消滅了。

▶ We have to eliminate the losing team from the competition.
我們必須把這支快輸的隊伍從比賽中淘汰掉。

---

11   **formula** [ˈfɔrmjələ] *n.* 配方；公式

複 formulas / formulae [ˈfɔrmjəli]

衍 (1) formulate [ˈfɔrmjəˌlet]
    vt. 構想；規劃 ⑥

(2) formulation [ˌfɔrmjəˈleʃən]
    n. 構想；規畫

▶ Mary never told anyone about the formula for her special lotion.
瑪莉未曾告訴任何人關於她特殊乳液的配方。

▶ We'll have to come up with a formula to solve this math problem.
我們得想出一條公式以解出這道數學題。

---

12   **instruct** [ɪnˈstrʌkt] *vt.* 教授，指導；指示，告知

片 (1) instruct sb in...
    教導某人學習……

(2) instruct sb to + V
    指示某人做……

衍 (1) instruction [ɪnˈstrʌkʃən]
    n. 教導 ②

(2) instructive [ɪnˈstrʌktɪv]
    a. 有教育性的，有益的

▶ To be a singer, you need someone to instruct you in singing.
你若想當歌手，就需要找個人教你唱歌。

▶ The captain instructed his crew to sail east.
船長指示所有船員往東航行。

---

instructor [ɪnˈstrʌktɚ]
n. 指導者，教練

似 coach [kotʃ] *n.* 教練 ③

▶ Sam works as a fitness instructor at that gym.
山姆在那家健身房擔任健身教練。

---

13   **eventual** [ɪˈvɛntʃʊəl] *a.* 終究的，最後的

似 (1) last [læst] *a.* 最後的 ①

(2) final [ˈfaɪnl̩] *a.* 最後的 ②

▶ No one suspected the eventual result of the decision.
沒有人懷疑那項決定的最終結果。

▶ I have confidence in our team's eventual victory.
我有信心我們的隊伍會贏得最後的勝利。

eventually [ɪˈvɛntʃʊəlɪ]
adv. 終究，到頭來

似 (1) finally [ˈfaɪnḷɪ] *adv.* 最後 ①
 (2) lastly [ˈlæstlɪ] *adv.* 最後

▶ The ship will have to be repainted eventually.
這艘船終究還是要重新上漆。

▶ Eventually everyone must die.
每個人到頭來都須一死。

14 demonstrate [ˈdɛmənˌstret] *vt.* 示範 & *vi.* 示威

片 demonstrate against...
示威反抗⋯⋯

似 display [dɪˈsple] *vt.* 展示 ②

▶ The salesman demonstrated how to work the machine to us.
該業務員向我們示範說明如何操作這部機器。

▶ Thousands of people demonstrated against the government this morning.
今天早上有好幾千人示威抗議政府。

demonstration [ˌdɛmənˈstreʃən]
n. 示範；示威活動

片 (1) give sb a demonstration
 向某人示範
 = give sb a demo
 (2) hold a demonstration
 舉行示威
 (3) launch a demonstration
 發動示威

衍 demo [ˈdɛmo] *n.* 試聽帶；示範
 (是 demonstration 的簡寫)

▶ The tennis coach gave us a demonstration of basic strokes.
該網球教練向我們示範了一些基本打法。
*stroke [strok] *n.* (網球) 揮球，一擊

▶ The teachers held a demonstration for a pay increase.
這些老師舉行示威要求加薪。

15 leisurely [ˈliʒəlɪ] *a.* 休閒的 & *adv.* 從容不迫地

片 lead a leisurely life 生活很悠閒
= live leisurely

衍 leisure [ˈliʒ&] *n.* 閒暇 ③

▶ Since the weather was nice, Gary went for a leisurely drive along the coast.
因為天氣不錯，蓋瑞就沿著海岸悠閒開車兜風。

▶ John has been living leisurely in the country since he retired.
約翰退休後在鄉下一直過得很悠閒。

16 adequate [ˈædɪkwət] *a.* 充分的，適當的

衍 adequately [ˈædɪkwətlɪ]
 adv. 充分地，適當地

▶ You need adequate sleep, or else your health will suffer.
你需要足夠的睡眠，否則你的健康會受損。

Level 4

Unit 05

似 **sufficient** [sə`fɪʃənt]
　a. 足夠的，充分的 ③

inadequate [ɪn`ædəkwət]
a. 不適當的

似 **insufficient** [ˌɪnsə`fɪʃənt]
　a. 不充分的；不勝任的

▶ Matt was fired because he was inadequate for the job.
麥特因為無法勝任工作而被開除。

---

17 **slight** [slaɪt] *a.* 輕微的 & *n.* & *vt.* 輕視；冷落

衍 **slightly** [`slaɪtlɪ]
　adv. 輕微地，稍微，好些
似 (1) little [`lɪtl̩] *a.* 輕微的 ①
　(2) small [smɔl] *a.* 微不足道的 ①
　(3) contempt [ˌkən`tɛmpt] *n.* 輕視 ⑤

▶ David had a slight headache after bumping his head into the wall.
大衛頭撞到牆壁後感到有點疼痛。

▶ Frank said he didn't mean to ignore me, but I took it as a slight.
法蘭克說他無意忽略我，但我認為受到輕視。

▶ I felt slighted when Angela bought everyone a drink except me. (slighted 為過去分詞作形容詞用)
安琪拉請大家喝飲料但沒請我，我覺得自己受到冷落。

---

18 **candidate** [`kændəˌdet] *n.* 候選人

似 (1) contestant [kən`tɛstənt]
　　n. 參與競賽者 ⑥
　(2) contender [kən`tɛndɚ] *n.* 競爭者

▶ There are two candidates running for chairman of our department.
本系有兩位候選人角逐系主任一職。

---

19 **bond** [bɑnd] *n.* 關係；債券 & *vt.* & *vi.* (使) 黏合 & *vi.* (與某人) 建立關係，培養感情

片 bond with... 與……建立關係
似 (1) connection [kə`nɛkʃən] *n.* 關係 ②
　(2) relationship [rɪ`leʃənʃɪp]
　　n. 關係 ②
　(3) join [dʒɔɪn] *vt.* 連接 ①
　(4) connect [kə`nɛkt]
　　vt. & *vi.* 連結；關聯 ③

▶ There is a special emotional bond between the mother and the newborn baby.
母親與新生兒之間存在一種特別的情感聯繫。

▶ I was so desperate for money that I cashed the bonds my grandmother gave me.
我急著要錢，因此把祖母給我的債券全拿去兌現了。
*desperate [`dɛspərɪt] *a.* 極度渴望的

▶ The glue promises to bond any metal to any surface.
這瓶膠水保證能把金屬黏在任何表面上。

▶ It's hard for Jim to bond with his co-workers.
吉姆很難和他同事打成一片。

---

20 **appropriate** [ə`proprɪət ] *a.* 適當的，合適的 & [ ə`proprɪˌet] *vt.* 撥 (款)

片 be appropriate for... 適合……
　= be suitable for...

▶ You should have taken more appropriate measures at that time.
當時你應該採取更合適的措施才是。

似 suitable [ˋsutəbḷ] *a.* 適當的 ②

▶ Jeans are obviously not appropriate for such formal occasions.
這樣正式的場合顯然不適合穿著牛仔褲。

▶ The government is going to appropriate $5 million for the project.
這項工程政府將撥款 5 百萬美元補助。

---

inappropriate [ˌɪnəˋproprɪət]
a. 不適當的，不妥當的

似 unsuitable [ʌnˋsutəbḷ] *a.* 不合適的

▶ Danny got drunk at the staff party and said something inappropriate to the boss.
丹尼在員工派對上喝醉，向老闆說了些不當的話。

---

21 revolution [ˌrɛvəˋluʃən] *n.* 革命；(星球) 運行，公轉

衍 (1) revolt [rɪˋvolt] *vi.* 叛亂，叛變 ⑥
(2) revolve [rɪˋvɑlv] *vi.* 旋轉 ⑥

似 rotation [roˋteʃən]
n. (地球) 自轉；旋轉 ⑥

▶ There is a revolution taking place in that country.
那個國家正發生一場革命。

▶ One revolution of the Earth around the sun takes a year.
地球繞太陽運轉一圈要花一年的時間。

---

revolutionary [ˌrɛvəˋluʃənˌɛrɪ]
a. 革命性的；創新的 & *n.* 革命家

似 (1) creative [krɪˋetɪv] *a.* 有創意的 ③
(2) original [əˋrɪdʒənḷ]
a. 有獨創性的 ③
(3) innovative [ˋɪnəˌvetɪv]
a. 創新的 ⑤

▶ Mr. Jackson's revolutionary ideas led to great change.
傑克遜先生革命性的觀念導致很大的改變。

▶ The computer is a revolutionary invention.
電腦是一項創新的發明。

▶ Dr. Sun Yat-sen was a great revolutionary, who led the revolution to overthrow the Manchurian government in 1911.
孫中山先生是一位偉大的革命家，他領導革命於 1911 年推翻了滿清政府。

---

22 emphasis [ˋɛmfəsɪs] *n.* 強調，重視

複 emphases [ˋɛmfəsiz]
片 lay / put / place emphasis on...
= lay / put / place stress on...
強調 / 重視……

衍 (1) emphasize [ˋɛmfəˌsaɪz]
vt. 強調，重視 ②
(2) emphatic [ɪmˋfætɪk] *a.* 強調的

▶ We lay great emphasis / stress on the quality of our products.
我們很重視我們產品的品質。

23 greasy [ˈgrisɪ] a. 油膩的

衍 grease [gris] n. 油脂；潤滑油 ⑥

▶ The floor in the kitchen is greasy, so you'd better be careful walking in there.
廚房地上很油膩，你在裡頭走動最好當心點。

24 reservation [ˌrɛzɚˈveʃən] n. 預訂；保留（意見）

片 (1) make a reservation for...
預訂……
= reserve...
(2) without reservation　毫不保留

衍 reserve [rɪˈzɝv] vt. 預訂 & n. 儲備 ③

▶ I'd like to make a reservation for a table of five people tonight.
我想預訂今晚一張 5 人座的桌位。

▶ I believe Mr. Wu is a competent young man, so I recommend him to you without reservation.
本人相信吳先生是個能幹的年輕人，因此本人毫不保留地把他推薦給閣下。

*competent [ˈkɑmpətənt] a. 能幹的

25 secure [səˈkjʊr] vt. 獲得；弄牢 & a. 安全的

片 (1) secure a contract / job
取得一份合約 / 工作
(2) be secure against / from...
安全免於……的

衍 security [sɪˈkjʊrətɪ] n. 安全 ③

似 safe [sef] a. 安全的 ①

反 insecure [ˌɪnsəˈkjʊr] a. 不安全的

▶ After beating France, Germany secured a place in the World Cup Finals.
打敗法國隊之後，德國隊取得了進入世界盃決賽的席位。

▶ The tables at this restaurant are all secured firmly to the floor.
這家餐廳的桌子都被緊緊地固定在地板上。

▶ Endangered species should be secure against poachers.
瀕臨絕種的物種應該要避免受到盜獵者所危害。

*poacher [ˈpotʃɚ] n. 盜獵者

26 suggestion [sə(g)ˈdʒɛstʃən] n. 建議；提議

片 make a suggestion　提出建議

衍 suggest [sə(g)ˈdʒɛst] vt. 建議 ②

似 (1) advice [ədˈvaɪs] n. 建議 (不可數) ②
(2) proposal [prəˈpozl]
n. 建議；提議 ④

▶ They accepted our suggestion and changed their plan.
他們接受我們的提議而改變計畫。

27 waken [ˈwekən] vi. 醒來 & vt. 喚醒

衍 (1) wake [wek] vt. & vi. 醒 ①
(2) awake [əˈwek]
vi. 醒來 & a. 清醒的 ③

▶ Zola wakened at the sound of her baby's crying.
左拉因她寶寶的哭聲而醒來。

▶ I was wakened by a phone call last night.
我昨晚被一通電話吵醒。

0528-0533

比 waken 與 wake 同義，前者較文雅，
後者則較普遍。
(1) waken　醒來
　 = wake up
(2) waken sb　將某人喚醒
　 = wake sb up

28　website [ˈwɛbˌsaɪt] *n.* 網站

片 visit a website　上某個網站

衍 web [wɛb] *n.* 全球資訊網 (大寫)
　 (= the World Wide Web)；蜘蛛網 ③

▶ Please visit our website for more information.
欲知更多詳情，請上我們的網站。

29　option [ˈɑpʃən] *n.* 選擇

片 have no option / choice /
alternative but to + V
除了……之外別無選擇

衍 optional [ˈɑpʃənl] *a.* 可選擇的 ⑤

似 (1) choice [tʃɔɪs] *n.* 選擇 ①
　 (2) alternative [ɔlˈtɚnətɪv] *n.* 選擇 ④

▶ Because of the rising flood waters, we had no option but to evacuate our home and head for higher ground.
由於洪水水位持續升高，我們除了離開家園前往地勢較高之處以外別無選擇。
＊evacuate [ɪˈvækjuˌet] *vt.* 撤離

30　incredible [ɪnˈkrɛdəbl̩] *a.* 難以置信的

衍 incredibly [ɪnˈkrɛdəblɪ]
adv. 難以置信地；極為

片 It is incredible that...
……是難以置信的

似 unbelievable [ˌʌnbɪˈlivəbl̩]
a. 難以置信的

▶ It's incredible that Victor speaks English so fluently without an accent.
維克多英文講得這麼流利又沒口音，真令人難以置信。

31　promotion [prəˈmoʃən] *n.* 促進，提倡；升遷；(產品的) 促銷

衍 promote [prəˈmot]
vt. 促進，提倡；升遷 ③

▶ Tourism in Taiwan is doing well thanks to recent promotions.
臺灣的旅遊業因為近來的推廣而正蓬勃發展。

▶ Lisa got a promotion last month, and now she can afford to buy a new car.
麗莎上個月升遷，現在她買得起新車了。

▶ The company is planning a big promotion for its newest product.
那間公司正為其最新產品籌劃一項大型促銷活動。

32 relevant [ˈrɛləvənt] *a.* 有關的 (與介詞 to 並用)

片 be relevant to... 和……有關

衍 relevance [ˈrɛləvəns] *n.* 相關性
(不可數，亦與介詞 to 並用)

▶ What you said has no direct relevance to the issue we were discussing.
你所說的和我們討論的議題沒有直接的相關性。

反 irrelevant [ɪˈrɛləvənt] *a.* 無關的
(亦與介詞 to 並用)

▶ Do you have any previous job experience relevant to this type of work?
你之前有沒有從事這種工作的相關經驗？

▶ I don't think your questions are directly relevant to our agenda.
我想你的問題與本議程沒有直接的關聯。

33 despite [dɪˈspaɪt] *prep.* 儘管

片 (1) despite + N/V-ing 儘管……
= in spite of + N/V-ing
= notwithstanding + N/V-ing
　＊notwithstanding
　　[ˌnɑtwɪθˈstændɪŋ] *prep.* 儘管
(2) despite the fact that... 儘管……

▶ Despite our best efforts, we couldn't save the dying man.

= In spite of our best efforts, we couldn't save the dying man.

= Notwithstanding our best efforts, we couldn't save the dying man.
儘管我們盡了最大的努力，還是無法挽救那位垂死的人。

▶ We failed to win the tug-of-war despite the fact that we had tried our best.
儘管我們盡了最大的努力，還是無法贏得這場拔河比賽。
＊tug-of-war [ˌtʌgəv ˈwɔr] *n.* 拔河比賽

1 assistance [əˈsɪstəns] n. 幫助，援助

片 come to sb's assistance
來幫助某人

衍 (1) assist [əˈsɪst] vt. 幫助 ③
(2) assistant [əˈsɪstənt] n. 助理 ③

似 help [hɛlp] n. 幫助 ①

▶ The needy family was grateful for the assistance given by their neighbors.
這個貧困的家庭對於鄰居給予的幫助感激不已。
*needy [ˈnidɪ] a. 貧困的

▶ We all came to John's assistance when we learned that he was in trouble.
我們知道約翰有困難時就前來幫助他。

2 gulf [gʌlf] n. 海灣；(意見等的) 差異

似 (1) bay [be] n. 海灣 ③
(2) gap [gæp] n. 裂縫；差異 ③
(3) difference [ˈdɪfərəns] n. 差異 ②

▶ The Gulf of Mexico is the ninth largest body of water in the world.
墨西哥灣是世界第 9 大海域。

▶ The gulf between the rich and the poor in that country is widening.

= The gap between the rich and the poor in that country is widening.

= The difference between the rich and the poor in that country is widening.
該國貧富之間的差距日益擴大。

3 intense [ɪnˈtɛns] a. 強烈的

衍 (1) tense [tɛns] a. 緊張的；繃緊的 ④
(2) intensive [ɪnˈtɛnsɪv] a. 密集的 ④
intensive training　密集訓練

似 (1) strong [strɔŋ] a. 強壯的 ①
(2) powerful [ˈpauɚˌfəl]
a. 強有力的 ②

反 moderate [ˈmɑdərət] a. 適度的 ④

▶ Mary's anger towards her husband was too intense for her to forgive him.
瑪莉對她丈夫的恨意強烈到她無法原諒他。

▶ I can't stand the intense heat waves during the summer.
我無法忍受夏日強烈的熱浪。

intensity [ɪnˈtɛnsətɪ] n. 強度；熱切

衍 intensify [ɪnˈtɛnsəˌfaɪ]
vt. 加強 & vi. 加劇 ⑤

▶ I can't stand the intensity of the heat.
我受不了高溫。

▶ The boss likes David because whatever he does, he does it with intensity.
老闆喜歡大衛，因為他不管做什麼都很投入。

intensive [ɪnˈtɛnsɪv] a. 徹底的，密集的

▶ The police began an intensive search for the missing child.
警方開始密集搜尋這個失蹤的小孩。

片 an intensive care unit
加護病房 (縮寫為 ICU)

衍 intensively [ɪnˋtɛnsɪvlɪ] *adv.* 密集地

似 concentrated [ˋkɑnsɛn͵tretɪd]
a. 集中的

---

4 **competition** [͵kɑmpəˋtɪʃən] *n.* 競爭 (不可數)；比賽 (可數)；(生意上競爭的) 同行 (集合名詞，不可數，之前置定冠詞 the)

片 be in competition with...
與……競爭

衍 (1) compete [kəmˋpit] *vi.* 競爭 ③
compete with... 與……競爭

▸ Unless we are prepared, we can't compete with them.
除非我們已經準備妥當，否則我們沒辦法跟他們競爭。

(2) competence [ˋkɑmpətəns]
n. 能力 ⑤

▸ Thirty students are in competition with each other for the tennis championship.
30 名學生競相爭奪網球比賽冠軍。

▸ Connie is the youngest contestant in the swimming competition.
康妮是游泳比賽中最年輕的參賽者。
＊contestant [kənˋtɛstənt] *n.* 參賽者

▸ Our prices are always lower than those of the competition.
我們的價格總是比同行來得低。

competitive [kəmˋpɛtɪtɪv]
a. 競爭的

衍 (1) competitiveness
[kəmˋpɛtɪtɪvnəs] *n.* 競爭力

(2) competent [ˋkɑmpətənt]
a. 能幹的 ⑤

▸ The boss admired Brian's competitive spirit.
老闆很賞識布萊恩的競爭精神。

▸ John became a college student through the highly competitive entrance examination.
約翰通過競爭激烈的入學考試成為大學生。

competitor [kəmˋpɛtətɚ]
n. 競爭者，參賽者

似 contestant [kənˋtɛstənt] *n.* 參賽者 ⑥

▸ There were 300 competitors in the marathon.
那場馬拉松共有 300 名參賽者。

---

5 **adjust** [əˋdʒʌst] *vt.* 調整，調節 & *vi.* 適應 (與介詞 to 並用)

片 adjust to + N/V-ing 使自己適應……
= adapt (oneself) to + N/V-ing
= accustom oneself to + N/V-ing

▸ Before the interview, the candidate spent several minutes adjusting his tie.
面試前，這位應徵者花了幾分鐘調整他的領帶。

▸ I'll adjust the window blinds because the sunlight is too bright.
我來調整卷簾，因為陽光太亮了。

▸ I'm having a hard time adjusting to the climate of this place.
我很難適應此地的氣候。

▶ Billy finds it very hard to adjust to the hustle and bustle of city life.
= Billy finds it very hard to adapt to the hustle and bustle of city life.
= Billy finds it very hard to accustom himself to the hustle and bustle of city life.
比利發現他很難使自己適應都市生活的繁忙。
＊hustle and bustle　繁忙

adjustment [əˈdʒʌstmənt]
n. 調整，調節；適應

片 make an adjustment　調整

似 (1) regulation [ˌrɛgjəˈleʃən]
　　　n. 調整 ④
　　(2) adaptation [ˌædæpˈteʃən]
　　　n. 適應，適合 ⑥

▶ After we made a few minor adjustments, the engine ran smoothly.
那臺引擎經過我們的些微調整後，運轉便順暢了。
▶ Some foreign students feel that it is a big adjustment living in Britain.
一些外籍學生認為要適應英國的生活很困難。

6　distribute [dɪˈstrɪbjut / ˈdɪstrɪbjut] *vt.* 分發，分配

似 deliver [dɪˈlɪvɚ] *vt.* 傳送 ②

▶ The professor is distributing the examination papers to the class.
該教授正在把考卷發給全班。

distribution [ˌdɪstrəˈbjuʃən]
n. 分配；分布

似 (1) delivery [dɪˈlɪvərɪ] *n.* 傳送 ②
　　(2) circulation [ˌsɝkjəˈleʃən]
　　　n. 發行 ④

▶ The distribution of wealth is uneven in that country.
該國財富分配不均。
▶ That magazine enjoys a wide distribution.
= That magazine enjoys a wide circulation.
那本雜誌的發行遍及各地。

7　criticize [ˈkrɪtɪˌsaɪz] *vt.* 批評

片 be criticized as...　被批評為……

似 (1) find fault with...　挑剔……
　　(2) comment [ˈkamɛnt] *vi.* 評論 ④
　　　comment on sth
　　　對……發表評論

▶ The plan was criticized as being too expensive.
這個計畫被批評為耗資過大。

▶ The politician refused to comment on that issue.
該政客拒絕對那議題發表評論。

反 praise [prez] *vt.* 稱讚 ②

criticism [`krɪtə,sɪzəm]
n. 批評，爭議；評論 (均不可數)

片 **constructive criticism**
建設性的批評

似 **comment** [`kamɛnt] *n.* 評語，批評
(可數) ④

▶ The new tax law has been the subject of criticism recently.
這條新稅法最近成為**爭議**的話題。

▶ This magazine is famous for its literary criticism.
= This magazine is famous for its literary comments.
這本雜誌因為它的**文學評論**而出名。

---

critical [`krɪtɪkl̩] *a.* 危急的；批評的

片 (1) **be in critical condition**
處於危急的情況
(2) **be critical of...**　批評……

似 (1) **dangerous** [`dɛndʒərəs]
a. 危險的 ①
(2) **risky** [`rɪskɪ] *a.* 危險的 ⑤

反 **stable** [`stebl̩] *a.* 穩定的 ③
be in stable condition
處於穩定的情況

▶ The patient is still in critical condition.
病人的情況仍然**危急**。

▶ Most environmentalists are critical of building a dam in that area.
大多數環保人士都對在那個地區建造水壩一事嚴加**批評**。
＊environmentalist [ɪn,vaɪrən`mɛntl̩ɪst] *n.* 環保人士

---

critic [`krɪtɪk] *n.* 評論家；愛挑剔的人

似 (1) **commentator** [`kamən,tetə]
n. 評論員 ⑤
(2) **faultfinder** [`fɔlt,faɪndə]
n. 吹毛求疵者

▶ T. S. Eliot was one of the greatest critics in Britain.
艾略特是英國最偉大的**評論家**之一。

▶ Mary is such a critic that no one likes to be around her.
瑪莉那麼**愛挑剔**，因此沒有人喜歡和她在一起。

8　largely [`lardʒlɪ] *adv.* 大大地；大部分

似 (1) **mostly** [`mostlɪ]
adv. 大多數地；主要地 ③
(2) **mainly** [`menlɪ] *adv.* 主要地
(3) **primarily** [praɪ`mɛrəlɪ]
adv. 主要地

▶ Our success is largely due to Kelly's help.
我們的成功要**大大地**歸功於凱莉的幫忙。

▶ Those who work in this field are largely women.
在這個領域工作的人**大半**是女性。

9　commit [kə`mɪt] *vt.* 犯 (罪)；奉獻

三 **commit, committed** [kə`mɪtɪd],
committed

片 (1) **commit a crime**　犯罪
(2) **commit robbery**　犯搶劫罪

▶ Lucas committed a serious crime and was sentenced to life imprisonment.
路卡斯**犯下**重罪，被判無期徒刑。

▶ Sherry commits an hour every day to studying English.
= Sherry devotes an hour a day to studying English.
= Sherry dedicates an hour a day to studying English.
雪莉每天**撥**一小時研讀英文。

(3) commit A to B　將 A 奉獻於 B
= devote A to B
= dedicate A to B
(4) commit oneself to + N/V-ing
致力於……

衍 commitment [kəˋmɪtmənt]
n. 委託，承諾 ⑤

make a commitment to + V
致力要……

▶ The mayor made a firm commitment to fight crime.
市長堅決地承諾要打擊犯罪。

▶ Mr. White has committed himself to teaching over the past 20 years.
懷特先生過去 20 年來都獻身於教育。

---

committed [kəˋmɪtɪd] *a.* 盡力的

片 be committed to...　致力於……

似 (1) devoted [dɪˋvotɪd] *a.* 致力的
(2) dedicated [ˋdɛdə,ketɪd] *a.* 奉獻的

反 uncommitted [ˌʌnkəˋmɪtɪd]
a. 未承諾的

▶ The new research center is committed to finding a cure for AIDS.
這家新的研究中心致力於找出治療愛滋病的方法。

---

10 **characteristic** [ˌkærəktəˋrɪstɪk] *n.* 特徵 & *a.* 典型的（皆與介詞 of 並用）

片 be characteristic of...
是……的特徵

衍 (1) character [ˋkærəktə] *n.* 個性（不可數）；人物（小說裡的角色）②

a man of noble character
有高尚品德的人

(2) characterize [ˋkærəktə,raɪz]
vt. 使具有……的特徵 ⑤

be characterized as...
被描述有……的特徵

▶ John is characterized as a man of principles.
約翰這個人的特徵就是很有原則。

▶ Genes determine the characteristics of every living thing.
基因決定了每樣生物的種種特徵。

▶ This usage is characteristic of American English.
這種用法是美式英語的特徵。

▶ This kind of hot and spicy food is very characteristic of the food in the country.
這種辛辣食物是該國非常典型的食物。

---

11 **retire** [rɪˋtaɪr] *vi.* 退休；睡覺，休息

片 retire from...　從……退休

▶ Jack retired from the military after 30 years of service.
在軍中服役 30 年後，傑克退休了。

> When did you retire last night?
= When did you go to bed last night?
你昨晚幾點睡覺？

---

retired [rɪˋtaɪrd] *a.* 已退休的

> Both Peter's parents are retired doctors.
彼得的雙親都是已退休的醫生。

---

retirement [rɪˋtaɪrmənt] *n.* 退休

> Ted became a volunteer after his retirement from business.
泰德自企業界退休後就成了一名義工。

---

12 **furnish** [ˋfɜnɪʃ] *vt.* 配備傢俱；提供（用於下列片語）

用 furnish sb with sth　提供某人某物
= provide sb with sth

衍 (1) furniture [ˋfɜnɪtʃə]
　n. 傢俱（集合名詞，不可數）②
(2) furnishings [ˋfɜnɪʃɪŋz] *n.* 傢俱、窗簾等裝飾物件（恆用複數）
(3) furnished [ˋfɜnɪʃt] *a.* 含有傢俱的

> I will not move into the house until it is fully furnished.
房子要到傢俱配置好之後我才會搬進去。

> This company furnishes you with all the equipment you'll need for camping.
= This company provides you with all the equipment you'll need for camping.
這家公司提供你露營所需的一切裝備。

---

13 **approval** [əˋpruvl] *n.* 贊成，同意

衍 approve [əˋpruv] *vt.* 批准，核可 &
　vi. 贊同（與介詞 of 並用）③
似 (1) agreement [əˋgrimənt] *n.* 同意 ①
(2) consent [kənˋsɛnt] *n.* 同意 ⑤

> The board of directors gave Bill final approval of his plan.
董事會最後同意了比爾的計畫。

---

14 **appoint** [əˋpɔɪnt] *vt.* 選定；指定；指派

用 (1) appoint sb to + V
　　指定某人從事……
= assign sb to + V
(2) appoint sb as + 職位
= assign sb (to be) + 職位
　　指派某人擔任……職位
似 (1) employ [ɪmˋplɔɪ] *vt.* 僱用 ②
(2) assign [əˋsaɪn] *vt.* 分派 ④

> Dave and I appointed our favorite restaurant as the place for the meeting.
我和戴夫選定在我們最喜歡的那家餐廳碰面。

> A date has been appointed for the important business meeting.
這場重要商務會議日期已定。

> Nancy's teacher appointed her to do the job.
南西的老師指派她負責這件工作。

> The coach appointed John as captain of the team.
= The coach appointed John captain of the team.
教練指派約翰擔任隊長。

Level 4　Unit 06

appointment [əˋpɔɪntmənt]
n. 約定，(公務上的) 約會；職位，職務；
任命

🈁 make an appointment with sb
與某人約會

▶ I already made an appointment with my doctor for seven this evening.
我已經和醫師約好今晚 7 點看診。

▶ David was thrilled about receiving an appointment as assistant professor at Cambridge.
大衛很興奮能獲聘到劍橋大學擔任助理教授一職。

▶ No one was pleased with Beth's appointment as group leader.
沒有人對貝絲獲任命為小組領導人一事感到高興。

---

15 panel [ˋpænl] *n.* 嵌版；儀表板；專題討論小組

🈁 (1) an instrument panel
(機器、設備等的) 儀表板 (正式說法)
(2) a solar panel　太陽能發電板

▶ There is a crack in one of the panels of the door.
這扇門的其中一塊嵌版有條裂縫。

▶ There's something wrong with the instrument panel.
儀表板有點問題。

▶ A panel of judges met to discuss the Carlson case.
裁判小組集會討論卡爾森案件。

---

16 expose [ɪkˋspoz] *vt.* 暴露；接觸

🈁 expose A to B
使 A 暴露於 B；使 A 接觸 B

▶ The politician's corruption was exposed by the press.
該政客的貪汙被新聞界披露了。
＊corruption [kəˋrʌpʃən] *n.* 貪汙

▶ The film was ruined by being exposed to light.
這捲底片因曝光而毀了。

▶ To learn English well, you should expose yourself more to this language.
要把英文學好，你就該多接觸這個語言。

exposure [ɪkˋspoʒɚ]
n. 暴露，曝晒；接觸 (與介詞 to 並用)

▶ Too much exposure to sunlight can cause skin problems.
過度曝晒於陽光下可能引發皮膚問題。

▶ Constant exposure to French is a must if you want to master the language.
多多接觸法文是想要精通這個語言的不二法門。

---

17 possess [pəˋzɛs] *vt.* 擁有，持有；(鬼魂) 附身於 (用於下列片語中)

🈁 (1) be possessed of sth
擁有 (能力、技能等)
＝ possess sth
(2) be possessed by a ghost
被鬼魂附身

▶ The man was arrested for possessing drugs when he arrived in the country.
這名男子抵達該國時，因持有毒品而被捕。

▶ Peter's father is possessed of a good sense of humor.

= Peter's father possesses a good sense of humor.

彼得的父親很有幽默感。

▶ The boy seemed to be possessed by evil spirits.

這男孩似乎被邪靈附身了。

possession [pə`zɛʃən]

n. 擁有 (不可數)；財產 (恆用複數)

Ħ (1) take possession of sth

取得某物的所有權

(2) be found in possession of...

被發現擁有……

▶ The possession of health is extremely valuable.

擁有健康是非常可貴的。

▶ The bank took possession of the debtor's home.

該銀行取得該債務人房子的所有權。

＊debtor [`dɛtə] *n.* 債務人

▶ The man was found in possession of guns.

該男子被發現持有槍枝。

▶ We lost all our possessions in the flood.

這次水災中我們失去所有的財產。

---

18 intellectual [ˌɪntḷ`ɛktʃuəl] *a.* 智力的 & *n.* 知識分子

Ħ intellectual ability   智力

衍 (1) intellectually [ˌɪntḷ`ɛktʃuəlɪ]

adv. 智力上

(2) intelligent [ɪn`tɛlədʒənt]

a. 聰明的 ③

(3) intellect [`ɪntḷˌɛkt] *n.* 智力 ⑥

▶ I was quite impressed with the boy's intellectual ability.

我對這男孩的智力感到很佩服。

▶ Mr. Bauer is one of the leading German intellectuals on environmental research.

包爾先生是德國在環境研究方面領先的知識分子之一。

---

intelligence [ɪn`tɛlədʒəns]

n. 聰明才智；情報

Ħ intelligence quotient

智商 (簡寫為 IQ)

▶ This job requires a high degree of intelligence.

這項工作需要高度的聰明才智。

▶ The woman used to work for the Central Intelligence Agency.

這名女子曾經替美國中央情報局工作過。

▶ Hank is a child with a high intelligence quotient.

漢克是個智商很高的孩子。

---

19 copper [`kɑpə] *n.* 紅銅 & *a.* 紅銅色的

比 (1) brass [bræs]

n. 黃銅 & *a.* 黃銅色的 ③

(2) bronze [brɑnz]

n. 青銅 & *a.* 青銅色的 ⑤

▶ Most coins are made of copper.

大部分的錢幣都是銅鑄的。

▶ Many homes today still get their water through copper pipes.

現今許多家庭仍使用紅銅水管取水。

Level 4   Unit 06

20 shift [ʃɪft] *vt.* 轉移，改變 & *n.* 輪班

片 (1) shift A to B　把 A 轉移給 B
(2) shift one's attention from A to B
　　把某人的注意力從 A 轉到 B
＝ change one's attention from A to B
(3) work on the day / night shift
　　上白 / 夜班

▶ Don't try to shift the blame to me.
不要試圖把責任推到我身上。
▶ What can I do to shift my son's attention from computer games to his studies?
我該怎麼做才能把我兒子的注意力從電動玩具轉移到課業上？
▶ I work on the night shift this week.
我這星期輪夜班。

21 resolve [rɪˈzɑlv] *vt.* 解決；下決心 & *n.* 決心 (不可數)

片 (1) resolve / solve the problem
　　解決問題
(2) resolve to + V　下定決心要……
(3) strengthen / weaken sb's resolve　增強 / 削減某人的決心
衍 resolute [ˈrɛzəˌlut] *a.* 堅決的；堅毅的

▶ The letter should resolve their doubts.
這封信應能解除他們的疑慮。
▶ We did all we could to resolve the dispute.
我們盡了全力去解決這個紛爭。
▶ It took me five hours to resolve this problem.
我花了 5 個小時解決這個問題。
▶ Kathy has resolved to marry Tony.
凱西已下定決心要嫁給東尼。
▶ The lack of a pay raise strengthened Jason's resolve to quit the job.
沒加薪加強了傑森辭掉工作的決心。

resolution [ˌrɛzəˈluʃən]
n. 志願，期望；決心

片 make a resolution to + V
　　下定決心要……
＝ make a promise to + V
＝ resolve to + V
＝ determine to + V
＝ make up one's mind to + V
似 promise [ˈprɑmɪs] *n.* 承諾 ②

▶ Have you made any New Year's resolutions?
你立定了任何新年新希望嗎？
▶ Cindy made a resolution to study abroad someday.
辛蒂下定決心有一天要出國念書。

22 determination [dɪˌtɜməˈneʃən] *n.* 決心

似 willpower [ˈwɪlˌpauɚ] *n.* 意志力
衍 determine [dɪˈtɜmɪn]
　　vt. 決定；確定 ③

▶ Ted's determination to quit smoking turned out to be in vain.
泰德戒菸的決心最後宣告失敗。

23 orchestra [ˈɔrkɪstrə] *n.* 管弦樂團

回 a symphony orchestra　交響樂團

▶ The great performance of the orchestra won everyone's applause.
管弦樂團出色的演出贏得一致的掌聲。
＊applause [əˈplɔz] *n.* 鼓掌喝采

24 compose [kəmˈpoz] *vt.* 組成，構成；譜 (曲)；寫 (詩、信等)

回 (1) A be composed of B
　　A 由 B 組成
　= A be made up of B
　= A consist of B
　= B compose A
　(2) compose oneself　使自己鎮定

▶ This class is composed of twenty boys and five girls.
= This class is made up of twenty boys and five girls.
= This class consists of twenty boys and five girls.
= Twenty boys and five girls compose this class.
這個班級是由 20 位男孩和 5 位女孩組成的。

▶ Beethoven composed nine symphonies.
貝多芬譜了 9 首交響樂。

▶ Charlie composed a love poem for his girlfriend.
查理為了他女友寫了一首情詩。

▶ Zack tried to compose himself before speaking to his girlfriend's parents.
在與他女友的父母談話前，查克設法讓自己鎮定下來。

composer [kəmˈpozɚ] *n.* 作曲家

▶ Who is your favorite composer?
你最喜歡的作曲家是哪位？

composition [ˌkɑmpəˈzɪʃən] *n.* 成分；(樂曲、畫、詩等) 作品；作文

衍 component [kəmˈponənt] *n.* 組件 ⑤

▶ The scientists analyzed the moon rock to determine its composition.
科學家們分析那塊月球岩石以確定它的成分。

▶ The composition of the sonata took Mozart only a few hours.
莫札特只花了幾個鐘頭就譜成了那首奏鳴曲。
＊sonata [səˈnɑtə] *n.* 奏鳴曲

▶ The teacher said my composition on honesty was excellent.
老師說我那篇關於誠實的作文寫得很棒。

25 colleague [ˈkɑlig] *n.* 同事

似 co-worker [ˈkoˌwɝkɚ] *n.* 同事

▶ Being ill-tempered, John has difficulty getting along with colleagues.
約翰脾氣不好，跟同事處不來。
＊ill-tempered [ˌɪlˈtɛmpɚd] *a.* 壞脾氣的

26 proposal [prəˋpozḷ] *n.* 提議，建議；求婚

片 approve / reject a proposal
贊成 / 反對某項提議

衍 (1) propose [prəˋpoz] *vt.* 計劃；建議
& *vi.* 求婚 (與介詞 to 並用) ②

(2) proposition [͵prɑpəˋzɪʃən]
n. (尤指商業上的) 提議 / 案

▶ The proposal to close the hospital was rejected.
關閉這家醫院的提議被否決了。

▶ Eve was thinking how to decline David's marriage proposal.
伊芙在想該怎麼婉拒大衛的求婚。

27 liar [ˋlaɪɚ] *n.* 說謊者

衍 lie [laɪ] *n.* 謊言 & *vi.* 說謊 ①

▶ I don't like to make friends with liars.
我不喜歡跟說謊的人做朋友。

 **Unit 07**

---

1 **pace** [pes] *n.* 步調 & *vt.* & *vi.* 在……來回走動 / 踱步

片 (1) keep pace with...
　　 與……並駕齊驅
= keep abreast of...
= keep up with...
(2) pace the floor
　　在地板上來回踱步

▶ Duncan likes the fast pace of life in the city.
鄧肯喜歡城市快的生活步調。

▶ Reading newspapers enables you to keep pace with the times.
閱讀報紙能使你跟上時代的步伐。

▶ Dad paced the floor as he waited for my sister to give birth to his first grandchild.
老爸在等候老姊生下他頭一個金孫時,一直在地板上來回踱步。

---

2 **acceptance** [ək`sɛptəns] *n.* 接受;答應 (邀請等)

衍 (1) accept [ək`sɛpt] *vt.* 接受 ②
(2) acceptable [ək`sɛptəbl]
　　 a. 可接受的 ③
似 agreement [ə`grimənt] *n.* 贊成 ①

▶ The new student found it hard to gain the acceptance of others.
那位新來的學生發現要被其他同學接納並不容易。

▶ So far we have had forty acceptances out of seventy invitations.
到目前為止,在 70 封發出的邀請函中,已有 40 封回函接受邀請。

---

3 **retain** [rɪ`ten] *vt.* 保留,保有

片 retain sb's title　衛冕;保留頭銜
似 (1) maintain [men`ten]
　　 vt. 維持 (某個狀況) ②
(2) sustain [sə`sten] *vt.* 維持 (生命) ⑤
(3) detain [dɪ`ten] *vt.* 扣留,拘留 ⑥

▶ You'd better retain copies of the documents for at least one year.
這幾份文件的副本你最好留著至少一年別丟。

▶ The boxer succeeded in retaining his title as the heavyweight champion.
那位拳擊手成功地衛冕重量級冠軍。

---

4 **content** [kən`tɛnt] *a.* 滿足的 (= satisfied) & *n.* 滿足 & *vt.* 使滿足 (= satisfy)

片 (1) be content with...
　　 對……感到滿意
= be contented with...
= be satisfied with...
= be pleased with...
(2) to one's heart's content
　　使某人心滿意足,盡情地

▶ Alex was content with his performance in the speech contest.
艾力克斯對他在演講比賽的表現很滿意。

▶ Ladies and gentlemen, let's drink to our hearts' content.
各位先生女士,我們開懷地暢飲吧。

0704-0708

反 discontent [ˌdɪskənˈtɛnt]
a. 不滿意的（= dissatisfied）
be discontent / dissatisfied with...
對……感到不滿意

▸ The father is discontent with his son's performance.
那位爸爸對他兒子的表現不滿意。

▸ Lounging on this beach all day contents me.
整天懶洋洋地躺在沙灘上讓我很滿足。
＊lounge [laʊndʒ] *vi.* (懶洋洋地) 躺著，靠著

---

content [ˈkɑntɛnt] *n.* (書、演講的)
內容 (不可數)；內容物 (恆用複數)；
目錄 (恆用複數)

片 the table of contents　目錄

▸ I don't like the content of this book.
我不喜歡這本書的內容。

▸ The policeman asked me to open my box in order to examine the contents in it.
警察要我把箱子打開，以便檢查其中的內容物。

---

contented [kənˈtɛntɪd]
a. 感到滿足的（= satisfied = content [kənˈtɛnt]）

片 be contented with...
　　對……感到滿意
= be content with...
= be satisfied with...
= be pleased with...

▸ The cat seems contented, just sitting in front of the fire.
這隻貓坐在爐火前，似乎很滿足的樣子。

▸ The boy is contented with what he has just got.
這個小男孩對剛剛拿到的東西很滿意。

---

contentment [kənˈtɛntmənt]
n. 滿意，知足

似 satisfaction [ˌsætɪsˈfækʃən]
　　n. 滿足 ④

▸ Happiness lies in contentment.
= Happiness lies in being content with what you have.
知足常樂。——諺語

5　abandon [əˈbændən] *vt.* 放棄

片 (1) abandon hope / a plan
　　　放棄希望 / 計畫
　　= give up hope / a plan
　　(2) abandon oneself to + N/V-ing
　　　沉溺於……

▸ The manager abandoned the plan to set up a new factory in Mexico.
經理放棄在墨西哥建立新廠的計畫。

▸ After his girlfriend left him, Peter abandoned himself to eating.
彼得的女友離他而去後，他就沉溺於暴食。

6　foundation [faʊnˈdeʃən] *n.* 地基；基礎；建立，創建；基金會

片 lay a foundation for...
= lay the foundation(s) for...
　　為……打好地基 / 奠下基礎

▸ First the workers laid the foundation. Then they built the walls.
首先工人們打好地基，然後把牆砌起來。

衍 found [faʊnd] vt. 建立，成立 ②
三態為：found, founded [ˈfaʊndɪd],
founded

▶ Our school was founded 85 years ago.
本校於 85 年前創立。

似 establishment [ɪsˈtæblɪʃmənt]
n. 建立 ④

▶ George's good command of English laid a solid foundation for his success as a businessman.
喬治流利的英文為做為一名成功的商人奠下紮實的基礎。

▶ The foundation of the university took place fifty years ago.
這所大學創立於 50 年前。

▶ My aunt works for the Save the Children Foundation.
我阿姨在《救助兒童基金會》工作。

founder [ˈfaʊndɚ] n. 創立者

▶ The founder of this charitable organization is a young entrepreneur.
該慈善機構的創辦人是一位年輕的實業家。
*charitable [ˈtʃærətəbḷ] a. 慈善的
entrepreneur [ˌɑntrəprəˈnɝ] n. 實 / 企業家

Level 4 Unit 07

---

7 assemble [əˈsɛmbḷ] vt. 組合 & vi. & vt. 集合

H assemble sth 組合某物
= put sth together

反 disassemble [ˌdɪsəˈsɛmbḷ] vt. 分解
disassemble sth 拆解某物
= take sth apart

▶ If you know how to assemble the computer yourself, you can save lots of money.
你自己若懂得組裝電腦，便可以省下很多錢。

▶ The boy can take the parts apart, but he can't assemble them.
那個小男生懂得把零件分解，卻無法將它們組合起來。

▶ The elderly people assembled in the hospital for free flu shots.
老人家們聚集在醫院裡打免費的流感疫苗。

assembly [əˈsɛmblɪ] n. 集會；裝配

H (1) the National Assembly
國民大會
(2) an assembly line 裝配線

▶ All the students went to the morning assembly in the auditorium.
所有的學生都去禮堂參加朝會。

▶ The factory has a fully automated assembly line.
這家工廠有一條全自動裝配線。
*automated [ˈɔtəˌmetɪd] a. 自動化的

---

8 shelter [ˈʃɛltɚ] n. 庇護所 (可數)；遮蔽物 (可數)；遮蔽，庇護 (不可數) & vt. 遮蔽；保護

H (1) take shelter 避難，尋求遮蔽物
(2) shelter A from B
保護 A 使免於 B 的侵襲

▶ I'd like to know how to donate clothing to a homeless shelter.
我想知道該如何捐助衣物到遊民庇護所。
*donate [ˈdonet / doˈnet] vt. 捐贈

▶ It's raining now. Let's take shelter in that temple over there.
現在要下雨了，我們到那裡的廟裡躲一下吧。

▶ It is against the law to shelter a criminal from the police.
包庇罪犯逃避警方追緝是犯法的。

▶ A big umbrella sheltered us from the sun.
一把大傘保護我們免於日曬。

9 encounter [ɪnˋkaʊntɚ] *vt.* 遭遇 & *vt.* & *n.* 與……不期而遇 (名詞時常與介詞 with 並用)

片 encounter a problem　遭遇到問題

似 bump / run into sb
與某 (認識的) 人不期而遇

▶ We encountered a small problem during the trial period.
我們在測試階段時遭遇到一個小問題。

▶ I first encountered my wife in Tokyo.
我和我太太第一次邂逅在東京。

▶ Arthur's first encounter with Alice was when he was in Taipei.
亞瑟和愛莉絲的第一次相會是他在臺北的時候。

10 theme [θim] *n.* 主題

片 a theme park　主題公園

▶ The theme of John's essay is water pollution in Taiwan.
約翰論文的主題是臺灣的水汙染問題。

11 phenomenon [fəˋnamə,nan] *n.* 現象 (單數)

複 phenomena [fəˋnamənə]

衍 phenomenal [fəˋnamən̩l]
a. 了不起的；令人印象深刻的

▶ TV violence is not a new phenomenon in Taiwan.
電視暴力在臺灣不是個新現象。

12 rural [ˋrʊrəl] *a.* 鄉下的

片 a rural area　鄉村地區

反 urban [ˋɝbən] *a.* 都市的 ③

▶ Some people like to live in urban areas for convenience, while others prefer rural areas for a quiet environment.
有些人因為便利性而喜歡住都會區，有些人因為環境安靜而喜歡住鄉下。

13 liquor [ˋlɪkɚ] *n.* 酒 (尤指蒸餾的烈酒或白酒，如威士忌及白蘭地)

似 (1) wine [waɪn]
n. 酒 (水果酒，大都由葡萄釀造) ②

(2) alcohol [ˋælkə,hɔl]
n. 酒類 (泛指各種含酒精的酒) ④

▶ You have to be 18 to drink liquor.
你必須滿 18 歲才能喝酒。

14 site [saɪt] *n.* 地點，位置；網站 & *vt.* 使位於，使設立於

片 (1) at the site of...　在……的現場
　　(2) a construction site　工地
　　= a building site
似 (1) website [ˈwɛbˌsaɪt] *n.* 網站 ④
　　(2) location [loˈkeʃən] *n.* 地點 ③
　　(3) locate [ˈloket / loˈket] *vt.* 使位於 ③
　　= situate [ˈsɪtʃuˌet] *vt.* 使位於

▶ There were several people at the site of the accident helping the survivors.
= There were several people at the scene of the accident helping the survivors.
意外發生的現場有好幾個人正在幫忙搶救生還者。

▶ Three friends founded the site youtube.com in February 2005.
三位好友於 2005 年 2 月創立了 YouTube 網站。

▶ The new office building will be sited near the train station.
這棟新辦公大樓將位於火車站附近。

▶ Mr. Johnson is going to site his new factory in that area.
強森先生將把他的新工廠設立在那個區域。

15 code [kod] *n.* 密碼 & *vt.* 編碼；加密碼

片 (1) break a code　破解密碼
　　(2) a dress code　服裝規定

▶ It took the specialist three years to break the code.
那位專家費時 3 年才將密碼破解。

▶ You have to obey the dress code if you want to work here.
如果你想在這邊工作，就必須遵守服裝規定。

▶ Each word on the list is coded to show the level of difficulty.
表上的所有字都加以編碼，以顯示其難度。

zip code [ˈzɪpˌkod] *n.* 郵遞區號
似 an area code　（電話的）區域號碼
延伸 ZIP　地區改進計畫
　　（= Zone Improvement Plan）

▶ If there's no zip code on it, the letter cannot be delivered.
如果信上沒有郵遞區號，信是無法投遞的。

16 lean [lin] *vi.* 斜靠 & *a.* 瘦的

片 lean against...　斜靠在……之上

▶ The young man was leaning against the wall, looking at the sky.
這年輕人斜靠著牆，仰望著天空。

▶ Matthew's brother is tall and lean.
馬修的弟弟又高又瘦。

▶ You should eat more vegetables and lean meat if you want to slim down.
如果你想瘦下來就應該多吃蔬菜及瘦肉。

17 pursue [pɚˋsu] vt. 追求

(1) pursue one's goals
　　追求某人的目標
(2) pursue one's dreams
　　追求某人的理想
(3) pursue a girl　追求女生
= chase a girl
= chase after a girl

▶ With my father's support, I have been able to pursue my dreams.
　有了我爸的支持，我才能夠去追尋我的夢想。

▶ Willy pursued the beautiful girl, who eventually fell in love with him.
　威利追求那位美眉，最後兩人墜入情網。

---

pursuit [pɚˋsut] n. 追求
in pursuit of...　追求……

▶ In pursuit of fame and wealth, the blossoming young actress neglects her old friends.
　為了追求名利，這名日漸走紅的年輕女演員忽視了老友。

▶ Peter is planning to study abroad in pursuit of a bright future.
　彼得計劃要出國留學，以追求光明的前途。

18 academic [ˌækəˋdɛmɪk] a. 學術的

(1) academically [ˌækəˋdɛmɪklɪ]
　　adv. 學術上
(2) academy [əˋkædəmɪ]
　　n. (專門培養專才的) 學院 (如藝術學院等)，專科學校 ⑥

▶ Laziness may be responsible for Timmy's bad academic performance.
　懶惰或許是提米學業成績不佳的原因。

19 maximum [ˋmæksəməm] n. 最大量 & a. 最大量的

a maximum of + 數字
　　最多不超過……
= at most + 數字

衍 maximize [ˋmæksəˌmaɪz]
　　vt. 使增加到最大極限

▶ To maximize your time, you should study on your way to and from school.
　為充分利用時間，你應該在往返學校途中念書。

▶ Give yourself a maximum of 20 minutes to read the questions.
　給自己最多 20 分鐘的時間讀完題目。

▶ The maximum capacity of this room is 300 people.
　這房間最多能容納 300 人。
　*capacity [kəˋpæsətɪ] n. 容量

---

minimum [ˋmɪnəməm]
n. 最小量 & a. 最小量的

a minimum of + 數字　最少……
= at least + 數字

▶ You must practice playing the piano for a minimum of two hours every day.
　你每天必須練習彈鋼琴至少兩個小時。

▶ Sarah prefers jobs that require minimum effort.
　莎拉喜歡最不費力的工作。

衍 **minimize** [ˈmɪnəˌmaɪz]
vt. 使降到最低 ⑤

▶ We should minimize our chances of making the same mistakes.
我們該儘量減少犯同樣錯誤的機會。

20 **manufacture** [ˌmænjəˈfæktʃɚ] *n. & vt.* (用機器大量) 生產，製造

似 **produce** [prəˈd(j)us] *vt.* 生產 ②

▶ The manufacture of newspapers requires a lot of wood pulp.
製造報紙需要許多木漿。
＊pulp [pʌlp] *n.* 紙漿

▶ Our company manufactures electronic devices.
我們公司生產電子儀器。
＊device [dɪˈvaɪs] *n.* 儀器，設備

manufacturer [ˌmænjəˈfæktʃərɚ]
n. 廠商；製造商

似 **producer** [prəˈd(j)usɚ] *n.* 製造者；
(影片／電視節目) 製作人 ③

▶ Manufacturers often introduce new products to keep their business booming.
廠商為了讓生意興隆，常推出新產品。
＊boom [bum] *vi.* 興盛

21 **cooperate** [koˈɑpəˌret] *vi.* 合作 (與介詞 with 並用)

片 **cooperate with...** 和⋯⋯合作
似 **collaborate** [kəˈlæbəˌret] *vi.* 合作
　collaborate with... 和⋯⋯合作

▶ We cooperated with the police to locate the suspects.
我們和警方合作找出嫌疑犯。
＊suspect [ˈsʌspɛkt] *n.* 嫌疑犯

cooperation [koˌɑpəˈreʃən] *n.* 合作
片 **in cooperation with...** 與⋯⋯合作
似 **collaboration** [kəˌlæbəˈreʃən]
　n. 合作 ⑤
　in collaboration with...
　與⋯⋯合作

▶ We made a film in cooperation with that big company.
我們和那家大公司合作拍一部電影。

cooperative [koˈɑpəˌretɪv]
a. 合作的 & *n.* 合作企業

衍 **cooperatively** [koˈɑpəˌretɪvlɪ]
　adv. 配合地

▶ Though Sandra didn't like the activity, she did her best to be cooperative.
雖然珊卓不喜歡這項活動，但她還是盡力去配合。

▶ The new national bank will be run as a cooperative.
這間新的國家銀行將由一間合作企業經營。

22 overcome [ˌovɚˈkʌm] *vt.* 克服

目 overcome, overcame [ˌovɚˈkem], overcome

似 (1) conquer [ˈkɑŋkɚ] *vt.* 征服 ④
(2) defeat [dɪˈfit] *vt.* 擊敗 ④

▶ I could not overcome the difficulty of learning French, so I changed my major.
我無法克服學法文的困難，因此我換了主修科系。

23 creation [krɪˈeʃən] *n.* 創造 (不可數)；創作品 (可數)

衍 (1) create [krɪˈet] *vt.* 創造 ②
(2) creator [krɪˈetɚ] *n.* 創造者 ③
(3) creature [ˈkritʃɚ] *n.* 生物 ③
(4) creative [krɪˈetɪv] *a.* 有創造力的 ③

似 recreation [ˌrɛkrɪˈeʃən] *n.* 消遣；休閒娛樂 ④

▶ This project will help foster the creation of new jobs.
本計畫將有助於創造新的就業機會。
*foster [ˈfɑstɚ / ˈfɔstɚ] *vt.* 培養，促進

▶ The bike was one of the company's new creations that hit the market recently.
這部自行車是該公司最近問市的新創作之一。

creativity [ˌkrɪeˈtɪvətɪ] *n.* 創造力

似 originality [əˌrɪdʒəˈnælətɪ] *n.* 獨創性 ⑤

▶ Without creativity, one can't be a successful artist.
一個人若是缺乏創意，就沒辦法成為成功的藝術家。

24 tragedy [ˈtrædʒədɪ] *n.* 悲劇；慘劇

反 comedy [ˈkɑmədɪ] *n.* 喜劇 ④

▶ I prefer comedies to tragedies.
我喜歡喜劇甚於悲劇。

▶ Jason's death was a tragedy to his family.
傑森的死對他的家庭是一個慘劇。

tragic [ˈtrædʒɪk]
a. 悲劇的；令人悲痛的

反 comic [ˈkɑmɪk]
a. 喜劇的；滑稽的 & *n.* 漫畫 ②

▶ I don't like stories with tragic endings.
我不喜歡悲劇性結局的故事。

▶ Rita's husband's sudden death was very tragic.
麗塔的先生突然撒手人寰令人悲痛不已。

25 comedy [ˈkɑmədɪ] *n.* 喜劇

衍 comedian [kəˈmidɪən] *n.* 喜劇演員 ⑤

反 tragedy [ˈtrædʒədɪ] *n.* 悲劇；慘劇 ④

▶ *The Taming of the Shrew* is one of Shakespeare's most famous comedies.
《馴悍記》是莎士比亞最著名的喜劇之一。
*shrew [ʃru] *n.* 潑婦

26 commerce [ˈkɑmɝs] *n.* 商業

衍 commercial [kəˈmɝʃəl] *a.* 商業的 & *n.* (廣播、電視的) 廣告 ②

▶ Taipei is Taiwan's center of commerce.
臺北是臺灣的商業中心。

似 trade [tred] *n.* 貿易 ②

延伸 the American Chamber of Commerce in Taipei 臺北市美國商會

▶ That company has always been promoting e-commerce.
那家公司一直都在推廣電子商務。

---

27 constitute [ˈkɑnstəˌt(j)ut] *vt.* 組成，構成

衍 constituent [kənˈstɪtʃuənt]
a. 組成的 & *n.* 成分，要素；選民

似 (1) form [fɔrm] *vt.* 形成 ②
(2) compose [kəmˈpoz] *vt.* 構成 ④
(3) comprise [kəmˈpraɪz]
vt. 構成，包含 ⑤

▶ Volunteers constitute one third of the hospital's workforce.
= Volunteers form one third of the hospital's workforce.
= Volunteers comprise one third of the hospital's workforce.
= Volunteers compose one third of the hospital's workforce.
= Volunteers account for one third of the hospital's workforce.
志工構成了這間醫院 3 分之 1 的人力。

---

constitution [ˌkɑnstəˈt(j)uʃən]
n. 憲法

衍 constitutional [ˌkɑnstəˈt(j)uʃn̩]
a. 憲法的 ⑤

▶ According to the US Constitution, people have the the right to speak freely.
根據美國憲法，人民享有言論自由權。

---

28 numerous [ˈn(j)umərəs] *a.* 極多的 (之後接複數可數名詞)

似 (1) plentiful [ˈplɛntɪfəl] *a.* 許多的 ④
(2) abundant [əˈbʌndənt]
a. 豐富的 ⑤
(3) many [ˈmɛnɪ] *a.* 許多的 ①

▶ I have numerous problems to solve and will need your help.
我有許多的問題必須解決，極需您的協助。

---

29 manual [ˈmænjuəl] *n.* 使用手冊 & *a.* 手工的；用手操作的

片 manual labor 勞力工作
似 (1) booklet [ˈbʊklɪt] *n.* 小冊子 ⑥
(2) handbook [ˈhændˌbʊk]
n. 手冊，指南

▶ You should read the manual before you use the copier.
在使用這部影印機之前，你應該先閱讀使用手冊。

▶ Mark doesn't like manual labor. He wants a desk job instead.
馬克不喜歡勞力工作。他反而想要一份坐辦公室的工作。

▶ My camera has manual and automatic functions.
我的相機有手動和自動功能。

30 **quarrel** [ˈkwɔrəl] *vi. & n.* 爭吵

片 quarrel with sb about / over sth
因某事與某人起爭執

= have a quarrel with sb about /
over sth

似 (1) squabble [ˈskwɑbl̩]
vi. & n. 爭吵，口角

(2) argument [ˈɑrgjəmənt]
n. 爭執 (尚未到吵架的地步) ②

(3) argue [ˈɑrgju] *vi.* 爭執，爭論 ②

▶ Terence is ill-tempered. He quarrels with his wife over almost everything.
泰倫斯的脾氣不好。他幾乎每件事都會和太太爭吵。

▶ I had a quarrel with Michelle over who should do the work.
我和蜜雪兒對誰該做這項工作起了爭執。

31 **renew** [rɪˈn(j)u] *vt.* 更新

衍 renewal [rɪˈn(j)uəl] *n.* 更新

▶ The boss decided to renew my contract for another year.
老闆決定和我再簽一年的合約。

32 **shade** [ʃed] *n.* 陰涼處 (不可數)；卷簾 (可數) & *vt.* 遮蔽 & *vi.* 逐漸改變

片 (1) in the shade of a tree   在樹蔭下
(2) pull up / down the shades
拉起 / 拉下卷簾
(3) shade into...   逐漸變成……
(4) put... in the shade
使……相形失色

衍 shady [ˈʃedɪ]
a. 陰涼的；令人起疑的 ④

▶ We took a rest in the shade of a large tree.
我們在一棵大樹的樹蔭下休息。

▶ I pulled down the shades and went to bed.
我拉下卷簾便睡覺去了。

▶ The tall trees shade the garden.
高大的樹將花園遮蔭了起來。

▶ The dusk shaded into night while I was driving home.
我開車回家時，不知不覺暮色已轉為黑夜。

▶ Monica's beauty and confidence put other contestants in the shade.
莫妮卡的美貌和自信使其他參賽者相形失色。

Unit **08**

0801-0803

---

1 **prominent** [`prɑmənənt] *a.* 重要的；顯著的，突出的 □

衍 prominence [`prɑmənəns] *n.* 傑出

似 (1) eminent [`ɛmənənt]
    a. 重要的，有影響力的
(2) outstanding [aʊt`stændɪŋ]
    a. 重要的，傑出的 ④

▶ Dr. Watson is one of the most prominent scientists in the United States.
華生博士是美國最重要的科學家之一。

▶ Richard has large eyes and a prominent nose.
理查有一對大眼睛及一個引人注目的鼻子。

---

2 **fundamental** [ˌfʌndə`mɛntḷ] *a.* 重要的；基本的 & *n.* 基礎 (常用複數) □

似 (1) basic [`besɪk] *a.* 基本的 ②
(2) essential [ɪ`sɛnʃəl]
    a. 必要的，不可或缺的 ④

延伸 1970 年代以來，全球興起人權運動，人權運動的活躍分子經常掛在嘴上的言詞就是『基本人權』，英文稱作 fundamental human rights。

▶ Clean food and proper exercise are fundamental to good health.
乾淨的食物及適當的運動對健康很重要。

▶ I don't see any fundamental difference between your proposal and his.
我看不出你的建議與他的建議有什麼基本上的差異。

▶ Learning to read is one of the fundamentals of education.
識字是教育的基礎之一。

---

3 **concentrate** [`kɑnsn̩ˌtret] *vt.* & *vi.* 集中 & *n.* 濃縮物 □

片 (1) concentrate on... 專注於……
    = focus on...
(2) concentrate A on B
    將 A 集中在 B 上面

▶ You should concentrate on what the teacher says.
你應當專心聽老師所說的話。

▶ Bob is concentrating his thoughts on writing the essay.
鮑伯將心思專注在寫論文上。

▶ I want fresh orange juice, not juice made from concentrate.
我要新鮮的柳橙汁，不是濃縮果汁。

---

concentration [ˌkɑnsən`treʃən]
n. 專心，專注；集中

片 a concentration camp 集中營
似 focus [`fokəs] *n.* 專注；焦距 ②

▶ A beautiful woman walked by and disturbed Joe's concentration. □
一位美女走過，使喬分心。
*disturb [dɪ`stɝb] *vi.* & *vt.* 干擾，打擾

▶ The researchers did a study on population concentration.
這些研究人員作了一項有關人口集中的研究。

▶ Six million Jews died in Nazi concentration camps during World War II.
二次大戰期間，有 6 百萬猶太人死於納粹集中營。

Level 4   Unit 08

4 incident [ˈɪnsədənt] n. 事件

衍 (1) incidental [ˌɪnsəˈdɛntl̩] a. 附帶的
(2) incidentally [ˌɪnsəˈdɛntl̩ɪ]
　　adv. 對了，附帶地；順帶一提

▶ I'll handle this problem immediately. Incidentally (= By the way), is Linda coming today?
我會立即處理這個問題。對了，今天琳達有來嗎？

比 incident 指的是有發生原因的事件，包括各種意志力所能控制的事件；但 accident [ˈæksədənt] 常指的是不可避免、無法預料或控制的意外事件。

▶ The incident that led to the mayor's resignation is now known to the public.
導致市長辭職下臺的那個事件現在人人皆知。

5 precise [prɪˈsaɪs] a. 正確的；精確的

衍 precision [prɪˈsɪʒən] n. 精確，精密 ⑥
with precision　精準地
= precisely

▶ The robot is able to carry out the task with precision.
該機器人可以十分精確地執行任務。

似 (1) correct [kəˈrɛkt] a. 正確的 ①
(2) exact [ɪgˈzækt] a. 準確的 ②

▶ Jeff double-checked the measurements to make sure they were precise.
傑夫再次檢驗測量結果，以確保它們是正確的。

▶ Our teacher gave us very precise instructions on how to conduct the experiment.
我們老師給我們非常精確的指示告訴我們如何進行這實驗。

precisely [prɪˈsaɪslɪ] adv. 精確地

似 (1) exactly [ɪgˈzæktlɪ] adv. 精準地，正好地
(2) sharp [ʃɑrp] adv. 準時地；整 &
　　a. 銳利的；敏銳的；劇烈的 (痛) ①
(3) on the dot　(幾點) 整

▶ The plane will take off at 10 o'clock precisely.
= The plane will take off at 10 o'clock exactly.
= The plane will take off at 10 o'clock sharp.
= The plane will take off at 10 o'clock on the dot.
飛機將在十點整起飛。

6 agreeable [əˈgriəbl̩] a. 可接受的，贊成的；令人喜悅的

衍 (1) agree [əˈgri]
　　vi. 意見一致，相符，相合 ①
(2) agreement [əˈgrimənt]
　　n. 同意；一致 ①
in agreement with...
　　與……意見一致

▶ What Johnny does is in agreement with what he says.
強尼言行一致。

▶ Can anyone come up with a solution that will be agreeable to all?
有誰能想出一個大家都覺得合適的解決之道呢？

▶ I'm glad that everyone here is agreeable to the plan.
= I'm glad that everyone here agrees to the plan.
我很高興這兒的每個人都贊成這項計畫。

▶ Mary is such an agreeable girl.
瑪莉真是討人喜歡的女孩。

似 (1) pleasant [ˈplɛznt]
　　 a. 令人愉快的，討人喜歡的 ②
　　 (2) acceptable [əkˈsɛptəbl]
　　 a. 可接受的 ③

7　convention [kənˈvɛnʃən] *n.* 慣例，習俗；大會，會議 (可數)

片 by convention　按慣例

似 (1) custom [ˈkʌstəm] *n.* 習俗 ②
　　 (2) tradition [trəˈdɪʃən] *n.* 傳統 ②

▶ By convention, it's usually the man who proposes to the woman.
按傳統，通常都是男人向女人求婚。

▶ Business people wear suits according to social convention.
生意人根據社會習俗穿西裝。

▶ Issues concerning the use of mercy killings are raised and discussed in the medical convention.
關於使用安樂死的數個議題在醫學會議上被提及與討論。
＊mercy killing　安樂死
＝euthanasia [ˌjuθəˈneʒ(ɪ)ə] *n.*

conventional [kənˈvɛnʃənl]
a. 傳統的，慣例的

似 traditional [trəˈdɪʃənl] *a.* 傳統的 ②

▶ It is conventional for Japanese to bow to one another.
日本人彼此鞠躬行禮是傳統。

8　detective [dɪˈtɛktɪv] *n.* 偵探；刑警 & *a.* 偵測的

片 (1) a detective novel　偵探小說
　　 (2) a detective movie / film　偵探片

衍 detect [dɪˈtɛkt] *vt.* 察覺 ③

▶ Patricia paid a detective to secretly follow her husband.
派翠西亞花錢僱了一位偵探偷偷跟蹤她老公。

▶ The scientist installed a detective device to prevent any gas leaks in the lab.
這位科學家裝設了偵測裝置以防實驗室裡的瓦斯外洩。

9　elsewhere [ˈɛls,(h)wɛr] *adv.* 在別處

似 in another place　在別處

▶ You can't find this bag for a lower price elsewhere.
這個包包的價格你在別的地方找不到比這裡更便宜的了。

10　percent [pɚˈsɛnt] *n.* 百分之 (幾)

用法 percent 須與數字並用，percent 之前置數字，之後接 of，若 of 之後的名詞為複數，則接複數動詞；若 of 之後的名詞為不可數名詞，則之後的動詞採單數動詞。

▶ One percent of the students in this school have passed the test.
該校有百分之一的學生通過測驗。

▶ Five percent of the gold in the world is found in this area.
該區擁有世界上百分之五的黃金。

percentage [pɚˋsɛntɪdʒ] *n.* 百分比

用法 percentage 通常與 large 或 small 並用，形成下列固定用法：

(1) a large percentage of...
   相當大百分比的……，大部分……
(2) a small percentage of...
   很小百分比的……，一小部分……

▶ The scientists expressed the figures as percentages.
   這科學家以百分比表示這些數據。

▶ A large percentage of prisoners come from poor families.
   大部分的囚犯來自窮苦家庭。

11 imply [ɪmˋplaɪ] *vt.* 暗示

衍 (1) implication [ˏɪmplɪˋkeʃən]
   n. 含意；暗示 ⑤
(2) implicit [ɪmˋplɪsɪt]
   a. 含蓄的，暗指的 ⑥

▶ Are you implying that I'm a hypocrite?
   你在暗示說我是個偽君子嗎？
   *hypocrite [ˋhɪpəkrɪt] *n.* 偽君子

12 chamber [ˋtʃembɚ] *n.* 房間；會議廳

片 chamber music　室內樂

▶ The princess retired to her chamber after the ball.
   舞會完畢後，公主回到她的房間。

▶ Mr. Evans left the council chamber shortly after the meeting started.
   伊凡斯先生在會議開始後沒多久就離開會議廳了。

13 sympathy [ˋsɪmpəθɪ] *n.* 慰問；同情，同感，共鳴

片 have sympathy for...　同情……
   = sympathize with...
衍 sympathize [ˋsɪmpəˏθaɪz] *vi.* 同情；
   有同感 (均與介詞 with 並用) ⑥

▶ My teacher wrote me a letter of sympathy after my father passed away.
   我父親過世後，老師便寫了一封慰問信給我。

▶ The rich man has no sympathy for the poor.
= The rich man doesn't sympathize with the poor.
   那位有錢人對窮人一點都沒同情心。

sympathetic [ˏsɪmpəˋθɛtɪk]
a. 同情的，憐憫的

片 be sympathetic to / towards...
   對……表示同情
衍 sympathetically [ˏsɪmpəˋθɛtɪkəlɪ]
   adv. 同情地

▶ We are all sympathetic to the COVID-19 patients.
= We all sympathize with the COVID-19 patients.
= We have great sympathy for the COVID-19 patients.
   我們對那些新冠肺炎病患相當同情。

14 absorb [əbˋsɔrb] *vt.* 吸收；理解

片 be absorbed in...　全神貫注於……
   = be buried in...

▶ Sponges are used to absorb liquids.
   海綿可用來吸收液體。

▸ I couldn't absorb everything I read.
所有讀過的東西我並非都能理解。

▸ I was so absorbed in my work that I didn't hear you calling me.
= I was so buried in my work that I didn't hear you calling me.
我太投入工作,因此沒聽到你在叫我。

15　attach [ə'tætʃ] vt. 繫住,連接(與介詞 to 並用)

片 (1) attach importance to sth
　　將某事物看得很重要
　(2) attach A to B　將 A 附著於 B 上

衍 attached [ə'tætʃt] a. 喜歡的,依戀的

▸ The little boy was very much attached to his mother.
小男孩很喜歡媽媽。

反 detach [dɪ'tætʃ] vt. 分開 ⑥

▸ Don't attach too much importance to what that guy said.
別把那傢伙說的話看得太重要。

▸ Tom attached the string to his kite.
湯姆把繩子綁在風箏上。

attachment [ə'tætʃmənt]
n. 附屬物,附加設備;愛慕

似 accessory [æk'sɛsərɪ]
n. 配件(常用複數)⑥

▸ This vacuum cleaner comes with various cleaning attachments.
這個真空吸塵器附有各種清潔配件。
*vacuum ['vækjuəm] n. 真空

▸ Maternal love nurtures a child's attachment to his or her mother.
母愛可孕育孩子對母親的依戀。
*maternal [mə'tɝnḷ] a. 母親的
　nurture ['nɝtʃɚ] vt. 培養

16　deserve [dɪ'zɝv] vt. 應得

片 (1) deserve + N　應 / 值得……
　= deserve to + V
　(2) Sb deserved it.　某人活該。
　= Sb asked for it.
　= It served sb right.

▸ Such a hardworking man really deserves a raise.
這麼努力工作的人值得加薪。

▸ Those who make more money deserve to pay higher taxes.
錢賺得較多的人理當付較多的稅。

▸ John was punished for cheating on the test. He deserved it.
= John was punished for cheating on the test. He asked for it.
= John was punished for cheating on the test. It served him right.
約翰因為考試作弊被懲罰。他活該。

17 spiritual [ˈspɪrɪtʃʊəl] *a.* 精神上的，心靈上的

衍 (1) spirit [ˈspɪrɪt] *n.* 精神；靈魂 ②
　　 be in high / low spirits
　　 精神、情緒很好 / 很差 (恆用複數)
　 = be in a good / bad mood
　 (2) spiritually [ˈspɪrɪtʃʊəlɪ]
　　 adv. 精神上

▶ I enjoy listening to music because it can fill up my spiritual emptiness.
我喜歡聽音樂，因為音樂能填補我心靈的空虛。

▶ The man was in spiritual torment after the incident.
事件發生後，這名男子心靈上很痛苦。
＊torment [ˈtɔrˌmɛnt] *n.* 折磨

18 definite [ˈdɛfənət] *a.* 明確的，肯定的

衍 (1) define [dɪˈfaɪn] *vt.* 下定義 ①
　　 define A as B 將 A 定義為 B
　 (2) definition [ˌdɛfəˈnɪʃən] *n.* 定義 ③
　 (3) definitive [dɪˈfɪnɪtɪv]
　　 a. 決定性的；最佳的 ⑥

似 (1) sure [ʃʊr] *a.* 確定的 ①
　 (2) certain [ˈsɝtn̩] *a.* 確定的 ①
　 (3) positive [ˈpɑzətɪv] *a.* 肯定的 ②
反 indefinite [ɪnˈdɛfənət] *a.* 不確定的

▶ The politician failed to give definite answers to many questions the press raised.
對於媒體提出的諸多問題，該政治人物均未給予明確答覆。

definitely [ˈdɛfənətlɪ]
adv. 絕對，非常

似 (1) absolutely
　　 [ˈæbsəlutlɪ / ˌæbsəˈlutlɪ]
　　 adv. 絕對地
　 (2) certainly [ˈsɝtənlɪ] *adv.* 必定地

▶ You're definitely right. I totally agree with you.
你說的非常對。我完全同意你。

19 resistance [rɪˈzɪstəns] *n.* 抗拒；(身體的) 抵抗力

衍 (1) resist [rɪˈzɪst]
　　 vt. 抗拒；耐 (熱等) & *vi.* 抵抗 ③
　 (2) resistant [rɪˈzɪstənt]
　　 a. 抵抗的；對⋯⋯抵抗力強的 ⑥

▶ The policy suffered strong resistance from the working class.
該政策遭受勞動階級強力反彈。

▶ Your body's resistance becomes low if you stay up frequently.
如果你經常熬夜，身體的抵抗力就會變差。

20 loan [lon] *n.* 貸款 & *vt.* 借給 (= lend)

片 (1) be on loan　已借出
　 (2) loan sb sth　把某物借給某人
　 = lend sb sth
　 = loan sth to sb
　 = lend sth to sb

▶ How soon can you pay off the loan?
你的貸款多久才能還清？

▶ "I'm sorry, but the book is out on loan," said the librarian.
圖書館管理員說：『很抱歉，這本書被借走了。』

► Could you loan me your car for the weekend?
週末你的車可以借我用嗎？

► Can you loan me some money?
= Can you lend me some money?
= Can you loan some money to me?
= Can you lend some money to me?
能借我一些錢嗎？

21 **formation** [fɔr`meʃən] *n.* 形成，構成；(軍語) 隊形

衍 (1) form [fɔrm] *n.* 格式；表格 &
　　vt. 塑造 & *vi.* 成形 ②
　　(2) format [`fɔrmæt]
　　vt. 格式化；編排 & *n.* 格式 ⑤

► The army played a part in the formation of the young man's character.
這位年輕人性格的形成有一部分受軍中的影響。

► The soldiers marched in parade formation.
這些士兵以閱兵隊形行進。
＊parade [pə`red] *n.* 閱兵；(慶祝重大日子等的) 遊行

22 **register** [`rɛdʒɪstɚ] *vt.* & *vi.* 登記，註冊；流露 & *n.* 登記 (本)，註冊 (本)

用 (1) register for...　　註冊……
　　= sign up for...
　　(2) a cash register　　收銀機

► I'm going to register for a course on English literature this semester.
= I'm going to sign up for a course on English literature this semester.
這學期我準備選修一門英國文學課程。

► Annie was shocked to see Bill, and her face registered it.
安妮看到比爾時非常驚訝，她的表情顯露無遺。

► If your name is not on the register, you won't be allowed into the building.
如果你的名字沒有在名單上，你就無法進入這棟建築物。

► The cashier opened the cash register and handed me my change.
收銀人員將收銀機打開，遞給我找的零錢。

registration [ˌrɛdʒɪs`treʃən]
n. 登記，註冊

似 enrollment [ɪn`rolmənt] *n.* 註冊 ⑥

► Student registration usually starts in mid-September.
學生註冊手續通常於 9 月中開始辦理。

23 **accuse** [ə`kjuz] *vt.* 指控

用 (1) accuse sb of...　　指控某人……
　　(2) be accused of...　　被指控……

► The clerk accused the customer of stealing.
店員指控這名顧客偷竊。

衍 accusation [,ækjə`zeʃən] *n.* 指控 ⑥ ▸ The boss was accused of harassing his secretary.
老闆被控騷擾祕書。

24 consult [kən`sʌlt] *vt.* 查閱 (字典、電話簿、書等)；請教，求教 & *vi.* 諮商，研討 (與介詞 with 並用)

片 (1) consult sb　請教某人
　(2) consult with sb
　　與某人商量 / 討論

▸ Consult a dictionary when you can't understand a word.
有不懂的字時就去查字典吧。

用法 表『查字典 / 電話簿』時，應說：consult / refer to the dictionary / phone book；表『在字典 / 電話簿內查某單字 / 號碼』時，應說：look up the word / number in the dictionary / phone book

▸ If you want the answer, you can consult Gina.
如果你要解答，可以請教吉娜。

▸ Go to consult that old man; there's nothing he doesn't know.
去請教那位老先生；他什麼事都懂。

▸ Sally consulted with a lawyer over the matter.
莎莉就這件事與某律師共同研討。

▸ If you want more advice, you can consult with Richard.
如果你要更多的建議，可以跟理查討論一下。

consultant [kən`sʌltənt]
n. 顧問 (與介詞 to 並用)

▸ Scott is a consultant to a software firm.
= Scott is an adviser to a software firm.
史考特是一家軟體公司的顧問。

衍 consultation [,kɑnsəl`teʃən]
　n. 請教，諮詢 ⑤

似 advisor [əd`vaɪzɚ]
　n. 顧問 (= adviser) ③

25 efficiency [ɪ`fɪʃənsɪ] *n.* 效率

衍 efficient [ɪ`fɪʃənt] *a.* 有效率的 ③ ▸ The manager was very satisfied with Taylor's efficiency.
經理很滿意泰勒的辦事效率。

26 universal [,junə`vɝsl] *a.* 普遍的，全宇宙的；全世界的 & *n.* 眾人皆知的概念或特色

衍 universe [`junə,vɝs] *n.* 宇宙 ②

似 international [,ɪntɚ`næʃənl]
　a. 國際的 ②

▸ It's a universal truth that people need to be loved.
人人皆需要愛，舉世皆然。

▸ Smiling is a universal expression.
微笑是全世界共通的語言。

▸ The philosophy professor talked about universals, such as the need to feel loved.
哲學教授談到了一些普遍的概念，如被愛的需要。

27　flee [fli] *vt. & vi.* 逃避，逃離

目 flee, fled [flɛd], fled
片 (1) flee the country　逃出國
　　(2) flee from...　逃離……
似 flea [fli] *n.* 跳蚤 ④
　　a flea market
　　跳蚤市場 (賣舊貨的市集)

▶ The criminal managed to flee the country.
該罪犯成功逃出國。

▶ Judy quit just to flee from the boring routine of a nine-to-five job.
茱蒂為了逃避每天朝九晚五的生活而辭職。

28　install [ɪnˈstɔl] *vt.* 裝設，安裝；使就任 (此意多用被動語態)

衍 (1) installation [ˌɪnstəˈleʃən]
　　n. 安裝，設置 ⑤
　　(2) installment [ɪnˈstɔlmənt]
　　n. 分期付款；一回，一集
　　by installments　以分期付款方式

▶ The mother paid off the washing machine by installments.
這位媽媽用分期付款的方式買了洗衣機。

▶ We have installed central heating in that building.
我們在那棟大樓安裝了中央暖氣系統。

▶ Mr. Pike was installed as mayor yesterday.
派克先生昨天就任市長。

29　isolate [ˈaɪsl̩ˌet] *vt.* 使隔離，使孤立

片 isolate A from B　將 A 與 B 隔離
似 separate [ˈsɛpəˌret] *vt.* 使隔離 ②
　　separate A from B　將 A 與 B 隔離

▶ After his wife died, John isolated himself from everyone.
妻子死後，約翰便過著與世隔絕的生活。

isolated [ˈaɪsl̩ˌetɪd]
a. 隔絕的，孤立的
似 secluded [sɪˈkludɪd] *a.* 與世隔絕的

▶ The lumberjack's cottage is rather isolated.
這名伐木工人的小屋位於相當偏僻的地方。
*lumberjack [ˈlʌmbəˌdʒæk] *n.* 伐木工人
　cottage [ˈkɑtɪdʒ] *n.* 小屋

isolation [ˌaɪsl̩ˈeʃən] *n.* 孤立，隔絕
片 live in isolation
　　過著與世隔絕的生活
= lead a secluded life

▶ Clare lives in isolation like Robinson Crusoe.
克蕾兒像魯賓遜‧克魯索一樣地離群索居。

30　route [rut / raut] *n.* 路線 & *vt.* 運送

片 sth be routed via / through + 地方
　　某物透過某地運送
似 way [we] *n.* 路線；方法 ①

▶ I'm not sure which route we should take to get back home.
我不確定我們該走哪條路線才能回到家。

▶ Most packages are routed via our Taipei office.
大多數的包裹都由我們的臺北辦公處運送。

31 welfare [ˈwɛl,fɛr] *n.* 幸福，福祉

似 well-being [,wɛlˈbiɪŋ] *n.* 福祉

▶ Parents always do whatever it takes to ensure their children's welfare.
父母總是盡力確保孩子的幸福。

32 appreciation [ə,priʃɪˈeʃən] *n.* 感激；欣賞

片 in appreciation of... 以感謝……

衍 (1) appreciate [əˈpriʃɪ,et]
　　vt. 感激；欣賞 & *vi.* (貨幣) 升值 ②

(2) appreciative [əˈpriʃɪ,etɪv]
　　a. 有欣賞能力的；感激的

▶ The company presented Jack with a gold watch in appreciation of his faithful service.
公司頒贈傑克一只金錶，以感謝他忠誠的服務。

▶ Appreciation of a variety of music will make your life more interesting.
欣賞各類音樂會使你的生活更有趣。

33 spark [spɑrk] *n.* 小火花 & *vt.* 激發，引發 & *vi.* 冒火花

片 spark sb's imagination
激發某人的想像力

▶ During a gas leak, any small spark could cause an explosion.
瓦斯漏氣時，一點小火花都會引起爆炸。

▶ Reading that famous writer's novels can spark my imagination and creativity.
閱讀那位名作家的小說可激發我的想像力及創造力。

▶ The movie sparked an interesting conversation.
這部電影引發了有趣的討論。

▶ Dad was fixing the car when something suddenly started sparking.
老爸正在修車時，某個東西突然冒出火花。

34 fax [fæks] *n.* & *vt.* 傳真

延伸 fax 是 facsimile [,fækˈsɪməlɪ] 的簡寫，由於 facsimile 過長，現均以 fax 取代。

▶ Did you get the fax from Mr. Wilson?
你收到威爾遜先生傳來的傳真了嗎？

▶ Could you fax me a copy of your report?
可以把你報告的副本傳真一份給我嗎？

35 impression [ɪmˈprɛʃən] *n.* 印象；想法，感覺；痕跡

片 (1) a first impression 第一印象
(2) an impression of... 對……印象
(3) be left with the impression (that)... 印象中記得……
(4) make a good / bad impression on sb 留給某人一個好 / 壞印象

▶ First impressions are often lasting impressions.
第一印象通常會持續很久。

▶ What's your impression of Penny's new boyfriend?
你對潘妮的新男友印象如何？

▶ After talking to the principal, I was left with the impression that it was a very good school.
和校長談過話後，我印象覺得這是一所很好的學校。

(5) have the impression that...
　　覺得……

(6) be under the impression
　　(that)...　以為……

衍 (1) impress [ɪmˋprɛs]
　　vt. 使印象深刻；使銘記 ③

(2) impressive [ɪmˋprɛsɪv]
　　a. 令人印象深刻的 ②

▶ Kent made a bad impression on Nelly's parents because he brought her home too late.
肯特給娜莉的父母留了壞印象，因為他太晚送她回家。

▶ I have the impression that you're not happy.
我覺得你並不快樂。

▶ I was under the impression that Emma was marrying Robert.
我還以為艾瑪要嫁給羅伯特。

▶ The kids left the impression of their hands in the wet cement.
這群小鬼在未乾的水泥上留下手印。

＊cement [səˋmɛnt / sɪˋmɛnt] *n.* 水泥

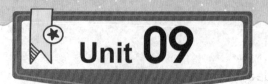

1 continuous [kənˈtɪnjʊəs] *a.* 連續的 (一直不中斷的)

衍 (1) continue [kənˈtɪnjʊ]
      vi. & *vt.* 持續，繼續 ②
(2) continuity [ˌkɑntəˈn(j)ʊətɪ]
      n. 連續性；持續 ⑥

似 (1) endless [ˈɛndləs] *a.* 不停的
(2) ceaseless [ˈsisləs] *a.* 不停的

▶ We've had continuous rain here for nearly a month.
我們這兒已連續下了將近一個月的雨。

continuously [kənˈtɪnjʊəslɪ]
adv. 持續不斷地

似 (1) endlessly [ˈɛndləslɪ] *adv.* 不停地
(2) ceaselessly [ˈsisləslɪ] *adv.* 不停地

▶ Jack drove continuously for 4 hours without a break.
= Jack drove for 4 consecutive hours without a break.
= Jack drove 4 hours in a row without a break.
傑克已經連續開了 4 小時的車都沒有休息。
*consecutive [kənˈsɛkjətɪv] *a.* 連續不斷地

continual [kənˈtɪnjʊəl]
a. 持續的 (偶有間歇的)，頻頻的；連續的

似 (1) frequent [ˈfrikwənt] *a.* 頻繁的 ③
(2) constant [ˈkɑnstənt] *a.* 持續的 ③

比 continual 和 continuous 可同時指『連續地』，但主要 continual 常指『持續的』，指在一段長時間內發生過許多次，停止後重新開始。而 continuous 常指『連續的』，指過程不中斷、持續進行。

▶ The sales report indicates a continual improvement of our products.
銷售報告顯示我們的產品不斷在進步。

2 plot [plɑt] *n.* 陰謀；(故事的) 情節 & *vt.* & *vi.* 圖謀

三 plot, plotted [ˈplɑtɪd], plotted
片 plot to + V   圖謀

▶ The terrorists' plot was uncovered in time.
恐怖分子的陰謀及時被揭發。

▶ The characters in the movie were good but the plot was terrible.
電影中的角色不錯，但是劇本卻很爛。

▶ The rebels plotted to overthrow their cruel ruler.
叛軍圖謀推翻殘暴的統治者。

3 consume [kənˈs(j)um] *vt.* 消費

片 be consumed by...   充滿 (某種情緒)

▶ Our bodies consume more energy in winter.
我們身體在冬天會消耗更多的能量。

衍 **consumption** [kənˈsʌmpʃən]
n. 消費，消耗量 ⑤

延伸 **time-consuming**
[ˈtaɪmˌkənˌs(j)umɪŋ] *a.* 耗時的

▸ This job is time-consuming, but it is worth doing.
這件工作很費時，但值得做。

▸ Helen was consumed by grief over her husband's sudden death.
海倫因丈夫的突然過世感到痛苦萬分。

consumer [kənˈs(j)umɚ]
n. 消費者 ④

▸ Finding out what the consumer really needs is the first step in marketing.
行銷的第一步就是要發現消費者真正的需求。

---

4   **crack** [kræk] *vi.* 破裂 & *vt.* 解開 (密碼) & *n.* 裂縫

片 crack down on...   取締 / 掃蕩……

▸ Most of the eggs Erin bought cracked when she dropped her basket.
大部分艾琳買的蛋在她的籃子掉到地上時都破了。

▸ After hours of trial and error, Ted cracked the code.
經過好幾個小時的反覆試驗後，泰迪終於解開密碼了。
＊trial and error　反覆試驗

▸ Dad won't allow me to go skating today because of the dangerous cracks in the ice.
老爸今天不讓我去溜冰，因為冰上有危險的裂縫。

▸ The police will spare no effort to crack down on the underworld.
警方將全力掃黑。

---

5   **invest** [ɪnˈvɛst] *vt.* & *vi.* 投資

片 (1) invest money in...
將錢投資於……
(2) invest in...   投資於……

▸ Jacob made a fortune by investing a large amount of money in the stock market.
雅各將大筆的錢投入股市，賺了一大筆錢。

▸ Oscar invested heavily in the property market in recent years.
近幾年來奧斯卡投資了很多錢在房市。

---

investment [ɪnˈvɛstmənt] *n.* 投資

片 make an investment in...
投資……

▸ Ryan lost a lot of money by making a poor investment in that lousy company.
萊恩在那家爛公司做了不好的投資，損失了不少錢。

▸ My father is going to buy some gold as an investment.
我爸爸準備購買一些黃金作為投資。

investor [ɪnˈvɛstə] *n.* 投資者

▶ The government will offer tax incentives to attract more foreign investors.
政府將提供租稅優惠鼓勵措施以吸引外國的投資者。
＊incentive [ɪnˈsɛntɪv] *n.* 刺激，鼓勵

6　calculate [ˈkælkjəˌlet] *vt.* 計算；估計

片 calculate / estimate that...
估計……

衍 calculator [ˈkælkjəˌletə]
n. 計算機 ⑥

似 (1) count [kaʊnt] *vt.* 計算 ①
　　(2) estimate [ˈɛstəˌmet] *vt.* 估計 ④

反 miscalculate [mɪsˈkælkjəˌlet]
vt. 算錯

▶ We need to calculate the overall costs before we make any decisions.
在做任何決定前，我們需要先計算一下全部的花費。

▶ The committee calculated that the project would cost at least one million dollars.
委員會推估該案子至少需花費一百萬美元。

---

calculation [ˌkælkjəˈleʃən]
n. 計算；計算結果

反 miscalculation [ˌmɪskælkjəˈleʃən]
n. 算錯

▶ Beth's calculations were never accurate.
貝絲的計算從沒正確過。
＊accurate [ˈækjərət] *a.* 正確的

▶ These calculations are based on the latest figures.
這些計算結果所根據的是最新的數據。

7　regulate [ˈrɛgjəˌlet] *vt.* 規範；調節，調整

片 regulate / adjust the temperature
調節溫度

衍 regular [ˈrɛgjələ] *a.* 規律的 ②

似 (1) control [kənˈtrol] *vt.* 控制 ②
　　(2) adjust [əˈdʒʌst] *vt.* 調節 ④

▶ With the number of cars increasing on a constant basis, the police are having a hard time regulating traffic in the city.
由於車輛數目不斷在增加，警方在管理市區交通上遇到很大的麻煩。

▶ Your health will be ruined if you do not regulate your life.
你生活再不規律點，健康都要給毀了。
＊ruin [ˈruɪn] *vt.* 毀滅

---

regulation [ˌrɛgjəˈleʃən]
n. 規定，法規

似 rule [rul] *n.* 規定 ①

▶ All staff must obey the new regulations.
所有同仁都要遵守新規定。

8　machinery [məˈʃinərɪ] *n.* 機器 (集合名詞，不可數)

衍 machine [məˈʃin] *n.* 機器 (可數) ①

▶ A lot of new machinery has been installed to cope with the increasing workload.
許多新機器已安裝妥當來應付日益漸增的工作量。

比 machine 與 machinery 皆為名詞，表『機器』，但 machinery 是集合名詞，故不可數。machine 則為普通名詞，單數存在時之前要加冠詞 a、an 或 the，否則應使用複數。

a machine　　　一臺機器
two machines　　兩臺機器
many machines　 許多臺機器
= a lot of machinery

▶ The general manager believes that more machinery / machines should be bought to increase productivity.
總經理認為應該買進更多機器來增加產值。

---

mechanic [məˈkænɪk]
n. 技工，機械士

似 technician [tɛkˈnɪʃən]
n. 技術人員，技師 ④

▶ The factory now has two job vacancies for auto mechanics. ☐
這間工廠現在有兩個汽車技師的職缺。
＊vacancy [ˈvekənsɪ] n. 空缺

---

mechanical [məˈkænɪkl̩]
a. 機械的；機械性的

衍 (1) mechanics [məˈkænɪks]
　　 n. 機械學 (不可數)
(2) mechanism [ˈmɛkəˌnɪzəm]
　　 n. 機械零件；機制 ⑤

▶ My brother is studying mechanical engineering in college. ☐
我哥哥目前在大學念機械工程。

▶ The flight was canceled due to mechanical problems.
航班因為機械問題而取消。

---

9 **witness** [ˈwɪtnəs] n. 證人 & vt. 目擊 ☐

片 (1) a witness to sth　是某事的證人
(2) bear witness to...　為……作證

衍 eyewitness [ˈaɪˌwɪtnɪs] n. 目擊者

▶ Vince is the only witness to the murder.
文斯是凶殺案唯一的證人。

▶ Will's success bears witness to his hard work over the past 10 years.
威爾的成功為他 10 年來的努力作了見證。

▶ Did you witness the car accident yourself?
你親眼目睹了這場車禍嗎？

---

10 **prime** [praɪm] a. 主要的；最好的 & n. 全盛時期 ☐

片 (1) prime time　（廣播電視）黃金時段
　　 a prime time show / program
　　 黃金時段節目
(2) prime minister　首相
(3) prime rib　特級牛肋排
(4) in one's prime
　　 某人處於顛峰 / 壯年
= in the prime of life

▶ The investigators are still unable to find the prime cause of that plane crash.
調查人員仍找不出那起飛機失事的主因。

▶ Matthew once played a part in the prime time television series.
馬修曾在黃金時段電視影集中擔任一角。

似 (1) **main** [men] *a.* 主要的 ①
(2) **primary** [`praɪ,mɛrɪ]
　　a. 主要的，首要的；初級的 ②

▶ Mr. Clinton was a very successful businessman in his prime.
= Mr. Clinton was a very successful businessman in the prime of life.
　柯林頓先生壯年時期是個非常成功的生意人。

11　**dominant** [`dɑmənənt] *a.* 支配的；重要的 (職位) ☐

似 (1) **bossy** [`bɑsɪ]
　　a. 跋扈的，頤指氣使的
(2) **domineering** [,dɑmə`nɪrɪŋ]
　　a. 跋扈的

▶ I don't like Vic because of his dominant personality.
　維克老愛支使別人的這種性格讓我很不喜歡他。
▶ John holds a dominant position in our company.
　約翰在我們公司的職位很高。

dominate [`dɑmə,net]
vt. 統治，支配；(山脈或建築物) 俯瞰

衍 **domination** [,dɑmə`neʃən]
　　n. 統治支配

似 **rule** [rul] *vt.* 統治 ①

▶ The strong animal dominated the weak animal. ☐
　這隻強壯的動物支配那隻弱小的動物。
▶ The big mountain dominates the landscape.
　這座大山俯瞰四周的景色。
▶ The house on the hilltop dominates the whole valley.
= The house on the hilltop overlooks the whole valley.
　山頂上的這間房子可俯瞰整座山谷。

12　**satisfaction** [,sætɪs`fækʃən] *n.* 滿足，滿意 ☐

片 (1) **a sense of satisfaction**　滿足感
(2) **To one's satisfaction, ...**
　　令某人滿意的是……

衍 (1) **satisfy** [`sætɪs,faɪ]
　　vt. 使滿足；符合 (要求、條件) ②
(2) **satisfied** [`sætɪs,faɪd]
　　a. (人) 感到滿意的
(3) **satisfying** [`sætɪs,faɪɪŋ]
　　a. (物) 令人滿意的
(4) **satisfactory** [,sætɪs`fæktərɪ]
　　a. 令人滿意的 ③
(5) **satisfactorily** [,sætɪs`fækt(ə)rəlɪ]
　　adv. 令人滿意地

▶ The success of the experiment gave the scientist a sense of satisfaction.
　這項實驗的成功帶給這位科學家滿足感。
▶ To the teacher's satisfaction, all her students have done their homework.
　令老師滿意的是，所有學生都寫了作業。

dissatisfaction
[,dɪsætɪs`fækʃən] *n.* 不滿，不平

衍 **dissatisfied** [dɪs`sætɪs,faɪd] *a.* 不滿的
be dissatisfied with...
　對……感到不滿

▶ All employees expressed great dissatisfaction with the company's new rules. ☐
　所有員工都對公司的新規定表達強烈不滿。
▶ A good leader should always pay attention to any signs of dissatisfaction.
　好的領導者要能隨時注意任何不滿的徵兆。

13 interpret [ɪnˋtɝprɪt] *vi. & vt.* 翻譯，口譯 & *vt.* 解釋，視為

Ⓗ interpret A as B 將 A 詮釋為 B

衍 (1) interpretation [ɪn͵tɝprɪˋteʃən]
n. 解釋；詮釋 ⑤

(2) interpreter [ɪnˋtɝprɪtɚ]
n. 口譯者，口譯員 ⑥

Ⓒ translator [trænsˋletɚ] 泛指一般翻譯員，主要指筆譯，而 interpreter 則專指口譯員。

▶ Mr. Lee interpreted the words of the French speaker for the American audience.
李先生為美國觀眾口譯這位法國演說者的話。

▶ I interpreted Stan's silence as acceptance.
我把史坦的沉默視為接受。

translate [trænsˋlet]
vi. & vt. 翻譯 (尤指筆譯)

Ⓗ translate A into B 將 A 翻譯為 B

▶ I translated the sentence into English.
我把這個句子翻譯成英文。

translation [trænsˋleʃən]
n. 翻譯本 (可數)；翻譯 (不可數)

Ⓗ a book in translation 翻譯本

▶ Shelly has read many of the author's books in translation.
雪莉看過許多這位作者著作的翻譯本。

▶ The translation of this book took Ron about a year.
這本書的翻譯花了朗恩將近一年的時間。

translator [trænsˋletɚ / ˋtræns͵letɚ]
n. 翻譯者 (尤指文字翻譯者)

▶ Being a translator is not an easy job.
當翻譯者不是項容易的工作。

14 virtue [ˋvɝtʃu] *n.* 美德；優點，長處

Ⓗ by virtue / means / way of...
憑著 / 藉由……

衍 virtuous [ˋvɝtʃʊəs]
a. 有品德的；清高的

▶ A man of virtue is a man of principle. He will never do anything against his conscience.
有美德的人即是有原則的人。他絕不會做任何違背良心的事。

▶ This plan has the virtue of being easy to carry out.
這個計畫的好處就是它容易實現。

▶ Robert was promoted to manager by virtue of his hard work.
羅伯特憑著工作勤奮而被晉升為經理。

15 permanent [ˋpɝmənənt] *a.* 永恆的；常設的

似 (1) endless [ˋɛndləs] *a.* 無盡的
(2) perpetual [pɚˋpɛtʃʊəl] *a.* 永遠的

反 temporary [ˋtɛmpə͵rɛrɪ]
a. 暫時的 ③

▶ The rich man has permanent residence in several countries.
這位有錢人擁有數個國家的永久居留權。

> Mandy is one of the five permanent members of our committee.
> 曼蒂是我們委員會的五位常設委員之一。

---

16 transfer [trænsˋfɝ / ˋtrænsfɝ] *vt. & vi.* 調離；移轉 & [ˋtrænsfɝ] *n.* 調任

目 transfer, transferred [trænsˋfɝd / ˋtrænsfɝd], transferred

用 transfer sb to + 地方　調至某地

> The CEO decided to transfer Neil to a Seattle-based law firm.
> 公司執行長決定要調任尼爾到總部設於西雅圖的律師事務所。

> Can you transfer $1,000 into my account by Friday?
> 你能否在週五前把 1,000 美元匯到我的帳戶呢？

> Sophie asked for a transfer to the company's branch office in Europe.
> 蘇菲請調至歐洲的分公司。

---

17 regarding [rɪˋgɑrdɪŋ] *prep.* 關於，有關 (= about)

衍 regard [rɪˋgɑrd] *vt.* 認為，視為……（與介詞 as 並用）& *n.* 尊重，重視 ②
hold sb in high regard　尊敬某人
= hold sb in high esteem

> Alfred Hitchcock is held in high regard by many film directors.
> 亞弗烈德・希區考克受諸多電影導演敬重。

> Regarding this issue, I'd like to hear your opinions.
> 針對這件事，我想聽聽諸位的意見。

---

18 fort [fɔrt] *n.* 要塞

衍 fortify [ˋfɔrtə͵faɪ] *vt.* 增強 ⑥
似 fortress [ˋfɔrtrɪs] *n.* 要塞

> Those soldiers were building a fort.
> 那些士兵正在建造一座要塞。

---

19 reception [rɪˋsɛpʃən] *n.* 招待會，宴會；接受，回應

衍 (1) receive [rɪˋsiv] *vt.* 收到 ②
(2) receiver [rɪˋsivɚ] *n.* (電話) 聽筒 ③
(3) receipt [rɪˋsit] *n.* 收據，發票 ③
(4) receptionist [rɪˋsɛpʃənɪst] *n.* (公司、醫院、辦公室的) 接待員 / 櫃檯人員

> The couple held the wedding reception in the garden.
> 這對夫妻在花園裡舉辦婚宴。

> The critics' chilly reception to his latest book made the author very disappointed.
> 評論家對該作者新書的冷淡回應令他很失望。
> *chilly [ˋtʃɪlɪ] *a.* 冷淡的，冰冷的

20 **genuine** [ˈdʒɛnjuɪn] *a.* 真的，真正的

▶ This is a genuine painting; in other words, it's not a fake.

這是一幅真畫；換而言之，不是假的。

authentic [ɔˈθɛntɪk] *a.* (物品) 真正的

衍 authenticity [ɔˈθɛntɪsətɪ] *n.* 真實性
似 genuine [ˈdʒɛnjuɪn] *a.* 真正的 ④
反 fake [fek] *a.* 假貨的 & *n.* 假貨 ③

▶ This restaurant offers a wide variety of authentic Japanese cuisine ranging from sushi to sukiyaki.

這家餐廳提供各式各樣的正宗日本菜餚，從壽司到壽喜燒都有。

21 **indication** [ˌɪndəˈkeʃən] *n.* 指示，顯示

衍 (1) indicate [ˈɪndə,ket]
　　vt. 指示，指出 ②
　(2) indicator [ˈɪndə,ketɚ]
　　n. 指標；指示器；方向燈

▶ There are clear indications that the war will soon be over.

有清楚的跡象顯示這場戰爭很快就會結束。

22 **laboratory** [ˈlæbrə,tɔrɪ] *n.* 實驗室

延伸 本字常縮寫成 lab [læb]。

▶ The great scientist spent most of his life in his small laboratory.

這位偉大的科學家大半輩子都待在他的小實驗室裡。

23 **horizon** [həˈraɪzn̩] *n.* 地平線 (單數)；範圍，範疇 (常用複數)

片 (1) broaden one's horizons
　　擴充某人領域 (本片語中 horizons
　　恆為複數)
　(2) be on the horizon　即將出現，
　　即將到來 (本片語中 horizon 恆為
　　單數)
衍 horizontal [ˌhɔrəˈzantl̩] *a.* 水平的 ⑤

▶ Traveling enables you to broaden your horizons.

旅行讓人增廣見聞。

▶ Don't look so sad. Good luck is on the horizon.
= Don't look so sad. Good luck is coming.

別氣餒。好運就要來了。

24 **primitive** [ˈprɪmətɪv] *a.* 原始的

似 primeval [praɪˈmivl̩] *a.* 原始的

▶ The tribespeople in the mountainous area still live a primitive life.

該山區的部落居民仍過著原始的生活。

*tribespeople [ˈtraɪbz,pipl̩] *n.* 部落居民

25 severe [sə'vɪr] a. 嚴厲的；十分嚴重的

似 (1) strict [strɪkt] a. 嚴格的 ②
(2) harsh [hɑrʃ] a. 嚴厲的 ④

反 gentle ['dʒɛntḷ] a. 柔順的，溫和的 ②

▶ The victim's family wanted the judge to give the murderer a severe sentence.
被害者家屬要求法官對兇手從重量刑。
＊victim ['vɪktɪm] n. 受害者
sentence ['sɛntəns] n. 判刑

▶ Without food and shelter, these animals will surely not survive the severe winter.
沒有食物和遮風避雨之處，這些動物肯定無法活過嚴冬。

26 annoy [ə'nɔɪ] vt. 煩擾；騷擾

衍 annoyance [ə'nɔɪəns]
n. 惱怒 (不可數)；令人困擾的事物 (可數) ⑥

▶ The noise from my neighbor's TV annoys me constantly.
我鄰居家電視的聲音經常令我不堪其擾。

▶ The poor horse was annoyed by flying insects.
那匹可憐的馬被飛蟲騷擾。

annoyed [ə'nɔɪd] a. 感到惱怒的

似 angry ['æŋgrɪ] a. 生氣的 ①

▶ Angela was annoyed when her boyfriend stood her up.
安琪拉被男友放鴿子時十分惱怒。

annoying [ə'nɔɪɪŋ]
a. 討厭的，煩人的

▶ It's really annoying that I need to have my car fixed again.
我的車子需要再送修，真是煩人。

▶ Jerry would be an attractive man were it not for that annoying habit of his.
要不是他那令人討厭的習慣，傑瑞會是個有魅力的男人。

27 millionaire [ˌmɪljən'ɛr] n. 百萬富翁，巨富

衍 million ['mɪljən] n. 百萬 ①

▶ Instead of relying on his father, the millionaire's son decided to start his own business.
這個百萬富翁的兒子決定不靠父親，要開創自己的事業。

28 category ['kætəˌgɔrɪ] n. 種類；範疇

片 fall into two / three... categories
分成兩 / 三……個種類

衍 categorize ['kætəgəˌraɪz]
vt. 將……分類

▶ Head injuries fall into two categories: external and internal.
頭部傷害可分成兩個種類：外部和內部傷害。

29 representation [ˌrɛprɪzɛn'teʃən] n. 代表；呈現

▶ Our company has sufficient representation in Europe.
我們公司在歐洲有代表機構可充分代表我們。

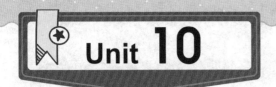

 1001-1004

1 **merit** [`mɛrɪt] *n.* 優點;功績

片 (1) the merits and demerits of sth
　　某件事情的優缺點
　(2) on merit　依績效
反 demerit [dɪ`mɛrɪt] *n.* 缺點

▶ What are the merits and demerits of living in the country?

= What are the advantages and disadvantages of living in the country?
住在鄉下的優缺點是什麼?

▶ In our company, people get promoted on merit rather than on seniority.
在我們公司,大家升遷是憑績效而不是以年資而論。
＊seniority [sin`ɔrətɪ] *n.* 年資,資歷

2 **curve** [kɝv] *n.* 曲線 & *vi.* 彎曲

片 throw sb a curve　給某人一個麻煩

▶ There are several curves on this road, so drive carefully.
這條路上有很多轉彎,小心駕駛。

▶ The sudden shower threw us a curve, and we had to cancel our outdoor party.
突然的大雨讓我們措手不及,不得不取消戶外派對。

▶ A sidewalk curves around the park.
人行步道沿著公園轉彎。

3 **license** [`laɪsn̩s] *n.* 執照(可數) & *vt.* 授權,批准

片 (1) a driver's license　駕駛執照
　(2) a fishing license　釣/捕魚執照

▶ Without a license, you can't drive.
沒有駕照不准開車。

▶ This company is licensed to produce Disney toys.
這間公司獲准生產迪士尼的玩具。

4 **dignity** [`dɪgnətɪ] *n.* 威嚴

衍 dignitary [`dɪgnə,tɛrɪ] *n.* 權貴顯要
= VIP (very important person)
似 self-esteem [,sɛlfəs`tim] *n.* 自尊

▶ With dignity and pride, our principal reached the end of his life.
我們校長帶著莊嚴與驕傲與世長辭了。

dignify [`dɪgnə,faɪ] *vt.* 使有尊嚴
三 dignify, dignified [`dɪgnə,faɪd], dignified

▶ The president dignified us with his presence.
董事長出席讓我們倍感榮耀。

5 differ [ˈdɪfɚ] vi. 不同，差異

片 differ from... 與……不同

衍 (1) different [ˈdɪfərənt] a. 不同的 ①
(2) differently [ˈdɪfərəntlɪ]
adv. 不同地
(3) difference [ˈdɪfərəns] n. 不同 ②
(4) differential [dɪfəˈrɛnʃəl]
a. 差異的
(5) differentiate [ˌdɪfəˈrɛnʃɪet]
vt. 使有差異 ⑥

似 vary [ˈvɛrɪ] vi. 不同 ③

▶ People differ from one another in their hobbies.
= Hobbies vary from person to person.
嗜好因人而異。

6 limitation [ˌlɪməˈteʃən] n. 限制；缺點 (可數)

片 impose a limitation on...
對……加以設限

衍 limit [ˈlɪmɪt] n. 限制；範圍
(恆用複數) ②

within limits 有限度地
know one's limits
某人了解自己的能力範圍

▶ I know my limits, so I'm afraid I can't help you with that job.
我知道我的能力範圍，因此很抱歉我可能無法幫你這個忙。

似 shortcoming [ˈʃɔrtˌkʌmɪŋ]
n. 缺點 (常用複數) ⑥

▶ The school authorities used to impose a limitation on the length of students' hair.
校方曾對學生頭髮的長度加以設限。
*impose [ɪmˈpoz] vt. 強制執行

▶ Basically, this is a good car, but it has its limitations.
= Basically, this is a good car, but it has its shortcomings.
基本上這輛車不賴，不過仍有缺點。

7 conscience [ˈkɑnʃəns] n. 良心

片 with a clear conscience 問心無愧

衍 conscientious [ˌkɑnʃɪˈɛnʃəs]
a. 守本分的，盡職的

▶ Everyone knows that Jim is a conscientious worker.
大家都知道吉姆是個負責盡職的員工。

▶ It makes one happy to complete a duty with a clear conscience.
問心無愧地完成責任會讓人快樂。

8 lecture [ˈlɛktʃɚ] n. 講課 & vi. 授課 & vt. 向 (某人) 說教

片 (1) lecture on... 講授有關……
(2) lecture sb about / on sth
因某事教訓某人；因某事向某人說教

▶ A good student always pays attention to his teachers' lectures.
好學生總是專心聽老師講課。

▶ Mr. Peterson lectures on British literature at Oxford University.
彼得森先生在牛津大學教授英國文學。

▶ Our boss often lectures us about the importance of being punctual.
老闆經常告誡我們準時的重要性。
＊punctual [ˋpʌŋktʃʊəl] *a.* 守時的

lecturer [ˋlɛktʃərə] *n.* 演講者；講師
似 speaker [ˋspikə]
　n. 演講者；(議會等) 議長 (s 要大寫) ②

▶ Tina is a lecturer in cultural studies at Lancaster University.
蒂娜是蘭開斯特大學教授文化研究的講師。

9　quilt [kwɪlt] *n.* 被子 & *vt.* 縫製 (成棉被)

似 blanket [ˋblæŋkɪt]
　n. 毯子 & *vt.* 覆蓋 ②

▶ Cover yourself with a quilt, or you'll catch a cold.
蓋上被子，不然你會感冒。

▶ We quilted the blanket with some beautiful patterns.
我們用美麗的圖案縫出那條被子。

10　disturb [dɪsˋtɝb] *vt.* & *vi.* 打擾，使煩惱

衍 disturbance [dɪsˋtɝbəns] *n.* 擾亂 ⑥
似 (1) bother [ˋbɑðə] *vt.* 打擾 ②
　(2) annoy [əˋnɔɪ] *vt.* 使煩惱 ④

▶ Don't disturb Dad while he is at work.
老爸工作時不要打擾他。

▶ The sign reads, "Please Do Not Disturb."
牌子上寫著『請勿打擾』。

disturbing [dɪsˋtɝbɪŋ]
a. 令人不安的

似 (1) troubling [ˋtrʌblɪŋ] *a.* 令人煩惱的
　(2) worrying [ˋwɝɪŋ] *a.* 令人擔憂的

▶ Please note that the following program contains language that may be disturbing to some viewers.
請注意，以下節目可能包含令某些觀眾感到不安的言語。
＊此處的 language 不是指語言，而是指『措辭、用語』，
　為不可數名詞；若表語言時，language 為可數名詞。

▶ Using disturbing language is forbidden.
禁止使用令人不安的辭彙。

11　aspirin [ˋæsprɪn] *n.* 阿斯匹靈

似 painkiller [ˋpen͵kɪlə] *n.* 止痛劑 / 藥

▶ Do you have some aspirin? My head is killing me.
你有沒有阿斯匹靈？我的頭快痛死了。

12　predict [prɪˋdɪkt] *vt.* 預測

衍 predictable [prɪˋdɪktəbl]
　a. 可預測的

▶ Dad predicted that I would win the contest, and he was right.
老爸預測我會贏得這次的比賽，結果他是對的。
＊contest [ˋkɑntɛst] *n.* 比賽

似 foretell [fɔrˈtɛl] *vt.* 預言
三態為：foretell, foretold [fɔrˈtold],
foretold

prediction [prɪˈdɪkʃən] *n.* 預測

片 make accurate predictions about
sth　對某事做出精確預測

▶ So far it's still very difficult for scientists to make accurate predictions about earthquakes.
到目前為止，科學家要對地震做出準確的預測仍然很困難。

forecast [ˈfɔrˌkæst]

vt. & n. 預測，預報

三 forecast, forecast / forecasted,
forecast / forecasted

▶ The weatherman forecast rain for the rest of the week.
氣象員預測，本週結束前還會有雨。

▶ According to the weather forecast, we are going to have snowstorms tomorrow.
根據氣象預測，明天會有暴風雪。

13　cease [sis] *vt. & vi. & n.* 停止

片 (1) cease to + V
　　不做……；停止做……
　= cease + V-ing
　(2) without cease　不停地

衍 ceaselessly [ˈsisləslɪ] *adv.* 不停地

▶ These factory workers worked ceaselessly throughout the Chinese New Year holidays.
這些工廠員工整個農曆新年假期都不停地在工作。

比 stop 與 cease 同義，但 stop 之後接不定詞片語或動名詞片語的意思完全不同：

① stop to + V
　停下某事去做另一件事

▶ I was late because I stopped to talk to Gina on my way home.
因為我在回家的路上停下來和吉娜交談，所以遲到了。

② stop + V-ing　停止做某事

▶ We stopped talking because the teacher came in.
因為老師進來了，所以我們便停止交談。

▶ If we could travel at the speed of light, time would cease to exist.
= If we could travel at the speed of light, time would cease existing.
倘若我們能以光速行進，那麼時間就會不存在了。

▶ The neighbor's dog barked without cease and kept me awake all night.
鄰居的狗叫個不停，害我整晚沒睡。

ceasefire [ˈsisˌfaɪr] *n.* 停戰，停火
▸ Both sides called a temporary ceasefire during the peace talks.
在和平談判中，雙方要求暫時停火。

---

14 **opera** [ˈɑpərə] *n.* 歌劇

延伸 (1) musical [ˈmjuzɪkl]
　　 a. 音樂的 & *n.* 音樂劇 ②
　(2) Chinese opera　京劇
　(3) a soap opera　肥皂劇，連續劇

▸ I enjoy listening to opera, but I don't really understand it.
我喜愛聽歌劇，但是聽不太懂。

ballet [bæˈle / ˈbæle] *n.* 芭蕾舞
衍 ballerina [ˌbæləˈrinə] *n.* 女芭蕾舞者
（danseur [danˈsɜ] *n.* 男芭蕾舞者）

▸ Erica's dream is to go to Russia and study ballet.
艾瑞卡的夢想是到俄羅斯學芭蕾。

gallery [ˈgælərɪ] *n.* 畫廊

▸ An impressionist painting exhibition is being held at the Paris Gallery.
巴黎畫廊正展出印象派畫作展。

---

15 **restriction** [rɪˈstrɪkʃən] *n.* 限制，約束

片 have restrictions on...
　　對……有限制
衍 restrict [rɪˈstrɪkt] *vt.* 限制，制止 ③
　restrict 當動詞與 confine [kənˈfaɪn]、
　limit [ˈlɪmɪt] 同義，皆與介詞 to 並用。
▸ John restricts / confines / limits his hobbies to singing and hiking only.
約翰的嗜好僅限於唱歌及健行。
似 limitation [ˌlɪməˈteʃən] *n.* 限制 ④

▸ That club has rigid restrictions on its membership.
= That club has rigid limitations on its membership.
那家俱樂部對它的會員資格限制很嚴。
＊rigid [ˈrɪdʒɪd] *a.* 嚴苛的
▸ The US asked Japan to reduce its import restrictions on cars.
美國要求日本減少車輛進口的限制。

---

16 **enforce** [ɪnˈfɔrs] *vt.* 實施，執行

似 (1) carry out...　執行……
　(2) implement [ˈɪmpləˌmɛnt]
　　 vt. 實施，執行 ⑤

▸ We would love to see the government enforce stricter regulations.
我們樂見政府實施更嚴格的法規。

enforcement [ɪnˈfɔrsmənt]
n. 實施，執行
似 implementation [ˌɪmpləmɛnˈteʃən]
　 n. 實施，執行

▸ Without a strict law enforcement system, society would become chaotic.
沒有實施嚴格的法制，這個社會會變得很亂。

17　complicate [ˋkɑmpləˏket] vt. 使複雜化

反 simplify [ˋsɪmpləˏfaɪ] vt. 單純化 ⑥

衍 complication [ˏkɑmpləˋkeʃən]
　　n. 複雜，困難；併發症（常用複數）⑤

▶ Even though we're behind on the project, asking John to help will just complicate our situation.
雖然這件案子我們進度已經落後了，請約翰幫忙只會讓情況複雜。

complicated [ˋkɑmpləˏketɪd]
a. 複雜的

似 complex [ˋkɑmplɛks / kəmˋplɛks]
　　a. 複雜的 ②

▶ The problem is too complicated to solve.
這個問題太複雜了，無法解決。

18　era [ˋɪrə] n. 年代，時代

似 epoch [ˋɛpək] n. 時代

▶ It is correct to say that we are in an era of computers.
說我們目前處於電腦時代並沒有錯。

19　dependent [dɪˋpɛndənt] a. 依賴的（與介詞 on 並用）& n. 扶養親屬，眷屬（= dependant〔英〕）

片 be dependent on...
　　依賴……；視……而定

衍 depend [dɪˋpɛnd]
　　vi. 依賴；視……而定 ②

反 independent [ˏɪndɪˋpɛndənt]
　　a. 獨立的 ②

be independent of...
不依賴……，獨立於……

▶ John is sixteen years old, yet he is independent of his parents.
約翰才 16 歲，卻已經不再依靠父母了。

▶ The elderly are often dependent on their children for many things.
老人在很多事情上時常依賴子女。

▶ Your success is dependent on your effort.
成功與否要視你的努力而定。

▶ While he was stationed in Germany, Colonel Smith took his dependents with him.
史密斯上校駐紮在德國時，他把家人一塊兒帶去。

dependence [dɪˋpɛndəns]
n. 依賴（與介詞 on 並用）

反 independence [ˏɪndɪˋpɛndəns]
　　n. 獨立 ②

▶ The government is planning to reduce its dependence on foreign oil.
政府正計劃要減少對外國石油的依賴。

dependable [dɪˋpɛndəbḷ]
a. 可靠的；穩定的

似 reliable [rɪˋlaɪəbḷ] a. 可依賴的 ③

▶ I'll marry a man who is always dependable.
我會嫁一個永遠可靠的男人。

▶ Do you have a dependable source of income?
你有一份穩定的收入嗎？

20 **frequency** [ˈfrikwənsɪ] *n.* 頻率；頻繁

(1) a high frequency sound 高頻聲 (2) a low frequency sound 低頻聲	▶ Dolphins are known to communicate via a high frequency sound they produce. 據了解，海豚會藉發出高頻率的聲音溝通。
衍 (1) frequent [ˈfrikwənt] *a.* 經常的 ③ (2) frequently [ˈfrikwəntlɪ] *adv.* 經常地	▶ The frequency of bank robberies in this area has declined. 該區銀行搶案的次數已降低。

21 **logic** [ˈlɑdʒɪk] *n.* 邏輯學；邏輯 (性)

似 (1) reasoning [ˈriznɪŋ] *n.* 推理 (2) judgment [ˈdʒʌdʒmənt] *n.* 判斷	▶ Bonnie studied some philosophy and logic when she was in college. 邦妮念大學時，曾念過哲學和邏輯學。 ▶ I couldn't follow the logic of John's argument. 我搞不懂約翰論調的邏輯。

logical [ˈlɑdʒɪkl̩] *a.* 邏輯的 似 (1) sensible [ˈsɛnsəbl̩] *a.* 理智的 ③ (2) reasonable [ˈriznəbl̩] *a.* 講道理的 ③ (3) rational [ˈræʃənl̩] *a.* 理智的 ⑤	▶ The man has a clear and logical mind. 這個人的思路清晰又合乎邏輯。

illogical [ɪˈlɑdʒɪkl̩] *a.* 不合邏輯的 衍 illogically [ɪˈlɑdʒɪklɪ] *adv.* 不合邏輯地 似 (1) irrational [ɪˈræʃənl̩] *a.* 無理的 (2) unreasonable [ʌnˈriznəbl̩] *a.* 不講理的	▶ It's quite illogical to assume that you will always be right. 你認為你總是對的，這種想法很不合邏輯。 *assume [əˈs(j)um] *vt.* 認定

22 **presentation** [ˌprɛzənˈteʃən] *n.* 授與，頒贈 (典禮)；口頭報告

片 give / make a presentation / report 做口頭報告 衍 present [prɪˈzɛnt] *vt.* 授與；提出；介紹；上演 ① **present sb with sth** 將某物授與某人 ▶ We would like to present you with an award in appreciation of your help. 我們將頒發給你一項獎座以感謝你的幫忙。	▶ The awards presentation ceremony will begin at two o'clock. 頒獎典禮將於兩點鐘開始。 ▶ Jerry will now give a short presentation on our product. 傑瑞現在將就本公司的產品做一個簡短的介紹。

23 admission [əd`mɪʃən] n. 入會；入場費；承認，供認

- apply for admission to + 學校
  申請某校就讀
- 衍 (1) admit [əd`mɪt] vt. 承認 ②
  (2) admittance [əd`mɪtəns]
  n. (常指實際或實體的) 進入 (非「抽象的」進入)

▶ We voted against the admission of new club members.
我們投票否決了俱樂部新會員的入會申請。

▶ Henry is applying for admission to Yale University.
亨利正在申請就讀耶魯大學。

▶ Admission to that zoo gets more expensive each year.
那家動物園的入場費一年比一年貴。

▶ The doctor's admission of his guilt surprised everyone.
那位醫生坦承罪行令每個人很驚訝。

24 guilt [gɪlt] n. 罪

- a sense of guilt   罪惡感

▶ I felt a sense of guilt about leaving my cat at home alone for so many days.
我把貓咪單獨留在家裡那麼多天，讓我有罪惡感。

guilty [`gɪltɪ] a. 有罪的
- be guilty of...   有……的罪
- 反 innocent [`ɪnəsnt]
  a. 無罪的；天真的 ③
  be innocent of...   無……的罪
- ▶ The woman believes that her son is innocent of the crime.
  女子相信她兒子是無罪的。

▶ The evidence shows that Peter is guilty of robbing the bank.
證據顯示彼得搶劫銀行有罪。

25 reform [rɪ`fɔrm] n. & vt. & vi. 改革

- 片 (1) economic reform   經濟改革
  (2) political reform   政治改革
- 似 (1) improve [ɪm`pruv] vt. 改善 ②
  (2) improvement [ɪm`pruvmənt]
  n. 改善 ②

▶ People have called for economic reforms to revive the economy.
民眾呼籲經濟改革以振興經濟。
＊revive [rɪ`vaɪv] vt. 使復甦

▶ The government is proposing plans to reform the health insurance system.
政府提出改革健保制度的計畫。

26 household [`haʊs,hold] n. 家庭 (= family)

- 片 a household name
  = a celebrity [sə`lɛbrətɪ]
  家喻戶曉的人物，名人

▶ A growing number of households have access to the internet.
越來越多的家庭都能上網。

housework [ˈhaʊsˌwɝk]

n. 家事（不可數）

片 do housework　做家事

▶ My brother and I take turns doing housework.
我哥哥和我輪流做家事。

27　celebration [ˌsɛləˈbreʃən] *n.* 慶祝

片 in celebration of...　慶祝……
衍 celebrate [ˈsɛləˌbret] *vt.* 慶祝 ①

▶ It has long been a tradition for the Chinese to set off firecrackers in celebration of the Lunar New Year.
中國人長久以來就有放鞭炮慶祝農曆新年的傳統。

28　issue [ˈɪʃu] *n.* 重大議題；爭議；期刊 & *vt.* 發行

片 (1) take issue with sb over sth
= disagree with sb over sth
　　與某人爭論某事
(2) be at issue　在爭論中
= be in disagreement
(3) issue sth　發行某物

用法 許多人關心的事用 issue，一般的問題用 problem。

▶ The issue of sexual discrimination in the office was widely discussed during the meeting.
會議中辦公室性別歧視的議題被廣泛討論。

▶ Susan took issue with Peter over who should be responsible for the mistake.
針對誰應對這個錯負責，蘇珊與彼得有所爭論。

▶ What is at issue now is when we should deal with the problem.
現在受爭議的問題是，我們應要何時處理這個問題。

▶ The latest issue of *Vogue* magazine featured an interview with Gal Gadot.
最新一期的《時尚》雜誌特刊出蓋兒·加朵的專訪。
＊feature [ˈfitʃɚ] *vt.* 以……為特色

▶ The government has issued a large number of booklets to explain its new policies.
政府發行很多手冊來解釋它的新政策。

29　lengthen [ˈlɛŋθən] *vt.* 使變長，加長

衍 length [lɛŋθ] *n.* 長度 ②
at length　詳細地

▶ Tell me the story at length.
= Tell me the story in detail.
把事情經過詳細告訴我。

反 shorten [ˈʃɔrtn̩] *vt.* 使變短；縮短 ③

▶ I need to have this skirt lengthened.
我得把這件裙子放長。

Level 4　Unit 10

319

Unit **11**

  1101-1108

---

1 favorable [ˈfevərəbl] *a.* 有利的

衍 favor [ˈfevə] *n.* 恩惠；贊同 &
    vt. 更喜愛；贊同 ②

比 favorable 和 favorite 皆為形容詞，
    favorable 表『有利的』，而 favorite 則
    表『最受喜愛的』。

▸ That's my favorite novel.
    那是我最喜歡的小說。

▸ Do not take any action until the situation is favorable to us.
= Do not take any action until the situation is in our favor.
    直到情況對我們有利之後再採取任何行動。

---

2 multiple [ˈmʌltəpl] *a.* 多重的，眾多的

衍 multiply [ˈmʌltəplaɪ]
    vt. & vi. 增加；(使相) 乘 ③

▸ Darren's latest album consists of multiple versions of the same songs.
    戴倫的最新專輯收錄了相同歌曲的許多版本。

---

3 psychology [saɪˈkɑlədʒɪ] *n.* 心理學

似 psychiatry [saɪˈkaɪətrɪ]
    n. 精神病學 ⑥

▸ Ross is an expert on social psychology.
    羅斯是社會心理學專家。

psychological [ˌsaɪkəˈlɑdʒɪkl]
a. 心理的，心理學的

衍 (1) psychologist [saɪˈkɑlədʒɪst]
       n. 心理學家 ④
   (2) psychology [saɪˈkɑlədʒɪ]
       n. 心理學 ④

▸ Psychological stress can lead to illness.
    心理上的壓力會讓人致病。

psychologist [saɪˈkɑlədʒɪst]
n. 心理學家

似 (1) psychiatrist [saɪˈkaɪətrɪst]
       n. 精神科醫師
   (2) shrink [ʃrɪŋk] *n.* 精神科醫師 (口語)
       & *vt. & vi.* 縮 ③

▸ My shrink says it's always a good idea to exercise whenever you feel stressed.
    我的心理醫師說你感到有壓力時就去運動，這個點子總是錯不了。

▸ Marcus has made a resolution to become a psychologist someday.
    馬克斯立志將來要當心理學家。

4 bracelet [ˈbreslɪt] n. 手鐲

延伸 (1) necklace [ˈnɛklɪs] n. 項鍊 ②
(2) earring [ˈɪr͵rɪŋ] n. 耳環 ②
(3) pendant [ˈpɛndənt]
　　 n. (項鍊上的) 墜飾

▶ Paul gave his girlfriend a bracelet for her birthday.
保羅送給女友一隻手鐲當作她的生日禮物。

5 strengthen [ˈstrɛŋθən] vt. 鞏固，加強

衍 strength [strɛŋθ] n. 力量 ③
反 weaken [ˈwikən]
　　 vt. & vi. 減弱，削弱 ③

▶ You can try watching English TV programs to strengthen your listening ability.
你可以試著看英語電視節目來增強聽力。

6 funeral [ˈfjunərəl] n. 葬禮

▶ A lot of people attended the hero's funeral.
大批民眾前往參加那位英雄的葬禮。

7 enthusiasm [ɪnˈθjuzɪ͵æzəm] n. 熱愛，熱衷

片 with enthusiasm　充滿熱情地
衍 (1) enthusiastic [ɪn͵θjuzɪˈæstɪk]
　　 a. 熱心的，熱誠的 ⑤
　　 be enthusiastic about +
　　 N/V-ing　對……充滿熱忱
▶ Peter is enthusiastic about helping the homeless.
彼得很熱心幫助無家可歸的人。
　　 (2) enthusiastically [ɪn͵θjuzɪˈæstɪklɪ]
　　　 adv. 熱衷地

▶ John showed little enthusiasm for jazz.
約翰對爵士樂沒有什麼熱忱。

▶ Stephen King greeted his readers with great enthusiasm.
史帝芬‧金熱情地和他的讀者打招呼。
＊Stephen King 是世界知名的美籍恐怖小說作者，諸多作品曾被改編成電影。

8 launch [lɔntʃ] vt. 發動 (活動)；發射 (火箭、飛彈)；發表 (新書、新作品、新產品) & n. 發表會；(船) 首次下水出航；(火箭) 首次發射升空

似 fire [faɪr] vt. & vi. 發射 ①

▶ To launch a legal demonstration, you must first obtain permission from the local government.
想要發起合法遊行，你們得先向地方政府申請許可。

▶ The space shuttle exploded soon after it was launched.
太空梭發射不久後便爆炸了。

▶ The troops launched missiles at the battleground, causing heavy casualties.
軍隊朝戰場發射了幾枚飛彈，造成嚴重的傷亡。
＊casualty [ˈkæʒjʊəltɪ] n. 死傷人員 (可數)

▶ Emma plans to launch her new novel next year.
艾瑪計劃在明年推出新的小說。

▶ The author herself will show up at the book launch ceremony.
作家本人會在她的新書發表會上現身。

▶ The astronauts were strapped in before the launch.
太空人在火箭發射前繫好安全帶。

9　inspire [ɪnˈspaɪr] *vt.* 鼓舞，激勵，啟發

片 inspire sb to + V　激發某人做……

衍 (1) inspiring [ɪnˈspaɪrɪŋ]
　　a. 激勵人心的

　　(2) inspired [ɪnˈspaɪrd]
　　a. 受到啟發的；卓越的

▶ Adam's father inspired him to become a writer.
亞當的父親激勵他要當作家。

---

inspiration [ˌɪnspəˈreʃən]
n. 靈感，啟示

片 (1) draw inspiration from...
　　從……獲得靈感

　　(2) a source of inspiration
　　靈感來源

▶ Nicholas often draws inspiration from art exhibitions.
尼可拉斯常從藝術展覽汲取靈感。

▶ Ordinary scenes are always a writer's best source of inspiration.
平凡的事件總是作家最佳的靈感來源。

10　allowance [əˈlaʊəns] *n.* 零用錢〔美〕(= pocket money〔英〕)；顧慮

片 make an allowance for...
　　考慮……

= take... into consideration

= take... into account

▶ Alan's mom gives him a monthly allowance of NT$5,000.
艾倫的媽媽一個月給他 5 千塊新臺幣的零用錢。

▶ You should make an allowance for Ben's young age before asking him to shoulder such a heavy burden.

= You should take Ben's young age into consideration before asking him to shoulder such a heavy burden.
你在要求班扛下如此沉重的負擔之前，應該要先顧慮到他年紀還小。

11　harmony [ˈhɑrmənɪ] *n.* 和諧

片 in harmony with...　與……和諧相處

▶ It is very important that people should learn to live in harmony with nature.
大家應該學習和大自然和諧相處，這點很重要。

harmonious [hɑr'monɪəs]
a. 和諧的

衍 harmoniously [hɑr'monɪəslɪ]
   adv. 和諧地

似 melodious [mə'lodɪəs] *a.* 悅耳的

▶ After Kim and Tom married, they moved to the country and led a harmonious life there.
小金和湯姆結婚之後搬到鄉下，小倆口在那裡過著和諧的生活。

---

12 **fortunate** ['fɔrtʃənɪt] *a.* 幸運的

片 It is fortunate that...　幸好……

衍 fortune ['fɔrtʃən]
   n. 命運 (不可數)；財富 (可數) ③

似 lucky ['lʌkɪ] *a.* 幸運的 ①

▶ It was fortunate that no one was hurt in the accident.
幸好沒有人在這起意外當中受傷。

---

fortunately ['fɔrtʃənɪtlɪ]
adv. 幸運地

似 luckily ['lʌkɪlɪ] *adv.* 幸運地

▶ Fortunately, Rex found the money he had lost.
很幸運地，雷克斯找到他遺失的錢。

---

unfortunate [ʌn'fɔrtʃənɪt]
a. 不幸的；倒楣的

片 the unfortunate　不幸的人

似 unlucky [ʌn'lʌkɪ] *a.* 不幸的

▶ Joanna has devoted herself to helping the unfortunate all her life.
喬安娜窮其一生都在致力於幫助不幸的人。

---

misfortune [mɪs'fɔrtʃən]
n. 不幸，災禍

片 have the misfortune to + V
   不幸遭遇……
 = have the misfortune of + V-ing

▶ I feel sorry for the misfortunes of those poor kids in Africa.
我對那些可憐的非洲孩子所遭遇的不幸深感遺憾。

▶ Annie had the misfortune to lose her baby in the car accident.
安妮不幸地在這場車禍中失去了她的孩子。

---

13 **cope** [kop] *vi.* 對抗，應付 (與介詞 with 並用)

片 cope with...　處理……

▶ This problem is hard to cope with.
= This problem is hard to deal with.
= This problem is hard to handle.
這個問題很難處理。

---

14 **realistic** [rɪə'lɪstɪk] *a.* 實際的；現實的

片 be realistic about...
   對……講求實際

衍 (1) real ['rɪəl] *a.* 真實的；道地的 ①
   (2) reality [rɪ'ælətɪ] *n.* 事實 ②

▶ It is not realistic to expect a promotion if you're not devoted to your work.
你不投入工作卻想升職是很不切實際的。

Level 4　Unit 11

▶ You have to be realistic about your level of proficiency in English.
你要對自己的英語造詣程度務實一點。
* proficiency [prəˋfɪʃənsɪ] *n.* 精通，造詣

---

15 thorough [ˋθɝo] *a.* 徹底的

似 through [θru] *prep.* 透過；遍及
& *adv.* 接通 & *a.* 做完的 ①

▶ The doctor gave June a thorough checkup.
醫生幫茱恩做了徹底的全身檢查。

---

16 insurance [ɪnˋʃʊrəns] *n.* 保險 (不可數)

片 (1) life insurance　　人壽保險
(2) health insurance　健康保險

▶ Ed gave me a brief introduction of the four types of life insurance provided by the company.
艾德為我簡略介紹這家公司提供的 4 種人壽保險。

---

insure [ɪnˋʃʊr] *vt.* & *vi.* 保險，投保

片 insure (sb/sth) against...
(為某人 / 某物) 投保……險

似 (1) ensure [ɪnˋʃʊr] *vt.* 確保 ④

▶ Hard work ensures success.
努力確保成功。

(2) assure [əˋʃʊr] *vt.* 保證 ④
assure sb of...　向某人保證……
= assure sb that...

▶ I can assure you of John's ability to handle the problem.
= I can assure you that John has the ability to handle the problem.
我能向你保證約翰具備處理這個問題的能力。

▶ Have you insured your house against fire?
你有幫你的房子投保火險嗎？

---

17 outstanding [aʊtˋstændɪŋ] *a.* 傑出的

似 (1) distinguished [dɪˋstɪŋgwɪʃt]
a. 卓越的 ④
(2) remarkable [rɪˋmɑrkəbl]
a. 卓越的 ④

▶ Mark is an outstanding young man. Nothing bad can be said about him.
馬克是個傑出的青年。他無可挑剔。

---

18 depart [dɪˋpɑrt] *vi.* 出發

片 depart for + 地點　　出發前往某地
= set out for + 地點
= leave for + 地點

▶ Stuart departed for France last night.
= Stuart set out for France last night.
= Stuart left for France last night.
史都華昨晚動身前往法國。

departure [dɪˋpɑrtʃə]
n. 出發，離開

▶ Please arrive at the airport two hours before your departure time.
請於飛機起飛前 2 小時到達機場。

19　visual [ˋvɪʒʊəl] *a.* 視覺的

衍 visible [ˋvɪzəbḷ] *a.* 可見的 ③

▶ Japanese food is not only delicious, but it has visual appeal as well.
日本食物不但好吃，視覺上也同樣誘人。
＊delicious [dɪˋlɪʃəs] *a.* 可口的
　appeal [əˋpil] *n.* 吸引力
　(= attraction [əˋtrækʃən])

audio [ˋɔdɪˏo] *a.* 聲音的
衍 audible [ˋɔdəbḷ] *a.* 可聽見的

▶ Roger is proud of his collection of audio cassettes.
羅傑以他收藏的錄音帶為傲。
＊cassette [kəˋsɛt] *n.* 卡式錄音帶

audio-visual [ˏɔdɪoˋvɪʒʊəl]
a. 視聽的

H audio-visual education　視聽教育

▶ Audio-visual education has long been emphasized in this country.
這個國家長久以來都很注重視聽教育。

20　rhythm [ˋrɪðəm] *n.* 節奏

衍 rhythmic [ˋrɪðmɪk] *a.* 有節奏的
似 melody [ˋmɛlədɪ] *n.* 旋律 ②

▶ Whenever it rains, I like to sit by the window, listening to the rhythm of the falling rain.
雨天的時候，我喜歡坐在窗邊聽下雨的旋律。

▶ Let's dance to the rhythm of the music.
我們跟著音樂的節奏跳舞吧。
＊dance to + 音樂 / 歌曲 / 節拍　隨著音樂 / 歌曲 / 節拍起舞

rhyme [raɪm] *n.* & *vi.* 押韻
H (1) a nursery rhyme　兒歌
　 (2) rhyme with...　與……押韻

▶ Most children can recite nursery rhymes, though they might not understand them.
大部分孩子都能背兒歌，不過他們也許並不了解其中內容。

▶ The word "led" rhymes with "bed", but they have different meanings.
『led』這個字與『bed』押韻，但字義不同。

21　volunteer [ˏvɑlənˋtɪr] *n.* 自願者，義工 & *vi.* 自告奮勇

H volunteer to + V　自願做……

▶ The city government is looking for volunteers to clean up the park.
市政府在徵求打掃公園的志工。

▶ The taxi driver volunteered to help.
這位計程車司機自告奮勇要幫忙。

1121-1127

voluntary [ˈvɑlənˌtɛrɪ]

a. 自願的，自動的

衍 voluntarily [ˈvɑlənˌtɛrəlɪ]
　　adv. 自願地，自動地

▶ All the funds of the group come from voluntary contributions.

這個團體所有的基金都來自於自願捐獻。

22　prompt [prɑmpt] *vt.* 促使 & *a.* 立刻的 & *n.* (演員) 提詞

片 (1) prompt sb to + V
　　促使某人決定做……
　 (2) prompt delivery　限時專送

▶ What prompted you to buy these flowers for me, Henry?

亨利，是什麼原因促使你買這些花給我？

▶ I was pleased with the prompt delivery of my items.
我很高興我的東西被快速寄送。

▶ When the actor forgot his line, one of his co-stars gave him a prompt.
那個演員忘詞時，聯合主演的另一個演員就幫他提詞。

23　fiction [ˈfɪkʃən] *n.* (虛構) 小說類 (集合名詞，不可數)

衍 fictional [ˈfɪkʃənl̩] *a.* 虛構的

反 nonfiction [nɑnˈfɪkʃən]
　　n. 非小說類 (集合名詞，不可數)

比 novel 和 fiction 皆表『小說』，但是 novel 為可數名詞，所以表示『一本小說』時要用 a novel；而 fiction 則為集合名詞，表『小說的總稱』，前面不可以置冠詞。

a fiction (×)
→ a novel (○)　一本小說

▶ The famous writer wrote 45 novels all his life.
那位名作家畢生總共寫了 45 本小說。

▶ That short story is a work of fiction. In other words, it is not true.

那則短篇故事是小說作品。也就是說，它不是真的。

24　forbid [fɚˈbɪd] *vt.* 禁止

三 forbid, forbade [fɚˈbæd]/[fɚˈbed], forbidden [fɚˈbɪdn̩]

片 (1) forbid + V-ing　禁止做……
　 (2) forbid sb to + V　禁止某人做某事
　 = forbid sb from + V-ing

▶ Smoking is forbidden in this building.
本大樓內禁止吸菸。

▶ Kimberly's parents absolutely forbid her to go out after midnight.
= Kimberly's parents absolutely forbid her from going out after midnight.
金柏莉的父母嚴禁她半夜出門。

25 entertain [ˌɛntɚˈten] *vt.* 娛樂

🅗 entertain sb with sth
　　用某物娛樂某人

衍 entertaining [ˌɛntɚˈtenɪŋ]
　　a. 有娛樂性，令人愉快的

▶ Martha entertained all the kids with interesting stories.
　　瑪莎用有趣的故事把全部的小朋友都逗得很開心。

---

entertainment [ˌɛntɚˈtenmənt]
n. 娛樂，樂趣 (不可數)；娛樂節目 (可數)

🅗 find entertainment in...
　　在……之中找到樂趣
= find fun in...

▶ The old man found entertainment in reading.
　　這位老先生從閱讀中找到樂趣。

▶ The food was great, but the entertainment was lousy.
　　食物很棒，但娛樂節目很糟。

---

26 restore [rɪˈstɔr] *vt.* 復原

🅗 (1) restore one's health
　　某人恢復健康

(2) restore A to B
　　將 A 恢復到 B 的狀態

衍 restoration [ˌrɛstəˈreʃən] *n.* 恢復 ⑥

▶ You must rest well to restore your health.
　　你必須好好休養才能恢復健康。

▶ The new government is trying hard to restore the country's economy to its full strength.
　　新政府正努力設法將該國的經濟回復到全盛狀態。

---

27 delicate [ˈdɛləkət] *a.* 脆弱的；精緻的

衍 delicately [ˈdɛləkətlɪ] *adv.* 精緻地
似 weak [wik] *a.* 柔弱的 ①

▶ The eye is a rather delicate organ.
　　眼睛是很脆弱的器官。

▶ Jonathan gave me a set of delicate china teacups for my birthday.
　　喬納森送了我一組精緻的陶瓷茶杯作為生日禮物。

---

delicacy [ˈdɛləkəsɪ] *n.* 美食 (可數)；
細緻 (不可數)；慎重 (不可數)

🅗 with great delicacy　很謹慎地
= with great caution
= very cautiously

▶ I'd like to eat some local delicacies.
　　我想要嚐點在地美食。

▶ Just feel the delicacy of this fabric.
　　摸摸看這塊布料細緻的質感。

▶ Todd talked to the patient with great delicacy.
　　陶德非常謹慎地與病人說話。

---

fragile [ˈfrædʒəl] *a.* 脆弱的
衍 frail [frel] *a.* 虛弱的

▶ Please handle these glasses with care. They're fragile.
　　請小心處理這些玻璃。它們很易碎。

Level 4　Unit 11

28 priority [praɪˈɔrətɪ] n. 優先考慮的事 (可數) ; 優先權 (不可數)

片 (1) one's top / first priority
　　某人最重要的事

(2) A have / take priority over B
　　A 比 B 更重要

▸ You need to get your priorities right / straight so you can get things done on time.
你得搞清楚事情的優先順序，以便能把事情準時完成。

▸ Our top priority is to improve quality control on the assembly line.
我們的首要任務就是提升裝配線上的品質控管。
*assembly [əˈsɛmblɪ] n. (機器的) 裝配

▸ Pedestrians at intersections have priority over vehicles.
相較於車輛，行人在十字路口有優先權。
*pedestrian [pəˈdɛstrɪən] n. 行人

29 recognition [ˌrɛkəɡˈnɪʃən] n. 認出 ; 承認，認可

片 win recognition　獲得認可

似 (1) credit [ˈkrɛdɪt] n. 讚揚 ③

(2) acknowledgement
　　[əkˈnɑlɪdʒmənt] n. 承認 ⑤

▸ There was no recognition in my old friend's eyes when he saw me.
我的老友見到我時沒有認出我來。

▸ The scholar has won international recognition for his great findings.
這位學者的重大發現獲得了國際認可。

30 pasta [ˈpɑstə] n. 義大利麵食 (總稱，不可數)

延伸 (1) spaghetti [spəˈɡɛtɪ]
　　n. 細條義大利麵 (不可數) ③

(2) macaroni [ˌmækəˈronɪ]
　　n. (義大利) 通心粉 / 麵

▸ The restaurant serves great Italian food like pizza and pasta.
這家餐廳提供很棒的義大利餐點，像披薩和義大利麵食。

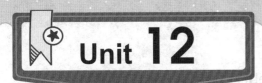 **Unit 12**

 1201-1204

---

1 anxiety [æŋˋzaɪɛtɪ] *n.* 焦慮

衍 anxious [ˋæŋkʃəs]
　a. 焦慮的；渴望的 ③

似 apprehension [ˌæprɪˋhɛnʃən] *n.* 憂慮

反 calmness [ˋkɑmnəs] *n.* 平靜

▶ Rosie's anxiety about unemployment is understandable.
蘿西對失業感到憂心忡忡，這點是可以理解的。

---

2 magnificent [mægˋnɪfəsənt] *a.* 非凡的，華麗的

衍 magnify [ˋmægnəˌfaɪ]
　vt. 擴大，放大 ⑥

▶ This microscope can magnify an object up to 1,000 times.
這部顯微鏡可將物體放大，最高可達 1 千倍。

似 (1) grand [grænd]
　a. 堂皇的，雄偉的 ②

(2) superb [suˋpɝb] *a.* 非凡的 ⑤

▶ Michael Jordan unveiled a magnificent statue of himself.
邁可・喬登為一尊他自己的雄偉雕像揭幕。
＊unveil [ʌnˋvel] *vt.* 揭幕，揭開……的面紗

▶ I was attracted to the magnificent view of the valley.
我被山谷壯麗的景觀給吸引住了。

---

splendid [ˋsplɛndɪd]
a. 富麗堂皇的；絕佳的

衍 splendor [ˋsplɛndə] *n.* 壯麗 ⑥

似 excellent [ˋɛksḷənt] *a.* 絕佳的 ①

▶ After the banker retired, he lived in a splendid house in the countryside.
那位銀行家退休後，便住進一棟位於鄉間富麗堂皇的宅邸。

▶ The bride looks splendid in her white wedding gown.
新娘穿著白色的婚紗看起來美極了。

---

3 discipline [ˋdɪsəplɪn] *n.* 紀律 (不可數) & *vt.* 訓練，管教

衍 (1) disciplined [ˋdɪsəplɪnd]
　a. (人) 有紀律的
　a disciplined army
　紀律嚴明的軍隊

(2) disciplinary [ˋdɪsəplɪnˌɛrɪ]
　a. 關於紀律的，懲戒的 ⑥
　a disciplinary committee
　懲戒委員會

▶ Discipline is what makes a soldier a soldier.
紀律是軍人之所以為軍人的要素。

▶ You must discipline your child, or he will grow up spoiled.
你一定要管教好你的孩子，否則他長大會被寵壞。
＊spoiled [spɔɪld] *a.* 被寵壞的

---

4 dismiss [dɪsˋmɪs] *vt.* 摒棄；開除

片 (1) dismiss A as B
　把 A 視為 B 而不予理會 / 考慮

(2) dismiss sb from his / her job
　開除某人的職位

▶ Mr. Warren dismissed the reports as ridiculous.
華倫先生將這些報導斥為無稽之談。
＊ridiculous [rɪˋdɪkjələs] *a.* 無稽的，荒謬的

329

Level 4 Unit 12

▶ The general **manager** dismissed Rachel from her job for incompetence.
總經理因瑞秋不適任而開除她。
*incompetence [ɪnˋkɑmpətəns] *n.* 不適任，無能力

5 **resemble** [rɪˋzɛmbl̩] *vt.* 和……相似

衍 resemblance [rɪˋzɛmbləns]
n. 相似 ⑤

bear a close resemblance to...
和……很相似
= look very much like...

用法 resemble 本身是及物動詞，故不得與
介詞 like 並用，無下列寫法：

▶ Jack resembles ~~like~~ his father. (×)
→ Jack resembles his father. (○)
= Jack looks like his father.
傑克長得像他父親。

▶ Kelly closely resembles her mother.
= Kelly bears a close resemblance to her mother.
= Kelly looks very much like her mother.
凱莉長得很像她媽媽。

▶ The two cars resemble each other.
這兩輛車彼此很相像。

▶ Your writing resembles your father's.
你的寫作和你父親的很像。

6 **protest** [prəˋtɛst / ˋprotɛst] *vt.* & *vi.* 抗議 & *vt.* 反駁 (用 that 子句作受詞)

片 protest against...   抗議 / 反對……

▶ Thousands of students took to the streets to protest high tuition fees.
數千名學生走上街頭抗議高學費。
*tuition [tjuˋɪʃən] *n.* 學費

▶ The villagers protested against the construction of the nuclear power plant in their neighborhood.
村民們抗議在他們住處附近興建核電廠。

▶ All the staff members in the company had the feeling that Peter was very lazy, but he protested that it was not the case at all.
公司所有員工都覺得彼得很懶惰，但他反駁事實根本不是那樣。

protest [ˋprotɛst] *n.* 抗議；抗議行動
片 in protest against...   以抗議……

▶ A neighbor's protest about the noise ended the party.
有位鄰居抗議太吵，致使派對結束。

▶ A large protest was held outside the building.
大樓外面舉行了一次大規模的抗議行動。

▶ The farmers launched a demonstration in protest against the new policy.
農民發動示威以抗議該項新政策。

7　drift [drɪft] *vi.* 漂流；遊蕩，漫遊 & *n.* (被風吹積起來的) 一堆 (雪、沙等)；(局面) 變化；漂流

似 (1) float [flot] *vi.* 漂浮 ③
　 (2) wander [ˈwɑndɚ] *vi.* 遊蕩 ③

▶ The boat drifted down the stream.
　船順著溪流漂流而下。

▶ I spent the whole summer vacation drifting around South America.
= I spent the whole summer vacation wandering around South America.
　我整個暑假都在南美漫遊。

▶ We couldn't drive down the road due to the deep snow drifts.
　因為雪積得很深，所以我們沒辦法把車開在路上。

▶ There has been a drift towards more liberal views in that age group.
　那個年齡層漸漸對比較自由開放的態度有了轉變。

▶ This ocean drift will lead us to land.
　這道洋流會將我們帶到陸地。

8　transportation [ˌtrænspɚˈteʃən] *n.* 交通運輸 (工具) (不可數)

衍 transport [ˈtræns͵port] *n.* 運輸 & *vt.* [trænsˈport] 運輸 ③

▶ All the articles will be transported to South Asia.
= All the articles will be shipped to South Asia.
　所有貨品都會被運送至南亞。

▶ All transportation came to a halt during the strike.
　這次罷工期間，所有交通運輸都停擺了。
＊come to a halt / stop　停頓下來
＝grind to a halt / stop

9　recovery [rɪˈkʌvərɪ] *n.* 找回；痊癒，復元

衍 recover [rɪˈkʌvɚ] *vi.* 恢復 & *vt.* 找回；恢復正常 ②
似 (1) retrieval [rɪˈtrivl̩] *n.* 找回
　 (2) recuperation [rɪ͵k(j)upəˈreʃən] *n.* 復元

▶ Mr. Anderson helped the police in the recovery of the stolen goods.
　安德森先生協助警方找回贓物。

▶ The doctor said that after careful treatment, the patient had a good chance of recovery.
　醫生說經過仔細治療後，該病患復元的機會很大。

10　terror [ˈtɛrɚ] *n.* 恐怖；可怕的人或物

片 in terror　惶恐地
衍 (1) terrible [ˈtɛrəbl̩] *a.* 可怕的；糟糕的，差勁的 ①
　 (2) terrorist [ˈtɛrərɪst] *n.* 恐怖分子 ②

▶ The sight of blood filled the woman with terror.
　見到血跡使那個女人心中充滿恐懼。

▶ We ran in terror from the scene of the explosion.
　我們驚恐地從爆炸現場逃離。

1210-1218

(3) **terrorism** [`tɛrə,rɪzəm]
　　n. 恐怖主義 ②

　▶ The criminal was the terror of the neighborhood.
　　這名罪犯是這附近一帶的可怕人物。

(4) **terrify** [`tɛrə,faɪ]
　　vt. 驚嚇，使恐懼 ⑤

似 (1) **fear** [fɪr] *n.* 害怕 ①
　 (2) **horror** [`hɔrɚ] *n.* 恐懼 ③

11　modest [`mɑdɪst] *a.* 謙虛的

似 **humble** [`hʌmbḷ] *a.* 謙虛的 ②
反 (1) **proud** [praʊd] *a.* 驕傲的 ①
　 (2) **arrogant** [`ærəgənt] *a.* 傲慢的 ⑤

　▶ The scholar was very modest about the prize he got.
　　這名學者對於他得獎一事非常謙虛。

modesty [`mɑdɪstɪ] *n.* 謙虛
片 **with modesty**　謙虛地
= **modestly** [`mɑdɪstlɪ] *adv.* 謙虛地

　▶ "I'm the chief of a small hospital," Dr. Walton said with modesty.
　　華頓醫師謙虛地說：『我是一家小醫院的主任』。

12　peculiar [pɪ`kjuljɚ] *a.* 奇怪的；獨特的

片 **be peculiar to + 地方**
　　是某地所獨有的
= **be native to + 地方**
= **be indigenous to + 地方**
　 *indigenous [ɪn`dɪdʒɪnəs]
　　a. 本地的；土產的
似 (1) **odd** [ɑd] *a.* 奇特的 ③
　 (2) **unusual** [ʌn`juʒʊəl] *a.* 不尋常的
　 (3) **strange** [strendʒ] *a.* 奇怪的 ①
　 (4) **weird** [wɪrd] *a.* 怪異的 ⑤

　▶ Don't you think that Kelly is a little bit peculiar today?
　　你不覺得凱莉今天有點兒怪怪的嗎？
　▶ This kind of bird is peculiar to that island.
= This kind of bird is native to that island.
= This kind of bird is indigenous to that island.
　　這種鳥是該島所獨有的。

13　reputation [,rɛpjə`teʃən] *n.* 名譽，名聲

衍 **repute** [rɪ`pjut] *n.* 名聲 (不可數)
a man of high / good repute
德高望重的人

　▶ The sex scandal has ruined the reputation of the politician.
　　這樁性醜聞毀了這位政治人物的名聲。
　　*scandal [`skændḷ] *n.* 醜聞

14　absolute [`æbsə,lut / ,æbsə`lut] *a.* 絕對的，完全的

片 **have absolute confidence in...**
　　對……絕對有信心
似 (1) **total** [`totḷ] *a.* 完全的 ①
　 (2) **complete** [kəm`plit] *a.* 徹底的 ②

　▶ You must tell me the absolute truth, or you'll be in big trouble.
　　你必須告訴我全部實情，否則你麻煩就大了。

▸ I have absolute confidence in your ability to handle such a problem.
我對你處理這種問題的能力有絕對的信心。

absolutely [ˈæbsəˌlutlɪ / ˌæbsəˈlutlɪ]
adv. 絕對地，完全地

⑭ completely [kəmˈplitlɪ] *adv.* 徹底地

▸ It is absolutely impossible to swim across the ocean.
想要游過那片海洋是絕對不可能的。

15　outcome [ˈautˌkʌm] *n.* 結果

⑭ (1) consequence [ˈkɑnsəˌkwəns]
　　n. 後果 ④
　 (2) result [rɪˈzʌlt] *n.* 結果 ②

▸ What was the outcome of the basketball game?
那場籃球賽的結果如何？

16　withdraw [wɪðˈdrɔ] *vt.* 提 (款) & *vt.* & *vi.* 退出；撤退

▤ withdraw, withdrew [wɪðˈdru], withdrawn [wɪðˈdrɔn]
▯ withdraw / deposit money
　提款 / 存款
⑭ withdrawal [wɪðˈdrɔəl]
　n. 提款；撤退；收回

▸ I used up all my spare money, so I'm going to withdraw some money from the bank this afternoon.
我身上已沒多餘的錢了，所以今天下午我要到銀行提款。

▸ The athlete's sore arm forced him to withdraw from the competition.
這位運動員的手臂疼痛，迫使他退出比賽。
＊sore [sɔr] *a.* 痠痛的

▸ John withdrew from school a year before he graduated.
約翰在畢業的前一年退學了。

17　monument [ˈmɑnjəmənt] *n.* 紀念碑

⑭ monumental [ˌmɑnjəˈmɛntl̩]
　a. 巨大的

▸ Mr. Lee made a monumental contribution to our company before he retired.
李先生在退休前對本公司有重大的貢獻。

⑭ memorial [məˈmorɪəl]
　n. 紀念物；紀念碑 ④

▸ A monument was built in honor of the late hero.
為記念這位已故的英雄建立了一座紀念碑。

18　artistic [ɑrˈtɪstɪk] *a.* 藝術的；美妙的

⑭ artist [ˈɑrtɪst] *n.* 畫家；藝術家 ②

▸ Henry's artistic ability began to shine when he was quite young.
亨利的藝術才能在很年輕時就已開始發光。

▶ The pianist gave a very artistic performance at the concert last night.
那位鋼琴家在昨晚的音樂會中有一場唯美的演出。

19　await [ə`wet] *vt.* 等候，等待

比 await 與 wait for 均表『等待』，但 await 之後須接抽象的事物作受詞，若接人為受詞，則帶有『預期某事會發生在某人身上』之意；而 wait for 可接任何表人或事物的名詞作受詞。例：

▶ I'm awaiting your answer.
= I'm waiting for your answer.
我在等候您的答覆。

▶ A scene of utter destruction awaited the rescue team at the bombed hotel.
= A scene of utter destruction waited for the rescue team at the bombed hotel.
在被炸毀的旅館處，等待著救援隊的是斷垣殘壁的景象。

▶ We are awaiting another chance to try again.
= We are waiting for another chance to try again.
我們正在等候另一次嘗試的機會。

20　convey [kən`ve] *vt.* 運送，運輸；傳達

片 a conveyor belt [kən`veə͈ ˏbɛlt]
n. 輸送帶
似 (1) deliver [dɪ`lɪvə] *vt.* 遞送 ②
(2) ship [ʃɪp] *vt.* 運送 ①

▶ Trucks convey cargo that used to be conveyed by train. 以前由火車運送的貨物現在都由卡車運送。
＊cargo [`kɑrgo] *n.* (船、飛機、車輛裝載的) 貨物

▶ The foreigner used gestures to convey his message.
那位外國人使用手勢來傳達他的意思。
＊gesture [`dʒɛstʃə] *n.* 手勢

21　grind [graɪnd] *vt. & vi.* 研磨，磨碎；磨 (牙) & *n.* 苦差事 (恆為單數)；書呆子

三 grind, ground [graʊnd], ground
片 (1) grind to a halt / stop　停頓下來
　= come to a halt / stop
(2) grind one's teeth　某人磨牙
延伸 grind 的過去式及過去分詞均為 ground，但 ground 另可作名詞表『土地』，或作動詞表『使某人禁足』或『使停飛』，此時的三態為：ground, grounded, grounded。例：

▶ The Mexican woman ground the corn into flour for tortillas.
那個墨西哥婦女將玉米磨成了粉，以便作成玉米薄餅。
＊tortilla [tɔr`tijə] *n.* 玉米薄餅

▶ Traffic ground to a halt during rush hour this morning. 今天早上在尖峰時刻交通陷於停頓。

▶ Dad has the habit of grinding his teeth in his sleep.
老爸睡覺時有磨牙的習慣。

▶ Sam is sick of the daily grind of working in the office.
山姆對於辦公室裡的日常苦差事感到厭煩。

▶ Nicole came back late last night, so her father grounded her for the weekend.

妮可昨晚太晚回家，所以她老爸罰她週末禁足。

▶ Because of the typhoon, all planes were grounded.

因為颱風的緣故，所有飛機航班都停飛了。

▶ Jack is such a grind; all he does is study.

傑克是個大書呆子，他只會念書。

---

22 exhibit [ɪɡˋzɪbɪt] *vt.* 顯示，現出；展示 & *vi.* 展示 & *n.* 展覽會 (= exhibition [ˌɛksəˋbɪʃən])

似 (1) display [dɪˋsple] *n.* & *vt.* 展覽 ②
　　(2) show [ʃo] *vt.* 顯示 ①

▶ The patient exhibited some early signs of the disease.

該名病患出現了這種疾病的若干早期症狀。

▶ The artists exhibited their paintings in the gallery.

這些藝術家在畫廊展示他們的畫作。

▶ We visited the calligraphy exhibit at the National Palace Museum.

我們參觀了在故宮博物院展出的書法展。

＊calligraphy [kəˋlɪɡrəfɪ] *n.* 書法 ⑤

---

23 grateful [ˋɡretfəl] *a.* 感激的

片 be grateful to sb for sth
　　就某事對某人表示感激
= be thankful to sb for sth
= be indebted [ɪnˋdɛtɪd] to sb for sth

▶ I'm grateful to you for your help.

對於你的幫助我非常感激。

---

gratitude [ˋɡrætəˌt(j)ud] *n.* 感激

片 (1) show one's gratitude　　表示謝意
　　(2) out of gratitude　　　　出於感激
似 (1) gratefulness [ˋɡretfəlnəs] *n.* 感激
　　(2) thankfulness [ˋθæŋkfəlnəs]
　　　　n. 感謝
　　(3) appreciation [əˌpriʃɪˋeʃən]
　　　　n. 感激 ④

▶ How can I express my gratitude for your help?

對於您的相助，我該如何表達我的謝意呢？

▶ John showed his gratitude by treating me to a movie.
= John treated me to a movie out of gratitude.

出於感激，約翰請我去看電影。

---

ungrateful [ʌnˋɡretfəl]
a. 不知感激的

▶ The ungrateful boy broke his parents' hearts by failing to do well in school.

這個不知感激的男孩在校表現不佳，傷透了父母的心。

24 grace [gres] n. 優雅；大方 & vt. 使增光；使美化

(1) with good grace　欣然地
(2) have the grace to + V
　　有做……的風度
(3) grace sb with your presence
　　駕臨而為某人增光

反 disgrace [dɪsˈgres]
n. 恥辱；令人可恥的事 & vt. 使丟臉 ⑥

▶ The members of the royal family conducted themselves with grace and dignity.
皇室成員的行事作風優雅尊貴。
*conduct oneself　舉止，表現

▶ John took my advice with good grace.
約翰欣然地接受我的建言。

▶ John hurt Mary's feelings by calling her an alien. And what's even worse, he didn't have the grace to apologize to her.
約翰叫瑪莉外星人而使她傷心。更糟的是，他甚至連向她道歉的風度都沒有。
*alien [ˈelɪən] n. 外星人；外國人

▶ Thank you for gracing us with your presence.
感謝您大駕光臨，使我們蓬蓽生輝。

▶ Peter's face has graced the cover of several men's magazines.
彼得在好幾本男性雜誌的封面露臉，讓雜誌更有看頭。

graceful [ˈgresfəl] a. 優雅的
似 elegant [ˈɛləgənt] a. 優雅的 ④

▶ The old gentleman talked with graceful manners.
這位老紳士的談吐非常溫文儒雅。
*manners [ˈmænɚz] n. 禮貌 (恆用複數)

gracious [ˈgreʃəs]
a. 親切的，仁慈的；富裕的
片 gracious living　優裕的生活
似 (1) kind [kaɪnd] a. 仁慈的 ①
　　(2) amicable [ˈæmɪkəbḷ] a. 親切的

▶ Ms. Mont is the kindest and most gracious lady I've ever met.
蒙特女士是我遇過最善良最親切的人。

▶ This new book is about gracious living in Monaco.
這本新書是有關於摩納哥的優裕生活。

25 alert [əˈlɝt] n. 警戒 & a. 警戒的 & vt. 提醒

(1) be on the alert for...
　　(隨時) 提防 / 注意……
(2) be alert to...　對……警覺 / 機敏
(3) alert sb to sth　提醒某人警覺某事
= awaken sb to sth

▶ On Christmas Eve, the children were on the alert for any sign of Santa Claus.
在耶誕夜，孩子們隨時注意聖誕老人出現的蛛絲馬跡。

▶ Police officers are always alert to possible danger.
警察對可能發生的危險隨時保持警覺。

▶ We should alert everyone to the dangers of smoking.
= We should awaken everyone to the dangers of smoking.
我們應該提醒每個人警覺抽菸的危險。

26　dispute [dɪˋspjut] n. & vt. 爭執；質疑 & vi. 爭執

(1) be in dispute with sb
　　與某人起衝突

(2) It is beyond dispute that...
　　……是毫無爭議的

▸ I was in dispute with my roommate over money.
　我跟室友因金錢起了爭執。

▸ It is beyond dispute that there's no free lunch.
　天下沒白吃的午餐是無可爭議的。

▸ Jack's loyalty to the company has never been disputed.
　傑克對公司的忠誠度從未被質疑過。

▸ The two countries disputed for years about / over where to set the border.
　這兩國對該於何處劃分疆界已爭執多年。

27　transform [trænsˋfɔrm] vt. 變化，改變

transform A into B　將 A 改變為 B
= convert A into B
= change A into B
= turn A into B
transformation [ˌtrænsfɚˋmeʃən]
　n. 轉型；轉變 ⑤

▸ The land owner transformed the old house into a hotel.
= The land owner converted the old house into a hotel.
= The land owner changed the old house into a hotel.
= The land owner turned the old house into a hotel.
　地主將這棟舊屋改成一家旅館。

28　maturity [məˋtʃurətɪ] n. 成熟

reach maturity　達到成熟
(1) mature [məˋtʃur] a. 成熟的 ②
(2) premature [ˌpriməˋtʃur]
　　a. 早熟的 ⑤
　　a premature baby　早產兒
immature [ˌɪməˋtʃur] a. 不成熟的

▸ Even though Penny is already 30, she lacks any maturity.
　雖然潘妮已經 30 歲了，她卻一點也不成熟。

▸ The last time I saw Mary was only three years ago. Now, she has reached her maturity as a beautiful woman.
　我上回見到瑪莉不過是三年前的事。如今她已成熟成為一位美麗的女人。

29　neglect [nɪˋglɛkt] vt. 忽視 & n. 疏忽

(1) neglectful [nɪˋglɛktfəl] a. 疏忽的
(2) negligent [ˋnɛglədʒənt] a. 疏忽的
　　be neglectful of...　對……疏忽
　= be negligent in...

▸ You should never be neglectful of your duties.
= You should never be negligent in your duties.
　你不能怠忽職守。

ignore [ɪgˋnɔr] vt. 忽視 ②

▸ A man who neglects his duties is not to be trusted.
= A man who overlooks his duties is not to be trusted.
　疏於職責的人是不會被信任的。

▸ This problem is the product of years of government neglect.
　這個問題是多年來政府怠忽所造成的結果。

overlook [ˌovəˈlʊk] *vt.* 忽略；俯瞰

▶ Do not overlook the rules of grammar when writing an English essay.
寫英文文章時，不要忽略文法規則。

▶ Our house is located on a hilltop overlooking the valley.
我們家就座落在小山頂上，可以俯瞰山谷。

---

30 split [splɪt] *vt.* 劈開；分裂 & *vi.* 分開 & *n.* 裂口；意見分歧

🔺 三態同形 (現在分詞為 splitting)

🔹 (1) split sth in two / in half
　　將某物分成兩塊
　　(2) split up with sb　與某人分手
　　= break up with sb
　　(3) a banana split
　　香蕉聖代，香蕉船 (冰淇淋)

▶ The cake was split into two parts.
這塊蛋糕被切成兩塊。

▶ My girlfriend split up with me because she thought I didn't really love her.
我女友和我分手了，因為她覺得我並沒有真心愛她。

▶ The sharp edges of the packaging created a large split in the plastic bag.
這個包裝的邊邊尖銳，把塑膠袋劃破了好大一個裂口。

▶ The issue of nuclear power has caused a split in the government.
核能議題在政府內部造成意見分歧。

▶ Let me have a banana split.
給我一份香蕉聖代。

---

31 accuracy [ˈækjərəsɪ] *n.* 準確性

衍 accurate [ˈækjərət] *a.* 準確的 ③
似 (1) precision [prɪˈsɪʒən] *n.* 準確 ⑥
　　(2) exactness [ɪgˈzæktnəs] *n.* 準確

▶ We cannot guarantee the accuracy of these statistics.
我們無法保證這些統計數據的準確性。
＊statistics [stəˈtɪstɪks]
　n. 統計數字 (恆用複數)；統計學 (不可數)

---

32 endure [ɪnˈd(j)ʊr] *vt.* 忍耐

衍 (1) endurance [ɪnˈd(j)ʊrəns]
　　n. 持久力；耐力 ⑥
　　(2) enduring [ɪnˈdjʊrɪŋ]
　　a. 持久的，永久的
　　(3) endurable [ɪnˈd(j)ʊrəbl̩]
　　a. 可忍受的
似 (1) stand [stænd] *vt.* 忍受 ①
　　(2) tolerate [ˈtɑləˌret] *vt.* 容忍 ④
　　(3) bear [bɛr] *vt.* 忍受 ①

▶ We must try to endure any pain in our quest for success.
在追求成功的過程中，我們必須設法忍受任何痛苦。
＊quest [kwɛst] *n.* 追尋 (= search)

---

33 reunion [riˈjunjən] *n.* 重聚，團圓

🔹 a family reunion　家庭團聚
衍 union [ˈjunjən] *n.* 工會；聯合 ③

▶ Our high school reunion is next Tuesday.
我們高中同學會在下星期二。

Level 4 Unit 12

34 romance [roˈmæns / ˈromæns] *n.* 戀情；浪漫；愛情小說

似 (1) love [lʌv] *n.* 愛情 ①
　 (2) passion [ˈpæʃən] *n.* 熱情 ③

▶ The couple wanted to keep their romance secret from their parents.
這對情侶想要把戀情瞞著父母。

▶ The fun and romance of the newlyweds' honeymoon was unforgettable.
蜜月期間的情趣與浪漫令這對新婚夫妻難忘。

＊寫本句時老外將 The fun and romance 視為一體，當作單數，故使用單數動詞 was。我們亦可將 The fun 及 the romance 視為兩個獨立的名詞，以 and 連接，此時就要使用複數動詞 were。

▶ Brandy enjoyed reading popular romances when she was in high school.
布蘭蒂上高中時很愛看愛情小說。

35 tremble [ˈtrɛmbḷ] *vi.* 顫抖

片 tremble with fear　嚇得發抖
似 (1) shiver [ˈʃɪvɚ] *vi.* 發抖 ⑤
　 (2) quiver [ˈkwɪvɚ]
　　 vi. & n. (因強烈情緒而) 顫抖 ⑤

▶ Lori began to tremble with fear when she saw the big dog.
蘿莉看到這隻大狗時，開始害怕地直發抖。

36 yawn [jɔn] *vi.* 打呵欠

似 yarn [jɑrn] *n.* 紗，紗線

▶ The man's speech was so boring that I couldn't help but yawn.
這位先生的演講很無聊，所以我忍不住打呵欠。

37 workout [ˈwɝkaʊt] *n.* (尤指運動的) 鍛鍊，訓練 (可數)

▶ A half hour of cycling can only be regarded as a light workout.
騎腳踏車一小時只能視為輕量訓練。

38 noble [ˈnobḷ] *a.* 高貴的；貴族的

似 (1) upright [ˈʌpˌraɪt] *a.* 正直的 ⑥
　 (2) virtuous [ˈvɝtʃʊəs] *a.* 道德高尚的
　 (3) aristocratic [əˌrɪstəˈkrætɪk]
　　 a. 貴族的

▶ We think highly of George because he is a man of noble character.
我們很敬重喬治，因為他是個品德高尚的人。

▶ My friend Charles claimed that he is a person of noble birth.
我的朋友查理宣稱自己有貴族血統。

1 privilege [ˋprɪvlɪdʒ] *n.* 特權；榮幸 & *vt.* 給予……特權

片 have the privilege of + V-ing
從事……感到很榮幸

= have the honor of + V-ing

似 honor [ˋɑnɚ] *n.* 榮幸 ③

▶ As a deputy director, you will be given certain privileges.
身為副主任，你將享有某些特權。
*deputy [ˋdɛpjətɪ] *a.* 副的 & *n.* 副手

▶ May I have the privilege of asking you for a dance, miss?

= May I have the honor of asking you for a dance, miss?
小姐，我有榮幸請妳跳支舞嗎？

▶ The government's policies privilege the rich and powerful.
政府的政策惠及有錢有勢的人。

privileged [ˋprɪvlɪdʒd]
a. 有特權的；感到榮幸的

片 be / feel privileged to + V
很榮幸能……

似 (1) lucky [ˋlʌkɪ] *a.* 幸運的 ①
(2) honored [ˋɑnɚd] *a.* 榮幸的

▶ In the past, only privileged people were allowed the opportunity to be educated.
過去，只有特權人士有接受教育的機會。

▶ I feel privileged to meet you, Dr. Johnson.
強森博士，能見到你是我的榮幸。

2 legend [ˋlɛdʒənd] *n.* 傳說

片 Legend has it that... 傳說………

衍 legendary [ˋlɛdʒənd‚ɛrɪ] *a.* 傳奇的 ⑤

似 (1) myth [mɪθ] *n.* 神話 ⑤
(2) Rumor has it that... 謠傳……
= Word has it that...
= It is said that...

▶ According to the legend, a fairy lives on the moon.
根據這則傳說，有一位仙女住在月亮上。

▶ Legend has it that in the mountains lived seven dwarfs.
傳說山裡頭住著 7 個小矮人。
*dwarf [dwɔrf] *n.* 矮子；侏儒

3 sketch [skɛtʃ] *n.* 素描；草圖 & *vt.* & *vi.* 素描；畫草圖 & *vt.* 概略

片 (1) do a sketch of... 將……作素描
(2) draw a sketch 畫草圖

延伸 a sketched map 簡要地圖

▶ James did a sketch of his girlfriend that looked just like her.
詹姆士為女友作素描，真是唯妙唯肖。

▶ Dan drew a sketch to show us what the new building would look like.
丹畫了一張草圖，告訴我們新大樓外觀的樣子。

▶ The artist sketched the mountains many times before making a painting of them.
藝術家將群山入畫前素描了很多次。

▶ Kevin likes to sit by the lake and sketch.
凱文喜歡坐在湖邊畫素描。

▶ I asked the lawyer to sketch the main points for us.
我請該律師概述重點給我們。

---

draft [dræft] *vt.* 草擬 & *n.* 草稿

卅 draft a plan　草擬計畫
= draw up a plan
= map out a plan

似 outline [`aʊt͵laɪn] *n.* 大綱 ③

▶ The athletic association drafted a contract for the new football player.
體育協會為新進足球員草擬了一份契約。

▶ The cartoonist turned in the final draft this morning.
今早那位漫畫家把最後的草稿交出去了。

4　namely [`nemlɪ] *adv.* 換言之，就是

似 That is (to say), …　也就是說，……

▶ We have only 2 days left. That is (to say), we are hard pressed for time to do the job.
我們只剩兩天了。換言之，我們做這件工作的時間非常緊迫。

▶ One group of people in particular will benefit from the proposal, namely the elderly.
這項提案特別會讓一組人受益，也就是老年人。

▶ I know someone who would be perfect for you. Namely, Bill.
我認識一個跟你很配的人。就是比爾。

5　humanity [hju`mænətɪ] *n.* 人類（總稱，不可數）；仁愛，慈悲

卅 a man / woman of humanity
慈悲的男性 / 女性

衍 (1) human [`hjumən]
　　　n. 人類 & *a.* 人類的，人性的 ②
　　(2) humane [hju`men] *a.* 人道的
　　(3) humanist [`hjumənɪst]
　　　n. 人道 / 文主義者
　　(4) humanitarian [hju͵mænə`tɛrɪən]
　　　a. 人道的 & *n.* 人道主義者

似 (1) human being　人類
　　(2) mankind [͵mæn`kaɪnd] *n.* 人類 ③

反 inhuman [ɪn`hjumən] *a.* 沒人性的

▶ We should do things for the welfare of all humanity.
= We should do things for the good of all mankind / humans.
我們應該做對全人類有益的事。

▶ Mother Teresa was a woman of great humanity.
德蕾莎修女是個非常慈悲的女性。

6　sacrifice [`sækrə͵faɪs] *vt.* & *n.* 犧牲

卅 at the sacrifice of...　犧牲了……
= at the cost of...

▶ Those martyrs sacrificed their lives for democracy.
那些烈士們為民主犧牲了生命。
*martyr [`mɑrtɚ] *n.* 烈士，殉道者

▶ Peter worked hard to build up his company at the sacrifice of his health.

= Peter worked hard to build up his company at the cost of his health.

彼得拚命努力創立公司卻犧牲了健康。

7 depression [dɪˋprɛʃən] n. 沮喪；憂鬱症；(經濟) 蕭條，不景氣

衍 (1) depress [dɪˋprɛs]
　　 vt. 使沮喪，使消沉 ⑤
　(2) depressed [dɪˋprɛst] a. 感到沮喪的
　(3) depressing [dɪˋprɛsɪŋ]
　　 a. 令人沮喪的

似 (1) sadness [ˋsædnəs] n. 悲傷
　(2) despair [dɪˋspɛr] n. 絕望 ⑤
　(3) recession [rɪˋsɛʃən] n. 蕭條 ⑤

▶ After losing my job, I experienced feelings of depression.

失業後，我感到消沉。

▶ Steve has been suffering from depression since his wife passed away.

自從太太過世後，史蒂夫便飽受憂鬱症的折磨。

▶ Many businesses failed to live through the Great Depression of the 1930s.

許多企業未能捱過 30 年代的經濟大蕭條時期。

8 loyal [ˋlɔɪəl] a. 忠誠的，忠實的

片 be loyal to sb 對某人忠實
= be devoted to sb
= be faithful to sb
= be true to sb

似 (1) devoted [dɪˋvotɪd] a. 忠誠的
　(2) true [tru] a. 忠誠的 ②

▶ The couple remained loyal to each other throughout their lives.

這對愛侶一生都對彼此忠實。

loyalty [ˋlɔɪəltɪ] n. 忠誠，忠實

似 (1) faithfulness [ˋfeθfəlnɪs] n. 忠誠
　(2) devotion [dɪˋvoʃən] n. 忠誠 ⑤

▶ The boss thanked the retiring employee for his hard work and loyalty.

老闆感謝這位即將退休的員工過去的努力和忠誠。

faithful [ˋfeθfəl] a. 忠實的；守信的

片 (1) be faithful to sb 對某人忠實
　　 = be devoted to sb
　　 = be loyal to sb
　　 = be true to sb
　(2) be faithful to sth
　　　 堅持遵守 (誓言、規則等)

似 honest [ˋɑnɪst] a. 誠實的 ①

▶ You are supposed to be faithful to your spouse once you get married.

一旦結婚後就應當對配偶忠實。

▶ Judy was always faithful to her word.

茱蒂總是言出必行。

★word [wɝd] n. 諾言

9 interfere [ˌɪntɚˈfɪr] vi. 干預；妨礙

片 (1) interfere in... 干預……
  = meddle in...
  = intervene in...
  (2) interfere with... 阻礙，妨礙……
  = hamper...
衍 interference [ˌɪntɚˈfɪrəns]
  n. 阻礙，干預⑤

▶ The government should not interfere in the stock market.
政府不該干預股市。

▶ Linda never allows her personal feelings to interfere with her work.
= Linda never allows her personal feelings to hamper her work.
琳達從不讓她個人的情緒妨礙到工作。

10 submarine [ˈsʌbməˌrin] n. 潛水艇

衍 marine [məˈrin] a. 海洋的⑤

▶ The Defense Department plans to purchase two more nuclear submarines.
國防部計劃多購買兩艘核子潛艇。

11 abstract [ˈæbstrækt] a. 抽象的

衍 abstraction [æbˈstrækʃən] n. 抽象⑥

▶ There are many abstract paintings in this museum.
這個博物館裡有許多抽象畫。

concrete [ˈkɑnkrit] a. 具體的 &
n. 混凝土 & vt. 用混凝土覆蓋

▶ A flower is concrete, but beauty is abstract.
花是有形的，而美麗是抽象的。

▶ Most of the houses are built using concrete.
大部分的房子是用混凝土蓋的。

▶ Mr. Yang chose to concrete over their front lawn.
楊先生決定在前院草坪鋪上混凝土。

12 landscape [ˈlændskep] n. 景色 (可數) & vt. 美化……的景觀

▶ There are many beautiful landscapes in that area.
該地區有許多美麗的風景。

▶ I have asked a professional to landscape our garden.
我請一名專業人士來設計自家花園的景觀。

scenery [ˈsinərɪ] n. 風景 (不可數)
衍 (1) scene [sin] n. 風景 (可數)；場景②
  (2) scenic [ˈsinɪk] a. 風景的⑥
比 landscape 特指有山有水的風景，為可數名詞；而 scenery 也表風景，但為不可數名詞。

▶ The island is noted for its beautiful scenery.
這座島嶼以美景聞名。

13 **context** [ˈkɑntɛkst] *n.* 上下文；背景

似 (1) **background** [ˈbækˌɡraʊnd]
    n. 背景 ③
(2) **content** [ˈkɑntɛnt]
    n. (書、演講的) 內容 (不可數) ④

▶ I have to know the context to tell you what this word means.
我必須知道上下文才能告訴你這個字的意思。

▶ To understand the novel better, you have to study its social context / background.
你若想更了解這部小說，就得研讀它的社會背景。

14 **pioneer** [ˌpaɪəˈnɪr] *n.* 開拓者，先驅 & *vt.* 率先發明 / 使用 / 倡導

似 (1) **forerunner** [ˈfɔrˌrʌnɚ] *n.* 先驅
(2) **initiate** [ɪˈnɪʃɪˌet] *vt.* 開始實施 ⑤

▶ Einstein was a pioneer in the field of nuclear physics.
愛因斯坦是核子物理學方面的先驅。

▶ Anyone who pioneers the use of a drug to cure victims of AIDS will be renowned.
任何率先發明藥物能治好愛滋病患者的人將會出名。

15 **access** [ˈæksɛs] *n.* (對人、地、物的) 接近或使用的權利或門徑 (與介詞 to 並用) & *vt.* 使用；(電腦) 存取 (資料)

片 **have access to...**
    接觸到……；利用……

衍 (1) **accessible** [ækˈsɛsəbl]
    a. (地或物) 可到達的，可進入的 ⑤
(2) **accessibility** [ækˌsɛsəˈbɪlətɪ]
    n. 易接近

▶ The only means of access to the building is along a muddy track.
沿著一條泥濘小路是到那棟大樓的唯一途徑。
＊muddy [ˈmʌdɪ] *a.* 泥濘的

▶ Students in this school have easy access to the lab.
該校的學生可隨時使用實驗室。

▶ You need a card to access the building at night.
晚上時，你需要用一張卡來進入那棟建築。

▶ Every time I access this file, my computer crashes.
每當我要讀取這個檔案時，我的電腦就會當機。

evaluate [ɪˈvæljuˌet] *vt.* 評估

似 (1) **size up...**   評估……
(2) **assess** [əˈsɛs] *vt.* 評估 ⑤
(3) **appraise** [əˈprez] *vt.* 評估

▶ We cannot make a final decision until the boss has evaluated the situation.

＝ We cannot make a final decision until the boss has sized up the situation.

＝ We cannot make a final decision until the boss has assessed the situation.

＝ We cannot make a final decision until the boss has appraised the situation.
直到老闆評估了這個情況後，我們才能做最後的決定。

evaluation [ɪˌvæljʊˈeʃən] *n.* 評估

似 (1) assessment [əˈsɛsmənt]
　　n. 評估 ⑤

　 (2) appraisal [əˈprezḷ] *n.* 評估

▶ The architects will have to do a thorough evaluation of the land before the project begins.
在這項案子開始之前,這些建築師要對這塊土地做一次完整的評估。
＊architect [ˈɑrkəˌtɛkt] *n.* 建築師

16　fulfill [fʊlˈfɪl] *vt.* 實現 (= fulfil〔英〕)

似 (1) realize [ˈrɪəˌlaɪz] *vt.* 實現 ②
　 (2) achieve [əˈtʃiv] *vt.* 完成,實現 ③
　 (3) accomplish [əˈkɑmplɪʃ]
　　vt. 完成,達到 ④

▶ Through hard work, my dreams were finally fulfilled.
= Through hard work, my dreams were finally achieved.
= Through hard work, my dreams were finally realized.
= Through hard work, my dreams finally came true.
透過努力我的夢想終於實現了。

---

fulfillment [fʊlˈfɪlmənt]
n. 實現;成就 (感) (= fulfilment〔英〕)

似 (1) achievement [əˈtʃivmənt]
　　n. 成就 ③
　 (2) accomplishment
　　[əˈkɑmplɪʃmənt] *n.* 實現;成就 ④
　 (3) realization
　　[ˌrɪələˈzeʃən / ˌrɪəlaɪˈzeʃən]
　　n. 實現 ⑥

▶ The release of this book marks the fulfillment of a lifelong ambition.
出版這本書代表實現了一生的抱負。

▶ Being a doctor gives me a sense of fulfillment.
當醫生讓我有成就感。

17　exhaust [ɪgˈzɔst] *vt.* 使筋疲力盡;耗盡 & *n.* 排出的氣體 (不可數)

似 (1) use up...　　用光……
　 (2) (a) waste gas　廢氣

▶ The traveler exhausted himself on the long walk.
這名旅行者走了這麼長的路而使自己筋疲力盡了。

▶ We overspent and exhausted our savings.
= We overspent and used up our savings.
我們過度花費而把儲蓄都耗盡了。

▶ The machine gave off noxious exhaust.
= The machine gave off noxious waste gases.
這部機器排放出有害廢氣。
＊give off... 　釋放 / 排放 (氣體)
　noxious [ˈnɑkʃəs] *a.* 有害的;有毒的

---

exhausted [ɪgˈzɔstɪd] *a.* 疲憊的

似 be tired out　累壞了
= be worn out

▶ After four games of badminton, Tom was exhausted.
= After four games of badminton, Tom was tired / worn out.
打了四場羽毛球後,湯姆筋疲力盡了。

exhausting [ɪgˋzɔstɪŋ]
a. 使人耗費精力的

似 (1) tiring [ˋtaɪərɪŋ] *a.* 累人的
   (2) grueling [ˋgruəlɪŋ]
     a. 使人耗費精力的

▶ I've worked eight hours without a break. It has been an exhausting day.
我一連工作 8 個小時沒有休息。真是累人的一天。

▶ Taking care of the baby is an exhausting job.
照顧小寶寶是件累人的工作。

---

exhaustion [ɪgˋzɔstʃən]
n. 筋疲力竭；耗盡

片 (1) be in a state of exhaustion
     處於筋疲力竭的狀態
   (2) with exhaustion   疲憊地

似 (1) tiredness [ˋtaɪrdnɪs] *n.* 疲勞
   (2) fatigue [fəˋtig] *n.* 疲勞 ⑤

▶ Running the marathon left Judy in a state of exhaustion.
跑這趟馬拉松使茱蒂陷入筋疲力竭的狀態。

▶ After weeks of hard work, the worker collapsed with exhaustion.
在拼命工作了好幾個禮拜之後,這名員工累倒了。
＊collapse [kəˋlæps] *vi.* 瓦解,崩潰

▶ We need to take action to prevent the exhaustion of our natural resources.
我們需要採取行動以防止自然資源被耗盡。

---

18   rebel [ˋrɛbl] *n.* 叛徒 & [rɪˋbɛl] *vi.* 反抗,造反(常與介詞 against 並用)

片 rebel against...   反 / 對抗……
衍 (1) rebellion [rɪˋbɛljən]
     n. 反叛,造反 ⑤
   (2) rebellious [rɪˋbɛljəs]
     a. 造反的;有叛逆性格的

▶ Most teenagers are rebellious.
大部分的青少年都有叛逆性格。

▶ The rebel took over the throne and declared himself king.
叛徒接管了王位,並宣稱自己就是國王。
＊throne [θron] *n.* 王位

▶ Adolescents tend to rebel against their parents.
青少年往往容易跟父母對立。
＊adolescent [ˌædlˋɛsn̩t] *n.* 青少年

---

19   discourage [dɪsˋkɝɪdʒ] *vt.* 使打消念頭,使氣餒

片 discourage sb from + V-ing
    打消某人做……的念頭
反 encourage [ɪnˋkɝɪdʒ] *vt.* 鼓勵 ②

▶ Carl tried to discourage his daughter from dating boys.
卡爾試圖打消他女兒想和男孩子約會的念頭。

---

discouragement
[dɪsˋkɝɪdʒmənt] *n.* 沮喪,失望;勸阻

似 (1) depression [dɪˋprɛʃən] *n.* 沮喪 ④
   (2) despair [dɪˋspɛr] *n.* 絕望 ⑤
   (3) dismay [dɪsˋme] *n.* 沮喪 ⑥
反 encouragement [ɪnˋkɝɪdʒmənt]
   n. 鼓勵 ②

▶ Flunking the test was a real discouragement for George.
考試被當使喬治非常沮喪。

▶ Despite her father's discouragement, Carl's daughter still went out on a date with her new boyfriend.
卡爾的女兒不顧父親的勸阻,仍然和新男友約會。

20　vessel [ˈvɛsḷ] *n.* 船艦；容器；血管 ☐

似 (1) boat [bot] *n.* 小船 ①
(2) ship [ʃɪp] *n.* 大船 ①
(3) container [kənˈtenɚ] *n.* 容器 ④

▸ The soldiers succeeded in sinking the enemy's supply vessel.
這些士兵成功地擊沉敵方的補給艦。

▸ Empty vessels make the most sound.
整瓶不響，半瓶響叮噹。—— 諺語，喻自我吹噓

▸ Blood vessels transport blood throughout the body.
血管將血液傳送到全身。

21　mysterious [mɪsˈtɪrɪəs] *a.* 神祕的 ☐

衍 (1) mystery [ˈmɪstərɪ] *n.* 神祕 ③
(2) mystical [ˈmɪstɪkḷ] *a.* 神祕的
= mystic [ˈmɪstɪk]

似 mythical [ˈmɪθɪkḷ] *a.* 神話的；虛構的

▸ David Copperfield's magic was so mysterious that everyone was amazed.
大衛·考柏菲的魔術很神祕，讓每個人都很著迷。

22　divine [dəˈvaɪn / dɪˈvaɪn] *a.* 神聖的，天堂般的 ☐

似 heavenly [ˈhɛvənlɪ] *a.* 天堂的

▸ Seeing my baby daughter for the first time gave me a divine feeling.
第一次看到我的女兒出生帶給我神聖的感覺。

▸ To err is human, to forgive divine.
犯錯是人，寬恕是神。—— 諺語
＊err [ɛr] *vi.* 犯錯

23　luxury [ˈlʌkʃərɪ] *n.* 奢侈 (不可數)；奢侈品 (可數) ☐

似 extravagance [ɪkˈstrævəgəns]
n. 奢侈，浪費

▸ All his life, the rich man led a life of luxury.
這名富豪終其一生都過著奢華的生活。

▸ A television was a luxury for me when I was young.
我年輕的時候，電視對我來說是奢侈品。

luxurious [lʌgˈʒʊrɪəs]
a. 豪華的，奢侈的

似 (1) extravagant [ɪkˈstrævəgənt]
a. 奢侈的，浪費的
(2) lavish [ˈlævɪʃ] *a.* 浪費的 ⑥

▸ The city boasts four luxurious hotels in the downtown area.
本市以在市中心擁有 4 家豪華的飯店而自豪。 ☐

24　stem [stɛm] *vt.* 阻止 & *vi.* 起因於 (與介詞 from 並用) & *n.* 莖 ☐

三 stem, stemmed [stɛmd], stemmed
片 stem from... 起因於……
似 hamper [ˈhæmpɚ] *vt.* 妨礙 ⑥

▸ The government should stem the rising crime rate.
政府應該阻止日益攀升的犯罪率。

▶ The riot that took place over the weekend stemmed from some immigration controversies.

週末的暴動起因於某些有爭議性的移民問題。

＊controversy [ˋkɑntrəˏvɝsɪ] *n.* 爭議

▶ The roses were too tall for the vase so Mary shortened the stems.

這些玫瑰花長度超過花瓶，所以瑪莉把它們的莖剪短。

---

25 earphone [ˋɪrˏfon] *n.* (塞在耳朵內的) 耳機 (之一)

片 a pair of earphones 一副耳機

似 headphones [ˋhɛdˏfonz]
n. (掛在頭上的) 耳機 (恆用複數) ⑥

▶ Marcie is wearing earphones and singing along to her favorite songs.

瑪西帶著耳機，跟著她最愛的歌曲一起哼唱。

---

26 choke [tʃok] *vt. & vi.* (使) 窒息；噎住

片 (1) choke sb to death
將某人窒息而死
(2) choke to death 窒息而死
(3) choke on sth 被某物噎住

▶ The old man was choking because of the heavy smoke from the burning building.

老伯伯被起火的大樓濃煙嗆得幾乎窒息。

▶ The family of six people all choked to death during the fire.

火災中一家六口全都被濃煙嗆死。

▶ Be careful when you eat fish, or you might choke on a fish bone.

你吃魚時要小心，否則可能會被魚刺噎到。

---

27 chew [tʃu] *vt. & vi.* 咀嚼

片 (1) chew the fat 閒聊
= shoot the breeze
= chitchat [ˋtʃɪtˏtʃæt] *vi. & n.* 閒聊
(2) bite off more than one can chew 不自量力

延伸 chewing gum 口香糖
a stick / pack of chewing gum
一片 / 包口香糖

▶ You should chew the food slowly to release all the flavors.

你應該要慢慢咀嚼這種食物，好讓所有味道發散出來。

▶ Amy likes to sit around and chew the fat with her friends.

艾咪喜歡和她朋友坐在一起閒聊。

▶ Peter bit off more than he could chew when he agreed to help.

彼得答應要幫助時，並沒有量力而為。

---

28 hesitation [ˏhɛzəˋteʃən] *n.* 猶豫

片 without hesitation 毫不猶豫

▶ Jane answered yes without a trace of hesitation when Charles proposed to her.

當查爾斯向珍求婚時，她毫不猶豫便答應了。

29 lifeguard [ˈlaɪfˌɡɑrd] *n.* 救生員

似 lifesaver [ˈlaɪfˌsevɚ] *n.* 救生員

▶ Three lifeguards are on duty at the pool at all times.
泳池邊隨時都有 3 名救生員執勤。

30 timetable [ˈtaɪmˌtebl] *n.* 時間表

似 schedule [ˈskɛdʒʊl]
n. 時間表；行程 ②

▶ We need a new train timetable to plan the trip.
我們需要新的火車時刻表來計劃這趟旅行。

31 summarize [ˈsʌməˌraɪz] *vt. & vi.* 概述，摘錄大意

片 To summarize, ... 總而言之，……

▶ Some of the students merely summarized the books they had read instead of writing a real review.
有些學生只是把他們讀過的書摘錄大意而不是寫下真正的心得。

▶ The boss summarized by saying that we needed to reduce costs.
作為總結，老闆說我們需要減少支出。

32 robber [ˈrɑbɚ] *n.* 強盜，搶匪

衍 (1) rob [rɑb] *vt. & vi.* 搶劫 ③
(2) robbery [ˈrɑbərɪ] *n.* 搶劫 ③

似 (1) thief [θif] *n.* 賊，小偷 ②
(2) burglar [ˈbɝɡlɚ] *n.* 夜賊 ④
(3) rubber [ˈrʌbɚ] *n.* 橡膠 ②

▶ The robbers escaped with the jewels.
這些強盜帶著珠寶逃走了。

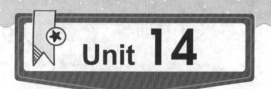 **Unit 14**

  1401-1407

---

1 partial [ˈpɑrʃəl] *a.* 偏心的 (與介詞 to 並用)；部分的 ☐

片 (1) be partial toward sb / sth
　　對某人 / 某物偏心
　(2) be partial to sb / sth
　　偏愛某人 / 某物

衍 part [pɑrt] *n.* 部分①

似 (1) incomplete [ˌɪnkəmˈplit]
　　a. 不完整的
　(2) limited [ˈlɪmɪtɪd] *a.* 有限的

▶ The umpire was accused of being partial toward one team.
　這名裁判被指控偏袒某一隊。

▶ Ron is partial to redheads.
　榮恩特別喜歡紅髮的女孩。

▶ There was only a partial truth in John's story.
　約翰講的故事只有部分是真的。

---

partially [ˈpɑrʃəlɪ] *adv.* 部分地 ☐

似 in part　部分地
= partly [ˈpɑrtlɪ] *adv.* 部分地⑤

▶ Sophie left her bedroom door partially open.
　蘇菲讓臥室房門部分開啟。

▶ Peter's success is partially due to our help.
= Peter's success is due in part to our help.
　彼得的成功有一部分要歸功我們的幫助。

---

impartial [ɪmˈpɑrʃəl]
a. 公平的，公正的 ☐

似 (1) fair [fɛr] *a.* 公正的②
　(2) unbiased [ʌnˈbaɪəst] *a.* 不偏袒的

▶ A judge must be impartial when deciding a case.
　法官在裁定案件時要公平無私才行。

---

2 disaster [dɪˈzæstɚ] *n.* 災害，災難 (尤指天災)；大失敗 ☐

衍 disastrous [dɪˈzæstrəs]
　a. 造成災害的；一團糟的⑥

似 catastrophe [kəˈtæstrəfɪ]
　n. 災難⑥

▶ That country is often hit by natural disasters.
　該國常遭天災襲擊。

▶ The party last night was really a disaster.
= The party last night was really disastrous.
　昨晚的派對真是一團亂。

---

3 defeat [dɪˈfit] *n.* 失敗 & *vt.* 擊敗 ☐

片 (1) admit defeat　承認失敗
　(2) defeat sb by...
　　以……之差擊敗某人

似 beat [bit] *vt.* 擊敗②

▶ The candidate admitted defeat in the presidential election.
　這位候選人承認在總統大選中敗選。

▶ We defeated the team by 2 points.
　我們以 2 分之差擊敗這支隊伍。

4 stroke [strok] *n.* 中風；(繪畫、寫字的) 一筆；游泳的方式；一擊 & *vt.* (用手) 撫摸

片 suffer a stroke　中風

衍 (1) sunstroke ['sʌn,strok] *n.* 中暑
= sun stroke

▸ I got sunstroke after playing on the beach for too long.
在沙灘上玩太久後，我中暑了。

(2) backstroke ['bæk,strok]
n. 仰式，仰泳

▸ My uncle's behavior changed after he suffered a stroke.
我叔叔中風之後，行為舉止都變了。

▸ With a stroke of his pen, Simon signed his name.
賽門一筆簽下他的名字。

▸ The champion swimmer's best stroke is definitely backstroke.
這名冠軍泳將最擅長的游法非仰式莫屬。

▸ The player hit a home run with one stroke of his bat.
這名球員用球棒一揮就擊出全壘打。

▸ Scientists say that stroking your pet can improve your mood.
科學家說撫摸寵物可以改善心情。

5 exaggerate [ɪg'zædʒə,ret] *vt.* & *vi.* 誇張，誇大

衍 exaggeration [ɪg,zædʒə'reʃən]
n. 誇大 ⑤

似 (1) overstate [,ovɚ'stet] *vt.* 過於誇大
(2) brag [bræg] *vi.* 吹牛
(3) boast [bost] *vi.* 吹牛 ④

▸ Andy always exaggerates how good he is at tennis.
安迪總是誇大他網球打得有多好。

▸ The politician's influence has been greatly exaggerated.
這名政客的影響力被過度誇大了。

6 clarify ['klærə,faɪ] *vt.* 澄清，說明

三 clarify, clarified ['klærə,faɪd],
clarified

衍 clarification [,klærəfə'keʃən]
n. 澄清，說明

似 explain [ɪk'splen] *vt.* 說明 ①

▸ The teacher asked the student to clarify what he meant.
這名老師請學生說明清楚他的意思。

7 diplomat ['dɪplo,mæt] *n.* 外交官

衍 (1) diplomatic [,dɪplə'mætɪk]
a. 外交的 ⑤

(2) diplomacy [dɪ'ploməsɪ]
n. 外交 ⑥

似 ambassador [æm'bæsədɚ]
n. 大使 (與介詞 to 並用) ③

▸ A diplomat needs to be persuasive.
外交官必須能言善道。

8 embassy [`ɛmbəsɪ] *n.* 大使館

似 consulate [`kɑnslɪt] *n.* 領事館

▶ Mr. Scott used to work for the US Embassy.
史考特先生曾為美國大使館工作過。

9 greeting [`gritɪŋ] *n.* 招呼，問候；祝賀詞，問候語 (此意恆用複數形)

用 (1) a greeting card 賀卡
(2) offer greetings to A for B
代 B 向 A 問好
= Remember B to A
衍 greet [grit] *vt.* 迎接，招呼 ②

▶ They exchanged brief greetings before getting down to business.
他們簡短互相打招呼後才開始談正事。

▶ Offer greetings to Evan for me when you see him.
= Remember me to Evan when you see him.
你看到艾凡時，代我向他問好。

10 desperate [`dɛspərət] *a.* 奮不顧身的；極度渴望的；絕望的

用 be desperate to + V / for + N
渴望想要 / 得到……
= be anxious to + V / for + N
= be dying to + V / for + N
= be eager to + V / for + N
= be longing to + V / for + N
似 (1) anxious [`æŋkʃəs] *a.* 渴望的 ③
(2) eager [`igə] *a.* 渴望的 ③

▶ The inventor was desperate to find potential sponsors.
這位發明家拚命尋找可能的贊助商。

▶ The couple are desperate for a child.
= The couple are anxious for a child.
= The couple are dying for a child.
= The couple are eager for a child.
= The couple are longing for a child.
這對夫妻渴望擁有孩子。

▶ With little food or water left, the situation was becoming desperate.
食物和水所剩不多，情況變得更加絕望。

11 conservative [kən`sɝvətɪv] *a.* 保守的 & *n.* 保守派人士

衍 (1) conserve [kən`sɝv]
vt. 保存，保護 ⑥
(2) conservation [ˌkɑnsə`veʃən]
n. 保存 ⑤

▶ The *Daily Mail* is a well-known conservative newspaper in the UK.
《每日郵報》是英國著名的保守主義報紙。

▶ A hot debate is going on between the reformers and conservatives about education.
改革派人士和保守派人士之間正進行一場有關教育的激烈辯論。
＊reformer [rɪ`fɔrmə] *n.* 改革派人士

12 mercy [`mɝsɪ] *n.* 仁慈

用 (1) have mercy on sb
可憐 / 饒了某人
= have pity on sb

▶ Please have mercy on me. I'll never do that again.
= Please have pity on me. I'll never do that again.
= Please forgive me. I'll never do that again.
請饒了我。我不會再犯了。

(2) be at the mercy of...
　　任由……的擺布

(3) mercy killing　安樂死
= euthanasia [ˌjuθə`neʒɪə]

衍 merciful [`mɝsɪfəl] *a.* 仁慈的

似 (1) kindness [`kaɪndnəs] *n.* 仁慈
(2) sympathy [`sɪmpəθɪ] *n.* 同情 ④
(3) compassion [kəm`pæʃən]
　　n. 同情 ⑤

反 (1) merciless [`mɝsɪləs] *a.* 無慈悲心的
(2) cold-blooded [ˌkold`blʌdɪd]
　　a. 冷血的
(3) heartless [`hɑrtləs] *a.* 無情的

▶ Each year between July and November, Taiwan is at the mercy of typhoons.
每年從 7 月到 11 月間，臺灣都受到颱風的侵襲。

13　mineral [`mɪnərəl] *n.* 礦物；礦物質 & *a.* 礦物的

片 (1) mineral water　礦泉水
(2) mineral resources　礦物資源

衍 (1) mine [maɪn] *n.* 礦 ①
(2) miner [`maɪnɚ] *n.* 礦工 ④

▶ There are precious minerals deep in the ground around here.
這附近的地底深處有珍貴的礦藏。

▶ This brand of mineral water contains many minerals that are good for our health.
這種牌子的礦泉水含有很多對我們健康有益的礦物質。

14　respectable [rɪ`spɛktəbḷ] *a.* 值得尊敬的；體面的，相當不錯的

衍 (1) respect [rɪ`spɛkt] *n.* & *vt.* 尊敬 ②
(2) respectably [rɪ`spɛktəblɪ]
　　adv. 可敬地；體面地

▶ Edward is really a respectable gentleman.
艾德華真是一位讓人尊敬的紳士。

▶ As a computer programmer, Lily earns a respectable income.
= As a computer programmer, Lily earns a decent income.
莉莉任職電腦程式設計師，薪水挺不錯的。
*decent [`disṇt] *a.* 像樣的，體面的

---

respectful [rɪ`spɛktfəl]
a. 尊重的，表示尊敬的

片 (1) be respectful to sb
　　對某人很尊敬
(2) be respectful of sth
　　對某事物很尊敬

▶ You should always be respectful to your elders.
你始終該對年長者很尊敬。

▶ Matt always tries to be respectful of others' opinions.
麥特一向試著尊重他人的意見。

1415-1422

衍 **respectfully** [rɪˋspɛktfəlɪ]
adv. 恭敬地，尊敬地

▶ Respectfully yours, Peter Lai
賴彼得敬上 —— 書信結尾用語

15 cherish [ˋtʃɛrɪʃ] *vt.* 珍惜，珍愛

似 (1) treasure [ˋtrɛʒɚ] *vt.* 珍愛 ②
　　(2) value [ˋvælju] *vt.* 珍惜 ②

▶ I promise I will cherish your love all my life.
= I promise I will treasure your love for the rest of my life.
= I promise I will value your love till the end of my life.
我承諾一輩子會好好珍惜妳的愛。

16 full-time [ˏfʊlˋtaɪm] *a.* 全職的 & *adv.* 全職地

用 (1) a full-time job　全職工作
　　(2) on a full-time basis　全職地

▶ Tammy is looking for a full-time job as an English teacher.
塔米正在找一份全職的英文教師工作。

▶ David is currently working full-time as a consultant in the publisher.
= David is currently working as a consultant on a full-time basis in the publisher.
大衛目前在這間出版社擔任全職顧問。
＊consultant [kənˋsʌltənt] *n.* 顧問

part-time [ˏpɑrtˋtaɪm]
a. 兼職的 & *adv.* 兼職地

用 (1) a part-time job　兼職工作
　　(2) on a part-time basis　兼職地

▶ After his surgery, Robert continued to work for the company, but only on a part-time basis.
手術後，羅伯特繼續替這家公司工作，不過是兼職。

17 recreation [ˏrɛkrɪˋeʃən] *n.* 消遣；休閒娛樂

衍 **recreational** [ˏrɛkrɪˋeʃən̩]
　 a. 娛樂的，休閒的 ⑥
似 **pastime** [ˋpæsˏtaɪm] *n.* 娛樂 ⑥

▶ Sally's favorite recreation is playing board games with her friends.
莎莉最喜愛的消遣是和朋友玩桌遊。

▶ Terry goes cycling for recreation.
泰瑞以騎腳踏車為娛樂。

18 blade [bled] *n.* 刀鋒

▶ Sharpen the blade before you cut the meat.
在切肉前先把刀刃磨利。

19 moderate [ˈmɑdərɪt] a. 適度的

反 excessive [ɪkˈsɛsɪv]
  a. 過度的，過量的 ⑤

▶ It's best to keep a moderate speed while driving.
  開車時最好保持適當的速度。

20 delight [dɪˈlaɪt] vt. 使喜悅 & n. 欣喜

冊 (1) take delight in... 喜愛……
  (2) To sb's delight, ...
    令某人高興的是，……
  = To sb's joy, ...

▶ The competition is sure to delight the audience.
  這場比賽肯定會讓觀眾很開心。

▶ Cole takes delight in cooking dinner for his family.
  柯爾喜歡為家人下廚做晚餐。

▶ To my delight, Charlie came back safe and sound from his journey.
  令我高興的是，查理安然無恙地旅遊回來。
  *safe and sound 安然無恙

delighted [dɪˈlaɪtɪd] a. 感到高興的

冊 (1) be delighted at / by / with...
    因……而感到高興
  (2) be delighted that... 很高興……
  = be glad that...

▶ Jack is delighted with his new iPad.
  傑克很喜歡他的新 iPad。

▶ The boy was delighted that his father gave him a bike.
  = The boy was glad that his father gave him a bike.
  男孩非常高興父親送他一輛腳踏車。

delightful [dɪˈlaɪtfəl]
a. 愉快的；漂亮迷人的

似 pleasant [ˈplɛzənt] a. 愉快的 ②

▶ My trip to Paris was a delightful experience.
  我的巴黎之旅是很愉快的經驗。

▶ You have such a delightful house, Helen!
  海倫，妳的房子真漂亮！

21 contest [ˈkɑntɛst] n. 比賽，競爭 & [kənˈtɛst] vt. 爭奪，角逐

冊 (1) a speech contest 演講比賽
  (2) a chess contest 西洋棋比賽
衍 contestant [kənˈtɛstənt]
  n. 競爭者，與賽者 ⑥

▶ Dad bought me a brand-new bike after I won the speech contest.
  我贏了演講比賽之後，爸爸買了一臺全新的腳踏車給我。

▶ Mr. Dole contested the presidency but lost.
  杜爾先生競選總統但是失敗了。
  *presidency [ˈprɛzədənsɪ] n. 總統職務

22 polish [ˈpɑlɪʃ] vt. 擦亮；改進 & n. 磨光，擦亮

冊 (1) polish (up)... 提升 (技巧、能力等)
  = improve...
  (2) polish off...
    狼吞虎嚥地快速吃掉……
  (3) give sth a polish 擦亮某物
  (4) nail polish 指甲油
似 shine [ʃaɪn] vt. 擦亮 ②

▶ To protect the leather, I polish my shoes once a month.
  = To protect the leather, I shine my shoes once a month.
  為了保護皮革，我每個月會擦一次皮鞋。

▶ You should polish up your English before traveling abroad.
  出國旅遊之前，你應該把英文磨練一下。

▶ Jim polished off his breakfast before he left for school.
吉姆匆匆吃完早餐後便上學去了。

▶ Nick gave his black shoes a polish before the formal dinner.
出席正式晚宴前，尼克把他的黑鞋擦亮。

23 craft [kræft] *n.* 手藝，工藝；手工藝品 (此意恆用複數)

囝 arts and crafts　手藝

似 handicraft [ˈhændɪ͵kræft]
　n. 手工藝；手工藝品 ⑥

▶ The furniture maker has been studying his craft for years.
該傢俱製造者研究這門工藝已好幾年了。

▶ I brought some traditional crafts home as souvenirs.
我帶了一些傳統手工藝品回家當作紀念品。
＊souvenir [͵suvəˈnɪr] *n.* 紀念品

24 bounce [baʊns] *vi.* 彈跳；(支票) 跳票 & *n.* 彈，跳 (可數)；彈性 (不可數)

囝 bounce up and down　跳上跳下

▶ When Kelly heard the news, she was so excited that she bounced up and down on the sofa.
凱莉聽到這個消息時，興奮地在沙發上跳上跳下。

▶ If the check bounces, the bank will charge you a fine.
如果支票跳票，銀行就會對你罰款。

▶ Ian gave the ball a bounce and then hit it with his racket.
伊恩讓球一彈，接著用球拍擊球。

▶ The beach ball has lost its bounce.
這顆海灘球失去彈性了。

25 foam [fom] *n.* 泡泡 (不可數) & *vi.* 起泡

囝 shaving foam　刮鬍泡沫

似 bubble [ˈbʌbl̩] *n.* 泡泡 ③

▶ I like cappuccino with a thick layer of foam.
我喜歡卡布其諾上面有厚厚的一層泡沫。

▶ We knew the dog was sick because it started to foam at the mouth.
這隻狗開始在嘴邊吐泡泡，所以我們知道牠病了。

26 negotiate [nɪˈgoʃɪ͵et] *vt.* & *vi.* 談判，交涉，協商

囝 negotiate (sth) with sb
　與某人協商 (某事物)

衍 (1) negotiable [nɪˈgoʃɪəbl̩]
　　a. 可商量的

　 (2) negotiation [nɪ͵goʃɪˈeʃən]
　　n. 協商 (常用複數) ⑤

▶ Hannah negotiated a pay raise with her boss.
漢娜與老闆商量加薪事宜。

▶ The boss negotiated with the sales manager about raising the price of the product.
老闆和業務經理商量有關提高產品價格之事宜。

似 compromise [ˈkɑmprəˌmaɪz]
　　 vt. 妥協 ⑤

27　orbit [ˈɔrbɪt] *n.* 軌道 & *vt.* 繞軌道運行

片 be in orbit　　在軌道中

▶ The satellite is in orbit around the Earth.
這顆衛星繞著地球運行。

▶ It takes the Earth 365 days to orbit the Sun.
地球繞太陽運行一周需時 365 天。

28　spare [spɛr] *vt.* 分出，騰出；節省；使避免 & *a.* 備用的 & *n.* 備用品

片 (1) spare no effort to + V
　　 不遺餘力……
　 (2) spare sb's feelings
　　 避免傷某人的感情
　 (3) a spare tire　　備胎

▶ Ashley asked her colleague to spare her a few minutes to discuss a matter.
艾希莉請她同事挪出幾分鐘給她來討論一件事。

▶ Spare the rod, spoil the child.
省了杆子，會寵壞孩子。── 諺語，喻不打不成器。

▶ David spared no effort to help us complete the project.
= David did his best to help us complete the project.
= David left no stone unturned to help us complete the project.
= David did all he could to help us complete the project.
= David did whatever he could to help us complete the project.
大衛不遺餘力幫助我們完成這項企畫。

▶ Tom wanted to spare Sue's feelings, so he lied about her new haircut.
湯姆為了不讓蘇難過，因此沒有對她的新髮型說實話。

▶ You really need a spare key. You're too forgetful.
你真的需要一把備用鑰匙。你太健忘了。

▶ David got a flat tire, but luckily he had a spare.
大衛的輪胎沒氣了，但幸好他有備用的。

29　barrier [ˈbærɪr] *n.* 障礙 (物)

片 be a barrier to...
　　 對……是個障礙 (物)
= be an obstacle to...
= be a hindrance to...
似 (1) obstacle [ˈɑbstəkl̩] *n.* 障礙 ④
　 (2) hindrance [ˈhɪndrəns] *n.* 阻礙

▶ Laziness is a barrier to success.
懶惰是成功的絆腳石。

Level 4　Unit 14

357

obstacle [ˋɑbstəkḷ] *n.* 障礙

片 be an obstacle to...
是……的絆腳石

似 barrier [ˋbærɪr] *n.* 障礙 ④

▶ Paul's stubbornness is an obstacle to his growth.
保羅的固執是阻礙他成長的絆腳石。

---

30 fantastic [fænˋtæstɪk] *a.* 極好的；幻想的

衍 fantasize [ˋfæntə͵saɪz] *vt. & vi.* 幻想

▶ Teddy fantasizes about being a millionaire all the time.
泰迪一天到晚都在幻想自己是百萬富翁。

似 (1) wonderful [ˋwʌndəfəl]
a. 很棒的 ①

(2) imaginary [ɪˋmædʒə͵nɛrɪ]
a. 幻想的 ④

▶ The dress looks fantastic on you, sis.
姊，妳穿那件洋裝真好看。

▶ Bruce's latest novel is a fantastic story set in a futuristic background.
布魯斯最新出的小說是在未來世界背景下的奇幻故事。
＊futuristic [͵fjutʃəˋɪstɪk] *a.* 幻想未來的

---

fantasy [ˋfæntəsɪ] *n.* 幻想

似 imagination [ɪ͵mædʒəˋneʃən]
n. 想像 ③

▶ Alice used to have fantasies about having a candlelit dinner with Harry Styles.

＝ Alice used to fantasize about having a candlelit dinner with Harry Styles.
愛麗絲曾幻想過和哈利・史泰爾斯共享燭光晚餐。
＊candlelit [ˋkændḷlɪt] *a.* 燭光的

---

31 sue [su] *vt. & vi.* 控告，對……提起訴訟

片 (1) sue sb for sth　控告某人某事
(2) sue for sth　因……而提起訴訟

▶ Danny sued the woman who insulted him in public.
丹尼控告了那位公然侮辱他的女子。

▶ They are going to sue the company for breaking the contract.
他們將控告那間公司毀約。

▶ When the newspaper published a false article about her, Megan threatened to sue.
報紙發表一篇有關梅根的錯誤報導，她揚言要提告。

---

32 stab [stæb] *vt.* 刺

三 stab, stabbed [stæbd], stabbed

片 (1) stab sb in the + 身體部位
刺中某人身體某處

(2) stab sb in the back
暗地中傷某人

▶ At the end of the story, the knight drew his sword and stabbed the villain in the chest.
故事的結尾是騎士亮出劍，刺進惡棍的胸口。
＊villain [ˋvɪlən] *n.* 壞人，惡棍

▶ I can't believe my best friend would stab me in the back.
我真不敢相信我最要好的朋友會在背後中傷我。

358

33　orphan [ˈɔrfən] n. 孤兒

衍 orphanage [ˈɔrfənɪdʒ] n. 孤兒院 ⑥

▶ Mr. James established the orphanage many years ago to help orphans whose parents had been killed during the war.
詹姆士先生多年前創建了該孤兒院以幫助父母在戰爭中喪生的孤兒們。

34　disadvantage [ˌdɪsədˈvæntɪdʒ] n. 缺點

反 advantage [ədˈvæntɪdʒ] n. 優點 ③

▶ What are the advantages and disadvantages to / of living in the country?
住在鄉下的利弊是什麼？

35　bridegroom [ˈbraɪdˌgrum] n. 新郎 (= groom [grum])

延伸 (1) a best man　　　伴郎
(2) a maid of honor　(首席) 伴娘
(3) bridesmaid [ˈbraɪdzˌmed] n. 伴娘

▶ The bridegroom was blushing as his bride came down the aisle.
新娘沿著走道走來時，新郎的臉都紅了。
*blush [blʌʃ] vi. (因害羞) 臉紅
　aisle [aɪl] n. (座席間的) 走道

36　apparent [əˈpærənt] a. 明顯的；表面上的

片 It is apparent that... 很顯然，……
似 (1) obvious [ˈɑbvɪəs] a. 明顯的 ②
(2) evident [ˈɛvədənt] a. 明顯的 ④

▶ It is apparent that the fitness center has serious financial problems.
很顯然，該健身中心有嚴重的財務問題。

▶ The girl's apparent innocence was just an act.
這女孩表面的天真不過是裝模作樣。

37　confidence [ˈkɑnfədəns] n. 信心

片 (1) have confidence in...
對……有信心
(2) lose confidence in...
對……失去信心
衍 confidential [ˌkɑnfəˈdɛnʃəl]
a. 機密的 ⑤

▶ We have confidence in the new product.
我們對這項新產品有信心。

▶ According to the report, many consumers have lost confidence in online shopping.
根據這項報告，許多消費者已對線上購物失去信心。

38　courageous [kəˈredʒəs] a. 勇敢的

衍 (1) courage [ˈkɜrɪdʒ] n. 勇氣 ②
(2) courageously [kəˈredʒəslɪ]
adv. 勇敢地
似 brave [brev] a. 勇敢的 ①

▶ It was a courageous action to speak out against unfair treatment.
公然反對不平等待遇是很勇敢的行為。

Level 4　Unit 14

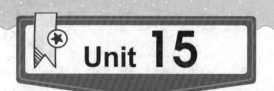
1 **insert** [ɪnˋsɝt] *vt.* 插入 & [ˋɪnsɝt] *n.* 插入物 (尤指插在書報雜誌內的廣告頁，可數)

片 insert A in / into B　將 A 投入 B

▶ Insert coins into the machine and press the button.
將錢幣投入機器，再按下按鈕。

▶ When Ken picked up the magazine, several inserts fell out.
肯撿起雜誌時，好幾份插頁廣告掉出。

2 **battery** [ˋbætərɪ] *n.* 電池

複 batteries [ˋbætəriz]
片 (1) a mercury battery　水銀電池
(2) a lithium [ˋlɪθɪəm] battery
鋰電池
(3) a rechargeable battery
充電電池

▶ The battery is dead. It needs to be recharged.
這顆電池沒電了，它需要充電。

3 **curiosity** [ˌkjʊrɪˋɑsətɪ] *n.* 好奇

片 out of curiosity　出於好奇
衍 curious [ˋkjʊrɪəs] *a.* 好奇的 ②

▶ The new girl in class attracted Jack's curiosity.
班上新來的女孩引起傑克的好奇心。

▶ Curiosity killed the cat.
好奇心殺害一隻貓。—— 諺語，喻過分好奇會惹禍上身

▶ Out of curiosity, I asked Denny how he could make so much money.
出於好奇，我問丹尼他怎麼能賺那麼多錢。

4 **protein** [ˋprotiɪn] *n.* 蛋白質

片 (1) be rich / high in protein
含有豐富的蛋白質
(2) be low in protein　蛋白質含量低

▶ Meat, milk and cheese are rich in protein.
肉類、牛奶及起司含有豐富的蛋白質。

▶ Doctors say that diets low in protein are bad for you.
醫生說蛋白質含量低的飲食對你有害。

5 **chorus** [ˋkɔrəs] *n.* 合唱團；(歌曲的) 副歌

似 choir [kwaɪr] *n.* 合唱團 ⑤

▶ The university chorus is giving a performance in the city hall.
大學合唱團要在市政聽舉行表演。

▶ The chorus of this song is easy to sing.
這首歌曲的副歌很容易唱。

6   **endless** [ˈɛndləs] *a.* 無窮盡的，不斷的

衍 end [ɛnd] *n.* 末端 ①

似 (1) unlimited [ʌnˈlɪmɪtɪd]
    a. 無限制的
  (2) boundless [ˈbaʊndləs] *a.* 無窮的
  (3) infinite [ˈɪnfənɪt] *a.* 無限的 ⑤
  (4) limitless [ˈlɪmɪtləs] *a.* 無限制的

▶ The line at the taxi stand looked endless.
計程車招呼站的排隊隊伍看起來沒有盡頭。

▶ My younger sister's endless talking really bothers me.
我妹妹嘮叨個不停讓我真的煩死了。

---

countless [ˈkaʊntləs] *a.* 數不盡的

衍 (1) count [kaʊnt] *vt.* 計算 ①
  (2) countable [ˈkaʊntəbl̩]
    a. (名詞) 可數的 ③

似 (1) innumerable [ɪˈn(j)umərəbl̩]
    a. 數不清的 ⑥
  (2) numerous [ˈn(j)umərəs]
    a. 眾多的 ④

▶ That movie has been on TV countless times.
那部電影在電視上播映無數次了。

---

restless [ˈrɛstləs]
a. 坐不住的；坐立不安的；得不到休息的

衍 restlessly [ˈrɛstləslɪ]
    adv. 不安地；不停地

似 edgy [ˈɛdʒɪ] *a.* 坐立不安的，急躁的

▶ Jamie is very restless. He can't stay in one place for very long.
傑米靜不下來，他無法在一個地方待很久。

▶ The man became restless while waiting for his test results.
這名男子等待化驗結果時坐立難安。

▶ During the days when Rebecca was critically ill, her parents spent many restless nights.
在蕾貝卡生重病期間，她的雙親度過許多不眠不休的夜晚。

---

hopeless [ˈhopləs]
a. 不抱希望的，絕望的

衍 hopelessly [ˈhopləslɪ] *adv.* 絕望地

似 (1) desperate [ˈdɛspərət] *a.* 絕望的 ④
  (2) unpromising [ʌnˈprɑmɪsɪŋ]
    a. 沒希望的

▶ I felt hopeless after my girlfriend dumped me.
我被女友甩了後感到很絕望。

▶ The financial situation of our company is hopeless, and we can do nothing about it.
我們公司的財務狀況已到了絕望的地步，我們也一點都使不上力。

7   **confess** [kənˈfɛs] *vt. & vi.* 坦承

用 (1) confess (to sb) that...
    (向某人) 坦承……
  (2) confess to + N/V-ing   坦承……
  = admit (to) + N/V-ing
  = own up to + N/V-ing

▶ Julia confessed that she broke the vase on purpose.
茱莉亞坦承她故意把花瓶打破。

▶ Peter confessed to his mom that he had stolen her money.
彼得向他媽媽坦承他偷了她的錢。

1507-1516

衍 confession [kənˈfɛʃən] *n.* 坦白 ⑤

▶ The suspect confessed to stealing the money.
= The suspect admitted (to) stealing the money.
= The suspect owned up to stealing the money.
這名嫌犯坦承他偷了錢。

▶ The suspect refused to confess to the crime.
這名嫌犯拒絕認罪。

8 innocence [ˈɪnəsn̩s] *n.* 無罪，清白；純真

衍 innocent [ˈɪnəsn̩t]
a. 無罪的，清白的 ③
反 guilt [gɪlt] *n.* 犯罪 ④

▶ Catherine pleaded her innocence; however, nobody believed her.
凱薩琳為自己的清白辯解，但是沒有人相信她。
*plead [plid] *vt.* 為……答辯

▶ The innocence of children should never be taken advantage of.
孩子的純真不應被拿來利用。

9 paragraph [ˈpærəˌgræf] *n.* (文章) 段落

似 passage [ˈpæsɪdʒ] *n.* 一段 (文字) ③

▶ The information you're looking for can be found in the third paragraph of the article.
你要的資訊可以在這篇文章的第 3 段找到。

10 species [ˈspiʃɪz] *n.* 物種 (單複數同形)

片 (1) a species of... 一種……
(2) two / three / four species of...
兩 / 三 / 四種……

▶ We found a strange species of bird on the island.
我們在這座島上發現了一種怪鳥。

▶ Many species of wild animals are endangered.
許多種野生動物都快要瀕臨絕種了。

11 wit [wɪt] *n.* 聰明機智

片 be at one's wit's end
(因擔憂、困惑而) 不知道下一步該怎麼做
衍 witty [ˈwɪtɪ] *a.* 機智的 ⑤

▶ George is known for his wit and humor.
喬治因他的機智與幽默聞名。

▶ I'm at my wits' end, so I can't come up with any good ideas to solve this problem.
我已經黔驢技窮，想不出任何點子來解決這個問題了。

12 carve [kɑrv] *vt.* 雕刻

片 carve out a bright future
開創光明的前途

▶ We carved the pumpkin for Halloween.
我們雕刻南瓜慶祝萬聖夜。

▶ Work hard, and you will carve out a bright future.
要努力，這樣你就會開創一片光明的前途。

13 **costume** [ˈkɑst(j)um] *n.* 服裝（尤指戲服或民族服裝）

▶ The kimono is the traditional costume of Japanese ladies.

和服是日本女性的傳統服裝。

＊kimono [kəˈmono] *n.* （日本女性穿的）和服

14 **revise** [rɪˈvaɪz] *vt.* 修正

似 (1) correct [kəˈrɛkt] *vt.* 改正 ①
(2) modify [ˈmɑdəˌfaɪ] *vt.* 修改 ⑤
(3) amend [əˈmɛnd] *vt.* 修正 ⑤

▶ This article has been revised several times, but there are still many errors.

這篇文章已修訂過好幾次，但仍有許多錯誤。

revision [rɪˈvɪʒən] *n.* 修訂，修正

似 (1) correction [kəˈrɛkʃən] *n.* 改正
(2) modification [ˌmɑdəfəˈkeʃən] *n.* 修改
(3) amendment [əˈmɛndmənt] *n.* 修正

▶ They're making some revisions to the dictionary for the new edition.

他們正在為新版字典進行修訂。

15 **handwriting** [ˈhændˌraɪtɪŋ] *n.* 書寫；字跡

▶ Although typing skills are important, handwriting should never be neglected.

打字技巧固然重要，但也不該忽略書寫技巧。

▶ I can't read your handwriting. Can you write more clearly?

我看不懂你寫的字跡。你可以寫清楚一點嗎？

16 **grave** [grev] *n.* 墳墓 & *a.* 嚴肅的；嚴重的，重大的

H from (the) cradle to (the) grave
從生到死，一輩子

衍 (1) gravestone [ˈgrevˌston] *n.* 墓碑
(2) graveyard [ˈgrevˌjɑrd] *n.* 墓地

▶ We went to our late teacher's grave to pay tribute to him.

我們到已逝的老師墓前向他致敬。

＊pay tribute to sb　向某人致敬

▶ Thanks to the welfare program, people in that country are taken care of by the government from cradle to grave.

由於這項福利措施，該國百姓一輩子都受政府照顧。

▶ Jim noticed that the boss had a grave expression on his face.

吉姆注意到老闆臉上嚴肅的表情。

▶ Such a rash decision could result in grave consequences.

如此草率的決定會導致嚴重的後果。

＊rash [ræʃ] *a.* 草率的

Level 4　Unit 15

tomb [tum] *n.* 墳墓

▶ The man accidentally discovered an old tomb in Egypt.
這名男子在埃及意外發現一座古老的墳墓。

17　ruin [`rʊɪn] *n.* 廢墟 (可數)；毀壞 (不可數) & *vt.* 毀掉，毀壞

片 be / lie in ruins　淪為廢墟

▶ The once prosperous city is now lying in ruins.
這座曾經繁華一時的城市現在成了廢墟。

▶ The owner had no money and let the house fall into ruin.
屋主沒有錢，讓房子陷入毀壞的狀態。

▶ An accident ruined Don's dream to be a sports star.
一場車禍毀了唐想當運動明星的美夢。

18　counter [`kaʊntɚ] *n.* 櫃檯 & *vt.* & *vi.* 反對，反擊 & *a.* 相反的 & *adv.* 相反地

片 (1) over the counter
(藥品無需處方可以) 直接透過櫃檯購買
(2) counter with...
用……來反擊 / 駁
(3) run counter to...
與……背道而馳

▶ Please pay at the counter.
請到櫃檯結帳。

▶ You can get most cold remedies over the counter.
大部分的感冒藥都可不用處方直接向櫃檯購買。

▶ When Mary called her a liar, Jane countered that she had proof she was telling the truth.
瑪莉稱珍為騙子時，珍以她有說實話的證據反擊。

▶ After Ryan saw the evidence, he could not counter with anything.
雷恩看到證據後，無法說出任何話來反擊。

▶ The politician did not come up with a counter argument.
這名政治人物沒有提出一個相反的論點。

▶ Sam's decision to quit his job ran counter to his wife's wishes.
山姆辭掉工作的決定與他老婆所希望的相反。

19　repetition [ˌrɛpə`tɪʃən] *n.* 重複，反覆

衍 repeat [rɪ`pit] *vt.* 重複 ①

▶ There is a lot of repetition in this class, and it's a little boring.
這堂課有很多地方一再重複，因此有點無聊。

---

repetitive [rɪ`pɛtətɪv]
a. (工作、動作等以乏味方式) 重複的

▶ John's job consists of dull, repetitive work.
約翰的職務盡是些乏味又重複的工作。

repeated [rɪˋpitɪd]
a. 重複的，屢次的

▶ After repeated **attempts**, Dan finally won a gold medal.
經過好幾次的努力，丹終於贏得一面金牌。

---

20 **triumph** [ˋtraɪəmf] *n.* 勝利，成功 & *vi.* 勝利，獲得成功

片 in triumph　勝利地
衍 (1) triumphant [traɪˋʌmfənt]
　　 a. 勝利的
　　(2) triumphantly [traɪˋʌmfəntlɪ]
　　 adv. 成功地
似 victory [ˋvɪktərɪ] *n.* 勝利，成功 ②

▶ The battle ended in triumph for the Greeks.
這場戰役最後由希臘人贏得勝利。

▶ Peter's horse triumphed in the big race of the day.
彼得的馬在比賽當天獲勝。

---

21 **mutual** [ˋmjutʃuəl] *a.* 相互的

片 mutual trust　互信
衍 mutually [ˋmjutʃuəlɪ] *adv.* 互相地
似 reciprocal [rɪˋsɪprək!] *a.* 互相的

▶ Linda and Mark's friendship is based on mutual trust.
琳達和馬克的友誼建立在互信上。

---

22 **invention** [ɪnˋvɛnʃən] *n.* 發明（不可數）；發明物（可數）

衍 (1) invent [ɪnˋvɛnt] *vt.* 發明；捏造 ③
　　(2) inventor [ɪnˋvɛntɚ]
　　 n. 發明者，發明家 ③

▶ Necessity is the mother of invention.
需要為發明之母。—— 諺語

▶ The airplane is an amazing invention. It allows people to travel the world in days.
飛機是一項驚人的發明。它讓人們可以在數天內環遊世界。

---

23 **adapt** [əˋdæpt] *vt.* & *vi.* (使) 適應 (與介詞 to 並用) & *vt.* 改編

片 (1) adapt (oneself) to + N/V-ing
　　 使自己適應於……
　= accustom oneself to + N/V-ing
　= get accustomed to + N/V-ing
　= get used to + N/V-ing
　= adjust to + N/V-ing
　　(2) be adapted from...
　　 由……改編而來
衍 adaptation [‚ædæpˋteʃən] *n.* 適應 ⑥

▶ It's hard for me to adapt myself to city life.
= It's hard for me to get accustomed to city life.
= It's hard for me to adjust to city life.
我很不適應都市生活。

▶ It took the new employee about a month to adapt to the new environment.
這名新進員工花了一個月左右的時間去適應新環境。

▶ The blockbuster movie was adapted from an original novel.
這部賣座鉅片改編自一本原創小說。

＊blockbuster [ˋblɑk‚bʌstɚ] *n.* 極為成功的影片／書

adopt [ə'dɑpt]

vt. 採用，採納 & *vt.* & *vi.* 收養

衍 (1) adoption [ə'dɑpʃən]
　　　n. 採用，採納；收養

　　(2) adopted [ə'dɑptɪd] *a.* 被領養的
　　　an adopted son / daughter
　　　養子 / 養女

　　(3) adoptive [ə'dɑptɪv]
　　　a. (主動) 領養的
　　　an adoptive father / mother
　　　養父 / 養母

似 accept [ək'sɛpt] *vt.* 接受 ②

▶ The general manager adopted my proposal without hesitation.
總經理毫不猶豫地採用了我的提案。

▶ Ben's wife is barren, so they've decided to adopt a baby boy.
班的太太不孕，因此他們決定領養一個小男嬰。
＊barren ['bærən] *a.* 不孕的，無法生育的

▶ As Nicole couldn't have a baby of her own, she decided to adopt.
因為妮可沒辦法懷有自己的小孩，她決定領養一個。

24　correspond [ˌkɔrə'spɑnd] *vi.* 符合；通信

片 (1) correspond to / with...
　　　符合……

　　(2) correspond with...　與……通信

衍 (1) correspondent [ˌkɔrə'spɑndənt]
　　　n. 報社 / 通訊社特派員 ⑤

　　(2) correspondence
　　　[ˌkɔrə'spɑndəns]
　　　n. 相符；書信 (皆不可數) ⑥

▶ Todd's actions don't correspond with his words.
陶德這個人言行不一致。

▶ Tom often corresponds with his foreign friends because he thinks it is a good way to practice his writing.
湯姆常和他的外國朋友通信，因為他認為這是一個練習寫作的好方法。

25　scarcely ['skɛrslɪ] *adv.* 幾乎不

片 主詞 + had scarcely + p.p. + when 引導的過去式子句
　　——……就……

衍 scarce [skɛrs] *a.* 稀少的 ③

似 (1) hardly ['hɑrdlɪ] *adv.* 幾乎不 ②
　　(2) barely ['bɛrlɪ] *adv.* 幾乎不 ③

▶ I can scarcely believe that the firm went bankrupt.
我幾乎不敢相信這家公司破產了。

▶ I had scarcely seen my father when I ran away.
= I had hardly seen my father when I ran away.
= As soon as I saw my father, I ran away.
= Upon / On seeing my father, I ran away.
我一看到我父親，拔腿就跑。

26　divorce [dɪ'vɔrs] *vt.* & *vi.* & *n.* 離婚

片 end in divorce　以離婚收場

衍 divorcee [dɪˌvɔr'si] *n.* 離婚者

▶ Believing that he could not live in harmony with his wife any longer, Larry finally divorced her.
賴瑞認為他無法繼續和他老婆和平共處，所以最後和她離婚。

▶ It is rumored that Harry and Abby are going to divorce.
謠傳哈利和艾比要離婚了。

▶ Brad and Jennifer's marriage ended in divorce.
布萊德和珍妮佛的婚姻最後以離婚收場。

divorced [dɪˋvɔrst]
a. 離婚的；脫離的

▶ Nancy is a divorced mother with two kids.
南希是一名離了婚、帶著兩個孩子的母親。

片 be divorced from reality　脫離現實

▶ Ray is acting crazy and seems divorced from reality these days.
雷最近行為怪異，似乎脫離現實了。

---

27 reward [rɪˋwɔrd] *n.* 報答，報償 & *vt.* 報答，獎賞

片 (1) give sb sth as a reward
　　給某人某物作報償

▶ I gave Vincent a watch as a reward for his help.
我送文森一只手錶以回報他的幫忙。

　(2) reward sb with sth
　　以某物獎勵某人

▶ The young mom rewards her children with cookies when they do well in school.
孩子在學校表現良好時，這位年輕媽媽會給他們餅乾作為獎勵。

衍 rewarding [rɪˋwɔrdɪŋ]
a. 有報酬的；值得的

---

28 empire [ˋɛmpaɪr] *n.* 帝國

衍 emperor [ˋɛmpərɚ] *n.* 皇帝 ③

▶ The British Empire consisted of several separate territories.
大英帝國由個別的幾塊領土組成。

---

dynasty [ˋdaɪnəstɪ] *n.* 朝代，王朝

▶ Those revolutionaries overthrew the Ching dynasty and built a republic in 1911.
那些革命分子在 1911 年推翻清朝，建立共和國。

---

29 gaze [gez] *vi.* & *n.* 凝視，注視

片 (1) gaze at...　凝視……
　　= stare at...
　(2) gaze out of the window
　　盯著窗外看
　(3) meet sb's gaze　與某人對視

衍 stare [stɛr] *vi.* & *n.* 凝視 ③

▶ Karen gazed at Johnson in amazement when he said that he would marry his elementary schoolmate, Joan.
強森說他要娶小學同學瓊安時，凱倫驚訝地盯著他看。

▶ When the woman looked over at him, Ben averted his gaze.
當女子看著班時，他移開視線。

▶ I met Judy's gaze across the crowded dance floor.
我和茱蒂在擁擠的舞池中目光相會。

---

30 aggressive [əˋgrɛsɪv] *a.* 有侵略性的；積極進取的

衍 aggression [əˋgrɛʃən] *n.* 侵略 ⑤
似 belligerent [bəˋlɪdʒərənt] *a.* 好鬥的

▶ Kim started to get aggressive and shouted at the policeman.
金開始凶起來並對警察大吼。

Level 4　Unit 15

▶ Tyler is an aggressive young man who aspires to achieve a lot.
泰勒是個積極進取的年輕人,他渴望有所成就。
* aspire [əˋspaɪr] *vi.* 渴望,嚮往

---

31 hydrogen [ˋhaɪdrədʒən] *n.* 氫

▶ Water consists of hydrogen and oxygen.
水由氫和氧組成。

oxygen [ˋɑksədʒən] *n.* 氧氣

▶ Without oxygen, we would die.
沒有氧氣我們就會死掉。

---

32 hatred [ˋhetrɪd] *n.* 厭惡,憎恨

片 (1) hatred of / for... 對……的厭惡
(2) out of hatred 出於厭惡
衍 (1) hate [het] *vt.* 仇恨 ①
(2) hateful [ˋhetfəl]
a. 可恨的,充滿恨意的 ③

▶ Philip made no secret of his hatred of politicians.
菲利普毫不掩飾他對政客的厭惡。

---

33 carrier [ˋkærɪɚ] *n.* 運送者 / 工具;運輸公司;(疾病) 帶原者

片 (1) a mail carrier 郵遞員
(2) an aircraft carrier 航空母艦
衍 (1) carry [ˋkærɪ] *vt.* 攜帶 ①
(2) carriage [ˋkærɪdʒ] *n.* 四輪馬車 ③

▶ Alice put her cat in the pet carrier and set off for the animal hospital.
艾莉絲把她的貓咪放在寵物籃內,並出發前往動物醫院。

▶ Our company is an international carrier.
我們公司是一家國際運輸公司。

▶ Some people are unaware that they are carriers of COVID-19 since they have no symptoms.
有些人因為沒有症狀而不知道他們是新冠肺炎的帶原者。

---

34 convenience [kənˋvinjəns] *n.* 方便 (不可數);便利設施 (可數)

片 (1) at sb's convenience
在某人方便之際
(2) a convenience store 便利商店
衍 convenient [kənˋvinjənt]
a. 方便的 ①
反 inconvenience [͵ɪnkənˋvinjəns]
n. 不便

▶ Please call me back at your convenience.
等你方便時請回我電話。

▶ The house is equipped with every modern convenience you could imagine.
這棟房子配有所有你想像得到的現代便利設施。

▶ Convenience stores are everywhere in Taiwan.
臺灣隨處可見便利商店。

35　concerning [kənˈsɝnɪŋ] *prep.* 關於 (= about)

似 (1) about [əˈbaʊt] *prep.* 關於 ①
(2) regarding [rɪˈgardɪŋ]
　　prep. 關於 ④

▶ Mr. Hu mentioned things concerning his boyhood.
= Mr. Hu mentioned things about his boyhood.
= Mr. Hu mentioned things regarding his boyhood.
胡先生提到有關他童年的往事。
＊boyhood [ˈbɔɪhʊd] *n.* (男性的) 童年

1601-1608

---

1 **cabinet** [ˈkæbənɪt] *n.* 櫥櫃；內閣

片 (1) a filing / file cabinet　檔案櫃
　　(2) a cabinet shuffle / reshuffle
　　= reshuffle a cabinet　內閣改組
比 (1) cupboard [ˈkʌbəd] *n.* 碗櫥 ③
　　(2) wardrobe [ˈwɔrˌdrob] *n.* 衣櫃 ⑥
　　(3) a chest of drawers
　　　　五斗櫃，(有抽屜的) 衣櫃

▶ Is there enough room for the new filing cabinet?
還有空間放新檔案櫃嗎？

▶ Every year the president reshuffles his cabinet for security reasons.
基於安全理由，總統每年都會將內閣重新改組。

---

2 **functional** [ˈfʌŋkʃənl] *a.* 功用的；實用的

衍 function [ˈfʌŋkʃən]
n. 功能 & *vi.* 產生功能；擔任⋯⋯的工作 ②

▶ The two machines look alike but have many functional differences.
這兩臺機器看起來很像，但是有許多功用上的不同點。

▶ The design of the chair is beautiful, but it is not very functional.
這張椅子的設計很漂亮，但是卻不很實用。

---

3 **classify** [ˈklæsəˌfaɪ] *vt.* 分類；歸類

三 classify, classified [ˈklæsəˌfaɪd], classified
片 classify A as B　將 A 歸類為 B
= categorize A as B
衍 classified [ˈklæsəˌfaɪd] *a.* 分類的
　　a classified ad　分類廣告
似 categorize [ˈkætəgəˌraɪz] *vt.* 分類

▶ Non-fiction books in the library are classified according to subject matter.
圖書館內非小說類的書籍是依主題內容來分類。

▶ Some classify this music as jazz while others call it pop.
有些人把這種音樂歸類為爵士樂，然而也有些人稱之為流行樂。

classification [ˌklæsəfəˈkeʃən] *n.* 分類 (不可數)；類別 (可數)

似 categorization [ˌkætəgəraɪˈzeʃən] *n.* 分類

▶ The classification of the wild flowers took several days.
這些野花的分類費時好幾天。

▶ In India, there is a strict classification of people based upon the caste system.
在印度，根據種姓制度的階級之分很嚴格。
*caste [kæst] *n.* (印度) 種姓制度

---

4 **crush** [krʌʃ] *n.* 迷戀 & *vt.* 擠壓

片 have a crush on sb　迷戀某人
= be infatuated with sb
　　*infatuated [ɪnˈfætʃuˌetɪd] *a.* 迷戀的

▶ Wayne has a crush on the beautiful girl who helped him today.
韋恩迷戀上今天幫他忙的美女。

似 crash [kræʃ] vi. 墜毀 ③

▶ The car crushed the bike in the accident.
這起車禍中，車子把腳踏車壓扁了。

clash [klæʃ] n. & vi. 衝突 &
vt. & vi. (使) 碰撞作響 & n. 碰撞聲

片 clash with... 　與……起衝突
= conflict with...

似 conflict [ˋkɑnflɪkt] n. &
[kənˋflɪkt] vi. 衝突 ②

▶ A clash between the union and the administration led to the fight.
工會與行政部門的衝突釀成打鬥場面。

▶ People with different opinions clashed with each other during the strike.
罷工期間，意見相左的人彼此發生衝突。

▶ Owen clashed the pans together on purpose.
歐文故意使平底鍋碰撞發出聲響。

▶ The metal containers clashed as they were piled into the sink.
金屬容器被堆放入洗碗槽時相互碰撞發出聲響。

▶ The first sound on the song is a clash of cymbals.
這首歌的第一個聲音是鈸的碰撞聲。
＊cymbal [ˋsɪmbl̩] n. 銅鈸

5　promising [ˋprɑmɪsɪŋ] a. 有為的，有前途的

衍 promise [ˋprɑmɪs]
vt. & vi. 答應 & n. 承諾；前途 ②

似 hopeful [ˋhopfəl] a. 有希望的 ③

▶ Jennifer is a promising young girl. I'm sure she will be a success someday.
珍妮佛是個年輕有為的女孩。我確信她將來會成功。

6　collapse [kəˋlæps] vi. & n. 崩塌

似 fall down 　倒塌

▶ Over 50 houses collapsed in the earthquake.
超過 50 棟房子在地震中倒塌。

▶ The collapse of the world's tallest building was a shock to everyone.
世界最高的建築物倒塌，讓大家很震驚。

7　strive [straɪv] vi. 力爭，奮鬥

≡ strive, strived [straɪvd] / strove
[strov], strived / striven [ˋstrɪvn̩]

片 strive to + V 　努力要……
= strive for sth 　努力爭取某物

似 thrive [θraɪv] vi. 繁榮 ⑤

▶ The coach encouraged his team to strive to win the championship.
= The coach encouraged his team to strive for the championship.
教練鼓勵他的球隊要努力爭取冠軍。

8　artificial [ˌɑrtəˋfɪʃəl] a. 人造的；虛偽的，不真誠的

片 artificial intelligence
人工智慧 (縮寫為 AI)

▶ Some artificial flowers are made of paper.
有些人造花是用紙做的。

1608-1615

衍 artifact [ˋɑrtɪˏfækt] *n.* 手工藝品

似 man-made [ˏmænˋmed] *a.* 人造的

反 natural [ˋnætʃərəl] *a.* 天然的 ②

▶ The official welcomed me with an artificial smile.
這位官員帶著虛偽的微笑歡迎我。

9　genius [ˋdʒinjəs] *n.* 天賦，天分；天才

複 geniuses [ˋdʒinjəsɪz]

用 (1) have a genius for...
在……方面有天分
= have a talent for...
(2) a man of genius
有天分的人

似 talent [ˋtælənt] *n.* 天分 ③

▶ Picasso is admired for his artistic genius.
畢卡索因藝術天賦而受到敬佩。

▶ Mozart was a musical genius.
= Mozart had a genius for music.
= Mozart had a talent for music.
= Mozart was talented in music.
莫札特是音樂天才。

▶ Genius is one percent inspiration and ninety-nine percent perspiration.
天才是百分之一的靈感，百分之九十九的努力。
—— 愛迪生名言
*perspiration [ˏpɝspəˋreʃən] *n.* 流汗，努力

10　violate [ˋvaɪəˏlet] *vt.* 違反；侵犯

用 (1) violate the law　犯法
= break the law
= disobey the law
(2) violate sb's privacy
侵犯某人的隱私

衍 violence [ˋvaɪələns] *n.* 暴力 ③

▶ Those who violate traffic laws will get a ticket.
違反交通規則的人將會接到罰單。

▶ Becky said her mother violated her privacy in reading her diary.
貝琪說她媽媽看她的日記是侵犯了她的隱私。

---

violation [ˏvaɪəˋleʃən] *n.* 違反

用 in violation of...　違反……

▶ Tim was fined for a traffic violation.
提姆因為交通違規而被罰款。

▶ Those found in violation of the regulations will be severely punished.
違反規定的人一經發現將會受到嚴懲。

11　conductor [kənˋdʌktɚ] *n.* (樂團) 指揮；(火車) 列車長；導體

衍 conduct [kənˋdʌkt] *vt.* 進行
& [ˋkɑndʌkt] *n.* 行為 (不可數) ⑤

延伸 semiconductor [ˏsɛmikənˋdʌktɚ]
n. 半導體

▶ George is the conductor of that symphony orchestra.
喬治是那個交響樂團的指揮。

▶ You can buy train tickets from the conductor.
你可以向列車長買火車票。

▶ Plastic is a poor conductor of electricity.
塑膠不容易導電。

12 guarantee [ˌgærənˈti] n. 保證 & vt. 保證，擔保

片 (1) be under guarantee
在保固期內
(2) come with / without a
guarantee 有 / 沒有保固

似 (1) assurance [əˈʃʊrəns] n. 保證 ④
(2) warranty [ˈwɔrəntɪ] n. 保證書 ⑥

▶ The guarantee from the manufacturer is valid for one year.
廠商的保證一年有效。
*valid [ˈvælɪd] a. 有效的

▶ The product comes with a three-year guarantee.
這項商品有三年的保固。

▶ I guarantee that everything will be fine. Just wait and see.
我保證一切將會沒事。等著瞧吧。

13 peer [pɪr] n. 同輩，同儕 & vi. 凝視 (與介詞 at 並用)

片 (1) peer pressure 同儕壓力
(2) peer at... 凝視……
= stare at...
= gaze at...

▶ When it comes to singing, Jane is a lot better than her peers.
說到唱歌，珍比同年齡的人強多了。

▶ The little boy peered at his birthday cake as his mother iced it.
小男孩的媽媽在他的生日蛋糕上加糖霜時，他盯著蛋糕看。

14 fatal [ˈfetl] a. 致命的；無可挽回的

片 deal sb a fatal blow
給某人致命的一擊

衍 (1) fate [fet] n. 命運 ②
(2) fatally [ˈfetlɪ] adv. 致命地
(3) fatality [fəˈtælətɪ]
n. (意外事故的) 死亡者 (可數)

似 (1) deadly [ˈdɛdlɪ] a. 致命的 ⑤
(2) lethal [ˈliθəl] a. 致命的 ⑥

▶ We dealt the enemy a fatal blow during the battle.
我們在這次戰役中給敵軍致命的一擊。

▶ The boss made a fatal mistake when he kicked out that competent manager.
老闆開除那名能幹的經理時犯了一個不可挽回的錯誤。

15 acquaintance [əˈkwentəns] n. 相識的人 (可數)；認識，結識 (不可數)

片 (1) a nodding acquaintance
點頭之交
(2) make sb's acquaintance
認識某人

衍 acquaint [əˈkwent]
vt. 使熟悉；使認識 (與介詞 with 並用)
⑤

▶ That man is no friend of mine. He's just a nodding acquaintance.
那個人不是我的朋友。他只是點頭之交。

▶ Dr. Brown is an acquaintance of mine.
布朗博士是我的一位相識。

▶ Hank is my business partner. I made his acquaintance 10 years ago.
漢克是我的事業伙伴。我 10 年前就認識他了。

16 penalty [ˈpɛn̩tɪ] n. 懲罰

片 the death penalty　死刑

衍 penalize [ˈpin̩aɪz] vt. 懲罰

似 punishment [ˈpʌnɪʃmənt] n. 處罰

▶ What is the penalty for paying your bills late?
帳單遲付會有什麼樣的處分？

▶ The judges are arguing whether the death penalty should be abolished.
法官們在爭論是否應廢除死刑。
＊abolish [əˈbɑlɪʃ] vt. 廢除

17 invade [ɪnˈved] vt. 侵入，侵略

似 (1) attack [əˈtæk] vt. 攻擊 ①
　(2) assault [əˈsɔlt] vt. 攻擊 ⑤

▶ The enemy invaded the town while everyone was sound asleep.
敵軍趁大家熟睡時入侵這個城鎮。

invasion [ɪnˈveʒən] n. 入侵

似 (1) attack [əˈtæk] n. 攻擊 ①
　(2) assault [əˈsɔlt] n. 攻擊 ⑤

▶ This film is about the invasion of strange creatures.
這部電影演的是有怪物入侵。

18 intimate [ˈɪntəmət] a. 親密的；私人的 & n. 知己，密友

片 an intimate friend　關係親密的朋友
= a very close friend

衍 (1) intimacy [ˈɪntəməsɪ]
　　n. 親密，親近 ⑥
　(2) intimately [ˈɪntəmətlɪ]
　　adv. 親暱地；詳細地

似 imitate [ˈɪməˌtet] vt. 模仿 ④

▶ Intimate communication is necessary for true friendship.
真正的友誼需要親密的相互溝通。

▶ The famous actor would not discuss the intimate details of his marriage.
該知名演員不願談論他婚姻的私人細節。

▶ Polly was one of Todd's greatest intimates.
波莉是陶德最好的摯友之一。

19 flexible [ˈflɛksəbl̩] a. 有彈性的，可變通的；可彎曲的

衍 flexibility [ˌflɛksəˈbɪlətɪ] n. 彈性 ⑤

反 inflexible [ɪnˈflɛksəbl̩]
　a. 無彈性的；不可彎曲的

▶ My schedule is flexible. In other words, we can meet any time you like.
我的時程很彈性。換句話說，我們可以在任何時間見面。

▶ Leather was chosen because it is strong and flexible.
選擇皮革的原因是它很堅固也有彈性。

elastic [ɪˈlæstɪk] a. 有彈性的
& n. 橡皮筋 (可數)；鬆緊帶 (不可數)

似 a rubber band　橡皮筋

▶ When making bread, your dough shouldn't be too elastic.
做麵包時麵糰不可以太有彈性。
＊dough [do] n. 生麵糰

▶ I wrapped an elastic around the box to keep the contents safe.
我在這個盒子上裹橡皮筋以確保盒內東西的安全。

▶ The elastic in the pants has snapped.
這條褲子內的鬆緊帶斷掉了。

20 **boast** [bost] *vi.* 自誇 & *vt.* 以擁有……而自豪 & *n.* 自誇；引以為榮的事物

片 (1) boast of / about...
　　自誇 / 吹噓……
　= brag of / about...
(2) an empty boast　瞎吹牛
(3) It is sb's proud boast that...
　　讓某人感到驕傲的是……

用法 boast 作不及物動詞表『自誇』時，主詞是人；作及物動詞表『以擁有……而自豪』時，主詞是地方（如城市、地區等）。

▶ That little girl likes to boast about her brother's abilities.
那個小女孩喜歡吹噓她哥哥的能力。

▶ The small town boasts the best hotel in the world.
這小鎮以擁有世上最棒的飯店自豪。

▶ When Justin told me how far he could run, I knew it was just an empty boast.
賈斯汀告訴我他可以跑多遠時，我知道他只是在瞎吹牛。

▶ It is Sophie's proud boast that she has been to every country in Europe.
蘇菲去過歐洲每一個國家這件事讓她引以為傲。

brag [bræg] *vi.* 自誇，吹噓 & *vt.* 吹噓說
目 brag, bragged [brægd], bragged
片 (1) brag about / of...　自誇 / 吹噓……
　= boast about / of...
(2) brag (that)...　自誇……

▶ Sam is always bragging about how much money he has.
山姆總是吹噓自己多有錢。

▶ Jennie bragged that her husband was the richest man in town.
珍妮吹噓她老公是鎮上最有錢的男子。

21 **earnest** [ˋɜnɪst] *a.* 認真的，誠摯的 & *n.* 認真，誠摯

片 in earnest　認真地
似 (1) serious [ˋsɪrɪəs] *a.* 認真的 ①
(2) sincere [sɪnˋsɪr] *a.* 真誠的 ③

▶ Because he is an earnest student, David is well liked by his teachers.
大衛是認真的學生，所以很受老師的喜愛。

▶ Aaron studied in earnest, but still failed the exam.
艾倫認真讀書，考試卻仍不及格。

22 **magnetic** [mægˋnɛtɪk] *a.* 磁的；磁性的；有吸引力的

片 (1) magnetic force　磁力
(2) a magnetic field　磁場
衍 (1) magnet [ˋmægnɪt] *n.* 磁鐵 ③
(2) magnify [ˋmægnəˌfaɪ] *vt.* 放大 ⑥
似 (1) attractive [əˋtræktɪv] *a.* 迷人的 ③
(2) charming [ˋtʃɑrmɪŋ] *a.* 迷人的
(3) charismatic [ˌkærɪzˋmætɪk]
　　a. 有魅力的

▶ A compass works according to the magnetic force of the Earth.
指南針依據地球的磁力而運作。

▶ John attached the important notice to the magnetic whiteboard.
約翰把那張重要告示貼在磁性白板上。

▶ The actor has a truly magnetic personality.
這個男演員的個性實在很有吸引力。

23 halt [hɔlt] *n.* 暫停，停止 & *vi.* & *vt.* (使) 停止，暫停

片 come to a halt　慢慢停頓下來
= grind to a halt

▶ The project came to a halt when we ran out of money.
我們錢用完時，計畫也就停頓了。

▶ The children halted when they saw a big dog.
孩子們看到一隻大狗時便停止行進。

▶ We have to halt production at the factory because the payment issue has not been settled.
我們必須停止工廠的生產，因為錢的事尚未解決。

24 chemistry [ˋkɛmɪstrɪ] *n.* 化學；(感情) 來電 (皆不可數)

衍 (1) chemical [ˋkɛmɪkḷ] *a.* 化學的 &
n. 化學藥品，化學產品 ②
(2) chemist [ˋkɛmɪst] *n.* 化學家 ⑥

▶ Chemistry is my favorite subject at school.
化學是我在學校裡最喜歡的科目。

▶ There's no chemistry between the two of us; I never think of Wendy as my girlfriend.
我倆不來電；我從未把溫蒂當作女友看待。

25 decoration [ˌdɛkəˋreʃən] *n.* 裝飾 (不可數)；裝飾物 (可數)

衍 decorate [ˋdɛkəˌret] *vt.* 裝飾 ③

▶ My friend David specializes in interior decoration.
我的朋友大衛專門從事室內裝潢。

▶ As Christmas was drawing near, every store put up beautiful decorations for the holiday.
聖誕節快到時，每家商店都擺出漂亮的裝飾物以慶祝這個佳節。

26 refusal [rɪˋfjuzḷ] *n.* 拒絕

片 shake one's head in refusal
某人搖頭表示拒絕
衍 refuse [rɪˋfjuz] *vt.* 拒絕 ②

▶ I asked Paul to go to the store, and I was surprised by his refusal.
我請保羅跑一趟商店，很驚訝他竟然拒絕了。

▶ Sue shook her head in refusal when I asked her to go to the movies with me.
我約蘇跟我去看電影時，她搖頭拒絕了。

27 enlarge [ɪnˋlɑrdʒ] *vt.* 放大 (照片)；擴大

片 (1) have a picture enlarged
(請人) 把照片放大
(2) enlarge one's vocabulary
增加某人的字彙量
似 magnify [ˋmægnəˌfaɪ] *vt.* 放大 ⑥

▶ I went to a photo shop to have my picture enlarged.
我到照相館把我的照片放大。

▶ To enlarge your vocabulary, you should read newspapers on a daily basis.
你若想增加字彙量，就該每天看報紙。

enlargement [ɪnˈlɑrdʒmənt]
n. 放大(照片)；擴大

▶ Jessy had an enlargement of one of her wedding photos done for her parents.
潔西把其中一張婚紗照放大送給她父母。

▶ The mayor proposed an enlargement of the city's main park.
該市長提議擴大市內的主公園。

28 curse [kɜs] *vt. & vi.* 詛咒，咒罵 & *n.* 咒語

片 (1) curse sb for sth　因某事咒罵某人
(2) put a curse on...　對……施咒

▶ The old man cursed the woman for almost running into him.
老伯伯咒罵那名女子差點撞到他。

▶ When the little boy started to curse, his parents told him off.
小男孩開口咒罵時，他父母便訓斥他。

▶ The witch put a curse on the beautiful princess.
巫婆對美麗的公主施咒。

blessing [ˈblɛsɪŋ]
n. 祝福；福氣 (可數)

片 (1) It is a blessing to + V...
………是種福氣
(2) a blessing in disguise
因禍得福；塞翁失馬，焉知非福

衍 bless [blɛs] *vt.* 祝福；保佑 ③

▶ It is a blessing to be taught by Mr. Wang.
能被王老師教到是一種福氣。

▶ John's girlfriend ran away with his best friend a year ago, but he soon met a rich and beautiful girl. They're planning to get married next week. It was indeed a blessing in disguise.
約翰的女友 1 年前跟他最好的朋友跑了，不過很快地他就遇到了一位多金又漂亮的美女。他們倆計劃下星期結婚。這真是因禍得福啊。

29 imaginary [ɪˈmædʒəˌnɛrɪ] *a.* 想像的，虛構的

衍 (1) imagine [ɪˈmædʒɪn] *vt.* 想像 ②
(2) image [ˈɪmɪdʒ] *n.* 形象；意象 ②
(3) imagination [ɪˌmædʒəˈneʃən]
n. 想像力 ③

似 fictional [ˈfɪkʃənḷ] *a.* 虛構的
反 real [ˈrɪəl] *a.* 真實的 ①

▶ All the events described in the story are imaginary.
這故事所描述的所有事件都是虛構的。

▶ As far as I'm concerned, real stories are much more fun to read than imaginary ones.
就我個人而言，閱讀真實的故事要比虛構的故事有趣多了。

imaginative [ɪˈmædʒəˌnetɪv]
a. 富有想像力的

似 (1) creative [krɪˈetɪv]
a. 有創造力的 ③
(2) innovative [ˈɪnəˌvetɪv]
a. 有創意的 ⑤

▶ Jennifer is good at thinking up new ideas. In other words, she is quite imaginative.
珍妮佛善於想出新點子。換句話說，她很有想像力。

imaginable [ɪˋmædʒɪnəbḷ]
a. 可想像的，可想見的

🔑 the + 最高級形容詞 + sb/sth imaginable
可想像得到最……的人 / 物

🔄 unimaginable [ˏʌnɪˋmædʒɪnəbḷ]
a. 難以想像的

▶ The brochure lists the most romantic resorts imaginable in Europe.
這本冊子列出全歐洲所想像得到最浪漫的渡假勝地。
*brochure [broˋʃur] *n.* 小冊子
resort [rɪˋzɔrt] *n.* 渡假勝地

30　coward [ˋkauɚd] *n.* 膽小鬼，懦夫

🔄 (1) cowardly [ˋkauɚdlɪ] *a.* 懦弱的 ⑥
(2) cowardice [ˋkauɚdɪs]
　　n. 膽小，懦弱 (不可數)

▶ Don't be such a coward. Just tell her how you feel.
不要當個膽小鬼。把你對她的感覺告訴她啊。

▶ As Shakespeare once put it, "A coward dies a thousand times, a hero only once."
莎翁曾云：『懦夫死千次，英雄只死一次。』(本句涵意為：英雄不懼死亡；而膽小鬼經歷過上千次的驚嚇，每次受到驚嚇時，他的感覺與死無兩樣。)

31　riddle [ˋrɪdḷ] *n.* 謎

🔑 solve a riddle　猜出謎底
🔄 puzzle [ˋpʌzḷ]
n. 謎，難題 & *vt.* 使困惑 ②

▶ Blair solved the riddle before Sam did.
布萊兒比山姆先猜出謎底。

32　suspicious [səˋspɪʃəs] *a.* 可疑的；多疑的，猜疑的

🔑 be suspicious of...　懷疑……
🔄 suspiciously [səˋspɪʃəslɪ]
adv. 可疑地，鬼鬼祟祟地；懷疑地

▶ We saw a suspicious man standing near the school.
我們在學校附近看到一名可疑男子。

▶ My girlfriend is a very suspicious person.
我女友是一個非常多疑的人。

▶ Ted said he came here just to say hello, but I was suspicious of his real intentions.
= Ted said he came here just to say hello, but I suspected his real intentions.
泰德說他來這裡只是打聲招呼，但我懷疑他真正的動機。

33　quotation [kwoˋteʃən] *n.* 引文

▶ Make sure this quotation is accurate.
請確定這段引文正確無誤。

34 **feedback** [ˋfid͵bæk] *n.* 反饋，回應 (不可數)

田 positive / negative feedback
正 / 反面回饋

似 criticism [ˋkrɪtə͵sɪzəm] *n.* 批評 ④

▸ Our company welcomes any feedback from our customers.
本公司歡迎顧客提供任何意見反映。

35 **disability** [͵dɪsəˋbɪlətɪ] *n.* 障礙，缺陷

田 a learning / physical / mental disability
學習障礙 / 身體殘疾 / 心理缺陷

衍 disable [dɪsˋebl̩] *vt.* 使失去能力 ⑥

反 ability [əˋbɪlətɪ] *n.* 能力 ①

▸ I was surprised to know that the accomplished scholar suffered from severe learning disability as a child.
得知那位傑出學者小時候曾有嚴重的學習障礙時，我很吃驚。

＊accomplished [əˋkɑmplɪʃt] *a.* 很有成就的

36 **engineering** [͵ɛndʒəˋnɪrɪŋ] *n.* 工程 (學) (不可數)

衍 engineer [͵ɛndʒəˋnɪr] *n.* 工程師 ①

▸ Ezra studied mechanical engineering at that university.
埃斯拉在那所大學念機械工程。

Level 4　Unit 16

1701-1705

1 **elementary** [ˌɛləˈmɛntərɪ] *a.* 基本的；初級的，基礎的

片 an elementary school　小學
= a primary school

衍 element [ˈɛləmənt]
　 n. 元素；要素，成分 ③

似 (1) basic [ˈbesɪk] *a.* 基本的 ②
　 (2) fundamental [ˌfʌndəˈmɛntl̩]
　　 a. 基礎的 ④

▶ There was an elementary error on the first page of the book.
這本書的第一頁出現很基本的錯誤。

▶ I took a course in elementary physics last semester.
我上學期修了一門初級物理學的課。

▶ Jacob and his family immigrated to Germany soon after he graduated from elementary school.
雅各小學畢業後沒多久便和家人移民德國。

---

intermediate [ˌɪntəˈmidɪɪt]
a. 中等程度的 & *n.* 中級程度的人
& [ˌɪntəˈmidɪ,et] *vi.* 作中間人

延伸 (1) a basic level　　　　　基礎級
　　 (2) an intermediate level　中級
　　 (3) an advanced level　　　高級

▶ The article is too difficult for intermediate students of English.
這篇文章對英文中等程度的學生來說太難了。

▶ This language program is especially designed to suit intermediates.
這個語言活動是特別為中級程度的人設計的。

▶ John was asked to intermediate between the two groups.
約翰被請來幫這兩組居中協調。

2 **circular** [ˈsɝkjələ] *a.* 圓形的 & *n.* 傳單，通知

衍 circle [ˈsɝkl̩] *n.* 圓，圓圈 &
　 vt. 環繞；圈選 & *vi.* 繞圈子，盤旋 ①

似 flyer [ˈflaɪə] *n.* 傳單

▶ The full moon has a circular shape.
滿月的形狀是圓的。

▶ More and more publishers distribute circulars to promote their new books.
越來越多出版社會發傳單宣傳他們的新書。

---

circulate [ˈsɝkjə,let]
vt. & *vi.* (使) 循環；(使) 散布，傳播

片 Rumors began circulating that...
　 ……的謠言開始散播

似 spread [sprɛd] *vt.* 傳播 ②

▶ Jessica turned on the fan to circulate the air around the room.
潔西卡打開電扇來讓房間內的空氣流通。

▶ Blood circulates through the veins and arteries.
血液循環流過靜脈和動脈。

▶ Rumors began circulating that the mayor would soon step down.
有關市長很快就要下臺的謠言開始四處散播。

▶ The affair quickly circulated around the office.
該事件在辦公室內快速散播。

circulation [ˌsɝkjəˈleʃən]
n. 循環；流通；發行量

- (1) in circulation   在流通
- (2) out of circulation   不再流通
- (3) enjoy wide circulation
  享有很大的發行量
- flow [flo] *n.* 流動 ②

- ▶ Good blood circulation is essential to good health.
  良好的血液循環對健康很重要。
- ▶ Connie complained that the circulation of air in the room was poor.
  康妮抱怨這房間裡的空氣流通不良。
- ▶ The bank reported that there was a lot of fake money in circulation.
  銀行舉報有許多假鈔在流通。
- ▶ Our two magazines enjoy wide circulation throughout Taiwan.
  我們的兩本雜誌在全臺的發行量很大。

3   reluctant [rɪˈlʌktənt] *a.* 勉強的；不情願的

- be reluctant to + V   不願意從事……
  = be unwilling to + V
- reluctantly [rɪˈlʌktəntlɪ]
  adv. 不情願地
- unwilling [ʌnˈwɪlɪŋ] *a.* 不願意的

- ▶ Feeling sad, Tanya gave me a reluctant smile.
  譚雅很難過，對著我苦笑。
- ▶ I knew there was something the matter with Dylan, but he was reluctant to tell me the truth.
  我知道狄倫出事了，不過他不願把真相告訴我。
  *something the matter with sb   某人出事了

reluctance [rɪˈlʌktəns]
n. 勉強；不情願

- with reluctance   勉強地；不情願地
  = reluctantly

- ▶ Jack has a reluctance to take part in any physical activity.
  傑克不想參加任何體育活動。
- ▶ With reluctance, little Johnny agreed to share his French fries with his brother.
  小強尼很勉強地同意與弟弟分享薯條。

4   fame [fem] *n.* 名氣，名聲 (不可數)

- (1) fame and wealth / fortune
  名利
- (2) rise to fame   成名
- famous [ˈfeməs] *a.* 出名的 ①

- ▶ Patrick achieved great fame as a photographer.
  派翠克成了聲名大噪的攝影師。
- ▶ All his life David pursued nothing but fame and wealth.
  大衛一輩子追求的只是名利。

5   frown [fraʊn] *vi.* & *n.* 皺眉頭

- (1) frown at sb
  對某人皺眉頭，表示不悅
- (2) frown on / upon sth
  不贊同某事，反對某事

- ▶ Mr. Roberts frowned at me for turning down his request.
  羅伯茲先生因我拒絕他的請求而對我皺眉表示不悅。
- ▶ Joy wanted to be a pop idol, but her parents frowned upon the idea.
  喬伊想要當流行偶像，不過她爸媽卻反對這樣的想法。

▶ Edward read his brother's letter with a frown.
愛德華看著他弟弟的信，面露不悅之色。

6 margin [ˈmɑrdʒɪn] *n.* 頁邊空白；邊緣；利潤；差數

片 (1) a profit margin　淨利率
(2) by a narrow margin
以些微之差；勉強地

衍 marginal [ˈmɑrdʒɪnl̩]
　　a. 頁邊的；邊緣的⑥

似 (1) edge [ɛdʒ] *n.* 邊緣②
(2) brim [brɪm] *n.* 邊緣

▶ Please write your contact information in the margin.
請把你的聯絡資料寫在紙邊空白處。

▶ The refugee camp lies at the margins of the city.
難民營在該市的邊緣地帶。

▶ The company tried to increase their profit margin by using poor-quality materials.
這間公司試圖使用低品質的物料來增加淨利率。

▶ The lucky boy escaped the car accident by a narrow margin.
這個幸運的男孩勉強逃過了車禍。

7 mild [maɪld] *a.* (天氣) 溫暖的；(個性) 溫和的；(食物) 味道淡的

似 gentle [ˈdʒɛntl̩] *a.* (個性) 溫柔的②

▶ The climate was rather mild when we visited Alaska.
我們在阿拉斯加時天氣特別溫暖。

▶ Our English teacher is a man of mild temper.
我們的英文老師是個脾氣很溫和的人。

▶ Ian prefers his curry to have a mild flavor.
伊恩偏好他的咖哩味道淡一點。

8 dynamic [daɪˈnæmɪk] *a.* 充滿活力的

似 energetic [ˌɛnɚˈdʒɛtɪk]
　　a. 充滿精力的③

▶ Stacey is so dynamic that she is able to work during the day and moonlight at night.
史黛西精力充沛，因此能白天工作晚上兼差。
*moonlight [ˈmun,laɪt] *vi.* 兼差

9 popularity [ˌpɑpjəˈlærətɪ] *n.* 聲望；普及，流行

衍 (1) popular [ˈpɑpjəlɚ]
　　a. 受歡迎的；大眾的，普遍的①
(2) popularize [ˈpɑpjələ,raɪz]
　　vt. 使流行，使大眾化

似 reputation [ˌrɛpjəˈteʃən] *n.* 名聲④

▶ The actor enjoyed great popularity for over twenty years.
這位演員享有很高的聲望達 20 多年之久。

▶ The popularity of the staycation continues to grow due to the pandemic.
由於此次疫情的緣故，宅度假越來越流行。
*staycation [steˈkeʃən] *n.* 在家 (或家附近) 度假
(由 stay 和 vacation 組成)
pandemic [pænˈdɛmɪk] *n.* 流行病

10 **accent** [ˈæksənt] *n.* 口音，腔調

片 with a(n)... accent 帶著……的口音	▶ Mr. Sato speaks English with a heavy Japanese accent. 佐藤先生講英語有濃厚的日本腔。

pronunciation [prəˌnʌnsɪˈeʃən] *n.* 發音

衍 pronounce [prəˈnauns]
   vt. 發出……的聲音 & *vi.* 發音 ③

▶ John doesn't like to speak English; he thinks his pronunciation is poor.
約翰不喜歡說英語；他認為他的發音很差。

syllable [ˈsɪləbl̩] *n.* 音節

▶ There are three syllables in the word "beautiful".
『beautiful』一字有 3 個音節。

11 **amateur** [ˈæməˌtʃɚ] *n.* 業餘人士 & *a.* 業餘的

反 professional [prəˈfɛʃənl̩]
   n. 專業人士 & *a.* 專業的 ④

▶ These photos were taken by amateurs.
這些照片都是業餘愛好者拍的。

▶ Phil is an amateur golfer, while Tiger Woods is a professional.
菲爾是業餘的高爾夫球選手，而老虎·伍茲則是職業選手。

12 **portray** [pɔrˈtre] *vt.* 描述，描繪

片 portray A as B   把 A 描述為 B
 = describe A as B
 = depict A as B

衍 portrait [ˈpɔrtrɪt] *n.* 肖像，畫像 ③

似 (1) depict [dɪˈpɪkt] *vt.* 描述 ⑤
   (2) describe [dɪˈskraɪb] *vt.* 描述 ②

▶ That movie portrays the famous writer as a very romantic man.
那部電影把該知名作家描述成一個浪漫的男子。

▶ This artist's painting vividly portrays what farm life is like in his hometown.
這位畫家的畫作生動地描繪他老家農村生活的模樣。

13 **catalog** [ˈkætəlɔg] *n.* (商品) 型錄 (= catalogue〔英〕) & *vt.* 為……編目

延伸 書中的目錄稱作 the table of contents。

▶ Please refer to our catalog for a complete list of our products.
我們完整的商品明細請參照我們的型錄。

▶ It was Helen's job to catalog all of the merchandise.
海倫的職務是替所有的商品編目。

14 **bulletin** [ˈbulətən] *n.* 告示，公告；新聞快報

片 a bulletin board   布告欄
似 notice [ˈnotɪs] *n.* 公告 ①

▶ The city government just released a bulletin, asking all the residents to practice social distancing.
市政府剛剛發布公告，要求所有居民保持社交距離。
*social distancing   社交距離

▶ There's an hourly news bulletin on this radio station.
這家廣播電臺每小時都有新聞播報。

---

15 instinct [ˋɪnstɪŋkt] *n.* 本性；本能；直覺

月 by instinct　本能地；直覺地
= instinctively [ɪnˋstɪŋktɪvlɪ] *adv.*

衍 instinctive [ɪnˋstɪŋktɪv]
　a. 本能的；直覺的 ⑥

▶ Fear of the unknown is a common instinct.
對未知的恐懼是人類共有的本性。

▶ Birds do not learn to build nests, but build them by instinct.
鳥類並沒有學習去築巢，而是依本能去築巢。

▶ Over the years, the explorer has learned to rely on his instincts.
多年來，這名探險家學會倚賴直覺。

---

16 surrender [səˋrɛndɚ] *n.* 投降 & *vi.* & *vt.* (使) 投降

月 (1) surrender to...　屈服於……
= yield to...
= concede to...
= give in to...
(2) surrender oneself (to...)
　某人 (向……) 投降 / 自首

▶ The general decided to negotiate a surrender.
將軍決定做投降的談判。

▶ After days of battle, the enemy troops finally surrendered.
經過連日交戰，敵軍終於投降了。

▶ He who never surrenders to fate stands a better chance of achieving success.
凡是不屈服於命運的人成功的機會都比較大。

▶ After committing a crime, the man decided to surrender himself to the police.
這名男子犯罪後，決定向警方自首。

---

17 glimpse [glɪmps] *n.* & *vt.* 瞥見

月 catch / get / have a glimpse of...
　瞥見……

似 a quick look　匆匆的看一眼

▶ Jack caught a glimpse of Ella out of the corner of his eye.
傑克用眼角餘光很快地看了艾拉一眼。

▶ I glimpsed my stomach in the mirror and frowned.
我在鏡中瞥見我的肚子，皺了皺眉頭。

---

18 memorize [ˋmɛməˏraɪz] *vt.* 背熟，熟記

衍 memory [ˋmɛmərɪ] *n.* 記憶；回憶 ②

▶ When learning English, do not memorize words only. What's even more important is that you know how to use these words.
學英文時，不要只背單字。更重要的是，你應懂得如何使用這些單字。

memorial [məˋmorɪəl]
n. 紀念碑 & *a.* 紀念的

衍 memoir [ˋmɛmwɑr]
   n. 傳記；回憶錄，自傳

似 monument [ˋmɑnjəmənt]
   n. 紀念碑；紀念館 ④

▶ In most English villages there is a war memorial.
英國大部分的村莊都有一個戰爭紀念碑。

▶ There's a memorial statue of Dr. Sun Yat-sen in front of the park.
公園前有座孫中山先生的紀念雕像。

---

memorable [ˋmɛmərəbļ]
a. 值得紀念的；難忘的

似 unforgettable [ˌʌnfɚˋgɛtəbļ]
   a. 難忘的

▶ The ceremony was memorable for its splendor.
這個儀式的隆重值得紀念。
＊splendor [ˋsplɛndɚ] *n.* 壯麗，隆重

▶ My parents and I spent a memorable vacation in the Alps last summer.
我和爸媽去年夏天在阿爾卑斯山度過一個難忘的假期。

---

19   oval [ˋovļ] *a.* 卵形的，橢圓形的 & *n.* 橢圓

片 an oval face   鵝蛋臉

▶ The most famous room in the White House is the Oval Office.
白宮最著名的辦公室就是橢圓形辦公室。

▶ The designer shaped the seat like an oval.
設計師把椅子設計成橢圓形。

---

20   explosion [ɪkˋsploʒən] *n.* 爆炸；(感情、笑聲等的) 爆發

衍 explode [ɪkˋsplod]
   vt. 炸掉 & *vi.* 爆炸 ③

▶ The men made preparations for the explosion of the dynamite.
這些人正準備引爆炸藥。
＊dynamite [ˋdaɪnəˌmaɪt] *n.* 炸藥 (不可數)

▶ The speaker's controversial comments prompted an explosion of anger from the crowd.
這名講者具爭議性的言論引發眾怒。

---

explosive [ɪkˋsplosɪv]
a. 爆炸 (性) 的；爆發的；(局面等) 一觸即發的 & *n.* 炸藥，爆炸物 (可數，常用複數)

似 dynamite [ˋdaɪnəˌmaɪt]
   n. 炸藥 (不可數)

▶ Be careful when handling these explosive substances.
處理這些會爆炸的東西時要小心。

▶ The police came in to handle the potentially explosive situation.
警方進來處理這個可能一觸即發的情況。

▶ Explosives must be handled with great care.
爆炸物必須要非常小心處理。

21 damp [dæmp] *a.* 潮溼的 & *n.* 溼氣 (不可數) & *vt.* 使潮溼

衍 (1) dampness [`dæmpnəs]
　　n. 潮溼，溼氣 (不可數)
　　(2) dampen [`dæmpən] *vt.* 弄溼
似 (1) moist [mɔɪst] *a.* 潮溼的 ③
　　(2) humid [`hjumɪd] *a.* 潮溼的 ③
反 dry [draɪ] *a.* 乾的 & *vt.* 使乾燥 ①

▸ The lawn was damp with dew.
　草地被露水弄得溼溼的。
▸ The clothes hadn't dried properly and still smelled of damp.
　這些衣服沒有全乾，仍聞得出溼氣的味道。
▸ The light rain shower had barely damped the ground.
= The light rain shower had barely dampened the ground.
　綿綿細雨幾乎沒怎麼弄溼地面。

22 rage [redʒ] *n.* 憤怒；狂熱 & *vi.* 發怒；肆虐

片 (1) be in a rage
　　火大，處於盛怒的情況
　　(2) be (all) the rage　大為流行
衍 (1) raging [`redʒɪŋ] *a.* 狂暴而又猛烈的
　　(2) outrage [`aʊt,redʒ] *vt.* 使憤慨 & *n.* 憤慨；令人憤慨的事 ⑥

▸ Never let your rage get the best of you.
　千萬不要讓你的憤怒戰勝你。
▸ Sandy was in a rage after she saw how much money her husband had spent at the mall.
　珊蒂看到她老公在購物商場花了多少錢之後大發雷霆。
▸ Mukbang videos are all the rage these days.
　吃播影片現正大為流行。
　＊mukbang [`mʌkbɑŋ] *n.* 吃播 (源自韓語)
▸ The storm raged throughout the night, keeping us all awake.
　暴風雨肆虐一整晚，讓我們無法入睡。

23 furious [`f(j)ʊrɪəs] *a.* 憤怒的

片 be furious about / at...
　　對……極為憤怒
衍 fury [`fjʊrɪ] *n.* 震怒 ⑥

▸ Mr. Miller was furious about being fooled by his students.
　米勒老師非常生氣被學生耍了。

24 frustrate [`frʌs,tret] *vt.* 使灰心，使氣餒

似 upset [ʌp`sɛt] *vt.* 使難過 ②

▸ The fact that Glen's company is going to shut down really frustrates him.
　葛倫的公司即將關閉一事使他心煩意亂。

frustrated [`frʌstretɪd]
a. 感到灰心的，感到沮喪的

似 (1) depressed [dɪ`prɛst] *a.* 沮喪的
　　(2) discouraged [dɪs`kɝɪdʒd]
　　　　a. 灰心的

▸ The fans felt really frustrated with the outfielder's repeated errors.
　那位外野手不斷失誤，令球迷感到灰心。

frustrating [ˈfrʌstretɪŋ]
a. 令人灰心的，令人沮喪的

似 (1) depressing [dɪˈprɛsɪŋ]
   a. 令人沮喪的
   (2) discouraging [dɪsˈkɜɪdʒɪŋ]
   a. 令人灰心的

▸ Handling customers' complaints can be very frustrating at times.
處理客戶的申訴有時真令人沮喪。

---

frustration [frʌˈstreʃən]
n. 挫折，挫敗

▸ If you can learn not to be knocked down by frustration, you'll get somewhere.
你若能學會不被挫折擊倒，就能成大器。

---

25 cruelty [ˈkruəltɪ] *n.* 虐待；殘酷，殘暴

衍 cruel [ˈkruəl] *a.* 殘酷的，無情的 ③
似 unkindness [ʌnˈkaɪndnəs]
   n. 不仁慈

▸ I can't stand to see cruelty inflicted upon animals.
我不忍心看到動物所受的虐待。
*inflict [ɪnˈflɪkt] *vt.* 使遭受

▸ The hunter aimed his crossbow at an antelope with cruelty.
這獵人殘酷地用十字弓對準一隻羚羊。
*crossbow [ˈkrɔsˌbo] *n.* 十字弓
 antelope [ˈæntḷop] *n.* 羚羊

---

26 scratch [skrætʃ] *vt.* 抓 & *n.* 抓痕

片 from scratch 從零開始；從無到有
= starting from the beginning
= starting with nothing

▸ If you scratch my back, I'll scratch yours.
如果你抓我的背，我也會抓你的。── 諺語，喻如果你幫助我，我也會幫助你。

▸ It's only a scratch. It'll heal very soon.
這只是抓傷而已。它很快就會好了。

▸ The old man built his business up from scratch.
老先生白手起家，創立了他的事業。

---

27 retreat [rɪˈtrit] *vi.* & *n.* 撤退

片 be in (full) retreat （全面）撤退
似 (1) withdraw [wɪðˈdrɔ] *vi.* 撤退 ④
   (2) move back 撤退

▸ The troops retreated when they knew they couldn't win the battle.
當部隊發覺打不贏戰爭後，便下令撤退。

▸ The general announced that the enemy forces were in retreat.
將軍宣告敵軍撤退中。

28 rescue [ˈrɛskju] *vt.* & *n.* 拯救

片 come to sb's rescue　營救某人
似 save [sev] *vt.* 拯救 ①

▶ The fireman died trying to rescue a child from the blaze.
那名消防員企圖拯救孩童時葬身火場。
＊blaze [blez] *n.* 火焰

29 globe [glob] *n.* 地球儀；地球

衍 global [ˈglobl̩] *a.* 全球的 ③

▶ We tried to find the tiny country on the globe.
我們試圖在地球儀上找到這個小國家。

▶ Dad has traveled all around the globe.
＝ Dad has traveled all around the world.
老爸到過全球各地。

30 profitable [ˈprɑfɪtəbl̩] *a.* 有利潤的；有益的

衍 (1) profit [ˈprɑfɪt] *n.* 利潤 & *vi.* 獲利
　　& *vt.* 對……有利 ③
　(2) profitably [ˈprɑfɪtəblɪ]
　　　adv. 有利地；有益地
似 lucrative [ˈlukrətɪv] *a.* 有利可圖的 ⑥

▶ That cram school is a highly profitable business.
那間補習班是間高利潤的事業。

▶ Mom spent a profitable day studying French.
媽媽善用一天的時間學法文。

31 prosper [ˈprɑspɚ] *vi.* 繁榮，興隆

似 (1) thrive [θraɪv] *vi.* 興盛 ⑤
　(2) flourish [ˈflɝɪʃ] *vi.* 茂盛 ⑥

▶ The store prospered under new management.
這家店在新的經營策略下生意興隆。

prosperous [ˈprɑspərəs]
a. 興隆的，繁榮的

似 (1) thriving [ˈθraɪvɪŋ] *a.* 興盛的
　(2) flourishing [ˈflɝɪʃɪŋ] *a.* 茂盛的

▶ My father was the owner of several prosperous hotels.
我父親擁有幾家生意興隆的旅館。

prosperity [prɑsˈpɛrətɪ] *n.* 繁榮

似 affluence [ˈæfluəns] *n.* 富裕
反 poverty [ˈpɑvɚtɪ] *n.* 貧窮 ③

▶ In times of prosperity, it is easy to find a job.
景氣好的時候找工作很容易。

32 infant [ˈɪnfənt] *n.* 嬰兒

似 baby [ˈbebɪ] *n.* 嬰兒，小寶寶 ①

▶ Infants should be lovingly cared for.
嬰兒應該以愛心來照顧。

Unit 18

1801-1804

1 satellite [ˈsætl̩ˌaɪt] *n.* 衛星

片 (1) by / via satellite　透過衛星
(2) a satellite dish　衛星天線
(3) a satellite town / city
　　衛星市鎮 / 城 (市) (指大城市附近的小型市鎮 / 城市，許多住於此的人是在該大城市上班)

▶ The Oscar ceremony was transmitted around the world by satellite.
奧斯卡頒獎典禮透過衛星向全球各地播送。

▶ It is not too much to say that Danshui is a satellite town of Taipei city.
淡水是臺北市的衛星城，這個說法並不為過。

2 preferable [ˈprɛfərəbl̩] *a.* 更合意的，更好的 (與介詞 to 並用)

衍 (1) prefer [prɪˈfɝ] *vt.* 比較喜歡 ②
(2) preference [ˈprɛfərəns]
　　n. 偏好，偏愛 ⑤

片 A is preferable to B　A 比 B 更合意

▶ A glass of iced tea is preferable to a cup of coffee on a hot day.
大熱天時，一杯冰茶比一杯咖啡來得更好。

3 ingredient [ɪnˈgridɪənt] *n.* (食品) 成分；(成功的) 要素

似 component [kəmˈponənt]
n. 構成要素；零件 ⑤

▶ What are the ingredients of the cake?
這個蛋糕的成分是什麼？

▶ Trust is an important ingredient in a successful relationship.
信任在一段成功的關係裡是很重要的要素。

4 herd [hɝd] *n.* 一群 & *vt.* 放牧

用法 herd 作名詞用時，與群居的草食性大型動物並用。

a herd of cattle / horses / elephants　一群牛 / 馬 / 象

延伸 (1) a flock of sheep　一群綿羊
(2) a pride of lions　一群獅子
(3) a pack of dogs / wolves
　　一群狗 / 狼
(4) a school of fish　一群魚
(5) a swarm of bees
　　一群在飛的蜜蜂
(6) a colony of bees / ants
　　一群蜜蜂 / 螞蟻

▶ A herd of cattle was quietly grazing on the grass.
一群牛在草地上正安靜地吃草。
*graze [grez] *vi.* (動物) 吃草

▶ The cowboys herded the cows with the help of their horses.
牛仔們的馬協助他們來放牧牛群。

5 curl [kɝl] n. (一根) 捲髮 & vt. 使捲曲

(1) have curls　有一頭捲髮
(2) wear one's hair in curls　留捲髮

curly [ˈkɝlɪ] a. 捲曲的

▶ One colleague of mine has nice, long curls.
　我的一位同事有一頭漂亮的長捲髮。

▶ The hairdresser curled Kathy's hair and styled it for the wedding.
　髮型師為凱西的婚禮將她的頭髮弄捲並做造型。

6 enclose [ɪnˈkloz] vt. 圍住；封入，附寄

Please find enclosed...
請隨函查收……

enclosure [ɪnˈkloʒɚ]
n. 圍住；(信函) 附件

include [ɪnˈklud] vt. 包含 ②

▶ A high wall with barbed wire encloses the celebrity's house.
　有帶刺鐵絲網的高牆把這位名人的家圍住。

▶ I enclosed a photo in my letter to my boyfriend.
　我在給男友的信中附上我的照片。

▶ Please find enclosed a check for $200.
　請隨函查收一張面額 200 美元的支票。

7 photography [fəˈtɑgrəfɪ] n. 攝影

(1) photograph [ˈfotəˌgræf]
　n. 照片 (= photo [ˈfoto]) ①
(2) photographer [fəˈtɑgrəfɚ]
　n. 攝影師 ③
(3) photographic [ˌfotəˈgræfɪk]
　a. 攝影的 ⑤
(4) photogenic [ˌfotəˈdʒɛnɪk]
　a. 很上相的，很適合拍照的

▶ Bob and I studied photography together in college.
　鮑伯和我大學時一起念攝影。

8 haste [hest] n. 匆忙，急促 (不可數)

in haste　匆忙地
= in a hurry
= in a rush

▶ John left in haste after hanging up the phone.
　掛電話後，約翰便匆匆離開了。

▶ Haste makes waste.
　欲速則不達。—— 諺語

hasten [ˈhesn̩] vt. 催促

hasten to + V
急忙 (說) ……；趕緊做……

hasty [ˈhestɪ] a. 急忙的 ③

▶ The father hastened his children off to bed.
　這個父親催促孩子們上床睡覺。

▶ For fear that the reporters didn't fully understand him, the politician hastened to add an explanation.
　這位政治人物擔心記者未能完全理解他的話，便急忙加了一句解釋。

9　nonsense [ˈnɑnsəns] n. 胡說八道，廢話 (不可數)

旬 talk nonsense　胡扯

▶ Nobody in our class likes Jim because he always talks nonsense.
我們班上沒有人喜歡吉姆，因為他總是胡說八道。

10　gifted [ˈɡɪftɪd] a. 有天賦的

旬 be gifted in...　有……的天賦
= be talented in...
= have a gift for...
= have a talent for...
衍 gift [ɡɪft] n. 天賦；禮物 ①
似 talented [ˈtæləntɪd] a. 有天賦的

▶ Jim Carrey is one of the most gifted comedians in Hollywood.
金‧凱瑞是好萊塢最有天分的喜劇演員之一。

▶ Believing that his son is gifted in painting, Josh has decided to send him to art school.
喬許相信他兒子有繪畫天賦，已決定送他到藝術學校念書。

11　brutal [ˈbrutl] a. 殘酷的，殘忍的

衍 brute [brut] n. 野獸 & a. 野蠻的
似 (1) cruel [ˈkruəl] a. 殘忍的 ③
　　(2) merciless [ˈmɜsɪləs] a. 殘酷的
反 (1) kind [kaɪnd] a. 仁慈的 ①
　　(2) benevolent [bəˈnɛvələnt]
　　　 a. 仁慈的，厚道的

▶ Murder is a brutal crime.
謀殺是殘忍的罪行。

▶ The government was accused of brutal treatment of political prisoners.
該政府被控告以殘忍的方式對待政治犯。

brutality [bruˈtælɪtɪ] n. 殘酷

旬 police brutality　警察暴行
似 cruelty [ˈkruəltɪ] n. 殘忍 ④
反 (1) benevolence [bəˈnɛvələns]
　　　 n. 仁慈，厚道
　　(2) kindness [ˈkaɪndnəs] n. 仁慈

▶ We should never forget the brutality of war.
我們永遠不該忘記戰爭的殘酷。

▶ The protesters accused the officer of police brutality.
抗議者控告那名警察施暴。
*protester [proˈtɛstɚ] n. 抗議者

12　acid [ˈæsɪd] a. 酸 (性) 的；尖酸苛薄的 & n. 酸 (性)

旬 acid rain　酸雨
反 alkaline [ˈælkəˌlaɪn] a. 鹼性的

▶ Acid rain is a result of air pollution.
酸雨是空氣汙染造成的。

▶ When Mira criticized their work, you could feel the acid tone in her words.
米拉批評他們的工作時，你可以感覺出她話中那股酸溜溜的語氣。

▶ If we mix these two chemicals together, they will form an acid.
如果我們把這兩種化學物混合在一起，他們會形成酸。

13 motivate [ˈmotəˌvet] vt. 促使，激發

月 motivate sb to + V　激發某人做……

衍 motive [ˈmotɪv] n. 動機 ⑤

似 (1) inspire [ɪnˈspaɪr] vt. 激勵 ④
(2) encourage [ɪnˈkɝɪdʒ] vt. 鼓勵 ②
(3) stimulate [ˈstɪmjəˌlet] vt. 刺激 ⑤

▶ Peter is rude to girls. We should do something to motivate him to change his attitude.
彼得對女孩子很粗魯。我們應有所作為以促使他改變態度。

▶ Encouragement can often motivate students to study harder.
鼓勵往往能激發學生更用功。

motivation [ˌmotəˈveʃən]
n. 動機；幹勁

似 (1) incentive [ɪnˈsɛntɪv] n. 動機 ⑤
(2) drive [draɪv] n. 幹勁，衝勁 ①

▶ You should make sure that your motivation for losing weight is healthy.
你應確保自己想減肥的動機是健康的。

▶ I have no motivation toward the project. I'm not interested in it.
我對這項企畫沒有動力。我對它不感興趣。

14 pessimistic [ˌpɛsəˈmɪstɪk] a. 悲觀的

月 be pessimistic about...
對……表示悲觀

衍 (1) pessimist [ˈpɛsəmɪst] n. 悲觀者 ④
(2) pessimism [ˈpɛsəmɪzəm]
n. 悲觀 ⑤

反 optimistic [ˌaptəˈmɪstɪk] a. 樂觀的 ③

▶ Instead of being pessimistic, you can learn from your mistakes.
與其感到悲觀，不如從錯誤中學習。

▶ Paul is pessimistic about his future. He should learn to look on the bright side of life.
保羅對他的未來持悲觀的態度。他應學習看人生的光明面。

15 frost [frɑst] n. 霜 & vt. & vi. 結霜

衍 (1) defrost [diˈfrɑst] vt. 將……除霜
(2) frosty [ˈfrɑstɪ] a. 結霜的

▶ In the place where we live, you see frost on the ground in winter.
冬天時，我們住的地方地面上會有霜。

▶ The cold weather had frosted the windshield of Nick's car.
寒冷的氣候使得尼克車子的擋風玻璃結霜了。

▶ The front lawn was frosted over when we awoke.
我們醒來時發現前院草坪結霜了。

16 container [kənˈtenɚ] n. 容器

衍 contain [kənˈten] vt. 包含 ②

▶ You should store these cookies in a container with a tight lid.
你應該把這些餅乾保存在一個有密閉蓋子的容器裡。

17　farewell [ˌfɛrˈwɛl] *n.* 告別；送別會

片 (1) say farewell to...　向……告別
= say goodbye to...
(2) a farewell party
歡送會，餞別會

▶ We said our last farewell to our good friend at her funeral.
我們在好友的喪禮中向她做最後一次的告別。

▶ We threw a farewell party for David, who is retiring tomorrow.
我們為大衛舉辦歡送會，他明天就要退休了。

18　capitalism [ˈkæpɪtḷˌɪzəm] *n.* 資本主義 (不可數)

衍 capital [ˈkæpətḷ] *n.* 首都，首府；
大寫字母；資本 & *a.* 大寫的 ②

▶ Many say that the US is a country founded on capitalism.
許多人說美國這個國家是以資本主義立國。

capitalist [ˈkæpɪtḷɪst]
n. 資本家；資本主義者

▶ Mr. Tate was labeled as a capitalist at a young age, but his beliefs have changed since then.
泰特先生年輕時被視為是資本主義者，但之後他的想法改變了。

19　imitate [ˈɪməˌtet] *vt.* 模仿，仿效

似 (1) copy [ˈkɑpɪ] *vt.* 模仿 ①
(2) mimic [ˈmɪmɪk] *n.* 模仿 ⑥

▶ The comedian is good at imitating famous people.
這名喜劇演員很擅長模仿名人。

imitation [ˌɪməˈteʃən]
n. 模仿 (不可數)；仿製品 (可數)

似 fake [fek]
n. 假貨，贗品，仿製品 (可數) ③

▶ The boy's imitation of the teacher made the teacher very angry.
男孩子模仿老師，使老師非常生氣。

▶ This watch is not a real Rolex; it's an imitation.
這只錶不是真的勞力士錶；它是山寨品。

20　disguise [dɪsˈɡaɪz] *vt.* & *n.* 假扮，喬裝

片 (1) be disguised as...　喬裝成……
= disguise oneself as...
(2) in disguise　偽裝
(3) a blessing in disguise　因禍得福

▶ The officer disguised himself as a hobo so he wouldn't be noticed.
那警官喬裝成遊民，這樣就沒有人會注意他。
*hobo [ˈhobo] *n.* 遊民

▶ Thomas went out in disguise to avoid being noticed by police officers.
湯瑪士變裝出門以免被警察注意到。

21　singular [ˈsɪŋɡjələ] *a.* 單數的；奇特的；非凡的 & *n.* (文法) 單數形

片 a singular success
= a remarkable success
無比的成功；非常成功

▶ The word "foot" is singular, while "feet" is plural.
『foot』這個字是單數，而『feet』則是複數。

衍 single [ˈsɪŋɡḷ] a. 單一的；單身的 & n. 單身者 ②

似 (1) strange [strendʒ] a. 奇怪的 ①
(2) remarkable [rɪˈmɑrkəbḷ]
　　a. 非凡的，了不起的 ④

反 plural [ˈplʊrəl] a. 複數的 & n. (文法) 複數形 ⑤

▶ I once had a singular experience during my short stay in Peru.
我在秘魯短暫停留期間經歷了一次奇特的經驗。

▶ The play we saw last night was a singular success.
我昨晚看的那齣戲非常成功。

▶ "Bacterium" is the singular of "bacteria."
『bacterium』是『bacteria』的單數形。

22　ancestor [ˈænsɛstɚ] n. 祖先；前身

衍 (1) ancient [ˈenʃənt] a. 古老的 ②
(2) ancestry [ˈænsɛstrɪ]
　　n. 祖先，祖宗；血統

似 forefather [ˈfɔrˌfɑðɚ]
　　n. 祖先 (常用複數)

▶ My ancestors came from Germany.
我的祖先們來自德國。

▶ This instrument is the ancestor of the modern guitar.
這種樂器是現代吉他的原型。

23　influential [ˌɪnfluˈɛnʃəl] a. 有影響力的

片 be influential in + N/V-ing
　　在……有影響力

衍 influence [ˈɪnfluəns] n. & vt. 影響 ②

▶ The non-profit organization is very influential in forming public opinion.
這個非營利組織對輿論的形成很有影響力。

24　tolerate [ˈtɑləˌret] vt. 容忍

似 (1) stand [stænd] vt. 忍耐 ①
(2) bear [bɛr] vt. 忍耐 ①
(3) endure [ɪnˈd(j)ʊr] vt. 忍耐 ④
(4) put up with... 容忍……

▶ I won't tolerate your rudeness any longer.
= I won't put up with your rudeness any longer.
我再也不會容忍你的粗魯了。

tolerance [ˈtɑlərəns] n. 容忍
似 endurance [ɪnˈd(j)ʊrəns] n. 忍耐 ⑥
反 intolerance [ɪnˈtɑlərəns]
　　n. 不寬容；無法容忍

▶ Try to show tolerance to your neighbors.
試著去包容你的鄰居們。

tolerant [ˈtɑlərənt] a. 容忍的
片 be tolerant of... 容忍……
反 intolerant [ɪnˈtɑlərənt]
　　a. 不寬容的，無法容忍的

▶ My father is a tolerant person on the whole.
大體上，我爸爸是個寬容的人。

▶ An open-minded person is tolerant of different opinions.
心胸開闊的人可以容忍不同的意見。

tolerable [ˋtɑlərəbḷ]
a. 可容忍的；尚可的

衍 **tolerably** [ˋtɑlərəblɪ] *adv.* 可容忍地

反 **intolerable** [ɪnˋtɑlərəbḷ]
　a. 不可容忍的

▸ The heat is high, but tolerable.
熱度雖高，但還可以忍受。

▸ Brad got tolerable marks in geography.
布萊德的地理成績尚可。

25　arch [ɑrtʃ] *n.* 拱門 & *vt.* & *vi.* (使) 成弓形

片 an arch bridge　拱橋

似 **curve** [kɝv] *vt.* & *vi.* (使) 彎曲 &
　n. 彎曲；曲線 ④

▸ They built the arch as a memorial to the general.
他們建造這座拱門以紀念這位將軍。

▸ The cat arched its back before it ran away.
這隻貓把背拱了起來然後就跑掉了。

▸ The willows arch over the riverbank.
柳樹沿著河岸邊垂下。

26　diverse [daɪˋvɝs] *a.* 多樣的

似 **various** [ˋvɛrɪəs] *a.* 各式各樣的 ③

▸ New York is well-known for its diverse cultures.
紐約因其多元文化著稱。

diversity [daɪˋvɝsətɪ]
n. 多樣性；差異

片 a wide diversity of...
　各式各樣的……
= a wide variety of...

似 **variety** [vəˋraɪətɪ] *n.* 多樣化 ③

▸ The makeup of the government does not reflect the ethnic diversity of the country.
該政府的組成結構並未反映出該國的種族多樣性。

▸ A wide diversity of ideas was presented at the meeting as to how to raise funds for the new school.
會議上提出了關於如何募款蓋新學校各種想法。

27　guardian [ˋgɑrdɪən] *n.* 守護者，保衛者；(法定) 監護人

片 a guardian angel
　守護者，守護天使

衍 **guard** [gɑrd] *n.* 守衛 ②

似 **defender** [dɪˋfɛndɚ] *n.* 防衛者

▸ The US views itself as the guardian of the values of democracy.
美國自許為民主價值的捍衛者。

▸ Nancy's uncle became her guardian after her parents died in an airplane crash.
父母死於空難之後，南希的叔叔成了她的監護人。

28　broom [brum] *n.* 掃把

衍 **broomstick** [ˋbrum͵stɪk] *n.* 帚柄

▸ Clean the floor with a broom.
用掃把將地板掃乾淨。

29 confusion [kən'fjuʒən] *n.* 混亂；混淆，困惑

片 be (left) in confusion　陷入混亂
= be (left) in chaos

▶ The whole city was in great confusion after the earthquake.
地震過後，整座城市陷入了一片混亂。

▶ The confusion of the word "borrow" for "lend" is a common mistake among English learners in Taiwan.
把『借入』一字誤以為是『借出』是臺灣學英文的學生常犯的錯。

30 destruction [dɪ'strʌkʃən] *n.* 破壞 (不可數)

▶ The destruction caused by the earthquake was immense.
這次地震引起的破壞很大。
*immense [ɪ'mɛns] *a.* 巨大的

31 diagram ['daɪə,græm] *n.* 圖解，示意圖

片 a diagram of sth　某物的示意圖

▶ The engineer showed us the diagram of the telephone circuit.
工程師讓我們看了電話線路的配置圖。

graph [græf]
n. (直線或曲線表示的) 圖表

片 (1) a bar graph　柱狀圖
(2) a line graph　線狀圖

似 chart [tʃɑrt] *n.* (塊狀) 圖表 ②
a pie chart　圓餅圖

▶ I made a line graph that showed sales increases since January.
我做了一份折線圖，圖中顯示自 1 月以來的業績成長。

statistic [stə'tɪstɪk]
n. 統計資料，統計數據 (常用複數)

片 (1) one statistic　一項統計數字
(2) two / many statistics
兩項 / 許多統計數字

▶ The latest statistics show that the amount of crime in this city is going down.
最新的統計數字顯示本市的犯罪量正在下跌中。

statistics [stə'tɪstɪks]
n. 統計學 (不可數)

▶ Statistics is a complicated science that may take years to master.
統計學是門複雜的學問，要花好幾年才能學通。

32 workplace ['wɜkples] *n.* 職場，工作場所

片 in a workplace　在職場上

▶ The meeting will tackle the issue of sexual harassment in the workplace.
這次會議將處理職場上性騷擾的議題。

▶ The speaker noted in his speech that discrimination based on sex, race, and religion is still a problem in the workplace.

演講者在演講中提到，工作場所裡性別、種族與宗教方面的歧視仍屢見不鮮。

---

33 torture [ˈtɔrtʃɚ] *vt. & n.* 折磨

似 **abuse** [əˈbjuz] *vt. &*
[əˈbjus] *n.* 虐待 ⑤

▶ Several prisoners claimed that they had been tortured both physically and mentally.

幾位囚犯聲稱他們身心遭受折磨。

▶ It was torture for me to hear you sing.

聽你唱歌真是一種酷刑。

---

34 sprinkle [ˈsprɪŋkl̩] *vt.* 撒

似 **spray** [spre] *vt.* 噴灑 ③

▶ I like to sprinkle pepper on my steak because it tastes better.

我喜歡在牛排上撒胡椒，因為那樣味道比較好。

---

35 loosen [ˈlusn̩] *vt.* 鬆開；放鬆（限制等）& *vi.* 變鬆

片 (1) loosen up　（心情）放鬆
(2) loosen one's hold / grip on...
放鬆對……的控制

似 **relax** [rɪˈlæks] *vt. & vi.* （使）放鬆 ③

反 **tighten** [ˈtaɪtn̩] *vt. & vi.* （使）變緊 ③

▶ Sean kicked off his shoes and loosened his collar and tie as soon as he got home.

尚恩一回到家便立刻踢掉鞋子、鬆開衣領和領帶。

▶ We see no sign that the government will loosen its hold on the media.

我們看不出政府會放鬆對媒體限制的跡象。

▶ Gina didn't notice that the knot in the rope had loosened.

吉娜沒注意到繩子上面的結已經鬆了。

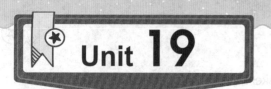

---

1 **immigrate** [`ɪməˌgret] *vi.* 移民（由外移入）

反 **emigrate** [`ɛməˌgret]
　vi. 移民（由內移出）⑥

▶ Trevor immigrated to Canada with his family when he was five.
崔佛 5 歲時和家人移民到加拿大。

immigrant [`ɪməgrənt]
n. 移民者（由外移入）

反 **emigrant** [`ɛməˌgrənt]
　n. 移民者（由內移出）⑥

▶ Canada has many immigrants from Europe.
加拿大有很多來自歐洲的移民。

▶ Mr. Wilson immigrated to Taiwan five years ago. In Taiwan, he is called an immigrant, while in the United States, his home country, he is called an emigrant.
魏爾遜先生 5 年前移民到臺灣。在臺灣，他被稱為外來移民，而在他祖國美國，他則被稱為移居國外的移民。

immigration [ˌɪmə`greʃən]
n. 移居（由外移入）

片 an immigration bureau　移民局

反 **emigration** [ˌɛmə`greʃən]
　n. 移居（由內移出）⑥

▶ Years of immigration brought many people to America.
多年的移民為美國帶來很多人。

▶ Frank went to the immigration bureau to pick up his work permit.
法蘭克去移民局領他的工作證。

---

2 **portable** [`pɔrtəbl] *a.* 可攜帶的，手提的

衍 **porter** [`pɔrtə] *n.* 搬運工，挑夫 ⑥
似 **potable** [`potəbl] *a.* 可飲用的
　potable water　飲用水

▶ Portable stereos used to be quite expensive back in the 1970s.
1970 年代手提音響相當昂貴。
*stereo [`stɛrɪo] *n.* 立體音響

---

3 **technological** [ˌtɛknə`lɑdʒɪkl] *a.* 科技的

衍 (1) **technology** [tɛk`nɑlədʒɪ]
　　n. 科技 ②
　(2) **technical** [`tɛknɪkl] *a.* 技術的 ③

▶ The steam engine was a major technological breakthrough of the 19th century.
蒸氣引擎是 19 世紀一項主要的科技突破。
*breakthrough [`brekˌθru] *n.* 突破

technician [tɛk`nɪʃən] *n.* 技師

似 (1) **engineer** [ˌɛndʒə`nɪr] *n.* 工程師 ①
　(2) **mechanic** [mə`kænɪk]
　　n. 機械工 ④

▶ I asked the receptionist to send a technician to my room to check on the heater.
我請櫃檯人員派一名技師到我房間檢查暖氣。

---

4 **hardship** [`hardʃɪp] *n.* 艱苦

片 **go through a lot of hardships**
經歷許多艱困

▶ John had gone through a lot of hardships before becoming what he is today.
約翰吃了許多苦才有今日的成就。

似 difficulty [ˈdɪfəˌkʌltɪ] *n.* 困難 ②

▶ Because of the pandemic, many people are facing financial hardship.
由於這場疫情，許多人正面臨財務困難。

5 glorious [ˈɡlɔrɪəs] *a.* 榮耀的

衍 (1) glory [ˈɡlɔrɪ] *n.* 榮耀 ③
(2) glorify [ˈɡlɔrəˌfaɪ]
vt. 頌揚，發揚光大

似 honorable [ˈɑnərəbḷ]
a. 光榮的；值得尊敬的 ⑤

▶ The nation celebrated its glorious victory with parades and speeches.
該國以遊行和演說的方式慶祝他們光榮的勝利。

6 usage [ˈjusɪdʒ] *n.* (字的) 用法

衍 use [ˈjus] *n.* (某物的) 用途 ①

▶ When trying to memorize new words, you should also know the usage of these words.
在試著記新單字時，你也應該要知道這些單字的用法。

7 sculpture [ˈskʌlptʃɚ] *n.* 雕刻 (不可數)；雕刻作品 (可數) & *vi.* 雕刻

衍 (1) sculpt [skʌlpt] *vi.* & *vt.* 雕刻
(2) sculptor [ˈskʌlptɚ]
n. 雕刻師；雕刻家 ⑥

▶ Tina is very good at sculpture and plans to pursue it as a career.
蒂娜非常擅長雕塑，並計劃將其變成職業。

▶ Hank has a large collection of sculptures by Rodin.
漢克有收藏大量羅丹的雕塑作品。

▶ Each chess piece is unique and has been carefully sculptured.
每一顆棋子都是獨一無二的，並經過精心雕刻。

8 bloom [blum] *n.* & *vi.* (觀賞植物的花) 開花

片 be in full bloom
(花) 在盛開之中；綻放著

▶ Spring is around the corner, and all the flowers in the garden are in full bloom.
春天就要來臨，花園裡的花都盛開中。

▶ Many plants bloom in spring, making gardens look beautiful.
許多植物都會在春天開花，使花園看起來很漂亮。

blossom [ˈblɑsəm]
n. & *vi.* (果樹的花) 開花

片 be in full blossom
(花) 在盛開之中；綻放著

▶ Look! The cherry trees are in full blossom.
瞧！這些櫻花樹正在盛開。

▶ The apple trees in the garden are blossoming.
花園內的蘋果樹開滿了花朵。

1909-1916

9　hardware [`hɑrd͵wɛr] *n.* 硬體（不可數）

用法　**a piece of hardware**
一件硬體（非 a hardware）

▶ We upgraded our computer hardware to improve our efficiency.
我們將電腦硬體升級以增進效率。
＊efficiency [ɪˋfɪʃənsɪ] *n.* 效率

software [ˋsɔft͵wɛr]
n. 軟體（不可數）

用法　**a piece of software**
一件軟體（非 a software）

▶ Could you assist me in installing the new software?
你能不能協助我安裝這套新軟體？
＊assist sb in + V-ing　幫助某人做……
＝ help sb (to) + V

10　idle [ˋaɪdl̩] *a.* 遊手好閒的 & *vt.* 虛度（光陰）（與副詞 away 並用）
& *vi.* 閒蕩（與副詞 around 並用）

片　(1) **idle away** one's time　閒度光陰
(2) **idle around**　鬼混，閒蕩

▶ Most clerks in the store sat idle because there were no customers.
由於沒顧客上門，店裡大部分的店員閒閒坐著沒事幹。

▶ An idle youth, a needy age.
閒蕩的青春會導致貧困的老年。/ 少壯不努力，老大徒傷悲。—— 諺語

▶ Bob idled away many hours watching baseball games.
鮑伯顧著看棒球而浪費了好幾個小時。

▶ Stop idling around and find something to do, Andy.
安迪，別再鬼混。找點事做。

idol [ˋaɪdl̩] *n.* 偶像

衍　**idolize** [ˋaɪdl̩͵aɪz]
vt. 把……當偶像崇拜

▶ The singer is an idol for many youngsters.
那歌手是許多年輕人的偶像。

11　durable [ˋd(j)ʊrəbl̩] *a.* 持久的；耐用的

衍　**duration** [d(j)ʊˋreʃən] *n.* 持久 ⑥
似　**hard-wearing** [͵hɑrdˋwɛrɪŋ]
a. 耐久的〔英〕

▶ This plastic is amazingly durable.
這種塑膠出奇地耐用。

12　elegant [ˋɛləgənt] *a.* 高雅的，有氣質的；漂亮的

衍　(1) **elegance** [ˋɛləgəns] *n.* 高雅
(2) **elegantly** [ˋɛləgəntlɪ] *adv.* 高雅地
＝ **gracefully** [ˋgresfəlɪ]
似　**graceful** [ˋgresfəl] *a.* 優雅的 ④

▶ Your aunt is one of the most elegant women I've ever met.
你的阿姨是我見過最有氣質的女士之一。

▶ Years have passed, but you are as elegant and beautiful as ever.
過了多年，妳卻高雅美麗如昔。

13　remedy [ˈrɛmədɪ] *n.* 治療法；補救（皆為可數，與介詞 for 並用）& *vt.* 補救

▶ The herb can be used as an effective remedy for headaches.
這種藥草可被用作治療頭痛的有效藥方。
＊herb [ɝb / hɝb] *n.* 藥草

▶ The politician thinks the remedy is to throw more money at the problem.
這政治家認為補救辦法是往這問題上砸更多的錢。

▶ We have taken steps to remedy the situation.
我們已採取措施來補救這情況。

14　thoughtful [ˈθɔtfəl] *a.* 體貼的；沉思的

田 It is thoughtful of sb to + V
某人做……很體貼

衍 thought [θɔt] *n.* 思想 ②

似 considerate [kənˈsɪdərət]
a. 體貼的 ⑤

▶ The thoughtful girl never forgets a friend's birthday.
這位體貼的女孩從不會忘記朋友的生日。

▶ It was thoughtful of you to assist me in installing these programs.
你人真體貼，還幫我安裝這些程式。

▶ Laura was in a thoughtful mood and didn't say much during the meeting.
蘿拉若有所思，在開會時沒說太多話。

15　youthful [ˈjuθfəl] *a.* 年輕人的；年輕的

衍 (1) young [jʌŋ] *a.* 青春的，年輕的 ①
　(2) youth [juθ] *n.* 青春，年輕；
　　青年時期；年輕人 ②
　(3) youngster [ˈjʌŋstɚ] *n.* 年輕人 ③

▶ Mrs. Jackson, though 70, still has a youthful complexion.
傑克遜夫人雖然已 70 歲，卻仍保有年輕人的膚色。
＊complexion [kəmˈplɛkʃən] *n.* 膚色

▶ This shirt is too youthful for a man of your age.
這件襯衫對像你這年紀的人來說是太年輕了。

16　breed [brid] *vt.* 繁殖；產生（惡果）& *vi.* 繁殖 & *n.* 品種

三 breed, bred [brɛd], bred
衍 (1) well-bred [ˌwɛlˈbrɛd] *a.* 有教養的
　(2) ill-bred [ˌɪlˈbrɛd] *a.* 沒教養的

▶ I'm planning on breeding horses someday.
我計劃有朝一日繁殖馬。

▶ Poverty breeds violence.
貧窮會滋生暴亂。

▶ Most animals breed in spring.
大部分動物都會在春天繁殖。

▶ My favorite breed of dog is the Akita.
我最愛的狗的品種是秋田狗。

17 drill [drɪl] *vi. & vt.* 鑽 (洞)；訓練 & *n.* 鑽頭；訓練

片 (1) drill through / into...
鑽孔鑽穿過 / 進……

(2) an electric drill　電鑽

似 (1) train [tren] *vi. & vt.* 訓練 ①

(2) exercise [ˈɛksəˌsaɪz] *n.* 練習 ①

▶ Bob drilled through the living room wall by accident.
鮑伯鑽孔不小心鑽穿過客廳的牆壁。

▶ Could you drill a hole in the wall for me?
你能不能幫我在牆上鑽個洞？

▶ Through constant practice, the coach drilled his baseball team to a high standard.
這位教練透過不斷的操練，把他的棒球隊訓練到高水準的地步。

▶ Every Wednesday, the soldiers drill from 8 a.m. to 3 p.m.
士兵們每週三從上午 8 點操練到下午 3 點。

▶ Only an electric drill is strong enough to do the job.
只有電鑽夠堅硬，可以進行這項工作。

▶ The coach said he is going to conduct another drill.
教練說他要再進行另一個訓練。

18 newcomer [ˈn(j)uˌkʌmə] *n.* 新手

似 novice [ˈnɑvɪs] *n.* 新手 ⑥

▶ Jennifer is a newcomer to the team, and that's why she has no idea about our plan yet.
珍妮佛是團隊的新人，這就是為什麼她還不知道我們的計畫。

19 infection [ɪnˈfɛkʃən] *n.* 感染

衍 (1) infect [ɪnˈfɛkt] *vt.* 感染 ⑤

(2) infectious [ɪnˈfɛkʃəs]
a. 傳染性的 ⑥

似 contagion [ˌkənˈtedʒən] *n.* 感染

▶ John hasn't recovered from his eye infection.
約翰的眼睛感染還沒復原。

20 ashamed [əˈʃemd] *a.* 感到可恥的

片 be ashamed of...　為……感到可恥
衍 shame [ʃem] *n.* 恥辱 ②

shameful [ˈʃemfəl]
a. 令人感到可恥的

比 使用 ashamed 時，主詞為人；而 shameful 則用以修飾事情。

▶ Why did you cheat on the test? I'm ashamed of you.
你考試為什麼要作弊？我真替你感到可恥。

▶ Your behavior is shameful. You really owe him an apology.
你的行為很可恥。你真應該向他道歉的。

shameless [ˈʃemləs] *a.* 無恥的

似 brazen [ˈbrezən] *a.* 肆無忌憚的

▸ I can't believe that girl is shameless enough to ask the old man to give up his seat.
真不敢相信那個女孩竟然臉皮厚到要那老人讓座。

---

21 athletic [æθˈlɛtɪk] *a.* 運動的

片 an athletic meet　運動會

衍 (1) athlete [ˈæθlit] *n.* 運動員 ③
(2) athletics [æθˈlɛtɪks]
　　n. 體育活動 (不可數) ⑤

▸ There was an athletic meet on our campus yesterday.
昨天我們校園有場運動會。

---

22 amuse [əˈmjuz] *vt.* 使娛樂，使快樂；使發笑

片 amuse sb with sth
　　以某物逗某人開心

衍 (1) entertain [ˌɛntəˈten] *vt.* 使娛樂 ④
(2) please [pliz] *vt.* 取悅 ①

▸ I was not at all amused when I heard Tom's joke.
當我聽了湯姆的笑話時，一點也不覺得好笑。

▸ The clown amused the children with magic tricks.
小丑用魔術把戲逗那些小朋友。

---

amusing [əˈmjuzɪŋ]
a. 好笑的；有趣的

似 (1) interesting [ˈɪnt(ə)rɪstɪŋ]
　　a. 有趣的 ①
(2) funny [ˈfʌnɪ] *a.* 滑稽逗笑的 ①

▸ At first I thought Dudley was boring, but as we talked, I found him very amusing.
一開始我以為杜德里很無趣，但當我們談過話後，我才發現他是個很寶的人。

▸ I read an amusing story in today's newspaper.
我在今天的報紙上看到一篇有趣的報導。

---

amusement [əˈmjuzmənt]
n. 娛樂；消遣，娛樂活動

片 an amusement park
　　遊樂園，兒童樂園

似 (1) pastime [ˈpæsˌtaɪm] *n.* 消遣 ⑥
(2) entertainment [ˌɛntəˈtenmənt]
　　n. 娛樂 ④

▸ The father pretended he was a dog for his children's amusement.
父親假裝自己是一隻狗，以逗孩子們玩。

▸ There are video games and other amusements at my uncle's house.
我叔叔家裡有很多電動玩具及其他可供娛樂的東西。

▸ The children are looking forward to going to the amusement park.
孩子們期待著去遊樂園。

---

23 dusty [ˈdʌstɪ] *a.* 蒙上灰塵的

衍 dust [dʌst] *n.* 灰塵 ③

▸ As we entered the old house, we saw dusty books all over the floor.
我們進入老房子時，看到地上到處都是蒙上灰塵的書。

24 telegraph [ˈtɛləˌgræf] n. 電報，電信 & vt. 用電報發送

囝 (1) by telegraph　透過 / 用電報 (傳)
(2) telegraph a letter / message to
sb
用電報傳一封信 / 訊息給某人

衍 telecommunications
[ˌtɛləkəˌmjunəˈkeʃənz]
n. 電信 / 訊 (恆用複數) ⑥

▶ As soon as Ben learned the news by telegraph, he
was flying high.
班一透過電報得知這個消息，他高興極了。

▶ Mr. Bell telegraphed an urgent message to me before
leaving for Boston.
貝爾先生啟程前往波士頓前，曾用電報傳給我一份緊急訊
息。

telegram [ˈtɛləˌgræm] n. 電報

▶ Years ago, sending a telegram was the only way of
communicating quickly with people that lived far
away.
多年前，與遠方的人快速聯絡只能靠打電報。

25 mislead [mɪsˈlid] vt. 誤導

目 mislead, misled [mɪsˈlɛd], misled
囝 mislead sb into + V-ing
誤導某人做……

▶ The salesperson misled the old man into believing
that this medicine can cure everything.
銷售員誤導老人相信這藥能治癒一切。

misleading [mɪsˈlidɪŋ] a. 誤導人的

似 false [fɔls] a. 錯誤的，不真實的 ②

▶ Misleading advertisements are prohibited by law.
誤導人的廣告為法律所禁止。
＊prohibit [prəˈhɪbɪt] vt. 禁止

26 sledge [slɛdʒ] n. 雪橇〔英〕(= sled [slɛd]〔美〕)

▶ Have you ever ridden on a sledge? It's quite exciting.
你坐過雪橇嗎？那很刺激。

sleigh [sle]
n. (由馬、馴鹿等拉的) 大型敞篷雪橇

▶ In the winter, we like to ride in old-fashioned
sleighs.
在冬天我們喜歡乘坐老式大型敞篷雪橇。

27 plumber [ˈplʌmɚ] n. 水管工 (人)

▶ Call the plumber and ask when he's coming to fix
our burst pipe.
打電話給水管工人，問問他什麼時候來修破掉的水管。
＊burst [bɝst] a. 破裂的

28 crunchy [ˈkrʌntʃɪ] a. 清脆的

衍 crunch [krʌntʃ] vt. 清脆的咬嚼

▶ I like to eat raw carrots because they are nice and
crunchy.
我喜歡吃生紅蘿蔔因為它們味美又脆。

29　alternative [ɔlˈtɝnətɪv] *n.* 選擇，替代方案 & *a.* 替代的

(1) have no alternative / option / choice but to + V
除做……外別無選擇

(2) an alternative way / route / method / approach
替代方法 / 路線 / 方法 / 辦法

(3) alternative energy
替代性能源 (非傳統性能源)

▶ A huge typhoon is coming, so we have no alternative but to cancel the trip.
強烈的颱風即將來臨，因此我們只有取消行程別無選擇了。

▶ An alternative way would be to travel by plane.
另一種可供選擇的方式就是搭飛機。

30　autograph [ˈɔtəˌɡræf] *n.* (尤指名人的) 親筆簽名 & *vt.* (名人) 簽名於

似 signature [ˈsɪɡnətʃɚ]
n. (簽在公文等上的) 簽名，簽署 ④

▶ The little boy asked that famous basketball player for his autograph.
小男孩向那位知名籃球員要簽名。

▶ I asked the famous author to autograph my copy of his book.
我請那位名作家在我買的他的書上簽名。

31　beggar [ˈbɛɡɚ] *n.* 乞丐

衍 beg [bɛɡ] *vi.* & *vt.* 乞求 ②

似 tramp [træmp] *n.* 流浪漢，乞丐

▶ I feel very sympathetic toward beggars on the street.
我對街上的乞丐感到很同情。

32　experimental [ɪkˌspɛrəˈmɛntl̩] *a.* 實驗性的

似 trial [ˈtraɪəl] *a.* 試驗的 ②

▶ The project is still in its experimental stages and won't be put into practice until next year.
該計畫仍處於實驗階段，要到明年後才會付諸實施。

33　muddy [ˈmʌdɪ] *a.* 泥濘的

▶ Our car got muddy when we went camping.
去露營的時候，我們的車變得泥濘不堪。

1 cube [kjub] *n.* 立方體；方塊物 & *vt.* 把(食物)切成小方塊 ☐

衍 an ice cube [ˈaɪs ˌkjub] *n.* 冰塊

▶ The mouse ate three cubes of cheese today.
這隻老鼠今天吃了 3 塊起司。

▶ Lauren cubed the cheese into bite-sized pieces.
羅倫把乳酪切成一口就能吃下去的大小。

cubic [ˈkjubɪk]
a. 立方體的；(數學) 立方的

片 a cubic meter   一立方公尺

延伸 a square meter   一平方公尺

▶ The artist's new creation is a cubic structure made out of shells.
這藝術家的新創作是一個由貝殼製成的立方體結構。

▶ We measure space in cubic meters.
我們以立方公尺的單位測量空間。

2 murmur [ˈmɝmɚ] *n.* 低語聲 & *vi.* & *vt.* 低語說 & *vi.* 私下抱怨 ☐

片 (1) in a(n) + 形容詞 + murmur
以……的方式低語

(2) murmur against...
私下抱怨……

似 (1) whisper [ˈ(h)wɪspɚ]
vt. & *vi.* 低語，耳語 ②

(2) complain [kəmˈplen]
vt. & *vi.* 抱怨 ③

▶ "I like you," John said in a low murmur.
約翰小聲地說:『我喜歡妳』。

▶ "I can't stand him," Joe murmured.
喬小聲地說:『我受不了他了』。

▶ Lisa murmured something to me, but I couldn't understand what she said.
麗莎對我喃喃低語，但我聽不懂她在說什麼。

▶ I was very angry when I found those guys were murmuring against me.
我發現這些人私下在抱怨我時我很火大。

3 biography [baɪˈɑgrəfɪ] *n.* 傳記 ☐

衍 (1) biographer [baɪˈɑgrəfɚ]
n. 傳記作家

(2) biographical [ˌbaɪəˈgræfɪkḷ] /
biographic [ˌbaɪəˈgræfɪk]
a. 傳記的
a biographical / biographic
story   傳記故事

▶ Dr. Wilson authorized Nick to write his biography.
威爾森博士授權尼克為他的傳記執筆。

＊authorize [ˈɔθəˌraɪz] *vt.* 授權

autobiography [ˌɔtəbaɪˈɑgrəfɪ]
n. 自傳

衍 (1) autobiographer [ˌɔtəbaɪˈɑgrəfɚ]
n. 自傳作者

▶ We laughed and told Sam that it was a bit early for him to write his autobiography.
我們笑著告訴山姆，現在寫自傳對他而言實在嫌早了點。

Level 4 Unit 20

(2) autobiographical
[ˌɔtəˌbaɪə`græfɪkḷ] /
autobiographic
[ˌɔtəˌbaɪə`græfɪk] *a.* 自傳的

4 interact [ˌɪntə`ækt] *vi.* 互動

🔒 interact with... 與……互動

▸ Tom interacts well with other kids at school.
湯姆在學校和其他的小朋友互動良好。

interaction [ˌɪntə`ækʃən] *n.* 互動
(常與介詞 with 或 between 並用)

▸ I don't know that man well, so I have little interaction with him.
我跟那人不是很熟，因此我跟他沒什麼互動。

▸ The problem is that there is not enough interaction between the couple.
問題在於這對夫妻間的互動不足。

interactive [ˌɪntə`æktɪv]
a. 相互作用的

▸ Kids can learn the importance of cooperation through interactive activities.
孩子可透過互動性的活動學到合作的重要性。

5 disorder [dɪs`ɔrdə] *n.* 無秩序，雜亂 & *vt.* 使混亂

🔒 be in disorder / chaos
陷入雜亂的狀況
= be a mess

衍 disorderly [dɪs`ɔrdəlɪ]
a. 混亂的，雜亂的

似 (1) mess [mɛs] *n.* 雜亂 ③
(2) chaos [`keas] *n.* 混亂，雜亂 ⑤

反 order [`ɔrdə] *n.* 秩序 ①

▸ How come your room is always in disorder?
= How come your room is always in chaos?
= How come your room is always a mess?
你的房間為何老是很雜亂？

▸ The newborn baby completely disordered their lives.
新生兒完全打亂了他們的生活。

6 learned [`lɜnɪd] *a.* 學問淵博的

衍 (1) learning [`lɜnɪŋ] *n.* 學識 ③
(2) learn [lɜn] *vt.* 學習 ①

似 knowledgeable [`nɑlɪdʒəbḷ]
a. 有知識的 ⑥

▸ Mr. Laurens is learned but modest, which is why we all respect him.
羅倫斯先生博學多聞卻虛懷若谷，這也是我們都很尊敬他的原因。

7 passive [`pæsɪv] *a.* 被動的

🔒 passive smoking 二手菸
衍 passively [`pæsɪvlɪ] *adv.* 被動地
反 active [`æktɪv] *a.* 主動的 ②

▸ Robert is too passive to take action.
羅伯特太被動了，以致於都不採取行動。

▶ Passive smoking is more detrimental to one's health than first-hand smoking.

二手菸危害個人健康要比直接吸菸還大。

＊detrimental [ˌdɛtrɪ'mɛntl̩] *a.* 有害的

＝harmful ['hɑrmfəl]

8　freshman ['frɛʃmən] *n.* 大一學生；高一學生

複 freshmen ['frɛʃmɛn]

延伸 (1) sophomore ['sɑfəˌmɔr]
　　n. 大二學生 ⑤

(2) junior ['dʒunjɚ] *n.* 大三學生；
　　年少者 & *a.* 資淺的 ③

(3) senior ['sinjɚ] *n.* 大四學生；
　　年長者 & *a.* 地位較高的 ③

▶ In the college where Willy studies, all freshmen are required to live in the dorms.

在威利念的那所大學，所有的大一學生規定都要住校。

＊dorm [dɔrm] *n.* 宿舍（是 dormitory 的縮寫）

▶ My sister is very excited because she is going to be a freshman in high school this year.

我妹妹很興奮，因為她今年將成為高一新生。

9　harsh [hɑrʃ] *a.* 嚴厲的

片 be harsh on sb　對某人很嚴苛
＝ be hard on sb
＝ be strict with sb

似 severe [sə'vɪr] *a.* 嚴厲的 ④

▶ The punishment for such a young student was too harsh.

這懲罰對這麼年輕的學生來說太嚴苛了些。

▶ Don't you think you're a little too harsh on your children?

你難道不覺得你對孩子太過嚴厲了嗎？

10　partnership ['pɑrtnɚˌʃɪp] *n.* 合夥關係

片 work / be in partnership with...
　　與……合夥

衍 partner ['pɑrtnɚ] *n.* 合夥人，搭檔 ②

▶ I have worked in partnership with Lydia for years, and we've been getting along very well.

我跟莉迪雅合夥共事了好幾年，一直相處得很好。

11　privacy ['praɪvəsɪ] *n.* 隱私，私生活

衍 (1) private ['praɪvɪt]
　　a. 私人的，個人的 ②

(2) privately ['praɪvɪtlɪ] *adv.* 私下

▶ Some media always violate the privacy of celebrities.

有些媒體一直侵犯名人的隱私。

12　ferry ['fɛrɪ] *n.* 渡輪 & *vt.* (定時) 運送

三 ferry, ferried ['fɛrɪd], ferried
片 take a ferry　搭渡輪

▶ If you want to go to that island, you have to take the ferry.

如果你想要去那座島，就要搭渡輪。

▶ The company used to ferry people across the river.

那家公司以前常載人過河。

13 sway [swe] vi. 搖擺 & vt. 影響 & n. 動搖，影響

片 (1) sway back and forth　來回搖擺
　　(2) be under sb's sway
　　　　受某人的影響

似 influence [ˈɪnfluəns] vt. & n. 影響 ②

▶ The palm trees are swaying back and forth in the wind.
棕櫚樹在風中來回搖擺。

▶ Don't let that politician's speech sway your decision.
別讓那政治人物的演講動搖你的決定。

▶ Mary has dated that handsome boy only three times, and she is completely under his sway now.
瑪莉跟那帥哥約會才 3 次，現在卻已完全受他擺布了。

14 nowadays [ˈnaʊəˌdez] adv. 現今

似 (1) these days　現今，這年頭
　　(2) today [təˈde] adv. & n. 今天 ①
　　(3) now [naʊ] adv. 現在 ①

▶ Yoga, which is helpful to one's body and mind, is very popular nowadays.
瑜珈對人的身心都很有幫助，現在非常流行。
*yoga [ˈjogə] n. 瑜珈

15 dense [dɛns] a. 稠密的

片 a dense population　人口稠密
衍 (1) densely [ˈdɛnslɪ] adv. 稠密地
　　(2) density [ˈdɛnsətɪ] n. 密度 ⑤
反 sparse [spɑrs] a. (人口) 稀少的

▶ We have a dense population in Taipei.
= Taipei is densely populated.
臺北人口稠密。

16 overnight [ˌovɚˈnaɪt] adv. & a. 一夕之間；整晚

似 (1) instantly [ˈɪnstəntlɪ] adv. 頃刻間
　　(2) suddenly [ˈsʌdn̩lɪ] adv. 突然間

▶ The lottery winner became a millionaire overnight.
這名樂透得主一夕之間成了百萬富翁。

▶ I stayed at my friend's house overnight doing homework.
我整晚待在我朋友家做功課。

▶ After Phoebe released that song, she became an overnight star.
菲比發行了那首歌之後，一夕之間成了明星。

▶ I am taking the overnight train to Moscow.
我要搭夜班火車去莫斯科。

17 socket [ˈsɑkɪt] n. 插座

片 put a plug into a socket
　　把插頭插入插座
延伸 plug [plʌg] n. 插頭 ③

▶ The light was not on because I forgot to put the plug into the socket.
這盞燈不亮，因為我忘了把插頭插入插座。

Level 4　Unit 20

18 alcohol [ˈælkəˌhɔl] *n.* 酒；酒精 (指各種含酒精的酒類，如啤酒、烈酒或葡萄酒)

衍 **alcoholic** [ˌælkəˈhɔlɪk]
　a. 含酒精的 & *n.* 酗酒者 ⑤

似 (1) **liquor** [ˈlɪkɚ] *n.* 烈酒
　　(如白蘭地、威士忌、金門高粱酒) ④
　(2) **wine** [waɪn] *n.* 葡萄酒，水果酒 ②

延伸 **low-alcohol** [ˌloˈælkəˌhɔl]
　a. 低酒精含量的

▶ I never drink alcohol because I get drunk easily.
　我從不喝酒因為我很容易醉。

▶ David drinks low-alcohol beer only.
　大衛只喝低酒精含量的啤酒。

19 messenger [ˈmɛsṇdʒɚ] *n.* 送信者

片 **a bike messenger**　腳踏車快遞 (尤指在大都會地區幫快遞公司用騎腳踏車的方式送信的人)

衍 **message** [ˈmɛsɪdʒ] *n.* 訊息 ②

▶ Vic has decided to get a part-time job as a bike messenger.
　維克決定兼職做腳踏車快遞。

20 settler [ˈsɛtlɚ] *n.* 墾荒者，移居者

衍 (1) **settle** [ˈsɛtḷ] *vt.* 解決 (糾紛) &
　vi. 定居；安頓 ②
　(2) **settlement** [ˈsɛtḷmənt]
　n. 定居點 ②

似 (1) **colonizer** [ˈkɑləˌnaɪzɚ]
　n. 殖民地開拓者
　(2) **pioneer** [ˌpaɪəˈnɪr] *n.* 拓荒者 ④

▶ Tommy's grandfather was one of the early settlers of Australia.
　湯米的祖父是澳洲早期拓荒者之一。

21 equality [ɪˈkwɑlətɪ] *n.* 平等，同等

衍 **equal** [ˈikwəl]
　a. 相等的 & *vt.* 匹敵，比得上；等於
　& *n.* 可與匹敵的人，地位相等的人 ②

▶ We should treat all people on the basis of equality.
　我們應以平等的基礎對待所有的人。

22 bargain [ˈbɑrgən] *n.* 很划算的東西 (可數) & *vi.* 講價，討價還價

片 (1) **a real bargain**　實在物超所值
　(2) **bargain with sb**　與某人討價還價

▶ The second-hand car Taylor bought the other day was a real bargain.
　泰勒前幾天買的那輛二手車實在是物超所值。

▶ Take it or leave it. I won't bargain with you.
　要就買，不要就拉倒。我不會跟你討價還價。

23　resign [rɪˋzaɪn] *vi.* 辭職 & *vt.* 順從

目 resign oneself to + N/V-ing
順從 / 接受……的命運

似 quit [kwɪt] *vi.* & *vt.* 辭職 (三態同形) ③

▶ Having been an editor for nearly ten years, Stan has decided to resign and try teaching for a change.
史坦做編輯快 10 年了，決定辭職並換跑道試試教書。

▶ My car broke down in the middle of nowhere, so I resigned myself to a long walk home.
我的車子在荒郊野外拋錨，因此我只好接受長途走路回家的命運了。

resignation [ˏrɛzɪgˋneʃən] *n.* 辭職

目 (1) a letter of resignation　辭職信
(2) accept sb's resignation
接受某人的辭職

▶ The employee handed in his letter of resignation to the boss.
這員工向老闆遞出了辭職信。

▶ The president accepted the minister's resignation after he was involved in a sex scandal.
部長捲入性醜聞後，總統接受了他的辭職。

24　miserable [ˋmɪzərəbḷ] *a.* 痛苦的，悲慘的；(天氣) 陰霾的，不好的

衍 misery [ˋmɪzərɪ] *n.* 不幸，悲慘 ③

▶ Little did I know that the famous actress had a miserable childhood.
我一點都不知道這位知名女演員童年過得很悲慘。

▶ It has been raining here for almost a month, and the low temperature is unbearable. I'm really sick of such miserable weather.
這裡連下了將近 1 個月的雨，低溫讓人受不了。這種爛天氣我真是受夠了。

25　perfume [ˋpɝfjum / pɝˋfjum] *n.* 香水 (不可數) & *vt.* 使充滿香氣

目 (1) a bottle of perfume　一瓶香水
(2) wear perfume　擦香水 (表狀態)

▶ I bought my wife a bottle of perfume for her birthday.
我買了一瓶香水給我太太當作她的生日禮物。

▶ Are you wearing the perfume I bought for you the other day?
你是擦我前幾天買給你的香水嗎？

▶ The lilies perfumed the air in the living room.
百合花讓客廳的空氣充滿了香味。

26　charity [ˋtʃærətɪ] *n.* 慈善 (不可數)；慈善機構 (可數)；慈善事業 (不可數)

衍 charitable [ˋtʃærətəbḷ]
a. 仁慈的，慈善的 ⑥

a charitable organization
慈善機構

= a charity

▶ Charity begins at home.
博愛始於家門，施捨先及親友。—— 諺語

▶ The football game will raise money for local charities.
這場足球賽將為地方慈善機構募款。

27 **civilian** [səˈvɪljən] *a.* 平民的 & *n.* 平民

衍 civil [ˈsɪvḷ] *a.* 平民的 ③
civil rights　公民權（恆用複數）

▶ After twenty years in the military, Jack returned to civilian life.
20 年軍旅生涯後，傑克回復平民的生活。

▶ The troops were accused of attacking unarmed civilians.
軍隊被指控攻擊沒有武裝的平民。

civilization [ˌsɪvḷaɪˈzeʃən]
n. 文明（不可數）

片 Western civilization　西方文明

衍 (1) civilize [ˈsɪvəˌlaɪz]
　　vt. 將……文明化 ⑥
(2) civilized [ˈsɪvəˌlaɪzd]
　　a. 文明的；開化的
(3) uncivilized [ʌnˈsɪvəˌlaɪzd]
　　a. 未開化的；不文明的

▶ These books are about the history of Western civilization.
這些書談的是西方文明史。

28 **refugee** [ˌrɛfjuˈdʒi] *n.* 難民

衍 refuge [ˈrɛfjudʒ] *n.* 避難；避難所 ⑤

▶ After the war, many refugees had no place to live.
戰爭後，許多難民無家可歸。

29 **solar** [ˈsolɚ] *a.* 太陽的；與太陽有關的

片 (1) solar energy　　　太陽能
(2) a solar calendar　陽曆
(3) solar electricity　太陽能發電
延伸 (1) a lunar calendar　農／陰曆
(2) (the) Lunar New Year
　　陰曆年，農曆新年

▶ Solar energy is a clean form of power.
太陽能是一種很乾淨的能源。

▶ Solar electricity is gaining in popularity.
太陽能發電日趨流行。

30 **spear** [spɪr] *n.* 矛 & *vt.* & *vi.* 刺

延伸 shield [ʃild] *n.* 盾 ⑤

▶ Some people still use spears when hunting.
有些人打獵時還是使用矛。

▶ Jane speared the last piece of steak with her fork.
珍用叉子叉了最後一塊牛排。

▶ The hunter speared and wounded the wild animal.
獵人用矛刺傷了野獸。

31 rusty [ˈrʌstɪ] *a.* 生鏽的；(技術等) 生疏的

▶ We can tell by the rusty iron gate that this house has been empty for years.
我們從生鏽的鐵門可以看出這棟房子已經空了好多年了。

▶ My badminton is rusty these days. I had better practice soon, or I might be beaten by my niece.
我的羽毛球球技現在很生疏。我最好儘快練習，否則我可能會打輸我侄女。

32 seize [siz] *vt.* 抓住；突然感到……；奪取，占領

片 be seized by fear / terror
突然感到害怕起來

用法 凡表『抓住』的動詞 (如 seize、hold、take、grab、grasp) 應與介詞 by 並用，用法如下：seize / hold /... sb by the + 部位　抓住某人的某部位

▶ I held Mary by the hand and said, "Will you marry me?"
我握住瑪莉的手說：『妳願意嫁給我嗎？』

▶ The bank robber was seized by the police when he tried to escape.
銀行搶匪想逃跑時，被警方一把抓住。

▶ The boy seized the girl by the arm and begged her not to leave.
男孩抓住女孩的手臂，求她不要離開。

▶ I was seized by fear when I noticed that a stranger was following me.
當我發覺有陌生人在跟蹤我時，我突然感到害怕起來。

▶ The rebels seized the capital and exiled the Prime Minister soon after the military coup.
軍事政變後，叛軍很快占領了首都並放逐總理。
　*exile [ˈɛgzaɪl / ˈɛksaɪl] *vt.* 放逐
　　coup [ku] *n.* 政變

33 bin [bɪn] *n.* 垃圾桶〔英〕(= trash can〔美〕)

▶ After reading the note, Ryan tossed it into the bin.
萊恩看完那張紙條後，就把它丟到垃圾桶裡。

34 commander [kəˈmændɚ] *n.* 指揮官

▶ The commander admitted defeat and decided to withdraw troops from the country.
該指揮官承認戰敗，並決定從該國撤軍。

35 overcoat [ˈovɚˌkot] *n.* 大衣

延伸 (1) windbreaker [ˈwɪndˌbrekɚ]
　　　 n. 風衣
　　 (2) raincoat [ˈrenˌkot] *n.* 雨衣 ②

▶ A witness said the suspect wore a heavy overcoat and sunglasses.
目擊者指出，嫌犯穿著大衣並戴著太陽眼鏡。

Level 4　Unit 20

413

36 orientation [ˌorɪɛnˈteʃən] n. 走向，目標；新生 / 新員工的訓練

片 an orientation ceremony
新生 / 人訓練

似 (1) aim [em] n. 目標 ②
(2) tendency [ˈtɛndənsɪ]
  n. 趨勢，走向 ④
(3) training [ˈtrenɪŋ] n. 訓練

▶ William was disappointed to find the non-profit organization has a commercial orientation.
威廉發現這間非營利組織是有商業導向時感到很失望。

▶ The orientation ceremony will be held a week before school officially starts.
新生訓練將於正式開學前一個星期舉行。

37 knob [nɑb] n. 門把

片 turn a knob　轉動門把

▶ The little girl didn't know there was a fantasy world behind the door before she turned the knob.
小女孩在轉動門把之前，並不知道門後面有個奇幻世界。

38 reduction [rɪˈdʌkʃən] n. 減少；折扣

似 (1) decrease [ˈdikris] n. 減少
  & vi. & vt. [dɪˈkris] 減少 ③
(2) discount [ˈdɪskaʊnt] n. 折扣 ③
反 increase [ˈɪnkris] n. 增加
& vi. & vt. [ɪnˈkris] 增加 ②

▶ The rapid reduction in rainforest has caused global warming to get worse.
雨林迅速減少使全球暖化更嚴重。

▶ The supermarket advertised many price reductions.
該超市做了許多減價活動的廣告。

39 gender [ˈdʒɛndɚ] n. 性別

片 a gender difference　性別差異
似 sex [sɛks] n. 性別；性 (愛) ②

▶ My sister and her husband don't want to know the gender of their baby because they want it to be a surprise.
我姊姊和她老公不想知道他們孩子的性別，因為他們希望這是個驚喜。

▶ Gender differences are not as solid as they appear to be.
性別差異並非如表面看來那般牢不可破。

40 librarian [laɪˈbrɛrɪən] n. 圖書館員

衍 library [ˈlaɪˌbrɛrɪ] n. 圖書館 ①

▶ The librarian helped the students check out books.
圖書館員協助學生借閱書籍。

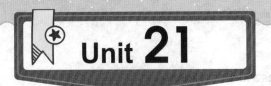

1 wreck [rɛk] *vt.* 毀壞；船難 & *n.* 失事的船隻／汽車／飛機（的殘骸）；車禍（事故）

衍 wreckage [ˋrɛkɪdʒ] *n.* 殘骸

似 (1) destroy [dɪˋstrɔɪ] *vt.* 毀壞 ③
(2) ruin [ˋruɪn] *vt.* 毀壞 ④
(3) shipwreck [ˋʃɪp͵rɛk]
　　n. 船難，海難

▶ I wrecked my car this morning, but luckily no one was injured.
今天早上我把車撞毀了，所幸無人受傷。

▶ The ship was wrecked by a fire on board.
這艘船被船上的一場大火給毀了。

▶ A team was sent to examine the wreck of the plane.
一個小組被派去檢查該飛機的殘骸。

▶ No survivors were found in the car wreck.
這場車禍沒有生還者。

2 grief [grif] *n.* 悲傷，悲痛

片 be overcome with grief
悲傷到無法控制

衍 grieve [griv] *vt. & vi.* (使) 悲痛 ⑤

似 (1) misery [ˋmɪzərɪ] *n.* 悲慘，痛苦 ③
(2) extreme sadness　極度悲傷

▶ Grief can be so strong that it prevents us from doing anything.
悲傷的情緒可以強烈到使我們無法做任何事情。

▶ The old woman was overcome with grief when she learned that her son had been killed on the battlefield.
老婆婆獲知兒子戰死沙場時，悲傷得痛不欲生。

3 sincerity [sɪnˋsɛrətɪ] *n.* 誠懇

片 a person of sincerity　很誠懇的人

衍 sincere [sɪnˋsɪr] *a.* 誠懇的 ③

▶ Peter is a person of sincerity and is well respected in the community.
彼得是個很誠懇的人，在社區內很受尊重。

4 witch [wɪtʃ] *n.* 女巫

似 sorceress [ˋsɔrsərɪs]
　　n. 女術士，女魔法師

▶ The witch cast a spell on the frog.
巫婆對青蛙施咒。
＊spell [spɛl] *n.* 咒語

wizard [ˋwɪzəd] *n.* 男巫

似 sorcerer [ˋsɔrsərə]
　　n. 男術士，男魔法師

▶ The wizard was wearing a black cloak and a pointed hat.
這巫師身穿黑披風，頭戴尖帽子。
＊cloak [klok] *n.* 披風，斗篷

5 keen [kin] *a.* 激烈的；敏銳的；渴望的

片 (1) have a keen eye for...
　　對……有敏銳的眼光
(2) be keen on + V-ing
　　渴望要做……

▶ Though the competition was keen, we kept going and finally succeeded.
雖然這場比賽競爭很激烈，但是我們不斷努力終於獲得成功。

> Marcie has a keen eye for beauty.
> 瑪西很有審美觀念。

> Sandy is keen on studying abroad someday.
> 珊蒂巴不得有一天能出國深造。

6 accountant [əˈkauntənt] n. 會計師

衍 (1) account [əˈkaunt] n. 帳戶 ②
    open an account at a bank
    在銀行開戶

(2) accounting [əˈkauntɪŋ]
    n. 會計學 ⑤

> That firm is seeking an experienced accountant to join their team.
> 那家公司正在物色一名經驗豐富的會計師加入他們的團隊。

7 admirable [ˈædmərəbl̩] a. 值得讚美的，令人欽佩的

衍 admire [ədˈmaɪr] vt. 欽佩；欣賞 ③

似 praiseworthy [ˈprezˌwɝðɪ]
   a. 值得稱讚的

> The boy's heroic behavior is admirable.
> 那男孩英勇的行為令人欽佩。

admiration [ˌædməˈreʃən] n. 讚賞

片 watch (...) in admiration
   讚賞地看著 (……)

> Barbara watched her son in admiration as he danced with his bride.
> 芭芭拉讚賞不已地看著她兒子與新娘共舞。

8 apology [əˈpɑlədʒɪ] n. 道歉，歉意

複 apologies [əˈpɑlədʒɪz]

片 (1) accept one's apology
       接受某人道歉

(2) make an apology to sb
    對某人表示歉意

衍 apologize [əˈpɑləˌdʒaɪz]
   vi. 道歉，賠罪 ③

> Please accept my apologies for keeping you waiting so long.
> 讓您等候那麼久，請接受我的道歉。

> You're so impolite. You should make an apology to the teacher.
> 你太沒禮貌了。你應該要向老師道歉。

9 arms [ɑrmz] n. 武器 (恆用複數)

片 arms talks 限武談判 (恆用複數)

衍 arm [ɑrm] n. 手臂 ①
   hold A in B's arms
   把 A 擁在 B 的懷中

> John held his girlfriend in his arms, gently kissing her.
> 約翰把他女友擁在懷裡，溫柔地吻著她。

> The police asked the robbers to lay down their arms.
> 警察要求搶匪放下武器。

> After three rounds of arms talks, both countries reached an agreement.
> 經過 3 回合的限武談判後，兩國終於達成協議。

10　clumsy [ˋklʌmzɪ] *a.* 笨拙的

似 awkward [ˋɔkwəd] *a.* 笨拙的 ③

▶ Randy is so clumsy that he cannot hold a cup of coffee without spilling it.
藍迪真是笨拙，所以手中拿著咖啡時，咖啡一定會濺出來。

11　germ [dʒɝm] *n.* 細菌，病菌

似 bacterium [bækˋtɪrɪəm] *n.* 細菌
（複數為 bacteria [bækˋtɪrɪə]）③

▶ Remember to wash your hands to get rid of any germs.
記得要洗手以去除細菌。

virus [ˋvaɪrəs] *n.* (濾過性) 病毒
片 a computer virus　電腦病毒

▶ Don't open any email that is sent by someone you don't know because it might contain computer viruses.
不要打開任何你不認識的人所發送的電子郵件，因為這郵件可能會有電腦病毒。

12　bald [bɔld] *a.* 禿頭的

片 go bald　逐漸變成禿頭
似 bold [bold] *a.* 大膽的 ③

▶ Duncan wears a toupee to cover his bald head.
鄧肯戴了頂假髮來蓋住他的禿頭。
＊toupee [tuˋpe] *n.* (男士用的) 假髮
　wig [wɪg] *n.* (多為女士用的) 假髮

▶ Jack is only twenty, but he is going bald.
傑克才 20 歲，卻漸漸禿頭了。

13　bankrupt [ˋbæŋkrʌpt] *a.* 破產的 & *vt.* 使破產 & *n.* (經法院宣告的) 破產者

片 go bankrupt　破產
= go into bankruptcy

▶ Because of a poor investment, Billy went bankrupt.
由於投資不當，比利破產了。

▶ Brian feared that the loss of his job would bankrupt him.
布萊恩擔心失去工作會使他身無分文。

▶ Emma was declared a bankrupt after the failure of her business.
艾瑪生意失敗後被宣告破產。

bankruptcy [ˋbæŋkrʌptsɪ] *n.* 破產
片 declare bankruptcy　宣布破產

▶ We thought that the big business would declare bankruptcy, but it didn't.
我們原本以為那家大公司會宣布破產，但卻沒有。

14　broke [brok] *a.* 身無分文的

片 go broke　破產的
= go bankrupt
似 broken [ˋbrokən] *a.* 破損的

▶ I can't lend you any money; I'm as broke as you.
我沒什麼錢可借你；我跟你一樣身無分文。

 2114-2121

> Many businesses went broke during the Great Depression.
> 許多公司於經濟大蕭條期間都破產了。

penniless [ˈpɛnɪləs] *a.* 身無分文的
> The old guy was penniless and had to sleep on the street.
> 那位老先生身無分文，必須露宿街頭。

15 basin [ˈbesn̩] *n.* 盆地；洗手臺〔英〕(= sink [sɪŋk]〔美〕)

> Taipei city is built on a basin.
> 臺北市建立在一個盆地上。

> You need to scrub the basin harder.
> 你刷這個洗手臺要更用力一點。
> *scrub [skrʌb] *vt.* 用力擦洗

16 biology [baɪˈɑlədʒɪ] *n.* 生物學

衍 (1) biological [ˌbaɪəˈlɑdʒɪkl̩]
　　a. 生物的 ⑤
(2) biologist [baɪˈɑlədʒɪst]
　　n. 生物學家

> Biology is the study of all living things.
> 生物學乃是研究所有生物的一門學問。

17 blend [blɛnd] *vi. & vt.* 混合；很協調 & *n.* 混合

片 (1) blend A with B　將 A 與 B 混合
　= mix A with B
(2) A blend well with B
　　A 與 B 很搭 / 協調
似 mix [mɪks] *vt. & vi. & n.* 混合 ②

> Just blend the flour with two cups of water.
> 就把麵粉和兩杯水混在一起。

> Mom likes to blend fruits together with milk.
> 媽媽喜歡把水果和牛奶混合在一起。

> To my surprise, the rap and the classical music blend together well.
> 令我驚訝的是，這饒舌音樂和古典音樂很搭。

> Your new hair color blends well with your skin.
> 妳新染的髮色和妳的皮膚很搭。

> This coffee is a blend of beans from Brazil and Colombia.
> 這咖啡是巴西和哥倫比亞的咖啡豆混合而成的。

18 blink [blɪŋk] *vi.* 眨眼睛；(光) 閃爍 & *vt.* 眨 (眼睛) & *n.* 眨眼睛

片 (1) blink one's eye(s)　眨眼
(2) in the blink of an eye
　　突然間，一剎那間
　= in an instant

> When I asked Lucy the question, she just looked at me and blinked.
> 當我問露西問題時，她只是看著我眨了眨眼。

▶ The Christmas lights blinked in the night.
聖誕裝飾燈在夜晚閃爍發光。

▶ I knew Jenny was lying because she blinked her eyes a lot.
我知道珍妮在說謊因為她不斷地眨眼睛。

▶ We watched the magician closely, but the rabbit disappeared in the blink of an eye.
我們緊盯著魔術師看,但兔子卻突然之間消失了。

wink [wɪŋk]

vi. 眨(眼) & *n.* 眨眼,使眼色

🔑 (1) wink at sb　對某人眨眼,使眼色
= give sb a wink
(2) not get a wink of sleep
沒闔過眼,沒睡覺
= not sleep a wink

▶ I thought John was being serious, but then he winked at me.
我以為約翰是認真的,但是他對我眨眼。

▶ Mary gave me a wink, asking me to stop talking.
瑪莉對我使眼色,要我別再說話。

▶ I was so worried about the test today that I didn't get a wink of sleep last night.
= I was so worried about the test today that I didn't sleep a wink last night.
我很擔心今天的考試,所以昨晚都沒睡。

19　**calorie** [ˈkælərɪ] *n.* 卡路里

🔲 calories

▶ I can't believe that Anna calculates how many calories she takes in every day.
我不敢相信安娜每天都會計算她攝取了多少卡路里。

20　**cargo** [ˈkɑrgo] *n.* 貨物

🔑 a cargo plane　貨機

▶ The ship's cargo will be unloaded tomorrow.
這艘船的貨物將於明天卸下。

▶ The cargo plane is carrying emergency equipment to the region.
貨機正向該區運送緊急設備。

21　**cliff** [klɪf] *n.* 懸崖

🔲 precipice [ˈprɛsəpɪs] *n.* 斷崖

▶ The car fell off the cliff, and the driver plunged to his death.
車子掉下懸崖,駕駛人墜落身亡。
*plunge [plʌndʒ] *vi.* 跳(入),衝(入)

◁)) 2122-2132

22 congratulate [kənˈɡrætʃəˌlet] vt. 道賀，慶賀

片 congratulate sb on sth
就某事恭賀某人

衍 congratulations [kənˌɡrætʃəˈleʃənz]
n. 恭賀 (恆用複數) ②

▶ Let's congratulate the boss on his marriage.
我們去向老闆道賀他的婚事吧。

23 conquer [ˈkɑŋkɚ] vt. 征服；克服

衍 conquest [ˈkɑŋkwɛst] n. 征服 ⑥

▶ When was England conquered by the Normans?
英格蘭是在何時被諾曼人征服的？

▶ We are still fighting to conquer cancer.
我們仍在為克服癌症而奮鬥。

24 cord [kɔrd] n. 線 (或細繩)；電線

似 chord [kɔrd] n. 合弦 ⑤

▶ Can I borrow some cord to tie these old books together?
我可以跟你借些繩子把這些舊書綁起來嗎？

▶ Where is the phone cord?
電話線在哪兒？

25 courtesy [ˈkɜtəsɪ] n. 禮貌

片 (by) courtesy of + 機構
由某機構免費提供

衍 courteous [ˈkɜtɪəs] a. 有禮貌的 ⑤

似 politeness [pəˈlaɪtnəs] n. 禮貌

▶ As a courtesy to other audience members, we ask that all cellphones be turned off during the performance.
基於尊重他人，請各位在表演期間將手機關機。

▶ Courtesy costs nothing.
禮貌不花錢 / 禮多人不怪。—— 諺語

▶ Everyone can get two bottles of wine at the end of the party, courtesy of the manufacturer.
派對結束時，每個人都可有兩瓶葡萄酒，由廠商免費提供。

26 troublesome [ˈtrʌblsəm] a. 棘手的；麻煩的

片 (1) a troublesome problem
棘手的問題
= a thorny problem
(2) a troublesome boy
(愛惹麻煩且) 令人頭疼的男孩

似 thorny [ˈθɔrnɪ] a. 棘手的

▶ The whole class was discussing the troublesome problem of air pollution.
全班正在討論空氣汙染這個棘手的問題。

▶ If it's not too troublesome, could you help me carry this suitcase?
如果不太麻煩的話，可不可以請你幫我提這只行李箱呢？

▶ Tom is such a troublesome boy and often creates problems.
湯姆是個令人頭疼的男孩，經常製造麻煩。

27 significance [sɪɡˈnɪfəkəns] *n.* 意義；重要性

🈁 be of great significance 很重要
= be of great importance
= be very important

▶ I did not understand the significance of my teacher's remark.
我不懂老師話中的含意。

▶ This letter was of great significance to my grandfather.
這封信對我爺爺很重要。

28 vacancy [ˈvekənsɪ] *n.* 空房；空缺

複 vacancies [ˈvekənsɪz]
🈁 a job vacancy 職缺
= a job opening
衍 vacant [ˈvekənt]
  a. 空缺的；有空房的 ③

▶ None of the hotels in downtown New York have any vacancies on New Year's Eve.
除夕夜紐約市中心的飯店都沒有空房了。

▶ Ben told me that there are some job vacancies in his company.
班告訴我說他的公司有一些職缺。

29 peep [pip] *vi.* 偷看

🈁 peep at... 偷看……

▶ Stop peeping at me like that. It embarrasses me.
不要那樣偷看我嘛。這令我怪難為情的。

30 merchant [ˈmɝtʃənt] *n.* 商人

比 businessman 及 merchant 均指
『商人』。businessman 的含意較廣，
任何從商的人均為 businessman。
而 merchant 專指從事大批貨物買賣
的商人，也就是批發商 (wholesaler
[ˈholˌselɚ])。

▶ Shakespeare's *The Merchant of Venice* is my favorite literary work.
莎翁的《威尼斯商人》是我最喜歡的文學作品。
*literary [ˈlɪtəˌrɛrɪ] *a.* 文學的

▶ John's father is a corn merchant.
約翰的爸爸是玉米批發商。

31 dodge [dɑdʒ] *vt.* 閃躲，迴避 (拳頭、子彈、問題等)

🈁 dodge a question 閃躲 / 迴避問題
衍 dodgeball [ˈdɑdʒˌbɔl] *n.* 躲避球
  play dodgeball 打躲避球

▶ Tom tried to hit me when I called him names, but I dodged the blow.
我罵湯姆時，他想打我，但我閃開了他的攻擊。
*call sb names 辱罵某人

▶ The actor dodged questions about his drug scandal.
這位演員迴避了有關他毒品醜聞的問題。

32 ambiguous [æmˈbɪɡjuəs] *a.* 模稜兩可的

似 vague [veg] *a.* 模糊的；含糊的 ⑤

▶ The wording of this contract is ambiguous. Thus, we shall not sign it.
這份合約的用字模稜兩可。因此，我們不應該簽約。
*wording [ˈwɝdɪŋ] *n.* 措詞

2133-2140

33 cane [ken] n. 手杖 & vt. 用杖打 (某人)

衍 (1) sugar cane / sugarcane
甘蔗 (不可數)
(2) cane sugar 蔗糖 (不可數)

▶ Oliver gave his father a cane as a gift for his 70th birthday.
奧利佛送給他老爸一根手杖，慶祝他 70 歲生日。

▶ In some countries, people who steal will be caned.
在某些國家，偷竊的人會被施以杖刑。

34 burglar [ˈbɝglɚ] n. 竊賊，破門盜竊者

衍 (1) burglary [ˈbɝglərɪ] n. 盜竊
(2) burglarize [ˈbɝglə,raɪz]
vt. 破門盜竊

似 (1) thief [θif] n. 賊 ②
(2) robber [ˈrabɚ] n. 搶匪 ④

▶ According to the police, burglars broke into the superstar's house last night.
據警方說法，昨晚竊賊闖入了這位超級巨星的房子。

35 coarse [kɔrs] a. 粗劣的；粗鄙的

片 coarse language 粗俗的言詞
= vulgar language

似 (1) inferior [ɪnˈfɪrɪɚ] a. 質量次等的 ③
(2) vulgar [ˈvʌlgɚ] a. 粗俗的，下流的

▶ Jerry bought a sweater made of coarse wool just because it is cheap.
傑瑞買了一件毛質粗劣的毛衣，只因為它很便宜。

▶ The boy never uses coarse language because he is afraid of being punished by his parents.
這男孩從不使用粗俗的語言，因為他害怕被父母懲罰。

36 kettle [ˈkɛtl̩] n. (煮開水用的) 水壺

似 teapot [ˈti,pat] n. 小茶壺 ②

▶ Is the kettle boiling, darling? Would you please take a look?
親愛的，水壺的水煮開了嗎？你能看一下嗎？

▶ You call him a fatty, but you're not exactly slim yourself. That's like the pot calling the kettle black.
你叫他小胖，但你自己也沒多瘦。那不過是五十步笑百步。
＊slim [slɪm] a. 苗條的

37 radar [ˈredar] n. 雷達

延伸 radar 是 Radio Detecting and Ranging 的縮寫。

▶ Our radar detected three enemy submarines in our waters just moments ago.
不久前在領海內我們的雷達偵測到 3 艘敵方潛水艇。
＊waters [ˈwatɚz] n. (某個國家的) 水域 (恆用複數)

38 intuition [ˌɪnt(j)ʊˈɪʃən] *n.* 直覺

衍 intuitive [ɪnˈt(j)ʊɪtɪv] *a.* 直覺的
似 instinct [ˈɪnstɪŋkt] *n.* 直覺 ④
   by instinct   藉由本能的

▸ Intuition told Sophia that her boyfriend had been cheating on her.
蘇菲亞的直覺告訴她，她的男友一直對她不忠。
*cheat on sb   對某人感情不忠

39 gown [ɡaʊn] *n.* 禮服；長袍

片 (1) a dressing gown
     (男女皆可穿的) 浴袍
   (2) an evening gown
     (女性穿的) 一般晚禮服
   (3) a ball gown
     (女性穿的) 舞會 / 最正式禮服 (為一種 evening gown)
   (4) a wedding gown
     (女性穿的) 婚紗禮服
   (5) a hospital gown   手術服

▸ Many Taiwanese people are not used to wearing a dressing gown at home.
許多臺灣人不習慣在家穿浴袍。

▸ Jessica was dressed in a gorgeous evening gown at the banquet.
潔西卡在宴會上穿了一襲迷人的晚禮服。
*banquet [ˈbæŋkwɪt] *n.* 盛宴

▸ You look so beautiful in that ball gown.
你穿那件舞會禮服看起來真漂亮。

▸ The patient was asked to put on a hospital gown before his operation.
手術前，該病患被要求換上手術服。

40 flea [fli] *n.* 跳蚤

片 a flea market
   跳蚤市場 (買賣舊貨的市場)
似 flee [fli] *vi.* & *vt.* 逃離 ④

▸ This shampoo should help get rid of my dog's fleas.
這個洗髮精應可幫助除去我的狗身上的跳蚤。

▸ Sometimes you can get a bargain at a flea market.
有時你可在跳蚤市場買到很划算的東西。

1　cue [kju] *n. & vt.* 暗示，提示

閂 miss a cue　錯過（提詞的）暗示

似 (1) clue [klu] *n.* 提示，線索 ③
　　(2) hint [hɪnt] *n.* 暗示 ③

▶ The actor missed his cue and said the lines at the wrong time.

這演員錯過暗示，接著說的時間、臺詞都不對。

▶ The director will cue you when it's your turn to say something.

輪到你說話時導播會給你提示。

2　cushion [ˈkuʃən] *n.* 軟墊，靠枕 & *vt.* 緩和衝擊

似 (1) soften [ˈsɔfn̩] *vt.* 緩和 ⑤
　　(2) lessen [ˈlɛsn̩] *vt.* 減少 ⑥

▶ I made a new cushion for the couch.

我為這張沙發做了個新靠枕。

▶ Luckily, the snow cushioned the climber's fall, so he was only slightly injured.

幸好，這堆雪緩衝了登山客墜落的衝擊力，因此他只受到輕傷。

3　deadline [ˈdɛdˌlaɪn] *n.* 截止日，最後期限

閂 meet a deadline
　　趕在截止日前完成

▶ Reporters always work under great pressure to meet the deadline.

記者總是在趕截稿時間的極大壓力下工作。

4　digest [daɪˈdʒɛst] *vt.* 消化 & [ˈdaɪˌdʒɛst] *n.* 摘要

衍 (1) digestive [dəˈdʒɛstɪv / daɪˈdʒɛstɪv]
　　　a. 消化的

　　　a digestive system　消化系統

　　(2) digestion [dəˈdʒɛstʃən]
　　　n. 消化作用 ⑤

▶ They say it takes eight hours to digest the food you've eaten.

據說食物要花 8 個小時才能消化完畢。

▶ The email contains a digest of the week's major news stories.

這封電子郵件包含了本週主要新聞的摘要。

5　digital [ˈdɪdʒɪtl̩] *a.* 數位的

閂 (1) a digital camera　　數位相機
　　(2) digital music　　　數位音樂

衍 (1) digitalize [ˈdɪdʒɪtl̩ˌaɪz] *vt.* 數位化
　　(2) digit [ˈdɪdʒɪt]
　　　n. （從 0 到 9 的任何一個）數字

▶ Young as he is, the engineer has a six-digit income.

這位工程師雖然年輕，收入卻達 6 位數。

▶ Nowadays, smartphones contain digital cameras, and that's why digital cameras themselves have become less popular.

如今，智慧手機包含了數位相機，這就是為什麼數位相機本身變得沒那麼受歡迎的原因。

▶ Sales of digital music albums greatly outnumber sales of physical albums.

數位音樂專輯的銷量大大超過了實體專輯的銷量。

6 diligent [ˈdɪlədʒnt] a. 勤勉的

似 (1) industrious [ɪnˈdʌstrɪəs]
　　　a. 勤勞的
　　(2) assiduous [əˈsɪdʒʊəs] a. 勤奮的
　　(3) hardworking [ˌhɑrdˈwɜkɪŋ]
　　　a. 努力的

▶ The diligent student received the highest grade on the math test.
這位用功的學生數學考了最高分。

---

diligence [ˈdɪlədʒəns] n. 勤勉

似 (1) hard work　努力 (視作名詞)
　　　work hard　努力 (work 是動詞)
　　(2) industry [ˈɪndʌstrɪ]
　　　n. 勤勉；工業 ②

▶ With diligence, you can master anything.
只要努力，什麼事你都能做得好。
*master [ˈmæstə] vt. 精通

Level 4　Unit 22

7 diploma [dɪˈplomə] n. (有學位的) 文憑

似 certificate [səˈtɪfəkɪt]
　n. 證明書；(沒有學位的) 結業證書 ⑤

似 (1) diplomat [ˈdɪpləmæt] n. 外交官 ④
　　(2) degree [dɪˈgri] n. 學位 ②
　　　a doctor's / master's /
　　　bachelor's degree
　　　博士 / 碩士 / 學士學位

▶ After receiving his diploma, Luke jumped for joy.
在接到文憑之後，路克高興得雀躍不已。

▶ These days, you can hardly find a decent job without a college diploma.
這年頭若是沒有大學文憑，要找到像樣的工作幾乎很難。
*decent [ˈdisn̩t] a. 像樣的，還不錯的

8 disgust [dɪsˈgʌst] n. 厭惡 & vt. 使人厭惡，使人噁心

片 with disgust　帶著厭惡的心情

似 (1) dislike [dɪsˈlaɪk]
　　　n. 厭惡，不喜歡 ③
　　(2) sicken [ˈsɪkən] vt. 使噁心，使厭惡

▶ The victim's parents looked at the murderer with disgust.
受害者的父母厭惡地看著那個兇手。

▶ Stay away from me. Your bad breath disgusts me.
別接近我。你的口臭令我反胃。

---

disgusted [dɪsˈgʌstɪd]
a. 感到厭惡的 (修飾人)

片 be disgusted with / by...
　對……感到厭惡

▶ We are all disgusted with the bad smell coming from the chemical factory.
化學工廠傳出來的惡臭令我們作嘔。

---

disgusting [dɪsˈgʌstɪŋ]
a. 令人厭惡的 (修飾事物)

似 sickening [ˈsɪkənɪŋ] a. 令人作嘔的

▶ The boy is picking his nose. It is disgusting.
那男孩在挖鼻孔。真是噁心。

9 dye [daɪ] vt. 將……染色 & n. 染料

- 目 dye, dyed, dyed (現在分詞為 dyeing)
- 片 (1) dye sth + 顏色　將某物染成……色
  (2) a tube of hair dye　一條染髮劑
- 似 die [daɪ] vi. 死亡 ①
  三態為：die, died, died (現在分詞為 dying)

▶ Sarah dyed her hair red, which looked awful.
莎拉把頭髮染紅，真難看。

▶ This brand of dye is the best for the fabric you chose.
這個品牌的染色劑對你挑的這塊布料是最好的。
＊fabric [ˈfæbrɪk] n. 織物，布料

10 endanger [ɪnˈdendʒɚ] vt. 使有危險，危及

- 衍 (1) danger [ˈdendʒɚ] n. 危險 ②
  put... in danger　使……陷入險境
  (2) dangerous [ˈdendʒərəs]
  a. 危險的 ①
  (3) endangered [ɪnˈdendʒɚd]
  a. 瀕臨絕種的
  an endangered species / animal　瀕臨絕種的物種 / 動物

▶ Drunk driving endangers everyone's life.
酒醉駕駛危及每個人的生命。

▶ We must protect all endangered animals, such as sea turtles.
我們必須要保護所有如海龜等瀕臨絕種的動物。

11 feast [fist] n. 宴會；饗宴 & vi. 大快朵頤

- 片 (1) feast on...　大快朵頤（食物）
  (2) feast one's eyes on...
  盡情欣賞……，飽覽……
- 似 banquet [ˈbæŋkwɪt] n. 饗宴 ⑥
  a state banquet　國宴

▶ We have a big Thanksgiving Day feast every year.
我們每年都有盛大的感恩節大餐宴會。

▶ The film festival should be a real feast for moviegoers.
電影節對愛看電影的人來說應該是一大樂事。

▶ Tonight we are going to feast on turkey and mashed potatoes.
今晚我們要吃一頓火雞和馬鈴薯泥大餐。
＊mashed [mæʃt] a. 搗成糊 / 泥狀的

▶ I feasted my eyes on the beauty of the valley, feeling as if I were in heaven.
我飽覽山谷之美，覺得自己彷彿置身於天堂般。

12 fierce [fɪrs] a. 激烈的

- 似 intense [ɪnˈtɛns] a. 激烈的 ④

▶ The price war sparked off fierce competition between the two companies.
價格戰引發了這兩家公司間的激烈競爭。
＊spark off...　激起……

13 fireplace [ˈfaɪrˌples] n. 壁爐

- sit by / around the fireplace
  坐在壁爐旁 / 附近

  ▶ I enjoy sitting by the fireplace, reading a novel.
  我喜歡坐在壁爐旁邊看小說。

14 flatter [ˈflætə] vt. 諂媚，拍……的馬屁；感到高興 / 榮幸，受寵若驚 (此意常用被動)

- flatter sb 拍某人馬屁，巴結某人
  = curry favor with sb
  = butter sb up
- flattery [ˈflætərɪ] n. 諂媚

  ▶ Don't trust people who flatter you.
  = Don't trust people who curry favor with you.
  = Don't trust people who butter you up.
  不要相信那些拍你馬屁的人。

  ▶ I was flattered when Sean said that I was handsome.
  當尚恩說我很帥時，我受寵若驚。

15 fluent [ˈfluənt] a. 流利的

- be fluent in + 語言 流利使用某語言
- (1) fluency [ˈfluənsɪ] n. 流利 ⑤
  (2) fluently [ˈfluəntlɪ] adv. 流利地

  ▶ "I'm afraid I'll never be fluent in Chinese," said Mack.
  梅克說：『恐怕我的中文永遠都說不流利。』

  ▶ Zora has never been to the States, but she speaks fluent English.
  卓拉從未去過美國，不過卻能說一口流利的英語。

16 stingy [ˈstɪndʒɪ] a. 小器的

- (1) miserly [ˈmaɪzəlɪ] a. 吝嗇的
  (2) cheap [tʃip] a. 小氣的 ①
- generous [ˈdʒɛnərəs] a. 慷慨的 ②

  ▶ The stingy old man won't give any money to charity.
  那個吝嗇的老頭一毛錢也不會捐給慈善事業。

17 flush [flʌʃ] vt. 沖 (馬桶) & vi. 沖 (馬桶)；臉紅 & n. 沖 (馬桶)；紅暈

- (1) flush a toilet 沖馬桶
  = give a toilet a flush
  (2) feel a flush of anger
  感到一陣憤怒
- blush [blʌʃ] vi. & n. 臉紅 ⑤

  ▶ Don't forget to flush the toilet after use.
  = Don't forget to give the toilet a flush after use.
  使用廁所後別忘了要沖馬桶。

  ▶ The toilet isn't working properly; it keeps flushing.
  馬桶不能正常運作；它一直在沖水。

  ▶ Anna flushed / blushed when Charles touched her hand.
  查爾斯碰她的手時，安娜臉紅了。

  ▶ I had to give the toilet another flush.
  我得要再沖馬桶一次。

  ▶ Rudy felt a flush of anger when he saw the man yell at his mother.
  魯迪看到那男子對他母親大叫時感到一陣憤怒。

18 fossil [ˈfɑsl̩] n. 化石 & a. 化石的

片 (1) a living fossil 　活化石
(2) an old fossil 　老頑固
(3) fossil fuel [ˈfɑsl̩ ˌfjuəl]
　 化石燃料 (如石油、煤、天然氣等)

▶ If you are lucky, you can find some animal fossils on the beach.
你運氣夠好的話，在海灘上會找到一些動物化石。

▶ The horseshoe crab is an example of a living fossil.
鱟是一個活化石的例子。

▶ Don't listen to Ricky; he's just an old fossil.
別聽瑞奇的，他只是個老頑固。

▶ Scientists recently discovered two new kinds of fossil plants.
科學家最近發現了兩種新的化石植物。

▶ Many scientists are now looking for energy sources that can replace fossil fuels.
科學家目前正在尋找能替代化石燃料的能源。

19 gene [dʒin] n. 基因，遺傳因子

衍 (1) genetics [dʒəˈnɛtɪks] n. 遺傳學 ⑤
(2) genetic [dʒəˈnɛtɪk]
　 a. 基因的，遺傳 (學) 的 ⑤

▶ Some people have genes that may put them at risk of cancer.
有些人的基因可能會使他們有罹癌的風險。
＊put sb at risk of＋疾病　使某人有得到某疾病的風險

20 goods [gʊdz] n. 貨品 (恆用複數)

似 article [ˈɑrtɪkl̩] n. 物品 (可數) ②

▶ As of next month, there will be tax increases on a wide range of goods.
從下個月開始，許多種貨物的課稅將會增加。

21 grammar [ˈɡræmɚ] n. 文法 (不可數)

片 a grammar school 　小學〔美〕；
　 重點中學，文法學校〔英〕

衍 grammarian [ɡrəˈmɛrɪən]
　 n. 文法家；研究文法的人

▶ English grammar is difficult to master without years of study.
沒有多年的研習，英文文法很難精通。

▶ My great-grandfather graduated from the grammar school in this town.
我曾祖父從這個鎮上的小學畢業。

grammatical [ɡrəˈmætɪkl̩]
a. 文法上的

片 make a grammatical error / mistake　犯文法錯誤
＝ make a grammar error / mistake

▶ The grammatical / grammar errors you made in your composition could have been avoided if you had been more careful.
你若更仔細一點的話，你作文中的那些文法錯誤原本是可以避免的。

22 **habitual** [hə'bɪtʃʊəl] *a.* 習慣的，慣常的

衍 habit ['hæbɪt] *n.* 習慣 ①
be in the habit of + V-ing
有做……的習慣

似 (1) regular ['rɛgjələ]
a. 規律的，常態的 ②
(2) routine [ru'tin] *a.* 常規的 ③

▶ Owen used to be a habitual smoker.
歐文以前是個菸癮大的人。

▶ The habitual thief was finally arrested by the police.
警方終於逮捕了這名慣竊。

23 **helicopter** ['hɛlə,kɑptə] *n.* 直昇機

似 (1) chopper ['tʃɑpə]
n. 直昇機 (非正式說法)
(2) copter ['kɑptə] *n.* 直昇機
(3) whirlybird ['(h)wɜlɪ,bɜd]
n. 直昇機

▶ The TV news helicopter flew above the traffic jam and reported the conditions to the public.
電視新聞採訪用的直昇機飛到塞車現場上空，把路況向民眾報導。

24 **honeymoon** ['hʌnɪ,mun] *n.* 蜜月 & *vi.* 度蜜月

片 go on (one's) honeymoon
(某人) 去度蜜月

衍 honey ['hʌnɪ] *n.* 蜂蜜 ①

▶ We spent our honeymoon on an island off the coast of Greece.
我們在希臘外海的一座島上度蜜月。

▶ The newlyweds are planning to go on their honeymoon to Phuket in Thailand.
這對新婚夫婦計劃要到泰國普吉島度蜜月。

▶ My brother and his wife honeymooned in Venice, Italy last month.
我哥哥和他老婆上個月在義大利威尼斯度蜜月。

25 **hook** [hʊk] *n.* 鉤子 & *vt.* 鉤住；用鉤 (釣魚)；(手臂等) 繞住

片 by hook or by crook   不擇手段
= one way or another
= no matter what
*crook [krʊk]
n. (牧羊人等用的) 曲柄杖

▶ Please hang your helmet on the hook by the door.
請將你的安全帽掛在門邊的鉤子上。

▶ The man vowed to attain his goal by hook or by crook.
這名男子誓言要不擇手段達到他的目的。

▶ Mark hooked the trailer onto the back of his car.
馬克把拖車掛在他的車子後面。

▶ I hooked some trout in the river behind our house.
我在我們家後面的河裡釣了幾條鱒魚。
*trout [traʊt] *n.* 鱒魚 (複數為 trout 或 trouts)

▶ Maggie hooked her arms around her boyfriend's neck and whispered something in his ear.
瑪姬雙手繞住她男友的脖子，在他耳邊講悄悄話。

Level 4　Unit 22

26 horrify [ˈhɔrəˌfaɪ] vt. 使恐懼

目 horrify, horrified [ˈhɔrəˌfaɪd], horrified

衍 (1) horror [ˈhɔrə] n. 恐懼 ③
(2) horrible [ˈhɔrəbḷ] a. 恐怖的 ③

似 (1) scare [skɛr] vt. 使害怕 ②
(2) terrify [ˈtɛrəˌfaɪ]
    vt. 使害怕，使恐懼 ⑤

▶ Jasmine's parents were horrified when she passed out.
潔思敏昏過去時，她父母都嚇壞了。
*pass out　昏倒
=faint [fent]

27 idiom [ˈɪdɪəm] n. 慣用語，成語

衍 idiomatic [ˌɪdɪəˈmætɪk] a. 慣用語的
    an idiomatic expression　慣用語
= an idiom

似 proverb [ˈprɑvɚb] n. 諺語 ⑥

▶ An idiom can be a group of words, a phrase, or an expression that has a different meaning from the one the individual words have.
慣用語指的是某詞組、片語或表達語，其意思與獨立單詞的意思不同。

▶ In English, "call it a day" is an idiom.
英文中的『call it a day』是慣用語。
*call it a day　到此收工 / 停工

▶ Occasional use of idioms adds fun to your writing, but don't overuse them.
偶爾使用慣用語會讓你的寫作平添趣味，不過不可過度使用它們。

28 inflation [ɪnˈfleʃən] n. 通貨膨脹，物價上漲

反 deflation [dɪˈfleʃən]
    n. 通貨緊縮，物價下跌

▶ The government carried out several policies to control inflation.
政府實施了幾項政策來控制通貨膨脹。

▶ The Minister of Economic Affairs called for an urgent meeting to discuss inflation.
經濟部長要求召開緊急會議討論通膨問題。

29 input [ˈɪnˌpʊt] vt. 輸入 & n. 輸入 (電腦等) 的資料 (不可數)；提供 (意見)

目 input, input / inputted, input / inputted

片 input sth into a computer
    將某物輸入電腦

反 output [ˈaʊtˌpʊt] vt. (自電腦) 輸出 & n. 生產量；(自電腦等) 輸出的資料 ⑤

似 store [stɔr] vt. 儲存 ①

▶ We will input your information into our computer.
我們會將你的資料輸入到我們的電腦中。

▶ We'll check the input and see what information we can use.
我們會查閱輸入的資料，看看有哪些資訊可供我們使用。

▶ The professor provided us with a lot of helpful advice. We're really grateful for his input.
教授給我們許多很有幫助的建議。我們真的很感激他提供的意見。

30 insult [ɪnˋsʌlt] vt. & [ˋɪnsʌlt] n. 侮辱

片 be an insult to sb/sth
對某人 / 某物而言是種侮辱

似 (1) offend [əˋfɛnd] vt. 冒犯 ④
(2) offense [əˋfɛns] n. 冒犯 ④

▶ Abby is very angry because Jennifer insulted her.
艾比非常生氣，因為珍妮佛侮辱了她。

▶ Your question is an insult to my intelligence.
你的問題對我的智力是種汙辱。

31 giggle [ˋgɪgḷ] vi. & n. 傻笑

片 burst into a fit of giggles
突然咯咯地笑個不停

▶ The girls giggled after Thomas told them a silly joke.
湯瑪士講完一個愚蠢的笑話後，女孩們各個都咯咯地笑。

▶ Ned burst into a fit of giggles while he was on the phone.
奈德講電話時突然咯咯地笑個不停。

32 mule [mjul] n. 騾子

片 be as stubborn as a mule
極為固執

▶ A mule is a cross between a horse and a donkey.
騾子是馬與驢子雜交所生的後代。

33 pickle [ˋpɪkḷ] n. 醃 / 泡菜；醃黃瓜 & vt. 醃

片 be in a pickle 陷於窘困，處於苦境
= be in a difficult situation

▶ Lee loves to eat pickles straight from the jar.
李喜歡直接從罐子裡吃醃菜。

▶ I had German sausage and a pickle for my main course tonight.
今晚我的主餐是德國香腸與醃黃瓜。
＊sausage [ˋsɔsɪdʒ] n. 香腸，臘腸

▶ Herman was in a pickle with a taxi driver after his motorcycle bumped into the cab.
赫曼的機車撞上計程車後，他就與那司機僵持不下。

▶ The chef pickled the fish in brine.
廚師用鹽水醃魚。

34 raisin [ˋrezṇ] n. 葡萄乾 (可數)

似 resin [ˋrɛzɪn] n. 樹脂 (不可數)

▶ Tina put raisins on the cheese cake.
蒂娜在起司蛋糕上放了葡萄乾。

35 skyscraper [ˋskaɪˌskrepɚ] n. 摩天高樓

似 a high-rise building 高聳的大樓

▶ Almost all big cities have skyscrapers.
幾乎各大都市都有摩天大樓。

36 scoop [skup] *n.* 勺子；一勺的量；獨家新聞

片 (1) a measuring scoop　量匙
(2) a scoop of...　一勺……
(3) an inside scoop　獨家內幕

似 exclusive [ɪkˋsklusɪv] *n.* 獨家新聞 ⑤

▶ Have you seen my measuring scoops? I'm going to make cookies tomorrow.
你有看到我的量匙嗎？我明天要做餅乾。

▶ I bought two scoops of ice cream from the old man.
我跟那個老伯伯買了兩球冰淇淋。

▶ Everyone's interested in the inside scoop on that scandal.
大家都很想知道那則醜聞的獨家內幕。

37 tickle [ˋtɪkl] *vt.* 搔……癢

▶ Jane tickled the baby's feet to make her laugh.
珍搔小寶寶的腳，想逗她笑。

38 aquarium [əˋkwɛrɪəm] *n.* 水族館；水族箱

似 (1) fishbowl [ˋfɪʃˌbol]
　　n. (小型如碗狀的) 魚缸
(2) a fish tank　（長方形）魚缸

▶ Harry went to the local aquarium and watched the shark feeding show.
哈利到當地的水族館看了鯊魚餵食秀。

▶ An aquarium is usually much bigger than a fish tank.
水族箱通常比魚缸大得多。

39 homeland [ˋhomˌlænd] *n.* 祖國，故鄉

似 (1) motherland [ˋmʌðəˌlænd]
　　n. 祖國
(2) fatherland [ˋfɑðəˌlænd] *n.* 祖國

▶ Many people appreciate their homeland more after living abroad for a while.
許多人在國外住過一陣子後，更懂得欣賞故鄉的好。

40 paw [pɔ] *n.* 爪 & *vi.* & *vt.* 用爪子抓

片 paw at...　用爪子抓……

▶ The tiger's huge paws and sharp teeth pose a great threat to other animals in the area.
這隻老虎的巨爪和利齒對這地區其他動物形成很大的威脅。
*pose a threat to sb/sth　對某人 / 某物構成威脅

▶ The cat was pawing at the window.
貓在用爪子抓窗戶。

▶ The dog pawed the bedroom door, but John wouldn't let him inside.
狗用爪子抓著臥室的門，但約翰不讓他進去。

41 creep [krip] vi. 爬行；緩慢前進

目 creep, crept [krɛpt], crept

似 crawl [krɔl] vi. 爬 ③

▶ Lisa screamed when she found a roach creeping down the wall.
麗莎看見蟑螂從牆上爬下來時，尖叫了一聲。
＊roach [rotʃ] n. 蟑螂（是 cockroach [ˋkɑk͵rotʃ] 的縮寫）

42 claw [klɔ] vi. & vt. (用爪子) 抓 & n. 爪子

用 (1) claw at...　用爪子抓……
(2) claw the way up...
用爪子爬上……

▶ The hungry cat clawed at his master's leg.
饑餓的貓咪抓著主人的腿。

▶ The cat clawed its way up the tree.
小貓爬上樹。

▶ Bears have big and scary claws.
熊的爪子既大又恐怖。

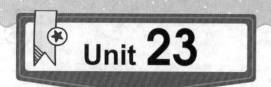

Unit 23

2301-2309

---

1 **makeup** [ˈmekˌʌp] *n.* 化妝 (不可數) ☐

片 wear makeup　上妝 (表「狀態」)

似 cosmetics [kɑzˈmɛtɪks]
　n. 化妝品 (恆用複數) ⑥

延伸 (1) a make-up (test)　補考
　(2) make up　和解 / 好

▶ Alice wore heavy makeup to hide her pimples.
愛麗絲化濃妝來掩蓋她的粉刺。
*pimple [ˈpɪmpl̩] *n.* 粉刺

---

2 **marathon** [ˈmærəˌθɑn] *n.* 馬拉松 (比賽) ☐

片 run a marathon　跑馬拉松

▶ I'm going to take part in the marathon in Osaka, Japan next year. Would you like to join me?
明年我會參加日本大阪的馬拉松比賽。你想加入我嗎？

---

3 **microscope** [ˈmaɪkrəˌskop] *n.* 顯微鏡 ☐

衍 scope [skop] *n.* 觀測器 ⑤

延伸 (1) binoculars [bɪˈnɑkjələz]
　n. 雙筒望遠鏡 (恆用複數)
　a pair of binoculars
　一副雙筒望遠鏡
　(2) a magnifying glass　放大鏡

▶ We used microscopes to study red blood cells in our class today.
我們今天課堂上用顯微鏡研究紅血球。

---

telescope [ˈtɛləˌskop]
n. (單筒) 望遠鏡

▶ As a child, I enjoyed seeing the stars through a telescope.
我小時候喜歡透過望遠鏡觀看星星。 ☐

---

4 **nationality** [ˌnæʃəˈnælətɪ] *n.* 國籍；民族 ☐

片 dual nationality　雙重國籍

衍 (1) nation [ˈneʃən] *n.* 國家 ②
　(2) national [ˈnæʃənl̩]
　　a. 全國的；國家的 ①
　(3) nationalism [ˈnæʃənl̩ˌɪzəm]
　　n. 民族主義 ⑥

▶ What's your nationality?
你的國籍是哪一國？

▶ A person with dual nationality is a citizen of two countries at the same time.
具有雙重國籍的人是同時為兩個國家的公民。

▶ You can see many different nationalities in London.
在倫敦你可以看到許多不同民族的人。

---

5 **recycle** [riˈsaɪkl̩] *vt.* 重複利用，回收 ☐

衍 recyclable [riˈsaɪkləbl̩]
　a. 可回收利用的

▶ Waste paper can be recycled into toilet tissue.
廢紙可以回收製成衛生紙。

6 revenge [rɪˈvɛndʒ] n. 報復 & vt. 為⋯⋯報仇

⑪ take revenge on sb 對某人報仇
= revenge / avenge oneself on sb

▶ That young man took revenge on the bad guy for his father's death.
= That young man revenged / avenged himself on the bad guy for his father's death.
那年輕人為父親的死亡向該壞蛋報仇。

avenge [əˈvɛndʒ] vt. 報仇

⑪ revenge 及 avenge 可作及物動詞，均指『報仇』。avenge 是直接接要報仇的事物。但 revenge 及 avenge 皆可用於以下此片語：revenge / avenge oneself on sb 對某人報仇

▶ I vow to avenge my wife's death.
我誓言要為妻子之死報仇。

7 sightseeing [ˈsaɪtˌsiɪŋ] n. 觀光，遊覽

⑪ go sightseeing 去觀光 (遊覽)
衍 sight [saɪt] n. 觀光地；視覺 ①
the sights 風景名勝 (恆用複數)

▶ Joanna and Luke love going sightseeing whenever they are on vacation.
瓊安娜和路克每次度假時喜歡去觀光遊覽。

8 signature [ˈsɪgnətʃɚ] n. 簽字 & a. 為 (某人) 所特有的

⑪ forge one's signature
偽造某人的簽名
衍 sign [saɪn] vt. 簽字 ①
似 autograph [ˈɔtəˌgræf] n. 親筆簽名 ④
⑪ signature 指在公文或支票等上的簽字，autograph 則指供作紀念的親筆簽名。我們拿書讓作者簽名時，
不可說：
May I have your signature? (✕)
應說：
May I have your autograph? (○)
我可以請您簽個名嗎？

▶ Irene was charged with forging her husband's signature on a check.
艾琳在支票上偽造丈夫的簽名，因而遭到起訴。
＊forge [fɔrdʒ] vt. 偽造 (簽名、字跡)

▶ The slow-cooked beef in chocolate sauce is that restaurant's signature dish.
慢火煮的牛肉佐巧克力醬是這家餐廳的招牌菜。

9 slogan [ˈslogən] n. 口號

⑪ (1) a political slogan　政治口號
(2) an economic slogan　經濟口號

▶ The demonstrators rallied in the square, shouting political slogans.
示威群眾在廣場集結，高喊政治口號。
＊demonstrator [ˈdɛmənˌstretɚ] n. 示威者
rally [ˈrælɪ] vi. 集結，集合

▶ The politician and his teammates are trying to think of an economic slogan for his campaign.

這位政治家和他的隊友正試圖為他的競選活動想出一個經濟口號。

10 surgeon [ˈsɝdʒən] n. 外科醫師

延伸 (1) physician [fɪˈzɪʃən]
  n. 醫師 (尤指內科醫師) ④
(2) dentist [ˈdɛntɪst] n. 牙科醫師 ②

▶ The woman plans to sue the surgeon for medical malpractice.

這名女子打算控告那外科醫師醫療疏失。

＊malpractice [mælˈpræktɪs] n. 誤診；不法行為

surgery [ˈsɝdʒərɪ]
n. 外科手術 (不可數)

片 (1) perform surgery on...
  對……動手術
  = perform an operation on...
(2) plastic surgery 整形外科手術

衍 surgical [ˈsɝdʒɪkl̩] a. (外科) 手術的 ⑥

似 operation [ˌɑpəˈreʃən]
  n. 手術 (可數) ③

▶ A team of doctors performed surgery on the Siamese twins.

一支由醫生組成的小組對這對連體雙胞胎動手術。

＊Siamese twins [ˌsaɪəmiz ˈtwɪnz] n. 連體嬰

▶ Ruby had plastic surgery in order to change the shape of her nose.

為了改變鼻形，露比去動了整形手術。

11 messy [ˈmɛsɪ] a. 雜亂的

衍 mess [mɛs] n. 雜亂 & vt. 弄亂 ③
  be a mess   很髒亂
  mess up a plan   把計畫打亂

反 tidy [ˈtaɪdɪ] a. 整潔的 &
  vi. & vt. 收拾，整理 ①

▶ How come your room is always messy?
= How come your room is always a mess?

你的房間為什麼老是很亂？

12 vain [ven] a. 空虛的，徒勞的；愛慕虛榮的，自負的

片 in vain   白費工夫
= to no avail
= to no purpose

▶ My father tried in vain to fix that broken fan.

我父親試圖要修復那臺壞掉的電扇，卻白費功夫。

▶ A vain person enjoys material comforts but has an empty soul.

愛慕虛榮的人貪圖物質享受，心靈卻很空虛。

＊comfort [ˈkʌmfɚt] n. 使生活舒適的東西 (常用複數)

13 vegetarian [ˌvɛdʒəˈtɛrɪən] n. 素食者

衍 vegetable [ˈvɛdʒ(ə)təbl̩] n. 蔬菜 ①

▶ I used to be a meat eater, but for my health's sake, I've become a vegetarian.

我以前是吃葷的，不過為了我的健康著想，我已改吃素了。

14 championship [ˈtʃæmpɪənˌʃɪp] *n.* 冠軍頭銜

> 片 win the championship　贏得冠軍
> 衍 champion [ˈtʃæmpɪən]
> 　*n.* 得冠軍者 ③

▶ Judging from Leo's performance, many of us think he will surely win the championship.
從利歐的表現看來，我們很多人都認為他一定會贏得冠軍。
＊judging from...　根據……判斷

15 voyage [ˈvɔɪɪdʒ] *n. & vi.* 航海旅行

> 似 (1) travel [ˈtrævl] *n. & vi. & vt.* 旅行 ②
> 　 (2) journey [ˈdʒɝnɪ] *n. & vi.* 旅行 ③

▶ The children are very excited about their first sea voyage.
孩子們對第一次出航感到很興奮。

▶ The cruiser is voyaging through the Caribbean Sea.
這艘遊艇正在航行經過加勒比海。
＊cruiser [ˈkruzɚ] *n.* 遊艇

16 converse [kənˈvɝs] *vi.* 交談 & [kənˈvɝs / ˈkɑnvɝs] *a.* 相反的

> 片 converse with sb　與某人交談
> ＝ have a conversation with sb
> 衍 conversation [ˌkɑnvɚˈseʃən]
> 　*n.* 談話 ②
> 似 opposite [ˈɑpəzɪt] *a.* 相反的 ③

▶ Who is that handsome guy Janet is conversing with?
正在跟珍妮特交談的那個帥哥是誰？

▶ Everyone thinks that Justin is honest, but I hold the converse view. I think he is a hypocrite.
大家都認為賈斯汀很老實，不過我卻持相反的看法。我認為他是偽君子。
＊hypocrite [ˈhɪpəkrɪt] *n.* 偽君子

17 recipe [ˈrɛsəpɪ] *n.* 食譜

> 片 a recipe for...　料理……的食譜

▶ Can you give me the recipe for the onion soup?
你能不能給我這道洋蔥湯的食譜？

cookbook [ˈkʊkˌbʊk]
n. 食譜書，烹飪手冊

▶ My mother's cookbook is full of old recipes.
我媽媽的烹飪手冊裡都是傳統的食譜。

18 cunning [ˈkʌnɪŋ] *a.* 狡猾的 & *n.* 狡猾，機靈

> 似 (1) sly [slaɪ] *a.* 狡猾的 ⑥
> 　 (2) crafty [ˈkræftɪ] *a.* 奸詐的
> 　 (3) foxy [ˈfɑksɪ] *a.* 狡猾的

▶ The fox is often portrayed as a cunning animal in fairy tales.
童話故事裡，狐狸通常被描述成狡猾的動物。
＊portray [pɔrˈtre] *vt.* 描繪
　portray A as B　把 A 描繪成 B

▶ Keep Paul at a distance. He is cunning and likes to take advantage of people.
跟保羅保持距離。他很狡猾，喜歡占大家便宜。

▶ The team displayed cunning and intelligence and went on to win the game.
這支隊伍展現機靈與智慧而贏得了比賽。

Level 4　Unit 23

19 hurricane [ˈhɝɪˌken] n. 颶風

比 hurricane、cyclone、typhoon 皆為颱風，惟在不同的地方有不同的名稱。在美國等稱 hurricane，印度洋附近區域稱 cyclone，東南亞、東北亞則稱 typhoon。

▶ The hurricane caused severe damage to the cities along the river.
這颶風對河岸的這些城市造成嚴重的損害。

cyclone [ˈsaɪklon] n. 旋風，氣旋
延伸 **tornado** [tɔrˈnedo] n. 龍捲風 ⑥

▶ The recent cyclone in Bangladesh was a real catastrophe.
最近在孟加拉的那場颶風真是場大災難。

20 dread [drɛd] vt. & n. 懼怕

用 dread + N/V-ing 懼怕……
衍 **dreadful** [ˈdrɛdfəl]
a. 可怕的；糟糕透頂的 ⑤
似 **fear** [fɪr] vt. & n. 害怕 ②

▶ Tony and some of his coworkers dreaded being laid off after the company announced a slump in profits.
在公司宣布利潤下滑後，湯尼和他的一些同事害怕會被解僱。
＊lay sb off 解僱某人 (lay 的三態為：lay, laid [led], laid)

▶ The dread of losing my girlfriend is making me crazy.
害怕失去我女友的想法逼得我快要發瘋了。

21 fertile [ˈfɝtl̩] a. 肥沃的；(動植物) 能生的，易受孕的

衍 (1) **fertilizer** [ˈfɝtl̩ˌaɪzɚ] n. 肥料 ⑥
(2) **fertility** [fɝˈtɪlətɪ]
n. 肥沃；生殖力 ⑥
反 **barren** [ˈbærən] a. 不孕的；貧瘠的 ⑤

▶ Anything can grow in this fertile land.
在這塊肥沃的土地上任何東西都可長出來。

▶ Mrs. Smith is fertile. She's had 8 children already, and she is pregnant again.
史密斯太太真能生。她已有 8 個孩子了，而現在肚子又有了。
＊pregnant [ˈprɛgnənt] a. 懷孕的

22 tumble [ˈtʌmbl̩] vi. 跌倒

用 tumble down... 滾落 / 跌落……

▶ Phil tumbled down the stairs and got a few bruises.
菲爾從樓梯跌下，身上帶了幾處瘀青。
＊bruise [bruz] n. 瘀青

23 sew [so] vt. 縫合

三 sew, sewed [sod], sewn [son] / sewed
似 **sow** [so] vt. 播 (種) ⑤
三態為：sow, sowed [sod], sown [son] / sowed

▶ Would you mind sewing this button on my jacket for me?
你介意幫我把這顆釦子縫到我的外套上嗎？

▶ As you sow, so shall you reap.
一分耕耘，一分收穫。── 諺語
*reap [rip] *vt.* 收穫

24 **shave** [ʃev] *vt. & vi.* 刮鬍子，剃毛髮

衍 shaver [ˈʃevɚ] *n.* 刮鬍刀 ⑥

▶ Eric looks younger after he shaved his beard.
艾瑞克把絡腮鬍刮掉後，看起來比較年輕。

▶ I got up late and didn't have time to shave this morning.
我今天起床起晚了，沒有時間刮鬍子。

25 **electronics** [ɪˌlɛkˈtrɑnɪks] *n.* 電子學

片 (1) an electronics industry
電子業

(2) an electronics company
電子公司

▶ The development of Korea's electronics industry should be attributed to supportive government policies.
韓國電子業的發展應該要歸功於政府政策的支持。
*attribute [əˈtrɪbjut] *vt.* 把⋯⋯歸因於
attribute A to B　將 A 歸因於 B

26 **bandage** [ˈbændɪdʒ] *n.* 繃帶 & *vt.* 用繃帶包紮

延伸 gauze [gɔz] *n.* 紗布

▶ Jason has a bandage on his knee because he fell down the stairs yesterday.
傑森的膝蓋上有繃帶，因為他昨天從樓梯上摔了下來了。

▶ The nurse bandaged John's sprained ankle.
護士用繃帶包紮約翰扭傷的腳踝。
*sprain [spren] *vt.* 扭傷

27 **stocking** [ˈstɑkɪŋ] *n.* (女用) 長襪

片 a pair of stockings　一雙長襪
似 sock [sɑk] *n.* 短襪 ②
a pair of socks　一雙短襪

▶ The store is offering large discounts; I just bought six pairs of silk stockings for the price of one.
這家店的折扣超優惠；我剛在那裡用一雙的錢買了六雙絲襪。

28 **plum** [plʌm] *n.* 李子

▶ Although the plums tasted a bit sour, I was so hungry that I ate three.
雖然李子嘗起來有點酸，但我餓到吃了三顆。

29 **hush** [hʌʃ] *vt. & vi.* (使) 安靜 & *n.* 寂靜

▣ hush sb　使某人安靜

㊝ silence [ˋsaɪləns]
　vt. 使安靜 & *n.* 寂靜 ②

▸ In the library, Alice's brother talked too loudly, and she immediately hushed him.

在圖書館裡，愛麗絲的弟弟說話太大聲了，她立刻要他安靜下來。

▸ Miss Wheaton told her students that if they didn't hush, she would give them a pop quiz immediately.

惠頓老師對學生說，如果他們再不安靜，她會馬上來個隨堂考。

＊a pop quiz　抽考，隨堂考

▸ A sudden hush followed the bad news.

壞消息傳來後，現場突然安靜了下來。

30 **kneel** [nil] *vi.* 跪下

▤ kneel, kneeled / knelt [nɛlt],
　kneeled / knelt

▣ kneel down　下跪

㊝ knee [ni] *n.* 膝蓋 ①

▸ The villain knelt down, begging for mercy.

那壞蛋跪下來請求寬恕他。

＊villain [ˋvɪlən] *n.* 壞蛋，惡棍

31 **stripe** [straɪp] *n.* 條紋

㊝ (1) strip [strɪp] *n.* 條，細長片 ③
　(2) streak [strik] *n.* 條紋 / 痕

▸ Charles likes that shirt with white and blue stripes.

查爾斯喜歡那件藍白條紋的襯衫。

32 **cottage** [ˋkɑtɪdʒ] *n.* (鄉間) 小屋

▸ The rich man used to live in a humble cottage in the country.

這有錢人曾住在鄉下一個簡陋的小屋裡。

＊humble [ˋhʌmbl̩] *a.* (物) 簡陋的；(人) 謙虛的

33 **lobster** [ˋlɑbstɚ] *n.* 龍蝦

㊀ (1) shrimp [ʃrɪmp] *n.* 小蝦 ③
　(2) prawn [prɔn] *n.* 大蝦

▸ Lobsters have two large claws and eight legs.

龍蝦有兩隻螯八隻腳。

＊claw [klɔ] *n.* (海洋動物等的) 螯

34 **refund** [ˋri͵fʌnd] *n.* 退貨還款 & [rɪˋfʌnd] *vt.* 退還

▣ demand a (full) refund
　要求 (全額) 退款

▸ Customers may demand a full refund if they find the products less effective than promised.

假如顧客覺得產品不符效果保證，他們可以要求全額退款。

> When Arthur told the clerk that he was not satisfied with the product, she offered to refund his money.
> 當亞瑟告訴店員他對這產品不滿意時，她主動提出要退還他的錢。

35 stereo [ˈstɛrɪo] *n.* 立體音響

戶 a stereo system　音響系統

> Turn down the stereo. The music is too loud.
> 把音響關小聲點。音樂太大聲了。

36 twig [twɪg] *n.* 細枝，嫩枝 & *vi.* & *vt.* 突然明白

目 twig, twigged [twɪgd], twigged
戶 twig (that)...　突然明白……

> We used some twigs and some larger branches to start a fire at the campsite.
> 我們在營區用一些細樹枝和較粗的樹枝生火。

> It was only after I explained to Linda for more than half an hour that she finally twigged.
> 直到我向琳達解釋了半個多小時後，她才終於突然明白了。

> I twigged that Matt was lying to me.
> 我突然明白麥特當時在對我撒謊。

37 miner [ˈmaɪnɚ] *n.* 礦工

似 (1) minor [ˈmaɪnɚ]
　　 n. 未成年人；副修 ②
　 (2) mineworker [ˈmaɪnˌwɝkɚ]
　　 n. 礦工

> Van Gogh presented the miserable life of miners in his paintings.
> 梵谷在其畫作中呈現礦工的悲慘生活。

38 hawk [hɔk] *n.* 鷹，隼；主戰派人士

衍 hawk-eyed [ˈhɔkˌaɪd] *a.* 目光銳利的

> The hawk successfully seized the field mouse.
> 老鷹成功抓住了田鼠。

> We don't need another hawk in the White House.
> 白宮不需要再添一名主戰派人士。

39 canoe [kəˈnu] *n.* 獨木舟

似 kayak [ˈkaɪæk]
　 n. (愛斯基摩人用的) 獨木舟

> We paddled the canoe down the river.
> 我們用槳划獨木舟沿河而下。
> *paddle [ˈpædl̩] *vt.* 用槳划 (船) & *n.* 槳

40 systematic [ˌsɪstəˈmætɪk] *a.* 有系統的

衍 systematically [ˌsɪstəˈmætɪklɪ]
　 adv. 有系統地
似 orderly [ˈɔrdɚlɪ] *a.* 有秩序的 ⑥

> I think the marketing department has organized this event in a systematic way.
> 我認為行銷部很有系統地辦了這次的活動。

Level 4　Unit 23

41 dew [d(j)u] *n.* 露水 (不可數)

片 **a drop of dew**　一滴露水，露珠

▸ The drops of dew on this petal evaporated after the sun came up.

太陽升起後，花瓣上的那些露珠就蒸發了。

*evaporate [ɪ`væpə,ret] *vi.* & *vt.* (使) 蒸發

42 hive [haɪv] *n.* 蜂巢

似 **beehive** [`bi,haɪv] *n.* 蜂巢

▸ Visitors are told to stay away from the hives.

遊客被告知要遠離蜂巢。

Unit 24

2401-2405

---

1 fetch [fɛtʃ] *vt.* 取來；售得，賣得 & *n.* 丟接遊戲（用於下列片語）

片 (1) fetch / bring sb sth
帶某物給某人

= fetch / bring sth for sb

(2) play fetch with...
和（狗）玩丟接遊戲

似 (1) bring [brɪŋ] *vt.* 帶來 ①

(2) sell for + 金錢　售得若干錢

▶ Would you mind fetching me a glass of water?

= Would you mind fetching a glass of water for me?
可以麻煩你幫我拿杯水嗎？

▶ The oil painting is expected to fetch at least one million dollars.
這幅油畫預計至少可賣得 100 萬元。

▶ My daughter likes to play fetch with our dog Max.
我女兒喜歡和我們的狗馬克斯一起玩丟接遊戲。

---

2 generosity [ˌdʒɛnəˈrasətɪ] *n.* 慷慨，大方

衍 (1) generous [ˈdʒɛnərəs]
a. 寬宏大量的；慷慨的 ②

(2) generously [ˈdʒɛnərəslɪ]
adv. 慷慨地

反 stinginess [ˈstɪndʒɪnɪs] *n.* 小器，吝嗇

▶ Grandfather is known for his kindness and generosity.
爺爺以善良和慷慨聞名。

---

3 graduation [ˌgrædʒʊˈeʃən] *n.* 畢業（與介詞 from 並用）

衍 graduate [ˈgrædʒʊˌet] *vi.* 畢業 ③
graduate from...　從……畢業

▶ What will you do upon graduation from college?
你大學畢業後要做什麼？

---

4 hose [hoz] *n.* 水管 & *vt.* 用水管沖洗 / 澆水

片 (1) a fire hose　消防水管

(2) a fire hose nozzle [ˈnazl̩]
消防水管噴嘴

(3) hose down...　用水管沖洗 / 澆水

▶ Use the hose to water the plants in front of the house.
用這條水管去澆屋前的那些植物。

▶ I don't see anything wrong. The fire hose is still securely attached to the fire truck.
我沒發現任何問題。消防水管仍牢固地接在消防車上。

▶ This fire hose nozzle is made of aluminum.
這消防水管噴嘴是鋁製的。

▶ Could you hose down the car for me?
能否請你替我沖洗車子？

---

5 humidity [hjuˈmɪdətɪ] *n.* 溼氣，溼度

衍 humid [ˈhjumɪd] *a.* 溼氣重的 ③

似 moisture [ˈmɔɪstʃɚ] *n.* 溼氣，水分 ③

▶ I hate summer because of the humidity.
我討厭夏天，因為溼氣太重。

6 ignorant [ˋɪgnərənt] *a.* 無知的；不知道的

片 **be ignorant of...**
　對……無知；對……不知

衍 **ignore** [ɪgˋnɔr] *vt.* 忽視；不理會 ②

▶ Without schooling, even naturally intelligent children grow up ignorant.
沒有學校教育，即使是天賦聰穎的小孩長大也會變無知。
＊schooling [ˋskulɪŋ] *n.* 學校教育（＝ school education）

▶ My grandfather is sad that many young people today are ignorant of the history of our tribe.
我的爺爺很難過，現今很多年輕人對我們部落的歷史一無所知。

▶ Don was completely ignorant of what had been going on that week.
唐恩完全不知道那個禮拜發生了什麼事。

ignorance [ˋɪgnərəns] *n.* 無知

▶ Those people's ignorance led them into a serious mistake.
那些人民的無知導致他們犯下一個嚴重的錯誤。

7 lag [læg] *vi.* 落後 & *n.* 時間差，間歇

三 lag, lagged [lægd], lagged

片 (1) **lag behind (sb/sth)**
　落後（某人／某物）
＝ **fall behind (sb/sth)**
(2) **jet lag** （乘坐飛機而造成的兩地）
　時差（反應）

▶ You're the one who wanted to go on a long hike, so don't lag behind and complain.
是你說要走這一大段路的，所以不要落後也不要抱怨。

▶ There was a long lag between two of our flights, but generally, the trip was pleasant.
我們兩段航程之間有一段很長等待的時間，但大致而言，整個行程很愉快。

▶ I have jet lag because I just arrived here after a 15-hour flight from New York.
我現在有時差，因為我從紐約飛了 15 個小時剛到這裡。

8 landmark [ˋlænd͵mɑrk] *n.* 地標；重要，重大（僅置名詞前）

片 **a landmark decision**　重大的決定

▶ The Statue of Liberty is a famous landmark in New York City.
自由女神像是紐約市著名的地標。

▶ The government made a landmark decision to build an industrial park in this area.
政府做出重大決定要在該區興建一座工業園區。

9 interruption [͵ɪntəˋrʌpʃən] *n.* 中斷；干擾

衍 **interrupt** [͵ɪntəˋrʌpt] *vt. & vi.* 中斷 ③

▶ The game resumed after the rain interruption.
比賽因雨中斷一陣子後繼續進行。
＊resume [rɪˋz(j)um] *vt. & vi.* 恢復

444

> ▶ I hate interruptions when I'm at work.
> 我工作時很討厭被干擾。

10 lawful [ˈlɔfəl] *a.* 合法的，正當的

衍 law [lɔ] *n.* 法律 ②

似 legal [ˈligl̩] *a.* 合法的 ②

反 (1) unlawful [ʌnˈlɔfəl] *a.* 不合法的
(2) illegal [ɪˈligl̩] *a.* 非法的

> ▶ It is not lawful to fish here unless you have a license.
> 除非你有執照，否則在此釣魚是不合法的。

> ▶ Gangsters hardly ever do lawful business.
> 幫派分子從事的幾乎都不是正當的生意。

> ▶ Ours is a lawful marriage.
> 我們的婚姻是合法的。

11 linen [ˈlɪnən] *n.* 亞麻布

片 wash one's dirty linen in public
家醜外揚

> ▶ The shirt is made of linen and cotton.
> 這件襯衫是亞麻布和棉製成的。

> ▶ The famous actress held a press conference to reveal her husband's love affairs yesterday. It just meant washing her dirty linen in public.
> 這位知名女演員昨天舉行了記者會，揭露了她丈夫有外遇。這只是讓家醜外揚而已。

nylon [ˈnaɪlɑn] *n.* 尼龍

延伸 polyester [ˌpɑlɪˈɛstɚ] *n.* 聚酯

> ▶ This nylon backpack is waterproof and light.
> 這個尼龍製背包既防水又很輕。
> *waterproof [ˈwɑtɚˌpruf] *a.* 防水的

12 lousy [ˈlauzɪ] *a.* 差勁的

似 (1) awful [ˈɔfəl] *a.* 差勁的 ④
(2) terrible [ˈtɛrəbl̩] *a.* 差勁的 ①

> ▶ That car of yours is lousy. You should buy a new one.
> 你那輛車太爛了。該買新車了。

13 mischief [ˈmɪstʃɪf] *n.* 淘氣，頑皮

片 be up to mischief　要搗蛋

衍 mischievous [ˈmɪstʃɪvəs]
a. 頑皮的 ⑥

a mischievous / naughty boy
頑皮的男孩，頑童

> ▶ Martha knew that the children were up to mischief when she saw them giggling.
> 瑪莎看到小孩們咯咯偷笑時，就知道他們要搗蛋了。
> *giggle [ˈgɪgl̩] *vi.* 咯咯地笑

14 monitor [ˈmɑnətɚ] *vt. & vi.* 監視 & *n.* 監視器；螢幕

片 a class monitor / leader　班長

似 screen [skrin]
n. (電影) 銀幕，(電視 / 電腦) 螢幕 ②

> ▶ The doctor will monitor the patient for two days after surgery.
> 手術後醫生會監控這位病患兩天。

▶ The nurse made sure that the patient was closely monitored.
護士確保該病人有受到嚴密監控。

▶ The monitor at the rich man's house showed that the thief broke in through a window at around 2 a.m.
這有錢人家的監視器顯示小偷在凌晨 2 點左右從窗戶闖入。

▶ The details of today's flights are displayed on the monitor.
今日班機的詳細資訊顯示在螢幕上。

▶ The teacher selected Ben as class monitor.
老師選班為班長。

15 mountainous [ˈmaʊntənəs] a. 多山的

衍 mountain [ˈmaʊntn̩] n. 山 ①

▶ The eastern part of Taiwan is mountainous and beautiful.
臺灣東部多山又美麗。

16 needy [ˈnidɪ] a. 非常貧窮的；極需大量關懷的

片 the needy 窮人

似 (1) poor [pʊr] a. 貧窮的 ①
(2) destitute [ˈdɛstə,t(j)ut] a. 貧困的

▶ Ivan dedicated his life to helping the needy.
艾凡奉獻一生幫助窮人。

▶ Rachel was a very needy child, but she grew up to be quite independent.
瑞秋是個非常需要別人關懷的孩子，但她長大後很獨立。

17 nightmare [ˈnaɪt,mɛr] n. 惡夢；可怕的情景

片 have a nightmare
做惡夢 (非 dream a nightmare)

反 a sweet dream 甜美的夢

▶ The little kid woke up from a nightmare, crying for his mom.
這個小孩從惡夢中驚醒，哭著要找媽媽。

▶ I had a nightmare last night. I dreamed I was being chased by a wolf.
我昨晚做惡夢。我夢到我正被一隻狼追趕。

▶ Driving home on the dark, rainy evening was a complete nightmare.
在漆黑又下雨的夜晚開車回家是非常可怕的。

18 nursery [ˈnɝsərɪ] n. 托兒所；育兒室，兒童房

似 a day care center
日托中心，托兒所

▶ This company has its own nursery, where employees' children can be taken care of during the day.
這家公司有自己的托兒所，員工的孩子白天在這裡可受到照顧。

| 延伸 | orphanage [`ɔrfənɪdʒ] *n.* 孤兒院 ⑥ | ▶ Amanda and Josh prepared a nursery for their unborn baby.
阿曼達與喬許為他們尚未出生的寶寶準備育兒室。 |

19 obedient [əˋbidɪənt] *a.* 服從的，遵守的

| 片 | be obedient to sb/sth
服從某人 / 某事 | ▶ Diane is an obedient child.
黛安是個很聽話的孩子。 |
| 衍 | obey [əˋbe] *vt.* 服從，遵守 ②
obey the law 守法
= abide by the law
= comply with the law | ▶ A good citizen is obedient to the law.
好國民都會守法。 |

| | **obedience** [əˋbidɪəns]
n. 服從，聽話
似 compliance [kəmˋplaɪəns] *n.* 順從 ⑤ | ▶ A good soldier is characterized by bravery, discipline, and obedience.
優秀軍人的本色就是勇敢、守紀律及服從。 |

20 offend [əˋfɛnd] *vt.* 觸怒，冒犯

| 似 | upset [ʌpˋsɛt] *vt.* 使不悅 ② | ▶ Barry's bad attitude deeply offended his boss.
貝瑞的不良態度嚴重觸怒了他的老闆。 |

| | **offense** [əˋfɛns]
n. 犯罪；攻擊；冒犯，得罪
片 (1) a weapon of offense 凶器
(2) take offense (at sth)
（因某事）而動怒 / 生氣
= be angered by / at sth
反 defense [dɪˋfɛns] *n.* 防禦 ④ | ▶ The young man was arrested for the offense of stealing.
這年輕人因犯了偷竊罪而被捕。
▶ Police were unable to find the weapon of offense used in the murder.
警方找不到謀殺用的凶器。
▶ Carol took offense at my comments about her.
我對卡蘿所作的評語令她不悅。 |

| | **offensive** [əˋfɛnsɪv]
a. 冒犯的，無禮的；攻擊性的 & *n.* 進攻
片 take the offensive 展開攻勢
似 (1) rude [rud] *a.* 粗魯的 ②
(2) distasteful [dɪsˋtestfəl]
a. 使人不愉快的
反 defensive [dɪˋfɛnsɪv] *a.* 防禦性的 ④ | ▶ Many Muslims regard the politician's comments as deeply offensive.
很多回教徒認為這政治家的評論很無禮。
▶ The government official thinks that to beef up our defense, we should buy more offensive weapons.
該政府官員認為若要加強我們的防禦，就應多購置攻擊性武器。
*beef up... 加強……
=strengthen...
▶ We took the offensive against the invading army.
我們對入侵的部隊展開攻勢。 |

Level 4　Unit 24

21 overthrow [ˌovɚˈθro] vt. 推翻

overthrow, overthrew [ˌovɚˈθru], overthrown [ˌovɚˈθron]

► The people cried with joy when they heard that the corrupt government had finally been overthrown.
當聽到腐敗的政府終於被推翻時，人們喜極而泣。

22 parachute [ˈpærəˌʃut] n. 降落傘 & vi. 跳傘

parachute into + 地方
跳傘進入某地

► Make sure to grab your parachute when exiting the plane.
離開飛機時務必要抓緊降落傘。

► The soldiers parachuted into the south of the country.
士兵們空降到該國南部。

23 perfection [pɚˈfɛkʃən] n. 完美

to perfection　完美地
= perfectly

(1) perfect [ˈpɝfɪkt / ˈpɝfɛkt]
　　a. 完美的 ②
(2) perfectly [ˈpɝfɪktlɪ / ˈpɝfɛktlɪ]
　　adv. 完美地
(3) perfectionist [pɚˈfɛkʃənɪst]
　　n. 完美主義者

► Mrs. Wilson expects perfection from all her students.
威爾森老師要求她所有的學生十全十美。

► The beef stew was cooked to perfection.
這道燉牛肉料理得好到沒話講。
*stew [st(j)u] n. 燉煮的菜餚

24 plentiful [ˈplɛntɪfəl] a. 大量的

plenty [ˈplɛntɪ] pron. 大量 ③
plenty of + 複數可數名詞 / 不可數名詞　許多的……

abundant [əˈbʌndənt]
　a. 大量的，豐富的 ⑤

► Fish are plentiful in this river.
= There are plenty of fish in this river.
= This river abounds in fish.
這條河有許多魚。
*abound [əˈbaʊnd] vi. 大量存在
　abound in / with... 有許多……

25 poisonous [ˈpɔɪznəs] a. 有毒的

poison [ˈpɔɪzn̩] n. 毒，毒藥 & vt. 下毒於 ②

► Not all mushrooms are edible; some are poisonous.
並非所有的菇類都可食用；有些是有毒的。
*edible [ˈɛdəbl̩] a. 可食用的

26 pregnant [ˈprɛgnənt] a. 懷孕的

be pregnant with...
肚子裡懷有……

► Sarah is pregnant with her third child.
莎拉的肚子裡懷了第 3 個孩子。

pregnancy [ˈprɛgnənsɪ] *n.* 懷孕

片 (1) during (a / the) pregnancy
懷孕期間

(2) a pregnancy test 驗孕 (測試)

▶ You shouldn't smoke or drink alcohol during pregnancy.
懷孕期間妳不應抽菸或喝酒。

▶ Ailsa did a pregnancy test at home.
艾莉莎在家做了驗孕測試。

---

27 rainfall [ˈrenˌfɔl] *n.* 降雨

似 precipitation [prɪˌsɪpəˈteʃən]
n. (雨或雪的) 降落

▶ The amount of rainfall in this area has become dangerously low.
這地區的降雨量已少到令人擔憂。

---

28 scold [skold] *vt.* 斥責 & *n.* 愛罵人的人

片 scold sb for + N/V-ing
因某事而斥責某人，因某人做某事而斥責某人
= tell sb off for + N/V-ing

▶ The boss scolded Kevin for breaking the company rules.
凱文因為違反公司規定而遭老闆斥責。

▶ Because Theo is such a scold, no one likes to talk to him.
因為西奧就是這樣愛罵人，所以沒人喜歡跟他說話。

---

29 tortoise [ˈtɔrtəs] *n.* 陸龜

似 turtle [ˈtɜtl̩] *n.* 海龜 ②

▶ Allen keeps a large tortoise as a pet.
亞倫養了一隻大陸龜當寵物。

---

30 spade [sped] *n.* 鏟子；(撲克牌) 黑桃

片 call a spade a spade
直言不諱，實話實說

似 shovel [ˈʃʌvl̩] *n.* 鏟子 ③

▶ Jason dug a deep hole with a spade.
傑森用鏟子挖了個很深的洞。

▶ Let's call a spade a spade. This song is absolutely terrible.
我們就實話實說吧。這首歌爛透了。

▶ I was happy when Bill played a spade because I was able to win the game.
我看到比爾出了一張黑桃時真開心，因為這樣一來我就穩贏了。

---

31 postage [ˈpostɪdʒ] *n.* 郵資，郵費

衍 post [post] *n.* 郵政〔英〕；職位 &
vt. 郵寄〔英〕②

▶ What's the postage for this letter to be sent to London?
這封信寄到倫敦的郵資要多少錢？

32 murderer [ˈmɝdərɚ] n. 凶手

似 killer [ˈkɪlɚ] n. 殺手

▶ Sadly, the cold-blooded murderer didn't show any remorse when he was arrested.
可悲的是這名冷血的凶手被逮捕時仍無懊悔之意。
＊remorse [rɪˈmɔrs] n. 懊悔；自責

33 lipstick [ˈlɪpˌstɪk] n. 口紅

片 wear lipstick 擦口紅（表「狀態」）

▶ Jenny looks beautiful and even sexy when she wears lipstick.
珍妮塗了口紅時模樣很美甚至還很性感。

34 impose [ɪmˈpoz] vt. 強加於

片 impose sth on sb
將某事強加於某人

▶ During the pandemic, the government imposed fines on those who didn't wear face masks.
在疫情期間，政府對沒戴口罩的人處以罰款。

35 ginger [ˈdʒɪndʒɚ] n. 薑

▶ I heard that ginger tea could help cure colds.
我聽說薑茶可以治療感冒。

36 ethnic [ˈɛθnɪk] a. 族群的

片 ethnic minority 少數民族
似 racial [ˈreʃəl] a. 種族的 ③

▶ The government launched a series of plans to protect the country's ethnic minorities.
政府啟動了一系列保護該國少數民族的計畫。

37 drowsy [ˈdraʊzɪ] a. 昏昏欲睡的

似 sleepy [ˈslipɪ] a. 想睡的 ②

▶ People often feel drowsy after eating lunch.
吃完午餐後，大家常會感到昏昏欲睡。

38 mill [mɪl] n. 磨坊 & vt. 碾碎

衍 windmill [ˈwɪndˌmɪl] n. 風車
似 (1) grind [graɪnd] vt. 磨碎 ④
三態為：grind, ground [graʊnd], ground
(2) crush [krʌʃ] vt. 壓碎 ④

▶ We brought the wheat to the mill to be crushed into flour.
我們把麥子帶到磨坊去讓它碾碎成麥粉。

▶ We have to mill the soybeans first to make soymilk.
做豆漿之前，要先把黃豆碾碎。

39 pest [pɛst] *n.* 害蟲;討厭鬼

似 (1) nuisance [ˈn(j)usn̩s]
   n. 令人討厭的人或事物

(2) a pain in the neck
   令人討厭的人或事物

▸ Mice are everywhere in this place. Let's call the pest control company right away.
這地方到處是老鼠。快打電話給防蟲公司。

▸ Brandon is a pest because he always interrupts others when they are talking.
布蘭登是個討厭鬼,因為別人說話時他老愛打岔。

40 nutritious [n(j)uˈtrɪʃəs] *a.* 營養的

似 nourishing [ˈnɝɪʃɪŋ] *a.* 營養的

▸ Do you know that soy milk is actually as nutritious as milk?
你知道其實豆漿和牛奶一樣有營養嗎?

Level 4

Unit 24

索引

索
引

索
引

索 引

索
引

索 引

索引

索引

索 引

索
引

索 引

索 引

索引

索引

☐ Cardinal Numbers　基數

❶ **one** [wʌn] 一
❷ **two** [tu] 二
❸ **three** [θri] 三
❹ **four** [fɔr] 四
❺ **five** [faɪv] 五
❻ **six** [sɪks] 六
❼ **seven** [ˈsɛvən] 七
❽ **eight** [et] 八
❾ **nine** [naɪn] 九
❿ **ten** [tɛn] 十
⓫ **eleven** [ɪˈlɛvən] 十一
⓬ **twelve** [twɛlv] 十二
⓭ **thirteen** [θɝˈtin] 十三
⓮ **fourteen** [fɔrˈtin] 十四
⓯ **fifteen** [fɪfˈtin] 十五
⓰ **sixteen** [sɪksˈtin] 十六
⓱ **seventeen** [ˌsɛvənˈtin] 十七
⓲ **eighteen** [eˈtin] 十八
⓳ **nineteen** [naɪnˈtin] 十九
⓴ **twenty** [ˈtwɛntɪ] 二十
㉑ **twenty-one** [ˈtwɛntɪˌwʌn] 二十一

㉒ **twenty-two** [ˈtwɛntɪˌtu] 二十二
㉓ **twenty-three** [ˈtwɛntɪˌθri] 二十三
㉔ **twenty-four** [ˈtwɛntɪˌfɔr] 二十四
㉕ **twenty-five** [ˈtwɛntɪˌfaɪv] 二十五
㉖ **thirty** [ˈθɝtɪ] 三十
㉗ **thirty-one** [ˈθɝtɪˌwʌn] 三十一
㉘ **thirty-two** [ˈθɝtɪˌtu] 三十二
㉙ **thirty-three** [ˈθɝtɪˌθri] 三十三
㉚ **thirty-four** [ˈθɝtɪˌfɔr] 三十四
㉛ **forty** [ˈfɔrtɪ] 四十
㉜ **fifty** [ˈfɪftɪ] 五十
㉝ **sixty** [ˈsɪkstɪ] 六十
㉞ **seventy** [ˈsɛvəntɪ] 七十
㉟ **eighty** [ˈetɪ] 八十
㊱ **ninety** [ˈnaɪntɪ] 九十
㊲ **one hundred** [wʌn ˈhʌndrəd] 一百
㊳ **one thousand** [wʌn ˈθauzn̩d] 一千
㊴ **one million** [wʌn ˈmɪljən] 一百萬
㊵ **one billion** [wʌn ˈbɪljən] 十億

☐ Ordinal Numbers　序數

❶ **first** [fɝst] 第一
❷ **second** [ˈsɛkənd] 第二
❸ **third** [θɝd] 第三
❹ **fourth** [fɔrθ] 第四
❺ **fifth** [fɪfθ] 第五
❻ **sixth** [sɪksθ] 第六
❼ **seventh** [ˈsɛvənθ] 第七
❽ **eighth** [eθ] 第八

❾ **ninth** [naɪnθ] 第九
❿ **tenth** [tɛnθ] 第十
⓫ **eleventh** [ɪˈlɛvənθ] 第十一
⓬ **twelfth** [twɛlfθ] 第十二
⓭ **thirteenth** [θɝˈtinθ] 第十三
⓮ **fourteenth** [fɔrˈtinθ] 第十四
⓯ **fifteenth** [fɪfˈtinθ] 第十五
⓰ **sixteenth** [sɪksˈtinθ] 第十六

⑰ **seventeenth** [ˌsɛvənˈtinθ] 第十七

⑱ **eighteenth** [eˈtinθ] 第十八

⑲ **nineteenth** [naɪnˈtinθ] 第十九

⑳ **twentieth** [ˈtwɛntɪɪθ] 第二十

㉑ **twenty-first** [ˈtwɛntɪˌfɝst] 第二十一

㉒ **twenty-second** [ˈtwɛntɪˌsɛkənd] 第二十二

㉓ **twenty-third** [ˈtwɛntɪˌθɝd] 第二十三

㉔ **twenty-fourth** [ˈtwɛntɪˌforθ] 第二十四

㉕ **twenty-fifth** [ˈtwɛntɪˌfɪfθ] 第二十五

㉖ **thirtieth** [ˈθɝtɪɪθ] 第三十

㉗ **fortieth** [ˈfɔrtɪɪθ] 第四十

㉘ **fiftieth** [ˈfɪftɪɪθ] 第五十

㉙ **sixtieth** [ˈsɪkstɪɪθ] 第六十

㉚ **seventieth** [ˈsɛvəntɪɪθ] 第七十

㉛ **eightieth** [ˈetɪɪθ] 第八十

㉜ **ninetieth** [ˈnaɪntɪɪθ] 第九十

㉝ **hundredth** [ˈhʌndrədθ] 第一百

㉞ **thousandth** [ˈθauzn̩dθ] 第一千

㉟ **millionth** [ˈmɪljənθ] 第一百萬

㊱ **billionth** [ˈbɪljənθ] 第十億

☐ Days of the Week　一星期

❶ **Monday** [ˈmʌnde] / **Mon.** 星期一

❷ **Tuesday** [ˈtjuzde] / **Tue.** 星期二

❸ **Wednesday** [ˈwɛnzde] / **Wed.** 星期三

❹ **Thursday** [ˈθɝzde] / **Thu.** 星期四

❺ **Friday** [ˈfraɪde] / **Fri.** 星期五

❻ **Saturday** [ˈsætɚde] / **Sat.** 星期六

❼ **Sunday** [ˈsʌnde] / **Sun.** 星期日

☐ Months　月份

❶ **January** [ˈdʒænjuˌɛrɪ] / **Jan.** 一月

❷ **February** [ˈfɛbruˌɛrɪ] / **Feb.** 二月

❸ **March** [martʃ] / **Mar.** 三月

❹ **April** [ˈeprəl] / **Apr.** 四月

❺ **May** [me] 五月

❻ **June** [dʒun] / **Jun.** 六月

❼ **July** [dʒuˈlaɪ] / **Jul.** 七月

❽ **August** [ˈɔgəst] / **Aug.** 八月

❾ **September** [sɛpˈtɛmbɚ] / **Sep.** 九月

❿ **October** [ɑkˈtobɚ] / **Oct.** 十月

⓫ **November** [noˈvɛmbɚ] / **Nov.** 十一月

⓬ **December** [dɪˈsɛmbɚ] / **Dec.** 十二月

附錄

☐ Seasons 季節

❶ spring [sprɪŋ] 春天

❷ summer [ˋsʌmɚ] 夏天

❸ autumn [ˋɔtəm] / fall [fɔl] 秋天

❹ winter [ˋwɪntɚ] 冬天

☐ Countries and Areas 國家與地區

❶ Argentina [ˌɑrdʒənˋtinə] 阿根廷

❷ Australia [ɔˋstrelɪə] 澳洲

❸ Brazil [brəˋzɪl] 巴西

❹ Canada [ˋkænədə] 加拿大

❺ China [ˋtʃaɪnə] 中國

❻ France [fræns] 法國

❼ Germany [ˋdʒɝmənɪ] 德國

❽ India [ˋɪndɪə] 印度

❾ Indonesia [ˌɪndoˋniʒə] 印尼

❿ Italy [ˋɪtəli] 義大利

⓫ Japan [dʒəˋpæn] 日本

⓬ Malaysia [məˋleʒə] 馬來西亞

⓭ Mexico [ˋmɛksɪˌko] 墨西哥

⓮ (the) Philippines [(ðə) ˋfɪləˌpinz] 菲律賓

⓯ Republic of China [rɪˋpʌblɪk əv ˋtʃaɪnə] 中華民國

⓰ Russia [ˋrʌʃə] 俄羅斯

⓱ Saudi Arabia [ˌsaudɪ əˋrebɪə] 沙烏地阿拉伯

⓲ Singapore [ˋsɪŋgəˌpor] 新加坡

⓳ South Africa [ˌsauθ ˋæfrɪkə] 南非

⓴ South Korea [ˌsauθ koˋrɪə] 南韓

㉑ Spain [spen] 西班牙

㉒ Taiwan [ˌtaɪˋwɑn] 臺灣

㉓ Thailand [ˋtaɪlənd] 泰國

㉔ Turkey [ˋtɝkɪ] 土耳其

㉕ (the) United Kingdom [(ðə) juˌnaɪtɪd ˋkɪŋdəm] 英國

㉖ (the) United States [(ðə) juˌnaɪtɪd ˋstets] 美國

㉗ Vietnam [ˌvjɛtˋnæm] 越南

☐ Continents 大陸；洲

❶ Africa [ˋæfrɪkə] 非洲

❷ Antarctica [ænˋtɑrktɪkə] 南極洲

❸ Asia [ˋeʒə] 亞洲

❹ Australia [ɔˋstrelɪə] 澳洲

❺ Europe [ˋjurəp] 歐洲

❻ North America [ˌnɔrθ əˋmɛrɪkə] 北美洲

❼ South America [ˌsauθ əˋmɛrɪkə] 南美洲

□ The Principal Oceans of the World　世界主要海洋

❶ (the) Arctic Ocean
[(ði) ˈɑrktɪk ˈoʃən] 北極海

❷ (the) Atlantic Ocean
[(ði) ətˈlæntɪk ˈoʃən] 大西洋

❸ (the) Indian Ocean
[(ði) ˈɪndɪən ˈoʃən] 印度洋

❹ (the) Pacific Ocean
[(ðə) pəˈsɪfɪk ˈoʃən] 太平洋

□ Religions　宗教

❶ Buddhism [ˈbʊdɪzəm] /
Buddhist [ˈbʊdɪst] 佛教 / 佛教的；
佛教徒

❷ Catholicism [kəˈθɑləˌsɪzəm] /
Catholic [ˈkæθəlɪk] 天主教 /
天主教的；天主教徒

❸ Christianity [ˌkrɪstʃɪˈænətɪ] /
Christian [ˈkrɪstʃən] 基督教 /
基督教的；基督徒

❹ Eastern Orthodoxy
[ˈistən ˈɔrθəˌdɑksɪ] /
Eastern Orthodox
[ˈistən ˈɔrθəˌdɑks] 東正教 / 東正教的

❺ Hinduism [ˈhɪnduˌɪzəm] /
Hindu [ˈhɪndu] 印度教 / 印度教的；
印度教徒

❻ Islam [ˈɪsləm] / **Muslim**
[ˈmʌzˌlɪm / ˈmʊzˌlɪm] 伊斯蘭教，回教 /
回教的；回教徒

❼ Judaism [ˈdʒudɪˌɪzəm] /
Jewish [ˈdʒuɪʃ] 猶太教 / 猶太教的；
猶太人

❽ Taoism [ˈtaʊˌɪzəm] / **Taoist**
[ˈtaʊɪst] 道教 / 道教的；道教徒

□ Parts of Speech　詞性

❶ adjective [ˈædʒɪktɪv] / *adj.* 形容詞

❷ adverb [ˈædvɚb] / *adv.* 副詞

❸ article [ˈɑrtɪkḷ] / *art.* 冠詞

❹ auxiliary [ɔgˈzɪljərɪ] / *aux.* 助動詞

❺ conjunction [kənˈdʒʌŋkʃən] /
conj. 連接詞

❻ noun [naʊn] / *n.* 名詞

❼ preposition [ˌprɛpəˈzɪʃən] / *prep.*
介詞

❽ pronoun [ˈpronaʊn] / *pron.* 代名詞

❾ verb [vɝb] / *v.* 動詞

附錄

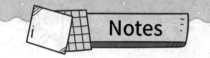

Notes

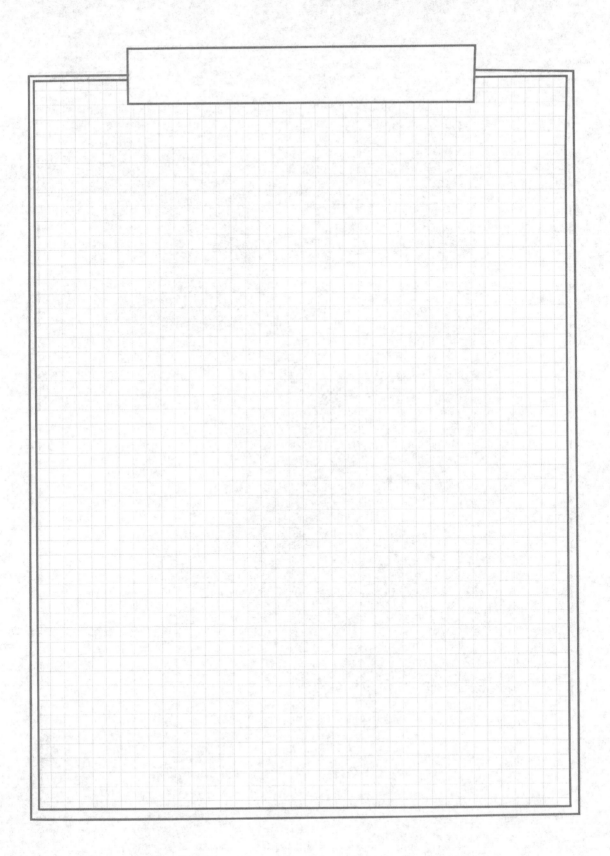

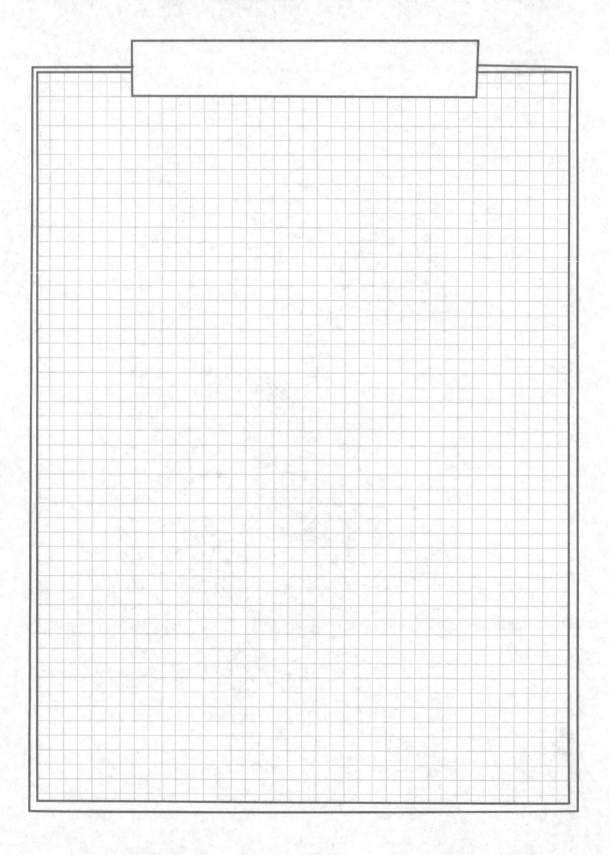

國家圖書館出版品預行編目（CIP）資料

英文字彙王：核心單字 2001-4000 Levels 3 & 4
／賴世雄作. -- 初版. -- 臺北市：
常春藤有聲出版股份有限公司, 2022.01
面；　公分.--（英文字彙王系列；E63）
ISBN 978-626-95430-3-8（平裝）
1. 英語　2. 詞彙
805.12　　　　　　　　　110020679

英文字彙王系列【E63】

英文字彙王：核心單字 2001-4000 Levels 3 & 4

總 編 審	賴世雄
終 　 審	李 端
執行編輯	許嘉華
編輯小組	常春藤中外編輯群
設計組長	王玥琦
封面設計	胡毓芸
排版設計	王穎緁・林桂旭
錄 　 音	李鳳君・劉書吟
播音老師	Leah Zimmermann・Jacob Roth・Michael Tennant Terri Pebsworth
法律顧問	北辰著作權事務所蕭雄淋律師
出 版 者	常春藤數位出版股份有限公司
地 　 址	臺北市忠孝西路一段 33 號 5 樓
電 　 話	(02) 2331-7600
傳 　 真	(02) 2381-0918
網 　 址	www.ivy.com.tw
電子信箱	service@ivy.com.tw
郵政劃撥	50463568
戶 　 名	常春藤數位出版股份有限公司
定 　 價	460 元

© 常春藤數位出版股份有限公司 (2022) All rights reserved.　　　X000083-3591
本書之封面、內文、編排等之著作財產權歸常春藤數位出版股份有限公司所有。未經本公司
書面同意，請勿翻印、轉載或為一切著作權法上利用行為，否則依法追究。

如有缺頁、裝訂錯誤或破損，請寄回本公司更換。　　【版權所有　翻印必究】